Pirates of the H

Pirates of

the Heart

JIM & TERRI
KRAUS

Tyndale House Publishers, Inc. WHEATON, ILLINOIS

Library of Congress Cataloging-in-Publication Data

Kraus, Jim.
 Pirates of the heart / Jim and Terri Kraus.
  p. cm. — (Treasures of the Caribbean ; 1)
 ISBN 0-8423-0381-2 (pbk. : alk. paper)
 I. Kraus, Terri, date. II. Title. III. Series: Kraus, Jim.
 Treasures of the Caribbean ; 1.
 PS3561.R2876P57 1996
 813'.54—dc20

                    96-23350

Printed in the United States of America

04 03 02 01 00 99 98 97 96
9 8 7 6 5 4 3 2 1

ACKNOWLEDGMENTS

England:
Mrs. Ann Partridge, Manor Farm, Yetminster,
  Dorset
The Dorset County Museum, Dorchester, Dorset
St. Peter's Church, Tawstock, Devon
Overbecks Museum and Garden (National Trust),
  Sharpitor, Salcombe, Devon
Royal Naval Museum, Portsmouth, Hampshire
The National Trust, London
Tower of London, Tower Hill, London
National Maritime Museum, Greenwich
Montacute House (National Trust), Somerset
Haddon Hall, Bakewell, Derbyshire
Townend (National Trust), Troutbeck, Cumbria

Barbados:
Barbados Museum and Historical Society
Barbados National Trust
Barbados National Cultural Foundation

Thanks to Jennifer Ochs and LuAnne Zaeske
for reading this book in manuscript form
and for their valuable advice

For our mothers
Anna and Anna

INTRODUCTION

17 February 1627
The Caribbean Sea

After tacking north, then south for several days in the warm turquoise waters, the crew of the small wooden ship *William and John* could hear the sounds of the island even before it could be seen. Twilight closed around them, enveloping them in the darkness of a moonless ocean. Waves crashed against rocks in the distance, a rumbling gnarled thunder roaring from the western shadows.

Forty-seven white men, all from England—the southern shires' port cities of Weymouth, Plymouth, and Falmouth—and three black men, slaves captured from the north coast of Africa, had set out to find the small island of Barbados. The island lay a hundred miles to the east of a submerged chain of volcanic mountains that marked the boundary of the Caribbean Sea, the islands of the Lesser Antilles. Barbados was so isolated, so far south of the ocean currents most ships naturally followed when setting out from Europe or Africa, that even Christopher Columbus, the famed navigator of the Caribbean, had never set eye upon its shores.

"'Tis like the Garden of Eden, and shaped most curiously like a leg of mutton," recounted early explorers. They had passed it by, calling it the "isle of the bearded" for its unusual bearded fig trees, and had charted its coastline a hundred years prior. It lay two thousand miles west of the Azores and nearly three hundred miles north of the Guyana coast. It was a small island, only fourteen miles wide and twenty-one miles in length. Living coral reefs, formed millennia ago, encircled its coast like fringed, protecting arms, a near uninterrupted natural barrier against conquest.

Barbados had a lower silhouette than most of the islands of the

Indies, a series of undulating coralline limestone plateaus some three hundred feet thick, rising from the sea to no more than eleven hundred feet above the waters. Its first inhabitants, their traces all but vanished now, had walked along the lush forest paths as Christ walked the dry and dusty streets of Jerusalem. The gentle Arawaks, who supplanted those first natives, were erased by the vengeful Caribs. By the time Europeans charted the coast in 1520, the Indians were gone, leaving behind only the forlorn remains of a bridge over an arm of the sea at what was to become Bridgetown.

The rich soil was blanketed with jungle in the lower valleys, which gave way to tulip, cedar, locust, mastic, fustic, logwood, and palmetto trees, then shrubs, then grasslands as the elevation increased, brilliantly green after the daily summer showers. The sultry island birthed no rivers and only a few surface streams—coral gullies formed by cracks in its coral cap filled with the waters of its brief rains. But birds were plentiful, dazzling in their plumage of vermilion, sapphire, yellow, and emerald. Great-throated pelicans nested there, and turtledoves sang their songs. Green sea turtles, brown and yellow whistling turtles, and fish of all shapes, colors, and sizes swam in the waters off the palm-fringed coast. The island was home as well to small black-and-white capuchin monkeys, squeaky lizards, pale yellow land crabs, stinging insects, and scores of wild hogs.

The craggy eastern coast, facing forward into the rolling Atlantic, was rocky, windy, and filled with the sounds of an angry surf. As the sun began to slip beyond the western horizon, the men on the ship saw a white line of breakers, sand, and rocks, and wooded hills rising steeply beyond. Sails were furled, the anchor splashed into the darkening sea, and the crew waited for the dawn. In the fading light, porpoises, dolphins, and grampuses played in the shadowy waters.

The crew slept fitfully that night, the echoes of the surf calling out their siren song of danger.

As the orange-red sun rose in an amethyst sky, the ship skirted north of the island, carried along by the strong and almost ever-present trade winds. By afternoon they had turned south and gently tacked along the island's leeward coast, enjoying the warmer, caressing breezes.

Hours before dusk would settle again, the ship anchored in a small bay, with a curving beach and swaying palms, equidistant from the northern and southern coastlines. The ship, a three-masted trader, drew a shallow draft and anchored within swimming distance of the shore.

A longboat was lowered and a dozen men—a couple with muskets, a few with sharpened pikes with irontips, most with swords—rowed toward the sandy beach. They jumped into clear, ankle-deep water and wrestled the boat to the shore. At the edge of the palm-fringed beach they gathered, listening, scanning the horizons, peering back at the men left on the ship and then forward at the lush vegetation. The air was filled with an orchestra of exotic smells; oranges, lemons, pineapples, peppers, papayas, cherries, guavas, plantain, cassava, figs, cloves, and cinnamon called out to the hungry crew.

A large, red-faced man reached into the longboat and pulled out a small flag from the court of His Majesty James I. He stepped onto the shore that bore no human footprint and pushed the oak staff into the coral sand until it stood upright. The flag, a blue and red velvet patch of bunting cloth, hung limp on the windless beach.

"For King, country, and God," he called out, then sank to his knees, bowed his head, and began a fervent prayer.

A few others joined him on their knees; the rest stood watch.

He prayed for a successful venture, for the Almighty's protection on their settlement, for guidance, for health, for strength.

After several moments, he arose to silence. "We sleep on firm ground tonight," he said. "On Barbados—our new home."

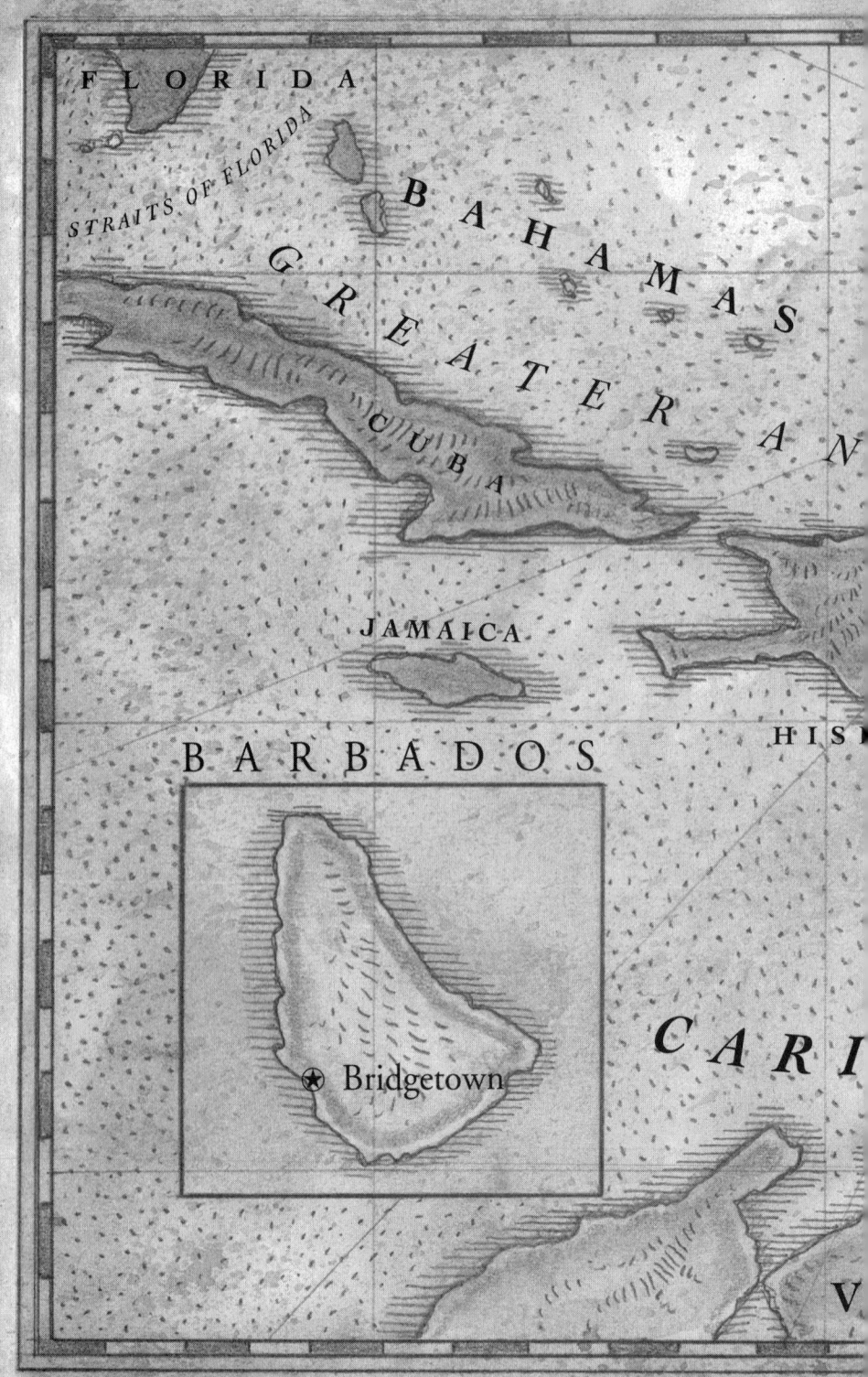

CHAPTER

I

April 1628
Hadenthorne, Devon
England

A light mist had settled over the Devonshire village of Hadenthorne, washing all of nature with a cooling glow. Droplets hung from the leaves of the berried hawthorn shrubs like ripened fruit. They dropped to earth as the tree branches stirred and rustled, drumming the ground with a liquid rhythm to the cadence of a slight spring breeze.

It was April in Hadenthorne, a month that could be cruel as easily as beautiful in the western shire of Devon. The nudgings of spring had just arrived, and the first shoots and tender fingers had pushed their greenings into the chilled air, seeking the sun. Patches of delicate anemone had begun to carpet the woodlands and shaded banks of the river Taw with their soft whiteness.

Hadenthorne had waited long for the stirrings of spring to arrive this year of 1628. For some, it held the magic of possibility, an intoxicating potion of *perhaps* and *might-be*. Perhaps this would be a truly good year, perhaps the fields would be fertile and the yields bountiful. The breeze carried along with it the scent of new growth, of new promise, a better future.

The farmers Brown, Arnold, and Cavendish had been in their fields nestled near the village church and cemetery. Now they gathered near the old stone wall and rusting iron gate at the north edge of the church. They stood in the misty afternoon, speaking in low tones.

Farmer Henry Brown, the youngest of a generation of yeomen in Hadenthorne, had pulled out a clay pipe from his pocket. Tenderly, carefully, he extracted a small pinch of brown leaf from a leather pouch and filled the bowl of the pipe. He pulled a small branch, with its end glowing red, from a small warming fire burning the winter stubble at the field's edge. He slowly touched it to the brown leaf in the pipe's bowl and drew the smoke into his mouth, his puffing the loudest sound for a hundred yards.

The smoke curled upward on the breeze, catching an updraft that carried it over the tile rooftop of St. Jerome's Parish Church, its high tower thrusting toward heaven. The tower was the highest point in the Taw Valley, named for the small river that gently meandered over its broad, green plains.

The vicar of St. Jerome's, Thomas Mayhew, had shuffled in anticipation across the cold stone floor of the dim church, his footsteps hushed echoes that drifted around its columns and arches, and climbed the narrow ladder inside the tower, cleaning out old birds' nests and clawing at the flimsy swags of cobwebs that formed in the still darkness.

The current vicar was not native to Hadenthorne, yet he had the longest tenure of the last four hundred years of vicars, all of whose names were inscribed on a plaque on the wall just inside the door of the church. Indeed, many of their remains, as well as those of nobles, soldiers, and the wealthy yeomen of the parish, along with their wives, lay buried under the floor of the church, now all but completely paved with engraved tablets in their memory, some worn down to illegibility over the centuries.

Vicar Mayhew stopped and looked down at his feet. Beneath them read the following:

Here lyeth in hopes of a joyful resurrection, the body of Reverend Sampson Bull of this parish, who departed this life the 8th day of January, in the year of our Lord 1481, aged 40

Vicar Mayhew couldn't help but wonder if his own body would finally rest here under such an epitaph. When that thought slipped into his being, a chilled shudder coursed down his spine.

He was a thin man, modestly tall at near five-and-a-half feet, but only ten stone in weight. Most of his hair had left him at an early age, and now, as he entered his third decade, he sported a thin thatch of fringe, more white than brown, above his ears and around the back of his head. He had eyes that were slightly narrow and of a thin blue color, and a wide mouth, which had seen few smiles in recent years. He had taken to wearing a closely cropped beard, which grew out nearly all white as well. Most of the day the vicar would squint ever so slightly, sun or not, to compensate for an almost imperceptible blurring of vision. From the pulpit it served him well, for each person in the pews would fall under his gaze during a sermon and feel pierced by it.

The church, a large structure of yellow oolite stone now mellowed to a warm golden tan, sat alone on a high knoll in the village, on the western bank of the river Taw. Each stone had been carried seventy miles from Ham Hill in the shire of Somerset and had been quarried, dressed, and shaped by hand by stone-dressers with rough, simple tools. As was the tradition of a Norman church, its floor was in the shape of a cross, and the large square tower hulked over the nave of the sanctuary, extending up from where Christ's heart would have been.

Church building was expensive and dangerous work, especially since it had begun being built well before the more modern conveniences, such as leather-thong belt drives and mechanical iron pulleys and winches, had been developed, which would have made the construction of the structure easier and safer. Most of the work had been done before 1348. That dark year marked the visit of the Black Death to the shire of Devon. Nearly a third of the population had died. The ornamentation in the nave had remained incomplete for fifty years. The loss of skilled craftsmen to the plague was so great that the carving of human faces and oak leaves on the stone corbels that finished the interior arches had been left undone for nearly two generations.

Each spring for the past seven years, the vicar would pick the earliest and brightest day, don his warmest cassock, and climb, cleaning his way through the web-filled darkness to be rewarded with a magnificent gift.

At the very top of the crenellated tower, and at the highest rung of a sturdy iron ladder, a small door could be opened, and a man with a delicate touch could step out onto a narrow parapet around the inside edge of the towering structure. No more than two foot-widths wide, it provided a breath-stealing view of the entire parish and town of Hadenthorne—from the low rise of the gentle hills of the northeast to the gently sloping yellow fields of rape flowers billowing like waves on the English Sea.

Each year the vicar would stand there for as long as he could in the chilled spring winds. He would slowly slide-step-slide the entire circumference of the tower's parapet. He told others it was to pray round the entire valley, but in reality it was to be filled with the handiwork of God.

As he stood there in the faint mist of spring, he drank in the view, then closed his eyes in prayer. *How I love this place and its beauty. But how I hate its distance from all that I knew before. I am enchanted by the loveliness of this parish, but I am embittered by how small my world has indeed become. Lord, I humbly ask that I be given a bigger task. . . .*

Off to the west stood imposing Hadenthorne Hall, the stately ances-
tral home of the earls and nobility that governed this quiet corner of
England since the time of William the Conqueror and the Magna Carta.

It was castlelike in its appearance, with its surrounding high walls
and gatehouse, its drawbridge, and its own tower, all punctuated with
great studded oak doors and elaborate tracery windows. The vicar
could take in its vast, precisely groomed knot gardens, the patterns of
twisting and overlapping borders forming outlines for a mass of brilliantly colored flowers within. Its current resident was the ninth earl of
Hadenthorne, Lord Robert Davis.

As often occurs with much inherited wealth, the earl was a pleasant
man, who Vicar Mayhew thought was soft in the middle of his being.
The earl enjoyed life at the massive estate with a quiet dignity, but his
manner was coupled with an air of expected entitlement.

"The common man," the earl had remarked after one church service,
"has no business dreaming about betterment. It would not suit him if
he found it. It is better for all if they just accept their lot in life. It is
where they should be, after all. Do not the Scriptures tell us we will
always have the poor with us? And should they not be content?"

Looking north, he saw that the valley met a low rise of foothills and
disappeared into the thickness of the Exmoor Forest—a dark, oak-filled
vastness that occupied virtually every acre from Hadenthorne to the
heather- and bracken-covered moors that edged to the Bristol Channel
beyond. It was a nobleman's private playground. Huge elk and red deer
made it their home, as well as did foxes, badgers, and game birds of all
types.

Now he was facing east, toward London. The vicar stared down at
the ground and shook his head. It had been more than seven years since
he had been in London, five days' journey to the east. It was not his
idea to be stationed so far from the radiant headquarters of the Church
of England, whose allure was felt strongly by the vicar. But it had been
so long that he was sure they had all but forgotten him and forgotten
why he had been sent here all those long years ago.

*Will I ever leave this place? Will I ever see more than this small corner
of England?* he thought.

Of all the directions he could see, his favorite was due south, to the
city of Plymouth, to the sea. The forty-mile distance was too great to
actually see the horizon of the water, but the vicar would imagine that
the thin blue-gray band off in the distance, just beyond the rolling
moors of Dartmoor, colored in purple and rust, was indeed the waters
of the English Sea. He would close his eyes and tilt toward it, listening

for the crash of surf on the rocks, the glistening rocks and salt spray of his childhood home in Peacehaven, in the Sussex Downs, near Brighton by the Sea.

He paused on his circuit to survey his parish. Nearly every structure could be seen from this perch—every cottager's hovel, every husbandman's cottage, every yeoman's house, and the imposing estate of the gentry that made up the church's geography. Miles and miles of precisely stacked ancient stones formed walls that crisscrossed the parish, dividing the land into tidy parcels.

He could see the small plot of ground that the Brown family had tended for generations, their garden appearing as a patchwork of neat squares of color from up above.

Over across the river was the smithy, the public house, and beyond them the few small shops housing a shoemaker, chandler, and victualler that made up the main road through the village. The small markets and buildings leaned hard together, as if seeking warmth on this chilled day. There was the miller-baker, who filled the town with the scent of fresh bread. Two homes further south was a small shop shared by a tailor-draper and a bodice-maker who sold hats, cloth, buttons, and thread. An apothecary shop had opened two years ago and did well, dispensing costly powders and curious dark and amber liquids. Capitalizing on another of his skills, the apothecary also served as the village barber and surgeon.

The Cavendish farm was the closest neighbor to the stone parsonage that Vicar Mayhew called home.

As the vicar looked straight down, just by the stand of evergreen and English pine, he could just see the corner of the parish school—one single room, built of half-timber, wattle, and daub. There, for three mornings each week, Vicar Mayhew would instruct the poor boys of the village, dressed in the drab grays and russets of the laboring class, in the basics of the English alphabet, the rudiments of mathematics, and a basic study of the Holy Scriptures.

He tried to instill in them a joy of the Lord, and a joy of learning, but the ground was hard and the fruit was sparse. *It is not their hearts that are small*, he reasoned, *it is their hopes. And how I feel impotent to help them.*

It was the church's own fault, the vicar mused. More than seven years ago the church had issued instructions—orders, to be precise—that all preaching should be limited to the text of the day. He could speak on the Catechism, the Creed, the Ten Commandments, and the Lord's Prayer, but that was all.

Where is my liberty? the vicar asked himself. *How can I tailor a message to these people who need so much when I am so limited?*

Even as recent as two years prior, in 1626, Parliament, nervous over religious turmoil in the land, commanded all preachers to avoid writing or speaking of controversial matters. "Discussion of such subjects does nothing but stir up the commoners," stated one lord, concerning their action.

And each spring the vicar would breathe great gulps of rain-cleansed air, filling his lungs with the newness of the season. He would hope that the air would cleanse and purify his soul as well. Then he would offer a short prayer of thanksgiving and ask the Lord's blessing on the small village. Almost unthinking, always unplanned, he would find himself asking God for a larger world in which to minister. *Lord, present to me a task that can fill me, a task that might envelop me,* he would pray silently, eyes narrowed to the view.

And every season he would turn, grasp the door's iron handle, pull it toward him, and scuttle back to the ladder, returning to the intimate darkness of the tower and the church below.

CHAPTER

2

April 1628
Hadenthorne, Devon
England

At first there was no alarm, as far as young William could discern. Her cough had begun just at the end of the cruel winter, but that was not uncommon. Homes were drafty and cold, and good nourishment was a rarity by the end of the season.

William's mother, Elizabeth Hawkes, had taken more ill than usual. She shrugged it off at first, but each day she awoke weaker and weaker. William tried to help, but the ten-year-old boy often felt as if he was in the way. He made himself busy by tending to the fire, sweeping the walk of the small half-timbered wattle-and-daub thatched cottage, fetching water—all things his mother would have done before. He stood by, feeling lost.

Women from the village came in a steady stream. The older ones brought their special concoctions, cures, family remedies, and poultices used to treat all types of ailments. A few of the younger women, Elizabeth's closest friends, came and held her hand. They fed her barley water and other herbed drinks made with borage and sea holly. The cottage smelled of wormwood and meadowsweet, which were thought to reduce fever and clear the lungs. Aromatic reed was mixed with syrup of violets to relieve the congestion.

But nothing seemed to turn the tide. Elizabeth's breathing had gone raspy and shallow.

"Mother," he asked in a mouse-soft voice, his deep blue eyes now nearing tears, "What can I do? Would you like me to get you some more of that warm drink Mrs. Rutley brought to you? I think there is some left from this morning."

Elizabeth reached over to her young son and smoothed his thatch of unruly blond hair, one small wisp always sticking up from the rest, and smiled.

"William, you are such a delight to me. Always thinking of others when you would be happier outside with your father." She smiled and lifted her head. "Perhaps you can fetch me some flowers. Are there any roses in the garden this early? It would be so terribly nice to look at a rose one more time."

It was only mid-April, William figured, who was not very keen on calendars. A rose this early would be so rare it would be a miracle. He seldom walked past the rosebushes since his mother had taken ill. They were his mother's roses, and the sight of them just reminded him of how dear they were to her.

He slipped open the rough wood door of the cottage, hurried outside, and closed the door tightly shut, keeping the chill of the April breeze outside and away from his mother. *She said "one more time,"* he thought, a sudden chill in his bones.

William knew that she was very ill, and that hope was not there. He did not despair from anything that a neighbor or villager had said— they had all done their best to keep their spirits joyful and light when visiting. But after seeing his mother's wan face through the glass, the boy suddenly knew.

He shuffled slowly to the edge of the garden nestled in a small patch of rich, black soil. Flowering plants shared this tiny plot with clumps of herbs.

Elizabeth would spend hours here, tending her flowers and roses. This was her small patch of English earth, she had said. "Vegetables are fine somewhere else, but I need my flowers for joy." Samuel would grouse and mumble, in a theatrical tone, that flowers served no useful purpose. "You can neither eat them nor wear them. So, Elizabeth, why do you spend your time with 'em? To attract the bees, perhaps?"

She would laugh and shoosh him from her patch with her small spade, and they both would laugh.

Every evening, from the earliest spring day to the latest fall afternoon, there would be flowers at the evening table. It might be roses, or asters, or pinks, or delphiniums. There was always a splash of color and a heady scent in Elizabeth's home as the three of them sat down to an evening meal of stew or vegetable soup flavored with her fresh herbs with flour biscuits or crusty bread.

William walked around to the garden, the small plot no bigger than three yards squared. *A rose,* he thought, . . . *a rose would be most unlikely. How could there be a rose so early?*

He carefully stepped between the tiny green heads of the daffodils that had just begun to peek out for the spring sunlight. He knelt down and lifted a fallen rosebush stem that must have been caught in last week's rain and wind.

She would never let this happen, William thought as he lifted the stem upright, hoping that it was merely bent, not broken.

As he lifted it, a flash of color caught his eye, lying near the earth itself. He bent down and brushed some loose soil aside. There at the end of the broken stem was a perfect red rose—small, but young and fresh.

For some in Hadenthorne, the spring of 1628 held little pleasure. It held little hope and little joy.

The dark door of the parish hall opened, and three figures slowly walked out, almost matching the rhythmic cadence of the drops of a spring mist. The small procession was led by Vicar Mayhew, followed by Samuel Hawkes and his young son, William. The two Hawkes men were dressed in their best breeches and short coats and had cleaned their boots.

The three of them walked slowly to the north end of the churchyard and stood by a fresh mound of moist, black earth.

The vicar placed his hand on the young boy's shoulder, leaned down, and whispered in his ear. Then the vicar straightened, took a small book from the folds of his cassock, flipped through the pages, and began to recite in Latin. William looked at his feet, hearing the words *spiritus* and *sanctus* and a few others that sounded familiar. The words of the vicar's recited prayer echoed off the thick stone walls of the church.

"William," said the Vicar Mayhew, "I have not always abided with the church dictums and the requirement for prayers for the dead to be in Latin. I believe our God is knowledgeable enough to understand more than just Latin. I know that we all need to hear words of comfort in a language that we can understand. William, it is true that you speak no Latin?"

William looked up and nodded silently to the vicar.

"Your mother was an extraordinary woman. Her death makes no sense to me. Perhaps, in time, God will show us why this has happened. I cannot believe that her spirit and kindness were needed more in heaven than they were in our humble little village."

William stood still, watching the vicar speak. His lower lip trembled, just slightly, and he struggled to prevent the tears from falling. His father reached over and laid his rough hand on the boy's shoulder.

"William, you have lost a loving mother," the vicar said. "Samuel, you have lost a loving wife. I know it now seems most difficult to understand, but there is a reason for her leaving us. And in time, we all will understand."

Samuel Hawkes knelt down by the mounded earth and wordlessly mouthed a prayer. After a few moments he stood and recited part of a poem that he and Elizabeth cherished.

> *Ask me no more where Jove bestows,*
> *When June is past, the fading rose;*
> *For in your beauty's orient deep*
> *These flowers, as in their causes, sleep.*
>
> *Ask me no more where those stars light*
> *That downwards fall in dead of night,*
> *For in your eyes they sit, and there*
> *Fixed become, as in their sphere.*

His son stood silently, listening and watching his father's face. William's eyes were still dry.

William's father reached into the pocket of his cloak and extracted a small golden locket on a thin rope of gold chain. His large fingers struggled with the clasp and finally popped it open. He stared at it one last time.

"William, I know that she would have wanted you to have this." He handed the small gold piece to his son.

William took it, opened the tiny clasp, and held it closer to his eye. On the right side of the locket was a small, delicate likeness of his mother, painted directly on the gold. The image was small, but it was his mother to be sure. Her long hair was curled around her throat and face, and her blue eyes were alive in the small locket.

He carefully turned it to see the back side, and on it, in the faintest of engraved lines, was the Scripture, *Be still and know that I am God, Psalm 46:10.*

He looked down at the locket and then back to the face of his father, a face grown old and sad in the afternoon mist. William snapped the locket back together gently and placed the chain over his head. The precious gold piece slipped comfortably beneath his shirt, the metal at

first cold against his skin, and then warming—heartbeat by heartbeat—
to the rhythms of the boy.

∎ ∎ ∎

Later that afternoon, William and his father sat on a rough oak bench
by the fire. It had been a very long day. Elizabeth Hawkes had been the
light of both men's lives, and in her absence the cottage had grown
thunderously quiet. Even the fire was muted. The smoke curled about
in the still air, filling the room with a thin gray wash. The mist of the
morning had given way to a gentle yet insistent rain.

They had eaten a few biscuits that morning and had some weak ale,
but now it was suppertime and both were hungry. This would be the first
test of their housekeeping skills, for up until now women from the village
had been in daily attendance, taking care of Elizabeth, and taking care
of William and Samuel as well.

Now William watched his father pour spring water into the cooking
pot, add a few whole turnips and a whole somewhat-shriveled carrot
taken from their meager store in a small cellar just near the rear edge
of the kitchen. William knew that his mother had always carefully
quartered each vegetable, allowing them to cook faster, but he recognized this as a time to be silent.

Samuel added some dried herbs and lowered the cooking pot nearer
the flames, placed the lid on, and sat back in the cottage's solitary
wooden chair. He stared at the flames as William stared at him.

After a few moments, Samuel leaned forward and placed his large,
calloused palms on the boy's shoulders. "William, 'tis you and I alone."

William nodded slightly.

"We can do this, but I know 'twill be not simple nor easy."

William nodded again.

"We'll miss her, but she would be sayin' to you that you must carry
on. You know that, do you not?"

William nodded again.

"Then 'twill be time enough tomorrow to teach you the trade of a
gamekeeper, just like me. You'll have to be makin' your way in the
world, with just me now. And that will be what you will be."

The quiet returned to the cottage. A faint hiss was emanating from
the cooking pot, the smell of vegetables filling the cottage. William's
stomach growled slightly.

And there was something else just near the edge of his awareness.
William turned and sniffed. The scent of a single red rose wafted
through the cottage, warming his heart with love.

May 1628
Hadenthorne, Devon
England

As a child, William had imagined the life of a gamekeeper for a powerful nobleman like the earl of Hadenthorne to be wonderfully exciting. His father would return at the end of a day and hang the massive musket he carried on a nail over the fireplace mantle. William would stare at the dark wood stock and iron-black barrel and flash pan. He imagined his father using the weapon to defend himself from the wild boars at the far north edge of the estate, or perhaps a wild stag charging at him through a dense thicket.

The reality of a gamekeeper's existence was much different, William discovered.

A few weeks after his mother's passing, Samuel instructed William to put on his best breeches and weskit and to clean every speck of mud from his shoes as well. It was still dawning as Samuel donned his felt hat, gathered up his son, and swung him into the saddle of the roan mare that was kept in the linhay, the small lean-to stable on the north side of their small home.

This must be a special event, William thought, for he had never dared to climb on the horse. The Suffolk horse was the earl's property, and no one could ride it except those authorized, such as his father.

Samuel walked alongside the horse, holding the reins in his heavy and practiced hands. The horse's hooves made rough scratchy sounds on the path, laid with hoggin, a mix of clay and gravel.

"Will, we are to be meetin' the master of the house this mornin'," Samuel said in a soft morning voice. "He has agreed to see if you can be learnin' the craft of bein' a gamekeeper from me. That way we can be together all the day, instead of just in the mornin's and evenin's. You would be likin' that, wouldn't you, Will?"

Will nodded swiftly. It would be a joy to be with his father.

Samuel smiled, knowing that his wife had spent long hours with the boy, instilling in him the respect of his elders and betters and instructing him how to behave civilly. She also placed a high regard for "a gentleman's tongue"—the ability to speak with the absence of the thick country accent of the western shires—and drilled the child as best she could to acquire and nurture a more refined style of speaking. Elizabeth often said, with a smile, that the mark of a good Christian was seen in their manners as well as their spirit.

"You remember what manners your mum taught you, Will?"

Will nodded. "Yes, sir. I remember."

Spring had come at last to the valley. And the rose gardens of the estate, their scarlets and vermilions and whites, stretched for miles, William thought. The explosion of hues and scents created a heady mix.

"Father," William said. "Meeting the earl will be such an honor."

His father laughed. It was not a happy laugh, but one closer to sadness. "We'll not be meetin' the earl, Will. Lord Davis would not be the one to be dealin' with the simple gamekeeper. We'll be meetin' the master of the house, the man that the earl employs to handle all the workin's of this estate. I daresay Lord Davis would be at a loss to know my name."

"But, I thought that . . . with our house on the estate . . . that being a gamekeeper was important."

"Will, it is important. A gamekeeper requires a good man—able to tend to the breedin' of the deer and foxes and quail and pheasants, to the trappin' of vermin, to keepin' poachers off the earl's property and take him and his noble friends out for the shoot. But I do not think that Lord Davis bothers himself with the smaller details. That's the job of the housemaster. That's who is important to you and me today. Now, let me help you down. 'Twill do no good if he thinks he'll be hirin' a gamekeeper apprentice who will not walk."

The housemaster was dressed in a fine green quilted velvet doublet, dazzling white linen shirt, and fine wool breeches. Each of his boots had a finely carved silver buckle.

"Mornin', sir. This be my son that I spoke to you about."

Housemaster Elger Mason pulled his shoulder back an inch or two, making himself appear even taller. He tilted his thin face back and stared down his nose at the small boy before him in his crudely made, shapeless clothing. Mason had a narrow, pinched face, with a tight, compressed mouth and lips. His dark eyes were deep set between his hawklike nose.

"Good morning, sir," William said in a bold voice.

Samuel winced and vowed to teach William that it is proper only to respond to such a superior, not initiate conversation.

Silence filled the courtyard.

After a moment or two, Mr. Mason snorted and gruffly said, "Do you think you could learn anything from your father?"

"Yes, sir. I believe I could."

"Are you prone to any sicknesses?"

"No, sir."

"You know the difference between right and wrong?"

"Yes, sir. My mother taught me about the Bible's commandments, and right and wrong."

"She did, did she?"

"Yes, sir."

"Well, you are a bit younger than I would prefer to have an apprentice gamekeeper."

William stared down at his scuffed and worn shoes.

"But as a favor to your father, I will allow you to begin to accompany him—at a reduced apprentice rate, of course."

"Thank you, sir," Samuel said quickly. "You will not be disappointed."

"See that I am not," Mr. Mason added with a sniff, and strode off toward the massive doors of the main house. He stopped, turned on his heel, and glared back at the pair.

"You realize that what I have allowed is a great gift and that anyone in your position would be most grateful for such a situation."

"Yes, sir," Samuel answered, his eyes focused on the ground.

"See that you remember who your benefactors are," Mason said in short, curt tones, and walked away.

William stared up at his father, and his father stared back down at his son. Both understood, in their own way, that this was a lesson in their social standing. William understood his father's averted face, understood that their place in the world was more common, less noble, than Will had ever imagined.

As they walked from the courtyard, the boy was silent. When they reached the dovecote, where the partridges of the estate were kept, Will looked up at his father. "Is Mr. Mason always that unpleasant?"

Samuel smiled and knelt down to William. "Actually, you met him on a particularly good day, Will. Most of the hands on the estate have stories that would make today seem as a Sunday sermon."

"Why would he be so . . . sour?"

"Will, his disposition may be caused, as I've heard rumored, by the raw lemons he eats for breakfast."

Will looked up, surprised, and saw a smile slip over his father's face. And Will struggled to hold his giggle, but couldn't help himself.

From that day on, William became a shadow to his father. Arising at the first dawning each morning, they would stoke the fire and make a small pot of porridge. They would sit in the quiet darkness, each with a steaming porringer and a few biscuits, preparing for the day.

Samuel was not an educated man, but he possessed a rudimentary ability to read. Each morning he carefully took the small bundle of papers that were stored in the uppermost cupboard near the cubbyholes by the fireplace. Samuel possessed an item of rare value—a portion of the Bible. It was a complete copy of the Psalms and much of the gospel of John. The priceless Scriptures, handwritten on thick, golden vellum, had been inherited from Elizabeth's father, William Gresham, who had cherished them as well. The words were hand-copied from one of the original manuscripts of the authorized King James version of the Scriptures from the beginning of the century. A complete Bible would have been too dear for a peasant to own.

Samuel would read a portion of a psalm, often getting no more than a few verses into it before it was time to head to the fields.

William would listen, sitting by his father's feet, as he heard God's Word. In his father's lined face he saw a man at peace, at least for a few minutes at the start of each day.

The verses completed, the sun rising, Samuel would gather up the loose pages and carefully return them to their hiding place of safety.

"Well, William, it does a man well to hear the Word of God every day, does it not?"

William always nodded vigorously.

Each day was filled with activity as Samuel struggled to impose a nobleman's order on nature's very different system of order. Encompassing more than one thousand acres, the estate would support perhaps four dozen wild doe and stags. More animals than that would increase pressure on the fields of grain and vegetables that ringed the forest and were owned by the earl as well. Rabbits were sought out as an inexpensive source of meat, but leave too many alive and one would court disaster as they ate through emerging crops or seedlings in the orchard. This day, Samuel counted four pair of foxes on the north edge of the land. That would be enough to supply the fall fox and hound games that the nobility so enjoyed. Samuel saw to it that rows of grain were left unharvested to supply food for the nesting pheasants and quail that were hunted in the fall as well.

Samuel spent long days tracking, spotting, and observing the wildlife on the estate. He knew that the earl greatly valued good hunting as well as a good yield from his fields. The gamekeeper's job was to see that neither side of the balance tipped in one direction, favoring not the hunted nor the hunter.

As summer came to Hadenthorne, William began to grasp the complexity of his father's tasks, as well as the risks.

Samuel and William had hidden most of a quiet morning in a stand of tall reeds that grew at the edge of one of the ponds that ringed the east edge of the property. They were watching several pairs of nesting geese. William watched his father peer through the thick reeds and stroke his chin.

"Well, Will, we may be havin' a few eggs for tonight's supper," he whispered.

"Eggs? How do you know that?"

"Will, you see these geese?"

"I see them," the boy answered softly.

"How many pairs have taken to nests by the ponds, do you reckon?"

William tried to count. After a moment or two, he said, "Two dozen?"

"Will, it be closer to three dozen, to be sure."

Samuel waited to see if William would speak. No answer came.

"Will, last year we had two dozen pairs nestin'. A goose means eggs to the fox, and last fall we had more than two dozen foxes in these fields. That is too many for the land to hold. 'Tis better to take their food now, so their kits will not grow up to cause the geese more problems. Understand?"

Will did not, but after a moment, he nodded.

"Will, you must always be ready to see a sign in nature. When there are too many geese, there will be too many foxes. A dry spring means fewer fish. A cool wind from the west means a storm to be brewin'. You understand all this, do you not, Will?"

Will nodded again. Some of it he did understand.

"God always portends his will for his earth through the seasons and nature. You must just look for the signs, and then you'll know what

God will be wantin' you to do. Nature is a way that God reveals his promise to his children."

"But how do you know what you are looking upon is God, or just something that . . . something that just happens?" asked the boy.

Samuel let a few moments pass as he considered his son's question. "Will, did I ever tell you of how I knew 'twas to be your mother I would marry?"

William shook his head, for he had never heard this tale from his father.

"I knew your mother since she was a babe. My family lived at one end of the village of Tawstock, and she at the other. Well, when she was of age, I had me eye set on her. She was the prettiest thing that I'd ever seen. Her voice was like . . . the song of a thrush in spring when the willows first green. I knew that we should be together. I wanted to ask for her hand, but I was full of doubt. One night I stood out in the clear dark at midnight and asked God for his help. And just as I prayed, a shootin' star sparkled in the heavens. That was God sayin' yes to my choice."

"A star said it was right?"

"Well, William, that star surely led the way. But it also helped that your mother said yes," Samuel said with a smile.

Will remembered the poem his father had spoken in his best formal voice at his mother's grave.

> *Ask me no more where those stars light*
> *That downwards fall in dead of night. . . .*

Samuel reached over and placed his arm around his son's shoulder and pulled him close. It was one of the few times he showed his affection in a physical way to his son.

On the way home, Samuel walked slower, to avoid breaking one of the dozen eggs he had collected that afternoon from as many nests.

"No sense in wastin' God's food, is there, Will?"

The next morning, following their evening feast on goose eggs, the master of the house summoned both Samuel and William.

They stood in the courtyard again as the precisely dressed Elger Mason slowly walked out from the great house, like an egret poised to spear fish in shallow waters, counting his steps, and stood before them.

"Samuel, were you at the ponds yesterday morning?" The housemaster's face was pinched and narrow.

Samuel hesitated only a second. "Yes, sir. We were."

"How many nests are there this year?" asked Mr. Mason.

"Nearly three dozen by my count."

"That may be too many. Is that correct, Samuel?"

"That is how I reckoned it."

"You'll be taking some of their eggs, won't you?"

William quickly looked up at his father. He thought he could detect the slightest flush around his ears.

"Yes, sir. We've done so already."

There was a pause. William heard a thrush cry in the distance.

"And Samuel, what happened to those eggs?"

Again, William looked up at his father. His answer came after only a breath of a delay.

"I pocketed a few, Mr. Mason, but I tripped later in the day and all were broken in my pocket. 'Twas before I had a chance to bring them here, sir."

"Slipped, did you?"

"Yes, sir." His voice was colder and firm.

"And William . . ." Mr. Mason peered around Samuel and stared down at the boy. "Your father slipped, did he?"

William did not hesitate. "Yes, sir. He slipped."

The housemaster paused and looked down at his hand and fingernails.

"And where did this tragic accident occur?" he sneered.

William looked up. "It was over by the river, near the bridge. We were looking to see if the muskrat had been burrowing by the supports and if we needed to set a snare. When we climbed back up, it was muddy, which caused my father to slip. He banged his side against his pocket with the eggs."

"By the bridge, you say?"

"Yes, sir."

William returned the housemaster's stare, moment for moment.

"Well, the two of you should be more careful." Elger Mason paused a moment. "You may go now," he said, dismissing them with an irritated wave of his hand.

Samuel reached down to place a hand on his son's shoulder, and the two turned and made their way out of the courtyard. As they neared the drawbridge, Elger Mason called after them.

"Glad to see that you cleaned your coat so well, Mr. Hawkes. And so quickly. Cleanliness is such an important virtue, don't you agree?"

"Yes, sir. It is," Samuel added without turning, and father and son slowly walked away, silent.

The senior Hawkes never mentioned the incident about the eggs again. But during the next two years, he never once stepped over the boundary of what was allowed to a gamekeeper. Every rabbit shot or snared, every egg collected, every game bird found, was dutifully and obediently brought back to the master of the house.

4

October 1630
Hadenthorne, Devon
England

Toward the middle of August most of London's titled noblemen and women left their fashionable London town houses to escape the oppressive heat of the city and headed to their country estates or the estates of friends and distant relatives. London was cramped and crowded, and many of the city's half-million people—most of them unwashed—lived shoulder to shoulder in dark hovels. The summer's sun fermented the sharp smells of so many bodies into a vast mix of unpleasantness. Sewage ran raw through the narrow streets—mere alleyways between tall buildings—and smoke poured from thousands of fires and chimneys, turning the mists of the Thames into poisonous fogs and creating a daily assault on the senses.

To occupy their time in the fresh air of the country, noble-born gentlemen sought out pleasures such as hunting and riding. Lord Davis, earl of Hadenthorne, planned his yearly foxhunt to coincide with the annual migration of noblemen from sweltering and foul summertime London to the cool and crisp air of the countryside. True, it was early into the hunting season for such an event—Michaelmas, the festival that celebrated the end of harvesting, had just passed—and some more royal of the royal class would snicker at Lord Davis's desire to have the first social gathering of the fall.

The guests would arrive at the appointed date and alight from fancy, gilded carriages, the gentlemen flamboyantly dressed in heavily brocaded doublets with slashed sleeves and elegantly cut breeches, and the ladies in elaborate layered silk gowns applied with yards of ribbon and lace. A stately doorkeeper would greet them and set out a footstool covered in fine French tapestry, on which they stepped down. A swarm of groomsmen, valets, ladies-in-waiting, and parlormaids would hover about each carriage, removing luggage and gifts. Butlers would supervise the escorting of each guest to his or her proper salon or guest room, offering relaxing drinks.

The gentlemen brought news of the continued struggles the king was having in London. King Charles—a monarch who saw kings to be divinely ordained by God—and Parliament had locked horns. They fought over the proper method of governing and the Crown's meddling in the Church of England, which itself was in turmoil between those of a more "Puritan" persuasion, who desired to maintain the spirit of the Reformation, and those who preferred practices their critics labeled a return to papism. The king's marriage to the Roman Catholic Princess Henrietta Maria of France brought widespread fear that Charles would bring back his new wife's religion.

Parliament tried to use the monarch's need for money to control his power. The Stuart king, with an air of petulance, dissolved the sitting assembly in June and determined to rule all of the Empire and the Church alone, without their help—or support. It was whispered in the halls and chambers of the empty Parliament that Charles saw himself as deputized by God to rule with complete and unquestioned power, answerable to no one but God himself.

Despite the turmoil in London over the King's arbitrary and faltering economic policies, and reports of scattered outbreaks of plague, the hunts stopped for no man. King Charles, while he may have thought highly of his own abilities, was not foolish enough to tamper with this bedrock of the nobility—the fall hunting season.

<hr />

The crest on the shining new hackney carriage was done in black, gold, and red. On a corner of the shield was drawn three gold coins and three three-masted sailing ships, reflecting the vocation of the current earl of Broadwinds, Lord Aidan Spenser. The carriage rolled to a slow stop after its journey of fifty miles from its home in the western adjacent shire of Dorset. The doorkeeper hustled to its door and opened it with a sweep. The groomsman rushed to the fine Spenser horses, taking the reins from the driver.

First out was Lord Spenser, who blinked sharply in the afternoon sun. He was not a large man, yet he possessed a regal air. People said it was his thick black hair, deep-set, penetrating hazel eyes, and strong jaw— an unusual and striking combination that commanded attention.

He turned and extended his hand back toward the door. A slim, gloved hand met his, and Lady Beatrice Spenser stepped out upon the stool and onto the drive of Hadenthorne Hall. She was an elegant beauty in a long cloak, with large radiant green eyes and a finely formed face. Her hair was pulled back with a series of green velvet bows and was plaited down her back. Almost as tall as Lord Aidan, she would be said to have a classic form—not voluptuous, but arresting. The earl's doorkeeper, groomsman, butler, valets, and maids all hesitated a moment as they saw her. Not only uncommonly beautiful, she possessed an inner grace that simply radiated from her being—and it was her soul that was most beautiful of all.

Lady Beatrice smiled at the assembled servants, who had seemed to have caught their breath in unison. She turned back to the carriage in time to watch ten-year-old Kathryne Spenser launch herself into the air from the top step of the carriage and tumble as she hit the gravel drive. She was attired as though a miniature version of her mother.

"Kathryne, must you behave as a barbarian?" Lady Beatrice whispered loudly as she helped her daughter to her feet, dusting and smoothing her elegant traveling cloak as she gently scolded.

Lord Aidan watched as the valet supervised the unloading of the luggage and trunks. Two servants had accompanied them on their journey and were helping sort out their traveling cases.

"How we need so much for such a short stay is beyond the powers of mortal man," he said quietly to the doorman, not expecting—nor receiving—an answer.

The trio made their way up the cool white stone steps of the grand entrance to Hadenthorne Hall.

Beatrice smoothed the dark curls of her daughter's hair. "Kathryne, you will try and remember all you've been taught about how a lady comports herself?"

"To say please and thank you?" asked Kathryne.

"Yes, and what else?"

"Um, not to run in the halls?"

"Yes, and what else?"

"Not to throw things out of the upper windows?"

"Kathryne, you are most impossible. I fear that I will spend a lifetime trying to tame your wildness." She smiled slightly at her daughter. "Please, just try to behave."

Kathryne looked up at her mother. "Mother, I will do my best to be proper."

Just then the young girl turned in time to see an older man in a tall, green felt hat ride up on a rough farm horse. Behind him, holding on, was a young boy, not much older than she. Their gaze met briefly.

His blue eyes were piercing, his demeanor adult. He was dressed in a plain brown belted waistcoat and breeches, which made the color of his eyes all the more noticeable. There was something about the boy, young Kathryne thought, as she struggled to define it. It was an implied promise about his bearing that she felt, more than saw or thought. It was the first time in her life that such an emotion washed over her. It was only for a moment, yet she knew—knew as certain as the sun would rise—that the young man with blue eyes felt the same thing, and that neither of them would forget this moment, this seminal awakening into adulthood.

"Mother, who might those two be?" she asked, her voice thick, almost grown. "Over there, on that chestnut horse."

Lady Beatrice looked over and casually replied, "They appear to be groundskeepers or gamekeepers, perhaps here to help with the hunt. They obviously are not guests. Come now."

Kathryne hated to take her eyes off of the young man, but she had promised her mother she would act like a lady. And she reluctantly followed her mother into Hadenthorne Hall.

■□■□■

The highlight of Lord Davis's social season was the actual hunt. At the first blush of dawn on the day of the hunt, the air about the estate was filled with the sounds of baying hounds and horses with braided manes and ribboned tails snorting in the crisp morning air. Most of the riders, intent on exhibiting good form to their companions, avoided spirits. Others, such as Lord Smithton of Sunderland Manor, chose to mount their horse fortified with as much as they could tolerate.

"'Tis a grand morning," Lord Smithton shouted. "Just be pitying the poor fox who wakes early today," he added, slurring just slightly.

Lord Smithton reigned his horse back; the horse retreated a few steps, and then the nobleman, with surprising grace, swooped down with only one foot remaining in the saddle and scooped up a full flagon of hot buttered brandy from a startled servant.

"No sense going dry on these godforsaken fields this morning," he shouted. Lord Smithton took another long swallow of the amber liquid.

Sir Thomas Brakeshire sidled his mount close by. "My lord, do be careful. We shall have a challenging ride today, and spirits have a way of making us all fools."

Just behind Lord Davis stood the master of the hunt, holding a polished gold horn. He raised it to his lips and sounded the notes that called for silence among the assembled.

The hounds would be split into small packs, making it easier to ride along the more narrow trails that ran through the oak stands on the northern edge of the estate. Each pack would be accompanied by one of three huntsmen, who had bred the hounds and who controlled them and kept them on the scent.

Early in the morning, the estate's gamekeeper—Samuel Hawkes, accompanied by his son—had gone on ahead and stopped up the holes of foxes in the hunt area. They did this to prevent the foxes, nocturnal animals, from returning to the safety of their dens.

When the hunt commenced, the master of the hunt would call out a loud "Halloo!" and riders would follow the huntsman and his hounds into a brush-filled covert in which a fox was thought to have sought refuge after finding the hole to its den stopped up. The hounds were sent in at one end of the covert and would sniff their way through it until they flushed the fox out into the open. Once the fox was spotted, the observer would shout "Tally-ho!" and the huntsman and the hounds would take off after the fox, with the riders following at a close distance.

From then on, the riders would gallop across the country at top speed, splashing through rivers and dashing across fields in pursuit of the hounds and the fox. It was hoped that the foxes, noted for their cunning, would test each rider to his fullest, heading over uneven terrain, through woods, over fences, thickets, and brush.

There was no official scoring to a foxhunt, no first place award or points scored. It was the thrill of a mass horse charge, galloping at breakneck speed down narrow trails. It was the thrill of jumps and the risks—all leading up to the delight of exchanging stories of derring-do and skill as a brandy was sipped by the evening fire.

■ ■ ■

Samuel, with Will snuggled behind, lurched off on their slow but sure-footed horse. William made sure that every fox hole he knew of was stopped up tight with a rag ball made from old wool cloth. After many minutes, William heard the horns cry in the distance and the dogs baying at a frantic pitch.

The hunt had begun.

Samuel and Will paused, dismounted, and stood in an open glen to watch the hunt.

From a distance it was great spectacle. They watched the small cavalry of riders in bloodred hunting jackets galloping across a green velvet field. Samuel smiled as he saw the pack of riders dodge right, then retreat and dodge left again. This fox was providing them with a serious test of dog and horse. He trusted that they were enjoying the challenge.

They mounted the horse and set off. The fox, well ahead of the snarling dogs, ran past and ducked under a fence and raced into the barren wheat field. Samuel, with William clinging to his back, rode up to a fence that the pack was now approaching. William wondered how many riders would leap the fence straight out and how many would ride along until a gateway was found. Most riders, despite their skill or ability, would shy from leaping a field fence. They realized there is little dignity in falling with a horse tangled beneath you. Far better to ride to a gate.

"We'll see who the skilled riders are, now won't we, Will?" Samuel remarked as they slowly rode along the fence line.

"Yes, sir," Will replied excitedly.

Out of the corner of Will's hearing there were hoofbeats, slight and echoed. It was not their own horse, to be sure, for they were making slower, quieter progress. Perhaps it was the wind, Will thought, that carried the hollow sounds along the fields.

Samuel dismounted and opened another gate that stretched between a cart path from the pasture to the edge of the wheat field. He motioned to Will to spur the horse through. Another fox den lay just over the next rise, in a rocky outcropping at the southern border of the wheat field. The area was a prime refuge for a fox. Its enemies could be seen at a distance and the wheat stubble and fallen grain supported many field mice, the fox's staple food source.

Will nicked at the horse's side. It whinnied a bit and nosed through the gate and then stopped. The horse lifted up its head and turned its great brown eyes, looking south along the rise of the pasture.

The sound of hoofbeats was clearly sharper now, but both William and Samuel knew that the riders were at least a mile or two behind them.

Samuel turned and muttered, "Gawblimey! Who in the blazes? . . ."

At the crest of the hillock at the close end of the pasture, just in front of Samuel and his son, came a crashing and roaring Lord Smithton, holding on to his horse with a fierce, drunken earnestness, his eyes unfocused, his movements unsure. It immediately appeared that the brandy was gone and the rider had little control over his mount.

"Get out of my way, you stupid git!" he shouted, waving an arm and tilting precariously to the side. "I'll be after the fox first!"

Samuel realized that Lord Smithton had not even seen William seated on the horse on the far side of the low fence. The nobleman's horse was trained well; he would jump whenever and wherever he was spurred. And Lord Smithton was spurring him directly at William.

Samuel lunged for his horse and slapped the animal as hard as he could on the haunches. The horse rose up and bolted forward, carrying William to safety. Samuel's rush stumbled him forward at the moment that the well-trained horse under Lord Smithton rose in an elegant arc over the fence. Most of Samuel had been hidden by the dense rails and vines of the fence. Samuel turned his head to see the animal and its drunken rider hurtling toward him in a chestnut-colored nightmare. The front hoof struck Samuel's forehead, and the rest of the heavy animal landed on top, dumping Lord Smithton in a collapsed heap. The horse screamed in pain, and it tumbled and rolled, then struggled to its feet, holding one foreleg dangling in the air. Great gasps of air bellowed from the horse. Lord Smithton lay to the side, moaning, his feet trying to find purchase in the damp grass. Samuel lay still, a small clot of blood appearing on his forehead, just below his hairline.

William leapt from the horse and ran to him, crying, "Father! Father!"

The boy cradled his father in his arms, struggling to lift his head to his lap.

The world had gone silent, cold, and gray. William did not hear the rest of the group as they rode to the fence line, nor did he see them as they gathered up the muddied and limp frame of Lord Smithton. William hardly noticed as they gathered round him as he stroked his father's damp hair. He only began to struggle as one of the noblemen knelt down and tried to pull William away from his lifeless father.

That is when the tears came. William's sobs echoed across the somber pastureland of Hadenthorne Hall.

▪ ▪ ▪ ▪ ▪

"It pains me, William. It is a pain I have never felt before, deep in my heart and creasing my very soul."

Vicar Mayhew stood beside William in the church graveyard and gently wrapped his arm around the boy. William stood silently, much as he had done for the last few days.

"I see no reason why your father should have been taken. But we must be assured that God knows his time."

The vicar paused. He knew full well about the cause. It was Lord Smithton, the fool, who should be here trying to comfort an orphaned twelve-year-old child. But it would do no good to harbor resentment. He knew from his past that fighting with nobility was a lost cause.

"William, you must know that God still loves you."

William stared at the freshly turned earth before him. "Thank you, Vicar. But I will speak no more of this. It is over. And I must be making my own way. What is done is done."

The village clergyman sighed. He knew the life that William faced—voluntary servitude to a farmer, no doubt, being much too young to assume the position of gamekeeper for Lord Davis and having no other training. It was a true sorrow that William had no relatives that could share the burdens of raising him.

In the hushed graveyard the rattling wheels of a carriage could be heard over the far wall of the church courtyard. A door was opened, and a horse snorted impatiently. The vicar and the young boy turned to face their visitor.

The gate opened and in marched Lord Davis, alone and most unexpected, dressed in his autumn finery, elegantly embroidered breeches and weskit. Perched on his hat was a huge white feathered plume that bobbed in the air as he walked toward them.

"Ah, the vicar . . . and the young boy. William, isn't it? Just the two I have been seeking," Lord Davis said.

The vicar's face registered surprise. "My lord, why seek us?"

Lord Davis extracted a blue velvet pouch from his topcoat. "This is from Lord Smithton. Not exactly from his own volition or generosity, but from his treasury nonetheless. It is a stipend that he has agreed to pay on a yearly basis for the care of the young boy."

Lord Davis paused and looked down at William, who returned the earl's gaze without compromise.

"After all, it was he who was partially to blame for this . . . unfortunate episode."

Partially to blame? thought the vicar with anger rising in his throat. *It was entirely his fault and totally his responsibility!*

William gritted his teeth at the reduction of the loss of his father to an "unfortunate episode."

"I cajoled him to part with such a sum for your care and upkeep," Lord Davis continued, looking directly at Will's face, finding the hardness in his blue eyes unsettling, almost unnerving. "It will do my standing in London no good to have such an incident unresolved, having occurred at my hunt and all. So I asked the master of the house who might be well suited for the task of overseeing the boy's care. And his answer was you, Vicar. He suggested that you be in charge of the boy's care. I agree that it is a capital idea. A most capital idea."

The vicar was stunned, his eyes wide. "But my lord, I have no experience as a parent. There must be other families who could use an extra pair of hands, or the extra money."

Lord Davis looked surprised that anyone would question his judgment. "Why, no, Vicar," he said slowly and deliberately. "There is no other than you who is as well suited. I believe you have an extra room in the parsonage for him?"

"But, my lord . . ."

Lord Davis cocked his head a few degrees to the right and narrowed his eyes. "And I believe that my annual tithe to the church is nearly due. I would want nothing to . . . jeopardize that gift."

Lord Davis looked first at the vicar, then his eyes swept along to the parish hall and sanctuary, and focused hard, back on the vicar. "Don't you agree, Vicar?" he said with an icy cold tone.

It was a threat, obvious and unveiled. But the vicar knew it was fruitless to argue. In the end, the only choice would be to house the lad and care for him.

The vicar looked at Lord Davis, then back to the boy. "Well, William, welcome to your new home."

In marriages and business partnerships there is a period of adjustment to be endured. The habits of one party either endear or enrage the other. It is a time of adapting and coping . . . and learning to accept.

William struggled those first few weeks of late autumn. Without parents, his life was adrift with no anchor, no cove in which to find security. *The vicar is a fine man,* William thought, *but this churchyard is no place for me.*

His last two years had been spent outdoors experiencing nature and learning from all of God's creatures. Now William spent afternoons sitting quietly as the vicar prepared his Sunday sermons or watching as the clergyman read through his library of theological tomes. William clearly felt ill at ease, the vicar noticed as he looked up from his desk in the parsonage. The house-place, the main living room in which he was studying, was the largest in the house, with wide oak floors and walls paneled halfway up to the beamed ceiling with polished oak planks and finished with white plaster. One wall of the house-place was entirely taken up with bookcases, filled with a wealth of rare and precious manuscripts and volumes, unusual for such a small parish.

The house-place was separated from the kitchen by a heck, a screen running floor to ceiling with built-in cupboards. Another heck separated the living room from the cross passage, a hall that led to two small sleeping chambers.

The boy sat on an old rough bench, his feet almost to the ground, and stared out the leaded glass window that looked out over the garden.

The vicar stopped his writing. He bowed his head and began to pray. His petitions were quiet and small. He began to ask God not for a miracle, just a direction, an open door, a path to follow with his new companion.

Dear God, I humbly beseech thee to provide a passage for young William. I am caught unawares as to how to deal with the boy. Wilt thou show me a way in which I may reach into young William?

The vicar lifted his head and asked himself, *Is this the larger task that I asked God for?*

Just then, in the silent dustiness of the house-place, a small feathery thump echoed against the leaded glass window.

William jumped up and looked outside, and the vicar rose from his desk as well. William ran to the door of the stone cottage, sprinted out to the garden, and knelt down, cupping his hands about a small tussle of feathers. He tenderly carried the small bundle into the parsonage.

"It's a Williamson thrush, Vicar," he explained. "You seldom see them this far west—and this late in the season. Mostly they like to spend time along the coast to the south. This one," Will said as he turned the still bird over in his palm, examining its markings, "being a male, must be looking for someone to . . . be with, I reckon."

"Williamson thrush, you say? I have never heard of such a species. Are you sure?"

"Sir, that I am. My father taught me."

The vicar peered down at the small, frightened creature. Tight bandings of reds and browns marked the edge of the wings and tail.

William gently extended one wing of the tiny bird, and then the other. He turned it over and felt, with a soft touch, each leg and along the ribs and breastbone. The bird's eyes were ablaze with life and fear, and its legs scrabbled in the air.

The vicar walked over to his bookshelf and slipped out a heavy volume covered in walnut-colored leather. He held it out and flipped slowly through the pages. He stopped midway through.

"Well, I'll be. It *is* a Williamson thrush."

William looked up puzzled. *Of course it is,* he thought. *What else could it be?*

The little bird began to struggle, its tiny wings pushing against Will's palm a bit, and chirped softly. William stroked its head with a thumb and walked slowly to the open door. He opened his hand and the thrush stood, perched on his palm, and flashed away, a feathered streak, into the afternoon sky.

"William, have you ever seen this book?"

"No, sir. Those books are yours. My mother used to tell me that unless invited, I was never to take from the possessions of others."

Vicar Mayhew placed the book on his desk, where it would catch the afternoon sun, and motioned for the boy to come closer to the desk.

William shuffled closer and sat in the vicar's chair. His eyes set upon a page filled with hand-colored engravings of dozens of species of English thrushes. His eyes widened. He extended a hand and with the utmost care and deliberateness, touched the page before him, gently stroking the artist's creations.

William was dumbfounded at the images that fluttered before his eyes.

The vicar turned a page to an explosion of starlings. The next page was hawks, then ospreys, then great sea birds.

William's jaw was open in amazement.

"My boy, do you know what this means, the writing under each plate?"

"I know they are letters, but my father never came to show me what they all meant." He turned the next page and saw a clutch of nesting geese and swans. "Vicar, could you show me what these letters might mean? I would like to know all the proper names of these birds."

"Why, of course I will show you, William," said Vicar Mayhew, and he pulled up a bench and sat down beside Will in the old wood chair, marveling at the God who used a tiny thrush to show him the path.

December 1630
Hadenthorne, Devon
England

By the time the fields had been gleaned that fall and the first light frost visited the hills around Taw Valley, William had learned more than most villagers would learn in a lifetime. He knew the alphabet, numbers to the century mark, and he was practicing at making the letters that spelled out his name.

Thomas was amazed. In such a short time William had swallowed a vast amount of complex knowledge and was using it to interpret and acquire more. The vicar had spelled out words on the slate writing tablet of the parish school, and William, with a slow and careful hand, copied each word, sounding it out as he wrote.

On this evening, William sat with his back to the fire, as his father had done, and tried to read through the vellum copy of Psalms. The crackling blaze jumped and flashed, shadows dancing across the page.

"William, do you have in those Scriptures a copy of the Sixty-First Psalm? It has always been one of my favorites. Do you think you may be able to reckon a few of the words?"

The boy moved closer to the tallow candles burning on the mantle and carefully thumbed through the pages. He found the number sixty-one, written in an elegant script.

In a halting voice he began to read, pointing out the letters with a small wooden fescue as his lips formed their sounds: "Hear my cry, O God: Attend to my prayer. From the ends of the earth I will cry to you. When my heart is over . . . over . . ."

"The word is *overwhelmed*, William. It means being swamped by your problems."

The boy continued: "When my heart is overwhelmed; Lead me to the rock that is higher than I. For you have been a shelter for me. A strong tower from the enemy. I will abide in your tab . . . tab . . . taber . . ."

"*Tabernacle*. It means temple or church," said the vicar.

"Tabernacle forever. I will trust in the shelter of your wings."

"Thank you, William. You have done well."

"But, Vicar, there is more to this part. Should I not read it?"

"Shall I read it again, then?"

"Yes, that would be lovely."

And William spoke the words firmly, with more assurance, and the vicar closed his eyes and marveled at the security of God's Word.

CHAPTER

5

May 1631
Broadwinds, Dorset
England

The spring brought little relief to the sufferings of most of the farmers around the Broadwinds estate, the home of Lord Aidan, his wife, Lady Beatrice, and their daughter, Kathryne. The noble family, of course, was well insulated. Vast stores of flour, parsnips, peas, turnips, barley, fruit, salted fish, smoked venison, hams, beef, cheeses, and pickled vegetables were laid up in the cool, dark larders of the estate.

The summer prior was dry, and what rain fell did so in great gusts filled with hailstones. Field after field of wheat lay rotting in the sun, broken at the stems by the weather. Much of the barley crop was afflicted with a blight that no one seemed able to stem. Turnip fields had produced only a portion of the normal yield. Most farmers went about their spring plantings with an air of desperation and panic. The skies were filled with troubling portents. Rains came heavy, washing seed away, or not at all, baking the seed until the sprouts withered and died.

For Kathryne, her family, and the staff at Broadwinds, life proceeded as always. In fact, Lord Aidan had turned a great profit by anticipating some of the problems and purchasing a great amount of animal feed, which he sold at healthy profits to farmers and other estate owners with shorter foresight.

Kathryne accompanied her mother in the Spenser carriage to the small village by the estate to supervise the production of new plush draperies for the great dining chamber of the manor. On this trip, even the normally talkative Mr. Biesty, their driver, rode silent as they passed by children with gaunt hollow faces and farmers scratching raw dirt in barren fields.

Lady Beatrice quickly concluded her business with her draperess, who was subdued and quiet. They hurried home, and Kathryne could hear her mother's voice, pinched and taut, as she spoke with her father behind a closed door of the library.

Lady Beatrice swung open the door, took Kathryne by the hand, and strode off toward the basement and the vast kitchens. She called out for Mr. Biesty, and within minutes he had his arms laden with smoked beef, flour, salted fish, and a heavy wheel of yellow cheese.

"You will come with me now, Kathryne," Lady Beatrice announced. "You will learn what God calls us to do."

They returned to the village and rapped on the door of the parsonage. The elderly Parson Pensworth opened the door and was properly shocked to see Lady Beatrice standing there with her driver behind with a carriageload of food.

"Reverend Pensworth, I have brought some of our provisions. Would you be kind enough to tell us which families are in the most dire circumstances?"

The parson sputtered and scratched his head, withdrew into the parsonage, came back with his wide-brimmed black hat, and simply said, "Follow me."

The four of them with armloads of food walked down the dusty streets of the village, tapping first at this door, then another, leaving behind a few pounds of beef, or a thick slice of cheese, or a portion of flour. Each gift was met with a stunned silence by the recipient.

On their way home after all the foodstuffs had been distributed, Lady Beatrice turned to Kathryne, who had said nary a word the entire day. "Kathryne, do you know what we did today?"

"Yes, Mama. We gave food to poor people who were hungry."

Lady Beatrice patted her daughter's head. "It was more than that, my dear child. 'And he said unto him, Lord, thou knowest all things; thou knowest that I love thee. Jesus saith unto him, Feed my sheep.' That is from the Gospel of Saint John, my child. It is what we are commanded to do. It is what we must do if we are to be called children of the living God."

"Even if we thought ahead, as Papa said, and the others did not?"

"Our Lord has used us to help those poor people. It makes no difference who thought in advance and who did not. You remember these acts of service, Kathryne. This is how a follower of the Almighty comports herself. Will you remember, child?"

Kathryne nodded enthusiastically, her dark curls dancing in youthful agreement. "I will remember, Mama. I promise."

CHAPTER

6

June 1632
Hadenthorne, Devon
England

Hadenthorne had been blessedly spared much of the pain that other villages suffered due to the famine. The local farmers had sufficient harvests, and while no one was boasting, few went to bed with empty stomachs.

As summer approached, most of the dozen boys in the vicar's school began to get restless and edgy. In a week school would be over for another year, and the vicar looked toward that date, as did most of his charges, who were there only out of pressure from their families who saw education as a means of eventually adding to their social and perhaps financial level as well.

All except William. He devoured as much knowledge as the vicar could feed him, thirsting and hungering for more. He had quickly mastered the alphabet, reading, and basic mathematics. He was now learning Latin and French, as well as the components of more advanced mathematics.

Will had turned fourteen that spring. The stipend from Lord Smithton provided him the luxury of not requiring additional funds, but being slothful was not of Will's nature. His mother had taught him the Puritan doctrine that labor was a duty to God, to one's family, to one's neighbor, and to society. So William hired himself out for a time each spring and summer to the Cavendish farm. He drove the horse-drawn harrow to break the clods of earth. He tilled the fields with a rough plow and stubborn oxen, enjoying the constant struggle of keeping the furrows straight and consistent. He weeded and tended the crops. The few coins he was paid for his help amounted to little, but Will was adamant in providing a portion of his own support.

William grew and learned and worked, yet he nurtured a small bitter streak in him. The vicar saw it grow as well, and it pained him.

"It was not right what that drunken nobleman did to my father. How could Lord Davis put a price on the value of a man's life?" Will often asked the vicar. Vicar Mayhew would always turn him to the Scriptures, trying to diffuse the boy's anger.

Even during the summer months, when farm work went on from first light to dusk, William found time to read from the vicar's—and the church's—library. He continued to make strides in all forms of learning, and the vicar considered himself a privileged teacher to have such a willing and rapt student.

It was unfortunate, the vicar mused, that such a sharp mind would be wasted in Hadenthorne. Oxford, Cambridge, and the rest of the English institutions of advanced studies would never allow a boy from such humble beginnings in attendance.

CHAPTER

7

November 1633
Broadwinds, Dorset
England

Kathryne Spenser stepped into the warm kitchen of Broadwinds, the cold breeze making her cheeks glow a light crimson. Her eyes were sparkling as well, deep green eyes set off by a graceful nose. On her lips, reddened by the cold, was a hint of the fullness they would possess as she matured.

"Take care, Kathryne. Stand aside," Mrs. Cole called as she made her way past from the scullery, where she had been overseeing the peeling of carrots, to the kitchen. With a *humph*, the scullery maid hoisted up a large tub of naked carrots to the table, sloshing a little water on the surface. Kathryne edged sideways, smiling.

"Are there any early treats before dinner?" Kathryne asked, happy to be in the large kitchen, filled with steam, scents, and activity. "Perhaps a flannel cake with cream—or a treacle sponge?"

Mrs. Cole turned to the girl with an expression of disapproval on her face. "They'll be no desserts before dinner, child. Not while I am in charge of the meals here."

Kathryne sidled up next to her and gave her a hug. "Not a crumb?"

"None. Now whoosh! You need to be washin' for dinner. It looks that you've been on a ramble and brought half the forest back with you. And out and about with your mother as ill as she is. And you shouldn't be disobeyin' the constable's decree to refrain from needless conversin', with the danger of spreadin' the plague about and all."

There was no other servant in the entire house who would speak as plainly and boldly as Mrs. Cole. For that, both mother and daughter loved her all the more.

"Now get up to see her. The surgeon has been with her all afternoon, though I do not trust that man one mite."

"The surgeon is here?" Kathryne asked, more alarmed. She tore up the stairs, discarding her heavy wool coat and leather gloves as she went.

As she rounded the first landing, she stopped a few steps short of the top. At the door to her mother's bedchamber stood her father, speaking in low tones to two others in a tight, confidential circle. She could smell the faint aroma of hyssop. Kathryne recognized Mrs. Deems as a woman from the village who dealt in herbs and cures, and the other was Mr. Acton Curvet, the surgeon and dentist from the village. When Kathryne stopped, they all turned to stare at her. Her father motioned her to come to him.

"She is asking to see you, Kathryne," Lord Aidan told his daughter as he opened the door to the dimly lit bedchamber. Kathryne slipped in, almost on tiptoe, and walked to the bed. Her mother lay still on the soft feather mattress, her head resting on a large bolster. A chambermaid was at her side, smoothing the crisp linen sheeting as she sat silently by.

"Daughter, is that you?" Lady Beatrice whispered weakly.

"Yes," Kathryne said, and stood near the dark carved-oak footboard.

"I seem to be at the bottom of my strength, dear Kathryne, and there are so many in the village that depend on me. I have asked your father and will now ask you—will you see to it that my promises are fulfilled?"

Kathryne nodded.

"Daughter, will you take my hand and sit with me a while?"

"Mama, will you be well soon? I do not like having you away from me."

"Kathryne," she said as she struggled to sit upright, "I will always be near you. And I believe that I will be well very soon."

Kathryne hugged her tenderly, and she felt the weakness in her mother's arms as they enfolded her. She sat on the large bed through that evening, finding sleep near the stroke of midnight.

Lord Aidan and a nursemaid came in and carried the sleeping child to her own bedchamber. When they returned, Lady Beatrice had slipped from the world, quiet and alone.

She was laid to rest under a beautifully carved stone tablet at a place of honor in the parish church. Kathryne refused to cry until that final moment, and when it came, she found she was unable to let a tear form in her eyes. The young girl stood at the graveside in the church, next to her father, her mouth pursed in pain, her eyes narrow slits, as she watched the coffin lowered into the cold, lonely dark.

Kathryne recalled the last words that her mother had spoken to her. "Could you read this, Daughter?"

She had pointed to Psalm 23, which Kathryne had read with a clear voice, breaking and halting only at the final few words. "Surely goodness and mercy shall follow me all the days of my life: and I will dwell in the house of the Lord for ever."

CHAPTER

8

November 1634
Hadenthorne, Devon
England

Will, now sixteen years old, was busy at the vicar's desk. It was piled high with books and papers. He had two books open; one a Latin text, the other a new English translation. The work was by the Roman historian Tacitus.

"Vicar, there appears to be some mistake in this new version. A whole paragraph has been omitted."

"William, there is another volume that references this material. I believe it is near the top shelf in the far corner . . . up there," he said, pointing to the uppermost shelf.

Even William could not reach it, and for that reason most of the books there were seldom, if ever used. He pulled a small stool in from the kitchen and, stretching, he pulled several books down.

"That's the one William, in the red cover."

As William returned the others to the shelf, he noticed behind the stack of books a brass object. William thought it odd that he had never noticed it before. Standing as tall as he could, he reached, his fingers barely managing to find purchase on the item. He carefully extracted it and brought it down. It was a triangular-shaped instrument, with an eyepiece mounted on a short tube and a compass with a swing line that acted as a marker along a scribed rule. There were two small mirrors that pivoted, and a set of degrees were marked along the curved bottom limb.

"Vicar, what might this be?"

Thomas looked up from the red volume, and his face broke into a broad smile.

"Well, I'll be. . . . I thought it had been forever lost. It must have been behind those books from the day I arrived at Hadenthorne and St. Jerome's."

"But what is it?"

"That, William, is a device that will allow you never to be lost."

"How does it work?"

"It is a sextant, a sailor's tool for discovering latitude, the distance north or south from the equator. It is most indispensable."

"How do you happen to have a sailor's tool?" William asked, curious as to this previously unknown aspect of the vicar's past.

"Well, my boy, in my youth, I managed to spend some time sailing the English Sea. My uncle was a fisherman in Peacehaven, as is my brother now, and I oft accompanied him out on his boat. It is through him that I learned of the use of such a device. It prevents us from being lost—in a physical sense, that is.

"Just as this will keep a sailor from physical danger, so is it that the *Holy Bible* will prevent us from running aground on spiritual reefs and shoals," the vicar said, as if delivering a sermon. "The sextant depends on the sun for guidance, just as we depend on God for guidance. But our spiritual sextant, the Holy Scriptures, works both day and night. It is always there to give direction."

The vicar turned to face William.

"Do you understand?"

"Oh yes, sir. It is most clear."

And waiting a moment, William, holding the sextant, politely asked, "Vicar, would it be possible to instruct me as to the proper workings of this sextant?"

"Of course, William," he said. "I would be most happy to." The vicar pointed to the small compass built into the base of the sextant. "It points to the true direction of north. No matter where you are in the world, the compass will point north for you, which will allow you to fix your position."

"Always?" Will asked.

"Yes, always."

A moment passed. "What makes it do that?" asked Will.

"It is attracted by magnetic forces that cause it to point that way, William. I am afraid that I know little more of the science of compasses than these few facts. But I trust it to be always so."

Will sat and stared at the arrow.

"It is something like our life as a believer in God. He is our compass, William." And as the vicar began speaking, he noticed for the first time a slight change in William's face, as if he stopped listening in these moments. The vicar proceeded, undaunted. "And if we trust in God and his provision, we will always be pointed in the right direction. Do you understand, Will?"

Will sighed. "Yes, sir. I understand." He sat at the table, staring at the compass, turning the sextant over in his hand. After several moments, he asked, "Sir, is your brother still alive?"

Do I look that old? the vicar thought.

"Yes he is, William. He is only a few years older than I, after all."

Without looking at the vicar, keeping his eyes on the sextant, Will struggled with his thoughts. "Does he still live near the sea?"

"Yes he does, William. A few days' ride from here. His home is on the east side of Brighton by the Sea."

William turned the sextant over again to look at the compass. Trying not to betray his growing excitement, William asked, "Does he still have a boat?"

"I believe that Barnaby still has a longboat."

And in a moment of clarity, the vicar realized the reason for William's questions. The vicar could not help William experience the sea, but his brother might.

Thomas closed his eyes for a moment and tried to remember the first time he had seen the ocean, the first time he set out in a small boat, the first time he felt the salt spray wash over him and cleanse him from the cares left on the shore. William knew nothing of the sea, other than what could be read of it in books. But those small words were a pale comparison to the reality of the waves and surf and sea-tinted skies.

The vicar leaned forward and put his hand on Will's shoulder. "Would you like to visit my brother in Peacehaven, William?"

Will's eyes opened wide, his features bright and lit with expectations. "Oh, yes, Vicar. That would be most glorious!"

"Well then, perhaps we can arrange it to be so."

"Would I be able to sail with him?"

"You would, William, but we will not undertake such a journey until spring. The waters would be too cold for an enjoyable sail this chilled season. And I must teach you how to navigate with a sextant and a map before I send you out on the wild waters of the English Sea."

William's face fell a bit, then grew studious. "Spring is only four months hence, is it not, sir?"

"Perhaps five, William."

"Does it take long to learn the sextant, sir?"

"In five months, you shall be expert with it."

CHAPTER

9

April 1635
The South Downs, Sussex
England

It was April, when the chaffinch began to sing for their paramours and the bramley apple trees in the valley began to bud with glorious pinks and whites. The vicar had sent word to his brother and his wife in Peacehaven, alerting them that he and his young charge would be journeying to meet them in the second week of the month.

It was noon as the pair climbed the last small hill of the windswept South Downs that stood between them and the waters of the English Sea. The vicar stopped and pointed into the distance to the band of blue-gray sea that slipped away from the land, no more than a mile distant. Will looked obediently to the south, following the vicar's pointed finger.

"That, my son, is the sea."

At first Will was simply puzzled, then a beguiled expression slipped across his face.

"Breathe deep, William."

Will filled his lungs with as much air as he could.

"It is the sea air that fills your lungs. There is no scent or aroma as sweet as this. I have forgotten how intoxicating it can be—and how much I regret not living near it," the vicar said, a hint of sadness in his voice. "Did you know they call the English Sea 'The Sleeve,' Will?"

"Why would they call it that?"

"From the French *la Manche,* because its shape resembles a sleeve."

The vicar put his finger to his mouth, calling for silence. "Can you hear it, William?"

Will nodded with enthusiasm.

In the distance both could hear the rumbling, echoing crashes of water to shore, the faint hiss of the waves, pierced occasionally with the call of the gulls.

"Let's find my brother's home."

Within the hour, they came upon a sturdy whitewashed, stone-built cottage with a roof made up of interlocking and curved red tiles. The door was painted a most pleasing shade of blue—the color of a robin's egg, Will thought. One wall, away from the sea, consisted almost entirely of a massive chimney, covered with vines. The cottage was no bigger than the parsonage, but looked stronger, more solid and permanent. It sat upon a small bluff, no more than two hundred yards from the rumbling surf, as if daring the sea to sweep it away, yet knowing that the sea would be unable to accomplish such a foolish task. Hung on a wooden post at the end of the walk was a small weathered plaque that read: BARNABY P. MAYHEW.

When the vicar knocked on the door, it swung open, and a hand shot out, grasped the vicar's arm, and pulled him inside with delight.

"As I live and breathe! It's Thomas!" Barnaby shouted and grabbed him about the waist in a bear hug.

Mary, Barnaby's wife, stood off in the corner in her apron, laughing in agreement.

"It has been too long, little brother. How grateful I am that you visited," Barnaby said affectionately.

And then he peered at the open doorway at William, who shied back at the welcome. Barnaby bent at the waist, his thick arms held cocked at his sides, his head tilted so his left eye came close to Will's face.

"And who might this be?"

"William Hawkes, sir," Will said, and stuck out his hand straight and long.

Barnaby grasped his hand, engulfing it, and pumped it vigorously.

"Welcome to the sea, Will. I understand that you've become an expert navigator with never havin' seen the sea."

"I do know how to use the sextant, sir. The vicar taught me."

Barnaby knelt in front of the boy.

"And I will teach you how to sail. However, I have one important task to accomplish first, and that is our midday meal. Mary has been cookin' all day. Come, come, both of you. Sit with us and tell us of the journey here."

By midafternoon, the meal was over and conversation had lulled a bit. Barnaby banged on the wooden table, causing cups and plates to rattle in place, and crumbs were set to dancing.

"Will, are you ready? Are you ready to take to the sea? The tide has slipped out though, so we'll have to do a wee bit of draggin'. You up for haulin' the boat along the sand?"

Will and Barnaby stripped down to their breeches, shirts, and caps, and Thomas helped them pull the old longboat from its mooring a few feet above the high water mark. As it first slid into the calmer waves of low tide, Will jumped up and over into the boat. Barnaby was at the stern, pushing into the surf until he could clamber aboard. The vicar, now in the water to his knees, gave one last hardy shove, and the small boat was afloat, oars pulling against the wind.

The vicar retreated to the shore, the water just lapping at his boots.

"You'll not be sailin' with us, then, Thomas?" called Barnaby.

"Not this time," Thomas called back. "I think William would best learn from a skilled sailor. Teach him well, Barnaby. Teach him well."

Barnaby waved, then returned to pulling on the oars, taking them beyond the unsettled waters of the shore and into the deeper water of the sea. They were perhaps two hundred yards into the water when Barnaby pulled on the ropes and raised the small sail. The wind listed the boat a few degrees, and the small craft took off like a dolphin. Thomas stood at the very edge of the sea, just beyond the lap of the small waves, and watched Will's face. That Thomas could see his smile from such a distance meant that the smile was a broad one indeed.

Barnaby pulled on the tiller, and the boat righted, then listed to the opposite side and continued to speed over the waters.

Thomas stood at the shore for a few more moments, happy for Will's experience. Then he turned slowly and made his way back to the cottage overlooking the waves.

Thomas and William stayed with Barnaby and Mary for almost four weeks. Barnaby and William would daily spend several hours sailing. One day, after many afternoons on the water, Barnaby looked fatigued. He helped William launch the boat and then set him free on the waters, with a hull full of admonitions and warnings.

William returned home, just as the sun settled over the western hills. He pulled and tugged the boat to its mooring and entered the house, looking burnished by the sun and most enthusiastically alive.

That night, he fell asleep quickly, almost during supper. Thomas helped him to bed and returned to share a small drop of port with his brother.

"Thomas, that is a remarkable lad you're helpin' raise."

"I realized that as well, Barnaby. He learns so quickly and almost without effort. His grasp of difficult subjects and arcane concepts is amazing."

Barnaby scratched at his whiskers. "Book learnin' is not what I was speakin' of. It is his freedom on the water. I have sailed with many a man, but I daresay I have not seen one that is more comfortable on the waves than William. He is a pure, natural-born sailor, Thomas. I swear to you that he knows more of the sextant and mappin' than I, and he simply knows when it is right to tack with the wind and when it is not. I have never seen that before, Thomas, never in all my days of sailin', to be God's truth. It is as if the sea talks to him, and he listens in a language I have not yet heard."

Barnaby took a long sip at the sweet, thick port. The wind whistled through the small leaded panes of the cottage windows, the candles' light flickering over his weathered face in the draft. "'Tis a shame he cannot return to the sea—Hadenthorne being such a distance and all. Any idea of what might become of him as he grows?"

Thomas looked uncomfortable, a little uneasy.

The lad does have a way of filling a room. I did not know I was lonely before he came—but I was, Thomas thought with affection.

"Could he be a sailor?" Barnaby asked again.

Thomas shook his head to clear the reverie. "I doubt that, Barnaby. He will have little means to do so, and the British navy is too harsh and inhospitable for any man with a soul. I know the navy would devour William in a single gulp."

Thomas paused and rubbed his hands down along his face, suddenly growing tired in the evening's dark. "I would imagine that he will stay in Hadenthorne and tenant farm for Lord Davis, perhaps buying a small plot of his own someday."

"A farmer," Barnaby snorted. "Such a waste of a boy born to the water."

Thomas sat silent. *Perhaps he is right,* Thomas thought with a tinge of sadness, *but I do not want to lose him just yet.*

CHAPTER

10

April 1636
Hadenthorne, Devon
England

"Vicar, may I ask you a favor?" William spoke over a steaming tankard of warm cider.

Both he and the boy had sat down to their breakfast, prepared by Mrs. Cavendish. She had been hired by the church less than a year previous, following the death of her husband, to do the cooking and help with the laundry and other household chores.

"Yes, William, what favor would you be needing from me?"

It had been five-and-a-half years since William first stepped through the door of the parsonage, and a lifetime of learning and experiences had occurred in that short span. William was indeed very skilled in learning; his Latin, French, and even Spanish would be the envy of most native speakers. His writing was fluid, and his knowledge of mathematics surpassed that of the vicar. William had decoded even the most complex arithmetic formulas relating to trigonometry, astronomy, and navigation. William learned about the Scriptures from his patient teacher as well. It was true that he knew the location of many verses, the meaning of each, their importance to believers. But in all this, he never once accepted the truth of the almighty God and his gift of salvation into his heart. There was a bitter wall there, the vicar imagined. It was first built by the two tragedies of the deaths of his mother and father. The divide was widened by an unsympathetic, rigid class system that worked to deny any future for a poor boy like William.

But as much as the vicar tried, William would not move a single stone of the wall around his heart. The vicar prayed every night for a softening, but saw no sign of such. Despite his unwillingness to yield to the Almighty, William, at eighteen, had grown to be a kind, gentle, and generous young man, willing to help those in need for the sheer pleasure of being able to. He possessed the boldest of natures, yet the most important attribute—knowing God—was absent.

Will sat at the table, a strange look of distance on his face, and stared at the vicar, his teacher and now his friend.

"Vicar, you know that I will be eternally grateful to you for all your love, care, instruction . . . for everything you have meant to me over the years."

It was the beginning of a conversation the vicar had anticipated for months now and had dreaded for a much longer time.

"I cannot see myself entering the way of the cloth, even though I believe that is the path you would prefer for me," William said. The vicar let a mask of pain slip over his face. William saw it, but continued nonetheless. "My heart will not allow me to live a facade. Nor can I become a farmer. My mind would surely rebel."

William swirled the last of the cider in his tankard. "I want you to ask Lord Davis, the Earl of Hadenthorne, for an extraordinary favor."

The vicar braced himself. Even with a nobleman's introduction, gaining entrance to any college would surely be no more than a dream.

"Vicar, if you would, ask Lord Davis for a letter . . . recommending me. I know that Sir Edmond from Plymouth is his friend, and I am sure that there are connections that can be exploited."

The vicar was confused. *Oxford is not near Plymouth. Sir Edmond is not associated with any college I am aware of. What could William want?*

"Sir, a letter from Lord Davis would be of most import." William paused, and his large blue eyes locked into the eyes of the vicar. "I would like to gain a posting with the British navy, with your kind prayers and blessing, if it is to be so."

"But, little Will, you canna leave Hadenthorne! This be your home. It be where your sainted mum is buried. You canna leave us. 'Twould be wrong for you to go."

William put his arm around Mrs. Cavendish and held her tight. "Mrs. Cavendish, I don't want to be leaving you, or Thomas, or Dugald or Philip . . . or anyone that I count on as my family. I do not desire it—but I must."

"But, Will, this be your home. How can you reckon leavin' is good?"

William turned and put both hands on the bulky shoulders of Mrs. Cavendish and steered her into the big wood and leather chair that the vicar had placed near the fire.

Tears had come easily as she considered the loss of William's presence in her life. "Will, you're such a bright lad, and such a help round the farm. I dunno if we can do it without you."

"Mrs. Cavendish, you have three healthy sons to run the farm. They do all the work. I have just been glad that you've allowed me a time to help out and earn a few shillings in the arrangement."

She sniffed loudly, pulled a damp kitchen cloth from a fold in her apron, and wiped her face with one swoop. "But, Will . . . ," is all she could get out before she burst into sobs again and buried her face in the cloth.

William stood by her and patted her shoulder. He looked over at the vicar with a look of panic on his face. He mouthed the words, "What do I do?"

The vicar rose from his seat at the dining table and walked over to the pair and spoke softly into Will's ear. "William, she is grieved. She is losing a boy she loves as much as her own sons."

Mrs. Cavendish sobbed even louder, as if agreement with the vicar's hushed words.

"Do not think you can leave this town untouched." And with that, the vicar turned and walked out, his hand reaching for his handkerchief to catch his own sudden and unexpected tears.

William stared after the vicar, and then down at Mrs. Cavendish, who continued to weep copiously. He stared up at the heavens and shook his head, bewildered.

Broadwinds, Dorset
England

"But Papa, I do not want to stay here. Staying here means I will stop growing. I will be sixteen in September, and I want to go to London to Lady Emily's school—the one for young ladies of the peerage—where I can study and learn of the classics, of science, of languages. I do not see why you say no. Why can I not go for just a year?"

Lord Aidan Spenser, face reddening, stood in the doorway of his daughter's bedchamber, glaring at his daughter. "My dear Kathryne, we have discussed this before, and I will not tolerate one more interminable discussion about it again. You are not going to any school this autumn. The entire idea of you leaving home for three years is preposterous!"

Kathryne stared back, green eyes blazing, mouth on the verge of trembling, fists clenched. A tear seeped from Kathryne's eye and glistened down her cheek.

Lord Aidan had more pressing business matters to attend to this day, and he was anxious to settle this aggravation with Kathryne. He had used some of the family wealth to finance several shipping concerns, each netting tidy profits. He owned a part of several trading ships, some sailing to India, where in the English colonies of Bengal and Madras the East India Company employed local women to make cotton cloth for export; some to China, where silk was woven and tea and spices were grown for export; and some to the West Indies, where tobacco and cocoa were produced. The risks were high, for pirates and storms often ate into the profits, but under Lord Aidan's guidance Broadwinds was financially sound, its future bright.

"My dear Kathryne, I will not have these tears! I insist that you remain calm!"

Kathryne's shoulders slumped and she fell, in a heap, on the massive canopied bed. "It is not fair, Papa. I want to learn of the great wide world outside Broadwinds," she cried between sobs, "and you will not let me." She lifted up her head, her cheeks wet with tears, and looked at her father standing above her.

"Daughter, I do not understand you. It is not a thing that a proper noble lady does—going to school—even such a thing as a . . . a . . . finishing school. You have had adequate tutoring here at Broadwinds. What will you do with anything that you learn there? A wife needs only to know how to meet the needs of her husband and tend to the raising of her children. What good will such schooling do you as a nobleman's wife?"

She broke into another chorus of sobs.

At that, Lord Aidan stopped, stared, and after a long moment, reached over and took her hand. "It is such a start to look into your face, my poppet. As you grow, everyday I see the face of your mother reflected in your image. It is as if she were here with me again—in you."

Kathryne continued to sniffle softly, her tears drying.

"It makes it so very difficult to argue with you. It is to her that I would be saying no."

Kathryne reached over and wrapped her arms about her father and hugged him tight. "I am sorry for causing you pain, darling Papa. I know I am headstrong." Kathryne sniffed once. "And I will do whatever it is you wish."

She leaned back and watched her father's face, then looked down at her folded hands, lying quietly in her lap.

"When did you say this school was to begin?"

Before she looked up, she hid all traces of the smile that edged at the corners of her mouth.

Hadenthorne, Devon
England

A light spring rain had drifted into Taw Valley, and as the last drops fell, the sun reappeared. The new greens and early flowers were so dazzling as to be blinding. The population had seen little color all winter, and when the crocuses broke through, it was as if their eyes had become unable to process the hues. There was a slight sense of delirium as the farmers set out to the fields and women set to cleaning. Shutters and doors were sprung open after months of shielding the cold and gray, and bedding was aired in the fresh breezes.

Will stood with his backside to the fire, warming his hands. His cup of ale and a biscuit were balanced on the rough oak beam that served as the mantle.

"I don't want to hurt anyone," Will explained, "but allow me to explain. Last fall as I tended the field out by the manor road, I watched as carriage after carriage drove along heading to the manor house for the hunt, and my soul started to stir. At first I was just angry—angry at the rich and their privileges and how they get the cream of everything and leave the dregs for the rest."

"William," cautioned the vicar, "remember what we spoke of in Paul's letter to the church at Philippi? He had found contentment with having nothing because God gave him the strength."

"Vicar, I understand those verses. And I am content. But I do not think that God has concern for my specific problem."

The vicar winced a bit, then added, "But, William, he does."

William looked off into the distance, out the window, and looked down the valley, south, towards the sea. "Perhaps he does, Thomas. Perhaps he does. And I also saw the young brother of the lord of Broadwinds—Radford, no, *Radcliffe* is his name—as he stopped at the smithy for care of his horse on his way to Bristol from Falmouth. He must be no more than a few years older than I, and already I have heard that he has been to India on Lord Spenser's ships. India! Can you imagine that?"

"And where might India be, Will? Is that very far from here?" Mrs. Cavendish asked.

"It's a journey around the tip of Africa and the Cape of Good Hope and past Arabia and . . ." William's voice faded off as he began to imagine what wonders he might see there, what worlds lay beyond the hills of Taw Valley.

"Mrs. Cavendish," the vicar answered, "India is a journey of several months' time—each way. When one journeys there, one prepares for every season."

"A year!" she wailed. "We would not see you for a year?"

Will stepped towards Mrs. Cavendish and put his hand gently on her shoulder. "And he's been to Gibraltar and through the Mediterranean!" William added. "He spoke of traveling to the Americas and to the West Indies in the Caribbean Sea, as well."

"Are any of those places a year away too?" moaned Mrs. Cavendish.

"William, I do not blame you for at times being in a frustrated state. It is not easy to be alone, although I hope that you have felt as if this poor parsonage has been your home."

"Vicar, you have been most kind and gracious to me. My heart does call this home. And it always will, most likely."

Vicar Mayhew smiled.

"But I want to make something of my life. And with the new ship money tax, King Charles will be building up the Royal Navy, and I want to be a part of it."

"William, with your knowledge and abilities, there are other things that you could do that are less drastic than signing up with His Majesty's navy."

"Vicar, with all due respect, what might those be?"

"You could stay with us on the farm," sniffed Mrs. Cavendish. "We could be makin' you part of the dividin' of things, as a partner with the land, as we are. We would do that for you, Will. And then there be Missy Holender. I hear that she was askin' 'bout you at the last market."

Will smiled back tenderly. He realized that she was seriously talking about dividing her most prized possessions—the bit of land and the farm—with a person who shared no blood with the family line. It was tantamount to giving away a birthright, a yeoman bestowing a rare privilege on a lowly born, landless cottager. It would be an immense sacrifice. And he knew Missy would be a rare privilege as well. She was the fine-boned daughter of Eugene Holender, the freeholder of a large farm a few minutes' walk to the west. Missy was perhaps the prettiest woman that Will had ever seen, and the thought of her interest caused him to pause a moment.

"Mrs. Cavendish, I am honored. Truly I am. Your love has given me strength. But I cannot be a farmer. I would turn to drink if I had to spend my life in the fields. It is not that I think lowly of you or your boys, but it is something I cannot do."

"Will, I know you spoke negatively about the life of a clergyman. But why? Cannot you see that God has your life in his hands? Would being part of my life, partners in spreading the Word of the Lord, be that horrible?"

"No, Vicar, it would not be horrible. I am grateful that you have taught me well of the Scriptures. I know how vital it is to you. I know the value of leading a good life, of doing right, of avoiding wrong. I know the import of being an example and of living your life in a moral way.

"But I cannot live a lie. It is important, and I appreciate your convictions, Vicar. But I cannot live your life any more than I could expect you to live mine. I cannot sit in a small village and hold hands with and whisper sweet verses at people. I would lie to my heart and to God at every turn."

William looked directly at the vicar and held out his hand towards him. "Is that what you would want for me? Is that how you think I should live my life? Doing something that I do not believe?"

It was now the vicar's turn to be near tears. He and William had had spirited discussions over the intricacies of the faith before, and the vicar had always hoped that William, beneath his attacks and parries against the hypocrisies of Christendom, had truly believed. William knew the truth, the vicar felt, and he had hoped that their battles had been mere intellectual sparring. But in William now, the vicar realized that it had been spiritual sparring instead, and that he had underestimated the position and the intent of the opponent.

"William, I will not hear of this! You are a fine Christian man. You would make a fine preacher. You could do great work for the Lord Christ."

Mrs. Cavendish chose at that moment to relapse into sobs. Perhaps intuitively, she sensed a rift, a chasm forming between the two men that if allowed to widen could grow to be unbridgeable. Her loud sobs distracted the pair, and they both turned to soothe her.

She enveloped both of them into her ample bosom and hugged tightly, hoping to embrace away the darkness she felt in each.

CHAPTER

II

May 1636
Broadwinds, Dorset
England

Kathryne spurred her gelding faster and faster. She was at full gallop, unusual for a young gentlewoman. She would not ride sidesaddle, as was the custom of the proper ladies of the court.

"How silly," she told the groomsman at her father's stable. "One cannot go faster than a trot, and if one does, one is at risk of continually slipping off the saddle. It is a most unwise position with a horse."

Just behind Kathryne on a dappled Arabian mare was her uncle Radcliffe, her father's younger brother, furiously spurring his horse in competition. They had started at a gentle canter from the rear stable of Broadwinds. As soon as they had passed from earshot, Kathryne called over her shoulder in a lilting voice, "Champion for this morning is the first at the village bridge."

And with that she heeled her horse sharply, crouched down behind the mane, and held on. Kathryne was slighter than her stronger uncle, but she possessed an elegant fluidity on her mount. The pair streaked along the muddy road. Radcliffe, never one to take besting well, pulled his riding crop out and slapped the horse's left haunch with a rhythmic count. Hoofbeats echoed up the narrow lane.

The bridge lay perhaps a mile away, but the road would carry them straight to the river Parrett, then turn at a right angle, continuing upriver to the wooden structure spanning it. Radcliffe's mare was nose to tail with Kathryne's gelding, with Radcliffe's strength and frenzied whipping yielding more speed.

A second or two later, Kathryne pulled the horse's bridle reins a touch to the left, reached up, and touched his neck. The horse veered left as well, straight for the high fence that bordered a field filled with wheat stubble. The horse drew to the fence at full gallop, lifted its front legs in a practiced motion, and kicked mightily with its rear legs, sailing over the fence with a half-foot to spare. They hit hard. Luckily the field had dried there or both horse and rider would have tumbled, mired in the soft earth.

As the bridge came into view, Radcliffe, who lacked the skill to jump such high fences, saw Kathryne and her horse running at full tilt across the field. Clumps of mud showered behind her steed, lifted off the soft black earth by the horse's massive hooves.

They both came at the objective in a blur. Kathryne neared her second jump and lifted slightly in the saddle to prepare the horse for just the right moment to leap.

Fall! Fall, Kathryne! Radcliffe urged silently.

The big Arabian horse lifted its front legs and soared again over the fence, landing with nary a misstep, and clattered across the wooden-decked bridge in triumph.

Kathryne pulled up on her horse, reached down, and stroked at its damp neck. Its sides were billowing in and out as it gasped for air. Kathryne shook back her voluminous dark hair and laughed, her deep green eyes flashing.

"Such a race, Uncle Radcliffe! But it appears that I have bested you once again."

Radcliffe had dismounted and knelt to the water's edge, splashing its coolness at his flushed face. "There would have been no contest if you had stayed on the true course, my dear. It is only through trickery that you arrived first!"

"Uncle Radcliffe!" she exclaimed in mock surprise. "We never discussed a proper course. I merely called the first to the bridge."

Radcliffe splashed more water and remained silent.

Kathryne dismounted, led her panting horse to the water's edge, and tied him off to a small tree. She walked up to the bridge rail and leaned against it.

Radcliffe had busied himself with a small tortoiseshell snuffbox and a clay pipe and was soon filling the air with great clouds of tobacco smoke. He puffed at the pipe, and Kathryne wrinkled her nose at the sharp, acrid smoke. How anyone could stand to be that close to such a noxious smell was an idea beyond her grasp.

"So tell me, my dear uncle," she said, fanning the smoke from her face, "where will you be off to next?"

Radcliffe pulled himself up on the edge of the bridge, spun about, and dangled his feet over the chilled waters of the river Parrett. He took a long puff from the pipe and blew the smoke out in a white stream that disappeared slowly in the moist spring air.

"Well," he said after taking the pipe from his mouth, "much of my itinerary depends on the planning of your dear father. I will attend to whatever business needs he has. It is he you should be asking about my destination. I am but a mere emissary for his lordship." Radcliffe broke into a smile, but after too long a pause, Kathryne thought.

Radcliffe continued, "I have been told that the next sailing of the *Plymouth Spirit* will be to the colony on the island of Barbados in the Lesser Antilles."

"Barbados," Kathryne replied. "I do not believe I have ever heard of that place. How far of a journey is it? What is the place like? What will you do there? Will you be buying or selling? How long will you be away from England?"

Radcliffe clapped his hands over his ears in mock surrender. "Kathryne, I do not know of such things. I go where my dear brother instructs, and I do what your enterprising father wants. It is easier to not understand much more of the plans than just that. All I know is that it will be warm, salty, and—if your father is involved—financially rewarding."

Kathryne twirled about, and faced her young uncle. "Barbados, you say. How terribly exciting! I wonder if I will ever see such sights as that."

Hadenthorne, Devon
England

"So, Vicar Mayhew, will you do me this favor?" William asked formally.

Thomas stood by the fire that spread flickering shadows across the small room. Mrs. Cavendish had just returned to her home after bringing up from the basement a fresh bottle of Somerset cider. Decanting a fresh cider bottle was an occasional treat, usually on holy days and for celebrations, and she was using every bit of food weaponry she could avail herself to in order to reverse William's decision to leave Hadenthorne.

He had calmed her by agreeing to think about it for a few more days, though William knew in his heart that there could be no turning back now.

"Vicar, I must know. Will you help me?"

The older vicar looked back at the young man, who had started in his life as a shy and timid child and was now poised on the precipice of adulthood.

It is so very curious, thought Thomas, as he looked up and considered again William's request. *For almost six years I have thought the arrangement to be temporary and that William would soon be gone. And now that it is about to happen, my heart beats frantically at the loss. I never considered him my son—not until this very moment. It is only now that I see how absolutely tight I have woven him into my heart and life. And how desperately I long for a family of my own.*

The vicar bent down, picked up the fireplace poker, and stabbed at the coal.

"Vicar, you did hear me, did you not?" William said softly.

Their eyes met briefly, and in that instant William understood part of the pain that beat in the vicar's heart. He dared but a glimpse, for he did not want to reconsider his hard-fought decision.

"Yes, William, I have heard you well. And I have thought of little else since the morning when you saddened the both of us by broaching the subject. Poor Mrs. Cavendish. I thought her tears would never stop and that our food would be forever salty." The vicar laughed, and William smiled broadly, feeling the tension decrease.

"And what have you decided?" Will asked evenly.

"William, your question deserves more than a rushed and thoughtless yea or nay response. You are talking about your *life*. It is a matter of the utmost import, not a trifling consideration!"

"Yes, Vicar, and it is precisely for that reason that I must have a positive response. It is *my* life. And as such, it should be my choice!"

"William, please," Thomas said, raising his hand to quiet the discussion. "We have more than this evening to speak of this. Lord Davis remains in London until midweek. Whatever my decision, it wouldn't be until then that I could act."

The sun dipped below the hills to the west, and the final oranges and golds of the day slipped from view. The colors at day's end were fleeting, and nature's hardest colors to hold. In a moment, the room was hidden in long shadows, and dark pools washed into the corners.

The vicar paced in front of the fireplace as he spoke. "William, I have a heavy heart since this morning. I will not further the debate at this time, for it pains me too greatly. I know you understand the fullness of God's Word. You would have been more than the equal of many of my classmates from the university. You have grasped much of the complexities of the Scriptures as well as the broad, yet simple meaning of

Christ's amazing gift to us. It is not your head that I argue with now—it is your heart. I have realized a grievous shortcoming this morning. You *know,* William, but yet you do not *believe."*

William began to mouth a reply, but the vicar held up his palm and silenced him. "You need not utter false protestations. I know where your heart is. And it is far from God right now."

"But Vicar, this is most unfair—to evaluate my request from a spiritual perspective."

"Unfair! That is hardly the proper response, William. Unfair, it is not. But rest assured, I will not hold you here in Hadenthorne because of a lacking in your soul. You are aware, as well as I, that I can no more force you to give your heart away as can I force you to change the color of your eyes. It is not something that can be done. Christ's gift awaits us all, and it is up to us to claim it and surrender to him.

"I know it is not done at the end of a blade or the threat of . . . a withheld recommendation. Whatever you would decide now would be a counterfeit act, an act of betrayal, and I will not call upon you to do such a disservice."

As the vicar stopped speaking, the stillness returned. The fire crackled weakly as embers sifted through the grate. The evening crickets were chirping in the garden, and the rolling bass notes of a bullfrog were heard from down by the river. The moments silently ticked by, neither man speaking.

William spoke first. "But Vicar, please understand that it is not because of you that my heart is where it is. It is because of *me.* I have tried. I truly have. But as I raise my eyes to the heavens, I once again see that horse leaping over the fence and the leering, ignorant face of a foolish, drunken nobleman and the broken body of my father. Perhaps if he had stayed alive I would be no more than a gamekeeper. Perhaps it was all I could ever be with him alive. But he is gone, and now I have the knowledge of a thousand books and no opportunity to use it. And my mother gone too soon as well, for the lack of proper medicine, most likely.

"So what am I to do? Stay a farmer? Live a lie as a clergyman? Tell me Thomas, where is my life destined? What would your God have me do?"

Silence returned in a flood. The vicar never had imagined that through knowledge he would have hurt William. But he had. He had laid out for William a banquet worthy of a king and then denied the starving boy the chance to sit at that overladen table. William had been denied parents, and now he had been denied freedom, denied a dream.

"William," the vicar said softly, "I am sorry. I did not willingly tantalize you and then remove the offer. I did not help you open a door to another world only to slam that door in your face. That was not my intention."

The vicar walked slowly to his desk, sat, and removed the writing quill from the ink. With his heart crying within him, Thomas Mayhew began to write. After a few moments, as the noise of a scribbling pen against parchment echoed in the stillness, the vicar looked up at William.

"My son," he said for the first time, "we will go at the week's end to see Lord Davis. This letter will make your desire clear and will list your abilities to your potential patron. I am sure that it will procure your freedom from our small village and give you the world you so desperately seek."

He laid down his pen and stared at the letter for a moment. He stood up and with as much cheer as he could muster, said, "Now, shall we partake of our evening meal?"

It was late evening two days later, the supper meal finished long before. After Mrs. Cavendish had gone home in sniffles again, the two men paced about the room, neither speaking.

For a few moments William had busied himself at the fire, prodding the peat and wood mixture to flame. He had noticed a deepening chill to the room and sat at the stone hearth.

As William occupied himself by the hearth, the vicar sat at his desk, reading through the second letter the apostle Paul had sent to his friend Timothy. Within the first few verses, the vicar had to stop and surreptitiously dab at his eyes. For the first time he understood how Paul had felt as he expressed his fondness for Timothy. "That without ceasing I have remembrance of thee in my prayers night and day; greatly desiring to see thee, being mindful of thy tears, that I may be filled with joy."

William hasn't even left yet, he thought, *and here I am becoming maudlin and weepy. It is true that I have become a weak old man,* he said to himself. With that, he flipped back into the Old Testament. *I will read a sterner, less emotional book.*

As the sun receded and stole the fading colors from the garden, William turned to the vicar's library, quietly, as he saw the clergyman deep in concentration over the Scriptures. He tilted his head a bit and let his eyes walk along the book titles: Homer's *Iliad* and *Odyssey,* works by Tacitus and Virgil. How thrilled he had been when the vicar helped make the first words understandable to him. *How long ago that seems,* Will thought.

He slowly pulled a large, brown, leather-bound book from the shelf. It was a dark walnut-colored tome, full of hand-colored prints of English birds. He tenderly opened the delicate pages. This was the first book William had held in his own hands, and the ideas as well as the colors were still a wonderment to him. *To grasp an entire world in my hand,* he thought. *To hold so many of God's creatures near my heart.*

The vicar coughed. William looked up and returned the book to the shelf. Neither had spoken further of William's request to meet with Lord Davis and of the vicar's intercession for him. William tugged at the collar of his dense woolen stomacher, a hand-knitted gift from Mrs. Cavendish last Christmas. He no longer felt chilled, but something akin to nervousness—or dread—had entered his thoughts.

He wants to keep me here, William thought in a panic. *He will change his mind and refuse to go with me to see Lord Davis because he thinks it a waste, or dangerous, or he needs companionship, or wants to force me to the ministry. . . .* His thoughts dissolved into a tangled mess.

Thomas stood up at his desk. He straightened his brown cassock and brushed at the crumbs on the collar left there from the evening meal, no doubt. His arms were relaxed at his side, and he looked as if he were about to begin on a new sermon to a crowded church full of expectant congregants.

William wondered if he should sit or cross himself.

"William," the vicar said, more loudly than needed, and both men looked a bit startled. "We have not talked about this for long enough, but Lord Davis returns home on the morrow, and I have made a promise to you."

An audible sigh escaped William's lips.

"I will not spend what precious time we have left together in anger and brooding melancholic silence. To remember each other with that as our last taste would be a grievous error."

William had been right. The vicar *was* giving a sermon. He had no notes, as was his habit, but it was a sermon nonetheless.

"I can only hope that you will find the leaving as difficult as I in allowing it to happen. For years I saw no image of myself as Paul when he wrote to Timothy and expressed his sadness at their parting. It was the words of a lonely servant, I thought. But no more. Now I am as he."

He paused. William took the opportunity to sit. *A sermon is not given or received as equals,* he thought.

"I have taken more pleasure than I could have ever acknowledged in your education. It has been a joy to be your teacher. You have surpassed my knowledge in so many areas. But there is one area that I will hold myself responsible for forever."

William knew what was coming, and he braced his soul against it.

"I have failed to pass along the eternal truth of God to your heart. From sunset yesterday when we spoke I have truly thought of little else. Why did I not see it? Why did I not do more?"

From his chair, William straightened as if to answer, but thought a moment and realized that the time for debate and discourse had passed.

Thomas bent to the desk and picked up the letter he had written days before. The rough linen paper held no more than a dozen black lines of elegantly scribed words.

"However, William, I will insist on one caveat—one condition for my delivering this letter explaining your petition and requesting an audience with Lord Davis."

William whispered in a mouse-quiet voice, "I will promise what I can provide, Thomas, and no more."

"That is fair and all that I will ask."

The vicar sat behind his desk, the sermon over. "William, I know that you have not been able to forgive others easily, and that may have stood in the way of allowing Christ to enter your life. I realize that I have been an imperfect model for you, and for that I will be forever regretful. Regardless of my shortcomings, I know the only important element in my life is my faith, the assurance that God indeed exists and that Jesus did indeed offer his life for ours."

"Vicar, how I wish I could offer those same words back to you. I cannot."

"I know I cannot force faith upon your heart, but, William, a decision delayed is a decision made. God will wait for you, but none of us knows just how long that will be. You are young, William, and you think that your time will be forever. It will not. God waits for you with outstretched arms and his free gift of salvation. I will not ask you to tell me a falsehood. But I will ask that you promise me one thing, and one thing only: that regardless of where you are and what you do in this world, you will continue to search for the truth. You must swear that you will never close your heart, that you will never stop asking that God reveal himself to you, that you never stop seeking his promise."

"But Vicar, I will of course seek knowledge and awareness—"

The vicar's harsh words cut through in mid-sentence. "No! *Not* just knowledge! Not just awareness! You must promise that you will seek *him!* I am not asking that you promise to find him—just to never give up on the search."

William bowed his head. *How hard would this promise be,* he thought. *I do not have to assure anyone that I will find anything. I just have to say I will be open to a sign from God. I can agree to that.* "Very well, Vicar Mayhew. I will agree. I promise that I will seek his truth."

The vicar took his Bible and closed it, carried it over to William, and placed his right hand on the leather cover. "Swear it." The vicar looked down at William's eyes, bluer now in the evening's darkness.

"I swear it."

And with this, the vicar placed his hand on William's.

"And I swear with you as well. We will both seek his promise."

Broadwinds, Dorset
England

The path back to Broadwinds weaved through the bucolic Dorset countryside. Along the way bright blue forget-me-nots were beginning to bloom. In the fields that flanked the road, the two riders, Kathryne and Radcliffe, were the audience of a dozen farmers out tending to their late spring chores. As they passed each, Kathryne would wave gaily and call out to them.

It was most obvious that Radcliffe would not suffer through such cloying familiarity with peasants and farmers.

The pair of horses stopped at the next crossroad. A mile to the north was the estate of Kathryne's ancestors, her beloved Broadwinds. The two riders pulled the horses to the left, toward home. The great house was situated off the road, several hundred yards from the muddy lane. The entrance was carefully groomed. Two large stone posts had been built to mark the way, and a wrought-iron archway had been constructed over the drive. At the apex of the arch, the family coat of arms was displayed, done in enameled metals and bronze. Without the riders' urging, the pair of horses plodded under the arch and headed to the stables behind the manor home.

Broadwinds was relatively new, compared to many other homes of the nobility. For more than six hundred years a Spenser had been lord of these lands and had always occupied the dwelling. The original structure, the stables, and chapel had been there since the 1300s. The main home had been lost to fire over eighty years earlier in a conflict during the brief reign of "Bloody Mary." Kathryne's great-grandfather

Black Spenser had stood against the Queen's attempt to overthrow the established reformed English Church, declared by her father, King Henry VIII, and to restore Roman Catholicism to the kingdom. Shortly thereafter, Black Spenser began rebuilding and had hired the best craftsmen of the day to complete the task.

The house was made from local Ham Hill stone, known for its warm buttery color. A sweeping stairway ascended from the drive up to the ground floor. There were large glazed sash windows, taller than the height of two men, evenly spaced across the front, back, and sides of the house.

Inside, the entry hall had two wide staircases providing a grand means of ascent that went up from the ground floor to the first floor on either side of the entry doors. The great parlor was on the ground floor behind the great entry hall, accessed through a richly carved arched doorway. Its walls were adorned with exquisite linenfold panels, on which were hung several Arras tapestries and trophies of the chase. To either side of the great parlor were wings with the withdrawing chamber on the left and the little parlor on the right, with offices and the library on either sides of those rooms.

The great dining chamber, with its enormous refectory table and dozens of finely turned chairs, was on the first floor, at the back side of the house, its windows overlooking the rear formal gardens and open to the two-story hall. It was flanked on either side by two wings of family bedchambers, all with sitting rooms, closets, and servants' quarters.

The wide corridor on this first floor was called the long gallery, where the family took its exercise in cold winter months by walking its length.

Throughout the house the decoration attested to the fact that the Spenser fortunes came from shipping concerns: rugs from Turkey on the oak floors; porcelains from the Far East; Flemish and Italian paintings prominently displayed; and rich textiles from Europe, India, and China at the windows and on the furniture.

The approach to the great house was magnificent in its subtle force. The road gave no real indication of incline, but the home sat perhaps fifty feet higher than the road. Flanked by two tightly planted columns of hemlock trees, the manor was hidden again from view as a guest would arrive. At the end of the drive, in the circle in front of the house, was a row of tall evergreens that just masked its facade. At the midway point of the drive the road elevated quickly, and in a sudden burst the entire manor house became visible. It was as if it did not exist, and then in an instant had magically appeared.

Kathryne loved that moment when the house shimmered into view. And in spring, the flowers along the wide circled drive were in mass profusion, the scents of white jasmine, primrose, honeysuckle, and Canterbury bells filling the air with delicate perfume.

Kathryne and Radcliffe rode around the house, past the orangery to the stable behind. A groomsman ran to meet them and carefully helped Kathryne dismount, obviously taking great pleasure in assisting the lady of the manor. But Kathryne had not noticed his attention. She had yet to consider herself a woman, nor a pretty woman if she had. Her long dark hair hung in natural curls along her shoulders, her deep emerald eyes were luminescent, and her lips and cheeks had a reddish glow, unneedful of artificial rouges or colors.

"Uncle Radcliffe, will you join me in the kitchens for a refreshment?" Kathryne asked.

"Most assuredly not," he snapped. "Have them send some ale to me in my room. I must say, Kathryne, I do not understand this fascination you have for peasants."

Broadwinds, like most manor homes of the day, had its kitchens located on the bottom floor of the home.

Kathryne loved spending time there, watching the cooks as they wrestled with huge serving platters of roasted game and simmering cauldrons full of soups, and eying the bakers as they rolled out their doughs for cakes, pies, and other tasty pastries.

The cavernous room occupied the entire east side of the basement level, back windows looking out over the formal gardens behind as the grounds sloped away from the house. In summer the huge windows would be opened, allowing the warm air in to provide much-needed circulation. Just outside the door was the herb garden, from whence came all the delicate flavors imbued into the foods of Broadwinds.

The west wall was dominated by a huge fireplace, its large opening roomy enough for a spit to roast an entire boar or side of venison. Split firewood was stacked in a large cubbyhole next to the firebox, replenished every day by one of the gardeners of the estate. Large bellows, long tongs, and an ash shovel were hung nearby. On each side of the fireplace hung two lanterns, on S-shaped wrought-iron sconces, swinging out from the wall. Along that same wall hung dozens of gleaming brass pots, each carefully polished by scullery maids until the kitchen was reflected in the bright metal. A thick oak chopping block also stood against the wall, a shallow depression in its center attesting to decades of use.

The focal point in the room was a large wooden oak tableboard in the center, with a loose top on a separate trestle frame, nearly a dozen feet long and almost six feet wide. It bore the cuts and scrapes of years of use by dozens of cooks, each using the area to cut and dress the meats and game used for an evening meal. Spices, flours, salts, and other condiments were kept fresh in large metal bins, and covered containers sat in the middle of the table on a raised shelf. Rushlights and tallow candles pinned to the beams all round the kitchen cast a warm glow over the vast room.

Next to the main kitchen was a small bakery with two domed ovens. Off the bakery was a small larder.

At the center of this beehive of activity stood the unflappable Mrs. Cole, head cook and clerk of the kitchen, who had been with Lord Aidan since he inherited Broadwinds. She had actually taken over the head position following the death of her husband, who had been managing the estate's kitchen for nearly twenty-five years. Her enveloping personality and warm smile drew Kathryne down to the friendly and welcoming room.

It had been three years since Kathryne's mother had died, and she naturally gravitated both to the warmth of the kitchen fires for solace and to the warmth and love of the dear Mrs. Cole. When Kathryne was still a child, she would come down to watch Mrs. Cole and her staff prepare meals for all the residents of the great house. On occasion the motherly head cook would slide a stool over to the edge of the table and lift the young girl up so she could help a baker roll out biscuits or rolls. "It never hurts a lass to know what it means to do a bit o' cookin', even a wealthy one like yourself, little missy," Mrs. Cole would tell Kathryne, and the little girl would nod in serious agreement as she rolled dough with a miniature rolling pin fashioned from a length of turned birch.

It was in this kitchen that Kathryne truly learned—learned the value of a heart, learned the value of a soul, learned the value of love. Her father, of course, loved her, she was sure of that, but it was not an easy thing for a man of his stature to bother himself with the needs of a young girl. He saw to it that she was always afforded the best that his money could buy. Mrs. Cole saw to it that she had everything else.

Kathryne entered the kitchen after trying to shake and sweep off as much of the caked-on mud from her skirts as possible. "May I have a tiny morsel of something to eat?" she asked Mrs. Cole.

Within a twinkling a pot of hot Somerset cider appeared on the rough wooden table that was the servant's eating area. A plate of toasted biscuits was taken from the warming chamber of one of the domed ovens, jellies brought out in blue-and-white china saucers, and clotted cream brought up from the cold cellar beneath the kitchen.

"Now, Lady Kathryne, what were you doing in the mud this mornin'? You know that the proper ladies in London will not look kindly upon a foolish little girl who still plays in the mud."

"Will they indeed be harsh, Mrs. Cole?"

"They had best not be, for if they are, I will be there to set them straight."

The older woman lifted her reddened and rough hand to Kathryne's face and gently pushed back a tendril or two of curled dark hair, smoothing it against her head, softly patting the hair against her temple. Kathryne's smile slipped away as she stared back into Mrs. Cole's broader, lined face.

"I will miss you, dear Kathryne. I truly will."

Kathryne placed her hand over Mrs. Cole's as she slid it to her cheek. "But I will be gone for only a season to start. I will return soon, for Yuletide," she said.

"I know, child, but this is the first time we have been apart for so long. Who will I have here to scold?"

Kathryne knew the pain she felt. Neither woman ever spoke of it, but to Kathryne Mrs. Cole was the mother she had lost as a child. In her was all the unconditional love, support, tenderness, and care that flowed from the best natural mother. In her Kathryne found solace and protection and security. She was always there with a kind word, a hug, a biscuit, a smile.

"I still do not understand why you must leave here to learn. Cannot your father merely hire tutors to explain things to you?"

"He has done so, but I cannot truly learn from those stuffy old men that used to visit my nursery when I was a child. True, they taught me French and Latin, but none of them were . . . men of experience."

"And goin' off to the wicked city of London will give you this experience?" Mrs. Cole said harshly. "You can learn what you need here!"

Kathryne smiled back at her dearest friend. How could she explain that she needed to see a bigger part of the world than was allowed her in the provincial village of her birth. She knew that her mother, the Lady Beatrice, was an amazingly unique woman, not well suited to the conventions of her age. Kathryne knew that Lady Beatrice had been educated by several teachers from Oxford, for women were not allowed to officially enter the college.

"Mrs. Cole, I must do all I can to embrace this world. If I merely stay at Broadwinds and wait, I will die as surely as would a hawk that is penned and never again allowed to fly into the clouds. I know it is hard for you to understand, but I feel that the very spirit of my mother is compelling me to do this."

It was Mrs. Cole's turn to stop and stare back at the beautiful girl who sat before her. She was the closest to a mirror image of her mother as one could imagine, without deviltry or a twinning. Her curled hair flowed around the delicate porcelain skin of her face and shoulders. That classic beauty was enhanced by a quick smile, sparkling green eyes, and a hearty, deep, from-the-soul laugh. As though to balance the precise line of her form, her heart was marked by the beat of adventure, spontaneity, and competition.

Mrs. Cole smiled, thinking about the handful any man would inherit if he consented to a marriage with Lady Kathryne. "I know, child, I know. Perhaps this finishin' school will smooth some of the rough edges off you after all. It just may do you some good in the end."

CHAPTER

12

June 1636
Broadwinds, Dorset
England

A velvet haze settled in the library of Broadwinds. Radcliffe had tucked himself into a golden brown leather chair, just by the two-story leaded glass window that overlooked the formal knot garden at the rear of the house. The smoke from his pipe drifted up, filling the room, diffusing the afternoon sun into a vague softness.

He lifted his head and squinted over at his older brother, Lord Aidan, who was furiously scribbling at some papers on his desk. Every few words or so, the earl would stab the quill back into the silver inkwell, clicking the nib on the bottom of the jar. The pen would be suspended between the inkwell and the paper as Lord Aidan half-closed his eyes composing another sentence. A few more lines and he was finished. He signed the single sheet with a flourish, sprinkled powder on the still-wet signature, and rocked a blotter pad across the name, to better preserve it.

"Now, that should solidify matters with Captain Blake and his eternal questions about ships' stores and provisions. I must say, I do not begin to understand his preoccupation with salt pork and hardtack. You'd think it was the only foodstuff available in all of England," Aidan said as he fastened the envelope with the Spenser seal and wax.

Radcliffe lifted his feet up, tucked them under himself, and brought his body upright. "My dear brother, it is not in England where he is worried about getting proper food. It is in the middle of the Indian Ocean that is of most concern." He paused as he relit his pipe, drawing in great gulps of smoke and exhaling them in a thick stream.

"When you have been at sea for three months and every bit of food you have seen for the past thirty days has been filled with maggots or weevils, a properly sealed barrel of hardtack and salt pork seems like the king's banquet. That's why he is concerned." Radcliffe paused, then said, "He has been there, dear brother."

Radcliffe exhaled another cloud of tobacco smoke towards Lord Aidan. "And you have not," he added dryly.

The elder Spenser sat motionless for a moment, staring at his younger brother. His face was not marked by anger nor disdain, but more of a curious look, owing to the inability of the two brothers to speak for more than a sentence or two without becoming disagreeable in some fashion.

"Well, yes, Radcliffe, that is true. And that is why you have gone in my stead. I expect you to keep me informed on these matters. And I thank you for setting me right."

"My pleasure indeed."

"Now then, I am glad to see from the ship's manifests that our most current voyage to Madras was indeed a remarkable success. Sir Evesham has estimated a near trebling of our original stakes in cotton cloth. And if Captain Blake and his *Plymouth Spirit* return from Cathay with the same sort of return on our investment—well, those of the company will be most properly appreciative."

"Your choice of the word *if* is most appropriate. It is a long voyage, with a thousand pirates hiding in as many ports along every league of the journey."

"Pirates. I must say it is almost unthinkable that they still exist. I would have thought by now the progress of our civilization would have driven them to the point of extinction."

Behind a veil of smoke and sunlight, Radcliffe watched his brother from his leather perch and smiled. An impartial observer would have called it a curious, sidelong smile.

13

July 1636
Hadenthorne, Devon
England

Vicar Mayhew and William set out early Wednesday morning as the fog slowly cleared from the valley. Their journey would end at Hadenthorne Hall and an appointment with Lord Davis. Neither man spoke much.

It was a modest walk, perhaps four miles, from the parsonage to the main house of Hadenthorne Hall. The sun was rising higher and the road turned left, then back again, as it followed the river Taw to the home of Lord Davis. William soberly remembered that he may not have the luxury of walking with his old friend for much longer. A small lump unexpectedly closed his throat for a breath or two.

To their left the hillside was covered with forest, nature's first greens showing as the trees began to bud with nascent leaves. The river gently drifted in the crook of the valley, and the opposite hillside was carefully tended and treeless. The earl's sheep were grazing there, small puffs of dull white speckled against the lush green spring grasses. The hogget lambs bleated plaintively by their mothers' sides.

A cloud slipped in front of the sun, and a deep shadow chased along the top of the hill, hastened down to the river, and washed over the silent pair in a darkening rush. Soon they were at the main gate, marked by several marble pillars, and turned in along the wide drive to Hadenthorne Hall. The fields along the main road were fenced by cob walls—layers of clay, chalk, and gravel, coated with a white veneer of plaster.

During the entire walk, neither man said a word. But if one had asked, they both would have said it was the most meaningful time they had spent together in many months.

The earl's huge brass doorknob squeaked as the vicar raised it and dropped it against its polished brass strike plate. The knock could be heard reverberating through the massive entry hall. The door swung open, revealing an aged butler, stiff and formal in his black suit.

"Yes?" he croaked softly, as he stood in the doorway and looked down on William and the vicar as they stood outside, uncomfortable, on the earl's marble steps.

"Vicar Thomas Mayhew and William Hawkes to see Lord Davis."

"Very well." The butler opened the door wider to allow the two visitors to enter the hall. "Wait here and I will announce you to his lordship."

With that, the butler spun on his heel and strode down the long hallway, his heels all but noiseless on the polished floor.

This marked the first time that William had set foot inside such a grand house. He had seen it from the outside often enough, and he remembered that he once had been allowed inside the smaller dwelling of the master of the house, which to William had been a wondrous occasion.

But this was far more grand—more heavenly. The entry hall was floored in huge squares of black and white marble. The room was flanked by a dozen two-story fluted columns with carved tops and huge, square pedestal bases. Dominating the hall was a massive carved alabaster table with a thick slab of white marble, veined with black, thicker than a man's leg, as a top. On this was a mammoth silver bowl. It stood on lion's paws and was perhaps the height of a small child; it was filled with a dazzling array of spring flowers and greenery. It was as if a miniature garden had been transported indoors, the color and the scents all but overwhelming.

In the quiet echoes of the room, both turned and watched as the butler returned, padding down the long hall, his image reflected in the shining black and white of the floor.

"The earl will see you now. Please follow me."

The butler slowly walked back down the long hall, with the two men in tow. William's head snapped from side to side as his attention shifted between huge portraits hanging in gilded frames to imposing statuary.

The library doors were open, and the trio walked in. "Your guests, my lord," the butler announced and then withdrew on silent footsteps, closing the doors swiftly, without even the sound of the latch snapping.

"Ah, Vicar. How nice to see you outside the church. You should make a habit of visiting your congregation more often," Lord Davis said with an oily tone to his voice as he sat in a large tooled-leather chair.

All three men knew the invitation to be false, but the vicar responded as expected, with warm acknowledgements of the earl's hospitality and kindness.

"Well, Vicar Mayhew, shall we discuss your note—your supplication, as it were—concerning your young charge here. . . . William, is it not?"

"Yes, Lord Davis. His name is William Hawkes, the son of your former gamekeeper."

"Oh, yes—and that unfortunate business with Lord Smithton and all. Most unpleasant." Lord Davis stared unemotionally at William. "Well, he seems to have turned out fine . . . under your careful tutelage, I assume."

The vicar was unsure of a proper response.

William spoke next. "Yes, my lord. I have been most blessed by your help and the vicar's patience. They have both been a godsend." William spoke as if on cue, as if he had known in advance which words were expected.

"Splendid. Now, Vicar—what was it that you required?"

The vicar outlined William's predicament and summed it up by explaining that a career at sea would make use of his talents, as well as be a true boon to the British Naval Force. He spoke of Will's intense study and mastery of all subjects in which he would be tested by the Royal Naval Seas Regulator, should Lord Davis choose to grant him the reference required. He finished by stating that without the earl's recommendation, William would find no open doors anywhere.

"Most well put, Vicar. You do have a gift for a pleasant and meaningful turn of the phrase, don't you?"

The vicar offered no answer. Silence descended on the room again, and the loudest sound was the slow click of the case clock's pendulum.

"Well, William, I take it this is an affair in which you will not be deterred?" Lord Davis said.

"Yes, my lord."

"And I understand that you seem to have a certain skill in sailing matters. You spent a few weeks on the sea some months ago, did you not?"

William could only nod. *How in the world would he have learned of that?* Will wondered.

"And that our vicar's brother called you the most natural sailor he had ever placed in a boat?"

"Yes, sir. He did indeed make that claim," said the vicar after more than a slight pause.

"Good, for I would never recommend a horse only fit for the knacker's yard. William—you are ready to get weaving, are you not—to get on and make something of yourself?"

"Yes, sir. I most assuredly am."

"Then I will make it so. I will scribe a letter to Sir Edmond in Plymouth. He has connections to most of the naval forces along the southern English coast and will be most kind to grant me this large favor—a personal recommendation. You both realize, of course, at what a cost this letter is being written."

His comment was addressed directly at the vicar, knowing that this would be a heavy debt to be carried by Thomas and repaid at Lord Davis's whim.

The vicar nodded solemnly.

"Very well. I will have the letter drafted and written by the morrow."

"Thank you, my lord," both Will and Thomas said together.

"By the way, William. You realize that this means the end of your yearly stipend. Lord Smithton will have no further obligations to you or the vicar. That has been made apparent to you, has it not?"

"Yes, my lord," William answered. "That has been most apparent."

Broadwinds, Dorset
England

Dorset was a cold and chilly place during the last week of July. Though Broadwinds was some twenty-five miles from the English Sea, an Atlantic storm had blown in and unsettled the air with a cold, driving rain and gusts of wind, each bearing the faintest traces of the sea from which the tempest was born.

Mrs. Cole stared out the kitchen windows to the fields beyond Broadwinds. The rain buffeted the thick leaded glass, the rivulets of water further distorting the view. She had a shawl about her shoulders and shivered.

"'Tis an unnatural thing, this cold summer wind," she remarked to the two scullery maids.

The bell marked "Orangery" rang once, and all three women turned to face it, then it rang again, and again, then once more in a furious succession of musical clangs.

Mrs. Cole smiled. In a moment Kathryne was heard running down the steps with remarkable dispatch, considering she was carrying her breakfast tray, a pot of now lukewarm tea, and several plates littered with crumbs and biscuit ends and dollops of jam. She skidded into the kitchen and banged the tray to the table, the rattle and crash of dishes unnerving the two young serving girls, who shrank in a fit of ill-hidden giggles.

"I thought I could make the run before the last ring had sounded. It seems as I have not," Kathryne panted.

"Kathryne, more and more each day I am absolutely convinced of the dire need of your attendance at this fancy finishin' school you'll be attendin' this autumn. If nothin' else 'twill teach you to behave as a proper society lady, not some rough peasant girl who is nothin' but elbows and knees."

"Why, Mrs. Cole, Lady Emily will do nothing of the sort. She will teach my mind how to behave, not me as a person."

"Then poor Lord Aidan will have wasted a bag full of guineas on the effort."

Kathryne giggled and reached for Mrs. Cole and gave her a hug. "May I stay here and have some warm tea, Mrs. Cole? It is so lonely upstairs with both Papa and Uncle Radcliffe away at Bournemouth and Weymouth."

"Of course, my child. You are always welcome here."

"Mrs. Cole, you are the dearest woman in all of Dorset. I had asked my father if I could accompany them to the ports. It seems as if some ship finally arrived back from China, of all places. But he actually shrank in horror at my suggestion. Why cannot a woman learn the pluses and minuses of trading and shipping?"

Kathryne had wanted to travel with her father and uncle, and she had wanted to see for herself the exotic goods with which the ship had returned. She had sensed the great excitement Lord Aidan had felt when he was informed of the ship's arrival. But when she made her request, he had laughed at the ludicrousness of her boldness. "Why, Kathryne," he had said, "A woman . . . being amidst the dealings of vital shipping matters. . . . My darling child, it just is not done, and that is truly final."

"And, Mrs. Cole, Uncle Radcliffe was almost livid that I had mentioned the idea. He fumed and sputtered and pouted the rest of the day. What would possess him to act that way? I actually think that his actions prevented me from going. I may have been able to cajole Papa into giving permission, but not with Uncle Radcliffe behaving so abominably."

Mrs. Cole took a deep breath and said a silent prayer. She prayed for a sense of peace at the mention of Radcliffe's name. She distrusted the man intensely and struggled with her less-than-Christian attitude. She tried so very hard not to influence the young Lady Spenser.

"Do you have any idea what comes over Uncle Radcliffe?" Kathryne asked.

Mrs. Cole wanted to say that it was because he was evil. She wanted to say that the man had hated Kathryne from the moment she opened her eyes to this world, for it meant that he no longer had any hope to claim Broadwinds as his own. Lord Aidan, as oldest of the family, inherited all the lands and holdings. Kathryne was then in line for the inheritance, and if she, as Aidan's child, married and produced a male heir, that firstborn son would inherit all of the Spenser fortune. Radcliffe would receive nothing. If he were included in the will, it would be at Lord Aidan's discretion. It gave him good cause to be overtly solicitous in his brother's presence. But Mrs. Cole had heard of his tirades and epithets hurled against his brother when none but a poor valet or maid was in the room. Kathryne was all that stood between Radcliffe and the Broadwinds estate—and its title and prestige.

"Why Kathryne, I believe your uncle just has much on his mind and does not wish to be distracted as he conducts his affairs. It is not malicious on his part." Mrs. Cole congratulated herself on her self-imposed civility.

Kathryne was surprised at the word *malicious*. She had never thought of that term while describing her uncle. And it was apparent that Mrs. Cole had.

"Do you think it not curious that Uncle Radcliffe has never married?" Kathryne asked innocently, deep in reflection.

Mrs. Cole looked at once angry and flustered, trying her best not to show either emotion, struggling to keep the images of Radcliffe's perversity unbidden. "I don't know, child. And perhaps some things are best left undiscussed," Mrs. Cole said with finality. "Besides, have you not better things to do, like prepare for your adventure in London? It may be the last few years before . . . well, before your father finds you an acceptable suitor."

The two scullery maids stopped their polishing in mid-stroke. Kathryne held her teacup midway between the saucer and her half-open mouth. "Suitor? What do you mean 'proper suitor'? Suitor for whom?"

"Why Kathryne, do not disappoint me. You are sixteen years old this next spring. You've not been locked up in an ivory tower these past dozen years. You know quite well what I mean when I mention 'proper suitor.'" Mrs. Cole stammered slightly, blushed a bit, and then asked

God why Kathryne's mother could not still be with them. How easy it would be for Lady Beatrice in this situation.

"Kathryne, most girls your age are soon to be wed. You may be old by the time your father finds a man willin' to settle for you."

Kathryne did not smile at Mrs. Cole's obvious attempt at levity.

"Surely your father and you must have discussed this at some time in the past."

"No. We never have had such a discussion. I would most assuredly have remembered if we had, Mrs. Cole. And we have not."

The two scullery maids exchanged abrupt glances with each other, both of their faces reddening slightly.

"My dear little Kathryne," Mrs. Cole said as she took a chair next to her and grasped at her hand. "This should not come as a shock to you. Have you not paid attention to the numerous weddin's and engagement galas you've attended? How do you think the bride and groom have come together?"

Kathryne, who was still a young child in so many ways, shook her head to clear her muddled thoughts. Her long thick hair swept the air around her face with each movement. "I am sure that I have never considered such a thought before, Mrs. Cole. I . . . suppose . . . I imagined that they . . . I guess that they just . . . arrived there together somehow."

Tucking a loose tendril of hair from Kathryne's face to behind her ear, Mrs. Cole tried to explain. "When 'tis time, your father will help select a suitable young man for you—for a husband. And he will take into account the fellow's social standin', and his peerage, and his holdin's, and his availability. When the match is right, it will be announced to you."

Kathryne shook her head in disbelief. "No, Mrs. Cole. I will pick the man. It will be the man that God brings me. Isn't that what you have taught me? That God is in control of our lives, but we must make the right decisions? Isn't that what you helped me believe in—a God who is concerned for me?"

"Yes, Kathryne. 'Tis true."

To Mrs. Cole's deepest satisfaction, Kathryne had, many years ago, professed that personal faith in her Savior. It was the conversion of a young girl, but it was real. Kathryne had placed her trust and her life in the hands of God. Mrs. Cole had helped her learn the Scriptures and the meaning of salvation by grace.

Here is a time that faith will be tested, Mrs. Cole thought.

"Well then, despite my father's wishes, I will find the proper man for me. It will not be a . . . business arrangement. I can assure you of that," stated Kathryne firmly with a toss of her head.

Mrs. Cole glanced over at the scullery maids, who had been silent. In a flash they both set back to work with a clattering. *How I wish that it could be that way,* Mrs. Cole thought. *It seems the poor, who can select their own mates, have a definite advantage over the nobility, who have no such freedom.*

"I will do the selection, Mrs. Cole. With God's help, I will," Kathryne repeated.

How I wish that to be true, my child, she thought as she pulled Kathryne close and enveloped her in her protecting embrace.

14

August 1636
Broadwinds, Dorset
England

The bright bedchamber was a tumult of activity. Trunks were open everywhere. Neatly folded clothing lay in short stacks on the high four-poster bed, on chests, on top of closed wardrobes. Kathryne had three flustered chambermaids frantically packing her belongings for the three-day journey into London to Lady Emily's finishing school—the Alexandrian. Lord Aidan had tried to avoid the whirlwind, but was drawn into the activity at Betsy, the head chambermaid's, insistence.

"Why, if she be left to her own choices, she'll be takin' the whole of her wardrobe with her, and half of her room's furnishin's. They'll be no room in London for all she's plannin' on bringin', my lord."

He reluctantly left his ledger book and walked down the hall and up the sweeping, curved staircase to the first floor. At the end of the hall he could hear Kathryne's voice giving orders, making decisions, asking advice.

He looked over at Betsy, who had been in his service for more than two dozen years. He shook his head slowly, as if in disbelief. Betsy smiled widely at him in return and commiseration.

"How difficult it has been without a lady of the house to keep all this on an even keel," he remarked to his faithful employee.

"Lord Aidan, beggin' your pardon for my boldness and all, my lord, but she is a lovely girl—just a bit headstrong at times."

Lord Aidan nodded as they neared the room and the noise level increased. "She'll be fine—with God's help, and yours."

Lord Aidan stood in the doorway, overwhelmed at the spectacle before him. All closet doors were open, every wardrobe stripped bare, chests open and drawers gaping.

He looked at the panicked faces of the three chambermaids, at the flushed face of his daughter, then back at Betsy.

Kathryne smiled first.

Lord Aidan smiled back. "She'll be needing all of God's help for sure."

Kathryne put her two hands on her hips and was about to begin explaining, when Lord Aidan held up an open palm. "No, Kathryne, I will not mediate in this. You have three trunks and one wardrobe to take. You are now in charge. Please see that it is all done with a minimum of fuss."

With that, he turned and went back to the comfort of his ledgers and books.

After all, she does have a full fortnight to accomplish the task, he said to himself with a grin.

Hadenthorne, Devon
England

The leather bag was on the table, waiting for William to awake for breakfast. The large pouch, carefully stitched together from thick cowhides, was polished a deep brown and rubbed until it glowed like a shiny chestnut warm from the coals. A heavy flap and clasp covered its deep pockets. All three of the Cavendish sons had labored on it, hand selecting the leather and hand sewing the pieces together.

As he rounded the corner dragging his hand through his long golden hair, he saw the beaming face of Mrs. Cavendish. The vicar, smiling more softly, was off to one side, and framed in the window overlooking the front garden were the faces of Dugald, Timothy, and Philip. The trio of Cavendish brothers had refused to enter the parsonage, claiming that their boots were too muddy. So they stood in the morning fog, hunched over, peering in as their friend strode to the table and picked up his gift.

William opened the bag and carefully ran his fingers along the seams, setting the long strap over his shoulder, trying it on for size.

Dugald was the first to speak. "It be for the boat, Will. You can pack your belongin's in it."

Thomas spoke next. "We made it for you, Will. To take with you."

Finally Philip spoke, halting, on the verge of tears. "'Tis so you'll have somethin' to recall us with. So you won't be forgettin' us."

Mrs. Cavendish, by that time, was awash with fresh tears. Will walked over and hugged her. And then he was out in the garden as well, trying to encircle all three of her sons in his arms.

"I would never forget my dearest friends. This bag will be something I will always treasure. Every time I lift it, I will feel closer to all of you."

The vicar stood in the shadows and watched as everyone blubbered and cried. It was not easy losing someone so dear. He stood dry-eyed, his tears spent from the days before.

■ ■ ■ ■ ■

Unwillingly the Cavendish clan had departed after many tears and suffocating hugs. The vicar watched William as he carefully folded his few possessions. The densely knit woolen stomacher and a thin worsted coat were folded and placed in the bag, along with two pairs of breeches, a simple doublet, a weskit, a few shirts, and several pairs of drawers and stockings. In no more than a few moments, William had finished. All of it fit within the expansive leather bag.

"Vicar, I am sorry I am leaving you in such a state. I wish there was something I could do or say. I know that my leaving has caused you great sorrow."

The vicar stood and placed his hands upon the broad shoulders of his soon-to-be-departing charge. "William, it will not do either of us well to remember this melancholic mood as our final time together. Yes, I admit that I will miss you greatly. I so enjoyed our conversations and discussions. I feel that I will miss those most of all.

"I will be honest with you, William. I am sad at your leaving, and yet I am sad that I will not see the world as you will. So you must promise me one more thing."

William nodded his yes.

"That I will be able to see the world through your eyes. You must keep me informed as to your travels and experiences. I will indeed see the world and its wonders through you. Promise me you will do that."

"Vicar, you have my word."

"And remember most of all William—be in the world, not of it," he half-whispered urgently as he gently shook William's shoulders.

"Vicar, I promise to remember."

CHAPTER

15

September 1636
London, England

Fall came early to London in 1636. A wintry wind blew from the north country and whistled through the narrow ways and alleys, pushing leaves and bits of trash along the cobbled streets. As dusk fell, the lantern lighters struggled to keep their flames lit, and the street lamps cast ghostly, flickering shadows as the sun dipped. The encroaching wisps of fog washed colors from sight.

An elegant carriage clattered down Lenox Street, and its driver pulled sharply at the reins. The horse slowed, its hooves sounding loud on the quiet street. Both sides of the street were lined with stately facades of imposing town houses, most entrances marked by thick columns, polished brass plaques, and ornate lamps.

The driver, Mr. Biesty, dressed in fine Spenser livery, jumped to the street and tapped at the window of the carriage. "Milady, we are here. Number 16 Lenox."

Kathryne leaned out of the carriage window, peering through the fading dusk at her new home.

"But do not unlock this door until I return!" cautioned Mr. Biesty, who looked both ways, up and down the street, twice, until he took one step forward. And with every two steps forward he took, he turned to see Kathryne's face, half-hidden in the darkness, safely behind the thick, locked carriage door.

Weymouth, Dorset
England

A slow, ox-driven vehicle clattered down the steep cobbled streets of Weymouth. This rough wagon carried a few barrels of ale, several cases of salt pork, and one passenger—William Hawkes.

The driver pulled up on the reins; the oxen raised their heads and stopped, mid-path. "There she is, lad. There be your vessel."

"Which one?" William called as he dismounted from the wagon, clutching at his bag and bundle of food, packed by Mrs. Cavendish.

"See there by the docks? The far pier? 'Tis the old boat at the end o' that pier. The ship with no center mast."

"Many thanks. I greatly appreciate your assistance."

William shouldered his bag and began to walk down the steps to the harbor and piers. He had been assigned as assistant navigator, linguist, and chart maker's helper on His Majesty's ship *Minion*. The vessel had a long history, most notably commanded by the famous John Hawkins in the battle of San Juan de Ulua almost forty years previous.

As he neared his new home, the sounds of shouts and derisive laughter filled the night air. He stopped, turned, and stared back once again at the slow cart plodding its way back to Hadenthorne.

■ ■ ■

The moon had begun to rise over the dead-quiet ripplings of the oil-black waters of Weymouth Harbor. The town—on the south coast of England—was built upon a long sweeping sound, and the land angled back steeply from the sea. A warren of wooden docks, piers, and crumbling stone-built jetties and breakwaters scuttled about the shoreline, dotted with drying nets and fishermen's dories and one-man coracles, looking like large sea turtles come in for a rest on shore. Along the quay, rickety shanties, taverns, alehouses, public houses, and run-down shops crowded from the water's edge to the first ridge. The dwellings and the parade of merchants became more substantial, more proper, more civilized, as they retreated from the offensive waters.

As William made his way down High Street toward the piers—toward his future—an abrasive mix of music, yells, laughter, and cries grew in volume and intensity. The cacophony emanated from both sides of the narrow street. On his left were a series of drinking establishments—The Sea Dog, The Spanish Main, The Eagle's Nest, Leeson and Son, and The Frog and the Frigate. On his right were a series of boardinghouses and cramped shops, now shuttered for the evening, offering all manner of supplies and necessary items for a sailing man.

Midway down the hill, William stopped short as two men flew out of The Sea Dog and landed with a *thud* onto the cobblestone street in front of him. The men were locked in a hostile ballet, each trying to hug the other's arms tight while battering at their opponent with a drunken fluidity. A crowd of patrons soon emerged from the smoky alehouse and shouted their encouragements to one or the other.

Where are the constables to put a stop to this? William thought incredulously as he edged his way further into the shadows, away from the combatants and the crowd. He was very leery of being jostled. Even though his money, what little he brought, was safely tucked in a belt drawn around his waist under his shirt and coat, he remembered the vicar's warnings about pickpockets and petty thieves.

William backed up, away from the catcalling crowd, until he bumped into a flickering street lamp. He leaned against it for a moment, trying to decide if he should wait for the fight to be over or seek out a side alley or street to get to pier sixteen and his new home, the *Minion.*

As he contemplated, he heard a soft voice from behind him. It was the honey-thick voice of a woman. William jumped, turning quickly.

Before him, standing uphill, was a tall, red-haired woman wrapped in a tight, red satin dress. Her gown had a thin band of white lace edging the deep-cut bodice, drawing one's eye to that spot, where she boldly displayed more white, delicate, and rounded flesh than William had seen in his entire life. William stared slack-mouthed for a long moment and then raised his eyes to her face. Her cheeks had been powdered a bright red, her lips an even darker color, and her hair was done in ringlets and bows that fell along her shoulders. He felt the blood rush to his ears and face. His heart began to thump, and his blood pulsed.

"I said, have you just come into town?" she said.

"I . . . I . . . I . . . um . . . yes . . . just in town this evening. Yes."

"Do ye have a place to stay?"

"I . . . I . . . am heading for my . . . ship. I am to report by tomorrow morning."

"Well, then—you have this evenin' free, don't you now?"

"I . . . I . . . I," William stuttered, unable to finish the sentence. The woman had reached over to him, placed her hand on his, drawing him towards her as if to guide him out of his dilemma. She placed his hand on her hip, soft and yielding. She placed her hand on his shoulder at first, then allowed it to slide, ever so slowly, down until it rested on his chest. It felt heavy and warm. She pressed hard against him, her palm pressing his mother's locket into his flesh.

A cry of bells and alarms was sounding—soft at first, then louder—in William's thoughts. He saw the image of a scowling vicar, then several Scriptures raced past, then an impression of the soft and caring face of his mother came to mind. He shook his head as if to clear the images dancing before him. The woman, who was pulling him toward a darkened doorway, had turned her face back to him, and he saw the faint wrinkles in her skin beneath the powder and paint. He stopped and pulled his hand back.

"I am sorry, madam, but I have to report to my ship now. I truly do." He backed away quickly.

"Don't go," she called after him. "There is no ship sailin' tomorrow. You have no need to be on ship this evenin'. Stay with me. It will be much more pleasant, I assure you. . . ."

The woman in the red dress watched as the tall, handsome young man walked off. She shook her head and with a wry smile and in a cold small voice, she said softly, to no one in particular, "He'll be back. They always come back." And then she turned and walked toward one of the alehouses at the top of the hill.

London, England

"Wait with the door locked till the valet fetches you," Mr. Biesty called as he neared the lower servant's door of the Alexandrian. "Take your hand from the handle, Lady Kathryne. You might slip, it would open, and you would tumble to the filthy street."

Kathryne raised her eyebrows in mock surprise. *That could never happen,* she thought.

"I have seen it happen many times, Lady Kathryne. And then a band of brigands set upon the young maiden, and she's pulled about to the back of beyond and never seen again. It happens more often than not, I daresay."

Kathryne obediently took her hand from the door handle of the new Spenser hackney carriage and waited impatiently to enter the cool evening air of London. Mr. Biesty had yet to tap at the door to announce her arrival, having stopped midway between carriage and entrance.

"No disrespect, milady, but you'll be needin' to take more care in London than at Broadwinds. London is a place that calls out for eternal caution."

But it is only a few feet from the carriage to the door, Kathryne thought. *What can happen in a dozen quick steps?*

"I tell you, Lady Kathryne," Mr. Biesty added as he stood midway between carriage and doorway. "I see dreadful crimes most often. There's a world of difference 'tween London—and every other place in England. It may take you a bit, but you'll see how it all is to work out."

Presently a young man of about fourteen years of age came out from a basement door and spoke softly to the driver.

"Indeed this is Lady Spenser," Mr. Biesty answered loudly. "See to it that her belongings are brought within—and that she is properly greeted and escorted inside."

In a flash, the valet ran back to the house and was followed out again by several other servants. As they each took a case or shared the opposite handles of a heavy trunk, the main door of the house swung open. From the entrance an elegant doorman, dressed in a deep blue, long-tailed night weskit, descended to the street and carefully opened the carriage door, extending his gloved hand to Kathryne.

Mr. Biesty eyed him critically, then surveyed the street for possible interference.

Behind the doorman, sweeping out into the street, was a tall, statuesque woman with light red hair and a smile-creased face.

"Kathryne!" she called out as she made her way to the door, "Welcome to London. I am so glad that you are here."

Kathryne felt herself being pulled from the street and enveloped in a warm and welcoming hug from the headmistress and proprietor of the Alexandrian, Boarding Home for Young Ladies of the Peerage—Lady Emily Bancroft.

Lady Emily held her by the shoulders at arm's length. "Let me look at you, my dear." She stared deep into Kathryne's young face and tentative smile. "You are an exact duplicate of your mother in virtually every manner. Oh, how I miss her—but oh, how much I am looking forward to your time with me!"

And with that, Lady Emily took her firmly by the hand and drew her into the warm, inviting glow of Number 16 Lenox Street.

Weymouth, Dorset, England

With each step away from the woman and the crowd, William felt safer. Would this type of encounter be a regular occurrence? Would he face such temptations every time in port? And if this was normal activity at a small harbor town such as Weymouth, what might happen in larger ports with infamous reputations? A portion of Will was terrified of the intoxicating allure of that woman in red satin, but he recognized as well the deep stirrings within him.

As William turned the corner at the base of the hill, the shops and buildings on his right—the water side of the street—gave way to piers, and the lively sounds were rolling over the area. Several ships, tied side by side, had lanterns strung on their pier side, away from their flammable canvas and pitch-covered ropes. In the distant glow he could make out several hundred men gathered on the main decks listening to music, dancing, singing, and apparently drinking from the ship's brandy and ale barrels.

At the end of the far long wooden pier were two small sentry huts at either side of the wooden planking that made up the wide deck. Between them was strung a thick rope, with three hanging lanterns illuminating the area. Sprawled in front of the two small huts were five Royal Marines, each wearing a scarlet coat, mostly unbuttoned. The men sat casually relaxing on the deck or on tall three-legged stools. William walked toward the lights, and as he approached from the shadows, one of the guards, a sharp-faced young man with a shock of black hair, nearly stumbled as he tried to leap from his chair. He grabbed his musket and swung it at William. Eyes wide, he barked out, "Halt there! Stop! Identify your person!"

William stopped dead in his tracks. After a moment, he took two steps forward and said loudly, "I am William Hawkes. I have been assigned a commission on the *Minion*. I understand she is berthed at this pier. I mean to present myself to Captain Lawrence for assignment."

He did not know what more information they needed, so he stood silent, arms at his sides. There was a momentary pause, then all the guards began to laugh, softly at first, then louder and more boisterous.

William was quite puzzled. *Is this not the right pier? Is it docked at another harbor? Did the* Minion *sink in the last few weeks?*

"Beggin' your pardon lad," the most senior of the guards finally said. "We not be laughin' at you in particular. 'Tis what you said we find most mirthful."

"But I do not understand. Am I not in the proper place? Is this not the fourth of September?"

"Indeed, laddy. You be correct on both accounts. The *Minion* is in port, and today be the fourth. But you'll find no captain of the ship on board. I would doubt if you would find any officer who would admit to bein' an officer of the *Minion* anywhere in Weymouth. You see, laddy—your good captain be in the gaols."

Standing in the darkness, listening to the alien sounds of drunken shouts and songs, and then hearing this most unsettling news, William had to fight the urge to turn around and return to Hadenthorne. Not just return, but *run* back home to the safety of the parsonage and the warmth of the vicar, Mrs. Cavendish, and all things familiar. An image of Missy Holender—pure and innocent, her soft lips open expectantly, his face against her silken hair—came to mind, and William's resolve seemed to ebb as the tide.

London, England

Kathryne followed Lady Emily over the butter-colored marble tiles that made up the grand entranceway of Number 16 Lenox Street. The house was one of a series of elegant four-story town houses.

On either side of the entry lay two rooms, a parlor on the right and a dining chamber on the left. The rooms were not formidable in size, yet were rich in decoration, topped with high white ceilings and delicately carved plaster trim. The walls were pannelled in linden wood, mellowed over the years to a warm tan. The floors were of gleaming oak, Kathryne noticed, and yet even in the dim evening light, she marveled at the lush, colorful Oriental carpets in each room.

The rooms were filled with a sense of gracefulness; none were formal or stuffy as one might expect of such a grand home. Arrangements of freshly cut flowers were placed about the rooms.

Lady Emily, with Kathryne in tow, walked down the long center hall, adorned with romantic paintings of landscapes and moody, yet grand portraits of people now long departed. They passed a breakfast room on their left, done in cheerful yellows, and then walked past a neatly kept office on the right, and up the sweeping staircase. As they ascended past the next level—the first floor—Lady Emily explained, "These are our meeting rooms and library."

On the next level—the second floor—two well-lit halls led off in opposite directions, each flanked with perhaps a dozen doors. Lady Emily walked down to the end of the west hallway and opened the door facing the rear of the house with a grand flourish.

"Now, Kathryne, this will be your room. The big bed by the window will be yours. Lucy Donnel will have this bed by the door." She paused, seeing the impassive look on Kathryne's face. "I know this is but a fraction of the room you have been accustomed to, but space in London is at a premium. I would be in the almshouse if I were to offer my students the likes of what you all have left behind."

Kathryne slowly walked to her bed. The room measured no more than five yards square. The walls were white, and the floors the same mellow wood she had seen in the ground floor rooms, but without a carpet. Pretty curtains in a delicate green fabric softened the expansive window. She ran her hand along the richly embroidered silk coverlet on the bed. She turned and watched as the servants began to stack her cases and trunks, making a small pyramid in the middle of the room.

Lady Emily had busied herself, fussing with the coverlet of the second bed and opening up the small door that held a tiny closet for dresses. She pointed to one of the two large, drawered chests in the room and exclaimed brightly, "And this will be for your things, Kathryne dear. I imagine that Lucy will be content with the other."

The valet had brought in the last of her belongings—a large hat box—and had stacked it at the very top of the mound of traveling boxes and cases. It tottered there, precariously for a moment, then tilted to one side and remained motionless.

"Well then, my dear. I will give you some time to get settled in. I trust that you will find this all to your liking. If you care to, I would love to have you join me for a late cup of tea," Lady Emily said, then added softer and conspiratorially, "or coffee, if you would prefer. I'll be down on the ground floor in the parlor at the front. Do come down."

With that, she spun on her heels, her satin dress flowing behind her, and she walked from the room. The door shut with a solid click, and her footsteps echoed as she walked down the polished wooden floors to the stairs.

Kathryne turned to the bed and hiked herself onto it, a much higher four-poster than she had at Broadwinds. She turned to the window to see the first sliver of the early autumn moon rise up over the small garden behind the house. Its pale light illuminated the row of homes behind her in ghostly fashion. A few windows had lanterns lit, and she thought she saw shadows moving behind the curtains. She drew the shutters closed. Her room was illuminated by the single beam of a tall tallow candle. The light of that small flame on the table on the far side of the room cast a jumbled shadow. She clasped her hands together in her lap and fought back the tears that had begun to form at the corners of her eyes.

"I will not cry," she told herself sternly. "I am made of stronger stuff than that."

And with those words the first tear fell and splashed warm against her folded hands, for Broadwinds seemed a lifetime distant.

16

September 1636
Weymouth, Dorset
England

"In the gaols? But what for?" Will asked, fighting his alarm. "Who will be the new captain?"

"Laddy, settle down. Come, sit here," the older guard said, indicating an empty stool near their small warming coal fire. "Have a cup of hot ale. 'Twill do you well."

William took the proffered cup and sipped at the weak, but warming drink. His thoughts were in a muddle. Was this the sign that the vicar had urged him to look for? Was God telling him to turn back before he even started?

"Where you be from?" asked one of the guards.

"Hadenthorne," William answered. "I have a letter from Sir Edmond and a commission from the Naval Board in London to begin serving aboard the *Minion* as assistant to the ship's master as his navigation aide. I also have the formal certification for the rank from the naval school in Plymouth."

After a moment of silence, Will asked, "Pray tell, Sergeant—what happened to Captain Lawrence? Is he to be removed from duty? Will my papers serve as well if there is a new captain?"

"For a poor boy from a tiny village, you ask a great many questions. Too many to suit us guards, who may not be very well informed."

The sergeant and the corporal smiled. The two lowest ranking members had already drifted back into a semislumber, each nodding off as they sat on the chilly dock.

"William, my boy, I would recommend that you stay here with us till the morrow. That's when, they tell me, the new captain of the *Minion* will be arrivin'. And that's when you can cozy up to 'im with your fancy learnin' and papers."

The hot ale felt good, and William's eyes had drooped a bit as well. Almost without thinking, he slid his one arm through the strap of his bag, and the other he rested on his fob, a small hidden pouch in the waistband of his breeches, where he kept his coins.

"Do not be fearin' us to be thieves, good William. We may be poor marines, but we be God fearin' and we'll not be stealin' from no one."

"That is a comfort to know, Sergeant." William thought for a moment, and then asked again, "What did you say Captain Lawrence was in the gaols for, anyhow? Is it some minor naval matter?"

"Naval, aye. Minor, no," answered the sergeant. "He be under lock and key for causin' the deaths of two dozen of his men."

William sat upright in a quickening, his eyes wide and his mind in a whirl.

London, England

For more than an hour, Kathryne opened cases and trunks, held up gowns, blouses, jackets, and skirts, trying to figure out what would be best kept where. It was soon clear to her that the small room had very limited storage and that, unless she was granted larger living quarters, she would have to leave the majority of her things still packed in their cases. It was strange, doing this for herself. At home, there would have been chambermaids to organize it all; the unpacking would have been done without Kathryne even considering how it happened.

She had filled the six large drawers of the chest with blouses, stockings, chemises, shifts, petticoats, and other items best kept from public view. The diminutive closet had held ten of her full dresses and suits, that is until she realized that it was a shared space. She then reduced the amount to five, folding away the others into one of the large trunks. She slipped several pairs of shoes and lacing boots onto the closet shelf along with a box of perfumed gloves smelling of musk and jasmine. She placed her gilt toilet set, her silver hand mirror, and a lacquer box with her hair ornaments on the top of the chest under the looking glass.

Looking about, she realized that there was no more room allotted. She was finished. She slid a few full cases into the corner, put the few empty cases under her bed, then slid the full cases that she felt she might need in front of them.

I am sure one of the servants will take the rest and place them in the attics in the morning. They can stay there until I have need of them.

Kathryne felt a sense of true accomplishment as she picked up the candle. Half-melted, it was dimming for need of snuffing. She picked off the charred wick without extinguishing the flame. The candle flickered a bit, then began to burn brighter. She opened the door and carefully headed down the half-dark corridor toward the ground floor parlor.

Perhaps it is time to try this coffee drink I have heard so much about, she thought with a smile. *I suppose if Lady Emily has tried it, it is no longer the domain of men.*

Weymouth, Dorset
England

"Deaths? How? What happened?"

William was wide awake now. The effects of the long journey and the ale had immediately vanished. He leaned toward Sergeant Linden.

"Scuttlebutt is that the good captain was a stern man and tolerated no infractions. The vessel was on her voyage back from the isle of Sicily, I believe, and the captain had heard rumors of a seditious group of sailors on board. I will tell for certain, laddy, as I have been on board durin' many sailin's, that there is *always* talk of mutiny in some quarters. But none on the *Minion* was confessed nor found out. Yet Captain Lawrence selected two dozen men at random from all the crews as examples. When none confessed or came forward, he had these men flogged—flogged till they died."

"Good God! Captain Lawrence must be some sort of madman to have that done," William said softly.

"No, lad, not really. It all be part of the discipline at sea. Sometimes it takes a bit more than others. You'll see. 'Tis just that Captain Lawrence went a bit too far this time."

"Well, Sergeant, perhaps the new captain will be a kinder man."

"Pray that he will, laddy. Pray that he will."

London, England

". . . The public has been treated by its rulers as a credulous and hapless herd, begotten to servility. . . ."

It was nearing midnight as Kathryne climbed the staircase back toward her small bedchamber. She had excused herself from the gathering; she could no longer keep her eyes open or her thoughts coherent. The talk and the ideas that were being discussed had been a new and wonderful sensation to her. The most interesting things discussed at Broadwinds had been the latest foxhunt, the impending ball, the expected shipping arrivals. No grand ideas and no glorious thoughts filled the chambers of her country home.

London life was so different than she had imagined. As she lay in her bed, her mind was awhirl with the conversation of the evening.

Just before falling asleep, Kathryne prayed to God, thanking him for this rare opportunity to learn, asking that she be given the discernment to know what is worthy and proper.

She put out the candle with her wetted fingers and closed her eyes to the first night in a new world.

Outside, the night street watchman, with his spear, his lantern, his bell, and his dog, could be heard crying out, "Maids in your smocks, look well to your lock, your fire, and your light. And God give you a good night!"

CHAPTER

17

September 1636
Weymouth, Dorset
England

William had nodded off a few times during the evening. The two officers had stayed the watch all night and were now barking orders to the few dozen groggy sailors who stumbled toward their ships. Each was made to show their leave papers. If it was past the time authorized, it meant a flogging. Some would face time in leg irons, remaining in chains pegged to the wooden deck, exposed to the elements. "That's what they get for returning three sheets in the wind," Sergeant Linden had said.

The sergeant had recommended to William that he present his commission to the harbormaster of Weymouth.

Harbormaster Herbert Dorling occupied a small, squalid office with windows that looked out over the entire harbor. An old battered trestle table that served as his massive desk was stacked with numerous ledger books and sea charts. One chart, almost as tall as a man standing, was posted on the far wall of the room. On it were drawn the piers and buoys and docks of the entire harbor. Large pieces of stiff Bristol board, cut to the shape of a vessel, were pinned at various points along the chart. Each was labeled with the name of a ship. William scanned the drawing and quickly saw the name *Minion* posted midway down Pier Number 16.

"William Hawkes, you say. Let me see yer papers!" Dorling said in a loud voice.

William quickly undid the ties of his leather bag, rummaged for the commission and the letters, and handed the parchment sheets to the harbormaster.

Dorling pushed a stack of ledgers to one side of his cluttered desk and unrolled the papers, smoothing them out with a greasy palm. As he read, he made small guttural noises, not unlike the growling of a dog who feels threatened at his evening meal.

"Seems to be in order," Dorling growled. "That is if Captain Lawrence were still the captain." Dorling let the edges of the parchment go, and they rolled themselves back into a tube. He handed it back to William. "But he ain't."

William looked about. "Is there someone else I should speak to?" He did not want to consider the humiliation of having to return to Hadenthorne and beg the earl a second time for another favor.

"Nah. There isn't another one who knows more than me. I hears the navy is sendin' over the new captain this afternoon. He'll be reportin' to me before he reports to anyone else. If I don't say he can board the *Minion*, he'll not be boardin' the *Minion*."

Herbert Dorling was unquestionably a man who enjoyed the power he wielded. "But I'll not be wantin' you in here all mornin', Hawkes," he said as he rustled through a stack of parchments. "Why not go for a stroll? Visit the church. Take a dander up High Street. Just be back here at eight bells—that be at noon to a landlubber as yourself."

William backed out of the office and walked down to the docks again. The sun was bright this morning, and William squinted into its brilliance. This was not the start he had anticipated. As he walked up High Street, part of him felt a sense of foreboding as gray as the clouds forming over the blue-black waters of the English Sea.

■ ■ ■ ■

William spent the next several hours rambling along the streets of Weymouth, looking at everything but seeing very little. Among the scores of small stores and stalls of the town he had stopped at only one. It was the store of Thomas Delby, whose sign outside his storefront read, T. H. DELBY, SHIP'S CHANDLERY; PURVEYOR OF NAVAL SUPPLIES FOR THE MERCHANTMAN AND PRIVATEER. Displayed in the main window of the store was a gleaming, brass-clad cannon, with intricate and delicate engraving along the barrel. It was supported on a rough oak carriage, with four stubby wooden wheels.

As William entered the darkened interior of the shop, he heard two men in heated exchange, apparently haggling over the price of canvas.

"Two quid for that amount of sailcloth is piracy!" the larger of the two men shouted.

The other man, smaller and older, held his palms up in a supplicant manner and replied in a softer tone, "But it is the fairest price in all of

England. Any less and I will be givin' you coins from me own purse to complete the sale."

"And perhaps you should at that, Mr. Delby. Your fairest price is still too dear for the materials offered."

And with that, the larger man turned and walked out without even a glance at William.

"He'll be back. He'll soon realize that two quid is indeed a fair amount," the smaller man said. He turned and faced William. "So then, my young fellow, what can I do for you this fine day? Some provisions for your vessel? Casks? Canvas? Pitch? Riggin'? Oakum? Perhaps some pistols, some personal armaments?"

William stammered a reply, "No, . . . nothing, thank you. You see, I am William Hawkes, and I am to be on board the *Minion* at noon. It is a new commission, and I had just . . . happened by that cannon there in your window and . . . merely wanted a closer inspection. I hope that this would be permitted."

Thomas Delby walked toward William with a curious thump-drag step. As the man came from the shadows toward the front of the shop, William stared down at his right leg. It ended just below his knee. The cloth of his trousers was gathered about a small leather cup, and a thick wooden peg extended to the floor.

Thomas saw William's eyes dart to the leg and then back to his face.

"It happened off the coast of the Azores more than a score of years ago," the man explained in a practiced manner. "And not even in battle to add to the spice o' the tale. 'Twas a poorly made Dutch cannon that blew up in gunnery practice one fine afternoon. Blew itself up, me leg off, and six of the crew up to their eternal rewards—or down to their eternal punishments, as it may be."

"I am sorry to hear of your misfortune. It must have been painful," William replied.

"Thank you, me lad. 'Twas for a time. But I managed. However, there is only one job on ship for a one-legged man. That be the cook. And owin' to the fact that I canna cook to save me life—or anyone else's—I decided that bein' a naval outfitter and a chandler was nearer to me likin'. So here I be. Thomas Delby at your service. For any provision you might be needin'."

Delby shuffled and thumped to the front of the store, where a tall stool with a canvas seat stood in the corner by the door. He hoisted himself up into it and rested the wooden peg on the latch of the door frame.

"This is so I can nap, and if anyone seeks to purchase, all they need do is knock," he said as he rapped on the solid wood of his artificial leg. "It means I only need awaken for customers."

William ran his hand over the cannon's carving. "And who might be buying such a grand weapon as this, Mr. Delby?"

"You've a good eye, mate. That be a cannon taken from a Spanish warship no more than a year ago in the Caribbean waters off Hispaniola by one of His Majesty's privateers with letters of marque. It was unneeded by the captain, so he sold it to me, and I will be sellin' it back to someone who is outfittin' a new vessel."

"Privateers?"

Delby looked hard at William, who bore a most perplexed look.

"Have ye never been at sea before, William?"

Was it that obvious? William winced. "No, sir. This will be my first sailing."

"Well, me lad, 'tis nothin' to be ashamed of. We all must start at some time, though you seem a bit long in the tooth for an apprentice. May I be offerin' a word of advice to you? Be aware of who you be askin' questions of. Some sea dogs don't take kindly to bein' thought of as a teacher to some fancy gentleman officer pretendin' to be a sailor."

"But I am not a gentleman. I am from simple cottager stock."

"That may be, lad. But still, you be startin' out with a fancy commission, with the help of some fancy lord or lady, most likely. Most sailors never even *see* the officers' deck."

"But they do get to see the world, do they not, Mr. Delby?"

"Aye, that they do." Then Delby shook his head. "If seein' the world means anythin'. They visit the ocean's finest rat holes and worst ports. To many of 'em, a sailor's lot—laborin' in fresh air—seems superior to a life of work sweatin' in the foul atmosphere of a mill or shiverin' in the dampness of a workhouse on land. They prefer to visit houses of dubious virtue and taverns that serve watery spirits and eat the rancid food aboard ship."

William imagined that Delby was doing his best to scare a novice sailor and impress him with his world-weary toughness.

"But are not some vessels different?" William asked.

"None that I've been aboard. The officers be revilin' the crew. The crew be hatin' the officers. Everybody be despisin' the ship, and they begin to loathe the ocean. Lad, I must tell you—'tis not a pretty nor heroic life for a man."

"Mr. Delby, I appreciate your cautions, but may I be so bold as to ask why you stay so near the sea and sailors, if it be such an abomination?"

"Laddy, you've asked the unanswerable question that I pose to meself at least once a day. And you know what me thinks? It be like asking why does God love us poor sinners? Why does the sun rise every day? Why do old sailors stare out to sea long after their limbs have failed 'em?"

Delby paused before answering his own question.

"William Hawkes, 'tis because the sea gets in your blood. You hate it, perhaps, but canna live without it. It be like a wife to you. A wife who harps and throws things when angered, who makes your life miserable at times, but one whose form is of such beauty and pleasure that you canna do without her."

William heard the church tower sound half past eleven and picked up his satchel and prepared to head back to the harbormaster's office.

"Mr. Delby, I thank you for your kind advice. I am sure that I will do my utmost to be a better officer than the ones you have encountered. I will try to make a difference on my vessel. It was a pleasure to have met you. I wish that we could speak at length, but alas, I must head straightaway to the harbormaster to meet the new captain of the *Minion*. I am sure that punctuality is to be expected."

Delby lifted his peg leg off the latch, unbarring the door as William walked through it.

"Perhaps we will meet again upon my return," he said as he headed out the door.

"Aye, William, perhaps we might. God speed your adventure, then."

William stepped out into the bright sunshine and took a few steps when Delby called out to him.

"Mr. Hawkes, wait. I have an item for you that you'll find handy on the voyage."

Delby jumped from his doorway perch and stumped to the back of the shop. In a moment he returned holding a small canvas bag.

William took the small pouch and hefted it carefully.

"It be lemons, Mr. Hawkes."

"Lemons?"

"Aye, lemons. There be a dozen in there. Do you see that I still have most of me teeth I was born with?" He opened his mouth wide.

"Indeed, Mr. Delby, most teeth are in place."

"Well, most sailors are not so fortunate, be they officers or not. You may not get the ship's doctor to agree with you, but I believes the tartness in these lemons keeps the scurvy away. Take the juice of one of those lemons every week, and you'll be the healthiest of the whole vessel, doctor included."

"Once a week, you say?"

"Aye. You can drink the juice in ale or water, or you can just eat the whole lemon. It will do a wondrous work, I swear on that."

"Mr. Delby, I thank you most kindly." He extended his hand, and Delby took it and shook it vigorously.

William waved to him as he turned the corner and headed downhill toward the piers.

Delby hoisted his peg leg back to the door latch, folded his arms over his chest, closed his eyes, and settled in for his morning nap.

London, England

Outside Kathryne's window she heard the sounds of a city coming awake. As the dawn crept over London, she arose, stretched, and slipped from the high bed to the floor. She went to the washbowl and splashed chilled water on her face, toweled herself dry, then splashed on the light scent of Hungary water purchased from a small shop in Dorset. It reminded Kathryne of the scent of spring at Broadwinds.

What to wear on her first full day in London was her next decision. She opened the closet and stuck her hand in the direct middle of her rack of gowns and dresses. She had arranged them the night before in order of fanciness. *About midway might be the best compromise,* she reasoned.

She pulled out a dress of deep blue lightweight wool, with a full skirt and lace hem. The bodice was modest, with lace underneath, buttoned to the throat. The sleeves were narrow, with ivory buttons up to the elbow. She selected a fine new pair of tan leather shoes with silk embroidery trim.

She styled her hair quickly with an ivory comb, carefully trying to emulate the method used by Betsy at home, put some light powder on her face, took one last look in the looking glass, and decided that, in style or not, appropriate or not, it would have to do for this first day.

And just before stepping out the bedchamber door, she slipped on a simple gold chain and delicate gold cross once worn by her mother. She looked down at it, said a quick prayer of thankfulness, and asked God to help guide her through this new day.

Weymouth, Dorset
England

The bell at the cathedral on the north side of town was pealing noon as William ran up the stairs to the office of the harbormaster. As he reached for the door latch, he looked into the bright office and saw a tall, dark man standing erect before Herbert Dorling. He was dressed in a bright red officer's coat with gold embroidered sleeves and gold epaulets with tassels on the shoulders. He held a plumed hat under his arm, his other hand resting on the polished gold handle of a long scabbard, its ebony case gleaming. Next to that was a small dirk with an ivory handle with several red jewels sparkling at the hilt.

He must be the new captain, William thought. He opened the door quietly and slipped into the far corner of the room.

"Captain Evan Blissmore," Dorling rasped, "why don't you turn around and meet your new master's aide. He'll be helpin' with all the mappin' yer vessel needs. Willy, come forward and meet your new captain." It was apparent that Dorling was enjoying making William uncomfortable.

"William Hawkes, sir, at your humble service. I am assigned as master's aide to assist with the navigation, sir." He stepped forward and extended his right hand.

Captain Blissmore turned slowly and did nothing except stare down his nose at William. Every button on his uniform gleamed in the morning sun. Captain Blissmore was a large man, standing more than six feet tall. His black hair was long, as was the custom, and tied in a long tail with a scarlet ribbon. His beard, as black as his hair, was full and reached almost to his chest. His eyes, dark brown to black, pierced William, causing him to shrivel at the man's gaze.

"And where might your uniform be?" the captain asked. It was a smooth, yet cruel voice—thick, low, and ominous.

"Sir, this is my commission," William stammered, as he fumbled for the parchment in his bag. "It is a new posting, and the orders state that all necessary supplies and provisions for my duties will be on board. It says that the uniform will be there as well."

"My Lord!" the captain cried. "This is your first posting?"

"Yes, sir, but I have passed all the admiralty testings."

"They have placed an untested assistant navigator—on his first posting—on *my* ship?"

The office had gone dead quiet. William glanced over the captain's shoulder and saw Dorling with a greasy smile on his face, barely able to contain his mirth.

William braced himself, trying to hold his face still, leaving no indication of the fear that ran in his soul.

"You had best pray that you do *not* direct my ship onto a sandbar or into another vessel, for if you do, I will see to it that you rue the very day you ever thought of seeking a life on the sea. You will curse the very heavens if you embarrass me or foul my ship with your incompetency. Do you understand!"

"Yes, sir. I understand," Will replied, trying to say the words with as much confidence as he could muster.

"Hawkes, get out of my vision and out of those rags and into a proper English uniform. *Now!*"

William took the steps three at a time on his way down and sprinted the entire distance to the *Minion,* not stopping to look so much as right nor left.

London, England

Outside her bedchamber, Kathryne quietly closed the door until she heard the latch close tight. She did not remember closing, nor latching, many doors back home. But here, with such a number of strangers to be living under one roof, she felt it oddly necessary. As the latch clicked, the face of Mr. Biesty floated before her thoughts.

On tentative steps she walked to the end of the hall, stopped at the top of the stairs, and leaned over, listening for voices. *Maybe it is too early for breakfast. Perhaps I will explore while I have the chance.*

She padded down the steps and stopped at the large landing on the first floor. Off to her right was the library she had whirled past last evening. The door was open, and sunlight illuminated the shelves of books. Kathryne walked in, selected one shelf at random, and ran her finger along the spines of the leather-bound volumes. Unsure of the policies of Lady Emily, she thought it best not to remove any of the volumes until she gained permission.

She stepped back into the hall and peered into one of the several meeting rooms. In the second room, there was an older harpsichord and next to it a smaller model of the keyboard instrument. *That is a new virginal,* Kathryne thought, impressed.

In the last room there was a large frame with a tapestry stretched out upon it. The design, a bucolic scene from what appeared to be the North Yorkshire Dales, was nearly three-quarters finished. Another smaller frame held a delicate linen sampler. Colorful wool and cotton threads and other sewing supplies were piled on a small table off to one side.

From downstairs, she made out the faint clatter of dishes and silver and the low mutterings of servants' voices.

She stepped to the stairway and quickly descended into the cheery breakfast room. Lady Emily sat reading at a small table nestled under a wide window overlooking the pleasant garden at the rear of the house. In front of her was a shiny silver tray with biscuits, jams, and a tea service for one.

As she saw Kathryne enter the room, Lady Emily brightly exclaimed, "My dear Kathryne, do come and join me. I can see you are likewise an early riser. How delightful!"

As Kathryne walked over to her, Lady Emily picked up a small bell, rang it, and almost immediately an elderly lady in a parlormaid's uniform delivered a second tray. As she sat down at the table, Kathryne could see that the book Lady Emily had been reading was a copy of the King James Bible, well worn from use.

"And how did you sleep last night?"

"Perfectly well, Lady Emily. I daresay that London is a bit more noisy than Broadwinds—or noisy in a different manner. I heard no owls or foxes during the night, but I did hear several voices calling out most persistently."

"Oh, yes. The delights of city dwelling," Lady Emily replied. "Most likely a few revelers from the public house nearby on Bourne Street. Occasionally a patron is too much into his cups, and we all hear about his progress as he makes his way past us."

"And then this morning, rather than a rooster, I heard the baker as he made his stop at the Alexandrian," Kathryne said as she picked up the buttery biscuit from the plate on her tray. "If they taste as good as they smell, I shall have no trouble forgetting the skills of Mrs. Cole, our cook at Broadwinds."

With that she spread the biscuit with a thick serving of plum jam and took a more than lady-sized bite.

"Ummm, I think I am already forgetting."

Lady Emily laughed and poured two cups of tea, a drink which was somewhat new to England.

"I know that tea is not the usual choice of beverage for breakfast for most of my young charges, but I tend to find it well suited for the meal. Having ale for breakfast seems so . . . uncivilized, and tea is the latest fascination here in London," she said with no hint of condescension.

In the country, the normal beverage was either weak ale, watered wine, or cider. They did drink tea at Broadwinds, brought from the Orient on Lord Aidan's ships, but for most it was too exotic, too recently introduced, and too costly to be widely accepted.

The two women sat, relaxing and enjoying the view of the garden. One of the cooks had spread out some crumbs, which were set upon by small birds, chirping and singing. One small creature, emboldened by familiarity or hunger, set down on the open windowsill just by Kathryne.

Lady Emily whispered, "Kathryne, put a small crumb in your hand. That's Willy. He's looking for a meal."

Kathryne broke off a small piece of biscuit and held it out. The brown bird with red and white markings hopped to her hand with a quick flash of wings, and with its dark eye it peered directly at Kathryne, then at Lady Emily.

Kathryne beamed at the experience, holding such a small, delicate creature.

"It's a Williamson thrush," Lady Emily said softly. "He's been coming here most mornings for several years—most often when I have my daily time in the Scriptures. I think he must be searching for the truth as well."

The tiny bird pecked gently at the crumbs Kathryne offered.

"I think he must know a friendly face when he sees one. He rarely does that for a stranger—or a person with an impure heart."

Weymouth, Dorset England

As he neared the end of the pier, William saw that a mass of pulleys and ropes had been assembled, some tied to mooring piers and pilings next to the ship, others stretched across several piers and tied to the masts and yardarms of ships berthed on adjacent piers. A gang of sailors, some with tan breech coats marking them as carpenters, were hoisting a new mainmast into place. Officers stood on deck with megaphones shouting instructions and commands to various teams of men, each team holding on to coarse ropes as thick as a man's wrist.

"Heave!" shouted one red-coated officer at a dozen men holding a rope at waist level.

As William neared the ship, the new mast, required to replace the mast that had broken in a storm off the Canary Islands more than a fortnight ago, was about to be lowered into the mainmast hole.

"Heave!"

The entire mast slid toward the hole, and then into it.

"Hold to!" several officers bellowed simultaneously.

Sailors began to climb the new mast, removing the stay ropes and pull lines, disassembling complex rigging, climbing the forward and rear masts, removing set lines and pulleys.

William felt purposeless in the whirlwind of activity as he stood on the pier, surrounded by the rush of sailors and officers, each with a clearly defined task in the mast raising. He walked to the cleated gangboard and stepped across the bouncing board from pier to ship's deck, stopping only for a quick glance at the calm waters of Weymouth Harbor. He stood on deck, feeling for the first time its gentle, almost imperceptible roll as the ship lay calm at mooring.

How curious of a sensation, he thought, *to be on such a hard surface that pitches ever so gently.*

An officer strode arrogantly up to William, eying him warily.

"William Hawkes, master's assistant navigator, reporting for service, sir," William said sharply, holding out his commission.

The officer, in his thick red coat, was sweating profusely. His deeply lined face, browned by the sun, was wet, and pools of perspiration had stained the back of his collar.

"Well, William Hawkes," he said as he wiped his brow on his sleeve. "You've been a navy man all of thirty seconds and you've already received your first promotion. It seems the old ship's master has gone on to his heavenly reward this very morning. How fortuitous for you."

William stared blankly, as if he could not comprehend the words he had just heard spoken.

"Come now, Mr. Hawkes. Do not look so surprised. Death will visit the *Minion* just as often as it visited wherever it is you've come from."

"Hadenthorne, sir."

"Have never heard of it, but that be of no matter. My name is Christopher Reed. I am First Lieutenant of the *Minion.* Let me introduce you to the ship's purser. I am sure he'll see to your uniform."

William meekly followed Lieutenant Reed toward the rear of the ship.

Reed stepped through a small doorway on the aft officers' deck. Being shorter than William, he ducked his head a practiced few inches. William, eager to keep up, misjudged the small frame and soundly banged the crown of his head in the beamed archway of the door.

"Welcome to the *Minion,* Mr. Hawkes," an amused Lieutenant Reed said. "Hatches are small here, and that will be but the first of many bruises—most likely a score more if you be a slow learner."

William rubbed his hand over the tender spot on his head. "Sir, I will learn the ways of this vessel with greater haste than you have ever seen," he stated.

"You'll need to. I hear we sail in two days with the night tide, for our new captain gets here tomorrow."

"Lieutenant, I must report that he will be here today. I have had the honor of meeting him at the harbormaster's office barely an hour past."

Reed stopped dead and spun and faced William in the dim light. He brought his face close. "What!? He'll be here this day? Hawkes, if you'd chosen a less suited way to make a favorable impression upon me of your analytical skills, you scarce could have thought up a more dismal response. He is on his way, and yet you neglected to inform me? How bloody wonderful, you simple-minded, grass-combing farmer!"

William stood silent again.

"You've chosen a unequivocally abysmal method of introducing yourself to His Majesty's navy. Please pray that your second day is less botched than your first."

Reed turned abruptly and began to climb the ladder they had just descended. "Hawkes, the purser is at the end of this passageway. Even *you* will not be able to mistake that fact."

London, England

As she sat and chatted with Lady Emily over tea, Kathryne discovered that most of the other young ladies would not arrive for several more days. In attendance at the Alexandrian, to date, was a Miss Elizabeth Murray of Ipswich, Henrietta de Keroulle of Portsmouth, both of whom Kathryne had met the previous evening, and the twins, Celia and Cecily Althorp of Bath.

Lady Emily explained, "As a general rule, breakfast, at about this same time each morning, is followed by lessons until our meal at early afternoon. Depending on the day, we will look at the classics—Cato, Varro, and the like—or more current writings. We will also study the French language as well as Latin."

Kathryne winced. "I must admit that those were not easy subjects. I have virtually no adroitness with tongues other than English, I am afraid."

"Your mother was much the same," Lady Emily related, "but she had a brief knowledge of both. We will also spend time with music. I understand from your father's letter that you do have a skill with scales?"

"Yes, and I am greatly pleased that I saw the music room on my way to breakfast."

"We will also call on some prominent ladies in London for conversation and perhaps a recital. This is the time that manners will be taught, and the proper method of meeting guests and running a mannered home. Like yourself, several of the young women here have grown up without the advantage of a mother for instruction in the art of being a proper lady of the house."

"I know," Kathryne giggled. "Mrs. Cole, my cook, said that you would throw up your hands in despair at the notion of teaching me to behave as a lady."

"I have never yet been confounded by such a task. And I know that your mother—and your father—have raised a God-fearing daughter. Those who understand the Scriptures are always so much more teachable. They have more the servant's heart."

Kathryne lowered her eyes. At times like this, the absence of a mother was sharp against her heart.

Lady Emily reached over and placed her hand atop Kathryne's. "I know how you feel, incomplete at times. I miss her as well, though my pain could not be as acute as yours." After a moment Lady Emily brightened, then added, "And I will have such amusement showing you London! There is so much to see and do—the monuments of Westminster, the shops on Bond Street. . . . Why shall we delay our first adventure? Let's let the sleepyheads slumber. We shall venture forth without them. Run and take a wrap, and I will summon a carriage."

Kathryne, excited by the prospect of adventure, rose and headed to her room. At the doorway, she stopped and turned back. "Lady Emily, I must ask you." She grasped the sides of her dress and billowed the skirt out and turned. "Is this a proper style to wear about the city? Is it what proper young ladies wear? Will they think me hopelessly provincial?"

Emily walked to her, took her hands in her own, then pulled her hair back from her shoulders, smoothing a few curls.

"My dear, with your angelic face and womanly form, there will be *no* one who will complain about your dressings."

Kathryne frowned. "That is what a parent says, Lady Emily. My father has said much the same on any number of formal occasions. But I came here to seek the truth. I must ask that you be truthful in all matters."

Emily took a step back and reviewed her young student with a slow, critical look.

"You are a most beautiful girl. That is the truth indeed. And this afternoon I hope you will allow me to introduce you to Mrs. Whilloughby."

Kathryne raised her eyebrows, puzzled.

"Mrs. Whilloughby is, by far, the most talented and stylish seamstress in all of London. We will match your form to its wrappings."

18

September 1636
The Atlantic Ocean

The *Minion* was two weeks out of Weymouth, and William Hawkes considered himself but a small cog in the enormous machine that was an oceangoing ship of His Majesty's navy. The *Minion* was not a top-of-the-line ship. She was only an older twenty-eight-gun frigate with three masts—foremast, mainmast, and mizzenmast—seven decks, and a complex birdcage of rigging, ropes, canvas, spars, lifts, davits, shrouds, lanyards, and deadeyes. The ship was 150 feet long, 40 feet wide at the widest, and had a draft of 20 feet. The *Minion* sailed well in heavy seas but was not quite as nimble in light winds. The cannons were split even on the port and starboard and occupied portions of the upper deck and main deck. It seemed a surprisingly small ship for the number of crew—each man seemed never to be more than an arm's length away from the other. But when the winds roughened, every man was needed to furl sails, to batten ledges and hatches, and to buckle the plugs into every porthole and opening.

William often stood on deck just to stare up into the maze of ropes and canvas, draped like vines from the masts. From the yardarms, Will watched as sailors let loose the sails when officers called "Let fall!"

More than 150 sailors, carpenters, marines, cooks, officers, doctors, clergymen, and servants made up their peaceful mission to the Azores and on to Venice. The *Minion* was to provide protection to a small convoy of merchant ships primarily hauling wool but also carrying some farm tools and muskets. It was an unusual assignment. Per standard operating procedures, a British navy vessel would not become involved in any protection of other English ships unless they happened upon an infraction as it occurred. The Crown, its treasuries now all but depleted from a recession of trade, was hard-pressed to spend additional monies providing insurance for merchants. But King Charles was committed to trade expansion. None of the experienced officers had any kind words for this duty.

William had eventually found his station and berth that first day, with little help from the other officers. His belongings were confined to a small sea chest bolted at the aft section below the quarterdeck. His narrow hammock would be hung between two beams. A scrutoire, a portable desk, folded down from the side of the hull and was large enough to spread out maps and charts. He spent most of his days poring over those charts, climbing to the quarterdeck every hour to take a new reading from the sun with his sextant, and consulting the large compass that hung level in the gimbals on the master's station. He quickly became proficient at the use of the ship's astrolabe and cross-staff and charted their change in position using the heavenly bodies as constants. These readings and consulting established charts would place the *Minion* more precisely along their route.

Lieutenant Reed, as well as the rest of his crew, had been incredulous at William's commission and assignment. "Never been at sea and you are our navigator?" Reed blustered, the gold buttons on his coat shaking in agitation.

Most other officers had complained bitterly, rolling their eyes and making comments that it would be a true miracle of God if they managed to make it out of the channel without running aground.

William felt every bit the fool and complete novice as he drew up the sailing charts for the first few days. He took comfort in the fact that, as tested by the Royal Naval Sea Regulator in Plymouth some months earlier, he had scored the highest of any candidate in navigational skills. The magistrate in charge of the testing had William repeat many parts of the examination, for he had been sure that Will had spirited a copy of the questions prior to the actual inquiry.

Now it was imperative that the fleet sail immediately, and there was no time for a replacement to be brought on board, so the *Minion* sailed with William at the navigator's station.

A week out of port she would reach first landfall at the Azores island chain. There the entire fleet would take on fresh water, and the merchants would conduct a portion of their business.

William had taken several readings with his sextant, transferring the information to his charts indicating depth of water. He peered out at the rolling sea from his perch in his small berth just below the quarter-deck, watching the color of the water change from the blue of a summer sky to the green of a pond in a meadow to the gray of a slate roof. He puzzled over the numbers, measuring the chart not twice, but three times. He picked up the sextant and reread the figures. He plotted backwards on the map with a compass and pen. He ran to the top deck and let out the log line, a long reel of rope with a small block of weighted wood at the end. As the ship sailed forward, William counted the knots in the rope that slipped past during a minute of counting, which indicated the speed of the ship. *Twelve knots.* He wound the rope back in and ran back to his station. The speed of the wind, nor the speed of the ship had varied more than a breath in the last few hours—making his dead reckoning of this position more certain.

This is wrong. This chart must be wrong, he thought.

He lifted the large linen sheet, carefully hand drawn by expert chart makers in London. It was done no more than six months prior.

"Can it be so misplaced?" he said to himself out loud.

William slipped the chart beneath a sturdy wooden arm to hold it in place and ran back to the top decks for one more sighting. He ran to a junior lieutenant and with a most polite tone, asked for a momentary use of his telescope. Telescopes were a new innovation and highly prized. As a result, most officers were loath to let these in the hands of a junior man. The lieutenant hesitated, then scowled and handed him the brass instrument.

William ran to the mainmast at the bow of the vessel and tucked the telescope into the belt of his breeches.

Pray that it does not drop into the sea, William told himself.

He grabbed the far rigging and made his way slowly, climbing the ropes as the ship pitched in the wind, making sure of each foothold before taking a step higher.

He found a handhold at the maintop, the small platform halfway up the foremast, some forty feet above the decking. Once situated in his lofty perch, he braced himself against the mast and opened the telescope, focusing it east toward land. At the crest of the wave William saw a faint touch of brown—a distant, low outline of the coast—just barely visible.

From the ship's deck, William could see a horizon of no more than a mile. From the maintop, Will could see nearly twelve miles. A ship's topsail could be spotted at twenty miles. But this was his first sighting of land, and he now could firmly triangulate his position. He tucked the telescope back in his belt and slipped down the ropes in haste. He ran back to the quarterdeck, gathered up his sextant, took a final reading, then charged back to his maps and charts.

After a third sighting and that first view of land, he knew that a grievous error had been made. Marking a thin triangle on the map, he realized that the chart maker had reversed a number and that the distances indicated on the revised chart were severely flawed.

The last accurate reading was two hours prior; his sighting and the chart matched. If they stayed on this course they would be at risk of running aground on a ridge of dangerous shoals no more than ten leagues north of their first port of call, Ponta Delgada, on the small island of São Miguel, due north of the island of Madeira—all Portuguese landings.

William knew his calculations were correct. *Do I dare tell Captain Blissmore?* he wondered. *Will he believe me?*

William knew he had no choice. In a moment, he was standing at the captain's door, softly tapping. Lieutenant Reed swung it open, and as he saw William, he rolled his eyes and muttered, "Enter."

William blinked at the rich wood paneling lining the walls, the dark red leather cushions on the chairs and benches. Off to the side, William saw the captain's bed, a boxlike cot, looking every bit like a coffin, hung from the deckhead. Lined with a thick white blanket, it was fitted to the captain's height exactly, for if he died while on the ocean, it would be nailed shut with a few cannon shot for weight and heaved overboard for a quick burial at sea. It creaked slowly with the listings of the ship. William looked back at the top of Blissmore's head.

"Sir, I . . ."

"Hawkes, I have little time for you," Captain Blissmore said as he glanced up from a stack of papers, invoices and shipping logs piled in great teetering stacks on his small desk. "State your business."

"Uh, sir, it appears that the map we are using has been mislabeled. The sighting at noon was correct, but the last two have been more than three degrees off. If we do not compensate, we will run aground on the shoals just north of the port of Angra do Heroismo on the island of Terceira."

Blissmore put down his quill and sighed. "Good God, man. I am to trust an entire convoy on the word of a navigator with two weeks' skill? Is that what you are asking me?"

William just stood, silent.

"Do you take me for a fool, Mr. Hawkes?" Blissmore said with ice in his voice.

"No sir, I most certainly do not."

"Do you think the admiralty is in the habit of making mistakes? Do you think your abilities are that much superior to chart makers who have devoted their lives to the task?"

"No, sir."

"Then you will do me the pleasure of removing your most unpleasant frame from my quarters."

"But, sir, the shoals are no more than a half hour's sail."

"I will not repeat myself again, Mr. Hawkes."

"But we need to rechart, sir."

"Mr. Hawkes, I will do no such thing. And if you say one more word of this, I will have you in leg irons on the deck for a fortnight."

William opened his mouth, and then caught himself as Blissmore rose sharply from his chair, standing almost face-to-face.

"Aye, sir," William said and turned to leave.

As Lieutenant Reed ushered him out, William whispered, "Lieutenant, it *is* true. Please come and see the charts. If we do nothing, we are in grave danger."

Reed knew that if the *Minion* struck those shoals, rescue at sea was difficult. And those officers who would be saved faced the humiliation of an investigation back in Weymouth. There would be little advancement opportunities for such an officer.

"You best pray to your God that you are indeed correct, Hawkes," Reed hissed back. "If you are drawing the long bow here and stretching the truth—I will have your hide, pure and simple. But you have me at a disadvantage, you stupid farmer. I cannot correct your questionable sighting errors now. But on the minuscule chance you are correct, I must take out insurance. Go up to the quarterdeck and tell Lieutenant Mallory that the *Tempest* is to take the lead for the next two hours. If we reach the shoals as you say, I would rather have her sunk than us. Now go!"

Returning to his charts after informing Lieutenant Mallory, William felt a sense of exhilaration coupled with a bit of panic. He knew he was correct in his calculations and felt helpless to prevent a tragedy to the *Tempest*. He rubbed the dull ache creeping up the back of his neck, then sat and stared out the small square window facing west. If he leaned toward the sea he could just make out the *Tempest* as she moved into position at the lead. William looked at his chart once more, made a few final calculations, and then set down his quill. He closed the inkwell, closed his eyes for a brief moment, then folded up his desk and made his way slowly to the poop deck, the highest deck on the ship and the one that offered the best visibility. Off in the distance, perhaps a half league in the lead, the *Tempest* sailed at full canvas, riding low in the waves, laden with cargo. William walked to the rail and leaned forward. Part of his soul hoped he was wrong.

Is it wrong to pray for the safety of those men, he asked himself, *when I myself doubt the effectiveness of such petitions?*

Nonetheless he mumbled a prayer he had learned by rote from the vicar. *Perhaps it will do some good, after all,* he said to himself. *I did promise to seek, and the vicar promised that God would look out for me as well.*

All was calm for the next hour, and William relaxed.

Perhaps I have made a miscalculation, he thought. *But if I have, Lieutenant Reed will be fit to tie.*

Both his expectations and fears were met a few moments later. William's eyes opened wide as he saw the *Tempest* rock stern end up and then list mightily to one side. The wind was broad into her sails, coming from the northeast, and the crew on deck saw the events unfold silently, terrifyingly mute, for the wind washed the screams of the *Tempest's* men away from their ears. The ship began to come about, her sails dipping into the salt waters, her mast nearly horizontal. William could see crewmen, tiny in the distance, leap from the ship, scrambling for small boats, clinging to cargo washed from the upper forecastle deck.

"Heave to!" bellowed the helmsman, who pulled the wheel to the right. An officer shouted "Away aloft!"

"Boats away!" screamed another officer, and as the *Minion* turned, sailors sprang to the small deck boats. Within minutes a half dozen were afloat and oars straining, headed to the floundering *Tempest.*

Other ships in the convoy had begun to heave to as well, lowering sails, pulling starboard into the wind, setting out rescue boats.

Captain Blissmore clamored up onto the quarterdeck, demanding the telescope. Through it he could see the gaping hole torn in the hull of the *Tempest,* her men paddling to stay alive in the heavy chop of the shoals. Cargo was strewn in a widening river from the vessel, following the current of the sea as it broke over the shallows.

He swung the telescope to his side. His face was red, his breathing labored. "See to it that what cargo is salvaged is distributed to the rest of the fleet," he ordered to Lieutenant Reed.

He walked woodenly to William and put his face no more than an inch from his ear.

"If one word of your initial request ever is heard by any man of this ship I will have your head," he hissed. "Is that understood? Your head will be speared on a pike at the front of this ship."

William nodded mutely.

"I *said,* Mr. Hawkes, is that understood?"

"Aye, Captain Blissmore. It is understood."

And with that the captain turned and fumed back to his cabin. At the top of the stairway, he stopped. "Mr. Hawkes, please plot us a new course for Ponta Delgada."

The *Minion* and the rest of the convoy arrived at the island of São Miguel, in the Azores, without further incident. Nearly three-fourths of the *Tempest*'s cargo was salvaged, the ship staying afloat for nearly an hour until she rolled and dipped beneath the waves. More than fifty crewmen were lost in her grounding. High swells and strong winds caused many weak swimmers to perish quickly. Not all sailors, William discovered to his amazement, knew anything about personal survival in water. He was glad for his summers by the river Taw and how he had taught himself to paddle, unaided, from one side to the other. But he was grieved at the loss of the fifty crewmen. *I tried to save them,* he consoled himself.

In Ponta Delgada a few goods were bought and sold from most of the ships in the fleet. Much wool was traded, and oil, olives, wine, cork, and port were bought in return, as well as fresh beef and a refreshed store of water. They then sailed south, past the Desertas Islands off Madeira's southern tip, and to the port of Funchal. The town was tucked into the southern coast of the island below terraced vineyards. What was not covered with vineyards, William noticed, was covered with scented fields of jasmine, veronica, salvia, and rosemary.

William accompanied one of the junior lieutenants of a smaller cargo ship of the fleet to help supervise the off-loading. Two native merchants were in a disagreement with the ship's captain. The two Portuguese islanders, a dark and shadowy pair, would speak with gestures and fast words in their native tongue, then slower, more halting, in English to the English captain.

William stood and listened. His knowledge of Portuguese was limited, and the pair spoke a fractured, country dialect, but he managed to follow most of their deliberations—private deliberating, they thought, in their own language.

Near the close of the transaction it appeared that only a few pounds separated both parties. "I think this feeble-minded English captain will take five hundred pounds for the entire hold of wool," one native trader said to the other. "It is cheap by half as to the real worth. And to think I was prepared to spend eight hundred pounds."

The ship's captain, frustrated over the slowness of the negotiations, was prepared to sign for the five-hundred-pound sum, thinking it was the upper limit of these "backward" traders.

William casually strolled over to the captain and remarked under his breath, "Raise the price to 750. It is within their resources."

The captain stared at William. *Who is this,* he thought, incredulous, *and how could he know the price of wool in the Azores? What does a backward-farmer-turned-sailor know about trading?*

The captain looked hard at William, who stood nearby, gazing out to the harbor, with no sign of nervousness. The captain then looked to the traders, who appeared a step more concerned than a few moments prior.

Let me take a chance, he thought, and paused. "Seven hundred fifty pounds," the captain said boldly. "That is the true price of the cargo."

A second round of haggling ensued, but a final price received for the wool was seven hundred twenty-five pounds.

The captain, in gratitude, sent William a one-pound coin in a leather pouch.

Daily activity on the *Minion* was both mind-numbing and exhilarating. William enjoyed charting out the route, reading maps, and setting the course. He was in love with the feel of the sea and the smell of the saltwater as he stood on the rear poop deck, riding high above the waves. He felt refreshed as the winds washed over him. Returning belowdecks afterward was difficult; the stench from the fouled seawater in the bilge, unbathed bodies, and rotting food was at times overwhelming. Sailors seemed to care little for bathing—most washed their stained hammocks only under an officer's order.

William felt comfortable speaking at leisure with only two or three of the officer corps. He often felt quite lonely, even in the midst of so many men, so tightly packed. The crowd of seamen that the vessel carried was the true engine of the ship. The total crew was made up of small subgroups: carpenters, stewards, and sail makers. The petty officers corps consisted of stewards, yeomen, quartermasters, boatswains' mates, gunners' mates, midshipmen, quarter gunners, chaplains, coxswains, cooks, a schoolmaster, a surgeon, purser, gunner, shipmaster, master-at-arms, a dozen lieutenants, and the captain. Seemingly apart from much of this was the navigator—William.

At night, in tighter waters, the ships of the fleet would lie with sails furled, not wanting to sail into any unseen obstructions. William would lie in his hammock, stretched out between two beams by his desk, and listen to the vessel around him splash softly in the dark, still waters.

Fire was a constant threat, so no lanterns, except those mounted at the aft deck and one per deck, were allowed. By day, deck prisms—small polished pyramids of thick glass—were set into the upper decks and allowed a bit of the sun's rays to penetrate the gloom. Beneath that, it was dark, dank, and foul. Belowdecks he could hear snoring and sometimes laughter echo up the gangways. Nights were often so lightless, so dark, so filled with blackness that William at times could not recall what light might look like. In these pools of pitch-black, William would close his eyes and try and recall the images of Hadenthorne; he would see the face of the vicar, Mrs. Cavendish's smile, her sons, the cool air of the garden in the morning, and Missy Holender. He felt a thousand leagues and a lifetime removed from all of that. It had been only a short time away, but each evening he had to struggle harder to conjure up their images. For every league they sailed, Will felt his memory of Hadenthorne and all his friends slip further and further into the graying fog of a past life.

His new experiences would have been more palatable, William thought, if only life were not so brutal on this vessel. The food was of abysmal quality most time—maggot-filled and often rancid. There was bread when in port, biscuits and hardtack when at sea, dried peas, salt pork, porridge, and cheese—and that was all. The meat had to be soaked to remove the salt, which made it tough, and when fried a yellow slush of grease floated to the top of the pan. Perhaps to dull the senses, the rations also included eight pints of ale per day, plus a full pint of brandy. William quickly began to dream of the meals prepared by Mrs. Cavendish, especially figgy-dowdy, his favorite pudding made with raisins.

He continued to consume lemons and other fruits at every chance, always buying an extra supply at every port. It was true what Master Delby said. For a sailor to have a full set of teeth was indeed a rarity. Scurvy, even worse an affliction, seemed to strike the ship no more than a few fortnights out of port. It would leave men pale and in pain. Wounds from old sword fights would open up after healing years prior. Too quickly their lungs would fill and their breathing would be labored until it stopped altogether. The dead of the lower classes were simply tossed overboard, a cannonball stitched into their hammock to weigh their journey to the bottom of the sea. A prayer was sometimes offered, sometimes not.

And civility was a rarity as well. Will saw that the average sailor on board slept in dirty, smelly surroundings, did dangerous work, suffered under despotic officers, endured harsh, often deadly punishments—for poor food, a pittance of a wage and, on occasion, a brandy-soaked adventure in a dangerous foreign port.

William resolved to not discipline fellow crewmen. It was not his station to come into much contact with them, but other officers took delight at brutalizing their fellowman. There were beatings and punishments for virtually any and every infraction of the rules, minor and major. Men were seized to the shrouds—hung from the rigging—for days in the wind and sea spray. Men were flogged near senseless by boatswains' mates; men found stealing were run the gauntlet of the entire crew who were armed with short, stout pieces of rough rope to lash out at them; men were placed in leg irons and left in the hot sun or freezing rain on deck for days as well.

It was so disturbing to William that he, despite his avoidance of spiritual matters, sought out the ship's chaplain one day as they sailed south along the African coast. All naval ships employed a clergyman because it was thought that a wholesome spiritual presence would encourage the crew to work harder, obey orders more closely, avoid mutiny, and generally make for a more successful journey.

"Chaplain," Will said, as they both stood by the rail of the quarter-deck, "why is it that no one is treated with respect on board? It seems to me that some officers actually enjoy meting out lashings and other corporal punishment."

The kindly chaplain, a portly Anglican priest from Norwich, replied, "Son, it is God's plan. He made the weak, and he made the strong. It is up to the strong to keep the weak in check. It is the godly way of the world."

"But that is not what Jesus taught," Will replied. "He said to treat others as we would ourselves. That is the Golden Rule of all faith. What the officers are doing is not following his teachings."

The chaplain stood for a moment. "Jesus was not speaking of the navy when he said those words. He would have phrased it different had he done so."

CHAPTER

19

December 1636
Weymouth, Dorset
England

"Mr. Biesty, if you please—stop the carriage here."

At the sound of his brother's voice, Radcliffe had opened his eyes and looked about, recognizing where they were—at the top of High Street in Weymouth.

"Aidan," he said with an icy tone, "I trust that you can handle the meeting with Captain Nance of the *Noble's Courage*. I have never liked him, and it has been a long journey. I believe I will refresh myself at one of these fine establishments."

Radcliffe sauntered into Percival's and walked boldly to the bar. He stopped, then turned and walked back to the doorway without asking for any refreshments. He watched as the Spenser hackney carriage turned the corner and spun away. But to be sure it was gone, he paused a moment more, filling his pipe with tobacco and puffing away.

No sense my being too anxious to meet with an old scapegallows like Dorling, Radcliffe thought, then began to chuckle quietly.

As Radcliffe waited patiently in the shadows of the tavern at the top of High Street, Lord Aidan was most anxious to arrive at Pier Number 12, where his shipping partner, Captain Nance, awaited him. His ship, the *Noble's Courage,* had at last returned from India, its cargo hold full of cotton, exotic spices, tea, silk, and pungent oils. On board, to Lord Aidan's surprise, was a group of six black men.

"Got 'em off the coast of Africa," Captain Nance declared proudly, as a few passersby on the pier gawked at them, staring at the unusual sight. Adding in a whisper to Lord Aidan, he said, "Traded my own personal musket for 'em and some powder and shot. Didn't cost you a shillin'."

"Captain, I am overjoyed that you have returned home safely, and with such a wonderful cargo, but trading guns for black men? What on earth are you thinking?"

Captain Nance placed his meaty hand on Lord Aidan's shoulder and drew closer. Lord Aidan tensed and thought of pulling back from the man, who smelled as if he had not bathed the entire six-month voyage. Soap, which was most dear to begin with, did not lather in seawater. Captain Nance may have had a visit to a Turkish bath in Gibraltar, their last stop, but that was several weeks prior.

"I know it's a little odd, perhaps. A little out o' the standard scheme o' things. But I know that there are ships on their way to the Caribbees. They all need slaves in the New World. Sellin' them at a tidy profit is what I plan."

At this statement, Lord Aidan did pull back and away. "Slaves? That, sir, is an abomination. I am sure that the Scriptures speak against the practice of one Christian enslaving another."

"Well, Lord Aidan, you would know that better than I, who remains woefully ignorant of such spiritual matters. I will say that these savages are not Christian but heathen, no doubt, and know not one word of God's Bible. Take that into accounts, and you'll have less of an effort to justify their purchase and sale. The Dutch call 'em black gold, for they'll be worth their weight in it when the sugar crops take hold in the Indies."

Lord Aidan was upset, and a scowl set upon his face.

"Now, my lord—there are other matters that need discussin'. To trifle over a few savages seems foolish. Let us not be misled. Not when you have so much other merchandise and stores to be accountin'," said Nance.

Slaves, Lord Aidan thought with a shudder. *How can a man sink so low?*

"Captain Nance, this is egregious, and you should know better of it. But as you say, other concerns are more pressing. Please—get them belowdecks and out of sight immediately. And do make plans to dispose of them at the earliest convenience. This whole matter is most unsettling."

As he walked up the gangway to the *Noble's Courage,* he stared hard at their pained and frightened faces. *'Tis a comfort that they are indeed mere savages,* he thought, and said to Captain Nance, "Now let us begin the counting."

And as the two watched assistants mark and tally each bale and carton of goods on the *Noble's Courage,* a more malevolent meeting was taking place, closer than a musket shot from that particular ship.

"Well, Dorling. I see that you have changed little since we met last. It appears that your jacket is indeed the same unlaundered rag as you wore last fall."

Harbormaster Dorling snarled back a guttural and vulgar retort at the elegantly attired Radcliffe Spenser.

Radcliffe looked shocked, then tilted his head back and laughed loudly. "I see that you have not lost your wit, my dear man. Such a civility about you."

Radcliffe and Dorling were standing in the shadows of the harbormaster's office. Dorling slumped into his chair by the desk. Radcliffe pulled up another and sat nearly face-to-face with Dorling.

"Are we agreed as to the accounting? An increase of two percent in all import levies on all items on board? And those additional funds are to be split evenly between your person and mine?"

"That's what we swore on last time," Dorling said.

"And that I must be shipboard as the counts and taxes are figured, agreed?"

"Agreed."

"It is most pleasant that we can handle such transactions with so little tumult, is it not, Mr. Dorling?"

"Aye, that it be, Mr. Spenser. That it be."

The pair watched as the crew of the *Noble's Courage* tended to repairs and unloading of empty barrels and rotten canvas.

"Dorling," asked Radcliffe, "where might a man dispose of black men in Weymouth?"

"Black men as in Moors, or be they heathens from the jungle?"

"Jungle black men, I would surmise."

"I would say but one man in Weymouth would be bold enough to offer purchase of slaves."

"And who might that be, my good man?"

"Why, it be Captain Blake, of the *Plymouth Spirit*."

CHAPTER

20

June 1637
London, England

"So tell me, Kathryne, what has been the most memorable event of your time at the Alexandrian this year?" Lady Emily asked as the entire class sat down together for one of their final meals of the term. It was a week prior to the summer season, and most of the young ladies would travel home to spend time with family and friends.

Kathryne had been packed for days. At first, the longing for home was slight. There was so much to learn, so many places in London to visit, such intriguing people to meet. But as the days became warmer, she thought of Broadwinds. She imagined the lime-green buds of the hawthorn, the furry blooms on the pussy willows by the river Parrett, and especially the carpet bluebells found in the forests and meadows of Broadwinds. And she also thought of Mrs. Cole, her father, and even Radcliffe, and when she did a corner of her heart would begin to ache. *I love what I am doing here and learning—but I miss them all so much,* she often thought, fighting the urge to weep.

But today the prospect of seeing them and her beloved Broadwinds again was cheering her soul.

"Well, Lady Emily, I have loved it all—every minute of every day. To choose the most eminent of them all—why, I daresay it would be impossible."

Lady Emily laughed. "Another method to avoid an answer, my dear, and I will not have it. If I have tried to do one thing these past months, it was to instill confidence in each of you—and an ability to *think.*" Her tone was nearing her strict teacher's voice that they all had grown accustomed to. "Now I want you to think! Prioritize! Evaluate! Choose!"

Kathryne pursed her lips, and the lines in her forehead creased. The rest of the women at the table were glad it was Kathryne that was called upon, not them.

"To be true, what most impacted me was hearing Reverend John Lilburne."

Lady Emily cocked her head to the side. "And why would he make such an impact?"

"By the power of his argument—that there are no *natural* justifications for the inequalities between different classes of men, that there is no *natural* justification for the inequalities between man and woman, but we are all one in Christ and equals in his eyes. I know it is quite the Puritanical notion of these matters, but they have stirred up my soul. It was indeed most memorable."

She paused again. "But that is only a small part of how I have changed. I see my life different than before. I have asked myself what the reason might be for this change in my heart. And my answer is always the same. I have changed because of those few minutes every morning that Lady Emily and I have spent reading the Holy Scriptures prior to breakfast and tea. I had considered myself Christian before, but I never knew the depth of God's Word until this year."

"And what have you learned from those early mornings with his Word?" Lady Emily asked softly.

Kathryne looked straight at her and answered in a bold voice. "I know that I have a purpose and that is to fulfill God's plan for me—whatever that may be and wherever that may be. Until this year, I truly believed that I would never leave Broadwinds, for I would have no reason to do so. I suppose I believed that God would use me there. But now I am not taking such a firm stand on my future. I will let God direct me. I am allowing him to use me as he sees fit. He has promised to direct my steps, and I will follow his path."

The table remained quiet after Kathryne spoke. She looked about at the young ladies she had grown so fond of. Some were smiling, some were staring uncomprehendingly, and Lady Emily was reaching for her napkin to wipe away a sudden tear.

The English Sea

A loud cheer erupted from the deck of the *Minion*. A keen-eyed sailor stationed on the foretop spotted a hint of green lying to the northeast.

"Ahoy! It be the Lizard ahead!" he shouted down.

Upon returning home to England, the first English soil a sailor would

see would be the small ridge tops, just east of Land's End, called the
Lizard—the most southerly bit of England's geography. Its beauty owed
to the rocks of which it was formed. Green serpentine, mixed with
black and red granite, often clothed with gorse and heather, gave the
steep and rugged landscape its colorful surface. From a distance it
appeared as a medley of blended hues and was a welcome sight after a
long sojourn at sea.

A great "Hurrah!" arose from the crew, glad to finally see their
homeland after nine months of journeying.

William was stationed on top watch that day and was nearly alone
on the quarterdeck, a true rarity amidst the tightly cramped quarters.
He had known that the Lizard would be spotted during the forenoon
watch. Men came streaming up from below ships and crowded about
on the foredecks, pointing at the headland, laughing, cheering, play-
fully tussling with a crewmate.

It had been a sailing of no major importance in nautical matters.
Goods and supplies had been sold and traded, bought and resold. The
Minion kept its distance from the merchantman, providing a discreet
level of guardianship. Each port was found handily, and other than the
first mishap in the Azores the voyage went smooth as a becalmed ocean.

William had made but few friends during the trip. Two or three
members of the officer corps were civil to Will, but most of them
seemed overly concerned with their prize share, their debauchery at
each port of call, and their ability to drink vast quantities of spirit and
still remain upright.

Captain Blissmore was barely civil to anyone on board. He seemed
to despise those in the seaman ranks and could barely tolerate even his
officers. The junior lieutenants spoke little to the petty officers, who
spoke little to the warrant officers, and so on. Every step of command
looked with disfavor at all those below and suspicion at all those above.

William stayed alone, read the books he had purchased in Italy, made
notes of words in other languages he was trying to learn, watched the
seas, and studied navigation and sailing techniques. He knew, with a
comfort, that his prize share would be larger than most, since he
declined his daily brandy ration in exchange for gold at the end of the
voyage.

For a man raised out of sight of the ocean, never really having seen
the water until less than a year prior, he and the sea were kindred spirits,
it seemed. *We are always in motion, always churning, always moving—
yet we never leave our containment. We seem to crash against the same
shores yet never leave those confines,* he thought.

He had but fifteen more months on his original commission. He knew that he would need serve on at least two more voyages, a prospect that did nothing to cheer his heart.

However, what was causing his heart to be glad was that he would soon be able to return to Hadenthorne to discuss his adventures with old friends again. How he had yearned to see their faces again and to be enfolded by the small, comforting realm of Hadenthorne.

London, England

"Isn't this the most amusing play, Kathryne?" asked Lucy Donnel.

The residents of the Alexandrian had a free afternoon before leaving for home for the summer and were spending it with Lady Emily at the Globe Theater, taking in a performance of *News from Plymouth*. The play was written by William Davenant, who collaborated with Inigo Jones, the architect and master designer, on its production.

"Indeed. I think it splendidly played," Kathryne answered as she purchased a Jaffa orange for refreshment.

"And the staging!" exclaimed Celia Althorp. "'Tis such a wonderful old theater. I especially enjoy seeing the actors pop up in the odd places about the stage, sometimes all at the same time—the platform, the inner stage, the balcony, the windows. Such inventiveness. Such creativity."

"And how the scenery was raised and lowered so quickly. No one was seen at the sides at all. And using candles with tinted glass!" said Lucy. "Such a marvelous effect. I was most completely surprised by everything."

"Done to perfection," added Cecily.

Kathryne removed a small folding fan from her sleeve. She gently fanned at her face as she stared off into the crowds.

A bell sounded and the group began to return to their seats. Kathryne held back. "Lady Emily," she said as she took her by the hand, "shall we take a stroll during this act? The heat has me most flustered today."

The two walked along the Thames, where a forest of England's merchant ships crowded the river's quays. A slight breeze came up, cooling the stale air.

"My dear," said Lady Emily, "are you unwell? Granted, the play is but a trifling, but you did not smile once. What is troubling you?"

"I . . . I am not sure."

"That is not what I have been instructing you to say."

"I know, Lady Emily. But I wish I knew what has caused me to be so perplexed. I am privileged—I know how few women have had the opportunity to learn what I have learned, or to have the experiences of the past year."

"And there is a difficulty in that?"

"No, not in the slightest. But I keep thinking that . . ."

"What?" Lady Emily asked.

"Well, that there is something more."

Lady Emily reached over and took Kathryne's hand in hers.

"Lady Emily, when did you know what you were meant to do with your life? I mean, did you receive clear direction from God as to how and where you were to live out your purpose in this world—the place and the way to make your life count for something?"

Lady Emily smiled and turned to face the young woman, who had the most perplexed look about her face. "Kathryne, how I see myself reflected within you. Your questions harken me to the time when I was but your age. Your mother and I would dream and plan and wonder and pray . . . seeking God's will, yet dreaming our own dreams."

She paused, thinking back. "Let me tell you a little story about her. We had both been at court for several months—a truly bewitching experience, indeed. Our aspiration was to become ladies-in-waiting. Our lives were dresses and flowers and social affairs—parties and masques and the like. It is almost humorous to admit to it now, but your mother's greatest desire was to have a red satin gown with ermine trim. She used all of her feminine wiles on her father, Lord Morgan, and at last she succeeded. Oh, she was magnificent in that dress! Noble men and ladies spoke to her differently when she wore it. But a curious thing happened. One night after a gala, when she readied herself for bed, she hung up the gown, stepped back, and realized it was empty. The dress was *empty!* She asked me that night as she put out our candle, 'Were they being cordial to the dress, or to me? Could anyone have worn it and seemed noble?' I think she knew all along that what made her heart sing was giving of herself, helping others, being a friend, showing her faith."

Emily leaned to Kathryne conspiratorially. "Not that she ever gave up her love of fine clothes completely," Lady Emily giggled, "but she saw what was truly important. In fact, that's how she made your father's acquaintance."

Lady Emily's voice took on a reminiscent tone. "It was at evening vespers that they first saw each other at a small parish church just outside Oxford—to be sure, one much below your mother's social standing. But she was drawn to it because its vicar had a passion to reach out to those among them in need . . . a passion shared by your father as well. Soon, it was our dear Lord Aidan that made her heart sing. So dashingly handsome he was, and with a wisdom beyond his years. . . ." As her voice trailed off, Kathryne was aware of a yearning in her mentor's eyes, a longing that Kathryne did not fully understand and that she dismissed as merely nostalgia.

"But Lady Emily," Kathryne confessed. "I haven't felt my heart sing about anything yet."

"My dear, you know so much more of the Scriptures than your mother or I did at your age. Do you not recall that verse about direction? It is promised that the Word will be the light on the path ahead of us. God will make his plan known to you. You are a prayerful girl, and you have inclined your ear to hear God speak. You must continue to trust that he will show you the way. It is indeed that simple. Trust in his promises."

"But, Lady Emily, until he shows me, what am I to do?" Kathryne asked.

"You continue to share the love of the living God with others. That is what the Scriptures call us to do."

Kathryne still seem perturbed, upset, and to some degree, confused. "That I understand, Lady Emily. And I will continue to share his love as I can. But what else is there? What do I do with my life besides that?"

Lady Emily nodded, as if for the first moment truly understanding Kathryne's real question. "Well, child, you have inherited your father's penchant for practicality. That is something your mother had less of."

Lady Emily held Kathryne at arm's length and appeared to be considering her afresh, for the first time. "My dear, I would say that of all your talents, you are most adept at figures, sums, and other mathematical, logical, and abstract concepts. You have an organizational mind . . . unusual abilities for a lady—and which must be acknowledged as a gift from God, just like all gifts are." Smiling, the older woman asked, "And what do these gifts indicate to you, Kathryne?"

"Well, . . . the only thing that comes to mind has to do with business affairs, and I know that is no arena for a gentlewoman."

Glowering at Kathryne, Lady Emily scolded, "I will not have you speak like this. God has blessed you with a fine intellect and a facility for such affairs. Why not consider them? After all, am I not in reality a business woman as well?"

Kathryne nodded, for the first time seeing Lady Emily in a different light.

"Why not learn of business? Become more acquainted with your father's enterprises. Perhaps that is where God has called you—to be a beacon of his light in the cold world of pounds and shillings."

Kathryne looked relieved. *Perhaps she is right . . . perhaps God has purposed this for me.* "Well," she said, "it does sound intriguing. I could be of assistance and benefit to my father, and I do seem to have a facility for figures and all." Kathryne remained perplexed for a moment. "But being a woman, that will most certainly be an enormous hindrance."

Lady Emily reached over and took Kathryne gently by the arm, and the two began to walk. "Child, if this is truly what God has given you to do, then no man will be an obstacle."

They left the river and began to slowly walk back to the theater. Both were quiet, deep in thought as they strolled. A few moments from their destination, Lady Emily stopped and spoke in a quiet, almost reverential tone.

"Kathryne, after my dear husband, Lord Caldwell, passed on, my dreams of having a 'quiver full' of children died with him. I thought my life had no meaning or purpose. Then God replaced those dreams and has given me a nurturing role in the lives of young women such as yourself who need a godly example. If God has allowed me to pursue my dream of teaching young women—much to the amazement of most men of my acquaintance—then you, my dear, can follow in your father's footsteps. Promise to be in prayer about this while we are apart this summer?"

Kathryne nodded. "Yes, if you promise as well."

CHAPTER

21

June 1638
Weymouth, Dorset
England

The day broke gray, windy, and damp. Rivulets of rain ran down the small window by William's head. He stretched his arms over his head and felt the beam that had been his headboard for the past many months. He looked out the small window by his hammock and sighed. A thin scud of gray clouds slipped under the rain.

You would think that after almost two years at sea I might have been given a sunny day on which to return.

The *Minion* had docked late the previous evening amidst a palpable sense of anticipation and excitement. It had been near dark as the ship slipped into Weymouth Harbor. With the ship tied and secure, the crew hurried to finish last-minute tasks. It had been a long, rough voyage; illness had taken more than five score of the crew, buried at sea from Spain to Bombay. To a man, the remaining seamen wanted off the vessel, to be able to turn about and see some other vista than the ship or the sea or canvas overhead. They wanted away from the harsh treatment, the bad food, the foul smells, and the ever-present fear of death.

A refrain came to mind.

> *When the rain's before a wind,*
> *Topsail halyards you must mind.*
> *When the wind's before the rain,*
> *Hoist your topsail up again.*

For the first time in many months, Will did not care whether the rain was before or after the wind. He was back at port, and his soul was silent, neither at peace nor anxious.

William reached to the window and opened a small movable pane of glass. The wind, cold and chilled, washed over Will like a shower. He tucked his blanket under his chin, breathing in the freshness of the air, feeling it wash the foulness from his lungs.

He closed his eyes. No one would be up and about while in port until midway through the morning watch, and Will estimated that to be more than an hour distant. While at sea, men were either working, eating, or sleeping. At least that is the way it felt to Will on this trip. Shorthanded since their stop in Bombay, the *Minion*'s crew had been pulling extra duty. Will looked forward to a time of rest.

As he lay in his hammock in the silent ship, his thoughts traveled back, reviewing the last two years of his life. . . .

■ ■ □ ■ ■

The first sailing to Africa and the Mediterranean seemed as if it were a decade in the past. His initial nine months aboard the *Minion* were a confusing mix of emotions. Will was scared, unsure of his abilities, homesick, and lonely the entire trip. He remembered his first visit back to Hadenthorne a year ago, last June, and how overjoyed they had all been to see him. Mrs. Cavendish had wept upon seeing him, started cooking, then wept again when Will had to return to his ship. It was a visit, he thought, bookended with tears.

It had helped to speak at length with the vicar. William had seriously considered asking Lord Davis if he would arrange to have his commission be terminated so that he could return to Hadenthorne to become a farmer or gamekeeper.

"Do you truly want to quit, William?" the vicar had asked.

"I know it would appear that I am seeking the coward's way out," Will had explained in his defense, "but life is so brutal on board. I would say that all but a handful of men have been flogged for mostly trivial breaches of a naval regulation. I am disheartened to find joyful ideas have become a rarity in my thoughts. I am afraid that I will not remain sound if I stay my commission."

What the vicar then had said was a shock to William. "The mark of a Christian—and I know you wish not to speak of faith and belief Will, but I must—the mark of a true child of God is how that person treats the trials in his life. You have spent but nine short months in an unpleasant situation, and now you want to leave? Is this how you deal with unpleasantness?"

The vicar's response had surprised Will. He had thought he would do almost anything to have William back in Hadenthorne and under his spiritual tutelage.

"You want me to return to the sea, to leave Hadenthorne?" he had asked incredulously.

"William, you have made a choice. You must live with the results of that choice. That is how character is refined. It is how the search for truth is continued. Would it be easy for you to stay? Yes, but that is not what you desired. I will not speak to Lord Davis on your behalf."

Returning to Weymouth and the *Minion* was not an ebullient experience, but William had solemnly packed up his bag a few days later and had returned to serve out his commission.

Upon his return, the refurbished ship had set sail for India, offering protection for a larger convoy of the East Indian Company. Enlisted men were not to be found for such an arduous journey, and most of the seamen had been taken in press-gangs. By law, British soldiers and naval officers had the power to take, by force, any able-bodied male needed to fill out the crew. For that sailing, more than three hundred men had been impressed into service.

This is not the way to build an able crew, Will had thought. *I imagine that the floggings will be on the increase.*

They were, and William had suffered in silence as men were punished for seemingly inconsequential infractions. It was difficult to smile at any time during the months at sea on the way to Bombay.

The fleet had been made up of thirty-five ships, all merchant vessels, save the *Minion* and a smaller frigate, the *Utopia.* Cargo on most ships consisted of wool, tin, and iron tools. They were to sell these items and then buy teas, china plates, silks, dyes, olives, wines, and spices.

The blistering port of Bombay was a vile stew of sewage and brackish water, compounded by a squalor unmatched in his experiences. The most miserable conditions of the teeming quarters about the harbor made the bottommost decks of the *Minion* seem delightful by comparison.

During their weeklong stay in Bombay William had spent much time in a small cafe overlooking the harbor and the *Minion.* For the men who would not get shore leave in this port, worldly diversions—wine, women, and entertainers—were allowed on board. A steady stream of gaudy females had entered and exited the ship in shifts. Will understood that frustrations were pent up aboard ship, but he was never at ease as the debauchery spun itself so close to his person. He had sipped at cool ale, tasted tea for the first time, conversed with other officers, and read—unwilling, perhaps unable, to turn a blind eye to what was going on throughout the ship.

The return sailing had taken an additional two months as the convoy encountered frail winds at the southern tip of Africa and storms causing them to delay near the equator. Heavily laden cargo ships did not sail well, and the *Minion* often sailed with only partial canvas in the wind, staying abreast with the fleet.

As the distance traveled in the slight breezes had diminished, William had not had much to do since navigational chores were lessened. He had taken advantage of the doldrums in the weather and had spent his time in an informal apprenticeship to the helmsman. He stood by him at the wheel, asking questions about technique. When was it proper to tack into the wind? At what angle of heel and list does speed diminish and danger increase? When to close into the wind? When can you set the twiddling line to the wheel and let the ship simply run free as a beast in the waters with no hand upon her?

On occasion the helmsman, glad for such an eager pupil, would stand aside from the great oak wheel and turn the ship over to William. The first time William had placed his hands on the great wheel he felt a surge of power, of tremendous energy pulsing through the polished ribs and spindles. At the helmsman's instruction, he pulled the wheel a quarter turn to the right with great effort, and as he did the vessel obeyed and heeled to the north a few degrees. An entire ship and an entire crew were in his command! After only a few minutes of the emotional surge, William had stepped down, bathed in sweat in the early morning coolness. Will loved learning this practical art of sailing, using the natural forces of wind and sea to create order and direction from relative chaos. It was an intoxicating experience.

As the return voyage had grown longer—the convoy had been sailing at no more than quarter speed for nearly a month—many of the crew had grown more and more restive. William had found it a perfect opportunity to learn. With the several Sicilian carpenters, he practiced his skill in Italian. He had done the same with several who spoke Dutch, French, and Spanish. One older Basque crewman, well-traveled and weathered, taught him words and phrases in Arawak and Carib, the language of the natives in the Caribbean. The Basque had been to the islands almost a decade ago and spent months fighting the natives in the dense jungles of Hispaniola.

Officers would often practice their skill in swordplay on the quarterdeck. The clang of sabers was a common sound. The men practiced with long swords, blades of medium length; cutlasses, short, heavy, curved cleavers with sharp edges; and rapiers, long, thin, flexible blades that were most elegant in action and most deadly because of their long reach.

Will had picked up a rapier one day and swiped at the air, flicking his wrist as he saw others do. The blade hissed in the air.

Lieutenant Reed, standing nearby, had laughed. "Only now, in extreme boredom, does our noble Mr. Hawkes take up a blade. I had thought your deep, spiritual nature was immune to frustrations. I must have misjudged you."

"Lieutenant Reed, I am not frustrated. It is merely that I wanted to see what the blade felt like," Will had answered evenly.

Lieutenant Reed had walked over to him, picked up another rapier, and placed the blade point against Will's chest.

"An incomplete lesson, Mr. Hawkes. A rapier is to be felt in opposition to a second rapier, not to the air."

A group of men had begun to gather. Reed was noted for his skills with a blade and his menace to practice partners.

"But, Lieutenant, I have no skill to match yours. It would be no contest," Will had demurred.

"Ah, Mr. Hawkes. Ever the diplomat," Reed had said. "True, my skill would find you skewered in a single thrust. So to make the odds at even, I will place the blade in my less-favored hand, my left. That should still be sport, do you not think?"

The circle of men had hooted their approval. William had had no reason to continue, but the heat and the languid pace had stirred something in his heart—a small stirring to lash out.

"Yes, Lieutenant, that would entail a fairer contest." William had sliced the air with the blade a few times, getting the feel of the weapon. "Shall we begin?"

Both men had placed thick tar and canvas tips on their blade points to prevent the accidental impaling or serious injury.

Reed had held his blade high, touched it to his forehead as a kind of salute, extended his wrist at shoulder level, then slashed at William in a flurry. William had but a moment to place his blade in position to parry the thrusts. He had watched combatants many times and saw, in his mind's eye, the moves that must be accomplished for defense. William met each thrust and advance with a parry and a dodge to the rear of sides. His moves were smaller than Reed's, flicking the blade away as it came at him in longer, sweeping arcs.

The crewmen had watched in silence. Most, for certain, felt that the contest would be over in a moment. Such was Lieutenant Reed's skill, even with his less-favored hand, for most polished practitioners of swordplay made every effort to learn the use of a weapon in either hand. And true, while William was offering a purely defensive strategy, Reed had not yet broken through it.

For many moments, upwards of a half hour, the two had circled each other as they fought. The lieutenant, working hard, had begun to sweat profusely in the tropical sun. He had begun to breathe heavier, and his initial smile was replaced by a grim visage and narrowed eyes.

Thrust was followed with parry, and Lieutenant Reed's blade would slide off, harmless, to the left or right. The tight, compact clinks, the long slide of metal to metal as the blades slid against each other, were loud in the hot sun.

"Mr. Hawkes, surely you toy with me. Have you practiced in the night?" Reed grumbled.

The men, standing about them in a circle, laughed nervously. Reed lunged forward once again, hoping to catch William off guard. William caught the blade and circled his wrist with a snap and the lieutenant fell forward, preventing a sprawling fall by catching his blade in the deck as a cane. He stumbled past Will, who turned to face him again. Reed, slowly and deliberately, transferred the blade from his left to his right hand. He smiled, a thin slash of teeth showing on his face.

Reed's blade point had been sticking through the canvas and tar tip, and when he removed the rapier from the deck, the protective tip came off completely. William looked down, expecting a time-out to be called. But Reed stepped back to confront him and thrust again at William. Their eyes locked. Both knew the tip of Reed's blade was off, but Reed was whipping the blade through the air like an angry wasp, seeking blood.

Reed slashed at William, again and again, with all the force he could muster, and William continued to meet and deflect each charge and thrust. Reed's face was glistening, his eyes blazing. After a moment's hesitation he slashed again. William raised his elbow, wrist at waist level, and caught the next thrust, raising the thrusting blade to carry over his body.

It was the lack of experience on William's part and the lieutenant's aggressive nature that caused the injury, the crew would say later. William did not have the time to duck, and Reed's blade creased the brow above his left eye, slicing through the soft flesh.

Another officer had called out "Halt!" and had stepped between the two men.

William had dropped to his knees on the deck with a hand over his eye, blood seeping through his fingers.

Lieutenant Reed had stood at one side, panting, with a small twisted smile on his face. "A thousand pardons, Mr. Hawkes. I do hope it is nothing serious," he had said in a coiled tone.

Most of the crew members watching had said nothing, no congratulations offered or applause as would have been normal.

Reed had scanned their faces, scowled, and turned, elbowing his way through the crowd, who quickly gave him a wide berth.

Robby MacCallister, an older seaman who had been a healer on the Isle of Jersey, had rushed to William. He had pulled away William's hand and saw the eye had been uncut, but the blood had blinded him for a moment.

"You'll be fine, Mr. William," MacCallister had said. "Let me get me poultice for this wee wound. I do not want to see this festerin' in the sun."

The afternoon following the rapier combat, the ship's chaplain had come to call on William as he lay in his hammock, resting.

"William, I am overjoyed that your eye will not be lost. A one-eyed navigator may find his duties quite taxing."

"Thank you, Chaplain Quilkton. I appreciate your concern."

"I must admit that I am most grieved that I missed your most entertaining duel in the sun. The men say that Lieutenant Reed was on course for a defeat."

"Reverend, I must correct you. It was *I* who faced defeat at every movement."

"Not the way I hear it, William. For every thrust, there was a more elegant parry." Chaplain Quilkton was animating his discussion with imagined thrusts, holding his hand at waist level and slashing at an imagined opponent. "Thrust, defense, advance, defense, parry, attack, defense." Quilkton lowered his arm, panting. "It must have been wondrous to view. To see Reed get a taste of his own! Half the crew believes you had practiced in secret at night. The other half imagines you as a man with a past who had learned these skills in some exotic land—seeing as how you speak near every language we encounter."

William had thought it curious that he was looked up to, or even talked about, by the crew. How could someone with as much self-doubt as he be an object of curiosity? "Reverend, may I ask you a question?" Will had asked.

Chaplain Quilkton had stopped and was bent at the waist, waiting.

"As I was out there this morning, with the steel in my hand, facing an opponent—no matter that I considered it a mock battle—I . . . felt something inside . . . stirring. I felt more alive than I have ever been. I do not understand it."

Chaplain Quilkton had stepped back to the window and stared out at the calm sea. "William, no man is more fully in life than when he faces death. It is the comparison between the darkness of death and the light of living in which we recognize what a rare gift life is. Only when you risk losing a precious item do you understand the true cost of it."

William was stunned, for he thought such insight was beyond the old chaplain.

"Only when we give up our lives, do we gain life—that's biblical, you know."

William had nodded in mute agreement.

"How I wish I had seen you in action," the chaplain had exclaimed brightly, breaking the mood. "Parry and thrust, thrust and parry—how bloody exciting."

■ ■ ■ ■

William shook his head to clear the images of the last twenty-four months. It was time to arise. It was time to face his decision reached on the last stretch of ocean between the Canary Islands and England.

I will revoke my commission, William had decided. *I will return home to Hadenthorne. That must be where my future lies.*

CHAPTER

22

June 1638
London, England

From the cobblestone street below, Baker Rupert called out a cheery "Until the morning!" as the scents of his fresh wares drifted through the open window by Kathryne's bed.

What a delicious way to arise every day, she thought. *How I will miss this when I return to Broadwinds.*

Every day for nearly the past two years, with the exception of a brief twelve-week span in summer and two weeks during the Advent season, Kathryne awoke to the same delightful sensations. On this morning she stretched out on her bed, the light blanket rustling softly. She burrowed her head into the satiny feather pillow and floated in that delicious state between waking and sleep.

What a grand adventure this has been! And one more term to come back to this fall, Kathryne thought, satisfied.

Lady Emily was the most patient and gracious of teachers. Since their discussion a year prior at the Globe Theater, and after that summer of mutual prayer, Lady Emily had embarked on a new mission. Feeling quite secure in Kathryne's grasp of literature, languages, the arts, and the social graces of a noblewoman, she now began a comprehensive instruction in the burgeoning business environment.

"Kathryne, my child," Lady Emily had explained, "We have spoken of this prior. You are aware that Radcliffe shall not inherit Broadwinds. You shall, and then your firstborn male heir. If that happy occasion arises, is there a guarantee that your future husband will be skilled in detailed business dealings? I daresay there is no such assurance. Many a noble-born son has no idea of money, securities, and paper holdings. Plenty of them are nestlings—too coddled, never having to fend for themselves. And many others are only acquainted with the ways of a gentleman farmer. In the modern world we live in that may not be enough to protect your future children, Kathryne. Since Broadwinds is no longer a working estate, you need be concerned about finance and capital. It is wise stewardship, indeed."

So Kathryne had indeed decided to devote herself to learning of business and commerce. Her second stay at the Alexandrian had focused on the skills and knowledge that would be necessary for her to follow in her father's footsteps as a manager of the Spenser shipping interests. It seemed to her that the more she learned, the more she needed to know.

How smart and cultured I felt on my first trip home at Christmas, Kathryne recalled with a snicker as she snuggled in her bed that morning. *And how ungracious I must have been,* she thought soberly as she remembered going home that first time. . . .

"Let me look at you, my child—it has been so long."

Mrs. Cole had taken Kathryne by the hands and had spun her around to fully evaluate the changes the last three months in London had caused to the little girl she considered as dear as a natural daughter.

"Such a smart gown, Kathryne. The color is most flattering to your eyes. It makes them seem a deeper green."

"Mrs. Cole, you have not lost your charm."

Mrs. Cole had stepped back and looked again with a more critical countenance. "They must be feedin' you well at that fancy school. It appears you've grown an inch or two." She had pulled the young girl close to her face and added in an intimate whisper, "You left Broadwinds a young girl and have returned a woman. You've added inches not only in height, my dear, but in other areas as well."

Mrs. Cole had given her an extra squeeze about the waist, Kathryne's hips full and pleasing.

Kathryne had blushed a deep scarlet. She had indeed blossomed in more ways than intellectually. The dress she had selected for the journey home did little to conceal the change.

"I am certain that a gentleman or two will stumble as they catch a glimpse of my little missy."

Kathryne had put a hand to her mouth and giggled.

"If those elegant London cooks can fatten up my Kathryne, so can I. Sit down, and I will set us out a plate of biscuits and Devonshire cream."

Kathryne had run to the table in anticipation, smiling and laughing. *How I missed this kitchen,* she had thought. *How I missed Mrs. Cole.*

The plate of tasty biscuits had been quickly reduced to crumbs.

Kathryne had chosen to ignore the dictums of how an elegant lady is to dine and had slathered jams and honey on them, taking great gulps of tea brewed from the leaves she brought back with her to Broadwinds, between bites.

I am so grateful Lady Emily cannot see me now, she had thought.

"Kathryne, so tell me. What is London like? Is it full of cosmopolitan affairs and ladies in silks and satin?"

Two kitchen maids had worked their way close, hoping to overhear all the details.

Kathryne had noticed the pair. "Please, sit with us. It will be all right."

"Oh, thank you, Lady Kathryne," they had said as they excitedly slipped onto the bench next to Mrs. Cole.

"London is the most exciting place in all of England," Kathryne had said as she started her story. "There is theater, and art salons, and teas with ladies of the court, as well as little musical evenings in the homes of Lady Emily's friends. Every week of the season is a whirl of royalty and society. We visited Pickadilly Hall, a fair house for entertainment and gaming where people of the best quality resort for exercise and pleasure, with handsome walks with shade, and an upper and lower bowling green. The game of tennis is played on roofed courtyards by the men. They dress in special taffeta tennis suits."

"Kathryne, did you not go there to study as well?" Mrs. Cole had asked with a smile. "Was your father's money spent purely on pleasure?"

Kathryne had smiled back. "Lady Emily seeks to produce a well-rounded lady," Kathryne had said, and blushed again slightly at her unintentional pun. "We at the Alexandrian do not spend *all* our time on frivolities—just a small portion of it. In the mornings, we study and learn from books mostly, such as the *Iliad,* the *Odyssey,* and *Beowulf.* On Wednesday mornings we would study Latin—how Englishmen abroad communicate in such a terribly difficult language is beyond me! I must admit that remaining awake was the true struggle those days."

The two kitchen maids had giggled at her honesty.

"Thursday mornings Lady Emily brought in Monsieur Culvette, who helped us with French. Since it is the language of diplomacy, and some of the girls will no doubt marry an ambassador or envoy, it will serve us well in the future."

Kathryne had giggled again and whispered, "Now I can order the most sumptuous repast in French—and not much else. That should serve me quite well—or shall I say, I will be well served."

The maids had giggled again.

"And Lady Emily instructed us as to how to maintain our 'rose and lily' complexion using techniques from the Continent, such as French face creams, and how to apply the new perfumes. The most fashionable ladies are wearing patches on their faces, some in the shape of the moon and stars, which looks most dreadful."

The kitchen maids' mouths had been agape as they listened.

"We spent some afternoon working on this immense tapestry of a scene in the North Yorkshire Dales. And we did fine sampler work as well. Lady Emily thinks that all young women should know some of the gracious arts. Actually, as we sew we talk of what one should wear to the musical consort that evening or how scandalous the new play at the Globe was."

The serving girls had appeared fascinated; Mrs. Cole had frowned.

"I trust that you have done nothing scandalous to sully your reputation as a fine Christian woman of faith!"

"No, Mrs. Cole. I have not. But my eyes have been opened to a whole world I was unaware of—the arts, drama! Dance and music! Painting and architecture! I know that had I stayed at Broadwinds, I would never have grown so."

"And what about God, Kathryne. Did you study about God as well? Did you spend time in the Word of our Lord?"

The question had been asked in a shriller tone, and while Kathryne had indeed found London to be a city where one could avail themselves to the brightest and best theologians and preachers of the day, she had felt like a wayward child, being scolded for wandering off.

"Yes, we spent some time with the Bible, Mrs. Cole. I have not yet become the heathen you might imagine. Just because I have been to a ball and attended the theater, it does not mean I have forgotten God. The world does not corrupt so quickly."

Kathryne had stood up and stared down at the woman she had considered to be a second mother. Afraid of what words she might utter in anger, she had turned and run from the room, angry tears about to flow.

The remaining weeks at Broadwinds had seen Kathryne chilled and moody. Indeed the weather had been unseasonably warm for December, but the spat between old friends had hurt. She had walked down the drafty hallways with a thick woolen shawl around her shoulders, avoiding the kitchen. She found it impossible to understand her own motives for the outburst. Mrs. Cole had spoken as she always had spoken, frankly and honestly. And up until that moment the confines of her love and care had felt secure and safe. But Kathryne chafed under it.

It will be good to return to London in January, she had thought. *It will be good to be out from her restrictions once again.*

■ ▓ ▓ ▢

Kathryne snuggled deeper into her bed, pulling the coverlet up tighter to her chin as she captured the memory.

It has been such a short time, she thought, *but it has been a lifetime of experiences. How much I have changed from the naive country girl to one who is breathing in the sophistication of London on a daily basis.*

The gentle waftings of breakfast slipped up the stairs, and Kathryne's stomach growled in response. She grinned broadly. *Well, perhaps not all of me has yet reached such a pinnacle of sophistication.*

CHAPTER

23

July 1638
Weymouth, Dorset
England

"You cannot be serious, Mr. Hawkes."

"Captain Blissmore, I must speak the truth. I am serious."

"But you have been the single most capable navigator I have ever sailed with. How can you justify withdrawing your commission and leaving the navy?"

"It is not an easy answer, sir. But as you must know, the sea is a very demanding taskmaster."

"Were you not satisfied with your portion of the prize?"

William, along with most of the officers, was awarded one hundred pounds as his share. In addition, by forsaking his brandy allotment, William had received an additional twenty-five pounds. With the monies he had earned on his first voyage, plus the charges he made for interpretation and consultation duties for some of the merchants, William had amassed a total of five hundred pounds, a truly princely sum, seeing as how the average yeoman farmer might earn twenty-five pounds per year and for much more toil.

"No, Captain, the award was fair—more than fair."

"Were you mistreated in any way?"

"No, Captain. You were fair with me."

"Then, William," he said in a more fatherly manner, "I do not fathom the reasons for your decision. In a matter of a few more years you could easily be advanced to a lieutenant position, or perhaps even to captain of a smaller vessel.

"This is not idle speculation. Even you, of common birth, could accomplish these things." William did not speak, and the captain continued, "I have a letter of commendation for your service, which you will receive regardless of the outcome of your dilemma. But I urge you—think hard on this. You have a rare gift for the sea, William. This is not something I would say lightly. You have that sense about you—you *know* where you are on the sea seemingly at every hour of every day. Few others can boast the same."

"Sir, I thank you for such high praise. I had no idea." William was indeed flustered by the plaudits.

"William, it pains me at times, but a captain of such a ship as the *Minion* can have no friends on board. It is not advisable to show any partiality. That is why I have not spoken of this before."

"Sir, I do appreciate all you have taught me. But it is time for me to depart. I plan on returning to Hadenthorne. I will know of what my future holds upon returning home."

Captain Blissmore stood up and removed a rolled parchment from his desk. He stepped toward William and extended his hand.

"Take this commendation, William. We will be berthed here for one month for repairs and refitting. If you return one week prior to the date of our sailing, you may return at full rank and privileges, and no more will be said of this."

William shook the captain's hand.

"I pray that you come to the right decision, Mr. Hawkes."

Hadenthorne, Devon
England

The door of the parsonage flew open, and Mrs. Cavendish threw herself out and embraced William in a fierce, loving hug, wrapping her arms tight around him and squeezing.

"Will, it's really you! After all this time, you're safe and home again. Praise be to the Almighty and all the saints above for your return."

William squirmed out and laughed, "You've been spending too much time with the vicar, Mrs. Cavendish. It seems as some of his piety has rubbed off on you."

Vicar Mayhew came running down the street, his cassock flowing in the breeze. "William! William! You are home!"

And behind the vicar, William could barely discern the three Cavendish brothers, at a slow gallop, running across a freshly mown field, arms and legs pumping wildly like clumsy draft horses in a race.

A moment later the brothers arrived, and as the three brothers at full stride intersected the same space as Will and the vicar, the five tumbled to the ground in a happy, tearful heap. Even Mrs. Cavendish could stand no more and tossed herself onto the group. William, near the bottom, felt as close to being crushed by love as he ever had in his life.

After dinner that evening William sat by the fire with a pint of warmed ale in his hand and shared the saga of his journey halfway round the world.

The Cavendish brothers sat near William's feet, looking like large sheepdogs. The vicar had to open the windows, for a small crowd of townspeople had gathered to welcome William home and to listen to his stories.

The Cavendish brothers shuddered in unison as Will spun tales of shipwrecks and drowning sailors. Their eyes widened as he told of the beauties of Italy and the Mediterranean. They thought he was spinning fairy tales as he spoke of Bombay and the images of snake charmers.

Enjoying his newfound fame, Will spoke on into the evening. When he again looked at his reclining friends, all three had drifted to sleep, arms tucked under heads, feet extending into the room. Even the vicar was slumped into his chair, with his chin resting against his chest.

It is such a pleasure to speak to civilized people, Will thought, *who are not three cups into their brandy allowance.*

He went from person to person, gently nudging them, bringing them back from their slumbers, assuring them that the stories would be continued on another day.

Early the following morning, Will awoke and walked through the quiet village. He walked by the river and sat tossing small pebbles into the deep pool by the bridge. From several farms he heard the cries of roosters as the village yawned and came awake. He heard some footsteps behind him, then the voice of a friend.

"William, I thought I might find you here," the vicar said. "Mrs. Cavendish wants you back momentarily for a full country breakfast. She has left no food untouched."

"It is an enchantment to eat at leisure, without a rolling deck beneath your feet or maggots in your food."

"Is life that difficult at sea, William?"

"It is, Thomas, but it seems to me that it doesn't have to be. It is harsh from the wickedness of men's hearts. It is unhealthy from the foolishness of the process. It is degrading from the pleasures they too often seek out." William quieted and tossed a small handful of stones into the deep waters. "It could be so much more tolerable if men were more decent."

"William, it is the same treatise I have been speaking to on *terra firma* as well."

"I dislike admitting this, Thomas," Will confided, "but I think your observations to be correct."

"William, how long can you stay in Hadenthorne? Will you be able to spend a few days with us this visit?"

William looked up and into the face of his friend. His eyes were wide, imploring. "Thomas, I have resigned my commission. If I choose, I may never set foot on a naval vessel again."

The vicar clasped his hands together and held them to his heart. He would have spoken, but his thoughts were a tangle of thanks and concern—thanks for Will's presence in his life and concern for the young man's future.

After a moment, William spoke again. "I am not sure of my future, but I think better of it here."

A rooster called on the far side of the bridge.

"Thomas, who might that man in the field by the bend be? The one with the ox and plow. His form looks familiar, and he waved to greet me, but I am not sure who it might be."

Without turning to look, the vicar replied, "That would be Mr. Holender. He purchased that land almost a year ago now, making him the largest landowner in Hadenthorne—next to Lord Davis, of course. You are acquainted with his daughter, I believe—Missy."

William watched as the farmer skillfully navigated the plow through the rich, black soil.

"Is she . . . ?"

"No, Will, she is still unspoken for."

William stood alone in the parsonage reviewing the books on the shelves. He had carefully unpacked the books he purchased on his voyages and unwrapped them from their oilskin covers, which were to prevent mildew.

As he arranged them there, he heard a sharp rap at the window. He turned and saw an unfamiliar face standing outside, wringing a crushed brown cap in his calloused hands.

"William, sir. Mr. Hawkes. . . . I was wondering if you would be so kind . . ."

"Ah, Mr. Holender, how good to see you. It has been a long time since we spoke," William said in greeting.

Mr. Holender stood there, unsure of what to say next.

"Please, come in. Let me serve you some cider—or ale if you prefer."

"Oh, no thank you, sir."

"And, please, do not call me sir. It is William. I am no different of a man now than when I left."

"William, then."

They both stood and stared.

"William, . . . would you be so kind as to pleasure my poor family with your presence at an evening meal? Perhaps a day past tomorrow?" This invitation had obviously been rehearsed.

"Why, of course. I would be most grateful to sit at your table."

"Well, then. We will prepare, then . . . for the day past tomorrow. At evening, then."

As he watched Mr. Holender walked away, back to his farm, William smiled. *I believe I am being courted,* he mused.

■ ■ ■ ■ ■

"Mrs. Holender, that was perhaps the most delectable meal I have ever tasted. Your lamb is most flavorful."

Margaret Holender, a small woman with sharp features, smiled broadly. She had once been beautiful, William thought, but the life of a yeoman's wife had hardened her softer edges.

Mr. and Mrs. Holender, Missy, and her two younger brothers had been enthralled as William told the story of how he came to have a scar above his left eye.

"Did you stab him, then, Will?" asked little Neal.

"Did you sneak up and toss him into the sea for the wrong he did you?" asked his brother, Nelson.

"No," Will answered. "It was not such a grievous injury. And Lieutenant Reed must live with his own demons—that may be punishment enough."

Mr. Holender leaned forward, elbows broad on the table. "So tell me, William. Are you back in Hadenthorne to purchase a farm? I have heard tell you came back with the wages of a prince."

His wife glared at him.

"What? 'Tis the truth I be tellin', is it not?"

And now his daughter glared at him as well.

"Women! I cannot determine if the error is in what I say or what I didn't say."

Will smiled. "Mr. Holender, do not be provoked. It is not a prince's wage, but I must admit that the sacrifices at sea have been rewarding."

"So, 'tis true then. You have your sights on the Arnold land," Mr. Holender stated with finality.

"It is too soon to know for sure what I am to do. I wish I had a firmer view of the future."

"Will, it will come in time. But don't be delayin'. The Arnold piece is fertile acreage," he cautioned.

At this, Mrs. Holender ushered their sons to bed. She broadly nudged her husband as she passed.

"What? . . . Oh, yes. William, 'tis a nice evenin' to enjoy. I think you and Missy should walk down to the village bridge to . . . speak of . . . things," he suggested.

As he finished his speech, Mrs. Holender passed again behind him, nudging him sharply in the back.

"What? What?"

Will held the door open for Missy, who smiled as she walked through, turning her head to keep William in view.

The moon had just risen, low and golden, above the southern horizon. The small stand of trees by the river was illuminated as if by a ghostly sun. The colors had disappeared from sight, but forms and textures were quite plain.

Missy had taken his arm to steady herself as they walked to the bridge. He felt his heart pound at her delicate touch. William turned his head ever so slightly, moving his eyes to one side, and then downward, to better view his companion's features.

Missy was always a fine girl, as he had recalled often on his long sojourn, but she had become fuller, riper over that same time.

Her hair was the color of flax, William thought, and he was fascinated by the way it poured along her shoulders in loose curls. Her lips were pale red and not as full as some, but they widened easily to display a fine set of white teeth. Her skin was as if dew-touched; her eyes blue as winter ice, dancing as she smiled.

"William, does this small village seem dreadfully dull after your sailing to so many far and exotic places?" Missy asked.

William paused, considering his reply.

"Help me up, please, William." Her back was to the low stone wall of the bridge. She took his hands and placed them at her waist.

How small it is, Will thought.

Without an effort, he boosted her so she could sit and watch the moon. Their faces were now at even level, their eyes matching gazes. His hands remained at her sides a trifle longer than necessary.

How delicate and light she is, Will thought.

She reached up and gently traced the scar above his left eye. "Is it, Will?"

"Is . . . what?" he stammered, his heart pounding, suddenly alive.

"Is the village dull . . . after seeing the world?"

Missy tilted her head ever so slightly, keeping her eyes locked on him. She reached out and gently took his hands in hers.

"Not tonight it isn't," he said, his throat going dry. "I can scarce remember the world or its charms."

Now why did I say that? he wondered. Missy smiled, lighting up the dark, her lips parting in invitation. *I think she knows why,* he thought.

Slowly, almost without measure, Missy began to lean forward toward Will. Will could scarcely detect her movement, yet there she was, suddenly it seemed, her head resting softly against his breastbone, her head turned, her breath sweet in the chilled night air.

Will stood stiff, unsure.

"Your arm about my shoulder would be lovely, Will," she whispered intimately.

Will gathered up his confidence and gently draped his arm over her shoulder, and she snuggled closer in the golden moonlight.

July 1638
Weymouth, Dorset
England

In the corner on a rough, oak, three-legged stool sat a small man with a fiddle. Oblivious to the noise of the crowd, he was playing a lonely song, its lyrics describing his home on the coast of Ireland.

As he played, he tilted his head back, closed his eyes, and in a strong tenor voice, sang out a sad refrain.

"Dorling, why are we punished at this tavern by such caterwauling?" Radcliffe sniffed.

Herbert Dorling considered Radcliffe Spenser's question. "'Cause I likes it here," the harbormaster belched with finality. "And no one will be overhearin' anythin' we says."

Captain Blake nodded in agreement. "Is not that a wise saying, Mr. Radcliffe? That discretion is the best part of valor? Mr. Dorling here is practicing discretion."

Radcliffe looked at both men, his face wearing a bleak expression. *How is it that I must deal with such people? The efforts I must take to protect my future,* he thought, annoyed.

"Very well," he snapped. "Now, shall we be about the terms of our . . . arrangements?"

He extracted several sheets of paper from an interior pocket of his fine woolen dress coat, and with a wave of his arm slid the pewter plates and tankards to one side of the small table the three men shared. He lifted his arm and shook it with disgust, trying to clear the crumbs and ale stains from the fabric.

"Captain Blake, this is a copy of the charter my dearest brother just received concerning some small island in the Lesser Antilles . . . called—" He slid his finger down the elegantly scribed text and said, "Ah, yes, called Barbados. It also contains the legal standing of the new West Indies Company—my brother is one of the major shareholders.

"Any planter who can first set up his claims on proper acreage for sugarcane will be the planter that will be best suited to reap a king's reward from sale of that commodity."

A comely serving girl by the name of Mandy came to the table carrying a tray of three full tankards of ale above her head, navigating through the crowded room with ease, her hips swaying slightly. Radcliffe saw his two companions openly leer at her as she moved toward them. She bent down to remove the empty tableware, and Radcliffe followed the eyes of Captain Blake and Dorling as the two of them stared intently at the young girl's revealing attire. She returned their smiles as she slowly straightened up. Radcliffe had no heart for such pleasures but was glad to see both his business associates could be so easily distracted.

"Gentlemen, if you please," Radcliffe said as the girl departed, "may we return to the business at hand?"

Dorling took a long swallow, belched, then grumbled, "If you say your brother holds claim, then he holds claim. Why involve us?"

Blake nodded.

And they wonder why they die poor and lost, Radcliffe mused. "My friends, I would attend to these matters personally. However, my dearest brother, in his wisdom, has contracted a voyage to Italy that I must serve upon. It will be perhaps a year until I can visit the island of Barbados in person."

Dorling finished his tankard and looked enviously at Radcliffe's untouched drink.

"Please, take mine," Radcliffe sneered. "It appears that your thirst is much greater."

With a wide smile, and unsteady hand, Dorling did so. "But what is my part in this arrangement?" Dorling asked between gulps. "As harbormaster, I cannot leave Weymouth to attend to any matters."

And a good thing you cannot, my fat friend, Radcliffe hissed to himself. "My dear Herbert, it is vital that you stay in your office. Our dear Captain Blake must undertake a short voyage to the northern shore of Africa. The land in Barbados is rough and needs taming. And how much easier to tame it with slaves than servants, or even indentured Irishmen or Scots. Blake will see to their transport there during his voyage."

Dorling's face opened up in surprise. "Slavin' not be legal in England—not without a charter from the King, and I hears he won't be assignin' any such charters for years," he stated.

"That is why your job is vital. All you need do is turn a blind eye as Captain Blake sails with a cargo of leg irons and muskets."

Dorling's eyes narrowed as he considered his task.

"It is not that difficult a mission, my friend. Your eyesight need only fail for a moment. And Captain Blake, you need to pick up proper cargo from your African port and deposit it on Barbados. Since I must be in Italy, I will send in my stead three emissaries who will select the most advantageous land allotments. After all, the island is hardly well-surveyed. A boundary or two may have to be . . . shall we say . . . realigned."

He paused. "The raw sugar would also need to be sold to the Dutch traders in Amsterdam to avoid the penurious English import levies."

Blake stroked his chin. "I suppose it could be accomplished," the captain replied in a cautious tone.

"For the right price," Dorling added.

"Assuredly," said Radcliffe. "For a mission requiring abilities such as those you possess, and this high degree of discretion, a new price might need to be agreed upon." Radcliffe placed both his hands on the table, palms up. "If I offer an increase of one percent over our usual arrangement, would that be of interest?"

Both Dorling and Blake looked sour and on the verge of backing away.

"And if I add, as a bonus, a dalliance with the serving girl, Mandy—would that be enticement enough?"

Smiles came and both men extended their hands.

"It be a deal done then, Lord Radcliffe," Dorling belched.

Lord Radcliffe, Radcliffe thought as he considered the term. *That salutation contains the most pleasing of sounds.*

CHAPTER

25

July 1638
Devon, England

A chorus of crickets offered up a serenade to the couple slowly strolling through the gentle and soft knee-length grasses along the bank of the shallow river. As a counterpoint, bullfrogs bellowed their deep bass calls in the dark, echoed by the hoot of owls swooping through the air on great feathered wings, colored gold by the warm summer moon.

Missy had taken Will's hand and held it close and tight at her side. She tried to match the rhythm of his longer strides, and he slowed a beat or two, letting her keep pace.

The two had spent most of the afternoon and much of the evening at the great market and fair at Barnstaple, celebrating St. James Day. The town was filled with visitors from the district and as far away as London—traveling merchants and peddlers, itinerant puppeteers, actors and balladeers, and local shopkeepers who rented stalls along the main road to offer their wares.

It was a long though pleasant walk from Hadenthorne, and when they arrived, Will had bought several Cornish pasties for lunch, as well as several tankards of cider from the stall of a local brewer.

After their midday meal, they had walked about the stalls, examining the pewter wares and amusing jestbooks and almanacs.

At midafternoon in a small meadow, a minute's walk from the eastern edge of the town, a group of actors had performed a series of selections from the comedies of Mr. William Shakespeare. Will and Missy sat off to the right of the acting troupe. Will had experience with the works of the playwright, having read two of his tragedies, being most impressed with his grasp of the complexities of motivation and character. But these actors specialized in his bawdy comedy scenes. The actors carried out their roles with great enthusiasm, and Missy blushed scarlet on two occasions, even while laughing, as a series of mistaken identifications involving lovers, wives, and cuckold husbands was acted out with loud, braying voices and sweeping gestures. Will, having spent much time at sea in the company of rough men, was less sensitive to such narration.

Missy had nestled herself back into the crook of his arm, leaning against him with the full of her side.

William had looked down at her over the crown of her golden curls. From this angle he saw but the tip of her nose and the swell of her lips, curling up and open in laughter. He had let his gaze drift lower and filled his eyes with a view of the rest of her body, feeling a turn towards wicked as he observed her at his leisure and without censor.

'Tis also true that Missy is a most beautiful woman. Her charms are most considerable, Will had thought with a warm feeling growing in the pit of his stomach.

Missy had laughed again, breathing in great gasps of air into her lungs, as Will watched, wide-eyed.

But I have time enough to ponder my future. I will not let it trouble me today.

And with that, he had reached up and stroked her hair, smoothing it to her, down her thin neck to her shoulder.

Feeling the pressure of his tender and tentative strokes, Missy had leaned in even closer and placed her right hand upon Will's knee.

Did she place her hand upon my leg? Will she leave it there? And what do I do in return?

It was not until later that afternoon, as the July sun slipped toward the rows of larch and ash trees on the west side of town, that William would feel his breath truly return to his chest and his heart beat as normal.

They had walked back through the town, and each had a cold cottage pie for their supper with a tart, lemon-flavored drink. Afterwards they had strolled through the town, spent a pleasant hour listening to a balladeer from the northlands, and purchased several sweetmeats to take with them on the journey back to Hadenthorne.

But Will had scarcely realized the position of the sun, his mind still reverberating from the softness of Missy as she lay against his side and the potency of Missy's simple touch upon his knee—and his heart. The sun had dropped below the horizon, the moon beginning to fill the dusk sky.

"It is best that we begin our journey home, Missy," Will had said with a hint of regret. "It will not be till past the midnight bells until we return back to Hadenthorne."

Missy had looked up at Will, her eyes shimmering in the fading light. "Will, we may take our time on the walk home. There will be no one waiting for my return—my father is at the market in Bideford and my mother will wake only for the dawn."

With that, Missy had squeezed his hand, placed her other on his forearm, and gently and with great deliberateness stroked his tanned skin from wrist to elbow. Will had felt himself tremble deep inside at her caress.

■ ■ ■ ■ ■

The moon had completed a quarter of its journey across the dark sky, and Will had estimated that they had traveled near halfway to Hadenthorne. They had spoken very little as they walked along, Will relishing the silence as well as Missy's velvet touch upon him. The loudest sounds in the summer night were the crickets, calling one to another, and the swish and hush of Missy's long gown as it slipped through the tall grass beside him.

"Perhaps," Will said after considering the proposition for several hundreds of steps, "we should tarry for a moment at the river's edge . . . to refresh ourselves and perhaps cool our feet in the shallow waters."

"Oh, William," Missy said, her unseen smile coloring her reply, "I would most enjoy a rest. It would be most delightful to tarry at the river with you."

He led her through the tall grass, and at the river's bank removed his weskit and set it on the ground as a dry seat for Missy. He took her hand and helped her to a sitting position at the riverbank. As he stood above her, her golden hair almost glowing in the darkness, she bent at the waist, lifted her dress to past her ankles, and began to unlace her short boots.

Will's eyes opened saucer-wide as he watched. He was convinced that Missy, when she looked up at his face, smiling, had heard the thunderous pounding of his heart.

She removed one shoe, then slowly the other, and a flash of ivory flesh up to midcalf was exposed to the cool evening air as she slid her feet, leisurely, an inch at a time, into the cooling waters of the river.

She turned to Will, lifted her hand toward him, opening her palm to the sky and to him. "Will, won't you join me? It feels quite delicious, I assure you."

He kicked off both his boots and stockings in a heartbeat and slid down next to Missy, the cool of the evening replaced by a curious fever that almost felt as a swoon to William.

She took his hand and drew his arm about her shoulder, and then lowered her head to his shoulder.

Will could not remember a time he felt more completely alive and aware.

"Go ahead, Will. It will feel delicious," Missy said, squeezing his hand.

For the next second, Will felt something akin to panic sweep over him, not knowing what she meant.

"The water feels so refreshing. You always know what I need, Will," Missy said.

Will felt a breath enter his lungs in relief, and he splashed his feet into the river, wetting the tops of his rolled-up breeches. He pulled her closer, and Missy willingly yielded.

She turned her face to his, the moon illuminating her eyes and mouth with a dark warmness.

In the back of Will's awareness, a small voice was clamoring to be heard. Blinking a few times, Will listened. *But is this right? Is this the face that will smile at me in all the mornings of my fiftieth year?*

Missy took her free hand and touched Will's face, her fingers tracing, softly brushing a line from his ear to his lips to his chin.

Will! Is this the woman?

Will blinked several more times in the darkness that seemed to gather about him and then bent to her, bringing his face to hers, his lips to hers.

<hr />

The sun stood at midmorning level in the sky, and William had yet to waken from his slumber. The breakfast table in the parsonage was spread with biscuits, apples, smoked fish, cheese, jam, honey, breads, a cottage loaf, and a plate of kedgeree, a wonderful mixture of fish, eggs, rice, curry, and cream. And it was topped with a potful of black coffee. William had returned from his journeys with a sack of the curious beans, and both Mrs. Cavendish and the vicar had taken a liking to the mildly bitter taste.

"Now, Vicar," Mrs. Cavendish remarked, sipping on her third cup of coffee, "I know that you preach against the sin of gossip. And I refuse to be counted as a busybody, knowing as to how much you are set against the practice, but I am bustin' to know what has happened to our sweet William. Have you talked with the poor boy? Are he and Missy Holender really to be betrothed?"

She paused to take another long sip. "Not that I be askin' you to repeat any gossip, mind you."

The vicar tried not to smile, but he shared her concerns. He took another sip of his coffee. "If you are asking if anyone's honor has been compromised, the answer is a firm no. Though Will is now a man of the world, I believe that he would not be taking advantage of a poor innocent like Missy."

"Vicar, I know you are a man of the cloth, but it be not William who would be taking advantage of anyone. I wish not to be speakin' ill of anyone, but I think it be the reverse. He's become such a handsome young man."

"Oh . . . ohhh, I see," the vicar said. "Well, that is a situation that I had not much considered."

"So what is our William plannin'? He has been back for almost a full moon cycle, yet he has made no move to purchase the Arnold acreage— or any other acreage for that matter. He does intend on stayin' in Hadenthorne, does he not?"

"He made that statement soon upon his return to us, but he has not spoken of it since then," the vicar replied. "I cannot see him as a farmer now, but he has said that he cannot see himself as a naval officer either. William is . . . in between different chapters in his life. I do not think that he has yet to fully decide."

"He has decided that in the whilst he'll be thinkin' things over with Missy," Mrs. Cavendish said hopefully.

"Yes, it does appear that they have become fast companions in a few short weeks."

"And his comin' and goin' at all hours—I am glad he does so without alertin' the neighbors. Why, if they had known he had come returnin' past moonrise last evenin', why, I do not know what they would say."

"And how did *you* know when he returned, Mrs. Cavendish?" the vicar asked, curious since she spent her nights back at her own house.

"Well, Mrs. Ogle saw him as her husband went off to the privy."

"And isn't she your neighbor? And now you know?"

"Oh, 'tis the truth, is it not, Vicar?"

■ ■ ■ ■ ■

William lay in his bed, no more than a dozen feet from the table where the two coffee drinkers sat, where his nights were filled with delicious dreams of Missy. Smiling, he listened to them speculate and revise speculations as to his plans. They continued until noon, when William finally arose from his bed. *Coffee can do that to a person,* Will mused.

When they heard him rustle, they quieted and noiselessly cleaned up some of their breakfast dishes. Since it was near time for the midday meal, they left most of the plates out, in case William awoke hungry.

He walked into the room, yawning and running his hand through his sandy hair. It had grown long and it now hung, untied, almost down to his muscled shoulders.

The kitchen had become quiet, yet busier. Mrs. Cavendish was in a whirl, laying food out, putting plates away, stoking the fire, moving pots, and stirring the soup kettle. The vicar had been out to the woodpile, had stocked the wood box, had opened the windows, and was now straightening items on tables and sliding chairs about.

William sat alone at the table, picking at a biscuit. He cleared his throat, and both the vicar and Mrs. Cavendish stopped in midstroke, staring at him in anticipation. He smiled and began to laugh.

"Are we that obvious, William?" the vicar asked, laughing now as well.

"It is the demon drink of coffee that has loosened your tongues, you two! I may be changed since my return, but the sea has not made me deaf."

It had been many years since Vicar Mayhew had blushed and felt oddly vulnerable, but he did so now. Mrs. Cavendish just giggled as she hid her face in her apron.

"I know that you have concerns for me. My heart is touched that you do. And I do so wish that I could answer your questions. But the answers are a bedevilment to me. Try as I might, as I approach a conclusion on one aspect, other questions run off, and I must spend my time reconsidering once again."

"Will you be stayin' in Hadenthorne? Will you be buyin' the Arnold land? 'Tis a select piece of ground."

"And your intentions to Missy Holender, Will," the vicar mentioned. "I do not want to see anyone's affections toyed with."

"And will you be lookin' to buy a home seein' as how the land is without? Will ye be needin' stone and lumber?"

Will held up his hands in surrender. "Please, please, you two. I am able to answer but one query at a time!"

The vicar pulled up a chair and sat at the other side of the table. Mrs. Cavendish leaned on her elbows on the tall cutting table she used to prepare meals.

"I would be able to purchase the land. I have the funds needed. But I am not certain my heart is ready for tilling the soil." Will paused. "If

I do not purchase the land, I will have no need for a house." Will looked over to Mrs. Cavendish, a little embarrassed.

"And I enjoy being with Missy," he said softly. "She has a most pleasing laugh, and she seems to genuinely care as to my happiness. And I will also admit that her form and appearance is totally without peer in this village—perhaps in the entire shire. A most pleasing form . . ." Will's voice trailed off, his eyes hazy, a smile creeping upon his face.

A concerned look spread across the vicar's face.

Will jumped back to reality upon seeing his mentor's visage. "Vicar, our relationship is pure," he said in a whisper, to avoid alarming Mrs. Cavendish. "But you know there are limits."

The room was silent, and it was as if a cloud had passed over Will's eyes.

Will looked as if on the verge of tears. "Vicar, I feel I am a ship becalmed. I can neither advance nor retreat."

CHAPTER

26

August 1638
Hadenthorne, Devon
England

Several days later, on his way to the village the vicar came upon William sitting under the bridge by the river Taw. He had been placing balsam leaves in the water, tying stem to tip so they formed a small boat with sail. A dozen ships floated there by William, their admiral, who absently tossed pebbles at each.

"William," the vicar called, "do you care for company?"

The two sat and watched the wind tug the leaves out into the current, to be swept from harm's way.

"Vicar, what should I do? I can renew my commission on the *Minion* and move up a rank, if I choose. But I must return to Weymouth by midweek to do so. If I do, Missy will be most hurt. If I ask for her hand, I will become, with just that single question, a yeoman farmer, a husband, and tied forever to this village. If I do not become a farmer and remain a naval man, then Missy becomes a widow of sorts, living alone by the sea, waiting always for my return."

He tossed another cannonade of pebbles at his tiny green ships, striking a few. "This is all so confusing, Vicar. What should I do?"

The vicar remained silent for a moment, then replied, "William, I know that this is not an approach that we agree upon." The vicar wiped the dust from his hands. "But have you prayed about this? I requested that you keep seeking the truth, and from many of the events you have related to us it appears that you have. But have you asked God to show his will? Have you asked our Lord to guide you?"

William looked out at his leaf boats and tossed the remaining handful of pebbles into the water. He rubbed his hands on his knees, then pushed his hair behind his ears.

"Vicar, I have searched. I have not found a God that seems concerned with the plight of the peasant or the squalid lives of so many I have seen. I would ask for guidance, but it is unmistakable that others have asked—and to my reckoning, all but a small few have been turned away with no answer."

"William, to judge our Lord by looking at a sinful man—or men—is unfair and unwise. If you look for God in man, you will find only man."

Tears had formed in William's eyes, and he made no attempt to conceal them or wipe them away. "The most difficult thing, Vicar, is that I have come to love the sea. I must confess that I feel a stranger on dry land. I have never felt so split."

The vicar put his hand on William's shoulder and pulled him close, as a parent would do to a frightened child. "The true believer feels much the same, Will. We are on earth, but our home is with Christ. You have come to understand that much, and that is a great thing."

Broadwinds, Dorset
England

"Papa, why is it that you have never fully discussed your business dealings with me? Should I not learn specifically of these matters?" Kathryne asked as her father was hunched over a stack of log sheets and letters at his desk. "After all, if I were to produce an heir, would not that child be in line for the Spenser estates?"

Lord Aidan looked up from his cluttered desk at his daughter who had just breezed in the room as if a cooling wisp from the northern hills. "Begging your pardon?" he asked.

"I take it you have paid no attention to my query, dear Papa?"

"I am in the midst of important work here. For you to come in like this, pleasant as your intrusion is, and ask a babble of questions at once and expect me to have paid strict attention to all of them is not within the realm of feasibility, now is it, dear daughter?"

Kathryne spun about and literally bounced into a large, leather-covered chair to the right of her father. The chair groaned and rocked back slightly.

"Kathryne! Do they teach you such manners at Lady Emily's? If so, perhaps we will need rethink our plans for this fall."

She exhaled in a gust and let her arms drop to the arms of the chair. "Papa! They do not teach proper sitting techniques at the Alexandrian. And that is exactly the point I am striving to make here."

"What point is that?"

"And that, as well—just another indication of what I speak about."

"Kathryne, of what are you speaking? You are trying my patience. It is as if you are conversing with someone other than me—and I must return to my work. So perhaps you might seek out Mrs. Cole. She might have some small task for the evening meal that you could busy yourself with."

Kathryne sighed loudly again, staring at her father, and made no attempt to move from her slouched position in the chair.

Her father returned to his papers, scratching out notes with a quill. After a few sentences, he looked up and saw Kathryne staring directly at him with a most curious expression on her face.

He set the quill back in the inkwell, powdered the last few lines of copy, and then rolled them with a thick blotter.

"I can see that I will be granted no peace until we discover what is irksome to you. Oh, you have so much of your mother's spirit in you! It would be days, on occasion, before I would grasp what words or actions I had done or said that caused her grief or anger. At least with you, Kathryne, the term of the sentence is much shorter. For that I am grateful."

Kathryne smiled for just a brief moment, then became serious again. She straightened in the chair, folded her hands and stared directly at her father. "I am your only child, correct?"

She paused.

Lord Aidan did not answer, but merely raised his eyebrows askance, for the question was too obvious.

"And as such, I, and then my child—a male offspring—would be in line to inherit Broadwinds, is that not also correct?"

Lord Aidan looked pained for a moment. It was a subject that did little to improve his disposition. He knew how much this manner of succession and inheritance inflamed Radcliffe. The situation vexed Lord Aidan as well.

"Yes, Kathryne. You will receive all of Broadwinds and the balance of my estate upon my death, to be passed on to your firstborn male offspring. I trust you are not too soon counting the coins, for I feel quite hale," Lord Aidan said with a little laugh, trying to release some of the tension that had settled in the warm room.

Kathryne made no reaction to his levity. "And, unless you designate another beneficiary, I—or my child—will assume your business affairs as well. That is correct?"

"Well, yes."

"And Uncle Radcliffe, unless designated, will have no say in how these business affairs are to be run?"

"True," Lord Aidan answered, with a puzzled look on his features. "But, Daughter, why are you asking now? What brings this subject up?"

"Papa, I am becoming quite facile in many disciplines—specifically matters of commerce. And with Lady Emily's assistance, I will be honing those skills this fall when I return."

Lord Aidan was about to speak, opened his mouth, then realized that Kathryne had ventured off on another subject. *Which subject am I to comment on?* he wondered and merely stared back at his most curious offspring.

"I am soon to be the age of marriage, Papa. I assume that you are aware of that as well."

My goodness, Lord Aidan thought, *here is a third—or perhaps fourth—subject she has started. I am completely confused.*

"I believe I understand the working of an estate such as Broadwinds. After all, I have grown up learning of its intricacies and requirements. If I were to take over its management, I would have no fears."

Now where is she going? Lord Aidan wondered.

"But your business affairs, Papa. Those require an entirely different process and methodology. I am generally aware of what it is that you occupy your energies with. If, God forbid, you were to fall ill tomorrow, who would be capable of administering your duties? Would you quickly turn to Radcliffe?"

Kathryne left this last statement hang, unwilling to provide an answer, even though she felt as if she knew her father would answer with a negative response.

"If not, dear Father, then I, as your only heir, need to be apprised of the specific functions that you handle. How else shall these skills be passed on to the next generation of Spensers?"

She leaned toward him, pulling the chair even to his desk, and placed her hands palm down on the edge. "Papa, I am asking that you teach me what I can know of this. I realize that for a woman I am asking for a great deal, for it is not often that a female is involved in such matters."

Lord Aidan pinched at the bridge of his nose with his fingers, nodding as he did, through tightly closed eyes.

"But, Papa, in Proverbs—I believe it to be in the thirty-first chapter— the Scriptures speak of a woman who trades with merchants from afar and buys land and develops it. It would appear that if a woman was capable, the Almighty is not mandating her to deny her using her talents. And you have told me proudly of Mama, who did many things that most women would never endeavor."

Lord Aidan considered the argument and nodded slightly.

"I want to ask if I may accompany either you or Uncle Radcliffe on a business journey to London or Weymouth or whatever destination may be upcoming prior to my returning to London for my last three-month term. I would respectfully ask that I be allowed to learn of the family business, Papa.

"If we are to be wise stewards of the resources we have been blessed with from above, does not the wise stewardship consist of a careful planning for the future?"

Lord Aidan nodded, and said after a long consideration, "Why, I imagine that it does."

"Then I am the future of the Spenser estate, Papa. I would deem it wise that I be trained to assure that future generations benefit from your wise legacy of fiscal prudence."

Her father sat back in his chair, seeing Kathryne anew. After several moments of quiet, when all that was heard was the slow ticking of the massive case clock standing by the far doorway, Lord Aidan leaned forward. "Kathryne, you have made good sense. Perhaps it would be advantageous to keep you apprised of our dealings."

Kathryne sat back, a faint smile on her lips.

"And who knows," her father added, "perhaps it will be a way to introduce you to an eligible man. After all, you are soon to be finished with your schooling. Perhaps there will be a way to multiply our blessings in this manner."

Lord Aidan leaned back and stroked his chin, thinking of ways that a marriage could double, or triple, his holdings.

Yes, if the right man from the right family were available . . . , he calculated.

Kathryne simply smiled.

Hadenthorne, Devon
England

Three days past the meeting by the river with Vicar Mayhew, William arose before dawn and, without making a sound, slipped into his clothing. He had packed his belongings into his leather bag without alerting anyone, leaving some things that he felt unnecessary to carry on ship.

He stopped at the kitchen table and placed two folded letters, each sealed with wax, on the table. One was addressed to the vicar; the other bore the name Missy. William turned once, briefly, as he passed through the front door, gathering as many memories as he could with the short glance.

He shuffled along the stone-flagged path, turned onto the road, and hurried toward Weymouth, toward the sea.

27

August 1638
Weymouth, Dorset
England

"Mr. Hawkes, as I live and breathe! It is you!" cried Thomas Delby as he pumped William's hand. "The *Minion* returned, and since I saw no sign o' you I presumed you'd been lost at sea. I am most grateful to the Lord in heaven for keepin' you safe."

"And with all my teeth, thanks to your gift of lemons. It proved to be the truth." Will smiled broadly to show his friend the results of his advice.

"Like I said, although I am sure you didn't listen to all I warned you 'bout."

"I am sorry that I did not stop upon my return, but I had other priorities."

"To be understood, Mr. Hawkes, to be understood."

The two spent a comfortable afternoon swapping tales of sea and sail.

"And what brings you back to Weymouth? Especially as you ended your tale with the turnin' in of the commission."

Shaking his head, William answered, "I am not for certain myself, Mr. Delby. The good Captain Blissmore promised that I may have the commission restored if I appear before the sailing date. And I have come to see if that be true."

Looking surprised, Delby answered, "Mr. Hawkes, you must not have heard. The *Minion* sailed two days prior—to an engagement in the Caribbees, I understand. I must be sayin' that you have come a day after the fair."

William slumped in his chair, crestfallen. "It must be true—that when a man is divided, there is no peace," he muttered.

"William, if you not mind me boldness—there is another choice. You can seek out the good Cap'n Waring of the *Artemisia*. He plans on sailin' for the same waters, and I hear he'll be seekin' out a second-in-command. 'Twould be a smaller ship, to be sure, but Waring is a decent, God-fearin' man."

Will's face brightened. "Would you introduce us, Mr. Delby? I would be most grateful."

Broadwinds, Dorset
England

Radcliffe threw his hat on Lord Aidan's desk in a pique of anger. The purple felt cap, decorated with a long gossamer feather, landed with a velvety thud on the papers strewn about the surface. A few letters leafed up, and a shipping manifest slipped from the desk and fluttered to the floor.

Through clenched teeth, Radcliffe hissed, "I do not see why I am beckoned to play nursemaid to Kathryne. To think that she may learn of our affairs is a most ludicrous thought! She is a woman, and a woman has no birthright in affairs of finance! My dear brother, this is a step too far—even for such a liberal as yourself."

Lord Aidan bent and retrieved the errant manifest, which had snuck under the desk chair. He sat back up and smoothed the papers, lifting Radcliffe's hat with a delicacy it did not deserve.

"Radcliffe, as much as it might gall you, I am the firstborn, and I am placed—by that birthright—as the head of this household. If I have determined that Kathryne is to learn some of the intricacies of our affairs," Lord Aidan exclaimed, and leaned further forward, almost rising to be at a level with Radcliffe's face, "then that is what will occur. There is no need—no, there is no allowance for further discussion. I trust that is clearly understood."

Aidan sat back down and grabbed at his pen and began to scribble at an unfinished letter before him.

Radcliffe's face had blanched to near white. Lord Aidan was a man who had seldom, if ever, raised his voice in his dealings. Radcliffe had been sure that if he merely pressed, his brother would have backed down from this scheme of teaching his daughter.

A moment or two passed, and Aidan looked up, his face set firm. "Radcliffe, we will not discuss this further. Kathryne is the brightest, most polished young woman I know—a sight more poised and educated than most of the men we do business with. She has been studying commerce and finance and seems to have an excellent grasp of the knowledge that would be required of her. In three months she will be back at Broadwinds permanently, and she is eager to begin using the skills she has learned."

Radcliffe was about to interrupt, had opened his mouth, and was near to beginning his second offensive attack, when a stern-faced Aidan glared at him and held his hand up, firmly demanding his silence.

"I did not consider this lightly, Radcliffe," Aidan continued. "But she is the only Spenser who may be capable of assuming greater responsibility if we were ever absent. Is there any other person who you would trust as much? Is there any other person who will be as loyal and as honest? Is there any other person who will consider our needs above her own? Kathryne is the logical choice to groom for greater accountability."

The room was silent.

"My dear brother, you are correct," Radcliffe admitted, with the greatest honesty he could muster. "Kathryne may indeed prove an asset."

And she is an asset that I believe I can control much easier than even my dear older brother, Radcliffe added to himself.

15 August 1638
Hadenthorne, Devon
England

Dear Thomas Mayhew,

It is with heavy heart that I write this. I am returning to the sea and the *Minion*. I have felt adrift these past weeks and it does no one well to have a person such as me about. You have provided more assistance than you will ever know. For that I will be eternally grateful.

Until my return, I remain, your most humble servant,

William Hawkes

My dearest Missy,

As you read these lines, I will be at sea heading to strange lands. My soul demands it and I can offer no recourse. The lonely wife of a sailor is no life for one as beautiful as you. I cherish the memories of our time together. I will dream of your lips when I wish to smile. Remember me when the moon is full and the breeze brushes your golden hair from your most beautiful face.

Your most humble,
William Hawkes

The vicar sat at the table, near tears, as he read the letter. *William, I trust that you will find peace. You will always find home with us,* his heart cried out.

Missy Holender wept copiously as the vicar read her letter to her. She cradled her head in her hands and wept, sobs shaking her body.

"When you write to him, Vicar," she said between gasps, "tell him that I will wait for him forever."

The vicar nodded and patted her hand.

"You tell him that," she cried. "Forever."

Windsor Castle,
Outside London,
England

"How silly this game seems to me at times," King Charles exclaimed after hitting a particularly bad shot. "To spend one's time marching about in a field, wielding a crooked lead club, attempting to maneuver a little leather ball filled with feathers into a hole in the ground—this should be deemed the occupation of fools!"

"I agree, Sire. However, the game does get into the blood, does it not?" replied Sir Adam Donnel as he squinted in the hot sun, removing a tussock of moist grass and earth from the horned end of his club.

"As does tennis. Except with golf, one needn't wear those ridiculous slippers required for play on a court," the king noted with obvious satisfaction.

"Speaking of court, Your Excellency, there is a matter that I've been meaning to discuss with you."

"Yes—what is it?" the king replied absently as he calculated the distance to the next hole. He looked over at Sir Donnel with an empty expression.

"As you know, with the death of Sir Henry Hawley—you know him, Sire . . . the late earl of Carlisle's governor, who had been serving as lord proprietor of the Lesser Antilles islands—I believe it would be most prudent if you quickly appointed a replacement, since that most important position includes the governorship of the island of Barbados," Sir Donnel explained.

"Hmm. . . . True enough, what with all of the Crown's interests in the planting of sugar there." He paused and appeared to be in deep thought. "It is most important to retain control. Have you any suggestions?"

Sir Donnel scratched his chin. "Well, it requires someone from whom we can expect the utmost loyalty to protect our considerable investment and one who has the necessary expertise to handle it all. I have given considerable thought, and I believe the logical choice would be a member of my syndicate—Lord Aidan Spenser, earl of Broadwinds."

King Charles paused and leaned on his club. "Spenser, you say. Well, he certainly has proved his fidelity—thanks to his money and large loans—to the Crown over the years."

"He is most seasoned in the affairs of foreign commerce. He is said to be upstanding and fair in all his dealings."

"Would he consider such an appointment?" the king asked as he centered himself over his club.

"I'm sure that he would."

"Then we shall make it so. See to it that the documents are prepared for my signature and seal."

King Charles hit the ball, which sailed only a few yards and hit the grass with a soft thud.

"Ah! This bloody game!"

28

August 1638
Weymouth, Dorset
England

The cabin for the ship's second officer on the *Artemisia* was small, even by naval standards, but was at the aft of the ship, just under the captain's more expansive lodging. It had a door—a door that locked, William noted. The room, measuring no more than eight feet long by five feet wide, had a cabinet for charts, a fold-down desktop, a hammock, and a wide expanse of windows that looked out to the water. The only element that stood between William and the sea were thin panes of glass.

Surveying his new quarters, William smiled. *It feels good to be home.*

■ ■ ■ ■

The day the *Artemisia* was scheduled to sail, carrying a cargo of machetes, plows, wooden timbers, and household wares, William took one last walk back up High Street.

It was early in the morning as he tapped at the door of one shuttered shop. "Mr. Delby, I need some lemons, if you please. Make it a large bag, so I can share them with the rest of the crew."

After the bag of fruit had been procured, the two friends exchanged farewells.

"I will be back in four months," said Will. "We will talk again."

"See that you come back, Master Will. I will look forward to that meetin'."

He picked up the sack of the yellow fruit and left to return to the *Artemisia*. It was a merchant ship, patterned after a galleon, but built with shorter lines and carrying a quarter of the crew.

"The smart merchant watches pennies as he can, William," Captain

Waring had told him as he accepted the position. "You will find that we sail with a different spirit than does the English navy."

"I had hoped we would," William had said. "I had hoped we would."

As he left Delby's shop, he stopped at the corner to look out over the harbor, drinking in the broad bay dotted with a dozen sailing vessels. It was as peaceful to William as the most bucolic scene in Devon.

At that instant, two men exited one of the local alehouses, blinking and squinting in the bright sunshine. The elder of the two, a ship's captain judging by his jacket, William perceived, waved his hand at him.

Puzzled, William looked about. *Who could he be hailing?*

"Son—you there—could I speak to you?"

He was a large man with a florid complexion. His coat, patterned after an admiral's jacket, had been tailored with great care and indicated that he was not a naval man, but a merchantman. The other fellow, William observed, was very well dressed, smaller but still tall, with a sharp chin and deep-set dark eyes. A thin beard, the color of ocher sandstone, framed his face. He stood a few paces from the captain and Will, almost hiding in the shadow of a nearby doorway.

The merchant sailor extended his hand. "Are you not William Hawkes? I was told by one of the patrons that it was you."

"Yes, I am William Hawkes."

"The William Hawkes that has just completed a tour aboard the *Minion* as navigator?"

"Yes, that would be me."

"Well, son, I am Captain Blake of the *Plymouth Spirit*. It happens that I would be needing a navigator on a trip to the Antilles. Would you be seeking a vessel to sail on?"

Before William could answer, a carriage clattered to a stop no more than a dozen feet away. The door swung open, and an agitated nobleman jumped out.

Under his breath, William heard the other man mutter, "Curse that Aidan Spenser. To follow his brother round like this."

"Radcliffe!" exclaimed Aidan Spenser. "I have searched half the town for you. I must speak with you immediately."

William watched Captain Blake's companion stride toward the man by the carriage.

"Please join Kathryne and me," said Aidan as he stood half in, half out of the carriage door. "We must be off at once."

Will's eyes followed the nobleman for a moment, then caught sight of a young woman leaning forward from the rear seat of the enclosed hackney carriage. Her hair was in loose waves, deep, rich brown, like the color of a red deer; her lips were full and rounded. Her eyes were deep set, piercing, alive with color and luminescent even from the shadows of the carriage.

She was visible for just a fleeting glance, and their eyes locked for a long spark of a moment.

A person might drown in those eyes, Will thought.

Kathryne leaned back against the leather-cushioned seat, placing her hand to her breast in an effort to calm the rapid beating of her heart. *Those eyes,* Kathryne thought between heartbeats. *I have seen those eyes before.*

And as she jumbled through her memories, an image of a foxhunt rippled into her consciousness. *The eyes of a fox?* Kathryne asked herself. *No, that's not it, but then again, maybe he . . .*

As the carriage rattled away, she tried to invoke the fleeting image of those potent eyes.

The Spenser carriage turned the corner, and William stared after it, slack-jawed.

Captain Blake's booming voice brought him back to the question of the moment. "Well, Mr. Hawkes, are you interested in my proposition? The voyage will be offering a substantial award to all officers and crew. It be worth your while." Draping his beefy arm around Will's shoulder, Captain Blake added, more softly, almost whispering into his ear, "We may not be the first to the island of Barbados with a land charter, but we have one for the most acreage, and if all goes as planned it could mean a small grant to you as well, if you care to be holding land."

Will continued to stare after the carriage. *Were her eyes green or blue? Have I seen those eyes before? Will I see them again?*

"Well, Mr. Hawkes? Do we have an understanding?"

Will turned, freeing himself from Captain Blake's embrace and facing him directly. "Captain Blake, I am most flattered that you have been made aware of my abilities as a navigator, but, most unfortunately, I have just agreed less than an hour previous to be the ship's second for Captain Waring of the *Artemisia*. Had we met earlier, perchance we may have struck a deal."

Captain Blake put his hand on Will's shoulder again, pulling him closer. "Tell him that a crisis has arisen and that you cannot sail. Then join with me. I will double his arrangement with you."

Will paused, his thoughts in a race. *Doubling would make me a rich man in Hadenthorne—on merely one voyage.*

"Well . . . ?"

After a moment or two of hesitation, William removed Blake's hand from his shoulder. "Captain Blake, your offer is most tempting, but I must be a man of my word. To do what you suggest would be a dishonoring of my character. And I cannot do that."

Captain Blake smiled. "That is indeed most admirable, Mr. Hawkes. Most admirable. An honorable man with a clear conscience is a rarity," Blake remarked, with the hint of a smirk upon his face. As he walked back into the alehouse, he turned and added, "Until we meet again. Godspeed on your voyage."

Radcliffe, with an angry sigh, removed his hat festooned with a great white plume and sat in a narrow-shouldered slouch on the forward seat of the carriage.

Lord Aidan was seated next to his daughter, Kathryne, who sat on the rear seat, facing forward.

My dear brother looks uncommonly agitated this morning, Radcliffe thought. *How enjoyable to see him in such a state.* He looked over at Kathryne, whose eyes were focused straight ahead, her hand still at her heart. *And the silly schoolgirl looks as if she has spotted a ghost. How curious.*

Lord Aidan was fumbling for a paper from his breastpocket. He pulled out a sheaf of several, then discarded all but one in a heap on the floor.

Now this is most curious indeed. Lord Aidan is never in such a state of disorder and confusion. "Pray tell, dear brother, what could be the cause of this most awful consternation?" Radcliffe asked in a voice thick with sarcasm. "Have we become bankrupt? Has King Charles announced war with France? Has our lovely schoolgirl, the Lady Kathryne, besmirched the family name?"

"Radcliffe, must you play the role of wastrel and cynic so majestically? Could you leave the theatrics to the actors at the Globe? This news is of major import to the Spenser family—which is all of us—including yourself," said an annoyed Lord Aidan.

Radcliffe pushed his hat to the side and leaned forward. *This indeed may be something worthy of my consideration.*

"The king you enjoy making sport of so often has altered our family history with a single signature," Lord Aidan said.

■ ■ ■ ■

"We will sail in three days, Mr. Hawkes. I suggest that you fully acquaint yourself with the *Artemisia*. It is not nearly as grand a vessel as what you have been accustomed to, but it has filled our requirements nicely."

Captain Waring and William were sitting in the captain's cabin of the *Artemisia*. A tidy and precise room, it was no more than four steps in breadth and the like in width. The cabin sat, snug and neat, below the stern lanterns one deck beneath the quarterdeck, occupying half the gallery at the stern.

Built into the center wall of the captain's cabin was a cozy bedchamber with a faded brown curtain hung by brass hooks and grommets. Underneath the bed were drawers containing the captain's personal effects. The port and stern walls were windowed, with window seats and storage beneath running their length. A round oak table sat solidly in the middle of the room, with one grand well-worn leather chair and several wooden benches positioned around it.

The captain had secured his astrolabe and cross-staff, along with his sextant and telescope in a wall-mounted cabinet. Underneath were hung two scabbards and a brace of pistols. There was a wooden cross mounted above the short door.

After his initial meeting on board with Captain Waring, Will retired to his cabin, which lay on the opposite side of the vessel from the captain's. It was narrower, and smaller in depth as well, but it was private.

To be alone will be such luxury, Will mused.

Will placed the few books he possessed in a small alcove by the door and laid out his clothing in two drawers by the chart cabinet.

The *Artemisia* was a three-masted ship with four decks and was a well-crafted merchantman vessel built in Antwerp a dozen years prior. William knew that this vessel's response to the tiller would be more graceful than that of the larger, ponderous *Minion*. Though ships of this class could carry upwards of fifty cannons and other large armaments, the *Artemisia* carried only six small ten-pound guns as well as a large cabinet full of pistols, muskets, and swords. Most of the crew of forty-five men had experience with a variety of weapons, but the ship was not sailed for battle nor built for offense.

William walked the main deck, watching as the muscled, sweating stevedores loaded cargo belowdecks for the voyage. The purser, Henry Kreble, stood by, holding a sheaf of papers and a long manifest of articles. As each item was loaded, he ticked them off his list.

The two introduced themselves, and Will inquired as to the bulk of the provisions to be carried on this voyage.

"Well, we always bring enough fresh supplies for the crew, of course, but on this trip we're supplying plows, axes, linen, wool, and a great deal of barreled beef, salted cod, flours, and the like. We are also contracted to carry a large supply of buttons, needles, and household utensils. It seems that all such materials quickly go to rust in the warm air of the tropics."

"But are not the islands self-sufficient in crops?" William asked. "I would have thought such an equatorial climate would provide a great bounty of provisions."

Henry laughed, "I am not a farmer, Mr. Hawkes, but I think there's a sight more money in tobacco and sugar than there is in cows and fishing. It must be easier to buy provisions than to grow one's own. At least that's what I hope is the case for our customers."

William slowly made his way to the bow of the vessel, and as he walked he carefully checked the tautness of the rigging, the condition of the netting and canvas, and the tightness of the oakum joints between deck planks. He made his way belowdecks, and while the fetid smells were similar to those of the *Minion,* it was not quite as overpowering on this ship.

At midafternoon, William was inspecting the pulley system of the rudder and wheel and the security of the tiller rope when a loud whistle called from above decks. Three shrill long reports followed by two short calls was the signal for assembly on deck. William crawled out from the pulley well and dusted off his breeches.

All the gearing and mechanisms are in perfect working order, Will determined as he made his way up ladders and gangways through the upper decks. *This ship has been tended to with loving care. It is much better maintained than any naval ship I have seen.*

As he arrived on the quarterdeck, the rest of the crew had gathered round Captain Waring. The captain had in his hand a small, black, leather-bound volume. He held up his hand to quiet the men, most of whom were sitting cross-legged in a semicircle about him.

William turned to a man with a shock of red hair standing next to him. "William Hawkes, the ship's new second. What goes on here?"

"Johnny Delacroix, boatswain. It's our daily prayer time."

Surprised, William asked a second question. "Prayer time, every day? Are all these men Christian?"

Delacroix, a tall and narrow man from the Isle of Wight, snorted under his breath, "Not bloody likely. I, for one, am not one of those hypocritical, smug, so-called holy men."

"Then why, pray tell, are you at a prayer gathering?" William asked in a whisper, as he strained to hear the words the captain was reading.

"'Cause our captain has made it a ship's rule. And I would hazard to guess that most of the crew loves this time."

William looked puzzled.

"'Cause we all can sit on the deck, sit back, and not work for a spell."

A breeze came up from the east, blowing against William's back. He watched as the captain read from the Scriptures. His words were carried in the wind, away from William in the strengthening breeze. Will saw only his mouth move and his hands gesture, but his ears discerned no sound.

▪▪▪▪

Kathryne's face showed the merest presence of a smile, knowing her part in the coup that she and her father were about to share with her Uncle Radcliffe.

"Kathryne—this schoolgirl, as you called her—had the good fortune to attend the Alexandrian with a young lady by the name of Lucy Donnel. Lucy happens to be the daughter of Sir Adam Donnel, a confidant of King Charles and one of the syndicate members who was a sponsor of a settlement on the island of Barbados. Kathryne was with Lucy at a social gathering not long ago when she picked up the most interesting tidbit of news. Lucy mentioned, in a most casual manner, that they had received recent news that Sir Henry Hawley, the late earl of Carlisle's governor, had died in a recent bout with yellow fever," said Lord Aidan.

Radcliffe looked confused. "So?"

"It appears that the good earl was lord proprietor of all the Lesser Antilles, including Barbados. As well as an employee of the syndicate, earning high wages."

"So?"

"He was governor of the island of Barbados as well. As you might imagine, that seat is currently unfilled."

The carriage just then struck a large hole in the rutted road, and the three inhabitants were pitched about, papers tossed in a heap on the floor.

Radcliffe ignored them all, not stooping to retrieve any. "Brother, you spin a wondrous tale of intrigue. But I have for certain no idea of what you seek to tell me."

Kathryne spoke up as her father rummaged through the pile of documents. "It seems, Uncle Radcliffe, that the filling of this gap in the government of such an island requires court approval—approval by King Charles himself. I spoke to Lucy, and we spoke to her most interesting and influential father, who in turn spoke to the king."

Radcliffe continued to stare. It was apparent that he thought that any complicated plans were beyond the skills of Kathryne and her father.

Kathryne looked down at the floor, bent to pick up one slip of parchment embellished with the royal seal of His Majesty King Charles, and with an elegant flourish, handed it to her uncle.

"Radcliffe, may I introduce the future governor and lord proprietor of all the Lesser Antilles—Lord Aidan Spenser."

"It appears that all the usurious taxes I have paid and all the loans I have made to the court suitors at Whitehall have finally been repaid," Lord Aidan added.

And as the carriage clattered away back to Broadwinds, Radcliffe sat, his mouth hung open in surprise, as Kathryne gleefully embraced her father, the soon-to-be governor of Barbados, the crown jewel of the Lesser Antilles.

29

September 1638
The English Sea, South of the
Land's End Peninsula

The *Artemisia* set sail at high tide. The water was calm as they slipped out to sea, the wind a mere whisper. Once into the English Sea, the winds freshened, and they were soon passing the last glimpses of English soil. William watched silently as the land receded from view.

"Are you the homesick type, Mr. Hawkes?" Captain Waring asked. "Or is it merely that you like to hold on to the view of land and home for as long as you can?"

"I would say neither, Captain. My first voyage was difficult, but since then I have realized that I am at home on the sea. I am satisfied here. I understand what the sea requires, and I am able to provide it. There is not much at home that draws me or calls out my name."

Waring looked at Will, then back to the land as the last ridge of the Lizard slipped from view. "'Tis no shame to admit missing home and hearth, William. I, like yourself, consider myself most free out on the oceans, but I also admit to finding much comfort back in Weymouth with my wife and children."

"You are married, Captain? I would not have surmised."

"Yes, 'tis true. After all, 'tis a biblical mandate. We are called to be fruitful and multiply, are we not?"

"That is indeed a scriptural calling," Will agreed, adding, "but do they not miss you terribly during your long absences?"

"Both parties have days of loneliness. But following this voyage, as with every voyage I have made as captain, I will spend upwards of a month or more at home. It provides a treasure of memories to all of us—and those have comforted me greatly. And that treasure is much more dear than a cold and heartless shilling or guinea."

Will nodded as he stared forward.

"Whom do you miss, Will?" the captain asked. "Is it the truth that there is no one at your home who holds you near their heart? Can it be that a most handsome young man as yourself has no one waiting for his return?"

William stared back at England. An image of Missy came first to mind, then was immediately replaced with a clouded image of an unknown beauty with blue—or green—eyes.

Did I hear the name Kathryne as the carriage stopped? Will struggled to remember.

"No, Captain. There be many friends at home, but none so closely embrace my heart."

"Well then, Will, I will offer in my prayers this evening a request that you will find that someone—and that our Lord will send you a sign to inform you of his choice for your life."

Will nodded in thanks, unwilling to discuss his true feeling as to God's direction and interest in his life. "I thank you, Captain, for your prayers. And I will look for such a sign."

London, England

"Lady Emily, are you sure that women are welcome in this coffee-house?"

"Of course, Kathryne. Lloyd's is a fine establishment. I have been to this place in the past—as a guest, of course—and I have made inquiries. A gentlewoman may enter, if she is indeed a gentlewoman."

Lady Emily surveyed the room, filled with fine wooden chairs, some covered in leather, an assortment of tables, and perhaps a dozen men standing in a half-circle by the fireplace, discussing some subject with much animation.

"And Kathryne—we *are* gentlewomen. So this will all be quite proper."

A uniformed butler, a man who looked incapable of smiling, seated them near the circle of men near the fireplace.

A gentleman whose face was framed in a full white beard and moustache had raised his arm and was exclaiming loudly, "I will undertake that assurance. I will offer that assurance."

Another pair, off to the side, were in heated discussion. "If the vessel makes it back with a full hold of silk, it will repay the venture at least tenfold. The ship and captain are sound—it is worth the risk," one man explained.

"If I offer a thousand-pound bond as assurance of its return, what multiplication of my funds are you proposing?" the other asked.

"A full doubling of your stake, Lord Weston. A full doubling."

"Then the deal is to be done. I will see that a draft for funds is placed in your backers' hands by the morrow."

Kathryne was watching faces, overhearing conversations, her eyes going from one group to the next. She understood the words, but try as she might, was unable to assess the importance of them.

"Lady Emily, I am quite baffled by all this," she whispered to her. "What manner of business is it?"

"Kathryne," Lady Emily whispered back, "these gentlemen are a syndicate of wealthy investors who are offering their funds as assurance that ships will return to England with full cargoes. Their funds permit others to raise additional monies to buy goods for sale. They are providing what is called insurance against catastrophic incidents—like sinkings or piracy."

Kathryne's eyes opened wide as the concept became clearer.

"The reason you are here is, that after your father announced the granting of charters and claims for the island of Barbados, two or three of his associates—his aides, truly—came here to indemnify his vessels. I wanted you to understand that process—just for insurance."

Kathryne smiled.

"Now, my dear, allow me to introduce you to Lord Arburton. He is the one who will be most pleased to meet the daughter of the noted Lord Aidan."

It was late into the afternoon when the two ladies sought their leave from Lloyd's. Kathryne had spoken at length with Lord Arburton about the intricacies of such arrangements as ship assurances and bonds. When he had discovered her lineage, he was most pleased to offer all manner of advice and counsel.

"After all, my dear," he had told her confidentially, "it has been public knowledge at court that Lord Aidan will be called to assume the office as the next governor of the island of Barbados. Your father would be most well-suited for such a task." He winked at her in a fatherly way. "And I would be most grateful if I might consider our meeting as but the first step in a long business association."

Kathryne smiled at him, took his hand, curtsied, and added, "Perhaps that is to be so, Lord Arburton, perhaps so." Suddenly she saw the light shining on the path ahead of her.

The Atlantic Ocean

For virtually all the vessels sailing from an English port the most frequently traveled route to the Caribbean was to head south from England, past Portugal and Madeira, stopping in the Canary Islands to take on fresh water. From there, the prevailing winds pushed ever stronger to the west and the Lesser Antilles through the area of the Atlantic known as the Sargasso Sea, named for sargassum seaweed filling vast areas of the salty water with its thick green tendrils. A mere mention of the name provoked fear, for there were many sailors who told stories of ships trapped in the seaweed never to see the open waters again. Indeed, it was a long expanse of empty ocean, and a major breeding ground for eels, but the trade winds were kind and sped vessels along their course.

The first leg of this journey to the Canaries was familiar to William, having sailed it three times. It was a simple matter to chart out the routes. He spent his time reading and studying a small book by Richard Hakluyt, *The Principall Navigations, Voiages and Discoveries of the English Nation*. It was a narrative of the author's experiences in the Caribbean, written thirty years prior and filled with naval battles, marches through jungles, attacks by wild natives, and sackings of Spanish towns. Included were pages of navigational instructions, detailing how to sail from island to island. The author supplied frustratingly few geographical details, and William surmised that much of the retelling had been embellished by time.

Their first day in the trade winds was a glorious day to sail, William thought. The sky was clear, the wind strong from the east. The *Artemisia* was not a grand sailing ship designed for speed, for her wide, fat hull sat low in the water. But in such wind as this, upwards of a hundred and eighty miles each day could be covered. If the moon was out, they would sail at night as well. A forty-day voyage would be considered rapid, indeed.

Will sat on the poop deck in the far starboard corner, the steering side of the vessel, with his book in hand. The crew, the majority of them having sailed together for several Caribbean journeys, was well trained. Sails were unfurled on first command. Men willingly spent time on hands and knees, scouring the deck with their holystones, soft Bible-shaped sandstones used to scour the decks with seawater and to take out splinters and stains from the decking. Sew-sew boys sat with yards of canvas in their laps, marlin spikes and thick thread at the ready, patching torn sails. Palm and picket men, with leather patches on their palms, spent hours splicing ropes, repairing rigging and cables. A six-man crew practiced with the small cannon on the port side.

If one could assign the demeanor of an animal to ships, Will contemplated, this ship would be a cow—pleasant, unruffled, unperturbed, but getting her business done efficiently. The *Minion,* on the other hand, would have been an injured bull—temperamental, hard to control, and prone to turn violent at a moment's notice. Will liked being on a cow much better.

The weather—strong winds, clear skies—repeated itself with great frequency during the voyage. On only three days did rain clouds form, and even then the *Artemisia* kept her sails unfurled, for it was not hard or driving rain that would place the masts or sails at risk of damage.

Frequently during the day, his official duties having been dispatched earlier, Will would be invited to man the wheel. As he felt the pull of the wind against the ship and the force of the water against the rudder, the helmsman, Griffin Edwards, would sit nearby and offer advice, counsel, and instruction.

"Don't fight her, Mr. Hawkes. Let her have free reign when she takes to the north on a gully of wind. A ship is like a woman, Will, and I'm sure you understand how to handle a woman—tenderly. Let her run free for a while, then bring her back in line."

Will nodded, even though he had precious little knowledge of the feelings or emotions of women. His only real experience had been with Missy, and for most every moment they shared Will had felt an overwhelming sense of puzzlement. He had often been quite baffled by her questions and requests. Most of her motives had seemed to make no sense to Will.

But this ship was a different matter. He turned on the wheel and felt the ship incline to his action, heel into the wind. Too much turn and the wind's power was lost and the ship cut too sharp an angle. Too slight a turn and the wind was immediately behind the vessel, and too much was taken into her sails, tipping them forward, driving the bow deeper into the waves. At just the right tack, a gentle angle off the direction of the wind, the ship rode as if on bone skates sliding across the thick ice of a hard winter. The swell felt like small ripples and the wake was slight. Will just knew when the angle, the wind, the seas, the heading were right—he just *knew* when all these elements were in the most perfect balance. He felt that he was born to handle such a vessel.

William cherished his times at the wheel. *If I had not chosen navigation, I would have chosen this,* he thought.

As William read the charts and sun, he reckoned that they were coming close to their destination. Any navigator could accurately place the ship as to the degree north and south at any point, the sextant near perfect for this information. But locating the distance east and west was not such an easy task. It could not be done by instrument readings alone. A sextant would position the ship at the right latitude. Longitude might be measured, if a landfall was near, by astrolabe and cross-staff. A triangulation was needed. But a ship on empty ocean seldom, if ever, had the luxury of a landfall at hand. A navigator had to practice dead reckoning, a mixture of guessing and science. Will had but to figure the speed of the ship, factor in the length of time under sail and the currents, and use that calculation to estimate the distance traveled. Every morning, Will consulted his charts and reviewed the log board on the quarterdeck, listing, hour-by-hour, the past day's worth of the ship's speed, wind direction, course, and sextant sightings.

William observed the sun and read the moon and stars, and armed with that knowledge—plus a sort of sixth sense of his location—always came within a quarter-day's sail of his target.

Lieutenant Reed of the *Minion* had labeled Will as part English goose, for he always seemed to know his exact position on the globe at any time. Captain Blissmore had echoed that sentiment.

"I have never liked Barbados," Captain Waring exclaimed as they neared the destination. "Trying to sail to it is like lying prone on the ground, looking for a coin tossed in the grass. One needs to run into it rather than see it."

If the *Artemisia* missed the island, sailing past by any distance, it would take days—perhaps a full week—of tedious tacking back and forth against the strong trade winds to return to the port of Bridgetown. It was found from the east, and lost from the west.

William was aware of the risk involved as he plotted out the final leg of the trip.

"Remember, Mr. Hawkes . . . last trip we tacked for five days until we saw the eastern coast of the island. It is no disgrace to be cautious."

William, by nature, was a cautious man—never revealing too much of himself to anyone, never making large leaps when little ones might do.

But on this sailing his feeling of security and confidence expanded, as if his heart itself was catching the full impact of the trades, filling full with a powerful wind of knowledge and assurance. He knew where to point the ship and how to bring her home. He just *knew*.

He stood by the helmsman, instructing him. "Keep her steady on south southwest, Mr. Edwards. We will need no tacking on this voyage."

"It be on your head, Mr. Hawkes, if we slip past our port and crash into the Guiana coast. And you know that I will not lie of your orders, William," he said in a leathery voice.

"There will be no need to lie, good friend."

And with that, carrying the captain's telescope, Will began to climb the center mast to the mainmast top. This time he took the outside path, and for a moment was suspended on a few small ropes, almost as free as a gull. Up in the wind he wrapped his strong legs about the slender pole of wood, sitting on a small platform and leaning against a spidery web of rigging.

He extended the scope and looked east. A dozen moments later, he folded the scope and scrambled down the mast. He walked slowly to the helmsman, leaned toward him, and whispered in his ear, smiling broadly, "Land ho."

In a few hours the ship had cleared the rough, windward, wave-tossed Atlantic coast of Barbados and was headed through the calm, leeward waters to Bridgetown.

It was a pleasant place with broad streets and wood and stone buildings that nestled around the port. Bridgetown was built in a shallow bowl, the land rising away gently, forming low hills.

Climbing up from the port through terraced hills and valleys, one could reach a steep escarpment four miles into the interior. At the top of this coral wall was the central plateau, a thousand feet above sea level, with constant and strong cooling breezes. At its eastern rim, Hackleton's Cliff dropped abruptly down to the wild Atlantic coast, edged with coral rocks and pounding surf. Understandably it was quickly christened the Scotland district. Here the air was bracing, with sweeping vistas, rugged hills, and narrow canyons, and at the bleak northern tip of the island the sea dashed high against the rocks.

On the southwest coast, Bridgetown had been established a decade previous on Carlisle Bay. The busy port was built around a thin finger of land that created a natural anchorage. On this point, called the Careenage, ships came to be beached, turned on their sides, and scraped clean of barnacles and worms. It was traversed by a rickety, primitive bridge there, built by the Carib Indians—hence the name Bridgetown.

As the *Artemisia* approached, the crew raised an English flag, a red cross and a white *X* splashed across a field of deep blue, signifying their ship as a friendly merchant and not a Spanish or French raider. In response, from a small wooden blockhouse on a bluff by the harbor, a cannon was fired.

"We be cleared to enter," cried the helmsman's mate. "Away aloft."

In the time it took to furl the sails and secure the anchor, several small boats from the town dock had reached the *Artemisia*.

One of the first men to scuttle up the side netting was William Hillard, owner of a three-hundred-acre plantation and importer of much of their cargo of barreled beef, pork, and salted cod. He and Captain Waring greeted each other with much fanfare, as old friends. An indentured servant accompanying Hillard produced a cask of brandy so a toast could be offered to the successful voyage.

Holding a large cup of spirits skyward, Hillard, in a loud and loose voice, offered the first of his many salutations. "This be for Captain Waring, the bravest and best sea trader in all the Antilles."

Hillard was the first to down his cup and request a second. Captain Waring, a man not given to excess with alcohol, sipped from his, and would not need more for another several toasts.

Hillard managed to salute most of the crew and then switched to the royal family. "And this be for Queen Henrietta Maria, though a Papist she be."

William reached the deck in time for the festivities and stood alongside Johnny Delacroix, who was combing back his long red hair and tying it into a tail at his neck with a colorful strip of ribbon.

"Is this standard formalities for a simple merchant ship's arrival in port?" he asked.

"This be Barbados, Will. I would hazard that the folks here look to any occasion to celebrate—especially with toasts and brandy."

Both men snickered as Hillard thought of one toast after another.

Delacroix nodded to William, then pointed with a thrust of his head. "Look over to the harbor, my friend. See how fast word of our arrival has spread."

There were a dozen boats, of all sizes, making their way out to the *Artemisia*. Some were obviously plantation owners of some note. One could make out the class distinctions by their hats. The more successful a man was, the broader and more elaborate his head covering—with feathers, fur, and jewels. One boat seemed to be populated with nothing but a flock of multicolored birds, so ornately feathered were the gentlemen's hats, save one poor man, nearly in rags, who struggled with the oars.

In a few moments the quarterdeck was filled with farmers, planters, plantation owners, and their servants. A few of the servants were black men. William had seen black men before on his first voyage, having encountered them in Venice and Gibraltar. But this was the first time he had seen one from such a close distance.

Johnny leaned over. "They be slaves, Will," he said quietly.

"I surmised as much. Would there be many of them on the island?"

"Quite a few by my understanding, and more are coming all the time. They say they be well suited to work in the sugar fields."

Captain Waring made his way to William, with a drunken Hillard in tow. "William Hawkes, meet Mr. Hillard. Mr. Hillard is the man who arranged for much of this cargo. Mr. Hillard, meet the man who got us to your fair island in record time—William Hawkes."

"Mr. Hawkes." Hillard slurred, "You, my boy, are a godsend. I don't know how much longer I could have managed without a fine piece of English beef. And here you be, with barrels of it right under our feet."

Hillard stumbled and William caught him, propping him back up. "Steady, Mr. Hillard. And it was my pleasure."

Hillard wrapped his arm around Will's shoulder and with his free hand still carrying the half-full cup of brandy, motioned to another planter to join them.

"George Reading, come here. Meet our Mr. Hawkes. He got here early with our beef, and he's a wonderful lad."

George Reading staggered towards the trio with an unsteady brandy-altered gait. "William Hawkes, pleased to meet you," he slurred, and draped his arm around Will's other shoulder.

"William, can I ask you a question?"

William, sagging under the weight of both men, gasped, "Most certainly, Mr. Reading."

"Have you brought us our new governor as well as our beef? I hear he's due here any time."

And with that, Reading slumped to the deck in a heap. Hillard thought it quite funny and pointed down at the prone figure, laughing and spilling the rest of his drink. Perhaps staring down was too much, for a moment later Hillard teetered a bit and then collapsed atop his unfortunate friend.

William stood in the middle of the collapsed pair with a helpless look, scanning the crowd for a sober face.

CHAPTER

30

November 1638
Island of Barbados
The Caribbean Sea

Barbados was a captivating place. From the rocky Atlantic coast to the lush jungles of the leeward side, magical and unexpected vistas seemed to hide behind each hillock and lurk beyond every twist in a forest path.

Nearly seven thousand souls now called this island home, not only those of English descent, but French, Dutch, Irish, Spanish, Jewish, and Indian as well, though not all with the same degree of enthusiasm.

Much of the land was untouched, pristine, and covered with luxuriant and exotic vegetation. Sweet-smelling frangipani and fragrant bougainvillea grew in profusion, their magenta and yellow flowers painting a colorful landscape against the turquoise bays of the coastline. Above, palm-fringed heights and secluded emerald forest glades were draped in lianas and ferns.

And amidst this primitive jungle a plantation society was struggling to be born. The first settlers, many of them the younger sons of the English gentry, carved out small parcels of farmland from the native foliage and experimented with various crops. They were seeking a profitable export, not being in line to inherit any of their family's wealth. The island was not as densely forested as some islands of the Antilles, and the planters quickly cleared the land by slashing through the native plants and burning the debris in huge bonfires that could be seen from miles out to sea.

The first crop was tobacco, then sea-island cotton, indigo, and ginger—all grew fairly well in the tropical climate. The Dutch introduced sugar as a crop and then sold the knowledge to grow and to process the thick green cane into raw sugars. Planters from Brazil, backed by Dutch traders, brought the know-how and the machinery required to make sugar profitable. The early land-grant holders and small farmers began to consolidate their small parcels into large plantations—some now more than two hundred acres. Many planters traveled to the Pernambuco region of northern Brazil for hands-on practice of the proven methods of running a sugar plantation.

But sugar needed slaves. Most of the early plantation workers were white indentured servants, but they were expensive, requiring more food and clothing than did the native Africans—blackamoors, as the slavers called them. The Brazilian planters preferred slaves, claiming that they were better suited to the backbreaking labor that sugarcane required.

In the ten years since its settlement, Bridgetown had grown from a raw, crude, and roisterous frontier community into a more civilized and picturesque harbor town. After a week in the harbor, the *Artemisia* was prepared to leave. Will would have welcomed more time to explore the island, yet he was glad to be getting under sail again. The ship's cargo was off-loaded, and they had taken on quantities of tobacco, cotton, salt from the salt flats of Aruba, and fustic, a dense, tropical wood that produced a rich and luxurious yellow dye. Captain Waring took on a quantity of boucan—strips of smoked wild hog—as well. They also contracted for a small shipment of sugar, which would bring a huge profit back in England if they could evade the customs tax. Since the Dutch brought the crop to the island, they also insisted on a monopoly in shipping it back to Europe. It was only a matter of time, the planters knew, until the English tax officials stepped in and asked for a share as well.

On the ship's final day in Bridgetown, their last act before putting out to sea was to search the holds for stowaways. It took three hours to scour the ship, revealing a dozen desperate men—indentured servants all—who were seeking escape to the American colonies or perhaps back home to England, Ireland, or Scotland.

They brought up anchor and unfurled the sails, beginning a three-hundred-mile voyage to St. Christopher, along what William thought to be the most beautiful seaway a mortal could imagine. The ship sailed past St. Lucia, Martinique, Dominica, Marie-Galante, Guadeloupe, Montserrat, Antigua, and Nevis. The islands were a chain of what appeared to be the tops of submerged mountains, forming a parade of dark green peaks rising dramatically from the turquoise sea at thirty-mile intervals. Each island appeared mist-covered, rugged, and densely wooded. And some, like Guadeloupe, thrust more than three thousand feet into the tropical sky.

Three hundred miles, with favorable winds, was a mere three-day sailing. For William, it was an invigorating and exhausting trip, a devilishly tricky voyage. When the sun went down, it was easy for a ship to veer close to any of these islands on the windward side. The winds were better on this the Atlantic side, but the risks of smashing into a submerged rock outcropping were great. And if a sudden squall were to whip down one of the steep mountainsides, the risk of a tragic beaching or a snapped mast was a serious threat.

It was safer, Captain Waring explained, to stick to the leeward side of the chain. Safer perhaps, but also slower. A ship could lose the trade winds altogether and sit becalmed for hours.

As they passed the island of Dominica, the captain ordered a cannon fired, and the *Artemisia* slowed. William charted a course close to shore, and the ship silently sailed past on half sail.

The Indians of Dominica were reported to weave excellent hammocks, and while the crew eagerly awaited the chance to trade with them, they were also wary, since these natives were Carib Indians, who sometimes greeted white traders cordially and sometimes shot at sailors with poisoned arrows. They were also known to build fires of dried pepper plants to windward, creating a burning gas that drove weeping and gasping invaders back to their ships.

On this voyage no Indians came paddling out, and William was disappointed that he would not yet see an island savage.

As the ship sailed along the breathtaking coastlines, Captain Waring increased the watch topside and posted a man to the top position of each mast. "We need to steer clear of any Spanish or Dutch raider that may be lurking near," Captain Waring remarked to William as they slid past Antigua, nearing the end of their trip. "We're beyond the line, you know, and anything might happen."

"Beyond the line, sir? I have not heard of that saying," William asked.

"It is not a written law, William, but once we pass west of the prime meridian in the center of the Atlantic, and south of the Tropic of Cancer, well, William, we are beyond the line."

"Sir, I understand the geography of the statement, but what does the admonition mean?"

"William, our diplomats and ambassadors have drawn up fancy peace treaties with France and Spain. Back home, we all agree to hold true to their conventions. But here, beyond the line, well . . . we are expected to take care of ourselves as best we can."

"But I thought we sailed under a gentleman's agreement?"

"On some days we do, William. Englishmen can trade with the Spaniards—and we do. Englishmen can settle on unoccupied islands—and we have. But if they choose to, the Spanish can pirate our ships and pillage our settlements—and they have. That is, if they have the strength to do so. Just as Englishmen are free to do the same to the Spanish."

Captain Waring looked topside to ensure that all three lookouts were still on duty and awake. "And while we have yet to encounter a Spanish raider on any of our voyages, there is no reason for us to be less cautious than needed."

William scanned the horizon with a renewed interest.

"And, William, as you have seen a small taste of in Barbados, living beyond the line is not just a matter of sailing agreements and peace treaties. I fear that the settlers see it as a chance to flout some basic Christian social conventions as well."

"As evidenced in the drinking and celebrating, Captain?"

"Aye, it is that, William, and much more. I fear that for many men in the tropics, it is their souls as well that are beyond the line."

CHAPTER

31

December 1638
Broadwinds, Dorset
England

Lord Aidan's office was a clutter of papers, sailing manifests, shipping orders, letters, correspondence, pamphlets, broadsheets, charts, ship's specifications, notes, and contracts. Both he and Radcliffe were off to London for a week's worth of social affairs and business appointments.

He knows where everything is without looking, thought Kathryne, *but how am I to make sense of this mountain of confusion?*

Upon her return home from the Alexandrian, it had taken Kathryne the best part of a week to organize the office, and she stopped only for brief meals and a few words with Mrs. Cole.

"I do not see why a lady would desire to do this," Mrs. Cole said as she brought in a small plate of cold cheese and meats to Kathryne, who had not left the office since sunrise.

"Mrs. Cole, this is a matter of great honor and responsibility. No one else would be concerned with the Spenser holdings. I owe this to Papa."

"What you owe to your father is grandchildren, Kathryne. He should be findin' you a husband instead of teachin' you shippin'."

Kathryne smiled as she returned to the stack of correspondence dealing with the latest voyage of the *Plymouth Spirit.*

I am so grateful to God that the decision of finding me a husband has been postponed for the interim, Kathryne thought.

"Thank you, Mrs. Cole, for the lunch," she said as the older woman left. "I am sure that God's timing will be perfect—as it always is—in these matters."

Island of St. Christopher
The Caribbean Sea

The *Artemisia* entered the small harbor of St. Christopher at dusk, three days since leaving Barbados. They had encountered no Spanish nor natives during the trip, both pleasing and oddly disappointing to William.

Fewer boats came out to met them here, William noted, and those that did conducted their business with much less brandy than on Barbados.

The island of St. Christopher was the "mother colony of the English West Indies"—the first permanent English settlement in the Lesser Antilles. It had survived because the English had joined forces with the French on this sixty-four-square-mile island to collaborate against Spanish and Carib Indian attacks. They had pooled their strengths and in so doing had been able to withstand both night raids by the Indians and Spanish attempts to run them off the island. They traded freely with the Dutch on the nearby island of St. Martin, who offered to join in warding off any Spanish attack. But neither the English nor the French were satisfied to divide St. Christopher permanently and were engaged in an ongoing battle for control of the small island. Even though they shared paths, roads, and salt ponds, there was always friction, and Will could feel the tension about the island.

From there they sailed west, heading south of Hispaniola, stopping only a day on its south coast at Petit Goave for fresh water. They then turned north, through the Windward Passage, and sailed to the long flat beach of Tortuga. It was there, after firmly securing all cargo and personal effects, that they beached the boat on the shore at high tide. As the tide receded, the men strung lines to the upper deck and pulled the ship to one side, careening the vessel. The crew could then scour the bottom hull, repairing any loose seams, removing oak worms that multiplied fast in warm water and if left unchecked, would eat through a wooden hull in a matter of months.

As the *Artemisia* lay on the white sands, a small group of black men in a curious three-hulled craft approached the same beach on which the ship rested. They were dressed in nothing more than loincloths. Their bodies were painted in bright colors, and they wore small ornaments of gold and shells in their noses, around their necks, and hanging from their ears. Most carried a small knife; some had machetes.

William looked about anxiously. He knew that the island of Tortuga was not an English settlement and that Caribs and Spanish pirates called some parts of the island home. He was surprised to see that no crewman made an effort to shoulder his musket nor unsheathe his sword. In fact, he thought, they all look relieved to see the natives appear.

Captain Waring walked out from the shadow of the rear of the ship, buttoning his coat. He extended his right hand high in greeting. He called out a few words in a language William recognized as Arawak. The three-hulled boat slid up the shoreline. One elderly black man extended his arm in a similar gesture and repeated the same few words and added a few more.

"Good, good, that be fine, then," Captain Waring called out, motioning to the crew. "Stand down men. We will allow our native friends to complete the work here."

And within a few moments, the entire crew of the *Artemisia* had retreated to the shade away from the beach, and the band of natives set on the ship—scraping, removing oak worms, and tapping in fresh oakum into the cracks between planks.

"We will be here for how long?" asked William.

"No shorter than three days, perhaps four."

"And the tide is not right until . . . perhaps the fifth day from now."

Captain Waring nodded.

"Captain, would it be asking too great a favor if I were to request that you ask one of this tribe to accompany me in our longboat and sail a bit farther around the north side of the island? I would be most appreciative if you were to agree, and I would pay the man from my own pocket."

Looking startled, Captain Waring asked, "Why would you want to do that, Mr. Hawkes?"

William had no firm answer in mind, but he knew that there was an entire island that he had yet to see, that he had an unnamed desire to take it all in. He stared back across the inviting waters while formulating a response. "It would be beneficial if I could chart these islands in a more detailed manner than our maps show," he finally said.

Captain Waring at first looked perturbed and on the verge of anger, but his visage softened as he saw the pleading look in Will's eyes.

"Very well, then. But return here in three days or we sail without you. Is that understood?"

"Yes, sir. It is indeed. Three days," William said as he got up and walked eagerly toward the ship.

32

January 1639
Broadwinds, Dorset
England

A single curl of gray-white smoke slowly snaked its way to the high ceiling of the library as Radcliffe and Aidan sat by the fire. The younger Spenser was reclining on a chair and ottoman with a lit pipe and a small snifter full of port.

"I must say, dear brother, that I am absolutely dumbfounded by this latest turn of events. I would have never thought such an appointment would be even a remote possibility for you," Radcliffe said while puffing.

Lord Aidan smiled. It was the first time in years—perhaps ever—that his younger brother regarded him with honest appreciation. He was enjoying the feeling.

"Well, Radcliffe, I would have thought it implausible as well. But all matters neatly fell into place."

"Of course, we will need to find a replacement for me on the East India Company's next voyage around the horn," explained Radcliffe. "I must accompany you, dear brother, to Barbados and assist in any way I can in your new leadership endeavors."

"I was trusting that you would propose such an arrangement. However, since both of us shall be in the New World for a time, we must place the Spenser's business matters with a person whose morals and honesty are above reproach."

Radcliffe nodded in agreement. He had yet considered the pressing need for continuity in such matters.

"It must be a person who has only our best interests at heart," Aidan continued. "It must be a person who seeks only to further our holdings, and not be looking to enlarge their own purse."

"I agree, brother. But where might we find such a person? I know of no one in which I could place such a high degree of trust."

"To be true, I can think of only one person who knows enough of our business to handle the needs that will arise and who I could trust with my very financial life."

Radcliffe was puzzled. "Who might that be?"

"I am suggesting that Kathryne be assigned as chief overseer of the Spenser holdings—for the time that we are in the New World, that is."

"Kathryne!"

"Yes. I think she would be outstanding at such an endeavor."

"Kathryne?"

"I believe it is again providential that she has undertaken to study and learn all sorts of business matters with Lady Emily over the last several months. Since I do not yet have a male heir, she will temporarily serve in that stead."

Radcliffe nodded his head, a slight smile working at the corners of his mouth. "As you wish, Brother."

Island of St. Christopher
The Caribbean Sea

On the evening of the fifth day, the *Artemisia*, now completely cleaned, was back to nearly upright and afloat, and the tide was increasing. In another two hours they could pole her from the sand and continue their voyage north through the Old Bahama Strait. From there, the ship would turn northwest through the Florida Channel, making a final stop in the port of Grand Bahama.

William stood in the surf holding his shirt. He shook the hand of the native guide and presented him with a small dagger that he had acquired in Venice, Italy. Tatum beamed as the elegant weapon was given to him. The rest of the Indian's group had been resting near the water's edge, waiting for Will and Tatum to return, drinking a type of ale they had brewed from maize. They quietly walked to their small boat and shoved it away from shore.

William called out a farewell in Arawak.

The native men turned to face him as they pushed the boat into the quiet surf. Tatum stood in the prow and waved a good-bye.

Sloshing through the waist-high surf, William, after securing the longboat to the ship, caught hold of the rope gallery ladder extending from the aft of the vessel and easily pulled himself on deck. His face, neck, and arms were burnished red from the tropical sun, his lips cracked from exposure, and he was bone weary.

Captain Waring stood on the quarterdeck, shaking his head as a parent would when scolding a child. "Mr. Hawkes, we have but two hours until the tide runs deep. You have returned with a very slight margin of error. You have tried my patience with this miscalculation."

"Captain Waring, I ask for your forgiveness. But when you discover what I have learned, it will all be worth your aggravation."

"And what could you have learned that will have import on our voyage?" helmsman Griffin Edwards asked in a snide manner.

William turned and pointed to the northwest. "If you sail in that direction—for no more than a half-day with good wind—you will come upon the island that is called the Great Inagua."

"That fact is hardly news," Captain Waring said. "That island has been on our charts for decades. We will be sailing past it at daybreak. Now, William, do you fancy yourself as a conquistador discovering new lands?"

"Not a discoverer of new lands, but of something else."

"And that might be?"

"A fleet of three Spanish frigates—all flying the flag of the skull and crossbones—lying in wait by the island called Great Inagua."

William waited a moment for the information to be fully comprehended. "I had thought that it may be of slight interest to you," he said quietly.

Broadwinds, Dorset
England

She knew she was on a ship, looking up at big, beautiful, puffy white clouds that drifted in the sky above her—so close, she thought, that she could reach out and touch them. She extended her arm and with a single finger she lightly pushed on one, amazed at the depth of its softness. Its whiteness dissipated, and above it was an endless sun-washed heaven of the clearest blue she had ever seen. She closed her eyes, feeling the warmth in the breeze on her skin, and breathed in the serenity. When she opened them again, he was standing there, smiling, his eyes bluer than the sky behind him. . . .

Island of St. Christopher
The Caribbean Sea

"Blast! Three privateers, you say. You are sure of this?"

William had finished gulping his third cup of water from the scuttle bucket on deck. He splashed a fourth over his face and neck.

"That I am sure of. Tatum sailed close enough to be hailed from their ships. They asked him if he sought to trade."

"And the Spaniards did not think it odd that a white man was sailing with a savage?" queried Diggory Dyer, chief petty officer.

"I remained hidden in the far hull, buried beneath ropes and leaves. I had a small slit arranged for vision, so I am sure that the skull and crossbones were unfurled on each vessel."

"Blast it to bloody Hades," ranted Captain Waring, "and may our Lord forgive my outrage."

Most of the officers turned, in shock, to see the captain throw his plumed cap against the deck in anger.

"We have been boxed into a corner, and I have a most unsettled feeling about it," the captain grumbled.

Helmsman Edwards said, "But there is a simple solution. We will need sail round the western edge of Cuba, by the looks of it—through the Yucatan Channel. And that adds only five or six days to our journey, sir. What be the harm in that?"

"It's in the air. Do you not smell the freshening winds?" Captain Waring shook his head, a troubled look spreading over his face.

The men looked about, some sniffing, some looking to the clouds and sails for evidence.

William spoke up as he tossed his shirt over his head. "I am concerned as well. Tatum tried to tell me that a storm was brewing—a hurricane, he called it. He pointed to the height of the clouds, and the smells, and the haze about the moon. To be honest, I would have thought him nervous as well, if natives of his type shared that emotion."

"Cannot we sail back to Petit Goave? The harbor is well protected and deep," one man asked.

The captain answered, "It is possible, but the time—we will encounter a delay of perhaps several weeks. And if I were those Spaniards, I would put into Petit Goave also, once the winds start to blow. It is the closest safe harbor for us as well as the Spaniards. No, we would not be safe there."

"Could we make it to Santo Domingo?"

"Perhaps, but it means sailing six full degrees latitude into the face of a strengthening trade wind. It may take a full week, if not longer."

The officers talked in low tones, in small groups of twos and threes.

William borrowed the captain's compass and straightedge and pulled from his desk his Gunter's scale of logarithms and tangents. He searched the map, placing the rule and compass at different points, consulting the scales and grids. "We may have one alternative—unproven perhaps—but an alternative."

"And what might that be, Mr. Hawkes?" Captain Waring asked.

"Rather than sailing northwest, there is an escape route to be had if we sail straight north, to the east of Great Inagua. From there, we head through the Mayaguana Passage, northwest through Crooked Island Passage, then south, just a few leagues, to the Old Bahama Straight and on to the Florida Channel and the port of Grand Bahama. It can be done in no more than two days."

"William," the captain said, in a grave voice, "it cannot be done. The channels are too shallow, and the widths too narrow."

"I would rather take my chances on a port in a storm, than to be drowned and shipwrecked on some landlubber's flight of fancy," cried Griffin Edwards.

"But I have just sailed it. Look on this chart." Will pointed to an unnamed island just north of their position. "This island does not exist. These shoals marked here," he said pointing again, "are marked at only ten fathoms on the chart, yet they are three times that deep. The depth is quite sufficient for this vessel." He turned to Captain Waring. "If we leave now, and take full use of the high tide, we can do it. I would not say so had I not been through the very same passage with Tatum. It can be done."

The officers, in a circle about the two men, remained quiet. Captain Waring scanned their faces, seeing doubt, anger, fear, but in most, a certain sense of confidence in William's words. Will stood, with his hand on the map, ready to chart out a new heading.

After a long pause, Captain Waring said in a somber voice, "Very well, Mr. Hawkes. Plot such a course," then walked through the circle and towards his cabin.

He stopped, turned, and added, "May God have mercy on your work."

Broadwinds, Dorset
England

. . . He knelt down next to her in one graceful movement. She could see in his eyes love as limitless as the heavens above them and as deep as the sea below. She felt the tenderness in him as his eyes searched her face, his long hair the color of the sand of a thousand beaches. . . .

Kathryne's eyes fluttered open, and she sat up abruptly as consciousness broke over her, and she found herself in the stillness of her bed at Broadwinds.

The chill in her room roused her further. Covering herself with her thick wool blanket, she laid back down. She could feel her heart pound wildly as she fought to hold on to the images in her mind. *Come back. . . . Oh, come back. . . .*

The Caribbean Sea

As dawn broke over the waters of the Florida Channel the *Artemisia* was in sight of the port of Grand Bahama. They would take on fresh water and a few scores of native cotton bales. It was a small settlement, like St. Christopher, and struggling to maintain a subsistence economy.

The winds had continued to increase, and the ship had battled a nasty squall for several hours, the rain pelting the ship, breakers crashing across the bow, and the winds whipping up a thick spoondrift mist from the waves. But the route was as safe and as deep as William had claimed. It had been a tight, confining sailing, and the hull and rock below were only separated by several dozen feet at a few locations. But they had made it safely, and they had sailed it quickly.

The *Artemisia* had traversed north of the Spanish raiders by several dozen leagues. During the two-day journey, the crew had been edgy and nervous. Watches during the day were doubled and tripled, and when possible sailing at night was attempted as well.

The ship stayed at Grand Bahama for only hours, and then, under full sail, exited and set a course for England.

Now the bow was empty of crewmen, except for Will. The sun was bright, but as the ship cut further north, the sea spray was more chilling. The water helped cool his reddened face and neck. Each time the ship ducked into the waves, Will leaned over to protect his personal navigational charts. He had begun to keep a journal of sorts—a combination of charts, maps, notes on the flora and fauna, and from this last journey several pages of Indian words and phrases.

During his time with Tatum he had learned some of the Arawak and Carib cultures. Will surmised that the Arawaks were a peaceable tribe. The Caribs, by contrast, were fierce warriors—cannibals, if Tatum spoke the truth. They were the most feared warriors in the Caribbees.

All Will's discoveries were recorded in his book. He had neatly copied from the ship's maps the details of what he knew through actual observation to be true and had added his own most recent sightings. He marked depths and currents, made notes on the weather and celestial observations, and added a few personal notes as well. In uncharted waters, a reliable map was more valuable than a hull full of Incan gold.

William felt the satisfaction of his skill. He closed the book and tucked it under his arm, and stared out to the eastern sea.

Broadwinds, Dorset
England

Is this what it feels like to be in love? Kathryne thought in awe as she snuggled under her coverlet, basking in the warmth of her evocative dream.

She remembered every detail of him . . . the searching look on that face, the probing need in those remarkable eyes.

Unwillingly, she got up and walked over to her washstand, dipped a towel into the cool water, and dabbed her face. She peered at her tousled reflection in her looking glass, her emotions stirring once more. She wondered if others felt that type of passion, that desire, that sensation of wanting someone so completely.

But most know who their special person is and can hold him and touch him. All I have is a dream. . . .

The Caribbean Sea

A small wave crested near the figurehead of the *Artemisia* and a heavy spray splashed over the bow. William wiped the spray from his face, making sure that his book had remained dry.

He looked to the sky, pocked with thick, darkening clouds. The next few days promised to be rough sailing, but these were not storm clouds. They had missed the hurricane, if that was what was developing, in the Bahamas by no more than a breath—escaping by the slightest margin.

William looked up, wondering if he should utter the words that were quiet and still on his lips, words that offered thanks to God for their deliverance.

As the moments flowed past William, that urge—at first so strong and insistent—grew slight and dim, and in a few moments, he turned and walked back toward his cabin, back to the shadows below.

33

June 1639
Weymouth, Dorset
England

The evening sky at Weymouth had begun to dissolve to purples and reds. The clouds on the western horizon had grown dark. Stevedores were wrestling the last barrels and cases of supplies aboard the *Queen Anne*. The vessel, a large, five-masted galleon, had been decommissioned by the British navy eighteen months prior. She still accommodated a full complement of weapons and fifty-four cannons.

Radcliffe thought it best to travel in safety, knowing full well what dangers lurked in distant waters.

He stood on deck with a shipping manifest in hand, ensuring that each item that had been selected and packed in London and at Broadwinds was indeed placed in the proper cargo hold.

Below him on the pier, Lord Aidan and his daughter, Kathryne, stood side by side as the last remnants of their current existence were hauled on board.

Radcliffe, half-hidden in the lengthening shadows, sneered at the pair.

All I must do, dearest niece, is play the game for a few more hours. When we leave England, the odds will shift in my favor. In due time, my reward will come. And I will wait, for I am a patient man.

Radcliffe turned from the dock, shouting to one of the stevedores to be more careful with the crates. "Whatever is in there is a bloody sight more valuable than your miserable life," he spat.

◼◻◼◻◼

"Kathryne, my dear, I trust that I have supplied to you all the information you will need to see our affairs to their proper—and profitable—

conclusions. However, I have these fears that there are ends left undone and questions left unasked."

Kathryne took her father's hand. She felt the warmth through the thin leather of her glove. "Papa, you have prepared me well. I am sure that every eventuality has been discussed."

Lord Aidan reached into his breastpocket and pulled out a small clump of papers. "I have made notes to myself on items that have been overlooked. Let us discuss them one more time."

"You must board soon, Papa. The ship will be casting off within the hour. Please, take courage. You have done a masterful job in teaching me."

"But I have neglected my duties as a father these last few months. We have spent so little time together as father and daughter."

"But we have spent weeks together," Kathryne replied, thinking of the endless hours, poring over the last several years' accumulation of shipping logs, orders, and plans.

"That was for commerce, my poppet. Those memories will warm neither of our hearts."

"Papa, you have loved me so much and have given me so much that a few weeks of 'mere business' can do little to disrupt a lifetime of wondrous memories," she assured him.

Lord Aidan reached out and smoothed his daughter's long silken hair. "How I wish your mother were with us. I have stolen a precious part of your life by denying you a mother."

"Do not speak foolishness. Mother is gone because of illness, not neglect. And you have provided more than enough love to suffice."

"But it was your mother who had the faith, Kathryne. She was always closer to our Lord. She always knew what a Christian should do. I fear that I have stumbled in your eyes on more than one occasion."

Kathryne squeezed her father's gentle hand. "We have all stumbled on some occasion, Papa. Please be assured that I know what a Christian man is by watching you."

"You look so much like her, Kathryne, that still, when I look at you in soft light of evening, I would swear . . ." He stopped, as tears touched the corners of his eyes. "Just before she left us, she called me to her bedside. She took my hand, as you have this evening, and said, 'Teach Kathryne well. She will need to know so much. She will need to know, for she is destined to accomplish much. Teach her well.'"

It was Kathryne's turn for tears. "You have taught me well, Papa. It is through you that I have known the love of God the Father. If you have given me nothing else, that would have been sufficient."

From the rail of the top deck, Radcliffe shouted down at the pair, "Aidan, was it three trunks of bedclothes we have brought, or was it four?"

Lord Aidan chose to ignore his brother and embraced his daughter tightly. "I will call for you, my dearest daughter. When we are settled and it is safe, I will call for you."

They broke apart. Kathryne had vowed not to weep, for a woman in business needs a stronger inner resolve, she told herself.

"Good-bye, Papa. I will pray for you continually."

He walked up the long gangplank, stopping halfway. "Perhaps there will be an eligible young plantation owner in Barbados for you. Perhaps it will take the warmth of the tropics to produce an heir."

Kathryne waved as he walked away, smiling through her tears and nodding. *Dear Lord, I had prayed that he had forgotten. Not all prayers are answered as we would like, it seems.* Then an image with blue eyes and sandy hair came to her as she gazed out upon the sea.

■ ■ ■

The darkness outside the carriage window was so complete, Kathryne thought, that one could almost cut it with a rapier.

Next to Mr. Biesty was a lantern that faintly illuminated the road ahead. The two horses had walked this way on many trips, and they plodded along, feeling the road more than seeing it. The night air was cold, and Kathryne had drawn a thick woolen blanket around her legs and waist, the only sound the rhythmic clop-clop of horses' hooves.

I am alone now, she thought, recalling the sight of her father and uncle slipping from view and from Weymouth Harbor. She had waved until the ship was no more than a speck in the darkening sunset.

Well, God, my Father in heaven, I have asked for this opportunity, Kathryne prayed, *and have sought thee to answer those prayers. I beseech thee, Lord, to grant me the wisdom to make not only the right decisions, but the decisions that honor thy Word. Please, dear God, keep me close to you. Keep my father from harm. Watch over my uncle. Thank you for allowing Mrs. Cole to be my angel.*

The rocking of the carriage was quieting, as a mother rocking her child to sleep. *And, dear God, please help me be a more obedient daughter, to you my heavenly Father and to my dear father here on this earth, no matter where I am—in all ways.*

In a few miles, Kathryne began to slump to one side, and as she fell asleep she had the Lord God's name on her lips.

▪ ▫ ▪ ▫ ▪

The *Queen Anne* edged out into the darkening waters of the English Sea. The full moon was due up in a hour, so the captain departed, taking advantage of the high tides.

The two Spenser brothers stood, silhouetted by the last rays of the sun, on top of the forward deck. Each held a Venetian crystal goblet filled with old—and potent—claret. Radcliffe extended his hand into the air.

"Join me, dear brother, in a toast to our good fortune," he said, then thought, *Although some of our futures appear to be healthier than others.*

Lord Aidan raised his glass as well and the two touched, chiming lightly in the evening air. "To our future on Barbados, Radcliffe. May we seek God's will, and may he prosper our enterprises."

With an odd smile on his lips, Radcliffe was thinking, *I am sure they will prosper, dear brother, but if I were you, I would ask for protection as well.* He said, however, "Yes, Aidan. To our future enterprises. And yes, may God's will be done."

CHAPTER

34

8 September 1639
Barbados

My dearest daughter Kathryne,

Please accept your poor father's apologies for the haste in which I wrote my last letter to you, telling of our safe arrival here. You have been so faithful in your correspondence. My predecessor, Gov. Hawley, has left such things as land grants and property division in a state of complete disarray, and much of my time has been spent in untangling the spider web of confusion left in his wake.

It has indeed been a most challenging time since my arrival. I am encouraged by the meeting of the first council, an assembly of more than three score of leading planters who will help me govern.

This wooded island is a most beautiful place. I cannot describe in words the sensation of first seeing it . . . the colors, Kathryne, are so very brilliant in the sunlight—the blue of the water, the green of the vegetation, the yellows and pinks of the flowers—bursting upon one's consciousness as if in a dream. The coastline is craggy, with tranquil beaches, and there are lovely birds with feathers as if borrowed from a rainbow. It seems to rain a little each day, but never in copious amounts. At night the stars are so radiant and sparkling they seem a mere stone's throw away.

Palmetto trees one hundred feet tall are abundant, the likes of which I have never seen, with leaves in the shape of a peacock's tail and fruit like a cabbage but tasting better. And that is but just one example of the strange and delicious foods growing here. Guava, cassava, plantain, soursop, papaya, and melons of all shapes and sizes are found in abundance. They are eaten fresh or are pickled and preserved. The juice of the pineapple is an especially tasty nectar. The

humid heat makes one exceedingly thirsty, and while I drink mostly
unfermented beverages, I am sorry to say that many of the island's
noble residents are overly fond of Madeira and brandy. The commoners also drink to excess a beverage called mobby, which is distilled
from sweet potatoes, or perino, made from cassava and plantain.
Thankfully, English ale and cider are shipped in regularly.

But what we lack is harder to purchase. We are much in need of
good Christian teaching, for I am afraid that many civilized,
God-fearing Englishmen have left the manners of their proper
upbringing at home. It is that nonsense of living "beyond the line"
that has fostered much of this loose behavior.

The abundance of exotic fish here is also quite amazing. I am
becoming especially fond of stewed turtle, but I could do with a succu-
lent sirloin of beef every now and then.

The largest nuisance I have found here are the mosquitoes—nasty
stinging insects so small in size you can hardly discern their presence,
but they make a curious sound and leave a knob on the skin that
lasts all day. I have been given a vial of the oil of peppermint, which
somewhat relieves the discomfort.

The number of colonists arriving here is on the increase. There are
few Indians, and the number of black slaves is rapidly rising. The
English planters here prefer them to the indentured servants.
Middling and lower-class young men, many from Scotland and
Ireland, have been arriving to clear and work the fields for a dozen
years now, with the promise of a small parcel of land at the end of
their tenure. They are now being replaced by the black slaves, who
require no such promise.

The establishment of an organized militia is also of primary importance. There is a watch house, but it is soon to be replaced by a fort,
whose construction is being supervised by Radcliffe. He is also overseeing the building of the governor's mansion, which I'm sure will be
a lovely and comfortable place in which to make our home. It is to
be called Shelworthy, meaning noble estate on the ledge, as it will sit
atop a cliff by the sea.

The planters' homes are built mostly of wood several stories high,
with low-ceilinged rooms on each story. The island remains largely
undeveloped but is more and more becoming a bona fide English
colony. The plantations appear to be one above another, rising up
the hills like several stories in stately buildings. Most hug the leeward
shore, and few are to be found in the interior of the island. Except
for one main thoroughfare, the roads out of the village of Bridge-

town are presently insufficient, often impassable after significant rainfall. I must procure crews of men to improve them before further development is feasible.

There are some five hundred planters, a few with sizable tracts of nearly a thousand acres, and many others with smaller parcels of under a hundred. You will recognize the merchant family names of Hothersall, Pears, Yeamans, and Codrington—all men with whom I have had commercial dealings at home and who are attempting to settle here. A much-needed house of worship, to be named St. Michael's Church, is to be built in Bridgetown.

The village itself has a mostly pleasing appearance. The buildings press as close as possible to the wharves along the waterside and are tall and narrow, very similar to buildings in London. There are taverns, alehouses, public houses, and shops aplenty, but no courthouse or town hall as of yet, and there are no local manufactures, so the importation of finished goods of all sorts is relied upon to sustain the life of an Englishman. Knives and swords and all things metal are continually rusting from the wet air.

I am enclosing a list of items that I hope you can procure and send at the earliest possible sailing. The linen clothing to replace my woolens and the shoes are of utmost importance. The building materials not locally available and needed for Shelworthy are arriving regularly. I am indebted to you for arranging for them. I am enclosing the carpenters' listing of items that you must order immediately from the ironmonger in Dorchester, since they cannot be manufactured here.

I pray constantly for your safety as well, amidst all the turmoil we hear tell of. I miss the sound of your sweet voice, my dear daughter, and the vision of you hard at work at my desk of my beloved Broadwinds is with me every hour. I send my fondest affection to you, and ask that you please give my warmest regards to all the loyal staff. And please pass along my fond regards to Lady Emily, should you correspond with her.

Your devoted,
Papa

CHAPTER

35

14 November 1639
Broadwinds, Dorset
England

My Dearest Father,

How I yearn to hear your voice and to have you near me. Loneliness is an affliction I am unaccustomed to dealing with. But, Papa, do not despair for me. I have Mrs. Cole and the occasional visit of Lady Emily. I have passed on your greetings to Lady Emily and was rewarded by a most wonderful smile in return. Often I take my dinner by the fire in the kitchen and eat among Mrs. Cole and the servants, for it is good to have company as one eats.

I admit to even missing the companionship of Uncle Radcliffe—and you dare not breathe a word of this comment to him.

It was so pleasurable to receive your last correspondence, and I thank you for including all the detailed descriptions for which I have been yearning. It is difficult to envision leaving here and coming there. But if God wills this as my future, then I shall have to pray even more for the grace to accept his plans for me and look upon it as a great adventure.

I have quickly dispatched a complete list of all the provisions you have requested. How distressing to hear that our fine fabrics decay and rot in the tropical heat!

Also, the foodstuffs have been procured and sent as well, and I trust shall be delivered with this correspondence. I understand that one must seek out proper English foods now and again.

Good news, Papa, concerning the *China Seas*. The vessel returned last month from Cathay after a fourteen-month voyage. Many of the insuring agents had been prepared to write the ship off as lost, but the fine captain brought it back to Weymouth. More than half of the crew had been lost to some sort of Asian illness, making progress difficult. The captain did not appear well himself, but the vessel's holds were filled with silks, spices, and some wonderful blue-and-white porcelains. From an initial accounting, a doubling of your original investment is anticipated.

I have contracted with the representative of a new concern in London to sell the bales of raw silk. It was purchased in Cathay for ten pounds and is being sold for one hundred. That will provide returns much better than our expected doubling. Of course, shipping costs must still be deducted, and I will wait until the total prize monies are distributed among the crew and their survivors, if there be any.

We have invested a small portion in the East India Company's latest sailing. I have taken 2,500 pounds from the profit on the *China Seas* and have purchased several shares in the voyage of the *Margaret Rose* bound for Madagascar at the end of this current month. Spices, vanilla, and turmeric will be its prime cargo. I trust that this arrangement meets with your approval.

The news from London continues to be disturbing. Lady Emily is to spend Christmas at Broadwinds. (She has instructed me to write how much she will miss you—and the annual foxhunt in Hadenthorne—as do I.) She has spoken of actual disturbances in the streets—large presses of men and boys calling for the end of the Ship Money taxes. I have heard Mr. Biesty call them riots, which were put down by uniformed soldiers. Lady Emily has not witnessed such events but cannot discount the story. Such news is indeed troubling.

The unrest has spread to our corner of England as well. A civilized person would think that such a small village would be immune from any political strife. But it is not to be.

The Reverend Pensworth, a godly man, as you know, has continued to preach from the Word with boldness. How you must miss the church services at St. Stephen's. Of course, the parson has used the Bible as a base for his readings and sermons. "How can a man change, if the Scriptures are not understood," he has often said. "And how can I preach, unless I use God's Word?" It appears that Bishop Laud is becoming much more powerful in the King's court. The Reverend Pensworth has claimed that the church is turning as to *eclesis anglais,* the English church. And to a belief that all man need concern himself with is the proper form—the proper prayers, the proper hymns, the proper liturgy—and then his obligations to God are met. The Reverend Pensworth was livid. "Not only does the king want to set our services, he wants to appoint all the bishops and clergy as well. No more will a congregation have a say in the matter."

Lady Emily fears a return to the practices of Rome—wearing crosses, kneeling for the sacraments, and swearing an allegiance to a church leader rather than to God himself. I do not know where such a path will take us, but I am at times fearful. I do so understand why many devout Christians have sailed to the New World—if only to protect their freedom to worship God in spirit and in truth.

Father, I do not write these lines to trouble or vex you. All goes well here. These are minor points, but I have greatly missed confiding their substance with you, so I have chosen to share them in this letter. Parliament is now in session, and perhaps great and godly men such as John Pym can turn their hearts toward the will of God. The Reverend Pensworth has heard tell of one of his keynote speeches in which he identified the royal government with the antichrist, and rumor is that Bishop Laud will be impeached!

We can only hope and pray for God's will in these matters. I pray every evening for peace, and I also pray every evening that you are safe. God has richly blessed me, and I know that he is guiding all my steps and is with me at every decision. I pray the same for our government.

> *Until your return, I remain,*
> *your most loving and obedient daughter,*
> *Kathryne*

36

10 January 1640
Bridgetown,
Barbados

My Dearest Daughter,

How I miss you, my Kathryne. Christmas was a long and lonely day for me, and 'twas an odd feeling to be here in the tropics on a holiday that belongs in winter! I had hoped, owing to the myriad of details needed to finish the official governor's residence, I would not have time to ponder your situation. But alas, it is not to be. Your welfare is at my mind daily—nay, hourly—and I pray that you are well.

I am gladdened of the successful voyages you have seen conclusion to. I am proud of your accomplishments beyond words. It is a blessing to know of your abilities.

You were right to invest in the new sailings. I believe that they should pay a handsome return.

Your loving uncle has also begun final construction of the fort to overlook the harbor at Bridgetown. Our island is difficult to reach from the west, but I fear that pirates one day will see our wealth and attack. I hear they have burnt to the ground several settlements along the Spanish main, as well as in the northern Caribbees.

Uncle Radcliffe has taken on the development of the estate with great enthusiasm. He has grown in spirit since his arrival. I think that he and you will be much less contentious in the future.

Shelworthy is nearly completed (your Uncle Radcliffe had the enclosed sketches of it drafted for you to see). It is of stone and wood and has three full stories, with a porch. There are seven rooms on the ground floor—an entry, a great hall, two parlours, a dining chamber, a library, and a service room—surrounded by a stately staircase with a handsomely carved balustrade. Our spacious bedchambers are all

on the first floor; they shall have four-poster bedsteads all with mos-
quito nets, a canopy overhead, and curtains hung at the sides to keep
out the bad night air. The guest bedchambers are on the second floor.
I'm afraid that the use of the new flocked wallpapers, as you suggested, is not possible here. I am told that in the humid tropic air it
would mold rapidly. The kitchen and bakery are in a separate back
building along with several service rooms. I am especially happy with
the great hall, which shall be done in cool green colours, with dozens
of chairs with floral satin coverings and a pair of harpsichords and a
harp for balls and receptions. I am very pleased with the selections of
china, crystal, and linens that you have made. I shall do my best to
select the remaining furnishings needed.

Please be careful of the turmoil that I hear spoken of by ships'
crews in port. Do not visit London if unrest is still in occurrence.
Send letters or postboys instead.

A new planter has arrived on the island on a ship from Weymouth.
He has obtained a grant of two hundred acres a half-day's walk from
the governor's residence. He is not married, and goes by the name of
Geoffrey Foxton. I believe it may be time that I address the issue of
your marital status.

Thank you for your prayers, my little poppet. How I covet God's
protection on you and your endeavors, and upon me as well.

Until we meet, your loving,
Papa

◼ ◻ ◼ ◻ ◼

Radcliffe spent much of his time dealing with unmanageable tradesmen
who were hard-pressed to complete Shelworthy, Radcliffe's home, and
the harbor fortifications. Aidan had no patience dealing with the
common man, and if the truth be known, Radcliffe had even less. But
it was his lot to do so, and the only facet of the process he enjoyed was
discovering the proper motivation to use with each tradesman. With
the foreman at Shelworthy, it was gold, clean and simple. The crew
leader at his home seemed to operate best with a steady supply of Irish
whiskey, and if it smoothed the way, Radcliffe was only too happy to
provide it. The foreman at the fort was a jumble of many vices, and
Radcliffe took grim satisfaction in seeking out solutions to his wants.

Radcliffe had been most adamant in one matter concerning the fort.
It was his handpicked crew that developed the foundation and seawalls
to the structure, and he personally inspected the progress. The work
was hard, backbreaking, and dangerous, yet Radcliffe insisted.

How else will I ensure that certain modifications to the plans are made, he rationalized. Such modifications included a widening of sewer tunnels that led to the sea—wide enough to permit the passage of a man. *One never knows,* Radcliffe assured himself as he watched his slaves dig through the hard rock, *when an unobserved escape might be needed.* He smiled, wiping his brow with a scarlet hanky. *Or even an unannounced entrance. Best to prepare for all eventualities.*

The crew turned and thought it most odd to see Radcliffe laughing loudly, with no one within a dozen yards of him.

37

February 1640
Barbados

The sun had just cleared the windward coast. It rose, yellow and glimmering, from the east. A lone figure could be seen at the casuarina-lined crest of Hackleton's Cliff, watching the crashing surf pound into the reef and rocks below.

Off to the north was a series of limestone caves, and to the south lay a series of rugged hills and narrow canyons, lush and green.

As the wind rippled the grasses and small shrubs that dotted this cool upland plateau, the solitary figure rose from his haunches, and the gulls scavenging around the cliffs flapped off, cawing. He stretched into the cool morning winds and made his way down the escarpment to the sea.

William Hawkes pulled his long hair back, now lightened by the tropical sun, and fumbled with a length of twine, trying to tie it into a manageable tail. *I must see the town's barber before we sail. A sailor has no business fussing with vanity.*

Just before he lowered himself onto the small and treacherous path, he turned back for one last look. His eyes took in the varied landscape of cool forest glades, gentle streams and hills, and steep ravines and gorges. *I can see why they call this land the Scottish Highlands. I cannot imagine a more beautiful spot.*

In a few minutes William was on a narrow, rocky outcropping on the shore, small waves curling about his feet. Pulled up onto the shore was a small sailboat, borrowed from one of the importers in Bridgetown. The *Artemisia* was scheduled to remain in port for nearly a week, awaiting a large consignment of sugar and molasses that was still being processed and packaged into barrels. They were early for their shipment, for William had caught too well the prevailing winds and crossed the Atlantic in a trifling thirty-nine days, the quickest of his six crossings thus far.

"It was not my doing," he had said as the captain and merchants had congratulated him. "It was just that the winds were favorable."

As was his custom in any port in which he had to wait on embarking, he would hire out a small sailing craft and explore the coastline. He had explored virtually every island in the Lesser Antilles, his favorites being Nevis, with its volcanic vents and high lushly green peaks, and the wild and foreboding Guadeloupe.

William knew that his livelihood depended on accuracy, so he spent much time revising his maps. He now had five full notebooks of maps, shorelines, bays, and coves. Pieced together, they formed a fairly complete mapping of the Lesser Antilles, plus Puerto Rico, Hispaniola, the eastern coast of Cuba, and many of the cays, lagoons, islets, channels, and sounds that formed the archipelago of the Bahama Islands. He had charted much of the eastern coast of the Florida peninsula as far north as St. Augustine. It was a world that, until two years prior, had been unknown, undreamed of by William. The sea, coves, bays, currents, shallows, and skies of the islands were now as familiar to him as the hills of Hadenthorne.

He had spent many days with the natives of the Caribbees, both the peaceable Arawaks and the more aggressive Caribs. Their populations had been in decline—especially on the islands where the Europeans had attempted to settle. William tried to learn their customs, their language, and their sensibilities as he sailed among them, exploring the nooks and crannies of the islands.

He reached down and undid the reef knot that held the craft secure to a bleached and wave-worn mangrove tree trunk. The wind ruffled the sails, the boat tipped, and William leaned to keep it upright. He could have reached out and touched the coralline rocks as he slipped past, farther out into the surf. In a few nervous minutes he had cleared the heavy surf and was several hundred yards to sea. He set the rudder and began to sail back north, on a close reach into the wind. The wind was steady, and the small craft plowed through the light chop, spraying a fine mist into the air.

William sat back against the transom and rested his arm on the tiller. After he had tied off the sail, he removed his linen shirt and reached into the small leather sack he had brought, taking out several bananas, biscuits, and cheese. He opened the cork on a small flagon of wine that he had procured in Madeira. William had grown quite fond of bananas.

It was a strange fruit, he observed, never having seen or even heard of them until his first voyage to the tropics.

As the small boat slipped further north and round the northeast corner of Barbados, William pushed the tiller a few inches and set the boat to at a square run with the wind.

It was times as this, when William's world was reduced to the sum of the wind, a small sail, and the empty ocean, that brought out a sense of deep sadness in his soul. On ship, his options were few and his tasks many, and his mind was kept in check. It was neither a time for sadness nor rejoicing. It simply was time, a simple duration containing neither past nor future—just the immediacy of the moment.

But alone there was a difference in feelings, in thoughts, in perspectives. On this fine day, sailing alone beneath God's skies, William sought to find peace.

He had been "beyond the line" six times in the short course of one-and-a-half years, and each time he crossed that watery boundary he felt more and more distant from the society that he called home. *I have promised good Vicar Mayhew that I would search for the truth,* William thought as he sailed along, *but the farther I travel, the further truth seems to be from me.*

He untied the sail from the gaff and let the canvas loose. As the end snapped in the light wind, he caught it and furled the canvas about the small mast.

I need time to drift, he thought. *Perhaps peace will come if I allow it time.*

Will bunched up a spare sail and tucked it under his head as it rested on the rear transom. He folded his arms across his chest and stared up into the tropical skies, the sun warm on his bare skin. The small locket on his chest caught the sun and glinted the light back into the heavens.

Perhaps the truth no longer travels beyond the line. Perhaps it is the absence of truth that allows evil to flourish—as with slaves being sold and Indians being slaughtered to make room for white men. How could things have gone so far wrong? Where could the truth be? It feels to me that God has turned a blind eye to these waters.

As he drifted in the turquoise water, William reviewed his last crossing. . . .

━━ ▪ ▪ ▪ ▪ ━━

Rain and fog had blanketed the southern coast of England for two weeks in September. The *Artemisia* had been readied for sail in the Weymouth harbor for that entire fortnight, and William had been impatient to leave. Each day he awoke to the fog and silently cursed the additional delay. He would have preferred to sail into harbor, unload their Caribbean cargo of cotton, tobacco, dye woods, silver, and sugar, then immediately take on new cargo.

William was most content when sailing out of harbor. When he stood on the piers of Weymouth, the nearness of Hadenthorne—a mere three-day journey north—was a painful reality. The village offered a silent, sirenlike summons. But for Will, the village held as much pain as pleasure. To see his friends would be so welcome, but that was not all that awaited him there. He did not relish having to face the questioning of Vicar Mayhew. He had not found the truth—nor had he truly searched, he knew—as he had promised. And could he ever return to face Missy Holender?

Not only was the weather presently inclement, the political climate was becoming bitter and hostile as well. There had been talk of war—this time not with France or Spain, countries that William had little feelings for, but with the Scots a few hundred miles to the north. And, as William understood it, the disagreement had begun over something as foolish as the choice of a prayer book.

King Charles had sought to impose a book of prayer—modeled after the one used in the English churches—on all the churches in Scotland.

The master-at-arms of the *Artemisia*, Matthew MacGregor, a temperamental Scotsman from near Edinburgh, became livid when he heard of the action when the crew had repaired to Percival's to catch up on the latest gossip and news.

"I dinna believe it," he wailed. "How foolish is that man to think a Scotsman will heed the English Crown when it comes to matters of the Almighty? It dinna make sense."

William added, "I have heard of a ruckus in Edinburgh, as some have taken to the streets."

Tommy nodded vigorously. "The king thinks too highly of himself, that be the problem. He be too happy ruling alone, without the benefit of Parliament." He swallowed a mouthful of whiskey, then grimaced. "I fear that the Scots'll be taking this matter to the field of battle afore too long."

As evidenced by the long faces around the table, each man echoed that sentiment.

Once in harbor, William had accompanied Captain Waring to the syndicate offices. They were housed in a large second floor suite of rooms in a building that overlooked the Weymouth harbor.

Captain Waring and William had been introduced to Sir Chester

Evesham, a tall gentlemen with a badly pocked face and an unctuous manner.

"Captain Waring, it is a pleasure to finally meet you. Your speed at ocean voyages has caused quite a stir in the sailing companies. I would daresay that most other syndicates desire to employ your services. How glad I am to have you in our employ."

"Sir Evesham, it is a pleasure to know that we have served you well."

"Your ship has not yet been fully provisioned nor loaded, is that not correct, Captain?"

"Aye, that be true. She's still taking on supplies and will wait for several shipments from London."

"Captain, you may not need to wait. See that assembly of machinery being unloaded from the transports near your vessel?"

Will and Captain Waring had looked out and watched as a team of deliverymen unloaded a series of rollers and wheels from three large, ox-driven wagons. Five men had shouldered a massive, ridged cylinder and were carrying it onto the pier where the *Artemisia* was docked.

"That will be your final cargo on this trip. It is a sugar mill, destined for a Mr. Radcliffe Spenser. I hear it whispered that any man who can install such a sugar refining mill on the island of Barbados will see a bountiful return on his investment. Well, good captain, you are looking at that man. You will need to make haste on this sailing."

Tied and bound on the center waist of the ship with some parts spilling out to the quarterdeck of the *Artemisia,* the disassembled sugar mill had taken up much of the open space on the vessel, in addition to the other machinery, foodstuffs, and household goods.

A cold squall had blown in at high tide, and the *Artemisia* had struggled out into the harbor. It was difficult and dangerous sailing in the rain. The decks would be less stable, it was more difficult to find a secure handhold for the ropes and yardarms, and one would become easily chilled in the biting rain. As the wind carried the ship forward, William had noticed—as did the captain—that the heavy sugar mill top-weighed the ship, making it harder to steer, and making her sit lower in the water, making the sailing slower.

If the sails would fill with a heavy gust, the entire ship could tip, the heavy top decks pulling her masts to the waterline. Helmsman Griffin Edwards had vowed to keep a double watch at all times, day and night, to be alert for sudden changes in the wind and weather.

By the time they had reached the Canaries, the crew had begun to relax a bit, becoming more accustomed to the vessel's altered performance. The sails caught a strong trade wind, and the ship began her journey west.

. . . William awoke from his remembering, sweaty and uncomfortable, having drowsed in the hot sun. The small boat in which he still lay bobbed peacefully in the light chop. A gull set down on the bow and called loudly. William sat up, dipped his hand in the warm waters, and splashed it over his tanned face and neck. He untied the sail and reset the tiller. The boat was nearing the northwestern corner of the island, and William set sail south, toward Bridgetown.

I now know what I must do, William thought. *I need to return at once to Hadenthorne.*

As the sun neared slipping into the western sea, Will kept his hand firm on the tiller. All afternoon he had battled a strong wind from the southeast, and now his ship, the *Artemisia*, resting in the main harbor at Bridgetown, was in sight. He aimed the tiny boat back into the quiet waters of the harbor.

Upon his return to the ship, as darkness covered all the ships resting at anchor in the harbor, William cautiously made his way toward his cabin. As he turned the handle, Captain Waring's voice boomed from behind the door of the captain's quarters. "Mr. Hawkes—if that be you—I request an audience!"

It was a sheepish and contrite William that entered the snug cabin of the captain. "Sir, I know that I have returned later than I had speculated. The winds picked up, and the leeward trip was devilishly tricky. I anticipated returning this day forenoon, but I was unable to fulfill that desire."

All that Will heard, as he stood at silent attention, was his own breathing and the gentle lap of the water against the ship's sides. The small lantern that lit the room was behind the table, hung on a small metal arm projecting from the rear wall, and it bathed the captain's face in deep shadow.

The seconds slipped by.

What was he planning to do? Would I be relieved of duty? Could I be set off ship here on Barbados? Will asked himself.

"William, how many times have you made this speech to me—in the darkness after you have failed to return to the ship as promised?"

William stared down at his feet. *There was Nevis during the second voyage, and then Hispaniola, on the third—no, that was the fourth. I was delayed at Tortuga by the storm, and then there was St. Christopher. . . .*

"Mr. Hawkes!" Captain Waring shouted.

William jumped at the sharpness of his words.

Slowly, speaking carefully, the captain added, "You have caused my heart to race at least once per voyage—and on several occasions twice. It does not do well for an old man like me to suffer such stress, William." He pointed to a stool and indicated that William should be seated. "You have caused me more worry than any crew member I have ever sailed with."

"Captain, I am sorry that I caused . . ."

The captain held up his hand, silencing William's answer.

He will terminate my position for certain this time. I have never seen him so anguished.

"My worry does not stem from the concern that I would need replace the most precise navigator I have ever sailed with. Nor does the worry stem from the truth of your uncanny business and trading acumen. Nor do I worry that I would be losing a fine translator."

William felt his face flush at the stream of perceived compliments.

"The ship would continue to sail, and the ship would continue to buy, sell, and trade."

A moment passed in quiet, until the captain spoke again. "I would be losing a friend, Mr. Hawkes, and that is an emotion I have yet to feel in all my days at sea. A good captain cannot be friendly with his crew. I may be called on to discipline them harshly, or watch them die in sick bay—and for those reasons I must be dispassionate and uninvolved. But with you, I could not."

William felt unsure of what was transpiring. *Am I being scolded, or is it that the captain is finding it difficult to tell me that my services are no longer required?*

"You have become my friend."

"Captain, I am honored, but—"

He held up his palm again, and William stopped his speech.

"I have not felt well on this voyage, William. Becoming your friend is a sign of my time passing. I have become softer. My years have made themselves known in my limbs. I am tired. I awake at dawn, desiring to remain at rest until noon. That is most unlike my habits of my youth."

"Perhaps a few weeks' rest back home," William suggested, "and then—"

"No. Sailing is a young man's occupation. I have funds enough to offer my family's security for many years. It would be so pleasant to have my dear wife at my side as I sleep. How I yearn for that tenderness now. Yes, William, it is time I leave the sea."

William was confused. *I am not being punished, and the captain is speaking of sailing no longer. But why is he sharing this plan with me?*

"William, I know that you have been amply rewarded on each voyage. You have deserved more, it is true, but you have been satisfied. I understand that your needs have been few, and because of such frugality there is a goodly sum held by barristers in Weymouth on your account. That is a fact, is it not, William?"

William nodded, but could not have been more puzzled by the line of the captain's conversation.

"I do not know your heart or your dreams, William. Perhaps you do not know them either." The captain placed both hands, palm down, on the table. "When we return to Weymouth, I would like you to consider a modest proposition. I would like you to consider purchasing the *Artemisia* from me and becoming its captain."

March 1640
The Atlantic Ocean

The *Artemisia* made additional stops at Nevis, Antigua, and St. Christopher, but William remembered scant little of the transactions and activity that transpired over those few weeks.

His charts continued to be produced with accurate detail, and the ship appeared to catch the currents and the winds at the correct time. Within a fortnight of William's discussion with Captain Waring concerning both their futures, the vessel was midway between the new and the old worlds. Winter was all but past, but William noticed an English crispness in the air.

This was not how I planned this trip to progress, William thought. *I had planned to leave the employ of this ship, return home to Hadenthorne, confess my shortcomings to the vicar, and ask Missy Holender to be wedded to me.*

It would have been so simple. I could have stopped this foolish search for the truth. I can scarce remember what truth it is that I had promised to be searching for. The truth is not in God's men, I can assure anyone of that. And what of old Captain Waring—a true Christian all his life—and here he finds himself tired, lonely, and ready to sleep in the arms of his wife at home. Has God really blessed him for his faithful service?

When I have seen all of the ill and evil that men have done on these tropic islands, I grow weary. It is too much to ask whether or not God cares for the common man. If he cares, how then could I explain the brutish squalor that slaves and servants must share? How can I explain that the rich care only for riches—and to the devil with their fellow-man?

Will took out his most recent notebook and thumbed through the pages, each carefully drawn and noted with readings and sightings. His friend Tatum, whom he had first met in Tortuga, had not been seen in three sailings. *Perhaps he had been captured as a slave, or succumbed to a new illness brought by the Europeans.*

He closed the book and held it to his chest. *I am tired on this journey, too. I am tired of being concerned for others.*

A few moments passed, and the sun came blistering out from behind a bank of clouds, causing William to squint. *Perhaps I should discuss this all with Vicar Mayhew. Perhaps he will be able to set my wrongs to right.*

CHAPTER

38

April 1640
Broadwinds, Dorset
England

"Kathryne! Obviously the climate here in Dorset agrees with you. You are no less than radiant."

Kathryne took Cecily's hand and pulled her close to provide a gentle hug. "Cecily, you too have grown more lovely. It is quite obvious that marriage agrees with your countenance."

Celia stepped forward, offering outstretched hands. "Kathryne! All alone in this big house by yourself. I cannot imagine what melancholy you must suffer."

"Celia, I suffer from no such ailment. I have traveled to London and Dorchester and Weymouth on several occasions—and I have much to do when I am here. It is not such a lonely existence."

Each woman stepped back, observing the other. After a moment, Kathryne said, "You must be quite fatigued after your long journey. Please, come inside out of this chilled air. I will have Mrs. Cole prepare us some coffee. That will do well to warm us all."

"Coffee? Kathryne, you are still the sophisticate," said Celia as they entered the house. "I would have thought that you, of all people, would treat such affectations as coffee with marked disdain."

Kathryne smiled wanly and reminded herself that despite any entreatments on Celia's part during this visit, she would not engage in any verbal sparring. At the Alexandrian, Celia, unlike her twin, Cecily, had not been a close friend, for she had a sharp, cutting way about her words.

"Celia, we will produce any drink you may care for. I merely suggested coffee for the warmth it provides."

"Why, Kathryne, we can sit by the fire if you find the climate chilling."

Both Kathryne and Cecily hesitated a step to allow Celia to enter first, and they caught each other's eye. Both women rolled their eyes heavenward, smiled briefly, and then returned to a more serious, civilized demeanor. Kathryne caught a giggle in her throat.

"Kathryne, did you say something?"

"No, Celia. It was just a cough."

"I would claim that these drafts would be enough to cause anyone to catch a goodly dose of consumption."

Cecily and Celia were each given large suites off the center hall of the second floor of Broadwinds. Kathryne had instructed her servants to keep a healthy fire blazing in Celia's rooms at all times.

"If we have to exhaust all the winter's wood to keep those rooms warm, then so be it," she had instructed. "She was cold the entire year in London, and she will be warm here."

Almost a year had passed since the three had been together. Kathryne had spoken to Cecily at a court function in London that she and her father attended just prior to his departure for the Antilles. They had promised that they would rejoin to speak of their school days and to catch up on current activities. As they promised to seek an agreeable date, Celia had come up and Kathryne and Cecily had felt forced, out of mere civility, to include her on their planning.

Kathryne had arranged the date, sent Mr. Biesty and a Spenser carriage for their travel, and had tried to arrange a pleasant five-day visit. Neither twin had ever been to Broadwinds, and Kathryne had planned to show them the countryside, perhaps attend church on the Sabbath, visit the Roman ruins a short distance away, and spend much time talking.

Lord, I pray that my tongue will remain civil and that you will guard my heart against malicious thoughts, prayed Kathryne as she escorted Celia to her suite.

Later that evening, after what Kathryne and Cecily thought to be a delicious meal prepared by Mrs. Cole—and at which Celia had merely picked—the three adjourned to the library.

The parlormaid followed them in and asked, "Would anyone care for a sherry, or coffee perhaps?"

Cecily asked for a small glass of sherry, and Celia agreed.

"Three glasses of the earl's finest sherry," Kathryne stated, sending the girl to fetch the refreshments.

Celia was wearing an elaborate gown of purple, with wide slits cut into the lace-edged sleeves, exposing a shimmery gold fabric. The skirt was trimmed in gold lace and was taken up in the front, showing several petticoats, adding a sense of voluminous elegance. The bodice was trimmed low—lower than Kathryne would ever feel comfortable in.

How ladies of the court feel secure with so much flesh exposed is a mystery to me, Kathryne thought.

"Do you like the gown, Kathryne?" asked Celia. "I noticed you eying it intently."

"Why, yes—it is very becoming. Purple does seem to be your color, Celia."

"Thank you. It was made for me by the most extraordinary tailor on Regent Street. I could have him do one up for you. Of course, you will have to draw up your measurements, for this size would be much too small for your larger frame."

Hold your tongue, Kathryne. You made a promise. "Why, that is a most gracious offer, Celia. But I have fewer needs for such gowns here at Broadwinds. And I must say that for my sensibilities, that style is more open and daring than I would feel comfortable wearing."

Celia screwed up her face in response and wagged her finger at Kathryne. "Kathryne, always the prude. It covers what needs covered— and besides, how will you ever attract a husband if all the treasures remain hidden?"

Cecily chimed in from a comfortable chair near the fire, "Celia, you promised to behave on this trip. You promised that no mention would be made of husbands and spinsters and the like. You promised!"

"Dear Sister, I made no hurtful remark. Did I, Kathryne?" she asked innocently.

"Cecily, I assure you that I have taken no offense."

"It is merely that one must do what is appropriate to attract a suitor's attentions," Celia said coyly as she adjusted her bodice even lower. "A dress such as this attracts their attentions, focuses their intentions, and speeds their enthusiasm." She giggled and took a long sip of sherry, which the maid had just brought in.

Cecily stood up and walked to Kathryne and sat by her on the couch. "Why haven't you been at court, Kathryne? Simply *everyone* is there."

Because being at court is a waste of time, Kathryne thought. *To wait in attendance of the queen or princess and hope to attract the attention of a noble-born wastrel would be a squandering of time and energy. And I have heard that many other "diversions" are practiced in the halls and rooms of the royal residences. I have other, more important things to do than simply chase a husband.*

She answered, however, "Cecily, my dear—I have no time. I must look after my father's interests here, and that is a demanding task that leaves few free hours."

"I do not see what you find interesting in all those numbers and figures," Celia remarked. "In a few years you *will* be old and alone and no man will want you."

"Celia!" cried Cecily. "You promised!"

"Cecily, you be quiet. Just because you have married well is no reason to look askew of my effort to find a proper suitor. And I would think you would want your dearest friend from the Alexandrian to be as happy as you."

Kathryne was perturbed. She had not wanted the conversation this evening—or any evening during the visit—to focus on her marital status. It was not a subject she favored discussing.

An uneasy silence filled the room, and the loudest noise was the crackling of the burning wood in the fireplace.

"Kathryne," Cecily asked in a mouse-small voice, "how *do* you propose to find a mate—stranded so far out here in the country and not having a father or mother to help you?"

"Yes, dear Kathryne," echoed Celia. "We would be most interested in your plans."

"After all," Cecily continued, "it is only a matter of time until Celia makes a suitable connection. And being married is quite nice. My dear Wesley Cheswick is a most pleasant fellow. I have a grand time arranging parties and visiting other ladies in Knightsbridge."

Kathryne leaned forward and placed her sherry, still nearly full, on the small end table. "Cecily, is that all that marriage is to you? It seems a matter of . . . convenience rather than passion."

Celia laughed, and Cecily blushed a bright vermilion.

"Kathryne, you wanton woman! How you have changed since Lady Emily's! Wesley can be most passionate indeed—when he chooses."

Now it was Kathryne's turn to blush. "Dear Cecily, I meant that I would hope to see marriage as a matter of love—not mere biological lines."

"Well, now, Kathryne . . . I could say that I have grown to love Wesley. He has his ways and demands his privacy. But I have begun to learn how to adapt to his manners. He is most successful. And he allows me two hundred pounds for a new wardrobe every season. And we attend the best balls, and he even has a reserved loge at the opera. And soon, I would trust, there will be children. What more is there to a woman's life than this?"

Kathryne stared at her friend. *She is serious. These are not just words. That life is a life she desires.*

"Besides, Kathryne," added Celia, "if Lord Cheswick has his private liaisons, there is no reason a wife cannot have hers. Isn't that right, dear Sister?"

Kathryne saw scarlet spread over Cecily's cheeks.

Celia looked back at Kathryne and smiled in the deepening silence.

May 1640
Weymouth, Dorset
England

The *Artemisia* sailed into home port on the high tide, and the persistent waves, misting rain, and fog had made docking the ship tricky. A crewman slipped from the foremast's yardarm to the deck below as they furled the sails. He broke his leg, and the wound was bloodied by a piece of bone cutting through the skin just below his knee.

Will was at the wheel as the crewman dropped to the deck, landing with a curious soft thump. Within moments all knew that the injury was severe. Others with similar injuries had lost the use of the limb or faced the bone saw of the surgeon.

The sailor's screaming, as the ship maneuvered to the pier, was unsettling. The rest of the crew went about its duties in the grayness with hardly a sound, lest someone break a spell of sorts and be the next one injured. Their worst fears were realized as a second injury soon followed. Another crewman had shouted from an open hatch for a rigging net to be sent down by rope and tackle. A sailor on the top deck tossed the rigging through the open hatch, just as the sailor below turned away. The heavy rope and block struck him from behind, knocking him to the ground. By midafternoon, he had begun to regain his senses, but he was in a dire state of confusion and agitation until then.

"It comes in threes, Mr. Hawkes," Johnny Delacroix whispered to him. "Bad happenings come in threes."

William had heard this often from Johnny and other crewmen, and he had scoffed at the improbability of any celestial plan that needed to operate with calamities always appearing in triplicate.

"Laugh if you will, Mr. Hawkes," Matthew MacGregor, the master-at-arms, said quietly in agreement. "But I awoke this morning to find a raven resting on the cathead. That is an omen, for sure. Someone on this vessel is doomed to be the third."

The ship was unloaded quickly, but the elation that often accompanied a shore leave at home port was absent.

Captain Waring distributed the prize awards to each man, and as they took the coins, he added that the ship would set sail once again at full moon—some three weeks hence.

Perhaps two dozen men had no homes nor family to return to and would remain on ship. Diggory Dyer, yeoman, would also remain to organize a detail of men to stand by as guards.

William was the last man in the captain's cabin. Captain Waring was at his table with a small stack of coins, a large ledger book, and quill and inkwell lying in front of him.

"Will, I am offering your normal award for this journey, but I will gladly keep it on account if your decision is to buy the *Artemisia*."

"Captain Waring, no thank you. I will take the coins with me. Not having the award in my purse may cloud the decision for me. But rest assured that I will return and inform you of my decision whether I accept it or decline it."

"Understood, Mr. Hawkes. I trust that you and your Vicar Mayhew will be able to set things right. Until your return, William, I pray that God will show you the way and guide your steps."

William shook his hand firmly and set out to his home of Hadenthorne with a bagful of possessions and a few remembrances from the Antilles.

It was at least a two-day journey by carriage or cart, three if on foot, from the sea to Hadenthorne. By the time the sun had disappeared, Will had arrived at Bridport and made arrangements to spend the night in a small room above a pleasant tavern. Throughout the night he dreamed of Missy's soft lips and small waist.

He arose early and walked the following day from dawn to dusk and reached Tiverton. On the third day he started out even earlier, determined to reach home by noon. Walking briskly in the dawning air, the fences and fields drifted past him in a soft blur.

After three days of walking, Will had reached the crossroads to the south of Hadenthorne. Soft rounded clouds rolled in the heavens, and shadows danced along the valley. To the west lay the sea, and to the north the forest of Exmoor. But ahead, in the gentle valley of the river Taw, lay Hadenthorne. There was the steeple marking the church and the parsonage of St. Jerome's. Further down the river was the Cavendish farm, and across the deep waters were the new Holender lands.

Off to the north was Hadenthorne Hall, its stately tan walls reflecting the golden spring sun.

Will stood there, drinking in the sight. He had hoped that his heart would have leaped at this spot, cheering him on, enabling him to feel assured as to his decision. *It is good to return,* he thought, *but my heart is unstirred, quiet.*

William looked about, and certifying that he was alone and unobserved, he dropped to his knees in the drying grass by the road's edge. *God, I have not bent my knee in prayer since I left this town. I do not want to be a deceiver nor a charlatan, but I am seeking your guidance. I have come home to stay. . . . I will seek to marry Missy Holender, and I will make peace with the vicar. I believe that is what you would have me to do. I ask that my heart be settled and I would be granted peace.*

He stood quickly and brushed at his knees. Without looking about, he set off for his home. There was a certain closure that he felt in his heart, like a door to the recent past shut and latched, not to be opened again.

I trust that this is what peace feels like, he thought as he walked slowly down the path, and with each step he felt that closed door recede even further into his past.

Broadwinds, Dorset
England

Kathryne sat at her desk and sighed, staring out at the greening landscape before her. The first signs of spring had not improved her mood. She looked back down at the note cards she had received from Cecily and Celia, her schoolmates who had visited Broadwinds only a few weeks prior. It had been an exhausting visit. Cecily, recently married, spoke of the wonders of wedded bliss, which, to her, were highlighted by new wardrobes and gay masques and pageants. Celia, the sharp-tongued twin, was now a lady-in-waiting at the royal court and spent much of her time nudging Kathryne to anger with her insistence that Kathryne needed a husband—and soon—or she would forever be an old maid.

Their note, full of gracious thanks, brought back to a boil the frustrations Kathryne had felt during many of their conversations.

Mrs. Cole had popped her head in the room and took one look at Kathryne's face. "It be the twins, no doubt," she said with a smile. "I have not seen that face on you since they left."

"Indeed, Mrs. Cole. They seem to have that effect."

"Would you like a pot of tea—or perhaps coffee?"

"Coffee please, dear Mrs. Cole. And please join me. It would do me well to speak to someone who causes me to smile rather than wince."

Soon Mrs. Cole returned with a steaming pot of tea, cream, sugar, and a plate of sweet biscuits.

"Child, be you troubled by their talk of marriage and all that again?"

"Mrs. Cole, am I wrong to think that marriage should be for love rather than for resources and connections? I must admit that Cecily's marriage seems cold and lifeless. If it wasn't for Sir Wesley Cheswick's success and social standing, they would have nothing in common."

Mrs. Cole poured a cup of coffee and stirred several heaping teaspoons of sugar into the thick, black drink. "Kathryne, how glad I am that your father is doing well on the island. I have grown quite fond of these two products of the tropics he has sent us. It almost makes his absence worth the pain."

Kathryne looked startled, then saw the broad smile on the woman's face. "Mrs. Cole, you are such a tease. But you have not answered my question."

"Kathryne, marriage is different for nobility such as yourself. There are more contingencies to consider—more entanglements and allegiances to be aware of. For a commoner such as myself . . ."

Kathryne winced as Mrs. Cole described herself as a commoner. She had admonished Mrs. Cole in the past that she was never to refer to herself as common.

". . . I know you find that troublin', but 'tis true. For a commoner, the requirements are simpler. Is the man a good man? Does he fear and honor God? Will he endeavor to meet the needs of his family before his own? Does he love the woman he courts? Is he pure?"

Mrs. Cole shook her head. She had overheard some of Celia's discussion of court gossip and was astonished at the cavalier manner in which she had described the morals of many of the ladies-in-waiting. She was astounded to hear that many couples of Kathryne's age considered it permissible to behave as man and wife with each other during the betrothal period as soon as the banns had been announced in the church.

"If you can answer in the affirmative to these questions, then 'twill be a good marriage—based on love and God's principles."

"Is that how you decided to marry Mr. Cole?"

"'Twas indeed. He was truly a good, gentle man and loved God with every fiber of his bein'. I wonder if that isn't the reason he was taken so early—because God wanted his goodness in heaven."

Kathryne reached over, took her hand, and squeezed it gently. Tears had formed at the corners of Mrs. Cole's eyes, and she looked down at her left hand where she wore an engraved gold mourning-ring in memory of Mr. Cole. She seldom spoke of her late husband, and Kathryne rarely mentioned him, for she knew that the pain of the loss was close to the surface even after all these years.

"I did indeed love that man. And he loved me," she half-whispered, the emotions never too far from her heart.

"But, Mrs. Cole, how will I love a man if I am not involved in his selection? How will I know if he is a good man deep down inside, a man that truly loves our Lord?"

"The Scriptures say to honor thy father and mother, Kathryne, but I do not know how they speak to this issue. You're an adult, but you need honor Lord Aidan. I know he will choose well for you."

"When I mentioned to Cecily and Celia that Papa had named a man in a previous letter that he thought might be a possible suitor in Barbados—that Geoffrey Foxton I told you of—they were beside themselves with glee. I do not understand this."

"Married women, or women that are seekin' marriage, think that all women should be as involved in the search as they are."

"But is that God's will? For me to marry a stranger?"

"Kathryne, I am not a theologian. I have no keen understandin' of these points. When I am confused in matters such as this, I pray to God for guidance. If you earnestly pray, he will show you the way."

Now tears formed in Kathryne's eyes. *How I wish my mother were here,* she thought with sadness. "Mrs. Cole, will you pray for me?"

She took Kathryne's hands in hers, lowered her head, and closed her eyes. "My Father, my God, I beseech thee to guide thy obedient child Kathryne. Show her thy ways, dear Lord. Protect her heart. Guide the actions of her dear father and give to him thy wisdom. Bring into her life a man that she may cherish and who may honor and love both thee and Kathryne. We ask that such a man be made known to her in the fullness of time. In the holy name of Jesus, Amen."

39

May 1640
Hadenthorne, Devon
England

William walked purposely as he made his way along the narrow road to the village. His strides were long, and he wanted to speak to no one until he had met with the vicar. He saw few people out, though some were working in fields more distant from the main road. Land rails sent their harsh, grating birdcalls across the corn and hay as he passed.

Will veered off by the oak grove near the river and came up on the parsonage from the east, along the lane that meandered past the church's graveyard. Here he walked slower, passing only a moment to acknowledge the graves of his father and mother, where roses were blooming in profusion.

> *HERE LYETH THE BODY OF*
> *SAMUEL BARTHOLOMEW HAWKES*
> *WHO DEPARTED THIS LIFE*
> *THE 15TH DAY OF OCTOBER*
> *IN THE YEAR OF OUR LORD 1630*
> *AGED 34*

He recalled the words of the poem his father had recited at his mother's burial, the words thick in his throat, constricted by the powerful rush of emotions.

> *Ask me no more where Jove bestows,*
> *When June is past, the fading rose.*

He stood by the small headstone bearing the words:

> *HERE LYETH THE BODY OF*
> *ELIZABETH GRESHAM HAWKES*
> *WHO DEPARTED THIS LIFE*
> *THE 20TH DAY OF APRIL*
> *IN THE YEAR OF OUR LORD 1628*
> *AGED 30*

How I still miss them. He reached to his heart and felt his mother's precious locket resting against his skin. That action was repeated perhaps a hundred times during the course of each day—William long since forgetting that he did so. When the familiar small ache came, it was a comforting reminder of his past.

The parsonage garden looked a great deal more precise this year. The elder bushes were trimmed short, and the box edging was cut neatly into the turf. A new arbor had been added since Will's last visit nearly two years ago and was already heavy with the blossoms of what would be fat, purple grapes. The double peonies were just past their bloom but looked tidy, the spent ones having been recently clipped off. *Has the vicar taken up an interest in the flower garden?* William wondered.

A small stone shed was built adjacent to the kitchen wall, and a large supply of split wood was stacked there. *Odd. Vicar Mayhew never used much wood for fires, but mostly peat or coal.*

He turned the handle of the gate and heard no squeak or rusty squeal. *Perhaps the vicar has hired a new man to repair such things.*

The fragrance of lilies of the valley wafted down the path to the parsonage. He peered in the window of the kitchen and saw an empty, darkened room. *Where would Mrs. Cavendish be? It is near time for the noon meal. Perhaps she was needed to help with the planting.*

He reached for the door and turned at the knob. The handle did not turn. *I have never known the vicar to lock this door.*

He rapped soundly at the door, hearing it echo through the parsonage. He waited and put his ear to the door. Perhaps he might hear the vicar's footsteps. Rather than footsteps, he heard a lock being turned and a bolt opened. William stood back a step from the door as he waited for it to open.

"Thomas, I have waited so—" William stopped in mid-sentence, his speech clipped to silence.

It was not Vicar Mayhew that appeared at the door, but a short, young man wearing long vestments. William looked down and saw bare feet peeking out from the bottom of his clerical garb.

"I . . . I . . . I am looking for Vicar Thomas . . ." William stuttered in surprise. "I mean to say that, I . . . that this is the parsonage of Thomas Mayhew, the vicar of this parish. Is he here?"

The young cleric glared at William. "He is not."

"Will he be returning this day?"

"He will not."

"Do you know when he shall be?"

"I do not."

A wave of dislocation swept over William. The face that he sought was gone, as was any trace of solace that the parsonage offered.

"Sir, I do not know who you are," William exclaimed rapidly, with a hint of desperation in his voice. "I am William Hawkes, and I lived with Vicar Mayhew at this home for most of my youth. Where might I find him? I need to speak with him."

"William Hawkes? I have never heard of you," the young cleric said blankly. He stared at Will for a long moment, then said, "I am Vicar Sheedy and have been the vicar of the church for fourteen months, since your old friend was removed by the church authorities."

"Removed?" Will asked, surprised and confused.

"Maybe *reassigned* is a more correct term."

"Where?"

"I have no idea—and I have learned better than to ask after him. The London bishopric did not think it wise that your old friend expressed such Puritanical notions so plainly. I am not one to gossip, especially to a stranger whom I do not know, but I hear it was said that your vicar was being sent away to a place where he could do little damage to the Church of England."

The young cleric remained solidly in the doorway and made no move to invite William inside. His thoughts in a whirl, William struggled to piece together what the new vicar was saying and to gain composure.

"Vicar Sheedy, do you know where the woman is who used to work for Vicar Mayhew? I expected to see her here as well."

"You mean old Mrs. Cavendish? She is most likely at her home with her somewhat oafish sons."

"Is she ill? Why is she no longer here?"

Vicar Sheedy squinted his eyes and pursed his lips. "She is no longer here because she was relieved of the position. She was much too aggressively familiar, and I daresay her culinary skills were that of a peasant farmer. I brought a servant with me from London who is much better suited to the requirements of life in a parsonage in such a backwards village as this."

Nearly stumbling over a loose stone in the walk as he backed away from the new vicar, William called out, "Thank you . . . for your help. I must visit the Cavendishes. . . . I must—" And with that William turned and began to run down the road along the river.

In a few breathless minutes William was at the front of the Cavendish homestead. He paused to calm his breathing, then loudly rapped on the front door. From the other side, he heard a quiet shuffling, and the door creaked open a narrow slit. From the darkness, Will could make out a single brown eye, peering at him from the darkness.

Had the Cavendishes left, too?

The door flew open, and Mrs. Cavendish raced out and embraced Will in a fierce bear hug, nearly squeezing the breath from his chest.

I am always amazed at the strength of this woman, Will thought, as her tears began to flow. *And I am amazed at the speed of her tears.*

"It is you, isn't it, Will? You're not bein' some sprite sent to fool me now, are you?" she cried.

"No, Mrs. Cavendish. It is I, William Hawkes—and I fear that I am as perplexed as you seem to be."

She held him at arm's length for a moment, staring at him, as the tears continued to stream down her cheeks. "Oh, Will," she said, her voice cracking, and pulled him close again, burying her sob in his chest.

"Mrs. Cavendish, everything will be fine. I am back, safe and healthy."

"I dreamt that you had taken sick and some savage illness had burnt you up, Will. I dreamt that you'd gone!"

"Mrs. Cavendish, please. I am well. I am standing before you, hale and healthy. Please take heart and allow your tears to cease."

She broke her embrace and dragged William into the kitchen, where a small fire smoked and warmed the tiny room. A window, two handbreadths wide, let a weak ray of light penetrate the hazy gloom. She pulled William in and sat him on a padded bench by the fire, opposite the cooking pots.

"You look famished. Sit here, Will," she said, pulling him down. "Let me look at you whilst I prepare some soup and cut some cheese and bread."

"Mrs. Cavendish, that is not needed, for I—"

She placed her hand over his mouth. "I knows when a man needs a meal and when he doesn't. And I say that you have a hungry look about you. I know you'll be wantin' some of my figgy-dowdy puddin', too."

William raised his hands in surrender and laughed—the first time in days. It felt good to be cared for, to be mothered. That persistent small ache in his heart felt soothed and quiet. He touched at his locket and it felt warm against his skin.

Mrs. Cavendish scurried to a small wooden locker at the base of a far wall and extracted a turnip, a parsnip, a carrot, and some peas. She took a ladle of water from a bucket and poured it into an empty cooking pot. She quickly quartered the vegetables and put them into the pot. She added a handful of flour, a small piece of tallow, and a dash of herbs and salt, then lowered the cooking pot close over the fire.

As she busied herself, preparing the meal, William felt at peace. It was good to be among a sense of the familiar. Her precise actions, her routine that William had observed a thousand times, warmed him in a way that no tropical sun could. He felt at home for the first time in years.

But even as William basked in this security of the known, questions bubbled up, pervading the silence, nudging and nipping at Will's peace.

"Mrs. Cavendish, what has happened at St. Jerome's in my absence? Where is the vicar? I stopped at the parsonage and was greeted by a most curious—and cold—stranger."

Mrs. Cavendish stopped in mid-stir. "William, I am not one to be speakin' ill of a man of God, but Vicar Sheedy is a devil—pure and simple. I scarce can bring myself to enter the church. 'Tis an abom . . . abim . . . abomi . . ."

"Abomination?"

"Yes, Will, it is that word." She caught herself, and her hand went to her throat.

"Will, that word be not a curse word in some foreign tongue, now, is it?"

"No, Mrs. Cavendish, but it is a strong admonition to call some-one—especially a man of the cloth."

"But it be the truth—what he has done and all."

"And what has he done?"

"They went and put a fancy carved altar at the front of the church—it must be twenty hands high. When the vicar speaks, you must twist your neck so as to look up in the heavens. 'Tisn't natural to look up that long."

William had heard, when the ship last docked in Weymouth, that William Laud, the bishop of London, had been instituting all manner of "improvements" to the church and the service style, regulating liturgical practice and imposing uniformity of worship in the manner of High Anglicanism.

"And then he passed out some sort of book that we all has to follow in the service."

William winced, knowing that so few people in the village could read and that such an action would be perceived as orders from a pompous head cleric who seemingly cared little for the common man.

"Well, we stand there listenin' to the few speak. And the words they use—even if I could do some readin', I would have no understandin'."

"But Mrs. Cavendish, perhaps Vicar Sheedy only means to teach believers—and this would be his way to accomplish that."

"William, that not be it. The new vicar uses all sorts of rituals and repeatin's to do the same thing that Vicar Mayhew used to do in common tongue. 'Tis become where a plain baptism is confusin'. I asks myself when the vicar is done talkin'—be the baby blessed or not?"

It was true William had been hearing that the split was deepening in the church between the followers of Bishop Laud and their quest for a formal, high church ceremony, and the clergy like Vicar Mayhew who sought to reach the common people by preaching biblically based sermons that sought to affect daily Christian living, a practice labelled Puritan by critics. Will had discounted much of the talk as harbor town gossip—most news he heard often seemed enlarged and inflamed. But Mrs. Cavendish's story was concrete evidence that the bishop of London's dogma had impacted a small, insignificant, country parish church.

"Mrs. Cavendish, did these changes cause Vicar Mayhew to leave as well? Where has he gone? I did so want to speak with him."

Tears welled up in the corners of her eyes again. "Will, my poor Will. Vicar Mayhew is gone as well, and I know not where he be."

She sobbed into her apron for several moments. "When the new vicar came, good Vicar Mayhew went back to London for a spell, and it was said that he would be returnin' to us. But as the season changed from winter to spring and still no Vicar, we was concerned. So Constable Markham went to the new vicar—as our town leader—to ask when we would expect to see the old vicar again. And he was told that Vicar Mayhew will never return here—he was sent on to another place and that we did not need to know where that might be."

She sobbed again, sat next to Will on the bench, and he wrapped his arm around her shoulder.

"Perhaps I could make inquiries for you. I have met a few influential people on my voyages. Perhaps they will know." Will knew that the vicar would not have gone without word, unless ordered to do so.

"Would you, Will? That would be an answer to me prayers," she said through her tears.

"Of course I will," he reassured.

"And then the new vicar comes and tells me that I am no longer to cook for the parish! That me cookin' be too simple and too common for the likes of him! Can you believe those evil words! And he said them to me, Will! To my face, that me cookin' was common!"

Will noticed that her sadness and tears had been replaced by a bitter anger. It was not enough for the bishop to remove her vicar, but his replacement insulted her cooking as well. It was a volatile mix, Will thought.

"Mrs. Cavendish, I will do my best to track down the vicar. I promise you that. I also have need to speak with him."

The soup began to bubble in the cooking pot. Mrs. Cavendish reached over, stirred it, and tasted a small spoonful.

"The soup is finished. We will eat now, after I asks the blessin'."

After a tearful prayer in which God was given praise for Will's safe return, they sat at the table, with a round of crusty bread between them and a large porringer of steaming soup for each. William recounted his last several voyages to Mrs. Cavendish.

Her eyes opened wide as he told her of the dark savages on the islands—and that some of them had been said to have practiced cannibalism. She shuddered when Will went on to tell of their body painting and jewelry and use of poisoned spears.

"Will, tell me no more of such things. I would not spend a peaceful evenin' again if I knew more of the dangers that you face."

Will smiled broadly. He anticipated that such stories would be troubling for the squeamish, and a part of him enjoyed it, as might a small boy enjoy tormenting a sister with a frog or snake.

"Well, Mrs. Cavendish, you may be able to sleep well for the rest of your days. That is why I have returned to Hadenthorne. I have finally decided. I have come back and am prepared to ask for Missy Holender's hand in marriage. I will buy a tract of free land in the valley and will build a small house for the two of us. I trust that Missy is well and as comely as ever."

Mrs. Cavendish put her spoon down and stared at Will. Her eyes began to fill with her watery tears, and her bottom lip began to tremble.

"Mrs. Cavendish, what is the matter? Do you feel unwell?" Will asked, nervous and alarmed.

"Will," she spoke, her voice shaking, "I wish I was not the one to say this to you, but Missy Holender is gone."

12 May 1640
Broadwinds, Dorset
England

My Dear Father,

Matters have gone well since my last correspondence. The shares of the latest East India Company voyages owned by the Spensers have returned a handsome fifty percent on the original sums. Your friends at Lloyd's have teased that their latest business partner—your obedient daughter—has a golden touch when dealing with arcane shipping matters and cargo choices. I take no real credit, for it is the Lord's blessing we share.

The mood of the countryside is yet unsettled. There is still much unrest in the north, and Parliament continues to battle over King Charles's questionable acts of policy. A local militia has been formed to ward off what some perceive to be coming troubles. I write this not to alarm you, Papa, but to keep you abreast of the news. I am told by many in our village that they see no disturbances here in the near future such as occur in London, and where many rebellious citizens take to the streets, tired of unemployment and being overly taxed, but they choose to be at the ready.

Cecily (Cheswick) Althorp and Celia Althorp have visited me from London and were most curious as to the nature of this Geoffrey Foxton you wrote of previous. What manner of suitor might he be? What work does he do, and what family, if any, does he call his own? I must say that I am curious as well, Papa. If it be not much trouble, perhaps you could tell me of his character and behaviors.

I will post this on the morrow. Perhaps it will sail with the *Artemisia* if not on a ship to depart sooner.

> *I remain, your obedient and loving daughter,*
> Kathryne

Hadenthorne, Devon
England

"Gone! To where? Or is she . . ." His voice trailed off in fear that she was not just gone from Hadenthorne—but dead.

His thoughts raced. *God, if this be your answer to my prayer, then you have a harsh side that I care little for. I need to speak to the vicar, and you have removed him from sight. I set my plans on marriage, and you remove the one woman for whom I have had feelings. Is this your way of caring for your creatures? Is this the God I am to respect and honor? My prayer has been in vain.*

Mrs. Cavendish had folded her thick arms on the table and buried her head in them, sobbing uncontrollably.

"What has happened to her?" William lowered his head closer to Mrs. Cavendish. He whispered, "Where has she gone?"

"'Tis all my fault!" she cried. "I have brought you ruination."

He reached out and stroked her arm. "It cannot be as dreadful as your tears portray it. Please, tell me what has happened?"

She wiped her face with her apron again and sniffed loudly. "Missy has married and sailed—a fortnight previous—to the New World—to a place called Jamestown."

"Married!" Will nearly shouted, incredulous. "But she said forever! She said she would wait forever—even though I didn't ask. She said forever! It has been a mere two years! That is not forever!"

Mrs. Cavendish's face looked ashen and pale.

"Whom did she marry? What caused her to break her vow?" Will snapped.

"Will, we thought you would never be returnin'. The vicar said the same. You said as much when you left last, in the letter."

That much is true, Will thought.

"So who convinced her of my desire never to return to this village?" he demanded.

"Oh, Will," she cried between sobs. "It was me. I made her break that vow. She married Dugald, me oldest—and they sailed off to the New World together."

Will stared at the woman, her face lined in tears and reddened from her sobs. He was silent, his mouth a thin slit. He took his hands from hers and in a slow motion, placed them folded on the table in front of him. He stared at her, then turned to stare at the dim light coming through the small window.

Thanks be to God—is that what you want me to say? Must I be grateful to you for answering my prayer in this manner?

He turned back to see Mrs. Cavendish's face, upturned and full of anguished pleading.

Well, I will not. If this be a sign from you I want little part of your blessings.

40

May 1640
Hadenthorne, Devon
England

William stayed only two more days in the small village of his birth.
He spent an evening with the two remaining Cavendish brothers,
Timothy and Philip, who reminded Will of how strongly opposed their
brother Dugald had always been to the religious restraints being insti-
tuted by the Church of England. After Vicar Mayhew had been taken
from St. Jerome's and replaced with Vicar Sheedy and all his Lau-
dian ways, Dugald had decided to seek religious freedom in Virginia.

"But did he have to marry Missy and take her away with him?" Will
had asked them.

Their only reply had been lowered heads and silence.

He had called on the Holenders and had gotten much the same
response from them.

The evening of his second day in Hadenthorne was cool; a quiet had
descended on the small village. William had taken a room and his meal
at the new public house in the village. He knew that his absence at the
Cavendish supper table would be a hurtful thing to Mrs. Cavendish, but
William felt hurt as well.

I would have married Missy. I never told the vicar that I would never
return. I had planned to come back. I would have married her had she
waited.

As William thought and reconsidered the recent events, a small voice
in the back of his awareness—the small voice that acts as a fair witness
to the events in one's life—kept calling for his attention.

You were only coming back to satisfy Vicar Mayhew and Missy. You were not coming back for your own needs, the voice called. *Do not leave these bridges burnt, William. You did not want to be a farmer, nor do you want to marry Missy. At the very least, be honest with your own feelings—even if you cannot be honest with others.*

William sat in the snuggery of the public house and had taken his fifth pint of dog's nose—a mixture of ale and rum. This was quite an unusual occurrence, for he seldom drank fermented beverages, even aboard ship. He never appreciated the splayed and reckless feelings it fostered. But this evening he wanted the potent drink to muffle that small voice in his heart. Besides the pints with his supper, he asked for a glass of brandy and was served a yeoman's portion—almost a full tankard of the strong spirit.

He ate and drank alone that evening, and after he finished, he tossed a few coins on the table—much more than the meal was worth—and carefully stepped into the cool evening air. He walked slowly and with great deliberation, being careful not to stumble in the rutted roadway and give indication to his loosened state.

Perhaps I shall never come back to this sorry little village. Perhaps I shall sail away on my own ship and never return to this common place. I think I just might take the good Captain Waring up on his solicitation.

He wandered in the dark, in a dense fog of his own making, down the north road of the village, the road that led to Hadenthorne Hall.

Perhaps I shall go visit his lordship in the fancy house. Perhaps I should thank him for helping me go to sea and lose everything else I have held dear. It is truly all his fault. And he should know that.

He picked up the pace of his steps, and he extended his arms for better balance. The night grew darker, and the moon was but a chip in the eastern sky. After William passed the home of Constable Markham at the edge of town, the road grew darker, and William's footfalls became more precarious and bumbling.

A half mile passed, and William was more determined than ever to reach Hadenthorne Hall. He stepped into a deep rut, full of thick, muddy water, and his foot slid forward. Struggling to regain his footing, he turned and stumbled further to the right. William lowered his head and, with a bang, went headfirst into the roughened bark of an old oak tree that was hidden in the darkness. He fell in an unconscious, deflated heap at the base of the tree, his legs sprawled, stretched across the first several shallow ruts of the road.

19 May 1640
Broadwinds, Dorset
England

My Dearest Emily,

It has only been a few short months since we last met, but my heart aches for the chance to sit with you on a sunny afternoon in the breakfast room of the Alexandrian, feeding poor Willy the thrush his twelfth biscuit of the day. How I cherish those memories.

Pray tell me what has been happening in London. We in the hinterlands do get some news of the civilized world of the city, but much of it comes to us from traders, itinerant merchants, and craftsmen. While good people all, no doubt, I must caution myself to consider their tales with some degree of skepticism.

I have heard of riots in the streets; some say they occur daily. And all of it stemming from disagreements over the divine right of kings and the authoritarianism with which King Charles is attempting to rule. The merchants with whom I have dealings were very optimistic when Parliament convened last month, for it was their hope that the Scots' threat of war would somehow be allayed. But now we hear that Parliament was dissolved a fortnight ago. I understand that passions often run hot, but one would think that intelligent men could come to some sort of compromise on the illegal taxation issue. Reverend Pensworth has told me that the assertions of unacceptable church policies by Bishop Laud have only added fuel to the fire. I spoke with some acquaintances at the Dorchester market last week, and it seems that the people of that village, at least, are refusing to pay any further their Ship Money tax. It seems that the public have lost all confidence in King Charles's ability to rule, and their disagreements are inflamed by a large mob protesting in the streets—but I scarce believe my ears. Is it as troubling as they say?

I trust and pray that this unpleasantness will soon pass and that England will return to a country undivided and one of civilized behavior and manners.

Despite nervousness of many financial backers, the Spenser business dealings continue to prosper. (I must confess, dear Emily, that I often must resort to signing documents with a simple K. Spenser, so as to not subject others in the trade to the troubling concept of dealing with a mere woman. How I long for the day that we may be considered as equal when it comes to matters of simple commerce.)

I have heard from my father often. All goes well. He is hard at work securing that the island's new legislative house continues to run smoothly. I am sure Papa is endeavoring to choose the Christian response to many of the problems he faces. And he claims that the weather is indeed beastly hot, but they are adapting as best they can. He asks, in a wry manner, if I might transport a few cooling English breezes to them.

He has made mention again of Geoffrey Foxton. I believe that part of me wishes that the issue would simply disappear. It appears that Mr. Foxton is a young planter with a large sugar plantation on the island. If all goes well, Mr. Foxton will be a very wealthy man—considering what prices for raw sugar are being quoted in the Amsterdam markets.

I know that my dear father wants to see me happy, which to him means married to this plantation gentleman. I am sure that Mr. Foxton is a nice man—Papa simply describes him as a man with great potential. What does a woman make of that? What sort of man is he? Is he a good Christian man? Papa simply says he seems to be a God-fearing man. That, simply put, may not be enough. It is not enough to merely fear the wrath of God and never experience his love and mercy. As the Scriptures say, even the demons know who Jesus is, but they don't obey him. My heart yearns for a husband who lives as the Scriptures require and who can be committed as I to sharing God's love with others.

Is that desire improper, dear Emily? I know that obeying one's father and mother, as the Bible calls us to do, does not mean we can sin if they ask us to. Would a marriage to an unbelieving man be sin? I think yes. Would it be wrong to marry a man who may not have placed his complete trust in God? I find that question much more difficult to answer.

If Papa says I must—what shall I do?

By the tone of my father's letters, it would appear that he is considering making Barbados the future home of the Spensers for the next generation.

Do I leave my beloved Broadwinds for that tropical isle? How do I leave England? And how could I leave you?

I have so many troubling and vexing questions. And even Reverend Pensworth can provide little solace. He just tells me to pray.

Please pray for wisdom and guidance for me, dear Emily. I covet that from you, such a dear friend.

I will perchance be in London for a meeting with other backers at

Lloyd's on or about the 24th of June. If it is so, I will call on you then.

Your most humble friend,
Kathryne

P.S. My father sends his fondest regards to you.

Hadenthorne, Devon
England

> *"All people that on earth do dwell,*
> *Sing to the Lord with cheerful voice;*
> *Him serve with fear, His praise forth tell,*
> *Come ye before Him and rejoice."*

Joshua Tempton's strong, clear baritone voice echoed across the still meadows, full of the glory of the words he sang.

> *"The Lord, ye know, is God indeed;*
> *Without our aid He did us make;*
> *We are His flock, He doth us feed,*
> *And for His sheep He doth us take."*

As he paused between the verses of the majestic hymn, he could hear the bleats of new lambs in a confused response to his singing. *They do not know great music when they hear it,* he chuckled to himself.

His song became even louder and more fervent as he sang the final verse.

> *"To Father, Son, and Holy Ghost,*
> *The God whom heaven and earth adore,*
> *From earth and from the angel host*
> *Be praise and glory evermore. A-men."*

Joshua, his mule, and his small cart containing all his worldly possessions were headed to the port of Weymouth. They had journeyed a full day from Ilfracombe. Joshua had sold all that he owned, packed what he needed, and was heading to the colony established by Roger Williams in America, called Rhode Island. Joshua was intrigued by the freedoms this settlement promised, as well as by the enticement of land and employment. He had no spare coins for lodging along the way and wanted to get to a small village before sleeping, thinking that the proximity to others would lessen the risk of encountering highwaymen in the dark. He traveled late into the night, for he had but two more days to reach Weymouth for the sailing of his ship, a vessel called the *Plymouth Spirit*.

Joshua held the reins of his small wooden cart loosely in his left hand. With his right hand he directed his imaginary choir, bringing them to a rousing, triumphant finish. The old mule pulling the cart was oblivious to the sound and kept up a slow, steady walk along the dark, pitted road. A small lantern was hung on the cart to illuminate their way.

Joshua brought his hand down, encouraging his illusory choir, and looked straight ahead into the flickering murkiness. He blinked his eyes sharply, and then pulled hard on the reins, back and to the right.

The mule picked its legs up higher and stumbled a bit to the right as well, trying to lift the cart over a large rut. Both driver and cart were jostled and tossed about as the cart harrumphed to the side of the road.

Joshua tossed the reins down, pulled the lantern from its hook on the cart, and cautiously made his way back up the road a few paces.

"Lord, I beseech thee that we did not inflict any damage to the poor person's legs," he prayed anxiously. With the flickering illumination held high, Joshua picked his way through the ruts and mud.

"Praise be!" he cried and bent to the prone figure lying at the road's edge. He turned the limp figure over and lifted him roughly by the arms, pulling him to a sitting position against the oak. His blond hair was matted with dried blood. Joshua looked carefully and found no open wound.

"By the look of you, it was either robbers or carelessness on your part that led thee here to end up in a stupor. And by the smell of you, I would say that a wee bit of spirits was involved in this as well," he said aloud.

Joshua went to his cart, rummaged through a jumble of things in the back, and pulled out a wooden pail. He walked to the river's edge and returned to gently splash the full bucket over the unconscious man. In a moment, the figure sputtered a bit, opened his eyes, and blinked several times.

"Are you hurt?" Joshua asked, peering down at the man. He held up his lantern above his head. "How did you get here? Who are you?"

"William . . . Hawkes. . . . And I was headin' to . . . mmm . . . to . . ." William's voice drifted off, and he slowly raised his hand to the wound on his forehead. He touched it gingerly and winced. "Mmm, . . . who did this to me?" he rasped.

Joshua stood up. "You were attacked? Might the brigands still be near?" Joshua turned about in a complete circle as he said this, holding his lantern up as high as he could, peering into the darkness.

William rolled to his right and propped himself up to a standing position. Joshua reached out to help steady him. Will turned and leaned back against the tree.

"No, kind sir, they are not. It becomes clearer now as I stand. It was no highwayman who bloodied me—just the dog's nose and ale that made me stupid, and this tree helped to prove the evils of drink."

"'Twill do that to a man, sir. 'Tis why I do not use the drink at all. Mr. Hawkes, I am Joshua Tempton, at your service," Joshua said with a small bow.

Both hands rubbing at his temples, Will looked up and answered, "Thank you, Joshua, for your help. You are a kind and wise man, sir."

Joshua nodded in thanks.

"Could you tell me where I might be?" William asked.

"Sir, I was about to ask you the very same question. I know that I passed through Barnstaple midafternoon, setting out for Exeter, and I had hoped to reach a village by moonset. But I may have missed a junction at some point. I am on my way to Weymouth—I must arrive there by evening of the day past tomorrow. Is Weymouth within two day's travel of here?"

William held up his hand and covered his ear with his other. "You speak too loud and too long, my friend. It appears that the drink has attacked not only my head, but my ears as well."

Joshua nodded again.

"I believe we are only a few miles from Hadenthorne," William reasoned. "I do not think I have traveled more than that. And yes, if one leaves with the dawn, with a fast cart Weymouth can be reached in two long days," Will replied.

"Then I shall stay here this night. Please, Mr. Hawkes. Allow me to share what I have with you. I will set a small fire for warmth. And I have some provisions with me as well."

William sat with his back against the cart's wheel and listened to Joshua as he gathered a few sticks for firewood. He struck his flint and steel into a small nest of twigs, and within minutes a small fire lit the evening.

"Allow me to brew some rose hips for you. My mother believed 'tis a wondrous herb that will cure many ills and ailments."

William sipped at the steaming hot cup of pungent liquid. He had heard of the drink's restorative powers from Robby MacCallister onboard the *Minion*.

"You are on your way to Weymouth?" William asked, as he chewed on a tough biscuit Joshua had insisted he take.

"To board the *Plymouth Spirit*. I will join Roger Williams's colony in Rhode Island. 'Tis said that he is establishing a new order of man—based on God's principles on earth. I would dare not miss this opportunity."

"Then you will sail with Captain Blake."

"Quite right. You are a pilgrim as well, Mr. Hawkes?"

He gulped at the hot drink. "Hardly. It seems as though God is quite selective as to which prayers and requests are answered and which are ignored."

Off in the distance a fox barked, and the soft hoot of an owl echoed across the river.

"Perhaps I am not a perfect witness," Joshua said in a small, yet firm voice, "but what you say, Mr. Hawkes, is untrue. If one believes and one petitions the Almighty, the Almighty will hear and respond. But one must believe, Mr. Hawkes. Do you believe?"

A frog croaked by the riverbank, then splashed into the still waters.

"I promised a friend that I would search for the truth—to search for the Almighty, as you call him. After many months I arrived at the answer. Armed with the decision, I came home—home to Hadenthorne. . . ." William's voice caught, and his eyes began to fill with tears. "And my answer was not good enough, for the two people I came home for are gone. God has neatly removed them from my life."

William sniffled and sipped at the drink. "Is that the response of a fair and just God?"

Joshua did not remain silent for more than a moment. "You came back with an answer of your own makin', Mr. Hawkes. God's answer may not be as tidy as you imagined."

Will sat silent now, and in a few minutes his eyes drooped, and he was softly snoring as he lay against the muddy cart's wheel.

"Dear Lord above," Joshua prayed in a quiet, honest voice. "Please be watchin' over Mr. Hawkes. I beseech thee to help him acknowledge that thy answer must have been no."

41

May 1640
Hadenthorne, Devon
England

William was awake at the first dawn. Roosters from the nearby Brown farm had just begun to call. He stretched, painfully and slowly, and rose to his feet. His head throbbed, and he felt a most unsettled feeling in his gut. Joshua, asleep under a worn blanket, was curled up near the cold fire.

William quietly walked the few paces to the river and looked about. Red clouds, dead level at their flat bottoms, their tops ragged and loose to the skies, slid by, following the winds like vast ships sailing over a gray and awakening landscape. He saw no other movement, so he removed his shirt, breeches, drawers, socks, and shoes and lowered himself into the cold water. He dunked under and gently washed at the tender bruise on his forehead.

What a stupid man I have become. To let a foolish young girl and a foolish old man vex me so. It is a fine thing that they have gone. I will be able to go on with my life without them—perhaps better now that I have no encumbrances here in Hadenthorne.

He splashed more water in his face and then snapped his head back and forth, like a dog shedding water. He stopped short. *How much that hurts. I think I will let the sun do the drying.*

He slipped back into his clothes, not minding the fact that he had no towel for drying. *A sailor gets used to wearing wet clothes for hours and days at a time. A few damp moments today,* Will mused, *shall prove no hardship.*

He walked back over to the fire and gently shook the shoulder of the sleeping Joshua. "Wake up, friend. We have little time to waste. I believe we both need get on the road to Weymouth this day. That town seems to hold both our destinies."

William stopped briefly at the public house and purchased a breakfast of cheese and bread for them both and then hired the son of the proprietor of the alehouse to run to the Cavendish home to fetch his bag and belongings.

"Tell Mrs. Cavendish I have found a friend who must return at once to Weymouth. I will write to her in care of the constable. Tell her that I would come myself but have urgent callings. Now run, lad, run!"

Will passed a small coin to the boy on his return with his leather bag, then mounted the small wagon and sat next to Joshua. With a flick of the reins, the mule stepped out, and they began their journey to Weymouth.

Weymouth, Dorset
England

By late afternoon of the second day they had arrived. To William's great surprise Joshua had made arrangements for portage of the mule and cart on ship as well as himself. He had stopped at a livery to purchase hay and oats for the mule's provisions during the voyage.

William walked with Joshua and his mule and cart to the *Plymouth Spirit*. He took a few moments to introduce him to Captain Blake and to ask that he be given special attentions as benefit a friend of a fellow sea captain.

"Captain, you say, Mr. Hawkes? I did not think there be but one captain aboard the *Artemisia,* and that be Captain Waring." Blake nudged Joshua in the side and smirked. "Or have you gone and mutinied on him?"

"No, although I have heard rumors that your crew has thought of the action on many voyages," Will replied.

Captain Blake looked hurt, then laughed and slapped him on the back, nearly knocking him to the ground. "Then the rumors I have heard be true? That you be buying the ship from the old dog Waring?"

William nodded and took Blake's extended hand in congratulations.

"Mr. Hawkes, I can tell a sharp sailor from a distance—and you are among the sharpest I have seen. 'Tis your killer instincts that may need honing, but you will soon learn the laws of the jungle."

"I trust that I will be an honorable captain," William stated firmly.

"Just not too honorable," Blake laughed, "for the honorable man gets the short end of most sticks. Oh, how I wish I could stay in port for just one more evening to celebrate with you—and perhaps plan a rendezvous or two."

Blake glanced over at Joshua, who was struggling to bring his very reluctant mule on board. The animal, his eyes wide with fear, was braying and scrabbling to gain a hoof hold on the slippery planking. Two crewmen were behind the mule, shoulder to haunch, giving it a shove toward the ship as Joshua pulled mightily on the reins.

"But, Mr. Hawkes, our celebration will have to be delayed. Your friend and his mule expect to get to the colonies in haste. And I promised a sailing this evening."

Captain Blake and the soon-to-be Captain Hawkes shook hands again and bid farewell.

So this is what it feels like to be a captain, Will thought. *Now all I need to do is visit with Captain Waring and settle on a purchase price.*

Will spent a few hours in the Hare and Hounds alehouse before heading to Captain Waring's home on the south side of Weymouth. He sat alone at a table overlooking the harbor and sipped at one weak ale for more than an hour.

He stepped out into the cool evening and watched the sun, a golden orange globe, drop into the steel-gray waters. He watched the *Plymouth Spirit* slip out of the calm harbor and for a moment saw it silhouetted against the sun, a composition of oranges, browns, reds, and purples that would shame most painters to stillness and mute the most wordy of poets.

For a moment the town was quiet. There was an absence of naval ships in harbor, and the public houses had not yet filled with revelers. When William stood just so, with his head craned to the water, he could hear the waves softly break against the rocky shore. William watched the sun, then sighed and made his way to the home of Captain Waring.

Broadwinds, Dorset
England

Kathryne's eyes snapped open and she struggled to focus her vision in the dark of the night. At last she was able to make out the familiar surroundings of her bedchamber in the faint light of the moon.

"I had the dream again," she said out loud in the stillness.

She closed her eyes again to see his exquisite face with its fathomless blue eyes as she lay alone, the warm spring breeze wafting in from the window her only caress. It was the dream of the man with the sandy hair. Kathryne sat up, her eyes wide, and gently, ever so gently, she touched her lip with her finger to see if a trace of his touch still remained.

Weymouth, Dorset
England

Captain Waring lived perhaps a mile south of Weymouth proper between the fort on the Bill of Portland and the harbor. Here, houses were not built cheek to jowl as in the town, but each modest cottage had a small garden and a stone fence or a row of shrubbery to separate it from its neighbors. It felt polite and civilized, each maintaining a dignified distance from the other.

After all the years at sea, I can understand why the old captain has looked for some elbow room, William thought.

His house, a sizable cottage, was bounded by rosebushes, and vines climbed and entwined over much of the stone facade in a green, leafy embrace. From a front window, the glow of a fire and lanterns spilled golden light into the tidy front garden. Captain Waring could be seen sitting by the fire, holding a pipe. At a dozen paces away, Will stopped short, for just a step.

This is what I thought I would have—had God not decided against me, he thought, feeling a strong sense of longing that seemed to cut to the core of his being.

Captain Waring greeted him warmly, inviting him in and calling out for his wife. "Alicia, please come down and meet the good Mr. Hawkes."

From an upper room—perhaps a bedchamber, Will imagined—Alicia descended the stairs. Will rose and turned to greet her, and his jaw dropped.

Will had expected a more matronly woman to emerge, as a visual counterpoint to the gruff, whiskery old sea captain. But the form that descended into the lit room from the darkness above was quite another matter. Alicia was young—perhaps no more than twenty and five summers old—and her eyes possessed a sleepy fire that Will felt more than saw. She was wearing a loose-fitting flannel dress that merely hinted at her form, but the hint was broadly taken. She extended her hand to William and smiled, her lips parting slowly and fully.

Although he was unsure of the reason, William's face reddened, and he stammered, "Good evening," as he took her firm hand in his. The longing he felt earlier became almost an ache.

"I am most pleased to meet the man who possibly holds the key to my husband's future, Mr. Hawkes. I trust you are here to discuss a way to allow your good captain to remain in port for more than a temporary refitting," she said, an evocative huskiness to her voice.

"Yes. . . . Yes I am, Mrs. Waring."

"Alicia," Captain Waring asked, "would you be so kind as to fetch us all a slight libation this evening? We will be in the parlor."

She turned to her husband and smiled. "Of course. Please, Mr. Hawkes, make yourself at home," she said, and walked slowly, with considered steps, to the kitchen.

Captain Waring must have noticed William's stare following his young and quite comely wife.

"I know that it seems unusual for an old goat such as myself to be paired with such a beautiful slip of a girl, but I do not challenge God's provision. She journeyed to Weymouth from York seven years prior as an indentured servant bound to a planter in Virginia. Her own family had lost three members due to the shortages in the north, and she saw this as her only way to a better life. I could not bear such a beautiful thing as her to be used as a mere tool by a rough farmer, so I bought her contract and asked for her hand. She acquiesced, and we have been man and wife since."

He ushered William into the well-furnished parlor and in a low, whispered voice added, "Now you also understand my desire to expedite a sale of the *Artemisia*? With how many more years will the Lord bless me and give me the health and strength to keep up with my young wife?" He snickered. "I would prefer to spend them here in the warmth of Alicia's arms rather than on a cold ship with the likes of you."

With that he laughed loudly and pulled up two stools around a small desk and extracted a sheaf of papers from a locked drawer.

"Mr. Hawkes," the captain said formally, "I am prepared to sell you the vessel bearing the registry of the *Artemisia* and sailing under the flag of England for the total price of . . ." He hesitated, watching William's face carefully. ". . . Seventy-five hundred pounds sterling."

William showed no emotion to the number. He stroked his chin and sat silent for many moments. "Sir, it is almost a fair offer, but since I am intimately acquainted with the needs of repair and refitting on the vessel, I would call a more accurate price to be twenty-five hundred pounds."

With that he sat back and waited, his face still.

This volley and serve of price and counteroffer continued for a full hour and was ended by Captain Waring pondering an offer and announcing loudly, "That be the price, Mr. Hawkes. That be the price."

William knew that his funds would not begin to cover the true cost of a ship like the *Artemisia*. It would be purchased on credit, although the sum of one thousand pounds, which William was prepared to advance to the captain, was a substantial sum.

"I accept your initial payment of a thousand pounds, William. I will not ask for your entire investment, for I know you will need capital to purchase provisions and supplies for your first voyage."

Captain Waring had had his barrister draw up a bill of sale and a contract for future payments. He inked in the agreed-upon amounts in the blanks provided. If William proved a shrewd trader, he might have the purchase price paid in full within a dozen voyages to the colonies of the Antilles.

"Captain Waring, I do have one further proposition to put before you this evening. I wish to make use of your sterling reputation and keen knowledge of the shippers and traders who have need of a vessel such as the *Artemisia*. Would you have interest in executing a role as a business agent for the ship? I will pay you a percentage of each cargo, in addition to the agreed-upon payments, of course, for the business that you arrange in my absence at sea."

Captain Waring pondered for a moment. "That is a capital idea, Mr. Hawkes. It will give me an activity to busy myself with and will provide a few extra shillings as well. Now let us have a drink to celebrate and seal the pacts. Alicia, would you bring in the fine port, please," the captain called.

As she arrived with the port and two glasses on a pewter tray, the two men became silent again, her image stilling all conversation as she poured each glass full.

"To the *Artemisia*," Captain Waring toasted, extending his glass high.

"To the *Artemisia*," William echoed.

One week later, as the new Captain Hawkes was hanging from the yardarm of the *Artemisia*, helping refit the sails of the mizzenmast on ship, Captain Waring came aboard.

"William, we have a part of your first cargo," he called.

William danced expertly down the rigging and leaped the last few yards. Captain Waring passed the papers to him—five sheets of a shipping manifest agreement.

"And what might we be shipping?" asked William, thumbing through the papers. "A consignment of windows and furniture to the governor's estate on Barbados, authorized by a K. Spenser."

William looked back up at his old mentor. "Captain Waring, I believe we are in business."

CHAPTER

42

June 1640
The Atlantic Ocean

William awoke in strange surroundings. He blinked his eyes a few times, adjusting them to the pale light. There was a dark brown felt curtain next to the bed, a few inches from his face. Almost fearfully, he parted it, exposing the room to the brilliant sunlight.

How many times will I be shocked that I have risen in the captain's quarters? William thought as he swung from his prone position and splashed cold water on his face from the basin at the foot of the bed. *It has been almost two weeks now, and every morning I awake with a start. Will I ever be fluent at being a captain so that my actions overcome the fear I have inside?*

William drew the curtain back and tied it, allowing the bed to receive a dose of fresh sea air. Will knew that most medical practitioners of the day viewed sea air as a negative medium, full of ill humors and disease. But to William the salt air was a natural tonic, invigorating and refreshing.

He dressed in a thin cotton shirt and light wool breeches. He thought a moment, then put on a red captain's coat, now beginning to fray at the cuffs and collars. It was the very coat that Captain Waring wore as a symbol of his office. He had left it in his closet for William's use—or perhaps as a reminder.

Even though I choose not to be a haughty leader, it is in my best interests to dress more the part. Besides, there is still a chill in the air. Perchance as we draw closer to the Canaries, the air will warm.

Will walked up to the quarterdeck casually chewing on a few biscuits and some cheese.

Johnny Delacroix, who had stayed on and became the ship's second-in-command, saw him emerge from the shadows of the lower decks and smartly saluted. "Top of the mornin', Captain Hawkes."

William returned the salute. "And a good morning to you as well, Mr. Delacroix."

Scanning the horizon, William saw nothing but the pale blue sky in all directions.

"The sky is not near pungent enough—the blue not thick enough—to hold this spell of clear sailing," Delacroix stated.

Griffin Edwards, the helmsman, nodded, as did William. Such a thin sky often augured a spell of squalls and rain. A thick, intense blue most often foretold of a day of clear, strong sailing.

William said quietly, "Navigator, what be the course for today?"

The new navigator, Ian St. Clair, brought up his charts. He was a hefty lad from the north York moors, with a full head of bright red hair. His last posting had been under His Majesty's service in the Indian Ocean.

"I reckon we be here, Captain, and if the winds aloft hold steady, we may reach the landfall of the Canaries by dusk."

William looked at the familiar charts, traced their route line with his finger, and nodded. The charts were first-rate and carefully prepared, but William withheld his smile. *Captain Waring always acted as if he expected excellence from me—and would not tolerate less—and I believe that I need do the same.*

The crew was all but identical to that of Captain Waring's. Will had lost three sailors to illness, and another five joined other ships with longer routes and the chance of higher rewards.

"Admirable job, Mr. St. Clair. We should be in the Antilles in good time," Will noted.

The weather held for the next two weeks, although rain and a heavy squall occurred three days out from Barbados. The winds were light, and the wave chop was modest.

The ship slipped into Bridgetown harbor on the evening of June thirtieth, a full week ahead of schedule.

The crew had gathered around the mainmast as they dropped anchor. Most bowed or dropped to their knees to offer a prayer of thanksgiving for a safe crossing. Even Mr. Delacroix said, "The day a man becomes a sailor is the day he learns to pray."

Navigator Ian St. Clair usually led prayer time aboard ship, a meeting that William seldom attended but encouraged others to do so.

To Mr. Delacroix, William had confided, "I will not be a hypocrite and pray to a God that cruelly takes parents from children and dashes the dreams of men so cavalierly."

"I agree with you, sir," Mr. Delacroix had said, "but I daresay many of the crew find the activity a blessing and would turn hostile if you tampered with the practice."

As the anchor splashed into the warm harbor waters, St. Clair prayed loudly, his voice filling the quiet harbor. "We thank thee, our most high Lord, for a blessed voyage and a safe crossing. We thank thee for all thy providence and provision, and ask that thou will continue to watch over thy children and obedient servants. Amen."

The rest of the crew mumbled "Amen," some crossing themselves silently.

William walked to the mast and grabbed hold of a swifting line and tackle, pulling himself up, a head above the crew. In a loud voice he addressed them.

"Men, I want to thank you for your help in making this a quick crossing. We will be in this port for two weeks, sailing on the favorable tide on the morning of the fourteenth of July. If this ship crosses back to England with the same quickness as our voyage here, I would predict a substantial reward to all."

The men cheered at the prospect of an extra reward share. Some were cheering as well for the extra week in port. It would be time to drink with their friends and spend their time and money in the taverns and brothels of Bridgetown.

"The standard leave policy will be in force. The afternoon watch may leave the ship at any time."

And with that dismissal, a third of the crew ran to lockers and began lowering the longboats to row into town.

"Will you be goin' to town tonight, Captain Hawkes?" asked Delacroix.

"Not this evening. I will take out the dress doublet and breeches and make a call on the new governor in the morning. After all, I do have a letter for him—and his windows—in my hold."

1 June 1640
Broadwinds, Dorset
England

My Dear Father,
How I miss you and Uncle Radcliffe! It has been only a year since you sailed off, and yet it seems as a lifetime. I wonder, do you ever

plan on returning to England? Or has your blood so thinned by the hot winds that a return is not foreseeable?

I trust that these windows will arrive in an unbroken state. I was told that there is a new captain commanding the ship called the *Artemisia* and that he and the crew are the finest in all of England and the Antilles. I will wait with bated breath until Uncle Radcliffe assures me that all panes arrived with no damage to them and all are installed at Shelworthy. (What a lovely name!)

I have disturbing news to report from Lady Emily. The Parliament that met in April dissolved in May after just three short weeks in session. The House of Commons refused to vote into law the huge subsidies King Charles demanded, and several members were sent to the gaol. It was even rumored that an apprentice was hanged, though there be no hard news of such. There was a great disturbance over Bishop Laud's reassertion of the position and nature of the altar in churches and the imposition of the Etcetera Oath on the clergy. Imagine, requiring them to pledge to accept the government of the Church as presently established. The Scots, never noted for placid temperaments, have had their ire further inflamed by these heavy-handed attempts by Charles to ensure allegiance. It is rumored that the Scots will invade if a negotiated solution proves unsuccessful. I am so troubled to hear of the anger and pain that these issues have caused within the body of Christ. I would pray that as Christians we could work out differences, no matter how large or small. Such diversions and distractions appear to be simply the work of man and not part of the Almighty's plan.

I have been speaking to Reverend Pensworth, and his calm assurance that you have only the best interests for me in mind as you speak of suitors and betrothals is comforting. I wish I could pry more information on this Geoffrey Foxton from you. As a man, you seem to speak a different tongue than do gentlewomen. I ask for a description and you respond, but I must admit that in no manner am I better informed than before I asked!

Is he an honorable man? Do you honestly perceive that he possesses the qualities of a Christian husband? Does he love our Lord? Does he laugh easily?

Can you answer these questions for me, Papa? Will you try?

I remain,

> *Your obedient daughter,*
> *Kathryne*

Before she closed the envelope, she picked up her pen and nearly added to the last paragraph of the letter, *And what color are his eyes?* But she just smiled to herself, thinking of the dream, and gently sealed the flap instead, an intriguing warmth washing over her.

43

July 1640
Barbados

"This is most uncomfortable," John Delacroix called out, lifting himself from the saddle, his feet firmly anchored in the stirrups. He reached back and rubbed his haunches. "How the nobility do this for pleasure is most odd indeed."

William laughed, then stretched as well. "My friend, it uses muscles that we have not trained."

The pair had rented horses to ride to the Carruthers plantation in order to collect a shipping debt owed from a previous sailing. Since it had lapsed and the usury escalated, a tidy profit was garnered and the reward was doubled. Sir Peter Carruthers had no ready cash to settle the owing and was forced to offer them a percentage of his soon-to-be-harvested sugar crop.

The ride back from the plantation was slower, hotter, and dustier. They rode from the Carruthers estate, which sat on a high plateau, down a steep ridge, across the St. George Valley, and now traveled along a dusty lane. Along the lane, the jungle reached to their sides, not yet cleared save for the roadway. Clinging and tangling vine tendrils reached out of the dense greenness, scraping and pulling at their arms and faces.

It's only a matter of time, Will thought, *until this too becomes sugar and tobacco fields.*

"Does it take a different temperament to be a farmer?" John asked several moments later as they rode past a green field of young tobacco plants. "It would seem to me that the life of a farmer would be that of constriction and utter dependence on the whims of the weather."

The horses clipped along, their hooves sounding muffled in the thick red dust of the road. The sun was hot, but fortunately the road dipped under scores of majestic tamarind trees along the way and out of the sun.

"It is similar to that of a sailor. We are both dependent on what God brings us—wind, rain, sun. We both remain tied to a small piece of real estate—the farmer to his land, and the sailor, his ship."

John nodded as William continued, softer now, in a smaller, quieter voice. "I almost became a farmer, Mr. Delacroix. If the woman I loved had waited for me, I would instead be behind a horse such as this, plowing a field in Hadenthorne."

"Is that true? I would have never guessed such a thing, Captain Hawkes, for you've kept your private life most private from us all."

The two paused by a small stone wall under a large canopy of almond trees that offered cooling shade.

"Was the woman beautiful?" John asked.

William pursed his lips and closed his eyes as if trying to remember Missy's features, which were always hovering near the edge of his thoughts.

Without opening them, he replied, "She was the most lovely creature in all of Devon. Full red lips, golden hair that curled and flowed about her face, a quick smile, and hearty laugh—and a wonderfully firm and endowed frame. She was quite beautiful."

"I do not wish to be bolder than I should, Captain Hawkes, but if I may, what happened to her? Why are you not a farmer? Sounds most like a woman I would have sacrificed everything in order to gain."

Will opened his eyes to the brilliant sun, blinked, and stared off to the western horizon. "She did not wait. I was undecided as to a life at sea or a life at the plow. I was prepared to purchase land and marry her—instead I purchased the *Artemisia* and therefore am sitting beside you now, Mr. Delacroix. Your company is pleasant, but not nearly as pleasant as hers."

John smiled. "Is she still in Hadenthorne? Was it difficult to face her when you last returned?"

William picked up a small stone from the dust and tossed it absently into the field of gently swaying tobacco plants. "No. She married an old friend, and the pair of them moved to Virginia to farm land there."

"Do you know where, exactly?"

"It is on the coast, a town by the name of Jamestown."

"Well, Captain, Jamestown is not that far. Perhaps we may visit there one voyage?" John replied.

Will pondered that for a moment, as if the idea had never crossed his mind. Then he smiled.

"Radcliffe, I am so glad to have you returned. I have the most wonderful news to report."

Radcliffe had just entered the room and was fanning himself with his large straw planter's hat. As was his custom, he had donned a waistcoat and breeches, with a white shirt and a cravat as well. His one concession to the weather was the broad-brimmed straw hat he purchased from an African slave on a nearby plantation.

"Aidan, why are these windows closed? Does not the sun bake me to a red-enough crisp while outdoors that I have to be baked in here as well?" Radcliffe fussed with the window latch and opened it, catching a slight afternoon breeze. They had rented rooms from Lord and Lady Wycliffe until Shelworthy was complete.

Lord Aidan stood and lowered the window back again. "Lady Wycliffe is sure that the sea breeze is the cause of her chilblains and her husband's gout. I will not upset our hosts any more than we have already."

Radcliffe slumped in a chair and increased his fanning speed. "Then, dear brother, tell me this supposed good news and let me return to your unfinished Shelworthy, where it is hopefully cooler by a substantial degree."

The earl shuffled through a stack of papers and extracted a single copy. He held it out toward Radcliffe. "Do you know what this is?"

Radcliffe sighed and let his hand holding the hat drop to his side and brush at the floor. "Dearest brother. I am hot. I have spent the morning arguing with the most incompetent land foreman, setting up the sugar mill. Our Dutch advisors must be from a very patient lineage to endure him. And this afternoon I have stopped at Shelworthy to inquire as to the final finishes and found no one there, save a few blackamoors who were sleeping in the drawing room of all places. It seems as the good Mr. Prudhome has started a second—or third—project. And now, after a long and dusty ride back to his jungle-hot rented office, my dear brother wants to play guessing games with me. I do not care what that paper is, nor do I wish to guess. Just tell me, Brother, before I do something rash."

The heat seemed to affect everyone. Some it made lazy and slow. For others it dulled the senses. And for still others it built a powerful thirst no beverage would slack. Radcliffe seemed to be energized in a negative, cruel way by the heat.

Lord Aidan sat down and calmly stated, "This is the bill of lading for the windows and furniture for Shelworthy. It has all arrived in total. It all came in a fine, unbroken state."

Radcliffe leapt out of the chair and tossed his straw hat in the air, bouncing it off the ceiling with a soft rustle. "This is most marvelous news! Yes! Yes! Most bloody and totally marvelous!"

He took Lord Aidan's hand, shook it, and slapped him on the back, a most uncharacteristic display of filial affection. "Have you arranged shipping to the estate? Is anyone supervising the off-loading? Have you sent word to Mr. Prudhome? Did you pay for the transit? Have you heard from our dear Kathryne?"

Lord Aidan smiled widely and wiped the perspiration from his forehead and lip. "Yes to all your questions, Radcliffe. I have actually spoken to Mr. Prudhome not more than an hour previous, and he assures me that we will be ensconced in Shelworthy in no more than a week from today. A livery crew has been sent to the harbor, and I had hoped we would both go and supervise the delivery."

Radcliffe bowed to his brother, in a mock salute.

"Praise be to our Lord for secure shipping, dear Radcliffe. I am grateful for his wise and careful protection of our possessions."

"Yes, Aidan, praise be to God. This was a day I have spent praying about for months."

And as Lord Aidan offered his praises, he knew that only one brother truly meant the offer of thanksgiving.

<hr />

The sun was high and hot as William and Johnny Delacroix walked closer to Bridgetown. They were leading their horses, as both men were suffering from the soreness that afflicted infrequent riders and which made for painful riding. Their progress was slow and deliberate, for the heat in the island's valleys was indeed more energy sapping than the heat on the ocean.

They stopped often in the shade and drank from the flagons of ale they had brought with them. Less than two miles from port, they stopped again.

"One last time," William gasped.

"Agreed," John replied. "It is curious. I am too sore to ride, and it is too hot to walk. It is a most unpleasant dilemma."

"If we rest just this one more time, we can make port by late afternoon. I have forgotten that riding a horse is an activity that one builds up a tolerance to. We should have arranged a carriage instead."

"Agreed. I will remember that for the next visit."

As they sat, a group of slaves were working in the field just next to the road. They were mostly naked in the sun; the men wore nothing more than crude linen loincloths or drawers, and the women wore smocks or skirts and top wrappings that preserved varying degrees of their modesty. None wore hats or shoes. A white overseer watched from a distance as they moved along the rows of tobacco, hoeing and cultivating the ground. The laborers looked fevered and hot, and their sweaty faces were stained with the red dust of the fields, their sweat etching lines in that dust, giving them painted, primitive visages.

As he passed close by, William called to a middle-aged black man in Yoruba. He had a smattering knowledge of the tongue, and the man, by his sharp features, looked to be of that African tribe from the Slave Coast, perhaps Dahomey.

The elderly man looked up, in great distress and puzzlement.

William thought he had understood and waved his arm. Perhaps the poor slave could not see well. "Over here," Will called in the native language.

"Who be sayin' that?" the slave called back in Yoruba. "This must be voodoo 'cause no white massa knows this way of speakin'."

William knew he was stumbling over the words and tenses, but realized that the frightened slave was not an educated man who would quibble with his grammar.

"Some white men do," he called. "What's your name?"

"I was named Luqua, but the massa, he call me Lucky."

"Luqua—what does that mean?"

"It mean 'healer.'"

"Can you heal sickness?"

"With the right plants and the right spirits."

"I will remember you, Luqua. If I ever need healing, I will call for you."

"Massa, I . . . I want to go. Can you take me. . . ?"

There were a few phrases Will had never heard, and as he was preparing to ask what they meant, the white foreman came over. He had a long mahogany staff in one hand and was wearing a single flintlock pistol. The pistol, showing slight signs of rust along the barrel, appeared to be loaded. The foreman's linen shirt was dark with a foul mix of dirt and sweat, and his face was darkened further by several days growth of beard, also stained by dust and perhaps by tobacco juices. He stood and stared at the two sailors, peering at them down his nose.

"Who might you be?"

"William Hawkes, captain of the *Artemisia*. And this is Mr.

Delacroix, my second-in-command. And yourself, good sir, who might you be?"

"I am John Gleeson, foreman for Master Carruthers. And I would be tellin' you true that it ain't wise to speak to them in their own language. It riles 'em up, makes 'em sort of crazy homesick."

"I meant no harm," Will said. His voice was neither pleasant nor warm, but had an edge. "And all I asked was his name."

"No matter to me, Mr. Hawkes, what you palavered about. But I don't want 'em getting riled up 'cause it just means I got to come down on 'em harder if they try to run."

He reached up and wiped at his beard with a greasy hand.

"And that happens often?" Will asked.

"Not so much—not with me here, that is," Gleeson said, patting his pistol.

"Excuse me, Mr. Gleeson, but if you work for Master Carruthers, isn't that a long way from the estate to walk every day to tend the fields? We have just completed business with your master and must admit that the long walk in this heat is most taxing."

Gleeson laughed. "Who says we be goin' home at nights? I stay in that tent over by the stand o' trees there. And as for the darkies, well, they be happy curlin' up on the ground. It what's they be used to back home, as me understands it."

Will looked over at Luqua. His sad eyes and prematurely bent frame indicated that perhaps it was not what they were used to back home.

William stood up, brushed at the seat of his trousers, and took the reins of his horse. "It was a pleasure to meet you, Mr. Gleeson. Perhaps we will see you again."

Will turned and walked a few steps, then called back a short sentence, over his shoulder, to the slave in Yoruba. Then to the foreman he added, "I merely said good-bye, Mr. Gleeson. A simple good-bye."

━ ━ ▪ ▪

Later that evening, after Radcliffe and Lord Aidan had spent the afternoon watching sailors and the local livery team load up several wagons of windows and furniture for Shelworthy, Radcliffe had excused himself from Lord Aidan's request to supper.

Radcliffe took his leave and hurried across the harbor road and down toward the small military garrison at the southern reach of town. The Crown had authorized a contingent of fifty naval marines to be housed at the new fort. It was important to those noblemen in London that their shipping interests be guarded and that the Spanish be prevented from looting the island. Fifty men were not nearly enough for the task, but it was a sufficient start.

It was the conventional wisdom that a seaborne attack was unlikely on Barbados, and Radcliffe agreed with that assessment. But there was another, more sinister reason that he viewed the marines as a clear and present advantage. Radcliffe often whispered to himself that those in control of the militia would be in control of the island, regardless of what the Crown or the governor might say.

And such a comfort, Radcliffe thought, *to be the commander of such a loyal garrison.*

Upon reaching the garrison, Radcliffe rapped at Colonel Westland's small hut with a hushed tap.

"Who is it!" rumbled a harsh bellow from behind the closed door.

"Radcliffe Spenser," he replied and heard the squeal of a lock being turned, and the door was slowly opened. He stepped into the shadowy room, blinking through the smoke, acclimating his eyes.

"Sit down, Lord Radcliffe. I was trusting that you had not forgotten our appointment."

"My dear Colonel, it would be most inopportune for me to overlook such a wise and cunning man as yourself. You hold a strategic position on this isle, and all would be wise to recognize the fact of your importance."

Some men have a weakness for drink, some women, Radcliffe thought. *The good colonel here has a weakness for flattery. I prefer his weakness—for it costs me much less.*

"Thank you for your kind attention, Lord Radcliffe. It would do most settlers here a good turn if they realized that it is the garrison that keeps them safe and is enabling them to be so successful."

Radcliffe pulled up a stool to the small plank table lit by a single candle, flickering in the thick, stale air.

"And the progress on the fort, Lord Radcliffe? I see that you have sent your laborers to finish the seawall. Is it all on schedule?"

"It is. And now my question to you: Did you meet the captain of the *Artemisia?* I am most curious to know how he reacted to our surcharge on the standard tariff and docking fees."

The colonel was the de facto harbormaster in the absence of a designated position. The governor had not yet waded through the flood of paperwork to create such a position; the depth of such paperwork and regulations was aided by Radcliffe, who sought to slow the affairs of state to suit his own needs.

"I did not assess him the extra," Colonel Westland calmly stated.

"What! It was agreed that we start our surcharge scheme on this date!" Radcliffe cried.

"Lord Radcliffe, I know that you value our partnership because I have a well-honed set of wits, as you stated yourself on many occasions. I chose not to announce our new taxing plan to this captain, for I knew he was heading straightaway to the governor himself. It would do us no good to have our operation nipped in the bud, as they say."

Radcliffe sat back in his chair. "Colonel Westland, I am amazed. I forgot for a moment how very dodgy you are. You are most correct, and I was in error. You have done the right thing in being so discreet. I commend your wise decision."

The colonel smiled and nodded.

He simply exists on flattery, Radcliffe thought, amused. "Tomorrow is a day soon enough to start our enterprise, Colonel Westland. Tomorrow is soon enough."

CHAPTER

44

July 1640
Barbados

The crystal pitcher, filled with "island punch"—a potent mixture of island rum, sugar, spices, and fruit juices—left a watery ring on the fine Honduran mahogany table as the vessel sweated in the afternoon. Lord Charles Carrington noticed the liquid seep onto the table and snapped his fingers for a servant. "Doily, here," he barked, pointing at the pitcher.

A few English planters of Barbados, such as Carrington, had learned how to distill molasses—a residue of the sugar curing process—into the potent drink with its sweet and burnished taste. Lord Carrington, a planter from the St. James Parish of the island, had invited Lord Aidan to dine with him and his wife and sample his newly fermented rum.

"So, Lord Charles. How does your plantation fare this season?" Lord Aidan inquired.

"Well, Governor, the cane that you see in the fields now was planted last September and December. That puts our harvesttime from January to April next."

"And you expect a large yield?" Lord Aidan asked.

"Perhaps a ton of sugar per acre, and we need employ one laborer for each acre. 'Tis a fair return on the investment. And instead of oxen for the grinding mills, those clever Dutch tell me that windmills are well suited to this island. It seems our low-lying hills catch both sea and land breezes," Lord Carrington replied.

"And windmills will increase production?"

"Well, of course. 'Tis a most promising prospect, as I was sharing with Radcliffe a few days previous. Using the Dutch techniques, I can plant my newly gained acreage and still maintain the schedule the cane processing requires. You see, Governor, the cane—once cut—must be crushed immediately or its sugar declines. And the juice, once ex-tracted, must be boiled within a few hours, or it begins to ferment. The windmills run themselves, night as well as day. And if I furnish the windmills with fireplaces for night illumination—why, it's day and night production." He took another sip of the punch.

"So does the taste of the rum please you, Lord Aidan?" asked Lady Carrington, a note of flirtation in her voice.

"I have never been much a fancier of spirits, my lady, however this does have an interesting flavor which I am hard-pressed to define," he answered politely, but added in his thoughts, *And I am hard-pressed to discern how this flavor could be causing such a demand here and abroad.* Taking the smallest sip on his drink, Aidan kept his face a mask of civility, masking the urge to grimace.

Following was a drawn-out feast of seven courses; the trio, trailed by three servants, entered the still air of the formal drawing room for drinks. The meal was quite elaborate, with oysters, olives and bacon, roast pork, mutton, and braised fowl, accompanied by potato pudding, custards, cream puffs, and fruit with a half-dozen varieties of strong drink to wash it all down. The more successful a planter became, noted Aidan, the more elaborate the dinners became. On the small island there was little else to spend one's entertainment resources on, so the midday dinners—the largest meal of the day, which began between noon and two o'clock—became more theater and status than simple nourishment, despite the fact that the hour was very hot for heavy eating in the Indies. Such gastronomic activity was oft followed by hours of drinking, smoking, and gossip.

Lord Carrington unbuttoned his wool waistcoat, loosened his cravat, and was about to unbuckle the belt of his breeches when a cough and stern look of reproach from his wife halted his activities.

Lord Aidan wondered why the man insisted on wearing the woolen garments of their homeland rather than adopt a mode of dress more suitable to the climate of the island as he had, switching to more lightweight linens and cottons.

"That was quite a meal," Aidan said in his most polished political manner. "Most inventive menu and preparation."

Lady Carrington beamed as she labored with a most diminutive fan to create a tiny breeze against her face and neck and down the skin left bare by her daring bodice. She fixed her eyes on his and replied, "Why, thank you so much, Governor. We do try our best to create a little bit of England on this foreign—and sultry—island."

"And you have succeeded well," he complimented her politely.

Lord Carrington offered a pipe to Lord Aidan, which he refused, and then took one himself. An attendant slave quickly appeared and filled it with tobacco. He puffed several times, and the smoke settled halfway up the room, held down by the heat near the ceiling. He patted his stomach absentmindedly.

"More punch?" Lady Carrington asked Aidan, bending just a bit too close and deep as she offered him the drink.

"No, thank you, my lady."

"So, Lord Aidan, how goes the governor's estate? I hear that your windows and furniture arrived?"

"Yes, they have, and we are in the process of moving our personal items from the Wycliffe residence to the house. The contractors have promised that within a fortnight, we will be able to host our first dinner party—an event I have looked forward to since my arrival."

"And then, Lord Aidan," bubbled Lady Carrington, "you will be sending for your daughter. I understand that a certain Mr. Foxton is most anxious. Best be done soon, for he is, without question, the choicest suitor in all the Antilles."

Aidan gaped at the woman. *How can news of such things travel so quickly? I have never made this common knowledge!*

Lady Carrington smiled coyly. "Do not be surprised, Lord Aidan. This is a small island, after all. There are very few secrets here."

"And even fewer worth knowing—or better yet, worth keeping!" guffawed Lord Carrington. As he laughed, great snorts of smoke erupted from his nose and mouth, and he began coughing as well.

Aidan smiled. "No doubt my daughter will visit us here, but I will not send for her quite yet. We still have no formal church and no school—and I think she would like to participate in instruction at a school, for she has been well-read and instructed in many areas."

Lady Carrington groaned. "But that may be a whole year—if not more—until she would deign come. Do you truly think Mr. Foxton, no doubt a man possessing a certain degree of . . . virility, will wait such an interminable time?" she asked, blushing.

"Lady Carrington, allow me to share with you a serious matter. Perhaps you may shed some understanding," Aidan said slowly.

The woman leaned forward, expectantly. Being asked advice was a novel experience for her, especially from someone so important and attractive as the new governor.

"You have been on this island for three years, am I correct?"

She nodded.

"And I have been here but a much shorter time. But in that time I have felt a degree of dismay that the planters here take a sort of pride in, as they say, living beyond the line. Are you familiar with that term?"

"Yes. It is well known to all of us."

"I am dismayed when I see the proper, civilized morality and conduct of sound Christian men and women so deliberately flouted. As with heavy drink, immorality, and other, even more unspeakable acts."

Lady Carrington tried her best not to blush again, for she knew of—and had occasionally been a participant in—such activities.

"It was not so back in England, and I am praying that this conduct is simply a matter of this island and its inhabitants existing under a previous governor who set no rules and saw no need for encouragement of proper, Christian activities and manners."

Both Lord and Lady Carrington raised their eyebrows, almost in unison, as if considering a new and novel concept. The attendant slave reappeared, sensing it was time that Lord Carrington's pipe needed refilling.

Lord Aidan continued, "I am praying that God will send additional numbers of churchmen and clergy upon this island and that the construction of proper church buildings will be what is needed to stem the tide of immoral and lascivious behavior among some planters. Do you think that my perception may prove true? I would hate to send for my innocent daughter Kathryne and expose her to such iniquity."

Lord Carrington nodded vigorously and laughed, "Well, a few more padres cannot hurt, can they? I say bring 'em on, and perhaps we'll all get holier."

Lady Carrington scowled. "Do not pay attention to him, Lord Aidan, for he has inherited a boorish streak from his family."

Her husband glared at her through unfocused eyes. She smoothed the fabric of her gown in her lap, allowing a silence to fall, hoping to reduce the tension in the room, as well as in her own heart.

After a few moments, she soberly pronounced, "You are right. More clerics will help. Perhaps they may bring a degree of English sensibility to this hot and torrid island."

A second, expectant hush settled on the room.

"But, Lord Aidan, how long will you wait?" she asked. "I mean, . . . that is, it is apparent that Mr. Foxton cannot be expected to tarry forever. Remember, eighteen months is a long period for any man."

And with that she looked directly at him, with a most brazen thought held behind her nearly closed eyes, but left unspoken.

In a fortnight plus two days, the *Artemisia* sailed from Bridgetown, its hold filled with raw sugar from the mill of Mr. Carruthers. William was conveying sugar without possessing a registered sugar license from London, a regulation set up to ensure that English tax collectors received their share of all cargoes—especially the valuable sugar cargo—from the Antilles.

It was not a complex matter to silence officials' inquiries. The governor was too busy to concern himself with simple shipping matters, and Colonel Westland, acting harbormaster, was all too happy to entertain Will's polite request—accompanied by an unofficial "honorarium"—that Westland personally handle such matters as official cargo inspections.

"What might you be hauling back to England, Captain Hawkes?" the colonel asked as he boarded Will's ship a day before sailing.

William and the colonel were alone on the quarterdeck, Will having given the crew a signal to depart quietly and quickly.

"Well, sir, it be nothing but simple agricultural products, some corn, and a few bales of tobacco. We will make port at several other islands to purchase other goods. Here is a copy of the manifest."

Will handed him a listing of all cargo, and sugar was not mentioned, despite the forty tons that rested belowdecks.

Tucked into a corner of a folded section of the list were two ten-pound gold sovereigns.

In a twinkling, the coins disappeared, just as the colonel was saying, "Everything here seems in order. I am authorizing you to set sail at your discretion."

The Caribbean Sea

Two weeks out of Barbados, after clearing the Antilles and racing through the Florida Channel ahead of a nasty summer storm, William awoke to cries of alarm from the crow's nest.

Running up the gangways with great dispatch, William grabbed the telescope that Mr. Delacroix handed to him.

"Over there!" Mr. Delacroix exclaimed as he pointed to the western horizon. "A set of sails at west southwest!"

Will focused his glass on the tiny speck perhaps three leagues off. Sailors were climbing the rigging with great haste, lowering every possible yard of canvas.

"Is it pirate or privateer, Mr. Delacroix?"

"We cannot be sure, Captain Hawkes. We know that as of sundown yesterday there was no ship behind us. Now there is. Perhaps word of our cargo was slipped to the wrong people?"

"Perhaps, Mr. Delacroix. Perhaps." William looked about the ship. "All sails lowered?"

"Aye, sir," Delacroix replied.

"Add a spar to the foremast," Will called. "Every inch of sail is needed."

He ran to the poop deck to face the winds that were coming from the southwest. It was a warm breeze, marking no hint of a storm. The skies were clear, and Will trusted that the breeze would hold until noon.

"Navigator!"

"Aye, sir!" cried Mr. St. Clair from the quarterdeck.

"Set our course ten more degrees to the east. This old ship sails best at broad reach from the wind."

"Aye, sir."

"Mr. Delacroix! Can you ascertain their speed or flag?"

"No, sir. She's still too distant. But I believe we have an edge in running speed."

"Mr. St. Clair!"

"Aye, Captain!"

William hesitated giving the next order. *Do I merely do this for impression? Do I think he will listen?*

"Mr. St. Clair, I think it would be proper to ask God for safety and protection. Do you not agree?"

"Aye, sir."

St. Clair quickly dropped to his knees, as did most of the crew, save Delacroix and William, who both maintained a vigilant eye on their pursuer.

"Almighty God," St. Clair prayed, "please keep us from harm. . . ."

The wind whipped much of the rest of the prayer from Will's hearing. *Perhaps this prayer will get through,* William hoped silently. *Perhaps Mr. St. Clair is more favored than I.*

And what began as a heart-stopping moment of terror ended with a whimper. As the sun rose, the winds settled a bit. The *Artemisia* sailed well in weak winds, for her hull rode nicely in the calmer water. By noon her pursuer was further behind. At dusk the waters in all directions were empty, save the *Artemisia.*

William ordered an increased watch that night and left all sails unfurled. It was wise, he thought, to continue putting as much distance between him and the other ship.

∎∎∎∎∎

Will had decided to sell the sugar in the Amsterdam market and thus avoid the high import duties if they docked first in Weymouth. It meant sneaking through the English Sea—either at night or by hugging the French coast—trying to avoid the English as well as the French authorities. Will had not come to the decision lightly, for it was serious breach of maritime law to do what he was proposing. He knew that his profits would near be doubled if the sugar reached Amsterdam untaxed. He also realized that he faced the gaols if discovered by an English ship. Mr. Delacroix, as well as Mr. Carruthers on Barbados, had argued strongly for a foreign sale. Will had been convinced.

If I make double my share, this ship becomes truly my own that much faster. And that is a good thing. I have been disadvantaged enough and have had my share of disappointments. So many other traders have done the same and gone on to glory and wealth. I see no overriding rationale why I should not do likewise.

The *Artemisia* entered the Amsterdam harbor at midnight on the twenty-first of July. As they lowered anchor, Will breathed a sigh of great relief.

How easy this has been, he thought. *And how nice the extra pounds will feel in my purse this evening. Perhaps I am becoming a true cutthroat businessman—and how coldly secure that feels.*

His mind kept saying, *All is well,* while his spirit was crying, *You are doomed.*

London, England

It was a simple letter of few lines, written with a bold, yet delicate pen.

Kathryne,
    Please come visit. I have most wondrous news.

Cecily

Kathryne had settled the most pressing matters at Broadwinds in quick fashion. Despite having visited London, Lady Emily, and Lloyd's only one month prior, she had heard so seldom from her friend Cecily that she attached great import to her request.

It was past noon of the second day of travel when Kathryne arrived at Cecily's elegant town house in Knightsbridge. Mr. Biesty held the door of the carriage and then ran to ring the front bell, all the time looking left and right. "Can never be too careful in this town, Lady Kathryne."

Kathryne smiled at his protection, overbearing as it could be at times. *It does feel nice to be looked after,* she thought as she waited for Cecily's butler to tend to the bell.

After a moment, the door opened, and Kathryne was escorted into the drawing room by the butler.

Kathryne took off her soft leather lace-trimmed gloves and walked about the room, examining the ornately framed paintings of the parents and grandparents of Cecily's husband. *Wesley comes from a very long line of dour-looking people,* Kathryne thought to herself, giggling silently.

The drawing room door opened a crack, and Cecily popped only her head into view. "Yoo-hoo!" she called gaily. "Kathryne!"

Kathryne turned and looked at the rounded face of Lady Cecily. *She has become weighty since we met last,* Kathryne noted. *And why does she not enter the room?*

"Are you ready for your first surprise?" Cecily chimed.

Surprise?

"Well?"

"I suppose I am, dear Cecily, but to be honest I have no idea of what you mean. And why are you hiding behind the door? Do come in so I may hug you."

Cecily giggled this time. "I will enter, but there may not be hugs."

Cecily walked into the room, and her stomach entered a half step before the rest of her frame.

How odd, Kathryne thought. *I have never known Cecily to be such a glutton.* Then Kathryne's eyes spread wide as plates. "Cecily! You are to be a mother!"

"Yes!" cried Cecily, and the two ran to each other, embracing awkwardly, Kathryne tentative for fear of threatening Cecily's condition.

Kathryne's eyes filled with tears as she took her friend by the hands.

"I know that a lady in this condition should remain in seclusion, but I just had to tell someone about this occasion," Cecily blurted.

"I am so overjoyed you did. I would have been disappointed beyond comprehension if you had kept this a secret from your dearest friend."

The two spoke until dinnertime concerning her progress, her emotions, her physical condition. It was apparent that she was quite thrilled, as was her husband, with the prospect of having an heir.

"I trust the child will not be quite as gloomy as his relatives hanging on the walls of this room," giggled Kathryne.

Cecily had half a biscuit in her mouth as Kathryne uttered this observation, and she almost collapsed in a fit of laughter, crumbs dribbling on the floor.

After the midday meal, Cecily had snacked on food all afternoon—biscuits, cheese, fruit, an herbal tea, a plum cake, petit fours, a Madeira rum loaf—so much food that Kathryne felt hard-pressed to match nibble for bite.

Then Cecily had taken Kathryne upstairs to the nursery, newly decorated for the upcoming event, where she displayed all the layettes for the expected child. Kathryne picked up one little white gown of the thinnest wool with delicate satin ribbon trimmings.

"Oh, Cecily—how sweet this will look on a baby!" she cooed.

"Well, we must have pretty things for the little one to wear over the swaddling bands," stated Cecily. Kathryne knew that long strips of cloth would be wound tightly around the newborn child for the first several months to help its limbs grow straight. "And it has a matching biggin," added Cecily as she showed Kathryne the tiny nightcap.

That evening, after supper had been served—an excellent gigot of lamb, of which Kathryne had but the smallest of portions—a quiet settled in the parlor where the two women sat. Cecily's husband, Lord Cheswick, was in York for a week attending to financial matters, and the two women had the room to themselves.

"Cecily, when I first arrived you spoke of this being your first surprise. Are there indeed others?" Kathryne inquired.

"There are indeed. Both are most intriguing, and I have been impatiently holding them in until you asked. But I do so much like talking of Baby."

Kathryne poured a small glass of sherry for them both.

"My second surprise has to do with our dear Celia," said Cecily as she nibbled on a marzipan confection.

"Surprising news from court, then?"

"Quite. It seems as though our dear Celia is now . . ."

"Now what? What?"

"Celia is . . . engaged to be married!"

"No!" cried Kathryne.

"It is true! And that is only the second of three surprises."

"And what could be more surprising than that?"

"She is betrothed to a perfectly splendid young man by the name of Maxwell Foxton, who just happens to have a dashing older brother named . . . Geoffrey!"

Poor Kathryne had trouble deciding on her response. It was a combination of shock, surprise, and amazement. And relief as well. Perhaps now she could find a bit more about this mysterious Geoffrey Foxton.

Cecily giggled and giggled as she told the tale of how Celia and Maxwell met—at Ascot during the horse racing season—and how Maxwell seemed to have tamed Celia's caustic tongue. Geoffrey's younger brother, Cecily explained, was a devilishly handsome man, and she produced a small miniature of his likeness to show Kathryne.

"It is said that the two brothers are most similar in looks and demeanor."

Kathryne carefully examined the painting, noting the strong jawline, the deep-set blue eyes, the abundance of chestnut hair, the engaging smile, and the sharp nose.

Are those the eyes of the man in my dream? she wondered.

45

August–December 1640
The Artemisia

Since anchoring the first time in the Amsterdam harbor, the *Artemisia* made two quick voyages between Weymouth and the Lesser Antilles. Each outbound trip saw them carry settlers, construction materials, foodstuffs, and metal tools to the island. On each return to Weymouth the ship returned empty, sneaking its sugar cargo into the Amsterdam harbor and selling it there, avoiding the English shipping regulations.

Despite their routine flouting of maritime law and the dangers it entailed, the crew had begun to idolize Captain Hawkes. He had proven a brave and fair captain, keeping them from harm on each sailing and rewarding them with almost double the going rate of pay. On two occasions he had outsailed a British naval ship, no doubt sent to forcibly impress members of his crew for the navy's use. He saw to it that the sailors' rations were the best that could be bought, and he even brought aboard a former schoolteacher to aid those who were interested in learning how to read and spell. He forbade gambling and fighting on board, often the scourge of a weak-spirited sailor. He encouraged the crew to attend prayer time, though he himself never attended.

They had yet to visit Charleston Harbor, with the weather or the urgency of the cargo preventing such a change in itinerary. Whether it be from pain or time's passing, Will never spoke of Missy Holender, who was now Missy Cavendish. He tried to keep his thoughts free from her as well.

But on each trip, William uttered a score fewer words to the crew, and when returning home from their unlawful destination of Amsterdam, he would sleep fitfully, if at all. Much of his time was spent on the forward decks, staring into the empty horizon of the sea.

Mr. St. Clair, at the end of each prayer gathering, would add—softly so Will would not hear, "And almighty God, please be with our captain and help soothe the pain he has in his soul."

1 December 1640
Barbados

Dearest Kathryne,

A brief note to let you know all is well here.

News has reached us of the Scots' invasion of the borders. Am I to believe the reports that the English army was routed by them at Newburn and that they also took Newcastle? Could it be that our forces are so inexperienced, so ill organized and ill supplied that this could happen? What do our business partners in London make of the whole thing? Do they feel it necessary to take any measures to secure any of our financial interests in light of these developments? The news we receive is so varied that one is hard-pressed to know what to believe. Some who arrive here on ships report business as usual. Others are doomsayers. I am concerned for your safety, above all. Please send word with the next sailing.

'Tis hard to believe that war could erupt within our own Commonwealth. I cannot blame the narrow dogmatism of Bishop Laud for this entire fiasco. Scotland has been slipping through King Charles's fingers ever since his accession. When the Church of Scotland entered this revolt against English domination, is it any wonder that King Charles mobilized the army? I say he was forced to consider the action—a reconquest of Scotland is the only manner in which to keep our country unified. All of that to say that I feared for many years that a peaceful future was but a dream. Perhaps it is well that we are considering Barbados as the permanent home of the Spenser family, if the situation worsens. I am told that Parliament has been called back into session and that Charles is to seek peace with the Scots.

We can only pray that God in his mercy will see fit to change the heart of the man in whom he has vested the governance of the people of England and that he will seek the will of the Almighty in his leadership.

I have received a most pleasant letter from Lady Emily with Yuletide greetings. I have responded in kind.

I send my love,
Papa

3 December 1640
Broadwinds, Dorset, England

Dearest Papa,

Happy Christmas! The lightest dusting of snow yesterday has put me in the mood for the holidays, and Mrs. Cole is already planning all her special delights. Lady Emily and I will have a quiet celebration.

I am safe, and all is well here. There has been little local trouble, and all business ventures seem unaffected by the current turmoil in Parliament.

Some startling turns of events to report, however. William Laud has been officially impeached as the bishop of London and has been imprisoned in the Tower for being the author of the disastrous intervention in Scotland. It is said that John Pym and other Puritan orators are convinced that a conspiracy had been formed by the king's ministers over the past two or three years, if not longer, to erect a despotism in England and return the nation to Rome. They again went so far as to identify the royal government with the antichrist and the devil!

Reverend Pensworth is, of course, elated at the prospect of clergymen being able to adopt or reject observances as they see fit, guided by the wills of their congregations rather than the will of the king, as Pym has been advocating. However, other respected leaders see this as the coming of religious anarchy and are calling it dangerous.

We must pray that our God will unite us and help us to see that the church remains *his* church and that mere mortals are not to be its head, but the Lord Christ. I take great comfort in the words of Saint Matthew, "Upon this rock I will build My church; and the gates of hell shall not prevail against it." Oh, Papa—why can't people just love God and love each other, as we are commanded to do first and foremost? That is the remedy for all the world's ills, is it not?

Amidst the confusion, I am aware of the peace we have as God's children and how thankful we must be for the precious gift of salvation as we celebrate Christmas—the coming of our Lord as human flesh to live among us and be our example, to die for our sins and be resurrected to conquer death. Our only hope is in the promise of eternal life!

Please send my good wishes to Uncle Radcliffe. Recently I have been impressed to pray for him all the more, that he also can fully

experience divine love and somehow be drawn closer to God. I shall
miss your presence at Christmas, as I do every day.

> *I send my fond love and affection,*
> *as does Lady Emily,*
> *Kathryne*

Christmas Eve 1640
Weymouth, Dorset
England

A weightless drizzle filled the salty air of Weymouth Harbor. Ship decks grew slick, and the water collected in the folds of furled sails. Gulls called out less in the cold rain, and the usual noises of the harbor were muted.

The crew of the *Artemisia* was completing the final preparations for yet another sailing to Barbados, with scheduled stops at St. Christopher and Nevis.

Herbert Dorling, the Weymouth harbormaster, at first was most puzzled when William's ship left port full and yet always returned empty. His curiosity was kept in check by a fresh ten-pound sovereign passed, unseen, from palm to palm each time William dropped anchor.

Captain Waring, who proved to be an excellent business manager for the *Artemisia,* had provisioned a third sugar mill to be shipped to the island, along with a full cargo of barreled meat, lightweight wool cloth, and furniture. Nearly at the last minute, Waring had contracted with the British navy to send a squad of fifty Royal Marines, which had been requested by the governor of Barbados and the Lesser Antilles to quell a native uprising on Antigua.

The military men, dressed in their red British uniforms, made a great display of loading their cases of muskets and shot. Dozens of barrels of gunpowder were brought aboard and stored in a far forward hold, well removed from any lanterns or fires on board.

It was nearing dusk, and the high tide was just beginning to recede. William and the crew had but a few minutes left to cast off ropes so as to catch the favorable sailing currents.

From the harbormaster's office along the pier, perhaps a quarter-league distance, William heard a muffled cry. He, as well as several of the crew, turned to face the sound. Dorling was seen, with a megaphone in his hand, shouting to delay any sailing of the *Artemisia*.

The game's up, thought William. *They have discovered our ruse and mean to arrest us. I suppose I knew that it would come to this. God's little plan of revenge, no doubt, on a poor man who is harming no one.*

William saw Dorling duck back inside and slam the window shut. A figure in a long black cassock and a wide-brimmed black hat slowly walked down the pier toward the ship. He carried a bulky leather bag over his shoulder and a shoulder-high wooden staff.

Will, now on the poop deck watching his progress, was greatly puzzled. *If it be a constable, it is the strangest one I have seen.*

"You there, on the pier," William called. "What is the nature of your call?"

The man called back, but William could not make out the words.

"Blessed injustice," William muttered and walked to midships and the gangboard between the pier and ship. William reached the top of the gangway at the same moment the stranger reached the bottom.

"What be your business here, stranger?" he asked.

"I seek passage on this ship for Nevis," he said. "I understand this is the fastest ship at sea, with the most skilled sailor at her helm—a Captain Hawkes, I believe."

William frowned. *Who was this person to speak so familiarly?*

The stranger tilted his head upwards, the fading sunlight illuminating his face. "Good evening, William. Are you not going to invite your old friend aboard?"

In front of a bewildered and reeling Captain William Hawkes stood none other than Vicar Thomas Mayhew.

"If this be your normal method of greeting paying passengers, I daresay that your mercantile skills need improving, lad," Vicar Mayhew said with a grin.

William was all but immobile at the top of the gangboard. When he finally took hold of his senses, he rushed down the narrow walkway in three steps and hugged the vicar fiercely, lifting him off the ground and spinning him about.

"Will!" the vicar cried. "Now you're taking greeting to a much higher level of enthusiasm—but I fear that it may be too much for most."

An assemblage of crewmen gathered at the rail to watch this most curious behavior of their captain.

"Vicar Mayhew! Thomas!" Will shouted. "How perfectly marvelous to lay eyes upon you! I was told you had been banished to the north country from Hadenthorne. I never knew how much I would miss you until I contemplated never seeing you again."

"I know, Will. It was most difficult for me as well. I felt ashamed for having been sent away and resolved not to complicate your life because of my indiscretions. It was not until this very moment that I realized how wrong that resolution was."

William grasped the vicar firmly around the shoulder and pulled him up the walkway toward the ship. "Come aboard, dear friend. We have much to speak of, and we have only a few minutes to cast off to meet the tide correctly."

Will gathered the vicar's single bag and tucked it easily under his arm. "Will you be waiting for additional trunks, Vicar? Even for a poor man of the cloth, these are meager provisions for a trip to the Caribbees."

The vicar smiled. "That is indeed all, I'm afraid. Moving three times in the last two years has necessitated a paring down of material things. Do not be afraid, Will. I have more than enough possessions to see me through."

Mr. Delacroix and Mr. St. Clair were at attention on the quarterdeck as Will and the vicar approached.

Mr. St. Clair saluted, then offered a firm handshake to the vicar. "Welcome aboard the *Artemisia,* good reverend. I hope that this voyage will prove pleasant for you."

"Welcome, Reverend," Mr. Delacroix said. "I would say that our good Captain Hawkes has told us much about you, but alas, he has kept most of his life before the sea a private thing from us. Perhaps you will tell us the real story of Captain Hawkes's consummate skill at *everything.*"

Vicar Mayhew greeted them both warmly and was escorted to the captain's berth and offered Will's bed.

"No, Will. I will not displace you."

"Vicar, see these two hooks on the opposite beams? The breadth between them is just suited for my favorite hammock. It is surprising how quickly the practice of swinging in one's sleep can become habitual. Please, Thomas. Let me offer you my best hospitality."

As the vicar unpacked his few belongings, William returned to the quarterdeck to marshal the crew for sailing. Lines were cast off, and within minutes the ship was well on its way out of the harbor and into the English Sea on the first leg of her trip west.

Will returned to his cabin to find the vicar trying to walk between the bed and door, and with each step he would sway in conjunction with the ship's roll and careen into the walls.

"It will take a few days to get your sea legs," Will laughed. "But in a short time you will no longer notice the pitching of the deck."

The vicar made it to the table and bent forward to brace himself. "I certainly hope so, Will. It has been many years since I have been aboard a sailing vessel, but I did not anticipate this violent reaction. It is the truth that I have never been on a ship this large. This is a most unsettling experience," the vicar said in a halting voice.

"The trip will become better," Will reassured his friend. He stopped speaking for a moment, then added in a quizzical voice, "Vicar, where *are* you traveling to? *Why* are you traveling?"

The vicar edged about the small room, holding exposed beams and clutching furniture as he could, and made his way to the small bench beneath the most stern-facing window. He fumbled with the latch and creaked it open, breathing deeply of the cool sea air.

"I trust that you do not mind, Will. The motions of this large ship and the closeness of the air here—well, I do not wish to become ill so quickly."

After a few minutes, the vicar's color was improving; the slight green tint, so common to sea illness, had vanished and was replaced by his normal, ruddy complexion.

After a long deep breath, the vicar said, "The fresh air seems to have done the trick, Will. Now, if you fetch me a drink of wine or ale, I will answer your questions as to how and why and where."

When Will returned, the vicar took a sustained swallow of the Madeira wine and began his story.

"It all began when you left, William, over three years ago. I knew you had to go, and when you left Hadenthorne, a certain hopeful light in my life was extinguished. I felt it. I know poor Mrs. Cavendish felt the same in her heart as well.

"I continued with my duties as parish vicar, of course, ministering as I could; baptizing, marrying, and burying as needed. But I felt cold inside, and I continued to petition London with requests to be involved in a different area of God's work.

"My sermons began to be more pointed, more direct. I told listeners that they alone were accountable to God for their commitment to him, or lack of it. They had to humble themselves, to come as children before the almighty God. They could not merely sit in the pews and allow their hearts to be hardened, for their eternal souls were in peril," the vicar recounted.

"I suppose I pointed too directly for some—our Lord Davis for one, I would imagine—and at last I received correspondence from the London bishopric. Rather than bringing me to a bigger, more active congregation, they assigned me to a very impoverished church on the Scottish border, and that amidst all the upheaval of the impending war against King Charles. The peoples' Scottish burr was so thick I could scarce understand it—and the people didn't welcome me. The English Book of Prayer had just been imposed on them by, in their eyes, a foreign king, and then comes Mayhew, a foreign vicar, being foisted upon them to boot. Looking back, I believe the bishopric had hoped I would leave the ministry quietly. But I have too stubborn a streak for quitting so easily, as you well know, William. My letters to London increased, not decreased.

"From there I was sent to a church in the Hebrides, then to replace a minister on the Isle of Man who had passed on. I thought I was destined to be the interim vicar in a series of small parishes in tiny, out-of-the-way island places.

"I know I was not doing God's will in any of those assignments—and I have asked for God's forgiveness, which I am overjoyed to say has been given to me. I cannot blame the church for diminishing my light. I allowed it to happen.

"And then, simply out of the blue, two months ago I received my current assignment. I am to be a missionary and schoolteacher on the island of St. Lucia—that is in the Lesser Antilles, Will, nearly on the same latitude as Barbados."

Will smiled and patted the vicar's hand. "Yes, Vicar. I know where St. Lucia is. We have been there numerous times."

"Oh, yes, yes. I had forgotten that you have made a specialty of shipping to the Caribbean."

Will sat facing the vicar. He lowered his head. "You should have written, Vicar. I lost my mother and father—and I thought I had lost you as well."

Tears had begun to form in the vicar's eyes, as well as in Will's.

"I know, William. But as the days turned to weeks and months, pride and humiliation stopped me. I knew it was wrong, but I could not stop. I beg your forgiveness as well. When I learned of my new posting, like Paul, scales fell from my eyes, and I could see again. Will you forgive me, William?"

The silence was loud, only broken by the splash of the water below.

"I could not hold a grudge against you, Thomas. I have found you, and I will never lose you again."

The pair embraced.

The vicar marveled at how William had matured in the two and a half years since they had seen each other. His grip, as well of the rest of him, had become strong, his demeanor deliberate. He had become a man.

It was nearing midnight and the change of watches when William finished his side of the story. As he related their close encounters with naval ships, skirting the coastline with a cargo of illegal sugar, the vicar looked on impassively, trying his best not to betray any emotion. Will searched his face for a hint of disapproval and to his relief saw none.

Just before they had drifted off to sleep, Will turned in his hammock. "Vicar, what happened with Missy? Mrs. Cavendish claimed it all her fault that Missy married Dugald. Is that true?"

The vicar had been dreading this question more than any other and had tried to rehearse an answer all evening.

"It was as much my responsibility as anyone's, Will. When we last spoke, in my soul I knew that you could never return to be a farmer or a shopkeeper in Hadenthorne. Perhaps you will call me a liar now, but your words then left little doubt. Missy was in a lamentable state following your departure. She would have waited for you, Will. She truly loved you. But I told her you would not return. She trusted me, and I instructed her to carry on with her life. And Mrs. Cavendish told you the rest."

"Vicar?"

"Yes, Will?"

"I understand. Perhaps it is all for the best. Isn't that what you have told me? That all things work together for good?"

"Yes, Will. That is what Paul writes in the eighth chapter of his letter to the Romans, the twenty-eighth verse, which ends 'to those who love God, to those who are the called according to His purpose.'"

There was a long silence as the qualification in Paul's words rang in the air.

"Happy Christmas, Thomas."

"Happy Christmas, Will."

The room grew silent again, and just before the vicar closed his eyes, he thought he heard a muffled sob, but perhaps it was just a wave.

CHAPTER

47

Christmas Eve 1640
Broadwinds, Dorset
England

Lady Emily spent most of late autumn and the Christmas holiday at Broadwinds, eager to escape the confusion and turmoil in the London streets since the calling of Parliament into session.

She had chosen not to open the Alexandrian in the fall. She had fewer students who had expressed a desire to enroll. Many of the families that would have sent their daughters or nieces had heard of the troubles in the city and selected tutors or closer establishments that offered scholastic instruction. She was not overly upset over closing. She had a substantial yearly income since her husband, Lord Caldwell, had passed on. She had shrewdly invested much of her earnings in real estate and a few syndicate offerings involving trade with the east, so her financial needs were easily met.

One of her dreams was to tour the sites of the English antiquities—especially the Roman ruins—and write a traveler's guide to them. Kathryne knew that this endeavor was partially inspired by her mentor's reading of *The Compleat Gentleman,* by Henry Peacham, published over a decade previous, wherein he placed travel for travel's sake high on this list of desirable pursuits, advocating self-education in topography, natural history, and sociology. "If it be desirable for a complete gentleman, then it must be desirable for a complete lady, also," Lady Emily had remarked to Kathryne, with whom she shared an insatiable curiosity about faraway places and an ever-present penchant to discover what was over the next hill.

So during her visit to Broadwinds, Lady Emily ventured forth on her own to begin to fulfill that dream and spent several days exploring, sketching the remains, speaking to local scholars, and digging up local history.

The Broadwinds staff had outdone themselves with Christmas preparations, all the more to ease the loneliness of the absence of Lord Aidan and his brother for Lady Kathryne. All was in readiness for the steamed Christmas pudding, the traditional cakes, and the feast that would be served in celebration of the birth of Christ.

Kathryne and Emily enjoyed decking the first-floor rooms of Broadwinds with branches of fir, holly, and ivy, freshly cut by the groundskeepers. They also decorated the bedchambers with wreaths of bay and rosemary—the latter being named after the Virgin Mary. It symbolized the cloak she wore on her flight to Egypt, white until the holy family rested by the wayside. Legend had it that Mary had placed it over a rosemary bush, and the color of the cloak used to enfold the baby king Jesus was transformed to purple. Lady Beatrice had always used rosemary at Yuletide, and Kathryne insisted on carrying on the tradition. During the days before Christmas, Broadwinds would be awash in a hurricane of scents of the holiday.

Kathryne was busy, even up till Christmas Eve, sorting through invoices and tariffs. One letter that gave her great pause was a request from two representatives of the East India Company requesting that her father assign letters of marque to deal with the growing threat of pirates in the Caribbean waters.

Not owing to the chill in the air, Kathryne shuddered. "Pirates . . . in this day and age."

Her work was interrupted by a soft rap on the door.

"Kathryne?" Lady Emily called. "Are you free for a spot of tea?"

Kathryne rang for service. Minutes later the hot liquid was poured and served with Mrs. Cole's treacle sponge cake and lemon curd spread.

The faint light of the winter's dusk had begun to ebb, and the room began to slip into darkness. The parlormaid padded over and stirred the fire. She also took several thick, white tallow candles out from the finely carved candle box, where they were kept so as not to attract vermin, inserted them into polished brass candlesticks, placed them about the room, and lit them. From outside, through the frosty panes of the windows, the strains of a Christmas carol could be faintly heard.

> *This endris night I saw a sight,*
> *Astar as bright as day;*
> *And e'er among a maiden sung,*
> *Lul-lay, bye bye, lul-lay.*

Kathryne put down her cup, jumped up, ran down the hall and through the entry hall to open the front door. Bathed in the soft glow of their tin lanterns and bundled in their warmest thick woolen greatcoats and cloaks, a small group of rosy-cheeked carolers had gathered. They scarce paused between songs, their sound a continuous strain of the heavenly music. As Kathryne stood, smiling out at them in the portal, Lady Emily joined her, and arm-in-arm the two sang along, their voices blending in harmony to the haunting melody of Kathryne's fondest Christmas carol.

> Lul-lay, Thou tiny little Child,
> Bye-bye, lul-le, lul-lay;
> Lul-lay, Thou tiny little Child,
> Bye-bye, lul-le, lul-lay.

When the singing ended, Kathryne, eyes sparkling with the wonder of Christmas, invited the carolers into the hall for hot, spicy mulled wine. Dusk had become darkness as they left, and they continued their traveling from house to house in the small hamlet.

Lady Emily stretched out to her fullest on the settee in the library and tossed a woolen shawl over her legs. Kathryne wrapped her own shawl around her shoulders and sat back down at her desk. The room was full of the scent from boughs of greens that draped the mantle.

"I was amazed to learn that caroling harkens back to the Nativity itself. How joyous must have been that first Christmas song the angels sang: 'Glory to God in the highest,'" said Kathryne as she sipped her tea.

"True, but the first song of praise to God was an eternity before that, even at the foundations of the world, when, as is written in the book of Job, 'The morning stars sang together, and all the sons of God shouted for joy.'"

"We have much for which to praise our Lord. This is my favorite night of the year," Kathryne responded. "I wonder how Papa will be spending this night. We've always so loved going to the midnight service together. And to matins on Christmas morning. But without a proper church in Bridgetown . . ."

Kathryne looked over at Lady Emily and saw that same curious look of longing in her mentor's eyes whenever they spoke Lord Aidan's name.

The crackle of the fire punctuated the silent coziness.

"So tell me, Kathryne, what other news—other than shipping and crop reports—comes from Barbados?" Lady Emily asked.

"Other news?"

"Perhaps from a certain handsome young man?"

"You have been communicating with Cecily, haven't you?"

"One has to in order to keep abreast of all the adorable antics of her delightful new son," Lady Emily replied.

"Cecily was never one to hold a secret well, I'm afraid," Kathryne said. She opened a bottom drawer of the desk and rummaged about for a moment, then extracted a thin pale envelope. "This may be what our friend Cecily is referring to." She waved a letter in the air.

"Kathryne, I am shocked that you could think I would ask to read your private correspondence."

Kathryne tilted her head and pursed her lips at her friend, trying not to smile.

"I just want you to read it to me," Lady Emily said, laughing.

Kathryne smiled as well. "I will not read it in its entirety, but will condense its content. Geoffrey appears to be a decent young man. He writes of his new sugar crop being planted. He tells me of his house being constructed—a smaller version of the one in which he grew up in Gloucestershire, in the Cotswold hills, though it will not be of Cotswold stone. He tells me a little of what transpires during the course of a normal day. He tells me of slaves being imported, although I do not find that as palatable as some."

"Have you written back?"

"Lady Emily, I am shocked at your forwardness!" Kathryne teased.

"Have you?"

Kathryne picked up a quill from the inkwell and twirled it a bit in her hand and stared at the papers on the desk in front of her. "Well, what do you think?"

Kathryne looked up to see Lady Emily's broad smile beaming back at her.

Christmas Day 1640
The Atlantic Ocean

Morning broke, and the sky looked as leaden as a wet slate. The crew wore canvas frocks with hoods over wool stomachers and woolen breeches. They, too, had gotten acclimated to the warmer weather of the southern latitudes, so the drizzly gray skies of English waters were doubly chilling to them.

Will and the vicar woke early and partook of a light breakfast. The vicar claimed the rolling was less noticeable this morning, but his stomach was still in slight distress.

"Then, Vicar, I recommend you stay in the cabin while I tend to my captain's duties. I will send a crewman down later to inquire as to your needs. And before I go, I will prepare a hot drink made with some of those herbs and powders I spoke of last eve. I don't wish you to spend the day of Christmas in an ill state."

"Thank you, William."

At midafternoon the skies remained dark, and the cold rain became more forceful and penetrating. Ian St. Clair, the navigator, approached the captain and inquired if he might spend a short time with the vicar since his charts had been updated a few moments prior. It had been many months since he had spoken with a seasoned man of the Word and had some inquiries concerning certain portions of the Scriptures.

The navigator brought a pot of hot coffee to the captain's cabin as well as his well-worn copy of the King James Bible.

The vicar was seated at the table, reading one of Will's books dealing with the islands, *The Principall Navigations, Voiages and Discoveries of the English Nation,* by Richard Haklyut.

"Please come in, Mr. . . . St. Clair, isn't it?"

"Please, call me Ian."

"Ian, then. I am being made quite nervous at the horrific actions the author describes in islands of the Caribbean."

Picking up the book, Ian laughed.

"Vicar, sir, this book contains nothing but fanciful stories. We all have had a laugh about his exploits. And since we have visited every locale he mentions, we know that his imagination played quite a large role in his writings."

"Thank heavens. I thought I might be taking on a more dangerous assignment than I thought," said the vicar, relieved.

"St. Lucia is a wonderful place, Reverend, and I believe I know of the school where you will be sent. It is a most beautiful spot, and the husband and wife who run it are a most gracious and dedicated pair."

"Good, comforting news then, Ian. Most appreciated."

"Vicar, I lead prayer time on the ship, and I have a few questions concerning several Scriptures that I thought you might advise me on."

"Prayer time—on Will's ship?"

"Yes, Vicar. Captain Hawkes does not participate, but he encourages others to."

"I see." The vicar picked up his Bible. "Before we start, Ian, may I ask you a question?"

"By all means."

"William mentioned that he buys sugar in the islands and sells it in Amsterdam."

"Yes."

"And that is illegal?"

"Yes, Reverend, quite illegal. If we were to be caught, Captain Hawkes could face a long spell in the gaols."

"Does Captain Hawkes know it is illegal?"

"Of course. Why do you ask?"

The vicar paused, then answered with a sigh. "I had hoped all my years of instruction would keep him from such nefarious activities. You are a good Christian man, correct? Why do you serve under him if he engages in such illegal activities?"

"Sir, I struggle with that as well. It is not for me to be making the decisions regarding the ship's business dealings, and I believe I must obey my master, as the Scriptures command. But I do pray that he will see the error of his ways."

"I will admit to you, my brother, that this is most distressing to know. I never imagined that my young charge Will would grow to become a . . . a smuggler. It does so cause my heart to ache."

"But, Vicar, in spite of this . . . shortcoming, Captain Hawkes is the bravest, most fair, and most generous captain I have ever known. The crew simply is devoted to him."

"Well, perhaps we need to continue to pray for Will's soul."

Neither the vicar nor the navigator heard any noise, but as they spoke, William turned away from the other side of the door, where he had been standing silently for several moments.

I do not want to see the vicar's heart ache, William thought, *but being a smuggler is how one earns the reward to keep this ship afloat. He just does not understand the ways of the world. A man must do what he must to get on in it.*

CHAPTER

48

January 1641
The Atlantic Ocean

The foul, gray weather persisted as they passed the Canary Islands. The wind was cool at best, and often filled with rain. The nights were dark, bleak, and cold. Dawn came, and the sky remained drab as slate. Crew members went about their business quickly and efficiently. No one liked spending time aloft in the rigging, setting sails, or repairing tears in such a wind. It cramped the fingers and made accidents more likely.

William walked to the helmsman, who so far this trip had had a rough time keeping the wheel in position. On a smooth crossing, the ship sailed itself. On a rougher trip as this, it was a struggle to maintain course.

"Good work, Edwards," he said. "We'll get there in due time."

"Aye, and I am glad for those marines on this voyage. I believes they'll be keen for our protection."

"What makes you say that?"

He shrugged. "Captain, I don't know. Just a feelin'. . . an itchin' in me gut is all. And then there was . . ."

"Was what, Edwards?" Will pressed.

"I feel almost foolish to mention it, sir. But since I've been on this ship, there's been a money spinner in her web just near my hammock. I looked forward to seeing that small red spider, knowing that her being there brings a dose of good fortune to us. Well, I set this voyage and the spider . . . well, she not be there."

William, uncharacteristically placed his hand on Edward's shoulder and squeezed. "'Twill be all right, Sailor. I'm sure she just ventured to a new part of the vessel where the hunting is better."

Edwards brightened a bit. "Aye, sir. Perhaps that is indeed what she has done."

Johnny Delacroix was on the quarterdeck with Mr. St. Clair. Both were working with the sextant. Sailing on days with thick clouds was difficult, for no sightings could be taken on the sun. Each man took the instrument and walked from one rail to the other, hoping to catch a glimpse of the yellow orb through the clouds. They ducked and squinted, but neither raised the instrument to his eyes. It was a time of dead reckoning. They had their compass, they knew their approximate speed, and they had a fair idea of how far west they had sailed—perhaps a week out from Barbados. But they had no firm idea on the degree north or south they had progressed. In spite of their detailed observations listed hourly on the log board, Will still imagined them to be nigh a little lost. This vexed him greatly. He had been uncanny in finding landfalls where he felt them to be. But on this trip that assuredness had ebbed. He felt unsure, uneasy, anxious.

Was it the vicar calling me a smuggler that has done it? he wondered.

Close to evening, a more needlelike rain had begun. It was warmer, which was welcome, but the rain made all aboard miserable and made their jobs more risky. As the sky began to darken, Matthew MacGregor was splicing a torn rope in the mizzenmast, the most stern-placed mast. He was hanging from the yardarm of the mizzen topgallant sail, as high as a sailor could climb.

"Captain!" came the scream from aloft.

Every eye turned, expecting to see a body hurtling down towards the deck. But no body fell.

"Over there—due east!" MacGregor screamed, pointing with a free arm.

His voice was lost in the wind, but William saw the direction he was pointing. Just at the horizon was the tip of a sail.

A quiet fell upon the ship. No one spoke.

This is it, then, Will thought.

A ship left harbor alone or as a member of a fleet or convoy. A ship did not greet strangers warmly in the open waters. Any ship's captain that did was soon called "victim."

Will smoothed his red officer's coat and turned to Mr. Delacroix, who was blanched white. "Mr. Delacroix, we have a good wind with us to the port side. See to it that all sails are let out, and set a course running broad reach with the wind. Perhaps we will wake on the morrow and see her gone. I will inform the vicar of our predicament. Perhaps he will offer to pray for us."

And with that he calmly walked from the quarterdeck to his cabin to inform the vicar of the presence of the strange ship nearby.

"Where?" the vicar asked, peering out the open window of the cabin.

Will took his telescope, nicked and dented, and opened it up. He sighted the sail, just clear against the dark eastern horizon. He handed it to the vicar and pointed again.

"Just there."

"You have better balance than I, William. For me the ship keeps bobbing, and I scarce get a glance of it before it moves again. Can you be sure they mean us harm?"

"No, I cannot, Vicar. But neither can I stay here and wait for them. We will travel under full sail all night, but it being moonless will make our jobs tricky. We will shift our compass direction several times after dark has settled, and perhaps she will veer a direction that we have not."

Through the door the vicar heard the sound of feet pounding on the walkways and heavy equipment squealing along the decking. This was the sound of cannons being moved. Most times they rested in their berth along the interior wall, but now they were slid to open gun ports. Other crewmen retrieved cannonballs from the cargo hold below. Bags of sand were brought up as well, for if a battle did ensue, the sand would sop up the pools of wet and sticky blood that would soon follow, allowing the remaining crew to handle the cannon without sliding.

"It is providential that we have the evening to prepare," Will said, as he pulled on a coat and soft, tight-fitting leather boots. "We will be ready if battle is called for in the morning."

"And you will go through all this furious preparation for an unknown ship that may not be there in the dawn? It seems that one should wait until its identity is known, Will."

William paused with his hand on the door latch. "Vicar, do you not study the Scriptures daily?"

"Yes, William. You know I do."

"Do you confront a person who is not Christian every day?"

"Well, I suppose not."

"Do you do battle with Satan every day?"

"In some ways, yes, but most times he remains hidden."

"Well, Vicar. We must prepare—just in case Satan does show up at the dawning."

As the door creaked shut, the vicar called after Will. "I will spend the night in prayer for us, William."

Is God really concerned as to my fate? Will asked himself. But he answered over his shoulder, "The crew will be comforted to hear of it."

Dawn broke, the horizon wearing the same flinty skies as the day previous. The winds were still fair, yet were not as strong or as full as Will needed. The *Artemisia* was running with full cargo and sat low and heavy in the swell. If a lighter pinnace or even a speedy fluyt was their pursuer, they would be in jeopardy.

All eyes were focused on the eastern horizon as the false dawn gave way to a fuller light.

Matthew MacGregor, who had first spotted the sail, was back on the mizzenmast yardarm. The crew listened and watched, and all turned when they heard him groan most pitifully.

"She's still there, Captain. A little farther to the north—but she has cut the distance between us in half."

"Can you spot her colors?" Mr. Delacroix shouted.

"It be a black flag riding above the flag of King Philip of Spain."

Delacroix, St. Clair, and several senior members of the crew gathered around Captain Hawkes.

"She's a privateer ship with letters of marque, no doubt."

"And swift."

"Can we toss cargo overboard?"

"Would speed us some, but not enough to escape. She's a fast ship."

"Do you think we can outrun her if we turn north with the winds?"

"Not likely. She'll be as swift as we with the same winds."

"Would we . . . consider a white flag? We do not have that much expensive cargo this sailing, true?"

"I say we sail as best we can then stand and fight when we must."

"What says you, Captain?"

Captain Hawkes listened carefully as the suggestions bandied back and forth. He stood silent, watching the sails to the east grow ever larger.

"There is only one tack. If we surrender, we will face their brutality. If we fight, we will face the same. We cannot outrun, but perhaps we can outfight."

The crew had gathered around him. Some looked angry, some calm, some looked close to tears, or perhaps panic.

"Gentlemen, you all know what to do. Mr. MacGregor and Mr. Dyer will be gunnery captains—Matthew on the starboard, Diggory on the port. Mr. Delacroix is my second, of course."

None of the men moved, as Will looked long at their faces, turning in a circle where he stood.

"May I say that this is the finest crew any captain has sailed with, and I know that we will do the *Artemisia* proud. Gentlemen, to your stations."

Before any man moved, Mr. St. Clair dropped to his knees and began to recite, loudly, his voice quivering in the slightest, "Our Father, who art in heaven . . ."

And as he voiced the words, the crew dropped to its knees and repeated the words with him.

The vicar had made his way to the deck and saw Will standing among the kneeling sailors.

"William," he said in a loud whisper. "Will you kneel with me if I ask?"

William hesitated, then bent on only one knee, beside his old friend. The first words he heard were the comforting call of Latin, learned an age ago in a small schoolroom in Hadenthorne.

"Kyrie eleison," the vicar began. "May the Lord have mercy upon us."

Broadwinds, Dorset
England

In southern England, the sun had remained absent from the sky for a fortnight after Christmas. Lady Emily had stayed for the new year and for Twelfth Night and Epiphany on the sixth of January, celebrating the coming of the Three Wise Men. She departed just after Plough Monday—the first Monday after Twelfth Night and the day marking the beginning of the agricultural year. The pagan custom of dragging a plough through the village and asking the gods to favor it had been made more Christian by the church, which now asked God to bless it instead.

After her mentor departed and the berried Christmas foliage that decked the grand house had been taken down, Kathryne had paced about Broadwinds, feeling oddly out of sorts.

Kathryne looked out the windows, now patterned with opalescent frost, out to the leafless trees, exposed in their naked beauty but for the ivy that covered their trunks. The landscape was bare and lonely, an accurate reflection of her mood. She remembered that her mother had always insisted that some yellow winter jasmine be cut and brought in, their starry branches bringing a pleasant scent and feeling of new life into the house at the beginning of the new year. *I shall have the groundskeepers cut some today,* she thought. *Perhaps that will cheer me.*

Thinking that the weather may improve later in the day, she called for her horse to be saddled, and when the sun was almost overhead she went riding in the great Mendip Hills, just north of Broadwinds. Just prior to her leaving, she donned her warmest riding attire and pocketed the letter she had received from Geoffrey Foxton. Perhaps she might read it again when she stopped for a rest.

The horse seemed delighted to run. They charged through the gray woods, with great gasps of vapor puffing from the horse's nostrils in the chilly air as Kathryne spurred him on. After several miles of hard riding, she slowed the pace. The underbrush became thicker, and Kathryne dismounted to lead the horse.

She pulled her way through a nasty section of thorns. The thick hedgerows were full of scarlet rose hips, silver teasels, and brambles, and the morning frost that dusted them was now melted away by the feeble winter sunlight. The horse whinnied behind her in displeasure.

"Oh, be quiet, Portia. I'm in as much of a jumble as you," she complained as she elbowed her way through the thorns and thistles.

Presently, the thicket thinned, and Kathryne found herself in a large meadow, at one end of which stood the ruins of an old abbey.

Kathryne tethered her horse, allowing him freedom to graze in the damp grass. She looked about at the grounds, overgrown with vines and green tendrils of ivy. She sat at the end of what was once a vast church, at the nave of the building. Behind her stretched the exterior walls, and a few pillars remained, no higher than a man. The rest of the stone was in great tumbles on the ground. A portion of roof remained at the nave of the church, where Kathryne sat. In front of her were three great arched openings, open to the wind and sky, that once framed huge stained-glass windows. She was sitting near where the altar once stood.

She looked through the empty windows. The clouds rolled through the southern English skies in great white and gray bales. At that moment a shaft of sunlight pierced the grayness and streamed through the arches, and the gentle mist was ablaze with its light. In another brief moment, the clouds closed, and it was like the door to a lit room being shut, and she was left in shadow again.

It is indeed more magnificent than any windows man can create, she thought.

She walked to the base of the windows and placed her hand on a smoothly rounded fluting of carved stone. Her hair was lifted by the breeze, and she looked up again to see the sun break through the clouds at the end of the meadow that ran from the church to woods beyond. The shifts in the wind allowed a tiny patch of sun, no more than a yard across, to run, as if a frightened deer, through the meadow. It streamed past and over Kathryne in a rush, filling her eyes with a sharp flash of light, then shadows returned again.

From an inside pocket of her jacket, next to her heart, she extracted the letter from Geoffrey Foxton. She opened it and read it again. She crossed her arms and inclined her head back, staring at the gray sky, and began to pray.

"Father, I feel pursued . . . hunted. Like I'm a young rabbit with my leg in a snare, and there's a fox in the hedgerow beyond, sniffing the air, sniffing for *me*. I would have hoped to know this man first. I have always desired a caring Christian man for a husband. I do not know if this is that man.

"My father has written that I should attempt to put all our business in order that I may sail to the island in less than a year's time. But I am so afraid that if I go it will be as a boulder tumbling down a mountain. And even if the path is dangerous for such a rock, there is no power on earth that will stop its progress."

And as Kathryne spoke those words, the skies, having darkened, opened, and a rush of rain squalled down, forcing her into the far corner of the ruins, seeking protection from the elements.

49

30 January 1641
The Atlantic Ocean

The skies remained close to the sea, and the winds stayed at medium force throughout the morning. By noon it was obvious to the entire crew that they would be overtaken during the daylight hours of this day. Unless a miraculous squall arose to save them, offering them shelter in the winds or fog, they would face the pirate ship, beam to beam, broadside to broadside, within hours.

A squad of sailors busied themselves gathering up all the hammocks from the crew's quarters, rolling them into tight bundles and stuffing them into the rigging nets on the upper deck. These breastworks would provide some protection from musket fire, but cannon shot would drive through them as a hot blade through cooked meat, easily separating flesh from bone.

The carpenters gathered their tools and made sure that the carpenter's walk—the corridor just below the waterline—was clear. If a shot hit there, they could quickly plug the hole with sheets of lead and timbers.

A half-dozen younger members of the crew would act as powder monkeys during combat. The explosive, chalklike substance was stored deep within the center of the ship, behind wetted fearnought curtains made of heavy protective wool, in the handling chamber. The charges, kept in canvas bags, would be quickly delivered one bag at a time to the cannon crews.

The vicar spent this time quietly going from man to man, praying for them, reassuring them, hearing confessions if they asked.

At midafternoon the privateer pursuers were no more than five hundred yards to the rear of the *Artemisia*. Within minutes the ship would be close for a broadside. Cannons of any type were terrifyingly destructive, but their accuracy diminished as their range increased.

Every man aboard the *Artemisia* was armed with a pistol, musket, a pike, a knife or sword, or even an ax.

William stood on the poop deck, just by the fluttering ensign—a faded and tattered British flag, watching the Spanish ship, the *Frontera Nueva*, draw closer. On the forecastle of that vessel stood a clump of a dozen or so sailors armed with a motley assortment of weapons, raising them above their heads, taunting their intended victims. Their shouts were lost to the wind, and after a few moments of staring at them impassively, William turned and walked to the quartermaster at the wheel of the ship.

"In a few minutes, when I give the order, turn her into the wind, to the north. That will be the signal for the cannon masters to fire. Perhaps we can get a broadside or two at the Spanish before she is able to turn and return fire."

"Godspeed, Captain," the quartermaster said. "I'm proud to have served with you."

The marines were loading their muskets and sharpening swords and pikes.

Will thought, *I wonder how I will react to the first time under fire? I must remain calm for the men, but it is not easy to mask the terror I feel in my heart.*

"Vicar, perhaps you should return to your cabin now," Will said. "I lost you once. I do not intend on losing you a second time."

"William, I will not abandon you again. I think that God will see us both through this."

"Vicar, I want to say that . . . I . . . I . . . love you, and you have meant the world to me."

The vicar embraced William for a brief moment.

Suddenly a musket sounded, loud and near. Then a second, and a third. Several of the marines, not used to sea battle, anxiously fired at the sailors on the *Frontera Nueva*. One of the pirates dropped to the deck, a red stain spreading from his waist.

"Marines! Hold your fire, you fools!" Will shouted. "Fire is to be on *my* orders!"

The captain of the *Frontera Nueva*, thinking that his victim was about to attack, called for his ship to turn into the wind first and screamed for his cannoneers to open fire.

A series of deafening roars emanated from the cannon ports of the *Frontera Nueva*, white billows of smoke pouring from the throat of each cannon.

No! Will screamed to himself. *Our only chance was to make the first move!*

The first angry volley tore across the water, the enemy gunners double-shotting each charge, using double powder and twin cannonballs. They fired a raking volley, not a full broadside, into the ship since they had turned first.

As their cannons roared, Will screamed to the quartermaster, "Turn! Turn!"

One shot splashed into the water at the bow, one hissed through the canvas of the spanker sail above Will's head, and one overshot the ship completely. The fourth gun had aimed at the marines on deck with a chain shot—two cannonballs connected by a length of chain. It ripped through the breastworks like a hand through water. A dozen men soon lay dead or injured.

The fifth shot hit midships, at the fourth gun position on the *Artemisia*. Splinters flew in every direction, killing the entire five-man crew in an instant. The hot cannonball ignited their charges, exploding the berth in a ball of angry orange flame that buckled the deck boards above and below it.

The sixth shot struck midships as well, at the waterline, punching a hole in the hull the size of a man's skull. A carpenter crew rushed to the gap with timbers to patch the breach.

The seventh shot hit a longboat stored just behind the forecastle deck, sending a deadly shower of wood splinters spraying about. William turned to see Mr. Delacroix drop to the deck with a splinter as thick as a baby's arm impaled in his thigh.

The eighth shot struck the mainmast dead center and cut through the thick oak shaft neatly, and the entire rigging, full of sail, began to tilt into the wind. It balanced upright for another few seconds, then dropped, slowly, toward the sea.

Will screamed again, "Fire! Fire!"

The *Artemisia* was matching the turn of the *Frontera Nueva,* but it was too late. The mainsail of Will's ship was collapsing into the sea between the ships, and three of her remaining four gunners could no longer see their target. They fired through the canvas and rigging, but only one shot hit the target, striking the *Frontera Nueva* near the bow, well above the waterline.

With the mainsail done in and dragging as an anchor in the water, Will realized that this fight was completed in the time it took one volley to be fired. The *Artemisia* could no longer maneuver, nor fire cannon effectively. Half the Royal Marines on deck were dead or badly wounded.

The *Frontera Nueva* turned back to mirror the movements of Will's crippled vessel and fired another volley from her eight cannon. These shots were aimed at the upper decks, and the chain shot hissed across them like a scythe, cutting down a score of sailors in an instant. The sand that was brought up from the hold was badly needed now, but Will had few crew left available to spread it into the blood.

Will could hear the screams and taunts of the Spanish privateers as they drew close to his ship. Several grappling hooks were tossed across the narrow gulf, and the Spanish sailors began to haul their prey close, like a spider retrieves a fluttering moth in its web. The Spanish snapped boarding axes at their lines and rigging.

A few marines fired back in defense, and two of the grappling lines were cut, but more were tossed back, finding a firm grip. The exploded cannon berth of the *Artemisia* was on fire, and a half dozen sailors were hauling water buckets to douse its spread.

The ships were now hull to hull, the wood shrieking as the ships scraped together in the waves, the *Artemisia's* cork fenders hit by shot and gone. The cannons were silent now, the enemy having done all the damage they needed to inflict. Any further firing would put both ships at risk of explosion. The top decks were no more than a man's height apart, and the Spanish privateers laid long planks between them. A few of Will's crewmen pushed a few of them back, but there were too many.

Will unsheathed his sword and removed his pistol from his belt. Since reloading was a time-consuming process, he would have but one shot, then would face hand-to-hand combat.

The Spanish crew huddled below their breastworks. Will heard the Spanish captain scream out in his native tongue, *"Ataque!"*

His men leaped to the planks and stormed across them into the smoke and confusion of the *Artemisia*. Will leveled his pistol at the privateers, and he fired, a swallow of smoke obscuring his vision. He could not know if the bullet found a target.

The Royal Marines on the *Artemisia*, for all their bravado, fought for only a moment, then scattered to aft and stern of the ship, many of them tossing down their muskets and holding hands high in the air.

Mr. Delacroix, lying on the bloody deck near Will's feet, shouted up through the din and screams, "Captain! The white flag! We will all perish if you don't."

A privateer had stormed up the gangway to the quarterdeck, and Will thrust his sword point deep into his shoulder. The man fell back screaming.

"Will! You must! We will live to fight another day!" Delacroix screamed.

Will's eyes burned from the smoke and haze filling the decks. He saw the vicar to one side, kneeling by a fallen sailor, cradling his head with his blood-covered hands.

Mr. Delacroix lay at Will's feet. A few marines had pikes lowered and were slowly retreating to the right of him.

"Will! It is not a disgrace!" Delacroix insisted.

"Mr. St. Clair! Hoist the white pennant. It is finished," Will called, his voice empty.

A few shots popped in the smoke, and men screamed from wounds they had received. But as the British flag was withdrawn and the white flag raised on the ensign pole, the tumult and furious activity began to slow.

In less than a quarter hour, it was over. A swarthy sailor from the *Frontera Nueva* grabbed Will's sword and tossed it into the sea.

In a moment the Spanish captain made his way over to the slippery deck of the *Artemisia*. He was a tall, arrogant man, with dark hair and eyes. A thin scar snaked down and marred the left cheek of his bronzed face.

"Captain? I am Diego San Martel, captain of the *Frontera Nueva*. We have letters of marque from King Philip to seize your ship and all that it contains. It is most legal."

Will answered in his native Spanish, "Does legal give you the right to murder half my crew? A letter from your pompous king gives permission to kill half my men?"

Will made a movement towards the Spanish captain, not realizing what he might do. Several Spanish sailors grabbed his arms, then struck him with a wooden belaying pin, knocking him to the deck.

"Brave man, this captain," San Martel called to his second, then with a louder voice said, "Begin to empty this ship of valuables. Leave nothing unturned," his eyes never leaving Will's.

San Martel motioned to a young sailor standing behind him. The sailor stepped forward and called out loudly, in English, accented with a Scottish brogue, "Our good captain San Martel asks any of you English sailors who care to join our ship that he will take as many as choose to go. He is a fair captain. That is true. I have sailed with him for two years and have been amply rewarded."

Will's lip had been bloodied, a wound on his forehead pulsed, and from his knees he cursed at the Spanish captain as he wiped at his bleeding mouth with the back of his hand. "None of this crew will leave. They will never join a pirate," he spat.

"Ah, my good English friend, do not be so sure," the captain replied in a knowing tone. "Sailors will swim to success, like sharks to a bleeding fish. You will see, my brave captain."

As the Spanish crew set about plundering Will's ship, a group of perhaps twenty men formed around the Scotsman from the *Frontera Nueva*. They gathered on the forecastle deck, well away from Will's piercing stare. Most kept their heads lowered.

Helmsman Griffin Edwards walked closer to the prostrate Will and spoke in a small voice. "It ain't that we think poorly of you, Captain Hawkes, for losin' and all, but this ship may not get anywhere without sinkin' first. I want no part of havin' a watery grave just yet. I hope you'll be forgivin' us, Captain. Besides, we already be smugglers in the eyes of King Charles. Bein' a privateer isn't much worse."

Will tried to salute the sailor back, but was butted again with the end of a musket.

Captain San Martel strolled towards Will again. "See, Captain? It is true what I have said about the nature of sailors, is it not? They will stay with the successful and abandon the weak."

Will looked up and saw the vicar being manhandled by two burly privateers at the base of the fallen mainmast.

"I tell you, I am but a poor vicar," he was saying. "I have no gold crosses or chalices. I simply am a poor man of God."

The Spanish captain walked over to Vicar Mayhew, whose arms were being held firmly.

"Priest, where is your gold?" he demanded.

"I am not a priest, my good man. I am a vicar of the Church of England. I do not have gold!"

The captain removed a leather glove from his hand, then swung about and with the back of his hand struck the vicar with his full force. The vicar all but collapsed. Will struggled to rise, but was struck a third time.

The Spanish captain grabbed the vicar by his lapels, pulled his bleeding face close to his own, and hissed, "Where is the gold, you old fool?"

The vicar's head lolled on his neck, and he sputtered weakly, "I do not have gold. I swear it on my life."

"Your life, eh?" San Martel said evilly. He motioned to a sailor standing nearby, holding a musket. "Perhaps with his life on the line, he may remember." He pointed at the sailor. "Shoot him."

Ian St. Clair was being held kneeling a few feet away, the sharp end of a sword placed against the nape of his neck. When he saw the Spanish sailor raise the musket, point it at the vicar's chest, and curl his finger around the trigger, he leapt forward, diving between the vicar and the musket. The gun sounded its loud roar, echoing across the waters. The bullet hit St. Clair square in the chest, knocking him like a lifeless doll, dead to the deck. His blood splattered in a terrible rain against the chest of the vicar who cried out, "No!"

The sailors stood for a moment, silent in the face of such sacrifice. It was the Spanish captain who spoke first.

"Perhaps he has no gold after all. But others in the church do. You there! The English captain! Do you hear me?"

Will nodded, his vision blurred with tears.

"We will take your vicar with us. If you make it to Barbados, tell the Church of England that we will hold him for ransom. Seek us out by the full moon four months hence at the leeward side of the island of Tobago. I want a hundred doubloon in gold for the man—or he will swim with the sharks!"

There was no sound from any man.

"English! Do you understand!"

William nodded, his tears falling on the deck, striking the locket that hung from his neck.

The captain saw the glint of gold, walked over to Will, reached down, and curled his fist about the locket, pulling it from Will's neck. The breaking chain cut a small slice near Will's throat. He felt as if the fist had clenched about his heart and torn it from him as well.

The Spanish captain knelt next to Will and whispered in his ear.

"Four full moons, English. Remember that Captain San Martel is a man of his word, a man of honor."

And with that he walked away.

Near Broadwinds, Dorset
England

When the rain stopped, Kathryne mounted Portia and rode east along a pretty lane for several miles until it led to the main road that ran to Salisbury between London and Broadwinds.

She looked up into the afternoon sky, now clearing following the rains. The sun was warm against her face, and she felt better than she had for weeks. She dismounted and walked alongside her horse for a mile or so, stretching her legs. She stopped under a large oak tree at the side of a small stream, allowing the horse to drink. The white, nodding heads of winter-flowering snowdrops dotted the damp shallow banks along the thin ribbon of water.

Kathryne looked about. She was alone. Her voice rang out into the quietness of the countryside, "Dear God, I trust thee to guide and protect me. I trust thee to lead me down thy paths. I trust thee to help me fulfill thy will, and not my own." She paused, then looked back up into the sky. "But, dearest God, would it be possible to show me . . . something . . . any little thing that might reassure my heart? I do not ask lightly for a sign, but my heart is so unsure. This is asked in the most precious name of Christ. Amen."

And as she opened her eyes, on the lowest branch of the tree beside her, flittered a small bird—a Williamson thrush. The bird looked directly at Kathryne, then burst into song.

The Atlantic Ocean

It was sunset by the time the crew had gathered up the dead and tended to the dying. The ship's surgeon had been killed by the explosion of the cannon, so several men had perished unnecessarily.

The dead were dropped, often unceremoniously, into the sea. William felt unable to mouth the words of any prayer, and the remaining crewmen walked about their tasks with silent, grim faces.

The mainmast had been cut away, the waterline holes patched. Mr. St. Clair, the navigator, was gone, so Will took a sextant reading, then set a course for where he thought Barbados might lie.

50

January 1641
The Atlantic Ocean

With only the foremast and the part of the mizzenmast remaining, the *Artemisia* was quickly transformed into a slow, lumbering vessel, leaking and lurching, almost floundering in the lightest of seas. The weather, gracefully, had turned clear and dry, though the wind kept the waves at a moderate chop.

They had no fish spar to rig a jury mast, so the sail that was left would be the sail that took them to their destination, regardless of its utility.

William sat, almost unmoving, on an empty crate left by the wheel stand. He was one of the few remaining officers with skills to pilot the vessel. The helmsman had left with the Spanish pirates. Mr. Delacroix was bandaged and in the small sick bay of the ship. The large splinter that pierced his thigh had missed the blood supply, and it did not appear that the wound would fester, and he claimed he would be back on deck within two days. Mr. St. Clair was dead. Three other officers who knew the rudiments of piloting had been cut down in the final broadside of the Spanish privateer's cannon.

In the quiet hours after the battle, William quantified and totaled his losses. Virtually all cargo, save the sugar mill, was either looted, tossed overboard, or destroyed. He would earn a few pounds by delivering the mill equipment, but much had been lost. More than forty men had died. Twenty-five men, all who he had thought were loyal to him and the English flag, had joined the Spanish ship. William was left with fewer than fifty men, and a score of them were injured in the battle. A few, so badly maimed, would never see land again.

Will sat on the cluttered quarterdeck amid the rubble and the destruction following the battle. He waved off the rest of the crew and sat alone that first desperate night, unmoving save for a minor correction in the wheel every few hours.

And his vicar was gone as well, as a hostage—or dead—at the whim of an angry Spanish captain.

He reached up and touched, without thinking, the spot on his chest that his mother's locket had once occupied. He found no comforting feel of gold and chain, just a hollow spot that was cold and empty.

The following morning Will and a few of the remaining carpenters walked the carpenters' walk around the interior hull of the ship. She had taken three shots below the waterline, and though all patches held, the ship was still taking on more water than she could stand. The bottom hold was near-filled with murky water, and the rats had been forced up to the upper decks. The pump that could have been used to empty the hull lay in ruins, shattered by the cannon explosion.

The small quiet group stood by the jumble of pumps, gears, and the long, broken sections of the pump dale, the mechanism's piping.

"It is beyond repair, is it not?" Will asked.

To a man they nodded yes, no one willing to voice the painful answer.

"We have too few men to bucket the water out, is that not right?"

Again, Will received a unison nod from the group.

"Well, then, it be time to get above decks and find port for this old ship. I expect you all to accomplish what repairs you can. I will see that none of us needs swim to Barbados. That much I will promise to you."

Before he made his way to the wheel stand, Will stopped in the crowded sick bay and spent a few minutes with his men, reassuring each that he would see England again.

He stood by the bed of Mr. Delacroix, who was covered in a thin sheen of sweat.

"Bit o' the fever from the wound, Captain. But the hole appears clean, and the herbs you gave me appear to be workin'."

"Good man," William said, and he put his hand on Delacroix's shoulder. "We'll be in port—hopefully Bridgetown—before too long. Then we can have all of you looked at by a proper surgeon."

"Rather be treated by you, Captain," John said in a fevered voice.

William squeezed the shoulder of his friend again and made his way back to the wheel stand.

Clouds filled the morning sky with a smattering of white and gray, and the wind was steady from the east. It had been a full day since Will had slept and longer than that since he had last eaten. Yet he was brisk and efficient, heading the slowly sinking vessel westward.

But in his chest his heart had stopped feeling, like a brick in cold water. *It is not worth all the salt in the sea to draw close to people,* he thought as he handled the massive wheel, fighting it, turning it to keep a steady course. *It seems as though God deigns me never to love anyone—for as I do, they are taken from me.*

He looked into the heavens and felt so very little. No tears had come to his eyes. Even as they had lowered Ian St. Clair into the water—and Will had insisted on a proper burial shroud for him—he felt a blankness, an empty pocket where his soul must have been.

It is better this way. Perhaps I will have less joy, but I will certainly have less pain as well. The vicar would say that all things work together for good and that God has a plan for our lives. Well, the Almighty must be laughing in his celestial throne, for I see no plan in my life—nothing but pain and loss.

At midday he retrieved his charts and personal maps, hidden behind a false panel in his cabin. The pirates had taken the ship's maps, three of their four sextants, and all their telescopes. He sighted the sun and read his charts, marking his progress with an inked quill.

A young crewman helped him steady a plank on which the map rested. The navigator's desk had been destroyed by a cannon shot; an empty, splintery hole remained by what was left of it at the quarterdeck railing.

"Well," Will pondered, staring at the nervous sailor, "do you have any idea of where we might be?"

The young man of no more than sixteen years was very frightened and a bit panicked. "No, I-I-I-I do not imagine I do, sir."

"You are honest. I like that in a sailor," Will said in a loud voice that bespoke false bravado. "If I have made my guesses correct and we sailed this far during the battle and the following night," he said tracing a thin black line northward, "then we should be . . . right here."

Will pointed to a spot in the open sea, a point some hundred leagues to the northeast of Barbados. "If we turn to the southwest now, we should run into our goal by tomorrow morning. And if we miss it, they'll be no turning back with this ship. We'll just keep our heading and sail to the coast of St. Lucia."

He looked up at the sailor, who still stood trembling at the verge of tears. "Son, we will make it to landfall. I may not have been a skilled enough sailor to avoid what happened, but I will not let this ship go down. Do you hear me? I will not lose another sailor on this voyage. Do you believe that?"

"Sir, I-I-I-I have always believed you. N-n-no captain has been more fair. And there is n-n-not a captain alive who could have outrun those p-p-p-privateers."

"You are a kind soul to have said that. Now let me be to steer this vessel home."

The young man withdrew. Will stood by the wheel, reading his only sextant. Something instinctual told him that he was indeed on the right course. Birds cawed from above, and Will looked up. It was a flock of brilliant blue-green parrots, flapping their wings furiously heading to the southwest.

"They'll be aiming for land as well," Will said softly. "All we need do is follow them there."

Broadwinds, Dorset
England

The desk in the library was a flurry of activity. There were two servants with dusters and mops cleaning the floor, dusting the shelves, and polishing the brass handles of the elegant chest-on-chest in the corner. Kathryne was directing their activities as she filed and refiled correspondence and made neat stacks of invoices and shipping manifests on the desk.

Mrs. Cole poked her head in a few minutes prior to one o'clock to inquire if Kathryne would be stopping her frenzy for a midday meal.

Kathryne pushed away a wisp of her dark hair that had loosened from the scarlet ribbon at her neck and tucked it behind her ear. She fanned her glistening face with the contract for a new shipment of linens and bedding bound for her father.

"If you do not eat, child, you will lose that attractive roundness that gentlemen are most partial to," Mrs. Cole warned. "Then it won't matter if they ship ye to China—no one will want you."

Kathryne wrinkled her nose at her old friend, then broke into giggles.

"It does my heart good to see you laugh, my dear," Mrs. Cole said as she stepped into the room and navigated around buckets and mops. She took another errant wisp of Kathryne's hair and tucked it back along the side of her head, smoothing it down and in place. "How long has it been since you've been anywhere other than this office, my child? This stuffy room is no life for a beautiful young woman. You should get out into the countryside more often—at least to sit in our gardens."

Kathryne sat back in the large leather chair that had been her father's.

She let her hands drop to her side. "But I have a house to run here," she protested.

"But no husband," Mrs. Cole answered.

"As soon as I sail for Barbados . . ."

"A year from now, child, a full year."

"I will have a hus—"

She stopped her sentence mid-word. She leaned back again in the chair and covered her face with her hands. As best she tried, she could not hide her emotions, and the tears started to come.

Mrs. Cole came over and sat on the arm of the chair, stroking Kathryne's hair. "There, there, my child," she said softly. "'Twill be all right. I did not mean to upset you so."

"It isn't your fault, Mrs. Cole," she sniffed. "It is mine." She took a handkerchief from her pocket and dabbed at her eyes, wet with salty water.

Mrs. Cole untied Kathryne's long dark hair, effortlessly formed in delicate curls, and retied it with the scarlet ribbon. "Then, my child, what is the reason for the tears?"

Kathryne turned and took her hands in her own. "What saddens me, Mrs. Cole, is that I will spend the greater part of a year merely waiting. Waiting until father writes and tells me Barbados has become 'civilized' enough for his little daughter. I do not want to spend the next twelve months waiting, never feeling rooted or secure. I had hoped that my life would mean more than just making money or waiting on a man who may be my husb—"

She seldom described Geoffrey Foxton as her actual, potential husband, for the thought still frightened her. He had sent a second letter, more expansive and personal than the first, full of little bits of news of his life as a planter. He wrote in a witty and charming style, and she had begun to believe that he was indeed a man of honor and good character. But she, in her heart, found it challenging to accept this man as her future mate for life without sampling the waters at any other part of the stream. What would her heart tell her when they met? Is this truly the man that God had chosen for her? Should she look about for other suitors during this year? Where would she find them if she did?

Mrs. Cole's voice interrupted her racing thoughts. "Kathryne, I know what the problem is, and I believe that I know how to solve it."

Kathryne looked up, the last of her tears drying on her cheeks, now flushed with a hint of rose. Her deep green eyes, luminescent with the tears, were open wide.

"You need somethin' to occupy thy time—no, something noble to redeem the time you have. And I know what would be perfect for you."

"What, Mrs. Cole? What?"

"There is a free school being formed in the town of Dorchester. The church reformers, Puritans if you like, have begun to outfit a buildin' on South Street and are assemblin' teachers for the trainin' up of the children of the town in religion, learnin', and civility—children who otherwise would remain ignorant. I heard the preacher John White at Trinity Church speak at the Sunday afternoon service with my Uncle Graham when I visited last. He asked the congregation to give very liberally to the endeavor. They are collectin' money for the support of teachers and for the purchase of Bibles, Testaments, primers, and other small books. Their program of godly reformation includes, along with feedin' and clothin' the poor, an interest in education first and foremost. I am sure that, with the breadth of your schoolin' and knowledge, you could find employ as a teacher in any number of disciplines."

"Me? Teach children?" Kathryne asked, skeptical.

"Yes. You'd be wonderful with 'em. 'Twould not be more than a few days per week, and your business here requires much less time than you spend on it. And now you would have a purpose. And the vicar who is organizin' it all is a very pleasant young man."

"And this is a church school?" she asked.

Mrs. Cole nodded. "The three churches in the town—St. Peter's, Trinity, and All Saints—have banded together to see it done."

Kathryne looked up at Mrs. Cole. Her eyes were even deeper now, as she began to imagine the possibilities. In a moment she responded. "Which church is organizing the effort? And who there shall I call upon to offer my services?"

The Atlantic Ocean

At dawn on the third day following the battle, the *Artemisia* was becoming an even slower, more ponderous vessel, to the dismay of all left aboard. Seawater was slowly filling the ship and now lapped at the stairs on the cargo deck—the second from the bottom. Another day and even the smallest of chop in the waves might swamp her.

Will had not left the wheel station for two days. He had food and drink brought to him. Even though no man could be spared, he assigned one sailor to remain perched in the forecastle mast crow's nest, telescope in hand, scanning the horizon for any sign of landfall. Will knew, as did most of the crew, that if land was not sighted by dusk, it might be the last sunset they would see.

A clump-thump on the deck behind William caused him to turn and face Mr. Delacroix, limping towards him on crude crutches made from a pair of discarded oars.

Will smiled at the sight of his friend, now up from his sickbed, then immediately reprimanded him. "You should not be here! This is no place for a man on crutches!"

He left the wheel and went to help. Delacroix tried to wave him off, but nearly lost his grip on a crutch and would have tumbled to the deck had Will not been there to steady him.

"You should not be here, my friend. You should stay in sick bay."

"The air is too foul there, and if it be true that I can walk, then it be true that I am well.

"I have a hunger for the fresh air of the top deck," Delacroix said as he was helped to the crate by the wheel. "How are our stocks, Will? Where is our position? Will this ship make it to landfall?"

Will returned to the wheel, noted that the compass had shifted a point, and corrected the drift with a slight turn.

"We have enough food for several weeks. We are somewhere northeast of Barbados. All the longboats have been destroyed. We will sink and drown if we do not find land by dusk."

Delacroix scanned the western horizon. "I am glad I did not ask for you to sweeten the news."

The pair of friends stared steadily out to sea over the bow of the ship, its deepening wake spraying a mist of seawater halfway to the back of the damaged vessel. They stood by each other for the next hour, not speaking, but concentrating on finding landfall, as if their thoughts and hopes might will it into sight.

And then, breaking their mutual reverie, from the forecastle crow's nest there came a loud shout. "Land ho! To the port bow! You've done it, Captain Hawkes! We are saved!"

The remaining crew ran excitedly to the forecastle deck, and within a moment or two the green sliver of Barbados slipped into view. It was the rough and rocky Atlantic side, offering no harbor, but it was land.

By dusk they had sailed about the island, and instead of docking the *Artemisia* in Bridgetown, William aimed the ship directly at a small, sandy beach just by the fort still being constructed.

"If we try to drop anchor, the ship may be lying at the bottom of the harbor by morning. We'll beach her and tie her down. Perhaps she can be repaired in place," Will informed his men.

As they neared the sand, the crew and all that could be carried quickly were placed at the stern of the ship, raising the bow, to effect a better grounding. Will steered straight for the sand, and as she caught some of the swell, the *Artemisia* lifted a bit, then scraped on the sandy bottom with a lurch. She tilted slightly at first, then listed twenty-five degrees out of horizontal and settled in the loose sands. The crew set about to securing the vessel with ropes to the rocks and tamarind trees along the beach. Will wanted no full tide to hoist her up and float her away.

As he jumped to the white sand, he looked at the battle damage, accented in the long shadows of the sunset. Long splits were visible along the hull, spider-webbing from the three waterline holes. William was not a carpenter nor a shipbuilder, but he knew without their advice that the damage was more serious than he had anticipated.

The following morning he and two junior officers set off to Bridge-town to arrange transport of the sugar mill, their one still-valuable piece of cargo. Mr. Delacroix, who had shown a remarkable recovery, was left in charge of the ship.

By midafternoon they had returned, Will looking pessimistic and glum.

Delacroix had fashioned a chair of empty cartons and trunks and had situated it under the hull, out of the sun.

"Captain, what be the news?"

"They'll be here for the mill by tomorrow. I managed to speak to an aide of the governor as well. I inquired as to what we might expect, as British citizens no less, as to compensation for the goods lost to the Spanish."

"And?"

"And! I am so pleased that you asked," Will nearly shouted, waving his arms about like a great flapping seabird. "It appears to me that the *Artemisia* is too badly damaged to be repaired. There are no skilled shipwrights on this island. And even if there were, there is no supply of the oak timbers that we would require. We, my friend, are out of a vessel."

"But what of the compensation?"

"I will be able to pay off the crew with the letter of credit I carry from my funds back in Weymouth."

"And what else? What about our cargo losses?"

Ignoring the question and pacing about the beach back and forth in front of Mr. Delacroix, Will cried, "Well, this is what I get for imagining that the government cares at all for insignificant peasants as we. I curse those nobles who keep us under heel with their rules and laws! What my heart would not give for a chance to strike back at those Spanish devils who raped my ship!"

"What did he say, William? And please leave your politicizin'—and sermonizin'—until later."

"I will get revenge, John," William shouted. "I swear to you that I will. I will get revenge on that Spanish dog."

"In due time, William. In due time. But first, might you calm down and tell me of today's events?"

William took a deep breath, nodded a bit, then dropped and sat cross-legged in the shade of his beached and canted vessel.

"Well, it appears that the attack was made in waters claimed by Spain. England has no quarrel with their claim, so, in essence, we were the ones trespassing on the Spanish. It was within their rights to kill forty of my men and steal everything we owned."

"But, William, every ship that crosses the Atlantic sails that route!" John was incredulous. "Spain has no rights to the entire ocean."

"But it allows the king in London to turn his royal back on us so as not to upset his friend, King Philip of Spain," Will said without emotion. "We should have known better than to put ourselves at risk."

"But, William, this is preposterous! Surely there is somethin' that can be done," John protested.

William lay back, reclining fully in the coolness of the sand. He looked up at the hull of the ship drying in the sun. The copper sheeting used to prevent worms and barnacles had turned a brilliant green. Will wondered if there was salvage potential in the raw materials of the ship—her wood and ropes and fittings. He tucked his arms under his head and closed his eyes. After a long moment, he spoke.

"There is nothing we can do, John," he said evenly, with no hint of emotion. "I have been abandoned yet one more time, and there is no one who will rescue me this time."

Delacroix bent and clasped his friend's shoulder. Both were startled to hear a stranger's voice.

"But that is where you are wrong, my dear Captain Hawkes. There is indeed someone who will rescue you."

Will sat up with a start, blinking at the bright sun.

A tall, willowy figure, dressed in an expensive blue jerkin over a shirt with ruffled collars and cuffs, stood before him, a wide straw hat with a matching blue plume shielding his face from the sun and hiding his eyes in shadows.

"I can offer you a most practical way out of your current dilemma."

Will was standing now, brushing the sand from his breeches. "And you, sir. Who might you be that is interested in my welfare?"

"I am Radcliffe Spenser," he said, taking off his straw hat.

Will peered at the man, who stood several inches taller than he, but thinner and harder-edged. His eyes were dark green, almost black in the shadows. *Those eyes,* William thought. *Where have I seen those eyes before?* Will felt a coldness creeping over him. He reached up to touch his mother's locket, then silently cursed again, feeling his chest empty.

"My brother is Lord Aidan Spenser, the governor of this island, who turned down your request for aid. He was correct in his interpretation of maritime law."

Will looked at him with a quizzical expression.

"I happened to be . . . nearby, shall I say, when the matters were discussed. You will soon understand who really controls the important issues here," stated Radcliffe.

"You being the power behind the throne?" Delacroix laughed.

Radcliffe's lips did not move, although his eyes focused sharply on the injured sailor. In a moment, Delacroix started to squirm a bit. "Yes, I suppose that is a correct assumption on your part," Radcliffe sneered.

"And you are offering us a solution to our problems?" Will asked, a hint of incredulity in his voice.

"Yes." Radcliffe took a step closer. "Actually, I offer a choice of three alternatives, and I believe I already know which course you will choose."

"Three choices?" Will asked.

"The first is to assume the captain's position of the *Lady Ivory.*"

Will cocked his head to one side. "That's the slaving ship that runs between here and Suriname, is it not? What happened to the captain?"

"A most unfortunate death," Radcliffe purred. "I believe some of his cargo got testy on this last voyage and did him in."

William looked at Delacroix, and unspoken words seemed to flow between them. They had been on a full ship outside of the Azores once, and the stench from so many packed bodies was all but overpowering. So many died en route from Africa and the Guiana coast that the lifeless bodies soon overcrowded the living. The moans and cries of the imprisoned men and women he heard were enough to turn Will's sleep troubled for days afterward.

"I think slaving is best left for others," Will said firmly, with Delacroix nodding emphatically.

"As I thought your answer would be," Radcliffe replied. "I know that your ship, the *Artemisia* will not be repaired. It appears that her name—meaning perfect—has outlived its descriptive value." He gave a short laugh. "But I would be willing to post transport for you and a small number of your crew to sail back to England to purchase a new craft and resume your trading activities—provided, of course, that you agree to sail to Amsterdam with sugar from my acreage and at my prices."

I could do that, Will thought. *But it sounds as if I will be indebted to this dubious man for many, many sailings.* "Sir, that does not, on its surface, seem to be attractive to me."

Radcliffe smiled his thin smile at Will. "Again, my supposition as to your choice was correct."

"And what is my third option?" inquired Will.

Radcliffe took a step into the sun and pointed to the harbor. "Do you see that pinnace at anchor by the larger merchant ship?"

Will stepped out into the sun and squinted. At anchor was a small vessel, no more than sixty feet in length, with three smallish sails. It rode high in the water. Will counted at least six cannon ports on the starboard side alone of the small ship. It meant she was carrying twelve cannons, eight more than most peaceable ships that size would carry. No flag was hung from its ensign.

"Yes, I see it," Will acknowledged.

Radcliffe rubbed his hands together as if to warm them. "My dear captain, I am willing to sell you that ship. I understand from the island's banker that your letter of credit is more than sufficient."

Will turned and glared. "That information is private. How do you know how much—"

Radcliffe held up his palm to silence Will's anger. "I know many things, Mr. Hawkes. I know that you are asking yourself, 'What good is a small ship such as that,' especially since you have experience with much larger vessels. Well, my friends, that vessel is equipped with an item of such rare value that all other ships in the harbor are put to shame."

Will and Delacroix stared at each other. *What could it have to be of such value?* Will thought.

Radcliffe leaned closer to Will. "My dear friends, that ship comes equipped with letters of marque signed by the governor of Barbados. She is the only ship to be so equipped. With her you will have every opportunity to seek your revenge on your Spanish tormentors. You will keep a full forty percent of all your plunder, share fifty percent with the Crown, which leaves me—let's see, now . . . a paltry ten percent. And all of this can be yours, William. To seek revenge, William. To strike back at a world that has given you nothing but pain, my dear captain. You alone can control your destiny. No one will be there to give orders—save yourself." Radcliffe stopped just short of cackling with glee. "Please speak about this with your second. I will offer you privacy."

Radcliffe paced several steps backwards and remained quiet, and the only sound was the crashing water on the rocks of the beach. The waves curled up the sand, hissing as they returned to the sea.

William looked again at the pinnace rocking gently in the breeze in the harbor. He looked at Delacroix, who had a curious look—one might call it gleeful anticipation—on his face. He looked at Radcliffe, whose thin-lipped smile told of the fact that this was the offer that he knew Will would accept.

"Mr. Spenser," said Will, extending his hand, "I am most interested in this third option."

"As expected, my dear captain. As expected," Radcliffe said as he took Will's hand and shook it.

Delacroix limped into the sun to view the vessel that Will had just purchased.

"And may I suggest a name for the craft, Captain Hawkes?" asked Radcliffe.

"Yes?"

"I suggest that you call it the *Reprisal*."

Will nodded. *Yes, that is a most fitting name. Most fitting*, he thought.

51

*February 1641
Dorchester,
England*

The last child filed out of the small building housing the free school on South Street in Dorchester, near St. Peter's Church.

The months that Kathryne had managed her father's business interests had never left her feeling as exhausted as did a morning with these children. And yet despite the exhaustion, she felt a keen sense of exhilaration as well.

She stood up to gather her few books together. St. Peter's was a ride of some ten miles from Broadwinds, and Kathryne needed to return early to finish several letters concerning the cargo for the latest sailing.

As she stood at the front of the small room, a figure stepped through the small doorway. "Lady Spenser, how delightful that I have caught you before you have left us. Would you care to have a glass of cider, or perhaps some of that new tea drink that I have heard you speak of? I have purchased a small quantity during my last visit to London."

"Why that would be most pleasant, Vicar Petley. Providing I may take my leave in perhaps a short hour's time, for I need to attend to pressing matters."

Vicar Giles Petley was indeed a pleasant man, as Mrs. Cole had said, and was, as yet, still unmarried. He was tall and angular, with thinning black hair and a wisp of a beard at his chin. His sharp brown eyes were set off by his soft face.

Kathryne picked up her satchel and closed the door to the room. She slipped her arm through his, as was proper for a lady to do when walking on uneven ground, such as a country walk. The vicar stiffened a bit as she did so. She glanced up at his face and saw a bright crimson edge to his cheeks and his ears. *Perhaps our Vicar Petley has limited experience dealing with proper ladies,* she thought.

When they reached the parsonage, a small suite of rooms just behind St. Peter's Church, he graciously opened the door and bid her enter. Of course his housekeeper was inside, for it would not have been proper to invite a lady—especially one of such noble stature as Kathryne—to the unchaperoned home of a bachelor gentleman, especially a man of the cloth.

The housekeeper bustled about at the vicar's request and in a few minutes brought forth a tray of steaming tea and cakes.

"Thank you, Mrs. Rice," said Vicar Petley.

Kathryne sipped at her tea and tried her best not to wince.

"Do you like it, Lady Spenser? The shopkeep claimed it had been imported from India."

"Why, yes, I do, Vicar. It is a blend I have yet to taste." *And will never taste again. Or perhaps it has just been boiled for several hours.* She nibbled on the end of a spice cake. *Have I become this jaded when all other food than Mrs. Cole's tastes of straw?*

The vicar was going on about the latest consort he had heard in London. "Do you enjoy music, Lady Spenser?"

"I do indeed, Vicar Petley."

"Perhaps at some date we may arrange a mutual time that we might attend a madrigal performance or chamber recital together—if I am not being too forward for asking."

"Of course not, Vicar. That would be most pleasant."

She looked over the simple table and her full teacup and uneaten cake to see the vicar begin to flush again. *I believe I am being courted,* Kathryne thought, and she smiled back at the red-faced vicar. *So this is what it feels like.*

She let her eyes remain on the vicar's face for a few moments. His countenance was a bit soft, unformed perhaps, but in all generally pleasing to the eye. *So far, I quite like this courting,* she mused.

18 February 1641
Broadwinds, Dorset
England

Dearest Cecily,

I am simply dashing this note to you. I am sure that your life with Baby keeps you quite occupied.

I understand that the London theaters have been closed for a time.

Despite that the order comes from men whose principles and judgment I find beyond reproach, I cannot understand what there is to be gained from such an action. If the play was licentious in an obvious way or horribly graphic, perhaps I would agree. But perhaps there is much I do not understand about the order.

I have begun to teach at the free school in Dorchester several mornings a week. It is most challenging and quite rewarding to see the young faces of the children light up with knowledge. It is such a noble thing that the church is endeavoring to do. I am glad that I may have some small part of it.

Oh, yes, and by the way—I am being courted (I believe) by the young vicar at St. Peter's Church, which is near the school. He wants me to take in a concert with him in London. There is an upcoming performance of the madrigals of John Ward and John Wilbye that we may be attending. I thought you might like to know.

> Your dear friend, as always—
> Kathryne

As she signed her name, Kathryne thought, *How this news of the vicar will tantalize her.*

Barbados

William stood on the tiny forecastle deck, watching the quarterboard painter dangle over the front railing. The sailor had repainted the background white a day previous, and all that was left to paint was the ship's new name: *Reprisal.* Virtually the entire remaining crew from his old ship had joined him in this new adventure. There was danger every league of the way on any voyage, they reasoned. Why not have the chance to reap the huge rewards of a privateer?

Privateer. William liked the way the word felt as he turned it over in his mind.

He looked about at the tidy ship, with its twelve gleaming sixteen-pound cannons lined up like prim yet deadly soldiers on the deck. His eyes took in the vessel's figurehead with its aquiline nose—the angry face of a great hawk.

Privateer. The word sounded most pleasing.

He felt for the locket, for the hundredth time since its taking, and his hand came up cold and empty. *But not for long,* Will thought. *Not for long.*

Will stood on the rear deck of the *Reprisal,* his new home and place of business. In no more than two dozen long steps he could walk from the stern plank to the bow spar of the vessel. The ship was perhaps a dozen short steps wide. She was three decks deep, not spacious enough for a tall man to stand without stooping. The vessel had three masts—one mainmast, standing forty feet high, plus a small mizzen course sail in the rear and an outer jib sail on the bow. His new crew of forty-five men had signed on gladly for the chance to serve under Captain Hawkes. Most were from the *Artemisia.*

"A privateer be no different than a naval ship," one old crewman explained as he scrawled his X on the ship's roster, "'cept on a privateer there be less floggin's, the food be a sight more palatable, and me share of the plunder be better."

William gathered his crew on the main deck a few hours after signing the letter that authorized his funds to be transferred from his barrister in Weymouth to the private account of Radcliffe Spenser, effectively transferring the ownership of the vessel to William. The deck was nearly cheek to jowl with sailors.

"Good men, I am privileged to have served with most of you previously. I welcome you to the *Reprisal.* She may not be a grand ship, but I believe she is sound and fast. Our voyages will not be as long as between here and England, for our hunting grounds be here in the waters of the Caribbees.

"I will do my utmost to run a decent and fair ship. As my standard, there will be no gambling or other games of chance on board this ship. Each man will have five ounces of brandy a day, and drunkenness will not be tolerated. There will be no floggings except as deigned by a council of crewmen, who will be chosen by their peers. I expect you to obey my orders or the orders of Mr. Delacroix, who is my second-in-command.

"As this ship is small, there be no place for fighting or ill feelings. If any man has a dispute, let him come to me first for disposition."

William stood there watching the faces of the crew as they listened intently to his words. *How many of these men have a family?* he thought. *How many have left wives and children back home? How many will die on my watch?*

"Do any of you have questions before we begin to learn how to sail this craft?"

A voice from the back cried out. "Will the shares be the same as before?"

"Yes, they will—double the standard rate."

"Will we ever sail back to England?" another asked.

William hesitated and looked to Mr. Delacroix for guidance. He merely shrugged, palms raised to the sky.

"No. Not on this ship," Will answered. "A sea crossing may be too much for this craft. I know that you with families would like to see them again. None of your marks on the roster means you must stay with this ship longer than you choose. Leave when you need. Stay as you need. There always are ships heading back to England."

"Who will be leading us in prayers, then, now that Mr. St. Clair has passed on?" a third man asked.

Will again looked at Delacroix, who shrugged emphatically.

"Who among the crew would like the position?" Will asked as he scanned the group.

There was silence. A few men shuffled about; most stared at their feet, and then at one another, avoiding eye contact.

Finally, a voice from the back called, "If no one else be willin', I'll give it a try. Just don't be expectin' me to be as good as Mr. St. Clair was, that's all." The man who spoke was Golder Ramsey, a carpenter from Chichester, in West Sussex. His uncle was a rector in that village, and he knew a goodly amount of the Scriptures.

"Fine. You will call the ship to prayer, then."

"Mr. Hawkes, will you be joinin' us then?" Golder asked.

Will was silent again. "It is a fair question," he said, hesitating. *And how do I answer it?* he thought.

"I will not attend as of now, for I have my personal reasons. But rest assured that I will defend, with my life, your right to do so. I believe that is compromise enough. Any others?"

The men stood silent.

"Very well, then. Let us raise the anchor and see if we can learn how she sails, shall we?"

■ ■ ■ ■ ■

Within two weeks, the *Reprisal* sailed twice around Barbados. William took her into the wind and against it. He sailed her close to beaches and over shallow reefs. The ship's draft was so shallow that as they crossed overtop a brightly colored coral reef the entire crew inhaled audibly as one, expecting to hear wood being ripped from the hull. But she slipped smoothly over with nary a scratch. They caught a strong wind from the west, and he tried his best to swamp her, tilting her into the wind. But she stood on the waves like a cork on the water. He would allow the helmsman to steer her on routine patrol, but when in battle, it was understood by all that William would be at the wheel.

From a calm sea and using several old longboats as targets, Will had each gunnery team practice with the new sixteen-pound cannon. He had barely enough men to set a minimum crew at each gun; rather than six men, he had four. It meant that each gun would need three, perhaps four, minutes to fire a second time.

The huge guns needed to be fed a great deal of powder and shot, and William called on his crews to make every practice shot count. Burning sticks would be held to flame pans, and the brass monsters would belch fire and smoke, lurching back and wrenching at the ropes that held them in place as if they were caged beasts struggling for freedom. If a cannon were to break free as it fired, becoming a loose cannon, the recoil could drive it across the narrow ship, where it would crash into the cannon on the opposite side.

After a few tries, an old longboat was struck midship by a single ball. It exploded into a thousand splinters in a plume of angry water. As the echo of the blast rolled back to them, riding the waves, the crew stood—mouths agape—at the destructive power of their newer, larger weapons.

When they returned to Bridgetown for a final provisioning, Will allowed the crew two days' freedom before their first hunting voyage. He walked into town, alone, and against the better judgment of his posterior, rented a horse. He rode at a leisurely pace to the plantation of Mr. Carruthers, who greeted Will with a wary look.

"I do not owe you any more crop, Mr. Hawkes. My debt is paid in full."

"True enough. Your debt has been marked canceled."

"And you no longer have a vessel that can haul our crops."

"That is true as well."

"Then what brings you here to the middle of this godforsaken oven box of an island?" Carruthers asked, wiping the sweat from his face.

"I came here to buy one of your slaves," Will stated.

"I'm not selling. I need all I have. Go to the slave market on St. Lucia if you want slaves," Carruthers replied.

"I do not want slaves," William said. "I want just one slave. A slave that you happen to own."

"None for sale, Mr. Hawkes. Very sorry. None for sale at all."

"He is a black man whom you call Lucky. I saw him working with the foreman Gleeson in your fields close to town."

"Lucky? Hmm, . . . Lucky. I am not sure that name is familiar to me."

Will looked out over the long front garden of the estate. A dozen black women were methodically working their way along the edge of the road, pulling weeds and trimming the bushes with small knives. All were bent at the waist, their backs burnished by the tropical sun.

"Mr. Carruthers, I want to buy a lone slave from you, a man who appears to have more than a hundred slaves. His name is Lucky. I will offer you twenty-five pounds for him."

Carruthers stood up straight. Twenty-five pounds was more than twice what he had paid for any slave. "Twenty-five pounds? Why didn't you say so, Mr. Hawkes? Of course I will sell him to you. Have a cup of planter's punch. I will send for him now. He'll be here within the hour."

And in an hour and a quarter Will and Lucky were walking back toward Bridgetown. The slave looked frightened, his eyes wide. Will, using the rudiments he had learned of Yoruba, the slave's native tongue, tried to reassure him.

"Lucky, all will be well. I need you to be the healer on my boat. Our healer died. Can you do that?"

"I can heal, Massa," Lucky stammered, "better dan any magic man der be."

William stopped as the black man stopped his slow, steady gait.

"You say I be da healer on boat?"

"Yes."

"It be like da boat dat brought me to dis angry place?"

"It is a boat, but it is small, and no black men are on it."

"No black men?"

"None, save you."

"And you want me be da healer?"

"I took you at your word that you are a healer. I saw the truth in your eyes when first we met, Lucky. A man's eyes do not lie."

"Massa, if you want me be da healer, I must gather da roots and da plants to make da powders. I get many on dis island—not all I need—but many."

"You will find them on the way to the harbor?"

"Yes, Massa. Dat I will."

Will pulled the horse, and the two walked along the narrow path. The slave darted off the road occasionally to grab a handful of the leaves or flowers of plants, or to dig up some roots. The sun was hot, and Will stopped to rest a moment by a small stream. The pair sat by the water, listening to its pleasant bubbling.

"There are three more things, Lucky, that you must know."

"Yes, Massa," he said, looking at Will with watery eyes.

"You must start to learn the white man's language. The men on my ship do not speak your tongue."

"Yes, Massa. I learn."

"Your name your parents gave you, it means healer, does it not?"

"Yes, Massa. Luqua it was."

"Then I will call you Luke. Luke was the name of a great healer in the Bible—a ship's doctor, he was. You will be the ship's doctor on the *Reprisal,* and you will be called Luke."

"Yes, Massa. Luke be my name."

"And, Luke, one more thing. You are now a free man again. There may be a black man on my ship, but there will be no slave under my flag."

Luke's lower lip started to tremble, like a butterfly trying his wings for the first time. William looked away, to spare Luke the embarrassment of showing his feelings so openly, yet he thought he heard the sound of his tears splash into the small, quiet pool at their feet.

28 February 1641
Knightsbridge, London

Dearest Kathryne,

I received your letter today, and although my activities as a new mother leave me little time, I felt I must write.

It is only my sincerest desire for your happiness that causes my concern. It is about this vicar whom you say is courting you. What more do you know of him besides his position at the church in Dorchester? What sort of family does he call his own? As the only Lady Spenser of Broadwinds, you have the responsibility of honoring your heritage by pairing up with a man of your class and breeding. I know that your faith is of utmost import to you, but having a partner with no more than a spiritual connection could be vexing in the long run. And you know I have only your best interests at heart when I say so.

Please come visit and see us the next time you are in London.

Fondly,
Cecily

Barbados

The evening before the anchored *Reprisal* was to set sail on its first hunting trip, Will took a small boat and rowed to the piers of Bridgetown. His crew had eaten its last fully cooked meal and was resting in clumps of twos and threes about the upper deck.

It is most foolish of me to do this, William told himself as he pulled smoothly on the oars in the still waters. *But I am sure that Vicar Mayhew would have wanted me to do so.*

He tied the boat to a moss-covered piling and walked up Broad Street to a small white clapboard house. A lantern at the front gate illuminated the walk. Will pushed open the gate, walked to the front door, and tapped soundly.

An elderly woman in a white bonnet opened the door. She squinted up at Will's face, pinching her features even more severely as she tried to focus her eyes. "Who might you be, and who might you want?" she cawed.

"I am William Hawkes, and I have come to ask if I may visit with the vicar for just a moment."

"Have you told 'im of your comin'?"

"No, I have not."

From the back room of the house a man's voice called. "Mrs. Kreble, who is it?"

She turned from Will and shouted, nearly at the top of her lungs. "I don't rightly know, Vicar. Some man says 'e's Hawkes and 'e wants to speak wi' you. Do you care to see 'im?"

From the shadows of the room, a small figure shuffled into the light of the front lantern, dusting crumbs from his lap. "Thank you, Mrs. Kreble," he said loudly, "I will handle this."

The old woman turned back to Will with a face full of suspicion and question, then scuttled off to the shadows from where the man had just appeared.

"Mr. Hawkes, is it? Are you the Captain Hawkes that Radcliffe Spenser has spoken about? Do come in."

He escorted William into a small drawing room with a small fireplace, containing only two weather-beaten and worn armchairs, and a small table nestled between them.

"Please, have a seat. I am Vicar Coates. But then, you must know that if you are visiting me. I would offer you a drink, but the parish house is so poorly supplied that I am sure you will not mind if I appear ungracious."

Will raised a hand. "I have eaten, Vicar Coates, and I require no libations, thank you."

"Radcliffe states that you have the first letters of marque penned by our new Governor Spenser and that you are off to seek revenge on the enemies of England. How jolly exciting."

"Yes, I have that letter, and yes, I do intend on sailing on the morrow."

"Do you think that you will see action soon? How I would love to join you for a hunting voyage. How very swashbuckling it all must be."

Will sat silent, thinking of the men nearly cut in two by cannon shot or run through at the end of a Spanish pike, watching in horror as their entrails spill, damp and with a sickening clump, to a bloody deck.

"Yes, at times it can be exciting," William said in a chilled voice.

The vicar wriggled in his chair, the toes of his feet barely touching the ground, dancing in the dust on the floor. "So, Mr. Hawkes, what is it that I can do for you? The church is at your disposal."

William wanted to get up and run, then leap into the cleansing seawater and swim furiously back to his ship.

"I do not know if this is proper, Vicar, for I have come to ask God's blessing on my venture. I would have come to you to ask for ransom money for Vicar Mayhew, my dear friend and mentor who is being held by the Spanish pirates that destroyed my ship, but I have learned from Radcliffe that such help was out of the question and that my vicar's life may be doomed. I came tonight to see if you may offer assistance, but I can see from this place that you cannot."

"All too true, Mr. Hawkes. If I had an extra pound, I would place it in our building funds for a proper church. I know that this may sound cruel, but God will see to it that your Vicar Mayhew is rewarded for his martyrdom."

Vicar Coates paused. "Actually, I believe I once knew a Thomas Mayhew in London. Wasn't he in trouble for some sort of business of impropriety in the pulpit? I seem to recall some fuss from some quarter over that name. No? Well, perhaps another man then."

"Vicar Coates," William said, in a narrow voice, "I have come to ask for God's blessing on our endeavors. And yet I must ask you, does God bless those who have lost sight of the Almighty?"

"Well, well, well . . . ," the vicar said as he fidgeted. "I suppose he must, since the Scriptures state that it does rain on the just as well as the unjust. And that if you are attempting to do something noble and honorable—such as rescuing a man of the cloth from the hands of the heathens, or worse yet, Papists—I suspect that the Almighty would prefer a favorable outcome. Am I correct to assume you are speaking about yourself?"

Will hung his head. "Yes."

"Well, nothing to be ashamed of. Many of us have lost sight of God for a moment or two."

The vicar waited for a reply and Will remained silent.

"But I am sure God will show you a sign of some sort. He always does, it seems."

Will remained silent.

"Well, then. You asked if the church might bless your sailing. By all means. Shall I do the prayer right here and now? Or would you rather I don my surplice?"

"Right here and now is fine," William said.

"Very well. Almighty God and most Sovereign Lord, I beseech thee that thy servant William Hawkes be provided a successful mission and that he be allowed to wreak havoc on his enemies and thine. I pray that he sails back to us with a bountiful cargo of gold and silver—in which we can build for thee a church worthy of thy blessing. I pray that Captain William return to us safely. In the name of the Father, Son, and Holy Spirit, amen and amen."

There was no sound save the scraping and shuffling of chairs in the room at the back of the house.

"Well then, that's it now," the vicar concluded, standing up. "You will return with news of how it all went, won't you? I would be so terribly interested in hearing of your exploits and all."

"Yes, Vicar," William said dryly. "I will inform you as to our success."

The door clicked behind Will as he walked into the warm night. He walked slowly to the street. Moths were scattering about the light holes in the tin lantern at the end of the walk.

From behind Will, a deep, calm voice spoke. "Be true to the God of your mother and father, William. Be true to that God."

Will spun around and faced a silent, empty street.

▪ ▫ ▪ ▫ ▪

At dawn, Will raised the *Reprisal*'s anchor, which was small enough to be lifted by two strong men, and called for the sails to be unfurled.

"Godspeed," a crewman called.

"Godspeed," echoed all along the deck among the men.

CHAPTER

52

March 1641
The Caribbean Sea

Luke was the first black man most of the crew had ever spoken to. Will waited until they were well under sail to bring him up on deck and tell the crew why Luke was with them.

"A black man can be no doctor."

"He'll be bad luck for us, to be sure, Captain."

"Won't be lettin' him touch me if I gets sick."

"Don't see why we won't get a proper doctor."

"Now listen to me, all of you. Luke is the best doctor on the island," Will said, knowing that he was making a huge assumption of Luke's abilities. "He was a skilled doctor in Dahomey, Africa, before he was taken captive and sold. He knows much of tropical illnesses—even more than surgeons from England. He does not speak much of our language, but I speak some of his. If there be any problems with this man—who is now as free as you or I—I want them noted now."

A murmur rushed through the crew, men leaning to other men, muttering softly.

"Anyone care to speak out?" asked Will.

"Captain, I for one am glad that he's here," Mr. Delacroix said. "It isn't wise to go to sea without a proper healer. Luke is a healer; it's only his skin that is a different color. The poultice he mixed for my leg is already havin' a good effect."

With that said, the crew nodded, collectively assenting to his presence.

Will showed Luke to a secluded spot to hang his hammock, near the bow cargo hold. He became upset and rocked back and forth, uttering a fast torrent of words that Will could not follow.

"What is it, Luke? What are you saying?"

Luke took Will by the hand and led him back to the small captain's cabin. He laid his thin blanket in front of the alcove that was Will's bed.

"Luke sleep here. Luke guard da man who gave freedom, gave life. I not let Evil One attack."

"Evil One, Luke? Who is that?"

"It be Evil One I hear da massa's preacha speak of. I keep him from troublin' captain."

Will placed a hand on Luke's shoulder. *I am not sure who he means,* Will thought. *But I am not willing to have a distraught black man running out of control on my ship the first day of a sailing. I will humor him for now.*

"Thank you, Luke. If that is where you choose to sleep, that is fine with me."

It will be like having a large watchdog asleep at my feet, Will thought with a smile.

8 March 1641
Broadwinds

Dearest Cecily,

How complicated life suddenly has become! And how I envy you for having your affairs in such tidy order—even now with your darling child.

Thank you for your most concerned letter. I know your desire to see me as happy as you are is your intention, and I love you for it. Let me set your heart at rest.

It was only months ago that I came to an understanding within myself. I did not know this Geoffrey Foxton of whom my father speaks, but he has written well of himself. He seems witty and sober and a true gentleman. I resigned myself to follow my dear father's wishes—to sail to Barbados and, unless the Almighty intervened, become betrothed to this Mr. Foxton.

My dear friend, how I struggled with this matter. Does the Scripture's admonition for children to obey one's parents imply that my father's will be done over mine?

And if that was not enough, dear Cecily, I have seen to it that my existence has become much more complex.

As you are aware, I have begun to teach at the free school in Dorchester. The vicar of the church near where the school is located, Giles Petley, is the most pleasant of young men. We have spent some time in conversation, and it thrills me to hear that he is considering a calling on the mission field—perhaps to the Americas, he says.

Giles Petley is most shy, and it was nearly a month that we spoke before he asked if I might accompany him on a trip to Salisbury to hear a chamber orchestra of some note.

We had the most marvelous of times. He is so amusing in a quiet way, and most obviously a man of God. He has never been to our parish, so he has never seen Broadwinds and may not even realize that Lord Aidan is my father. How refreshing.

To set your mind somewhat at ease, know that his father is the earl of Ipswich, who, they say, is quite successful and well connected. You may have heard of the eldest son, Giles's brother Corwin Petley, at court. I understand he has completed his studies of law at one of the finest inns of the court.

But, Cecily, what to do? I enjoy his company, yet I know that I am rebelling against my father's wishes, for he would also say that the vicar was beneath my station. I suspect he may be right, but I still desire to spend time with Giles. I am in such a quandary.

I may not speak of this to Mrs. Cole, who would be scandalized— nor to Lady Emily, who possibly could inform my father.

Please respond, dear friend, with words of counsel.

> As always, your friend,
> Kathryne

The Caribbean Sea

William stood by the wheel station. On this voyage it was he, Mr. Delacroix, and two other mates that had experience behind the wheel of the sailing ship. The *Reprisal* was an easy craft to handle, Will thought, and for that he was gladdened.

The crew was relaxing on deck, the few work details having accomplished their tasks quickly. Since the ship was so small, the vile air—and the rats and rancid waters—had little place to collect and spoil the smell of the ship. Their food could often be foraged from any of the small islands they sailed by. Much of the Antilles was populated by wild hogs, which were most delectable when roasted on an open fire—boucan, it was called. It was a simple matter to spend a calm night—Will simply found a smooth beach, one without too many dangerous rocks, and beached the craft. It was required that he do so at low tide, so the ship wouldn't be stranded if the tide went out.

On their first night on a beach, Will and Johnny Delacroix sat by the fire, enjoying strips of boucan. Afterwards, they walked to the water's edge, near the ship that sat bobbing in the shallows.

"Do you think that a privateer needs to have a set mapping of a route, Mr. Delacroix?" Will asked.

"Well, I have never been one before, so this is all a novel situation, Captain Hawkes," he replied. "Perhaps we merely sail along the trade routes and wait."

"That seems to be haphazard, but I cannot imagine any other way of accomplishing our purpose, short of following a prize ship out of safe harbor. I am certain that that is like the fox who waits for the hare by the front door—it will have a long wait."

"Perhaps, Captain, we will be smiled on by Providence. Perhaps our prey will cross in front of our front door." He smiled.

The following morning they began their sail to a small island just south of St. Vincent, an island in the Grenadines. They sailed the circumference of the island in part of an afternoon. It was without a proper name, since it was small and uninhabited; at least that is what Will surmised from previous trips. In the middle of the island rose a muted volcanic mass. The thick forest and jungle between the beach and the black interior bespoke of it having been hundreds of years since the volcano had last sent ash and lava into the ocean. He had desired to use it as his base—his home island—as they hunted these waters. He had wanted a place to build shelters and store their plunder. Barbados was too far away to be convenient, and Will knew that this small island offered a special convenience.

Will had spotted on a previous reconnaissance a small, secluded, almost hidden cove. It was reached by sailing through a breach in the shore no wider than the height of four men combined. The *Reprisal* slipped through, palm branches and limbs of trees rustling against both sides of the vessel. The cove then opened up to a shallow body of water no more than twenty acres in surface area. It was deep and wide enough for the ship to be poled or rowed about.

As the ship grounded, the men began to jump to the sands, swords at the ready.

"There is no one on this deserted beach," Will called out. "There is no need for defense."

He walked toward a line of palms about forty paces away. A short, pointed wooden object came hurtling from the thick jungle growth and impaled itself with a deadly thump no more than a pace in front of Will.

Everyone stopped dead, eyes alert. Mr. Delacroix motioned to a crewman on deck for his musket.

Will waved that order off.

"Perhaps I spoke a moment too quickly." He looked about, squinting into the thick brush.

"No firearms yet," he loudly whispered. "Whoever threw this easily could have placed the spear in my heart if he chose to. It is apparent that it was merely a warning."

Will took one step backward toward the water's edge.

"Hello!" he called out loudly, with what he hoped was a friendly tone in his voice. "I am Captain William Hawkes of the *Reprisal*. We only seek to anchor here. We come in peace. May I speak to your chief?"

He repeated the greeting and question in French, Spanish, rudimentary Arawak, and Sranan, the Creole language of Suriname. And Luke, who was immediately behind Will, called out in his own tongue, Yoruba, and two other African tongues that he understood.

There was no sound save the cawing of a parrot and the gentle lapping of the water on the beach.

After perhaps a full three minutes in which the entire crew stood motionless and at risk of sudden attack, Will thought he detected a rustling off to his right, and then he saw a few palm fronds bend.

From out of the green barrier a small black man emerged, followed by several of his scrawny tribesmen. He looked to be quite elderly and was clad only in a ragged loincloth. "I am Sapua. I live here with my tribe," he stated.

He spoke the words of one of the African languages Luke had called out in. Luke translated to Will, who translated back to the crew.

"We have lived here for many seasons after the ship we sailed in sank in the waters out there," he said, pointing back to the ocean. "Have you brought us food?"

Will turned and called to Delacroix to bring him some bread or biscuits. In a few moments Delacroix brought Will a handful of small, sweet, molasses cakes, and Will in turn handed them to the chief.

"Here, this is an offering for you and your people for letting us stay with you."

The chief nibbled politely at the edge of one of the strange cakes, then broke out into a wide smile and inserted an entire cake into his mouth.

Through the crumbs, the chief called, "Welcome, Hawkes tribe," and motioned for the rest of his own tribe to join him.

Perhaps fifty black men, women, and a few children gathered around William, hands outstretched, asking for a taste of the molasses cakes.

Mr. Delacroix returned with the ship's entire supply and passed it out, distributing the cakes as equitably as he could.

After several hours of translation, Will discovered that it had been three years since they had been washed ashore on the island. At first they were twice their number, but a white sailing ship had returned and gathered many of them up and sailed off. Those who remained hid in the jungles, and no more ships had come since. It had been difficult— they had no implements or supplies, but they had fashioned a cluster of small huts just beyond the palms in a small clearing. They survived on fish, berries, papaya, cassava, maize, and peanuts. Occasionally they would trap a wild boar. Most of them were wearing but tatters, or nothing at all. Will had an extra canvas sail brought out, with a few knives and sewing supplies.

"It isn't decent for them to be naked," he said, justifying his gift. "And we can ingratiate ourselves with them. We need this cove to be a secure spot for our hiding place—and we need them to be friendly."

Two days later, after supplying the castaways, as Will called them, with a crate full of old tools, fishhooks, lines, and nets, the *Reprisal* set off again, rowing through the narrow opening and catching the tide as it pulled from shore.

By noon they were between St. Vincent and St. Lucia, sailing with only the mizzen sail and jib unfurled. The sky was blue and translucent as bone china, and the waters were edged in deep turquoise. A series of clouds floated by high in the heavens, portending several days of fine, clear sailing. The wind blew strongly from the southeast. Three crewmen with telescopes on deck scouted in every direction. One sailor sat in a small basket at the top of the mainmast.

Standing on the rear deck by the wheel, Will turned to Mr. Delacroix and whispered, "Do you imagine that this is what a privateer does?"

"It must be so, Captain. For this is what *we* do—and we are privateers."

Both men smiled and turned away to scan opposite horizons.

10 March 1641
Broadwinds, Dorset
England

My Dear Papa,
I am so distressed to hear of the storm that has lengthened the completion date of the island's first church. It seems as if the weather

has conspired with the devil to prevent me from sailing sooner. I trust that your latest estimation of completion by Christmas will hold true. I do so want to see you again—and to meet Mr. Foxton. He writes the most delightful letters.

I have not invested in any sailing this season. I heard reports of increased pirate activity in the oceans around Madagascar and wanted no resources of ours to end up at the bottom of the sea. Pirates! I do not understand how any man—heathen or Christian—would allow himself to stoop so low as to scavenge from innocent sailors. I have placed funds in the Crown banks, which will return a full two percent after taxes are collected. It is less rewarding, Father, but more secure.

Again, I am most saddened to hear that my departure from home may be delayed. I am sure that Vicar Petley will be heartened to know that I may continue to teach at the free school for one more term.

Lady Emily has replied to my letter and for now will remain in London, but she plans a visit in the near future.

> Your loving daughter,
> Kathryne

As she pressed her monogram seal into the sealing wax, she paused, then thought to herself, *I trust that he cannot read the lack of sincerity in this correspondence. And that Vicar Petley will be more than glad concerning this delay.*

The Caribbean Sea

It had been three days that the *Reprisal* lay in the waters between St. Vincent and St. Lucia. The time slipped past slowly. If no prey showed within the week, Will told the crew, they would sail north to the St. Lucia Channel to wait.

Will knew that in less than two months he would need to be on the leeward side of the island of Tobago, in case the Spanish captain and his privateers made good on their hostage demands for Vicar Mayhew.

Most crewmen laughed at the possibility.

Will knew they were probably correct in their prediction, but he would have to try. He reached up, and for the thousandth time, felt the empty spot under his shirt, the spot that once held his mother's locket. *If for no other reason than that,* Will thought.

Hunting was tedious, uneventful work—until the first moment that a sail was spotted.

On the fourth day, an hour after dawn and in the middle of breakfast preparations, the mainmast spotter shouted in a shrill voice, "Sails! Captain! Sails to the west!"

Indeed, off due west were three mainsails. *A slow and unwary merchant ship by the looks of her,* Will thought.

"Set a course, Mr. Delacroix. Unfurl all sails. Unlimber the cannons. Set muskets at the ready. Extinguish all fires."

In a moment the deck was alive with scrambling sailors climbing rigging to release sails, closing clamping ports, setting muskets on deck racks, and untying cannons.

"Well, Mr. Delacroix, the hunt is on."

"Aye, sir, it is. And may the winds be with us."

Within five minutes Will knew the chase was won. The merchant ship was sailing under full sails, but the *Reprisal* began to quickly close the gap. Within thirty minutes the spotter could see that the other ship was under the Spanish flag.

Will called out, "Gentlemen! It is fair game!"

A cheer arose from every man.

As the merchantman spotted Will's vessel, her crew raised the ensign calling for identification. Off the stern, the black flag with three chevrons was raised above the flag of both England and Barbados.

It was the first time the *Reprisal* had publicly claimed herself to be a privateer—a hunter. As the black material topped the ensign pole and began to snap and flutter in the wind, a cold chill ran up Will's spine and into his heart.

It was nothing, he told himself. *It was just a surge of excitement, is all.*

But deep in his heart, where only truth could live, Will knew that a part of him—the part of him he truly liked—was ebbing away. It was the part of himself—his core—that was always good and honorable. It was the part of his soul that called itself Christian.

That part of his heart called out, *Can a privateer call himself a good and honorable man?*

Will pushed those thoughts aside and conjured up the images of Vicar Mayhew being dragged off his ship and the dirty hands of the Spanish captain as they curled around his locket, wrenching it from his neck.

The Spanish trader was less than two thousand yards away, and Will called on his first cannon team to prepare to fire a warning shot if the other vessel did not heed to stop. Slowly, with each wave, the *Reprisal* drew closer, narrowing the gap from fifteen hundred to fourteen hundred to a close thousand yards. During this time, the crew was closed-mouthed, speaking in nipped sentences and terse responses.

The Spanish trader kept her flag high on the ensign, not responding to Will's flag requesting them to furl their sails. Will had the black-and-gold checkerboard ensign raised, calling for the Spanish ship to slow, but they did not respond.

No white flag was seen.

"Cannon one!" Will shouted.

"Aye, Captain."

"Prepare to fire at your discretion—a shot across their bow as we turn broad reach into the wind."

In a moment, the lead man on the first cannon crew on the port side looked to Will, who nodded back. He lowered his fuse stick to the flash pan, and the giant gun roared and leapt back, tugging violently at its ropes. The smoke billowed out from the gun, and the shot whistled across the gulf between the ships.

But rather than splashing across its bow, the shot crashed into the Spanish ship's forecastle deck, and Will watched as the debris and lumber was scattered in a huge arc from the impact and men were tossed in several directions. At the moment of impact, as Will watched with a dread curiosity, he spied a small boy running a white flag up the ensign pole in the rear.

"All cannons stand down!" Will shouted, almost frantic. "They've surrendered, Mr. Delacroix—even as we fired! They've surrendered."

Within moments the Spanish mainsail was being raised, and the ship began to slow. The *Reprisal* quickly moved beside the larger ship, and Will's crew threw grappling hooks to secure them together. A small squad, including Will, scrambled up rope netting, watched carefully by a full complement of muskets aimed from the *Reprisal*'s bow and stern. Her cannons remained loaded and could fire an incredibly deadly broadside into the very heart of the Spanish ship.

Will walked, with his men in tow, to the Spanish captain, elegant in a rich purple coat traced with gold trim and lace. All eyes of the merchant crew followed his progress in silence, save the moans of the injured still prone on deck.

"Sir, I am William Hawkes," he explained in Spanish, "a privateer for the governor of Barbados and the Crowned Head of England. These are my letters of marque declaring this boarding as legal under the law. I command you to relinquish all goods and supplies as we see proper."

"Señor Hawkes, why did you fire? We were raising the flag of surrender."

"It was not done quickly enough. We anticipated a defense. And we intended on sending that shot across your bow. These are new cannons, and the crew is yet unsure of their power."

"Then by God's grace, Señor Hawkes, have them practice before you approach the next poor merchant with death in your eyes."

Will stood eye-to-eye with the imperial-looking man, having no words to reply. *The language of regret is leaving me silent,* he thought.

"I will send my doctor to tend to your wounded, if you permit," Will finally said.

"I would, for we have no ship's doctor."

Will called to Mr. Delacroix to send over Luke and to have a full crew search the Spanish ship's cargo.

"I will take my leave, sir," Will said, almost bowing. "I have pressing business to attend."

The Spanish crew parted like a plow through soft earth as Luke walked aboard. With a slow dignity, he carried his bundle of plants and potions and walked to the injured. Will was right behind, ready to translate.

Luke bent close to the first man, an angry red stain filling his shirt. "No, he be gone."

He bent to the next, who had large splinters protruding from his leg and arm. He looked the injured man in the eye. Both were silent, yet the injured man's breath could be heard rasping in his chest. While their eyes were locked, the injured man relaxed, and Luke wrapped his long fingers about the splinter. With a smooth, practiced move, he pulled it out in the blink of an eye. The second was extracted the same way, and into each open wound, Luke sprinkled a mixture of finely ground cloves and comfrey, eucalyptus oil, and the juice of citron. For the next hour, as the raiding party of the *Reprisal* scoured the holds, lockers, and officers' quarters for valuables, Will and Luke tended to the injured and dying on deck.

Within another hour Will's crew had done its work. The *Reprisal* claimed food, several silver ingots that were hidden beneath a floorboard of the captain's cabin, five drums of sugary molasses, and a wealth of gold and silver amulets, looted from descendants of the Aztecs and Incas of Peru and Mexico.

William was the last to leave the Spanish ship. As he made his way down the rigging, he saw the Spanish crew grab one of their dead by the arms and legs and simply fling the body into the sea.

Such an improper last impression, he thought.

Later that night, as they sailed south towards St. Vincent, the men of the *Reprisal* were celebrating noisily. One crewman, a Frenchman from Normandy, was playing a jaunty tune on a fiddle, and several crewmen were dancing to the happy refrain. Will was alone at the stern, perched on a little platform that overhung the water. It was as far from the crew as he might get, short of climbing the mainmast. Luke was on the deck, just in front of Will, squatting, watching the men dance and sing, bobbing his head in cadence to the rhythm.

"You can join them, Luke. You need not stay by me."

"No, I must. Dis was important day."

It does not feel important to me. I have caused the deaths of more than a dozen men. I can take no pride in that—and what's the curse is that it was all done for naught. Those men died in vain. Because of me.

"Massa feel pain?"

"Yes, Luke. I do. Those men should not have died."

"Every man dies. Some today. Some tomorrow. We all die," Luke said, explaining it in a childlike manner.

"But these men would have lived if we had not killed them," Will said softly.

Luke sat, at first looking forward to the men celebrating on deck, then starboard to the icy darkness of the ocean at night, then back over his shoulder to see Will's face, faintly illuminated by the glow of the ship's lanterns.

"Massa in pain?"

"Yes."

"Massa know de Great Spirit?"

"Great Spirit?"

"Luke heard of dis Spirit from massa's preacha on de ship to de islands. He say Great Spirit sent de Son to die so we will not."

"Are you speaking of God and Jesus?"

"Yes, Massa. Dat be him. You know him?"

"I know of whom you speak."

"Men on ship who die today know him, too. I see cross 'round necks. Dey know him, so dey not die. Dat what Great Spirit do."

"Yes, Luke. That is what the Almighty does."

"Den de men not die. No need feel pain, Massa."

With that, Luke turned away, curled himself into a round form, tucked his head on his arm, and within minutes was softly snoring.

Will wanted to cry, then shout, and then leap into the dark waters of the Caribbean to hide from that sliver of conscience that pounded in his heart.

53

*April 1641
Dorchester,
England*

The moon was high over the fields near St. Peter's Church. Kathryne had stayed late to witness the "graduation" of her class from the free school. The proud parents, virtually all of whom lacked the skills to read or write, stood in an uneven line at the rear of the simple room and watched Vicar Petley, then Kathryne, bend and shake each student's hand in turn.

Later that night, after the parents had left, Vicar Petley and Kathryne strolled under the bright moonlight by the river Frome. It was no wider than a stream at this point, and the waters filled the evening with its rolling, liquid sound.

I could listen to this forever, Kathryne thought.

At that instant Vicar Petley tentatively, and ever so slowly, reached out and took her hand in his. She felt a tremble echo up his palm and noticed a stiffness develop in his gait.

"This has been a most pleasant evening, Kathryne," he whispered shyly.

"Yes, it has," Kathryne said softly.

They walked in the moonlight for several moments, neither willing to speak. They stopped in the nodding darkness, and both spoke almost in unison.

"Vicar—"

"Kathryne—"

"Please, Vicar, you first. I do not know what I had wished to say."

The vicar took one tentative step forward. Kathryne remained absolutely still. He bent slowly at the waist, Kathryne still unmoving. Slowly, and then slower yet, his face neared hers, his lips nearing hers. In a brief moment, they touched.

How warm they are, Kathryne thought, *and how soft and giving.* She closed her eyes and titled her head back.

After perhaps a dozen heartbeats, of which the vicar was sure sounded as loud as cannon shots, he gently pulled away and stepped back. He had both her hands in his.

"Kathryne, I want to speak to you." And with that he let her hands drop, took a step backward to regain his composure, and caught his heel on an exposed tree root on the stream bank. His arms shot up to catch himself as his one leg tipped forward and his other slipped further toward the stream, and with a huge splash he crashed into the shallow waters of the Frome.

Kathryne's hands flew to cover her eyes, and when she opened them, Vicar Petley was seated, water swirling about his waist, his arms behind him to brace himself up.

And in another moment they both began to laugh—at first a giggle, then a full-out, doubling-over laugh. Kathryne extended her hand to help Vicar Petley back to dry land.

CHAPTER

54

April 1641
The Caribbean Sea

From its first victim, fifty percent of the *Reprisal*'s plunder was set aside for the Crown, ten percent for Radcliffe Spenser, and forty percent split among the crew. Even with this smaller amount, every man would receive twenty pounds, William calculated as he recorded the worth of their plunder in the cracked leather-bound ledger book stored in a secret cabinet behind his bed. That amount was nearly half a year's wages in His Majesty's navy. Most of the crew was at once dumbfounded by the great fortune and then quite anxious to be able to begin spending the windfall.

For the next week the *Reprisal* cruised the waters of the Straits of Florida, the narrow body of water between the northern tip of the island of Cuba and the southern tip of the vast continent of the Americas called Florida. The warm current from the gulf flowed swiftly north and east through the channel, and it could easily sweep an unsuspecting or inexperienced sailor to ruin on the many shallow reefs and shoals.

On a blistering hot afternoon, precisely a week following their first encounter, a call was heard from the lookout perched on the mainmast.

"Sails to the east!" he shouted.

Mr. Delacroix quickly spun the wheel, and Will called for the second low jib sail to be set. Its use would add to their speed.

"Can you make out her flag?"

"Not yet, Captain. Wait . . . wait . . . aye! She be a Spanish ship!"

"Set to all cannons!"

"Set to all muskets on deck!"

"Batten down the port covers!"

Within a few minutes, the cannon had been unlimbered, loaded, and primed, and Will had taken the wheel.

The sails had caught a healthy stream of wind, and the *Reprisal* tacked, inclining deeply in its face. The bow splashed into the swells, and the vessel took off like a shark after a meal.

The Spanish ship, smaller than their last prey, was not giving ground as quickly. She was lighter by several tons and had a fuller complement of sails. The Spanish ship took a broad reach tack with the wind, and Will matched the effort, letting the wind carry them due north. As the sun rose directly overhead, the wind slackened, and both ships slowed. The *Reprisal* was better suited at sailing with just a light wind and slowly began to narrow the gap on its begrudging victim.

As was the atmosphere before their first encounter, the crewmen were silent, save a few necessary orders. All that would be heard by an observer to the action was the steady hiss of the ship's bow in the light waves and the groan and flap of the canvas in the wind.

"Captain, she be takin' a tack to the east."

"Why would she turn there? The waters begin to shallow over reefs in half a league. They'll be grounded in a moment."

"Perhaps she has no navigator as skilled as you, Captain," explained Mr. Delacroix. "I have seen other English sailors blindly follow their charts into rocks and reefs before. Why should the Spanish be any more clever than we?"

And true to Will's prediction the Spanish ship lurched, its stern rising from the water slightly. The stern then began to come about, as the currents pivoted the ship against the reef. In another moment the sails began to tilt, and the ship listed to half from perpendicular.

"We've captured another!" William shouted to the crew, who responded with a hearty "Hurrah!"

Owing to her very shallow draft, the *Reprisal* sailed directly up to the Spanish ship. They kept the cannons primed, not knowing what awaited. As they came within hailing distance, Will saw two sailors waving the white flag on a long pike.

"Strike up the black-and-gold ensign. Prepare to board," Will ordered.

Will hailed to them in Spanish. "Ahoy! We will now board you to take our plunder! I advise you most strongly that armed resistance is futile as our cannons would send you all to your deaths if we are provoked!"

"Our arms are down, sir. We will not resist, but we have little of value to raiders such as yourselves," came the reply.

A small boarding party climbed the tilted deck and made their way belowdecks. Within less than a half hour they returned, shouldering two small trunks between them.

"It be all tobacco bales belowdecks, Captain Hawkes," said Mr. Dyer. "We found a few trinkets and a few gold coins."

Mr. Delacroix turned to Captain Hawkes. "It may not be as rich as our first, but it was less deadly."

"To be sure," Will replied. "Very well. We will take what you have found."

"Mr. Delacroix, set a course back to base."

"Aye, sir, Captain Hawkes."

On their way home they almost stumbled over a large merchant vessel flying Dutch, French, and Spanish flags—in a vain effort to declare allegiance to each country.

"Which flag is at the top?" Will called.

"It be the Spanish flag."

"Then prepare to set chase."

Within an hour they drew close enough for a warning shot to be fired—and this one cleared the bow cleanly. The huge splash it created resulted in a white flag immediately being raised.

The *Reprisal*'s boarding party searched throughout the ship, carrying mostly cotton, sugar, and tobacco. The sugar was the lightest and most expensive of the cargo, and the raiders spent much of the afternoon loading it onto the deck of their ship. A small chest full of gold doubloons was found hidden away in the captain's berth.

It was not a huge prize, William knew, though the smaller amounts would quickly add up.

On their way back to their hidden cove, they came across yet another Spanish ship, sailing alone in the waters just north of Hispaniola. They, too, surrendered without a shot being fired, and the boarding party from the *Reprisal* did not find much gold or silver, yet each small plunder was adding to their growing treasure.

"Captain Hawkes," one of the crewmen called as they sailed away from their last victim, "you have the Midas touch when it comes to huntin' plunder. We are most blessed to have you as captain."

Blessed? To have me as captain? How I wish I could agree, Will thought.

⬛⬛⬜⬛⬜⬛

The *Reprisal* sailed back through a scenic series of narrow channels and passages, then across more open water to her hidden cove south of St. Vincent.

As she neared the shore, Will was astounded by the sight that greeted his ship. An entire width of palm-fronted beach had been cleared of trees and brush, and in its place a dozen small huts had been constructed.

As the ship glided in onto the sand, the chief of the tribe came to the water's edge to greet them. "We have built you houses," Sapua said proudly. "We now have the axes and other tools you gave us, and we knew you would need a place to sleep. So we built them."

Around him were a dozen children, hiding from the blond-haired white man who stumbled through a tortured version of their own language.

"That is most . . ." Will paused, knowing no word for gracious or generous, ". . . loving of you."

The chief giggled and looked to the ground.

Luke, behind Will by a step, whispered in his ear, "Dat means love in a . . . husband-wife way, Massa."

It was Will's turn to blush. "Then tell them, Luke, how much we appreciate their work."

Again the chief beamed, and the children giggled behind him. Most of them were wearing a new piece of clothing fashioned from the canvas Will had left behind.

Will said in a loud voice, "Luke, tell Sapua that as thanks we will feast tonight."

A cheer rose up from both the sailors and their black benefactors.

"Mr. Delacroix, might you gather up a few men with muskets and locate a wild hog or two for tonight's table?"

"Right away, Captain! You'll soon be tasting some fine boucan!"

The chief extended his bony hand and wrapped it around William's wrist, pulling him toward the newly constructed huts. The children followed them. Sapua stopped in front of the largest of the huts, perhaps a dozen feet across. It was neatly crafted, with wooden poles at the corners between which were walls of woven wattle and mud well hardened in the sun. The thatched roof was of palm fronds. This particular one had a true door, fashioned from limbs and palm woven together and tied with green vines to the frame.

Sapua began to chatter most excitedly.

"Luke, he speaks too fast. What is he saying?"

"Dis be your hut. It be de biggest of all—for de great warrior who has given dem new life."

Will looked down at the black chief, whose eyes were alive and vibrant with happiness—the happiness that comes from giving.

"Tell him thank you. This is the best house I have ever had."

And with that, he opened the door and walked in. The inside was light; under the eaves of the roof were openings for air and illumination. The floor was hard and dry—a mixture of mud, pebbles, and lime that had been well pounded and cleanly swept.

In the corner were two large piles of palm fronds covered by an expanse of canvas that had been scrubbed and bleached in the sun. The chief pointed to the largest, then to William, who nodded. He then pointed to Luke, and then to the smaller cot.

I am glad they prepared him a cot as well, for if they didn't he would be sleeping, no doubt, on the floor at the foot of the bed.

After crowding into the interior with Sapua and Will, the parade of children followed them as they circled the outside of the hut, Will expressing his admiration of their work. Some of the crewmen were already busy constructing a wooden gridiron on which to roast the hogs.

Will looked out over the flurry of activity of the small, pleasant island village. Instead of contentment, he felt a restlessness at the core of his being.

▪ ▪ ▪ ▪

That evening, after feasting on roasted roots and boucan and drinking nearly a full barrel of borrowed Spanish ale, a quiet descended on the small band. William rose from his honored seat around the fire and walked to the water's edge. The tide was rising, and small waves lapped at his feet.

"Massa tired?"

"Yes, Luke, I am tired, and more than a little hot and dirty."

But it is more than that, William thought, as he waded into the warm water. *It is not just fatigue that I feel. I wish I knew what malaise is troubling me.*

The sea at night, he thought as he looked out over the blackened water, *so dark, so mysterious . . . a vast realm of the unknown in its fathomless depths, just as a man's heart.*

He turned to face inland and could see the towering outline of the volcanic mountain peak, now in silhouette against the near-dark sky.

"*Hear my cry, O God; attend unto my prayer. From the end of the earth I will cry unto thee, when my heart is over . . . over . . .*"

"*The word is* overwhelmed, *William. It means being swamped by your problems.*"

"*When my heart is overwhelmed: lead me to the rock that is higher than I.*"

The voice of a younger William and Vicar Mayhew, from what

seemed so long ago, echoed inside him as he stood chest deep in the gentle waves.

"*For thou hast been a shelter for me, and a strong tower from the enemy.*"

A small sob caught in Will's throat as he let the rolling tide wash over his head.

∎∎□∎

The following afternoon the crew set to making repairs to the *Reprisal*—small items mostly—and doing a thorough careening as well, scraping barnacles and removing sea worms from the hull.

Will sat and watched them work from a small cluster of smooth rocks by the shore, a vantage point a little removed from the vessel. A gaggle of children had followed him, laughing shyly, watching every move he made. One of the young ones slowly made his way to a position just below his feet. Gingerly his hand went to touch Will's foot. The little finger rubbed at his ankle for just a moment, then withdrew. He looked down to see an amazed look on the young boy.

"The white does not come off, lad," Will said in English.

The boy returned his words with a curious stare.

Will thought for a moment, then called out. "Mr. Delacroix! Would you be so kind as to retrieve my aviary volumes from my cabin?"

Soon Will had two dozen children at his shoulder, neck, and waist, all staring without uttering a sound as he turned the pages of the book, the first he himself had read as a child with Vicar Mayhew. On each page was an explosion of color plates, featuring birds of England and the Continent. Will knew that this was the first book these children would have ever seen, and he slowly read the names beneath each bird.

And in their quiet voices the choir of children repeated them back to Will.

"Tufted titmouse."

"Rufous hummingbird."

"Williamson thrush."

As their voices echoed about the small cove, Will wondered about his oldest friend. Was he safe? Was the vicar still alive?

By the time Will finished with his third volume, it had grown to dusk. He picked up the smallest of the children, who had been asleep for several minutes, and carried him back to his mother. She had waited, just removed from the circle, until Will had finished. As he handed her the child, she bowed and smiled and bowed again.

There is goodness in this, Will thought. *Goodness that is pure. Why cannot the rest of the world feel the same to me?*

Broadwinds, Dorset
England

The great house was as quiet as a tomb. Kathryne had stayed in her bedchamber the entire day following her return from the graduation party. Mrs. Cole had slipped upstairs to find Kathryne, still dressed in her sleeping robe, sitting on her window seat, staring out into the distance toward the gentle hills beyond the Broadwinds estate.

She tapped ever so lightly at the doorframe. "Kathryne?"

Kathryne slowly turned her head, hardly moving at all, until she saw Mrs. Cole out of the corner of her eyes. "Mrs. Cole, do come in. Would you know what time it is?"

"Child, 'tis midafternoon. Are you ill?"

Mrs. Cole reached out and stroked her hair, as a mother would do for a child frightened by a troubling dream or midnight thunder. Kathryne responded by leaning into her and circling her waist with her arms, as a child seeking that protection.

Poor lamb, Mrs. Cole thought. *How I wish on these times that her sainted mother was still alive. Or that her father was in England. 'Tis so hard for her to navigate life all alone.*

"Did somethin' bad happen, Kathryne?" Mrs. Cole stiffened as she spoke the words, the thought never occurring to her until she spoke out loud.

"No, Mrs. Cole, nothing bad—no bandits or ravishers of young women set upon me."

Mrs. Cole breathed a sigh of relief, trying hard not to let Kathryne know. "But then, child, what did happen? You have never remained in bed all day. You're not some slovenly wastrel who needs to recuperate from a night of debauchery."

It was Kathryne's turn to stiffen. She held herself at arm's length from Mrs. Cole. "Surely you cannot think I would do anything immoral or immodest!" Kathryne exclaimed.

"No, child. I did not think you would."

"After all the Scriptures you've quoted me, after all the Bible stories you told me as a little girl, after all the prayers we have prayed together, after all that—there is never one chance I would do anything to disappoint you or our Lord."

With that she snuggled closer, and Mrs. Cole held her tight.

"Although if I had, I am certain that your punishment would be far more everlasting than the Almighty's retribution."

They both giggled and pulled each other closer.

"Then, child, what can be the matter to have you lie in bed all day?"

"I wish I had my mother here to discuss this. For even as close as we are, Mrs. Cole, it seems almost too intimate to talk about."

Dear God, Mrs. Cole thought, in a panic, *she will not be askin' me of where God brings babies from? I am sure that she understands that at her age.*

"Too intimate, dear? Perhaps I . . . I mean, are you sure . . . that I am . . ."

Kathryne sat up, breaking their embrace again. She looked at Mrs. Cole with a look of mock indignation. "Mrs. Cole! Surely you did not think I was attempting to ask you of . . . those matters of such a personal nature, did you?"

It was Mrs. Cole's turn to be flustered. "Child, all I know is you're not right. And I do not know what you might ask me."

"Well, it is not that," Kathryne stated with finality and returned to Mrs. Cole's motherly hug.

After a moment, she added with a sly whisper, "Lady Emily spoke of it to me and was flushed, red as a beet, for nearly two weeks after every time she looked at my innocent face."

Mrs. Cole giggled, thanking the heavens that she would not have to explain such concepts.

"But, Mrs. Cole, perhaps I am facing something much more complex and confusing than all that."

"What could possibly be more confusin' than that?" Mrs. Cole asked innocently, causing Kathryne to laugh again.

"Well, I am faced with the horns of a dilemma in which I see no resolution. And rather than dance about the situation, as we have in past conversation, I will plainly state it to you."

Kathryne sat back up, as straight as she could, and smoothed her sleeping gown out with her hands, then folded them in her lap, preparing to deliver her problem to a waiting advisor.

"I am now twenty-one years old. It is at my age that most women are . . . married. I know this. On the island of Barbados there waits a perfectly fine young gentleman my father has . . . selected to be a suitor. If he turned out to be a drunkard, or in reality a cruel heathen, perhaps no nuptials would proceed. But I am sure my father has chosen carefully, with my best interests in mind, as well as my sensibilities. So unless fate intervenes, my future . . . betrothed waits for my hand—a mere ocean between us."

Mrs. Cole had nodded throughout. This was ground that had been thoroughly discussed.

"And I have come to accept this . . . fate as proper. Love is most likely an overrated emotion—at least the headlong, rhapsody of love that poets and balladeers speak of. I think Christian love is different, and two can grow to love each other. It does not need occur as in poems and songs."

Mrs. Cole continued to nod.

"My heart has begun to say yes," Kathryne stated softly.

"Child, that is good. It will be best for you. You'll see."

Kathryne continued as if she had not heard. "And I have been teaching at the free school for these many months."

"And it has helped your disposition greatly, Kathryne," Mrs. Cole responded.

"I have loved every moment of passing knowledge onto the children. It was so wonderful to see how proud the parents of these children were. One might feel the heat from their beating hearts."

Kathryne reached and touched the pane of window glass in front of her, tracing along the mullion. "And Vicar Petley is such a noble man. He wants to go to the colonies to preach the gospel, did you know that?"

"No child, I did not." *What is she tryin' to say?* Mrs. Cole wondered.

"He does. And he is so knowledgeable of the Holy Scriptures. Much greater depth than I would even hope for."

"Yes, child, but what is the problem?"

"Last night, we walked by the river after our little graduation ceremony. . . ."

The hairs on the back of Mrs. Cole's neck began to prickle and stand on end.

"And he took my hand in the moonlight, and we stopped to talk."

Mrs. Cole held her breath, fearing the worst.

"And then he leaned toward me and kissed me . . . on the lips."

Mrs. Cole exhaled and slumped.

"And then he fell into the river."

"God's punishment, no doubt, for takin' such liberties with such an innocent young woman!" Mrs. Cole cried out.

"But what shall I do now? I believe I may be falling in love with Vicar Petley," wailed Kathryne as she burrowed into the arms of a bewildered Mrs. Cole.

Kathryne's eyes filled with tears as Mrs. Cole smoothed her hair and cradled her head in her arms. "I never intended this to happen, but he is such a kind and gentle man," Kathryne cried.

Mrs. Cole held back her anger. *A man of the cloth has no business tamperin' with the affections of naive, innocent girls,* she thought. *What is becomin' of today's young people—kissin' by the river in the dark. And a vicar—what licentiousness.*

The Caribbean Sea

The *Reprisal* laid up a week at the hidden cove. The crew settled into their new huts, quickly completed the most major repairs on the ship, and then they sailed again.

On their second venture, two more vessels came under their guns. Only one shot was fired in both attempts. The plunder returned was not a king's ransom, but it added to the treasury.

In between sailings, the crew was glad to remain holed up at their cove. Much of the crew spent their days lazing about, sleeping in hammocks stretched between palm trees near the shore. Some carved the dense wood of the tropics into intricate scenes and objects. Others sat idly by, talking and smoking tobacco, reveling in their leisure. Johnny Delacroix taught the boys of the village how to harvest oysters that encrusted themselves on the tangled branches of mangrove trees that stood in the shallow saltwater at the edges of the bay. Some of their time was spent maintaining the vessel as well, sealing loose joints with oakum, replacing worn ropes with new, mending sails, and splicing rigging.

The crew agreed that this time, as the Tambor brothers claimed, was a "bit of paradise for sailors not used to bein' happy."

But for their captain, no happiness was to be found.

May 1641
Broadwinds, Dorset
England

After a famished Kathryne had finished her third plate of stew, bread, and cheese, she asked if Mrs. Cole might sit and join her at table. Kathryne had eaten in the kitchen, still in her sleeping gown, although she covered herself with a full satin robe.

"Well, Mrs. Cole, have you decided what I should do?"

"Me, child? Why, 'tis a decision for only you to be makin'."

"But I cannot decide."

"You must. For if I were to instruct you, you may blame a bad outcome on me—and that cannot be. These are the decisions of life that one person alone must make."

"So you are stating that I should follow my father's wishes, sail to Barbados, and marry Mr. Foxton?"

"I've not stated that."

"So you want me to follow my heart and choose Vicar Petley, obviously a more godly man, and ignore my father's wishes."

"Child, I've not claimed that opinion either."

"Then I do not know what to do. I never thought I could be in such a shilly-shally state."

"Have you prayed about this?"

"But Mrs. Cole, it happened only two nights ago."

"Time enough to pray."

"I have, Mrs. Cole, and I think that is what is most frightening."

"Frightenin' child? How could God's will be frightenin'?"

Kathryne folded her arms in front of her and rested her chin on her wrists. "Because I believe God is telling me—telling me to follow my heart."

Mrs. Cole placed a tender hand on her arm. "If the message is from God, child, then that is indeed what you should do."

But his eyes are not blue, a small, insistent voice intoned in her head. And with that Kathryne cradled her head in her folded arms and began to quietly weep.

May 1641
The Caribbean Sea

"Six weeks, Captain Hawkes, and a clean dozen trophies. No injuries on the *Reprisal,* a full chest of gold hidden, full bellies, and enough to share with King Charles and Radcliffe Spenser. I believe that this may be a crownin' achievement."

Will stood by the wheel, steering the ship on a sharp tack to the west. "Thank you, Mr. Delacroix. It has been a successful voyage. I do think we will surprise Mr. Radcliffe with our returns."

The fourth full moon was approaching, and Will was heading directly to the leeward side of the island of Tobago.

"I hate to be the one to be bringin' the skeleton to the feast, Captain, but your vicar won't be there," said Delacroix.

"We'll sail with you to China if you ask, sir, but the Spanish won't be waitin' for us with your vicar, and that's a fact," echoed Diggory Dyer.

Will shrugged off all the negative comments. He had set aside a hundred gold pound coins as a ransom settlement, for insurance.

He'll be there, Will thought. *He'll be there, and somehow he'll make all of this good and noble again. He'll be able to stop this pain in my heart. I know he will.*

At sunset they cleared the leeward side, and Will had expected to see a full complement of sails waiting for him. Instead, there was an empty and dark ocean, with a cool, almost chilling breeze flowing from the north.

"We will anchor here for tonight," Will called. "We'll be in proper position to hunt for them at the dawning."

Dawn came, and the *Reprisal* waited at anchor till noon. Will ordered the anchor raised and the sails set and headed south, along the leeward coast. The winds were weak there, and progress into a weak headwind was slow and tedious.

At dusk, the lookout thought he spotted a small sail at a dozen leagues, but it was too far to give chase in the fading light, with the reefs and shoals a constant threat. They anchored again, and Will waited out the night on deck, listening for the groan or splash of a foreign ship.

Dawn broke empty. By late afternoon they came upon a small fishing vessel, plying its nets in a wide lagoon near the southern tip of the island. They hailed it, and in a moment it was broadside, hoping to sell some of its catch. Will did indeed purchase reef fish and turtles, enough for the next two evening's meals.

"Have you seen the *Frontera Nueva*, a Spanish pirate ship, in these waters?" Will called to the five-man crew.

A stocky, deeply bronzed man called out an answer. "We know 'em Captain. Have seen 'em plenty of times in these waters. Always buy from us, too."

Will's heart leaped. "Where are they now? How long have they been gone? Where were they headed?"

"Captain, you ask a lot of questions."

"I am searching for a clergyman they have as hostage. I want him back."

The fishermen laughed. "We won't be makin' fun of you, Captain. But with all due respect, that poor clergyman is most likely dead a long time now."

Will felt his spirits plummet. "We seen 'em do it before. But we haven't seen 'em in these waters for more than two months."

"And you are sure they are not here, hidden in some cove?"

"We knows every cove on this island and have been here for a week, sailin' up and down this coast. Your pirates'll not be here, Captain. Most sorry to have to give you bad news."

The *Reprisal*'s crew tossed a few coins to them and retrieved their fish and turtles.

Will sat at the edge of the stern, quiet. "Set a course due north," he finally said. "But make the sailing slow this trip. Make the sailing slow."

London, England

The next few weeks were a blur to Kathryne. In a few short months she would have to sail across a vast ocean to the island of Barbados to meet

her father and Mr. Foxton. She had spent several days in London with
the barristers representing her father's business dealings. She was arranging to pass on the responsibility, at least until one of the Spensers
returned to England, for maintenance of the Spenser business affairs.

As she reviewed the standing of all the family's accounts and assets,
she realized that a great deal of wealth would someday come to her and
her line as heir to the Spenser estate.

"Your father may indeed set up his will in a different manner than
this, but conventional wisdom dictates a male heir of your line," Mr.
Cochrane stated.

*Perhaps indeed that is the primary reason for Uncle Radcliffe's
ill-mannered behavior to me all these years. Or perhaps it is just human
nature, after all,* she thought, unwilling to assign such uncivilized
behavior to a blood relative.

Upon her return to Broadwinds, she began settling the matters of the
manor as well. In a few short months she would be leaving for an
undetermined length of time. She engaged a local man of high moral
repute to manage the house and grounds in the family's absence. He
was assigned the small home at the rear of the property for the use of
his family. Mrs. Cole, as well as a groundskeeper, head butler, and the
necessary kitchen and parlor maids, would be engaged in perpetuity as
well. The house would run and be occupied as before, with the
exception that no Spensers would be in residence for an unknown
period of time, perhaps for several years.

The thought disquieted Kathryne, and she spent the rest of the day
wandering about the house, touching gilt-framed paintings, examining
the curious bric-a-brac that filled shelves, running her hands over the
bindings of old books—filling her senses with the sights, colors, smells,
and sounds of the place that had been her home since birth.

Barbados

Will and the crew of the *Reprisal* had made their second trip back to
Barbados to present Radcliffe with the Crown's share, as well as his
"unofficial" ten percent of the plunder.

Radcliffe had been most congratulatory over the success of Will's
privateering, calling him the best hope for the quick completion of the
church being built in Bridgetown.

"Best hope for the church? What do you mean?" Will asked.

"My dear Mr. Hawkes, a large portion of the Crown's share of your plunder has been assigned to be used for the construction of the new cathedral. If you continue to be successful, the quicker the good citizens of Barbados will have St. Michael's, their place of worship, completed. That should spur you on to more daring exploits," Radcliffe laughed with a sneer.

"Plunder used to build a house of worship?" Will asked, surprised. "That does not seem a fitting way to spend these gains, especially since the church has chosen to abandon one of their own, my vicar."

Radcliffe laughed. "A pirate with a conscience. How novel."

"I am not a pirate," Will snapped loudly, almost as a shout. "I have a legal charter. We are privateers—not pirates."

Radcliffe had waved him off with a lace handkerchief in his hand. "Pirate, privateer, honest sailor—none of these titles makes any difference to me. You may call yourself what you will. If being described a privateer comforts your soul, then by all means, describe yourself a privateer."

The Caribbean Sea

The *Reprisal* spent a week in Bridgetown provisioning, the crew enjoying its freedom on shore. At the full moon and high tide, Captain Hawkes gathered his crew and set sail again.

In the next three months, they took a series of a dozen ships, some surrendering immediately, others after a long chase. Some required one cannon shot, others required a dozen broadsides. In boarding and battling, Will lost a total of six of his crew to injury. But to offset those losses he added a dozen sailors willing to abandon their ships to join the triumphant privateers. Most important, the *Reprisal* secured a great amount of silver from one of her prey, a large quantity of muskets, a chest of doubloons, and all manner of jewels and heathen artifacts.

It was making Will a rich man. Each victim added numbers to the ledger entry by William's name. *But without any worthy cause to spend these riches on, what good will they provide for me?* whispered the voice in his head.

Broadwinds, Dorset
England

The sun had just edged into the sky and peeked above the sill of the windows in the kitchen. The room was tinted red from the glow, and

Mrs. Cole opened the door to begin supervising the breakfast preparations. She moved slowly, as she always had, until the day seeped into her bones and her pace increased.

She took two steps into the room and gasped, her hand flying to her chest in surprise. Kathryne was sitting at the massive table at the center of the room, eating a large slice of bread spread thick with honey. Her eyes were wide and innocent, looking directly at her old friend.

"Kathryne, you've given me such a start! What on earth has brought you down here so early?"

Kathryne poured another dollop of honey on the bread and mashed a large bite into her mouth. She began to chew and nodded her head, indicating Mrs. Cole was to wait a moment for her answer. Her voice muffled slightly by the last few chews, she said, "Mrs. Cole, I have come to a decision. And I wanted to celebrate. And all that I found to eat was this bread and honey. I do hope that you were not saving it for dinner, or perhaps supper."

"Good heavens, child, of course not. This is your house, after all."

"Yes, well, perhaps," she said with a wave of her hand. "Would you care to join me?"

"No, child, but I would like to hear of your decision," Mrs. Cole said as she pulled up a chair next to Kathryne.

"Do I follow my heart, which has led me to Vicar Petley, or do I follow God, who has, through my obedience to my father, led me to Mr. Foxton?"

"Yes, child. That is a most brief recap, but accurate."

"Well, I cannot follow a course of action that brings me in direct opposition to my father's wishes. I would be acting against God's dictums. I cannot do that."

Mrs. Cole took Kathryne's hand. "Child, I am sure the Almighty will honor your obedience. I am sure that Mr. Foxton is best suited for you. I am sure."

"As am I, Mrs. Cole. As am I. But, Mrs. Cole, . . . how do I tell Vicar Petley?"

CHAPTER

56

August 1641
The Caribbean Sea

On the first of August, following a weeklong spell of squalls and rains that drove the *Reprisal* back to her hidden cove, the crew sailed to the calm waters south of the island of Jamaica. It was a pleasant area of anchorage for many Spanish ships on their journey from the treasure mines of Mexico back to the royal treasuries of Spain.

"I have an unsettled feelin' about these huntin' grounds, Captain," Mr. Delacroix confided in Will during their first night at anchor.

"Have you been speaking to Luke? Has he been filling your head with stories of visions and warnings too?"

"William, I do not state my fears easily nor cavalierly. But these waters feel bewitched. I have the most strong feelin' that we will regret sailin' into them."

"And I say that you are quite mistaken. There is no God watching over us to see us do well, so how can one be waiting to cause us ill?"

Delacroix turned to walk away, then paused and said, "Captain, 'tis true that I share no devout belief in God, but when I hear those words from your mouth, even *I* am shamed. Perhaps I have no faith, but there is a Creator. I am sure he watches over what he has created."

Will had no reply and stood silent as Delacroix went belowdecks.

■ ■ ■ ■ ■

It was warm by the time the sun cleared the eastern horizon. The day promised to be brutally hot, with no clouds in sight.

The lookout shouted, "Sails to the south!"

Will, without even taking time to put up a telescope to his eye to confirm the sighting, spun the wheel as he called for all sails to be lowered.

"Set to all cannons! Unlimber them, gentlemen!"

The crew, well practiced at the deadly dance, swarmed to post and assignment with a fluidity that indicated their practice.

"She be a Spanish ship of the fleet, Captain!"

A chill ran through Will, as it did many of the crew. A ship of the fleet meant a standard naval ship, with better trained crews, more cannons with practiced gunners, faster sails, and better techniques.

Will set a grim look on his face. *We can take her. I know we can take her.*

It may have been a deliberate tempting of the hands of fate. The *Reprisal* and her men had not yet tasted defeat in any of their hunts and had begun to think of themselves as more than mortal, incapable of being defeated by any opponent, no matter how large.

Odd that such a ship is sailing alone, a solitary prey. Spanish naval ships usually travel in convoys. Perhaps she has floundered and will be easier to take, Will thought as he hoped that his boldness was not mere false bravado.

The die had been cast as Will set to the chase. No matter that the odds were not in favor of a successful resolution—the *Reprisal* was a hunter and William was hunting.

The chase was long—all that day Will followed the Spanish ship's tacks in the wind with his. Dusk came, and both ships were lit with the light of a three-quarters moon, both sets of sails ghostly apparitions in the silvery waters. If his prey could be kept in sight, Will could catch them with the dawn.

Dawn broke hot, with a thin wind from the south. The sparse breeze favored the small ship, with less bulk to carry through the waves and a shallower draft than her Spanish prey. The sun, just at the eastern horizon, slipped up to a cloudless sky. The first rays had already caused men to begin to sweat—some from heat, some from tension.

As the sun rose, the *Reprisal* gained ground slowly. Soon the distance was quartered, then halved, then she drew within twenty-five hundred yards—too far for effective cannon shot, but well within sight.

I'll catch her before noon, Will told himself with pride. *And we'll have her stores for our dinner.*

Will did not anticipate the turn of events that transpired.

At two thousand yards, Will called his steward to raise the black flag with the three chevrons, indicating they were privateers. On a higher standard, they raised the black-and-yellow signal flag that called for the Spanish ship to stop and be boarded.

From the stern, Will saw no flag in reply. "Perhaps we shall get their attention in another manner," he said with a thin smile.

"Make ready cannon one! Turn her as far forward as you can."

In a few minutes, the cannon had been repositioned so her line of fire was almost facing forward, and she was loaded and primed.

"Please, if you would, Cannon Master, fire your shot off her stern as I turn away for a moment."

Will cut the wheel a half turn, the *Reprisal* slid to starboard a few degrees, and the cannon had a clear shot to hit just behind the Spanish ship.

The mighty gun roared and the shot splashed a few yards to the rear of the enemy ship. William settled the *Reprisal* again just off the starboard rear of the Spanish ship, waiting to see a white flag raised.

Why are they not responding? And why would a Spanish fleet ship be left behind like this? Is it a trap?

Will began to doubt his decision and turned his head to look behind him for a second Spanish ship in case he was being followed. In doing so he did not see the Spanish ship in front of him execute a slight turn to starboard as well, opening up a clear shot from several of her forward guns. Their cannons roared in reply, smoke belching from the first four cannon ports. All shots were fired and fell short, thankfully, though landing close to the *Reprisal*'s bow. The thick spray from those shots, no more than a dozen yards in front, sluiced across the forward deck at ankle depth.

William quickly turned back to sit at the rear right corner of the Spanish ship to avoid her side cannons. At the distance he followed, the small cannon and side arms mounted at the stern were too distant to be effective.

Will caught a rough wave of her wake, and the *Reprisal* sloshed to port for a bit, coming nearly perpendicular to her prey for a few seconds, until Will righted the wheel and set her straight again.

Some warships carried a full complement of large cannons at the rear, but most often it was protected with smaller armament, stern chasers of small bore and weight.

Will kept his ship in the enemy's shadows, planning his next move. The crew was silent, save the occasional order given and quickly carried out, for his men were practiced at this ballet of death.

After perhaps a league of distance had been covered with neither side showing any movement except forward, Will called out. "Cannon masters and lead crew, come to the wheel."

At an instant, Will was joined by twelve men.

"What is the fastest time that your cannons can be fired, then loaded again?"

The cannon master answered, "Perhaps three minutes between firings, sir."

"That would be too long. Can your men do the task in two minutes a shot?"

"If we had one crewman assigned as powder monkey, sir, to fetch the fresh powder."

"Make that order so, Cannon Master. Select your men as powder monkeys. We'll sail with full sails."

The powder monkeys were selected, and the cannon master motioned to the captain that all was ready. The cannons were loaded and primed.

"Men, this be the plan. I will cut across her wake at right angles to her. You will fire into her stern at your best opportunity. It will be a difficult shot for the roughness of the waves and that the firing side will be descended downward as we pass. You will need to elevate the cannons to the maximum. Do you understand?"

Silent nods were seen by all crew.

"Very well. Cannon Master, are you ready?"

"Aye, sir."

"Then let the hunt begin."

Will angled the ship a bit to starboard, then cut sharply back across her wake, turning the *Reprisal* almost perpendicular to the Spanish ship. Without waiting for an order, all six guns sounded, bellowing across the waves, smoke billowing out from six roaring beasts. As soon as they fired, Will spun the wheel back to right the ship before making a second tack, reversing her direction. The six shots all fell short, but barely, splashing huge waves against the stern windows of the hunted ship.

"Increase the elevation, Cannon Master!"

The wheel spun again, and the ship veered to port. As they tracked across the narrow wake, Will attempted to place the ship level as they cleared the first wake. The cannons on the port side roared out again, and this time three of the shots found their mark. One hit directly at what Will took to be the captain's quarters, and it exploded in a ball of splinters and glass shards. Two other shots hit lower, near the waterline, just above the rudder.

Perhaps we can easily disable her by nipping at her heels, Will thought. *After all, a small dog can sometimes bring down a wild stag by staying away from its horns and biting at its rear legs.*

The ship was brought to the rear port side and straightened out, following the Spanish ship as a shadow that moved from left to right.

The cannon master was smiling from the thrill of the battle, and he nodded broadly. Will turned the wheel and cut back against the wake. As she cleared the first wake and settled into the narrow trough between the two, the cannon announced again, and this time all six gunners sent all six home with their second attempt. The gallery running the width of the Spanish ship's stern was struck and partially destroyed. Two shots crashed through the windows of the stern quarter gallery. The fourth, fifth, and sixth shots struck heavy at the rudder chain and stern post, creating neat holes in the long oak strakes of the ship's rear. Will spun the wheel, and his small pinnace turned to sit at the starboard far rear.

It is a simple matter to bring down such a Goliath. All it takes is skill and bravery, Will thought.

Two more passes were made, and the stern of the Spanish ship was devastated. A small fire had broken out on her third or fourth decks, and the entire stern section was a mass of broken and charred wood, splinters, and wreckage. The ship was turning slowly; apparently her rudder had been struck and disabled as well.

Will was about to congratulate his cannon master on bringing down such a prey with such dispatch. He looked up at the poop deck of his victim and saw the glint of brass in the sun. He squinted, and in the briefest moment the brass glint bellowed out a roar. In a half heartbeat a cannonball broke across the *Reprisal*'s quarterdeck. Wood was rent from its place, and men shrieked in pain. The Spanish sailors had removed a sixteen-pounder from their main deck and carried it to the aftercastle deck and opened fire. Will turned to his left and saw that gun number five had been cleanly knocked through the rail, carrying half the gun crew with it. An angry red stain on the torn decking was all that remained of four men.

The crew all turned, slowly, as if paralyzed by the shot, then one man broke into a wail, while grabbing a full pail of water to throw on a small fire that had started. Will looked back up and saw a second glint.

From his right, he heard a crewman say over the bellowing cannons, "Holy Mother of God," just as a second enemy cannon roared.

This shot hissed through the mainmast of the *Reprisal*, making the sound as when a blacksmith lowers a red-hot pike tip into a bucket of cold water.

The *Reprisal*'s port side cannons, except the one just destroyed, were primed, and Will had no choice but to turn back into the wake and fire again. The cannon master did his job well, and one of the Spanish cannons—or at least the decking around it—was hit. The splinters and debris created a deadly rain. The lucky victims were impaled by large splinters and quickly died; those less fortunate would be left on the decks, writhing in agony from a hundred smaller wounds.

As they passed by the stern, the Spanish cannon fired a single shot, which cleanly tore the *Reprisal*'s bowsprit and some of the forecastle deck off. Three men disappeared, and a portion of the deck was all but destroyed. Then all six cannons from the *Reprisal* fired again, and three shots struck at the Spanish vessel's thick rudder assembly, crippling its effectiveness. The three other shots went higher, into the gaping wound that was the stern of the Spanish ship. Explosions could be heard, as well as the screams of the Spanish crew.

Will was near panic. *It was not supposed to be like this. There is too much blood and death and destruction.*

If he did nothing, they would eventually be sunk. The combined firepower of the *Reprisal* was no match for the Spanish ship. But to back down now and retreat like a beaten dog with its tail tucked between his legs was almost as unthinkable. Will had lost at least a dozen men so far, and if they came away with nothing, what would their deaths have accomplished?

In a sudden flash of awareness, Will knew what he must do.

He turned his ship again, and the five remaining port guns sounded, firing their charges into what was left of the stern of the Spanish ship.

One shot was graced, for it struck a small rear magazine full of small arms and gunpowder. From the rear, it looked as if the starboard side of the Spanish vessel was growing, expanding, taking a large breath of sea air. But then fire, smoke, debris, and men were expelled from the ship, as if the devil himself were sneezing destruction into the world.

The crew stood slack-mouthed as they watched the detritus rain over the ocean around them.

As the smoke and mist carried about the *Reprisal,* hiding it from the Spanish ship, Will turned the wheel one last time.

"Set to forward decks with hooks!" he shouted. "Set to muskets from quarterdeck! Pikes, boarding axes, and swords at the ready!"

The small pinnace was following on the wake of the greater ship, coming closer and closer. A hundred yards, then seventy-five, then fifty, then twenty-five. The fire aboard the Spanish ship was still raging, and the smoke obscured much of Will's vision. He kept steering into the worst of the smoke, his eyes filled with tears from the acrid atmosphere.

A few seconds later the *Reprisal* rode its bow into the very stern of the Spanish ship. With a wooden crunch the two ships met.

"Hooks off!" Will cried, and a dozen grappling hooks sailed up into the stern of the Spanish ship. When the hooks found purchase, they were tied off on cleats on the rail and deck.

"Secure hooks!"

A few Spanish sailors came to the top of the stern or made their way through the wreckage of the officers' cabins at the stern. A dozen sailors on the *Reprisal*, each armed with muskets, opened fire, dropping most of their targets.

There were sixty-five able crewmen when the *Reprisal* met the Spanish ship the previous evening. There were now fifty left. Those men, armed with pikes, swords, knives, pistols, and clubs, leaped from the forecastle of their ship into the smoke-filled rubble and damage of the Spanish vessel.

They were met with surprising little resistance on the lower decks. As Will and his men ran from there to the middle decks to the upper gun decks, only a scattering of opposition was encountered.

Will was at the lead of one group of men making their way up the gangways to the rear quarterdeck. His eyes were filled with smoke, and he could see no more than a few feet in front of him. He had met only one Spanish sailor, who was dispatched easily with a thump on the head with the rounded brass pommel on the hilt of Will's cutlass.

At last they reached the deck just rear of the mizzenmast. The explosion had splintered the deck there, and the mast was cracked and leaning toward the bow. Will could hear the rigging and the ropes shriek as the crew tried to hold it from falling.

The deck was a shambles of wounded men, smoke, burning canvas and pitch, blood, and dead or dying sailors. The explosion had been more intense than Will had suspected. Nearly half the quarterdeck had been blown away, and a gaping hole punched into the ship down to her middle deck. What Will had thought had been the rear magazine had turned out to have been the main magazine for the entire ship.

Will had captured a destroyed ship, and in the swirling smoke, he was unsure of what to do next.

A tall, elegant Spanish captain, with soot and ash smeared across his sweat-lined face, came toward William with his sword held at the ready. Will pulled the pistol from his belt and aimed the weapon at the captain's chest. As he pulled the trigger, he closed his eyes, unwilling to see the moment when the bullet crashed into his enemy.

But there was no sound, no recoil from the shot. Will looked in surprise at the pistol and realized that in the tension of the battle he had forgotten to load it with powder. Before Will could drop his gun, the Spanish captain lunged at Will.

Combat, at arm's length, is a strange and deadly intimate dance. To Will the action seemed to take place in another realm—a realm where speed was lengthened and each movement occupied not seconds, but long moments.

Will saw the Spanish blade flickering in the noon sun as it began its long, graceful arc up, away, and then toward his shoulder. Will bent at the waist and pulled his cutlass to chest height to parry the blow. Will was late, and the Spanish blade found purchase in the soft flesh of Will's left upper arm. Blood ran in thick rivulets down his arm. No main vessels had been cut, Will imagined, but the pain spun out from the cut like ripples from a cannon shot into the sea.

Will backed up a step and lashed back. He lifted his cutlass, held first at chest level, and rotated the blade in a wide circle, its goal the left, unprotected side of his attacker.

The captain was skilled and brought his weapon up quickly to deflect the blow. The swords clanged together loudly. Rather than pull the weapon back close to his body, Will left his own front unguarded and sliced again with the cutlass, this time lower, aiming at his opponent's thigh.

The captain did not expect Will's continued aggression, and the blade dug deeply into the flesh, easily cutting through his fine blue felt breeches. The blade was buried deep as Will extracted it again. His opponent, with a shocked look on his face, stumbled backwards a step. He put his left hand to the wound and pulled it back covered with scarlet.

Will, breathing deeply, called out in Spanish, "Please sir, I ask that you surrender. I have letters of marque, and this ship is my treasure. You have fought bravely. I ask for your surrender."

The Spanish captain shook his head slowly and with lips tightly pursed, either from the pain or determination, lunged again. Will deflected his attack, a sweeping long overhead blow that Will saw develop from a distance. The two blades met with a sounding clatter. The Spanish captain's blade bounced back from Will's, who had a firmer grip. Again, the Spaniard stepped back, then with another long overhand swipe, charged at Will. Almost as if by instinct, Will lowered his cutlass, the point aimed directly at the gut of his opponent.

Whether it was a sudden swell of the sea, or the loss of blood, or perhaps the injured leg, Will would not know. His opponent took a sudden lurch and charged forward, as if not seeing Will's extended blade. As the Spanish captain stopped almost at arm's length from Will, he looked down at his chest, as if annoyed, as he stared at the blade impaling him. His eyes turned from there to Will's face, then grew soft and unfocused as he dropped to the deck at Will's feet.

The fight now subsided from all corners. A few combatants were still engaged, but most stopped to look as the two captains finalized their fight.

Will looked about, his faced streaked with blood, ash, and smoke. He was panting hard. *I did not mean to see his death. Now what shall I do? Now what is proper?*

A spirited "Hurrah!" arose from his attacking crew members, and the remaining Spanish sailors, as if taking cues in this battle, tossed down their arms with a clattering surrender and held hands skyward.

Will called out loudly in Spanish, "Who is the second-in-command on this vessel?"

A figure stepped forward from the far side of the shattered deck. "I am, sir. I am Lieutenant Escobar. What shall you do with us? In the name of the Almighty, I request that you do not put us all to the sword."

Do we appear to be bloodthirsty devils? Will thought.

"Lieutenant Escobar, we will do no such thing. Unless your men resist our search, no further injuries will result. I do ask, however, for the location of the ship's treasury and valuables."

"Sorrowfully, some was lost when the magazine exploded. But there is a forward cargo hold that contains silver bars."

William organized a crew to extract what cargo of value remained. Following the explosion and the heavy cannon damage, much had been lost or destroyed. The crew searched with haste, for the Spanish ship, named *El Diablo,* William discovered—an appropriate name, he thought—was still burning at several points. Most of the Spanish crew was pulling up buckets of seawater to extinguish the flames, but as the last silver bar was extracted from the forward hold, Will saw that their cause was most hopeless.

"Lieutenant Escobar. I suggest that you take your remaining crew off in longboats. I see you have enough for all members. The island of Haiti is no more than two days sail east."

The lieutenant looked about at the dying ship, now starting to roll to the starboard side. "Yes, we will evacuate."

"Well . . ." Will stood there, with his cutlass held in his left hand, while he held firm pressure on his injury with his right hand, trying to close the wound. "Well, Godspeed then. You were a most worthy opponent," he said.

The *Reprisal* shoved off from the burning Spanish ship and then set sail to the south. As the crew turned to see the *El Diablo* for a last time, they saw the scores of Spanish sailors lower their longboats and sail from the fiery wreck.

A quick tally showed that the *Reprisal* had lost one cannon to the ocean floor and a second had been badly damaged by enemy fire. At least twenty men had been lost, and another dozen had been injured in the attack—some slight, others of such injury that they would not breathe long. The ship had been struck a dozen times, yet she still held her seaworthiness. Sections of her deck were gone, her bow beam was split, her jib sail and mast were gone, her mainmast was a shroud of holes, and the railing about the aft deck was a splintered remnant.

Will climbed slowly through the wreckage, using the cutlass he held with a death grip in his left hand as a cane. Mr. Delacroix had a severe cut across the forearm of his right arm, caught while deflecting a blow with his bare skin. Luke had stayed behind and was prepared for the onslaught of injured and wounded.

Will turned from him as they began to sail south. "You will treat me last, Luke. There will be no arguments. Tend to the others before."

"But massa, you cut deep. I must now—"

"No. I will be fine. Tend to Mr. Delacroix first."

For the next two hours, Luke treated cuts and musket wounds. He had no training for amputations, but it was a necessity for shattered limbs. With a bucket of hot pitch to seal the limb, he neatly cut through tendons and bone with a saw. When they returned to the hidden base, there would be two sailors needing to be fitted with wooden stumps for legs. Two others lost arms. Three died as Luke treated them.

As Will steered the ship, his right hand still clutching at the wound, he stared straight ahead without hearing the screams and moans of the wounded and dying. Those that escaped injury altogether were quiet, but took small comfort in that they had just come upon a fortune of gold and silver.

Was this fight worth it? Will asked himself. *Is all the gold of the seven seas worth dying for? Is being an instrument of revenge voiding my soul in the process?*

The sun had turned orange at the western horizon as Luke returned to Will. "I done as Massa say. I tend all de others first. Now I tend Massa."

Luke pulled away Will's hand from the wound. It was black at the edges, where the blood had dried. The flesh had parted to the bone and was an angry red color.

"Massa hurt deep."

Luke pulled a small leather pouch from a belt at his waist and sprinkled witch hazel into the opening. Will winced as he did it, staring out to sea, ignoring the process. Luke then poured rainwater from a gourd into a small wooden cup and added a handful of fine yellow powder, his own special blend of herbs, which he mixed to a thick paste. He applied that to Will's arm, wrapped a leaf from an aloe plant around it, then tied it closed with thin strips of canvas.

"Massa rest. Much blood spilled."

"I will rest when we get back to base, Luke. I am weary, but I cannot rest."

The *Reprisal* sailed all that night and two days until it reached home. By the end of the second day, William was bathed in sweat from a fever. He trembled as the ship rolled with the swells of the sea, but refused to relinquish the wheel.

As they neared their hidden cove, perhaps an hour's sail to the south side of the small island, Will wavered, then collapsed like a rag doll to the deck. Luke cradled his head in his lap until they landed, with Mr. Delacroix at the wheel. The crewmen gingerly placed him on a thick blanket and carried him, as men might carry a casket, to his hut by the beach.

A crowd of natives and crewmen gathered about Will's hut, silent, heads down. Luke came out.

"Massa Will sleep. He be better. He be better."

From the shaky tone of Luke's voice, all knew that he was unsettled and most anxious about the captain's chance at recovery. A man who suffered the trancelike condition of catalepsy, such as William, oft never returned.

As that night turned to day, and then night again, Will slumbered in his fever. He tossed fitfully. He sweated, and Luke wiped the sweat from his body with cool water. He moaned and called out and began to thrash about. Luke called for help, and two crewmen came to hold him still lest he injure himself as he battered himself about the hut in his delirium.

▪ ▪ ▪ ▪ ▪

Who is that calling me? Will dreamed. *Who is there?*

He was in a vast field of red poppies surrounded by a sea of green trees with thick trunks. From the far side of the field, he looked, and through the clouds he saw the image of a woman. It was his mother. Beside her stood his father, and beside them was the vicar. They reached out to him, their arms floating over the field of poppies. He saw their mouths open, calling to him, talking to him. From behind him and to the sides were roaring, bellowing, claps of rolling thunder, with clouds of black smoke billowing across the field.

"Mother," he called out in his dream. "Father. Vicar." They continued to call for him, but he could not hear their voices over the roar at his sides.

"What is it, Mother? What are you telling me?"

And as he heard but a thin wisp of her voice, the booms would start again, and her soft voice would be drowned out by the noise.

"What are you telling me? Don't leave me! Don't go!"

The poppy fields began to spread, and the trees fled, and the faces of his loved ones vanished in the field of red, waving flowers.

CHAPTER

57

August 1641
Dorchester, England

The house-place in the parsonage of St. Peter's was still as Kathryne entered. She had tethered her horse outside by the gate and had walked slowly to the door. Tapping, at first softly, then louder, had drawn no response from inside. She tested the latch, and it was unlocked.

Is this too forward? she wondered. Opening the door a narrow crack, she called out, "Vicar? Mrs. Rice? Is anyone at home?"

She stood back again and heard no activity. The weather had grown squally, and Kathryne felt the first few drops of rain on her forehead. Her horse, Portia, was nestled under an oak tree, so her saddle would receive little moisture from the light shower, but Kathryne was standing in the open with no protection.

Well, if it is too forward, then so be it.

She opened the door and boldly stepped into the house-place. The small kitchen and eating room that was off the living room was dark as well, and smelled of . . . *cauliflower,* Kathryne thought, as she sniffed the air. The firebox needed cleaning, and the small pots of herbs on the windowsill needed water and pinching back. There was also a thin layer of dust on the eating table.

She dusted off a bench in the house-place and sat by the fireplace to wait. Within an hour she was rewarded. She heard the vicar's voice from outside, excitedly calling, "Kathryne! Are you here, Kathryne?"

She leapt from her chair to the door, swung it open, and ran outside. As she did, the thought struck her solid as a club, *I could be doing this as a wife—waiting for a husband to return home. How joyous my heart would be.*

And as the thought entered her mind, a second thought quickly followed. *But it will never be with the good vicar. That possibility is over, for I am leaving.*

And her heart began to ache. It was a pain that Kathryne had thought had ended with her decision. She had been wrong, and the tears that threatened to come convinced her of that.

"Dear Kathryne, what a tender surprise! What brings you to St. Peter's on a Monday morning such as this?" The vicar took her hands in his and looked deep into her green eyes.

"Let us go inside, for I have news of great import to tell you," she said.

He looked about to see if anyone was watching. He saw no one.

The pair entered the kitchen, and the vicar removed his surplice and shook off the moisture. He hung it with great care on a peg on the back of the door. He was dressed in black, as was his custom, but he was wearing his best, and most solemn looking, cassock and upturned collar. It was what he wore to funerals and weddings. Kathryne puzzled over his choice of outfit but remained silent. The two sat in the two chairs by the cold fireplace.

The vicar seemed excited this morning, his actions carrying a sense of imminent promise. He took her hands in his.

"Kathryne, how I love to gaze upon your features. It does my heart well to see you in the mornings like this."

"Vicar Petley, I am flattered—"

"Please call me Giles."

Kathryne blushed, from the compliment and suggestion of familiarity as well as the impending task.

"I must share with you some news of an unpleasant nature," Kathryne continued. "I thought it best to see you as soon as arrangements had been made. It seemed to me to be the proper path to follow, Vicar, . . . er, Giles, and one in which my father would be most honored."

The vicar looked bewildered. "Kathryne, I must confess, I find no logic to what you are saying. Might you restate your news?"

Kathryne placed her hands, folded together as if two intertwined animals, in her lap. She stared at the floor. "You know my father is governor of Barbados in the Lesser Antilles."

"Yes, and I am very proud of his accomplishment. And I am impressed that I know you . . . as well as I do. The church officials in London were also most delighted that such a connection has developed—if I may put it in those terms."

Kathryne hardly heard his words, though if she had, she may have been more distressed than she was at the moment.

"Yes, I am glad for you, but what I have been dreading to tell you is that my father and I have been corresponding. He has finished the governor's estate. The church is nearing completion, and the needed funds continue to be received. The social life on the island is slowly but certainly adapting to the proper English sense of order and morality. My father thinks it would be an opportune circumstance if I journeyed there to visit with him and . . ."

She let her voice trail off, unable to breach the news of Mr. Foxton just yet.

"Kathryne, as long as I live I shall never understand the Almighty and his plans!"

To Kathryne, the vicar's words were correct, but the tone in which he spoke them was much too joyful and excited to be understood.

"And Vicar Petley, . . . Giles, it pains me to say that I shall soon sail for the Caribbean. How I am grieved—"

The smile on the vicar's face was so disconcerting and bewildering that Kathryne stopped in mid-sentence. "Giles Petley! I do not purport to understand the workings of the male sensibilities, but I am announcing that I shall be leaving England shortly and journeying nearly halfway about the globe, and you sit there grinning like a jester. If you are happy to see me depart, I suggest that you hide your feelings, as would a true gentleman. To see you smile as my heart breaks is too much for me to bear." Kathryne's words came in a torrent, and she was close to tears.

The vicar looked distraught, then smiled and moved to Kathryne, embracing her in a full, encompassing hug. She was so taken aback, she neither returned his embrace nor pushed him off.

"Kathryne—darling girl—your news is remarkable and wonderful and amazing all at the same time."

He broke the embrace, and Kathryne sat back, stunned to silence. He reached into his breastpocket and extracted a folded sheet of parchment. "Do you know what this is?"

Kathryne numbly shook her head no.

"It is what I have been hoping for, and praying about, for months," he said, his excitement very apparent.

"This small sheet of paper holds out such promise for me, Kathryne—for *us*, now as well. This is an assignment from Bishop Halifax in London. He has requested that I assist in the final stages of construction and dedication of a new cathedral—in Bridgetown—on the island of Barbados! I have been assigned to travel there as well! We will be on the same island!"

Kathryne's jaw dropped as she gaped at him in astonishment. "But how? When? But I . . ."

"I shall leave in two months time."

"As will I."

"And the bishop has arranged travel for me on a ship called . . . let me find its name here . . . called the *Plymouth Spirit*."

Kathryne felt herself go faint. Just before she slipped into the curious state, she uttered the words, "It is the same ship upon which I will travel."

The vicar caught her and began fanning her face, cooling her brow as best he could. He had no practice with the frailties of women and felt at a loss to know how to treat her delicate condition.

Her eyelids fluttered, and after only a few minutes of unconsciousness she opened them tentatively. The vicar had her head cradled in his arms, his face was no more than inches from hers.

She reached up and touched his cheek with her palm, allowing it to linger there a moment. *How smooth his cheek is,* she thought. She let her hand slip slowly to his chin, and then cupping the chin softly, she pulled his face to hers, their lips meeting in a warm kiss.

At that moment, Mrs. Rice returned from the market in town, her apron filled with muddy turnips she had purchased for supper. She struggled with the latch and entered the room, seeing her employer, the moral and upstanding vicar, in a most amorous embrace with that libertine woman from his school. She shrieked, let go of the apron corners, spilling the dozen turnips in a noisy clump on the floor, and hid her eyes with her hands.

One of the turnips rolled across the floor and nudged against Kathryne's foot. She thought it to be a mouse or rat and jumped up, shrieking as well, spilling the vicar into a heap at her feet.

58

August 1641
The Caribbean Sea

It had been almost a month since the *Reprisal* limped back to her secret base, full of silver and gold—four times the total plunder from its first voyage in one capture.

Four more sailors had died by then from their wounds. Their deaths were expected, though Luke did all that he could for them. Will recovered, slowly healing from the gash in his arm and the fever that followed. The wound scarred over, and no tenderness remained, save an occasional twinge at night.

He regained consciousness a day after his dreamlike vision and spent the next several weeks sitting at the threshold of his hut, staring out to sea with a blank countenance on his features. The only time he was animated and expressive was the daily time he took to teach English to the village children. He would read to them from the books he had and show them letters and words, written in the sand with a thin stick.

The children were easy students, absorbing all the knowledge that Will could impart. When they left to return to the tasks of island living, Will would slowly walk back to his hut and stare in silence again.

By the third week, Will was healed sufficiently, and the ship was repaired adequately to continue her hunting.

As they slipped out into the open sea, Will paused and looked skyward. *You have kept me alive. You have given us much plunder and treasure. I am not sure you listen to sinners such as I, but I heard my mother and father call to me—is that a sign from you? Are they calling for me to quit this path I am on? What am I to do? All I feel inside is cold and empty. Please, if you are there, almighty God, I am asking for a sign.*

Three days later the *Reprisal* came upon a lone Spanish ship with a crippled mast. She responded with a white flag of surrender. As the *Reprisal* sailed close, a large squad of Spanish marines, hidden behind a level of breastworks, leaped to the ready and fired a volley of musket shot at Will's crew. Four men fell in that first volley fired under guise of a surrender.

Will ordered his cannons fired—point-blank into her sides. The Spanish ship was brutalized as the five sixteen-pound shells ripped into the hull from a distance of a few yards. Will risked the explosions damaging the *Reprisal* as well, for the sweet taste of revenge was too rewarding.

William leaped to the Spanish ship's deck, a pistol at the ready and a cutlass in his left hand. He pointed his pistol at whom he thought was the captain and fired, hitting him on the right shoulder and spinning him about before he dropped to the deck, clutching at the wound.

"Who else will toy with me?" Will shouted in Spanish and English, flailing his cutlass over his head. "Who else here is willing to risk his life over a few gold coins? Who will raise his blade against us?"

The Spanish crew, numbering perhaps three score sailors and marines, stood still and dropped their arms in a pile on the deck.

"Belowdecks! Find what they were protecting. If you find nothing, we'll set fire to the hull," Will shouted.

In five minutes, Will heard a crash from belowdecks, and a moment later four sailors came up from belowdecks grinning—and straining mightily. They pulled and dragged two huge chests, thumping up the gangway. They huffed and struggled them to in front of where William stood, then collapsed at his feet from the exertion.

"Captain," one sailor panted, "these be their treasure. And there be two more just like 'em in the captain's quarters. But we cannot carry 'em any further."

Will nudged them with his foot. Whatever was inside was heavy, for the chest was all but immobile. The sailor at his feet smiled and reached at the latch that had been broken off. He lifted it slowly and the sun, hitting the interior of the chest, glinted off in a hundred directions, like a golden prism. Will actually had to shield his eyes from the reflection.

"They be gold bars, Captain William! I figure there be near four dozen of 'em!"

Will whistled softly.

"We be rich men, Captain. We be very rich men."

The *Reprisal* took no chances after looting the Spanish treasure ship. They set a course directly back to their hidden cove. Mr. Delacroix and Will spent an hour in the captain's cabin estimating the worth of the treasure seized.

"Well, William, you are a wealthy man with the captain's share," Mr. Delacroix said expansively. "I should think you are pleased with your success." It was enough for Will to easily pay back his debt to Captain Waring fourfold and have ample funds to retire in a cottage by the sea, if he chose.

Will looked vaguely about the small cabin. "I have a mission now, you know, and I should be happy with that."

"Mission?"

"When we left base, I prayed, Johnny. I prayed to the Almighty for a sign. Do I continue to practice the art of privateering? Or shall I surrender all to his will and leave this life to others? And you know what he said, Mr. Delacroix? He presented me with these riches. I take it that stealing from the enemies of England is my mission. I am rewarded. I answer to no man. I have all that I can want. I have a small village where I can live in peace. And the church on Barbados will be built with the fruits of my labor. I can see that privateering is what God wants me to do."

"William, it does no one well to speak in such blasphemous terms," Mr. Delacroix said firmly.

"Blasphemous, am I? God takes my parents. He takes the woman I loved. He takes my vicar. He nearly takes my life. And then he rewards me with gold and silver. I think it not blasphemous at all, John. I think it most appropriate thinking."

"I cannot agree with you, William Hawkes. I will follow you as captain, for I think of you as an honest and moral person. But this is a side of you that is disturbin', indeed. I cannot—no, I will not—allow you to continue."

Mr. Delacroix was about to place his hand on William's shoulder, but looking at the coldness in Will's eyes caused him stop. "Perhaps it is just time for a rest," he said quietly.

"Rest? As if rest will fill my heart," Will said in a bitter voice. "No, Mr. Delacroix, I know what I must do. I will seek revenge, and I will be set free. I will teach the Almighty to abandon me. I will seek my revenge. That is what I must do."

Mr. Delacroix shook his head sadly. "Perhaps a rest is what we all need, Captain. I will take my leave now, if you please."

Will slumped into his sleeping berth and waved him off.

Luke stepped out into the darkened passageway with Mr. Delacroix. He grabbed John by the arm and pulled him close, whispering in his ear. "Massa Will be fine. Be fine soon."

"And how are you sure of this, Luke?"

"I pray and ask dat Massa Will be healed of de pain. And de Great Spirit—God—tell me yes."

"Have ye had a vision of this?" Mr. Delacroix asked, always having high regard for dreams and interpretations.

"No. But God say he help if we ask. If I ask—he come. And I ask he come to Massa Will."

"Would that you'd be right, Luke. Would that you'd be right."

CHAPTER

59

21 August 1641
Broadwinds, Dorset
England

Dearest Lady Emily,

I write only days prior to my trip to Weymouth and beyond. My heart leaps when I tell it that my father waits for me there. It also leaps at the adventure of it all—and you have taught me that it is good to seek out adventure. "A Christian must lead an adventuresome life filled with joy" is a phrase I oft remember hearing you utter. "For without the joy of life only God can give, one is not truly a Christian." I believe that, Lady Emily, and I will try to be a joyful witness for the faith—always.

I write this to thank you for what you have taught me.

You have been a most worthy example of what a Christian woman should be. From the morning I first awoke at the Alexandrian you have shown to me the need for a daily reading of the Holy Scriptures and prayer. Without your encouragement I would never have considered handling my father's business affairs. I would have thought a woman most unfit for such activities. You believed in me, and that has made the difference. Without your guidance and support I would have remained ignorant of my God-given abilities.

To write what is on my heart would consume volumes and years, and I have so little precious time left in my beloved England. I make one final request, Lady Emily, and that is for your prayers. My future is still seen as through a glass darkly, as the Scriptures say, but my heart is at peace. God will indeed open doors that are meant to be opened for me. He will lead and guide me along the proper path—of that I have no doubt. But still, your prayers would be most welcome.

I will never again have such a mentor as you. Perhaps, in the years to come, I will be able to be the same for another rambunctious young lady who is full of odd ideas and energy, and I will have the task of setting her to the path of God, as you have for me.

I remain, forever your friend,
Kathryne Spenser

P.S. Perhaps . . . perhaps someday in the not distant future you might journey to these islands? What wondrous pleasure your visit would provide.

Tucked beneath that missive was a short note to Cecily. And the last note, written after several others, was written through a mist of tears in her eyes.

My Dear Mrs. Cole,
I have delayed writing this, for I am fearful that my emotions will overtake my sensibilities. I am fearful that I will decide that I am unwilling to leave your side and refuse to board the ship sailing in two short days from this day.

I am incapable of expressing your worth to me, Mrs. Cole. You became my mother and closest friend. Without you I would have wandered from God's path many times. You have always loved me and cared for me—more than any other person alive. For that there are no words strong enough to describe the reality of my gratitude. Suffice it to say that in my heart you will always be. I cannot thank you enough, nor express my love to you adequately—so I will say simply that I love you—I always have and I always will. If the Almighty allows a child to ever enter my life, the role of mother will be patterned on your model and example, Mrs. Cole. I think no other praise is high enough for that gift you have given me.

I shall pray for you every day, for I shall never cease seeing your smiling face in my mind's eye, knowing you shall pray unceasingly for me as well.

I remain, your faithful,
Kathryne

The ink had smudged a word or two near the end, as a tear or two slipped out and splashed over the ink.

The moon had begun to rise by the time Kathryne gathered her letters and walked slowly to her darkened bedchamber.

1 September 1641
Weymouth, Dorset
England

The carriage, driven by Mr. Biesty, had jarred and rumbled to a stop at the entrance of the docks in Weymouth. It was to be Kathryne's last journey on the land of her birth for perhaps forever, she had thought as they rambled through the pastoral beauty of the English countryside.

How I will miss the way the soft, rounded hills fairly fold in on themselves, and how the curlews' calls of "jer jer" *cut through the velvet-green stillness as they fly overhead,* she thought with a piercing sadness as she gazed out the window. *The gentle meander of the river, the sun slipping behind that billow of gray clouds as a chill spills across the valley . . .*

"Lady Kathryne, you must stay inside this carriage till I return. I will see as to which ship shall be yours."

"Yes, Mr. Biesty. I will stay here."

He turned away, then pivoted around after taking only one step. "And please lock the carriage door from the inside, my lady. 'Tis an area where anythin' may happen."

"Yes, Mr. Biesty. I am locking it now."

He stepped away and then spun back again. "And please do not be conversin' with anyone save myself. I have heard of pretty girls as yourself bein' literally seduced by the words of smooth-speakin' sailors."

"Yes, Mr. Biesty. I will speak to no person but yourself."

He turned and then turned back again.

Kathryne spoke first this time. "Mr. Biesty! I will be fine in this locked carriage in the middle of the day! You will never be out of eyesight. Please, if you delay longer with your instructions my ship will have sailed without me—and then you will have to answer to my father."

She smiled at his face, lined with years of concern and worry. He smiled a brief smile, then turned to find her ship, worrying that his carriage would not fit on the narrow piers.

Kathryne shook her head slowly as she smiled. *Such a dear man,* she thought. *How I will miss his faithful concern.*

She looked back up the hill, past the shops and alehouses to the high, white steeple at the very crest of the hill.

Dearest God, how afraid I am. And how excited. And how confused.

I am trusting you to help it all fit into your grand plan for my life. I know it is beyond my frail abilities.

Her thoughts wandered back to the last few frenzied months at Broadwinds. . . .

⬛⬜⬛⬜⬛

She and Mrs. Cole had spent two weeks packing her dozen trunks and numerous containers. Kathryne, at first, had desired to take every piece of clothing that she possessed with her.

"But is it not hot on the island?" Mrs. Cole had asked.

It was as if Kathryne had not yet considered the climate. "Why, yes it is, Mrs. Cole. You know, as I think on this, Father has written of the insufferable heat at times. I suppose that any of the woolen greatcoats and worsted jackets may be superfluous."

"Child, I am sure that they are."

"Then perhaps I shall need to unpack and to repack again."

"Let me help you, Kathryne. 'Twill be my pleasure."

Mrs. Cole knew little of the proper way to pack, fold, and store clothing for travel—that had always been the task of the upstairs chambermaids—but her little Kathryne would soon be gone, and she had desired to spend as much time with her as possible. It was as if her daughter were leaving the nest.

They had finished repacking Kathryne's third trunk, a large wood and leather piece, and a small mound of woolens had grown on Kathryne's bed. Mrs. Cole stopped and looked about, as if mentally preparing a tally sheet. "I do not see the—" Tears had filled her eyes as she spoke.

"Mrs. Cole, whatever is the matter? I am not leaving for weeks. It is not time to be as distraught as this."

"It was just that I . . . I was lookin' for the bolt of white silk for the weddin' gown—and I knew I would never see you wearin' it," Mrs. Cole had sobbed. "I wanted so much to be present on that day."

Kathryne had wrapped Mrs. Cole in her arms and had said, "I know, Mrs. Cole—and it grieves me, too. But our hearts will never be separated. And I may not care for Mr. Foxton. He may not care for me. I may be taken captive by a gang of cutthroats on the voyage—or left on a tropical island with black-skinned natives who run about in fig leaves!"

Kathryne's trick had worked. The sorrow that was welling up in Mrs. Cole was now replaced with apprehension—an emotion more easily dealt with.

"Or perhaps I shall jump ship and spend my days alone, marooned on a small island, with no one to bother me again—no business matters, no arranged marriages, nothing at all but quiet."

"Now you're makin' sport of me, child, and I do not like that one bit," Mrs. Cole had scolded with more than a hint of false anger. "Come. We need to finish packin'."

Kathryne hugged her close. "I have the silk and lace and ribbons tucked in the bottom of that trunk by the window, along with the patterns I received from Mrs. Willoughby in London. If the day happens, I will commission a painting of me to be sent home to hang in the great hall of Broadwinds—and I will write a small epoch poem in commemoration of the event. You shall feel transported, Mrs. Cole."

Both women had started giggling.

■ ■ □ ■

Mr. Biesty tapped at the window, and a startled Kathryne jumped a bit, being roused out of her reverie.

"Lady Kathryne, the ship called the *Plymouth Spirit* is at the end of this pier, and the captain has said 'twould be fine if you chose to board now. I've gotten some stevedores to be cartin' the luggage."

Kathryne stepped out of the carriage and into the gusty winds of the Weymouth harbor. The salt from the waves tinted the air with its flavor. "Very well, Mr. Biesty. I thank you so much for your help. I shall miss you as well. Please take good care of Mrs. Cole and all the rest for me." *I know he will,* she thought. Tears formed in her eyes, and she began to weep silently.

Mrs. Biesty stood there, holding Kathryne's hand and looking as flustered and confused as a man could be in the face of such a squall of emotions. In a few moments, the tears passed, and he escorted her down to her ship, all the while glancing back at the carriage for fear that strangers would leap from the alleyways, bent on tampering with its workings.

60

September 1641
The Caribbean Sea

A different William Hawkes boarded ship for the *Reprisal*'s next voyage. The light that had been in his eyes was gone. Those eyes, once bright and kind, seemed sunken, distant.

He had allowed the crew several weeks to rest. The time had been therapeutic—they looked well-fed, healthy, and ready for action. Will had spent most of his time, save what he spent with the island children, in his hut alone or down at the water's edge staring out to sea. He spoke little to anyone, and most kept their distance.

The first leg of this September voyage was to be to Barbados, to split the gold with Radcliffe Spenser. The plunder had been weighed and recorded, and before the *Reprisal* left her hidden cove, Will took a healthy amount of his gold and buried it near the foot of the mountain. "If you need it, it is here," Will had told the chief in confidence. "Perhaps in time you will need to leave this place. This gold will buy much freedom."

Near midnight of the second day, the *Reprisal* slipped into Bridgetown harbor. Will and Johnny Delacroix, with John and Bryne Tambor, set out in their longboat, stroking to the piers. The Tambor brothers were brought along as rowers as well as guards. Will had known them since his time on the *Minion,* and no sailors had greater loyalty than the two. Nor did many sailors possess the sheer size and strength of the brothers, who towered more than six feet tall and wore long, shaggy beards that increased the ferocity of their visages.

Despite the lateness of the hour, nearing three hours past midnight, two alehouses remained open. Will and Johnny Delacroix slipped into the first, leaving the gold and the Tambor brothers bobbing in the waters by the pier.

Even though their entrance was quiet, all eyes turned to them and stared. William had established a firm reputation as a skilled privateer—one noted for his mastery of technique in sailing and attacking—and he was known well within that sailing fraternity. They sat at a dark booth in a far corner. A serving girl, no doubt an indentured servant from Ireland from the looks of her long red hair, sidled over and asked, in a nut-brown voice, what pleasures they might be looking for.

William was all business. "Two ales, miss. And we would like to hire a trustworthy messenger; I need to summon someone immediately."

The ale arrived a few moments before a young man walked up and sat next to Mr. Delacroix. "Who might you be needin' at this late hour?" the man asked.

William noted his slightly unsteady gait and looked at his sun-darkened face and into his red and watery eyes. *At this hour, one may not have the choice of messengers,* Will thought. "Do you know of Radcliffe Spenser? I need him summoned. And I will pay a half sovereign when he arrives."

"Half sovereign," he repeated, impressed at the amount. "I will have 'im back before you've finished your ale, gentlemen."

Will and Delacroix exchanged glances, and as the messenger left, Will whispered, "Are you prepared to wait until dawn?"

"Perhaps we should draw lots to determine who has the first watch," Delacroix replied.

But before they had sipped a third of their ale, in walked the messenger with Radcliffe Spenser in tow. "He was next door at the Eagle's Nest. I seen 'im enter nary an hour before," the messenger said with a toothless grin. He extended his open palm. "Now where's me sovereign?"

"Half sovereign," Will said and tossed the coin to him. The messenger smiled and scuttled back toward the bar.

"I continue to be surprised by you, Mr. Hawkes," Radcliffe said with an officious air. "I had heard you've developed some sort of secret hideaway. 'Radcliffe,' I told myself, ''tis the last you have heard of Mr. Hawkes and his plunder for the Crown.' But as I live and breathe, here you are again."

"We made an agreement, Mr. Spenser," Will said, stating the obvious, as if to a child. "And with William Hawkes, his word is his bond."

Radcliffe shook his head slowly in disbelief. "Again you delight me—a pirate with honor."

Before Will could offer his protestations, Radcliffe held up his hands. "A thousand pardons, Mr. Hawkes. Not a pirate—a *privateer*. I was making light of your profession, and I remember that you are sensitive about such titles."

Radcliffe cared little for feelings or emotions but knew that mere words were a trifling to pay for a man's continued complicity.

"And what draws you back to Bridgetown? I have heard news of several attacks and plunder. Perhaps you have come to share the spoils?"

"We have indeed, Mr. Spenser. We have returned with the treasure from several boardings. I have brought you the Crown's half and your ten percent. I have already distributed the crew's portions."

"And you have been honest with this division? Am I to trust you on this? I would have assumed you would bring it all back to Barbados to be divided."

"I did not, for every movement of it increases the risk. And if you choose not to believe my divisions—well, you are free to turn me away with all shares in my possession."

"No, no, Mr. Hawkes. I speak too frankly at times. You must forgive me. It is the heat of this miserable place that dilutes one's civility. I will accept your divisions as accurate." Radcliffe placed his hands, palm down, on the dark tabletop, stained with a thousands rings from wet tankards. "And how much is the Crown due?" he asked.

"We have, in a small longboat at the pier, gold ingots worth forty thousand pounds."

Radcliffe tried hard not to demonstrate his shock, but failed. "Forty thousand pounds! With one small ship! Did you sink the Spanish treasure fleet? Such a plunder!"

He noticed he was speaking too loudly, and several patrons turned boozily to make out the cause of his astonishment. Radcliffe looked about, leaned closer, and whispered, "How much gold are we speaking of here?"

"Forty gold bars."

This pirate is most amazing, Radcliffe thought. *I expected never to see him again, and here he is with a fortune in gold! My share is four gold bars! And who knows? Perhaps there may be a method to increase my share even more.*

"Mr. Hawkes," Radcliffe said in an oily tone, "you are a true gentleman. I am amazed at your talent. Perhaps it is time to speak of a larger ship. Perhaps I may seize a galleon for you? What size would you like?"

"Our small pinnace is well suited to our needs, Mr. Spenser. Now, if you would make arrangements for the gold, we shall be on our way. We have hunting to accomplish."

William stood to leave, and Radcliffe grabbed his sleeve, pulling him back.

Radcliffe struggled for the trigger to this curious man before him. *Is his weakness women? I have never seen him with one of the loose women of this port. Is it gold? I think not, for he has returned to this island with honest shares. Could it be flattery? Or perhaps power?*

Radcliffe looked up into William's eyes, lit by the glow of a single candle. There was coldness there, and a deep thirst, or perhaps a low desire.

Ahh. . . . Perhaps there is something else, Radcliffe mused. *Perhaps he desires the sweetest of all tastes—the taste of revenge.*

"Mr. Hawkes, please stay," Radcliffe pleaded theatrically. "I have a most interesting proposition to make. Perhaps you may find it interesting."

"Proposition?"

"I have news of a ship—the *Plymouth Spirit*—that may prove rewarding for the pair of us," he confided in low tones.

The Atlantic Ocean

Kathryne woke to a the sound of drops splattering against the small glass window of her cabin aboard the *Plymouth Spirit*. She pulled back the baize curtains to the sight of a gray, driving rain. The ship had just turned west, clearing the nine volcanic islands of the Azores, some eight hundred miles off the coast of Portugal, after stopping there. She sat up in bed and hugged her knees, trying to remember all the sights and sounds of the harbor of Ponta Delgada on the island of São Miguel as their ship docked for a day, purchasing provisions and taking on fresh water.

The colors were bright, she thought—vibrant and alive. At the dock there were a score of peddlers and merchants to greet them, offering wide straw hats, fruits of all description, woven shawls, carved icons, and strange, exotic birds. Innumerable stone bottles of Passada wine were stacked next to huge wooden casks of St. George's wine on the piers, awaiting the ships that would transport them to a thousand distant sea ports.

Kathryne had ventured down the gangway for a closer look, accompanied at arm's length by an ogling, burly sailor and Vicar Petley. The vicar had not taken to ocean travel well and had yearned to set foot on a surface that did not pitch and yaw, though his first few minutes off ship were so disconcerting that he felt the illness rise again in his throat.

Kathryne had carried a few small coins and purchased a wide-brimmed straw hat decorated in bold-colored ribbons from a small boy. She had presented the boy with the coin that he asked for when the sailor accompanying her shouted loudly and snatched it away. The boy and sailor had argued for several moments in a foreign tongue.

"Milady, may I have a half shilling?" the sailor had asked.

Kathryne had given him one, which was half the coin she originally presented for the hat.

"You needs to bargain with these heathens. Their first price is always double what they'll take. No need to be throwin' good money away, milady."

Kathryne had thanked him, but to her a half shilling was so small a sum as to be negligible.

Toward the end of the dock, Kathryne fancied upon a man selling birds, most of which were a type unknown in England—popinjays—with bright bold green plumage and long yellow beaks just as likely to crack a walnut as a finger. Some were on perches with small chains on their legs; other smaller birds were in cages.

Many sailors returned home with such birds, for she had seen such birds and the like in Weymouth public houses, their bright feathers in obvious contrast against the dark walls of such establishments. A birdcage seemed to be an integral part of seamen's luggage.

In one cage however, a small brown bird with odd markings had hopped from perch to perch. Kathryne had pointed to it with a quizzical look on her face.

"English," the merchant had called out. "English bird." He had handed the small cage to Kathryne. "You like? Songbird. Pretty songs."

I cannot be sure, but it looks most like that small bird from Lady Emily's—a Williamson thrush, Kathryne had thought.

The bird excitedly trilled.

"Rare bird—five shillings!"

Kathryne's sailor escort and the merchant had exploded into a battle of offer and counteroffer for the next quarter hour as Kathryne cooed at the small creature.

When the dust had settled, the sailor had asked her, "Do you wish to purchase the bird, milady?"

"I would like to, unless Captain Blake has a rule against such animals on board."

The sailor had snorted rudely. "Rules! Not bloody likely, pardon me language, milady. On one trip to the Caribbees we 'ad a pair of bloody camels on board! Some chap wantin' to try 'is luck wi' 'em in the islands. If you want the bird, you can get it."

"And how much did you negotiate?"

"You can 'ave it for three shillin's."

She had placed three coins in the merchant's hand and gaily accepted her new purchase. As she had walked away, back toward the ship, from the corner of her eye Kathryne had seen the merchant slip a shilling coin back to the sailor, but she said not a word about it.

Perhaps it was all rehearsed, she thought, *but at three shillings for such a sweet little thing, who would argue?*

As they walked back to the *Plymouth Spirit,* Vicar Petley caught up with them. "A thrush? Why would you purchase a common thrush when you could have purchased a grand and gaudy parrot?"

"It will remind me of home," Kathryne had stated firmly as she whistled to her new pet. "And I shall name him Willy—after the thrush at Lady Emily's."

Barbados

"The *Plymouth Spirit?* That is Captain Blake's ship, is it not?" asked Will.

"Yes it is. I believe he attempted to lure you from Captain Waring's ship at one point, did he not?" answered Radcliffe.

William nodded.

"'Tis a good thing you chose loyalty, William, for I have heard evil things about Blake in the interim. He has dealt with slaves, then wenches, and on one voyage his ship was full of Papist missionaries to the Yucatan. I understand that he will do anything for gold."

Neither William nor Mr. Delacroix made comment, for they both knew most sea captains, save for Captain Waring, were cut from much the same cloth as Blake.

"And on this voyage is my brother's daughter, Kathryne—a prissy and snobbish girl of the worst character you might imagine a noble-born woman to have," Radcliffe sneered.

"You speak so ill of your own niece?" asked Will.

"Mr. Hawkes, I must be honest as I see the facts. She has that attitude of . . . entitlement. She would look down upon a poor peasant such as yourself and, literally, have no words to speak to you," he added.

"Surely you paint too bleak a picture," Will protested.

"I am afraid I do not. She is journeying here to marry some noble-born fop—all by her father's arrangement. As much as I loathe to speak ill of blood, I feel I must. I would have spoken of this earlier, but it was not my place."

"Spoken of what?" Will asked, a hint of anger in his voice.

Radcliffe paused dramatically. "It was my own dear brother that would not offer ransom for your vicar. I heard him issue that decision to our Vicar Coates."

Will looked as if he were struck. "What right has a mere governor to dictate the workings of the church?"

Radcliffe called for more ale, as he shook his head. "Mr. Hawkes, how innocent of the world you are. It has always been the prerogative of the ruling class to determine such things."

"You mean that Lord Aidan could have set search for Vicar Mayhew?"

"Not only could he have, but should have. Yet he determined that the cost was simply too great for such an unimportant man as an unknown vicar."

William reached over and grabbed Radcliffe by the arm.

Ye gads, Radcliffe thought as he looked at the powerful hand encircling his forearm, *how strong his hand is. And how bruised this arm will be on the morrow.*

"Mr. Radcliffe, are you speaking the truth of this? That Governor Aidan sentenced Vicar Mayhew to die because it was too much expense to search for him?" Will hissed.

"Too expensive by a few pounds. More than that, he was too busy building his new estate to be bothered with such a trifling affair."

William tightened his grip on Radcliffe's arm, who tried not to wince and squirm in his chair. "And you swear that this is the truth?" Will demanded.

"Mr. Hawkes, had I a Bible I would swear upon that sacred Book in front of witnesses." Radcliffe hung his head to his chest and counted to ten silently, as a measure of theatrics, knowing that the pause would add to the drama. "You do not know how relieved my soul is for having this unburdened," he added. "Perhaps nothing can stop the evil of my brother. But I feel cleansed of my part in the affair."

The alehouse grew silent. A clatter arose from the opposite corner as a patron, too far into his cups, slipped off his bar seat and collapsed in a rummy heap on the filth-encrusted floor. Before anyone had moved, he started to snore loudly, and the barman and serving girl shrugged and left him lie.

"You say the *Plymouth Spirit* left Weymouth recently?" asked Will.

"On the first of September."

"And they will sail directly here?"

"Yes, following the normal routes, of course."

Mr. Delacroix looked a shade uncomfortable. "Will they be sailing under the English flag, Mr. Radcliffe?" he asked tentatively.

"Captain Blake will sail under any flag that is most convenient. It may be the English flag, or Dutch, or Spanish for that matter. He has no permanent allegiance to any one country."

Delacroix squirmed. "But no doubt this voyage will be under the English ensign?" Delacroix asked again, firmer, wanting to be certain what options they were being presented with—and just what the true risks might be.

"I would hesitate to wager," Radcliffe said, sliding past his concern. "It might be English, it might not. In truth, does it truly matter?"

William looked off into the dim interior, his eyes unfocused, thinking. "The first of September, which means they have cleared the Azores," calculated Will.

Radcliffe massaged his arm where William's hand had been, barely able to contain his excitement. *Be careful now,* Radcliffe said to himself. *It is most difficult to know the proper time to set the hook.*

William kept staring off into the darkened tavern. Mr. Delacroix was silent, but uneasy.

Grab the fishing rod and jerk cleanly up, with the hook ever so sharp, Radcliffe thought and said, "And the governor's daughter is coming here with a small fortune—the church wants to see the sanctuary finished for Lady Kathryne's wedding. A small fortune, Mr. Hawkes. Gold they were unwilling to use for your . . ." He left the rest of the sentence unsaid. *The hook is set,* Radcliffe thought with immense pleasure. *And the fish doesn't even realize it.*

"Mr. Delacroix, let us return to the ship," William said. "I am afraid we have little time to waste, for we will be sailing against the trades. It is the first of October, and with two-thirds of their journey covered . . . if we sail upon the morrow . . . given the wind at their back and in our face . . . and a fortnight of hard sailing on our part . . . that should place our meeting with the *Plymouth Spirit* some one hundred leagues west of where we sit tonight."

■ ■ ▯ ■ ■

"But, Will, an English ship?" John Delacroix asked, his voice tight and nervous.

Radcliffe had scuttled off to the Eagle's Nest next door to locate a few able-bodied men to haul his gold. Will and Delacroix left the alehouse and stood in the quiet darkness at the end of the street.

Delacroix reached over and put a hand tenderly on Will's shoulder. "Will, it be an English ship," he repeated.

"It will be a ship of no flag. You heard Radcliffe. It is time that someone paid for these transgressions," Will said.

"Will, you have been the bravest and most generous captain I have ever served with—or could hope to serve with. If you say that this is the deserved course of conduct, then I will serve at your side. All the crew will. They will follow you to the gates of hell if you asked. But I must inquire of you now—*is this right?*"

Will stared back, fury evident in his eyes. *Right? Who are you to ask of right?*

Will stepped back and stood still, his face lost in the dark, his features hidden. After a moment, he replied softly, with an edge of malice to his voice. It was an edge that Mr. Delacroix had never before heard.

"You ask what is right? We are right to kill Spaniards with our letters of marque. We are right to steal their gold for King Charles, and the governor of Barbados says it meets with royal approval. We are privateers, we tell ourselves. John, we are pirates—pure and simple. We have been so from the beginning. Do not wince in the darkness, my friend, for it is the truth that I say. Everything dear to me in my life dies or is killed by a drunken nobleman or is torn from me—and the church does nothing to help. I ask God for a sign, and he rewards me—beyond my wildest expectations—for being a pirate. Do you honestly believe that such a deity exists—that snuffs out the wise and loving and good in life and lets vile people like myself be rewarded with gold far in excess of my most fanciful dreams?"

Will paused, breathing hard, his face close to Delacroix's. John could see his wide eyes, the vein at his temple, the taut muscles in his neck. "If there be a God in the heavens who permits such things, John, I want no part of him. I am now seeking only to settle this fire in my belly that calls out for revenge. And I shall have it, John. I shall." Will's voice was venomous and high-pitched.

William stepped toward Delacroix and placed a hand on his shoulder. In the smallest of voices, somewhere between desperation and a soulless pain, he asked, "Will you be with me, John. Will you follow me?"

And in a smaller voice, near cracking, John answered, "I will follow you, William. And may God, if there be one, have mercy on both our wretched souls."

CHAPTER

61

17 October 1641
The Atlantic Ocean

The *Plymouth Spirit* had crossed the unmarked boundary between the civilized world and the world that was "beyond the line." The crossing was unmarked by fanfare or announcement, yet each day the ship sailed deeper into this sea of changed sensibilities.

Kathryne sat on a stool on the high quarterdeck, feeling the cleansing winds. As the weather warmed, the smells from belowdeck had intensified. The heady mix of sweat, rancid food, animals, fouled water, and cooking stoves so permeated the cabins that at times Kathryne found the purchase of a breath to be difficult.

The atmosphere did decidedly little to help Vicar Petley's disposition and well-being. Regardless of his desire, his body would not adapt to the roll of the waves, a motion Kathryne found comforting.

The sea was empty yet, in Kathryne's opinion, full of life and vital energy. The horizons appeared calm, yet the waters were in constant motion. Small peaks of white dotted the waves, and the bow broke through deep troughs, spraying the ship with the bitter tang of saltwater.

The captain ordered Kathryne to remain on the quarterdeck for her safety. If she had been allowed, she would have perched at the very bow of the vessel—to be the first to plow through the green waves. *It is said the sea air is full of malignancies,* she thought, *but it fills my lungs with a glow.* Terns and gulls cruised the air behind the ship, Kathryne marveling at God's design that enabled a mere bird to transport itself across such a trackless ocean. At her feet, half-protected by a knitted woolen shawl, was her small Williamson thrush. When a large bird approached, Willy shouted out a joyously defiant song, lest the predator come near.

Every sunset was a rhapsody of colors and brilliance and brought her closer to the island that held the promise of her future. The decision resting between the vicar and Geoffrey Foxton seemed curiously distant and removed. Kathryne knew it was still there, but its import was lost as the ship cut through the magnificent waters.

■ ■ ■ ■ ■

On the small table in the captain's quarters aboard the *Reprisal,* Will had spread out every chart he had concerning the crossing of the Atlantic. How difficult it was to estimate one's progress in the best of conditions, yet Will was estimating the progress of a ship that may or may not have sailed on time. *Did she stay in Madeira?* he contemplated. *Or perhaps she took a landfall in the Canary Islands as well.*

But it was October, and most wise sailors would be in haste to cross, since it was the season of storms. From the late summer until well into autumn, the waters in the warm Caribbean could be sent boiling by hurricanes and immense tropical depressions. *No, she will stop only a day—two at most—then take the fastest path to the islands,* Will imagined as he drew those courses on map after map.

After hours of tracing and considering, and factoring in their tortured progress against the wind, Will stood up from his desk. He drew out a small dagger and with a flick of his wrist, he tossed it with an expert's eye at the map on the table. It stuck soundly, and Will looked close at its point. *That is where we shall meet Captain Blake's good sailing ship from Weymouth. That small voice inside me says it will be so.*

With that feeling of assurance, Will walked out, closing the door behind him, and took his place at the wheel station for the third watch—from midnight until false dawn. Sailors called it the death watch, for more sailors died, more ships were left to be swallowed by the sea, and more vessels ground to their death on sharp rocks and hidden reefs than during any other watch.

To William it felt like the right watch for him. In the darkness, when no one could see his face—and his soul—he felt a small sliver of peace in his heart. It was fleeting, yet it was all the peace he possessed, and he cherished those few moments as if jewels.

■ ■ ■ ■ ■

On the bridge of the *Plymouth Spirit,* most eyes were on the western horizon. The voyage had been uneventful, but as they entered the warmer waters, which were favored by pirates and privateers, the watch was increased from two men to four, both day and night, scanning the horizons in every direction for the white spot of an enemy's sail. As she neared her destination, Bridgetown, on the island of Barbados, the crew grew more restive. Privateers, cutthroats, and pirates splashed in the waters all about these islands, hiding in secluded coves in the Caribbees, in the rocky shoals and coral reefs of the Bahamas, and in the mouths of rivers of the Guiana coast, hidden by dense, protective jungle.

On the aft deck, a solitary figure stood, silhouetted by the morning sun. Lady Kathryne Spenser watched the sea dance beneath the ship's rudder and bow with her deep green eyes. The light, at that low angle, illuminated each drop of the spray, turning it to liquid gold. She lifted her head to the western horizon, toward Barbados, toward her family and new home. It had been a long trip, alien, uncomfortable, and exotic. The crossing of an ocean was never a simple thing, and even though she had few of her accustomed luxuries, she was joyful.

What a glorious day this is, she thought. *How gracious is our God who creates such a masterpiece every morning.*

The islands held out a promise to her, and each day brought her closer to a new life. Thrilled with the adventure of the trip, she was more exhilarated with the thought of being reunited with her dear father in the new governor's mansion called Shelworthy. It was strange to think of her loving papa as the man possessing ultimate authority, except for King Charles, over the many islands of the Lesser Antilles.

It will be good to stand on firm, dry ground, Kathryne mused. *And the absolute decadence of a long bath laced with lavender, of well-cooked food, of freedom from the preying eyes of all the sailors.*

She turned and faced southeast, into the wind. Her long dark hair billowed out, as if a sail, catching the cool breeze. She shook her head, letting the wind lift her hair from her neck, feeling the air against the ivory bare skin of her throat and shoulders.

At the edge of her vision she glimpsed a small spot of white. *A curious spot for a cloud, and a most curious shape as well,* she thought. Taking a step forward, she put her right hand on the rail, steadying herself, to afford a sharper view. This was a most unusual little cloud. Her white hand grasped the sun- and salt-bleached rail, and she leaned forward, squinting in the blaze of the sun, trying to peer through the brilliance of the morning.

Her hand jumped to her throat and then to her small mouth as she stifled the urge to scream. She had no desire to be thought of as an easily frightened, foolish woman. It is only a merchant ship, she told herself.

After all, none of the crew has noticed, nor seemed upset. She congratulated herself on her composure, and she smiled.

Moments later Kathryne, still watching the ship, heard the lookout call excitedly, "Sails ho!"

Captain Blake rushed out of his cabin in his shirtsleeves. "What standard she be showing?" he called to the lookout.

"I cannot make her out, for she be a shadow against the sun from up here."

The first officer had pulled out his telescope and trained it on the quickly approaching vessel. "Not to worry, Captain," he reported. "She's English!"

Kathryne saw the tension drain from Blake's face at the news. He quickly put on a smile and called to the crew, which had frozen at the prospect of a sea battle, "Continue with your duties, men. It looks like we'll have company as we finish our voyage." As the crew returned to its assigned tasks, Blake said to his first officer, "I'll be in me quarters. Let me know if she hails us."

The bleached sails billowed overhead as the morning winds quickened. Loose canvas ends snapped in the wind, and the sails billowed out, fat and full. The mainmast groaned under the strain. Along the yardarms, the ropes tightened, the wood joints squealing with the pressure.

To a man, the crew of the *Reprisal* was silent—silent as death. Will muttered an order, just under his breath. His men scuttled along the open deck, moving to position, hunched slightly, making a lower silhouette against the sun.

"Make ready the starboard cannons," whispered Johnny Delacroix. He wiped at the beads of sweat on his bare forehead.

On the cannon deck, the cannoneers lurched the gleaming sixteen-pound cannons into firing position. The gunnery crews eyed their prey, alone in the ocean. She was the *Plymouth Spirit*, sailing innocently westward. She was growing larger in their sights, soon to be within range of the large guns. The cannon crew of the *Reprisal* tested the wind and watched the waves, mentally reviewing the flight of their cannon shot. Each gun was loaded, black powder was drizzled on the flash pan, and burning embers were held inches from the shock of explosion.

The men on deck inhaled audibly as Will nodded to the quartermaster. He spun the massive wheel a quarter turn to the right. The sails caught a fuller gulp of the track winds. The deck inclined a degree or two at first, then a sharper list followed. The gunners wound down the adjusting wheels, lowering the cannon barrels to compensate for the change.

The small pinnace, a three-masted ship, was wonderfully suited for plying the shallow shoals and tight waters of the Antilles. It was built with two goals in mind—speed and stealth. She splashed a few compass points more to the west, into the freshening southern winds. She was leeward now, running at broad reach with the wind. The vessel was poised to make a long sweeping arc, intersecting with her intended victim in a matter of moments. The ship was swiftest at a degree or two starboard of running with the wind—the winds just off her starboard rear. The water was sparkling past the front bow and the dark, menacing hawk of the ship's figurehead.

Will squinted into the eyepiece of his fancy new telescope, a recent acquisition from the Spanish merchantman who happened to cross William's path on her way home to Barcelona. *An unexpected gift,* he thought to himself, *but ever so beautiful.* He lowered the scope and compacted it together, taking great pleasure in the metallic clinks and hisses, the mother-of-pearl inlay, and the polished brass, all glinting in the wash of the morning's sun.

The *Plymouth Spirit*'s holds would be filled with supplies, provisions, and perhaps cannon and muskets. *And much more important cargo,* Will thought with a thin smile.

Captain Hawkes filled his lungs with fresh, cool air, tinted with the sea spray, and smiled widely at his exceptional fortune. His penetrating blue eyes were on his prey. He raised his bronzed right arm to the sky, his muscles highlighted in the sun. In a mere moment the ship would be running before the wind, cutting the waves like a fox—a fox running to the slow, helpless, and unsuspecting hen.

With a wide sweeping flourish, Will slashed him arm down to the deck and shouted to the crew his one word command: *"Fire!"*

A billowy roar emanated from the approaching ship. First a small puff of smoke was seen from the *Plymouth Spirit,* then the combined roar of four sixteen-pound cannons rolled across the waves. The noise broke over the ship like a waterspout. In an instant, every crewman pivoted on his heels to the south. In that moment they knew.

The cannon shot streaked past the bow of the *Plymouth Spirit* and hissed into the waters no more than a stone's toss away. The spray plumed up and washed over the bow and front decking in an angry wave. It was a warning shot from the *Reprisal*—an intentional miss. The next ones would find their mark easily.

As the shot tore past their bow, and every eye was locked on that ship, they saw the English flag pulled down, to be replaced with a flag of black and three chevrons—a pirate's flag, to be sure.

It is odd what men do in times of danger and crisis. Some genuflected, crossing themselves solemnly, repeating Latin words they learned long ago and barely understood. Some cursed the heavens; others cursed the captain or the seaborne fates. Yet they all began to move as if one single entity. They scrambled to add sail and canvas to seek the wind, to unfurl jib sails, to raise spinnakers. They scurried to armament lockers and powder kegs, unlocking cannon from their deck pinions, filling swabbing buckets with seawater.

The wind held out the barest of hope. If the *Plymouth Spirit* could catch a solid stream of wind before her pursuer, she had a whisper of a chance of escape. Perhaps, just perhaps, she could outrun them. If not, it was a matter of time until the swifter pirate vessel overtook the poorly armed merchantman and began the slaughter.

Captain Blake of the *Plymouth Spirit* clamored up on the rear deck. He was buttoning his scarlet officers' coat, buckling the gold clasp of his cutlass. "My dear Kathryne, you must leave this deck at once. It appears this ship has deceived us. It is the evil face of the pirate that we now see."

Barely meeting his eyes, paying little attention to his request, Kathryne stared at the ship growing larger against the southern horizon.

"Why do you not return his fire, Captain Blake? Are we not a bigger vessel?"

Captain Blake finished buckling and set his hand to the hilt of his cutlass. "Would that I could, my lady," he answered with a forced calmness. "We have only six cannon and would need to turn from the wind to fire. He would be upon us in a flashing. Our only hope is to outrun him."

Kathryne held fast to the rail.

"My lady, I must insist! You must go belowdecks now! You are in most particular danger if they see you here!" His voice was loud and just shy of cracking.

Kathryne turned to him, her eyes wide in fear.

The captain took her hand from the rail, gently, as if trapping a frightened baby bird who had fallen from the nest. He looked down at his lovely young passenger. "Lady Kathryne, your uncle Radcliffe and

I have been doing business for many years. The Spensers are a family that honors honesty. So I will tell you no falsehood now. We are all in grave danger. We will attempt to outsail them, but ours is a slower vessel, less maneuverable. I, as well as the pirate captain, know this to be true."

"But Captain Blake," she said in a half-whisper, "we can offer them our goods and cargo. Will they not take that and sail off?"

"How I wish it could be as that." Captain Blake paused. He averted his eyes from her beautiful form. "You are a woman, and it is not wise for a woman to be here. I could not have spoken more forcibly to your uncle concerning this foolish trip."

Captain Blake took her hand, now with more force than necessary, and led her from the rail. He drew her to the hatch leading to belowdecks. "My crewman will take you to my cabin. There is a disguised closet there, hidden in the wardrobe. You shall remain there, safely out of harm's way. I will send Vicar Petley to stay in the cabin—for God's protection. Perhaps there is still a chance to win this footrace." Captain Blake's words contained little hope. "But you must go—now!"

The crewman, a leering young man, took hold of Kathryne's wrist and led her into the dimness of the decks below. She looked one last time at the pirate ship bearing closer and closer, then stepped boldly into the darkness.

■ ▫ ■ ▫ ■

"Lower the English flag and raise our ensign, sailor. Let us see if they will fight or attempt to flee," Will said coldly.

The black flag with the three chevrons was pulled to the top of the mast, and the signal flags calling on the *Plymouth Spirit* to heave to were also raised. The English ship kept plowing ahead, straight west.

"Mr. Delacroix," called William, "what is their armament? Can you see the crew size?"

"Captain, it appears they have three twelve-pounders on each side— perhaps another small six-pounder on each side as well," he replied. He stood near the bow, trying to brace himself in the rolling of the ship. Spotting an enemy and determining his strength was a difficult task through a telescope from a pitching deck. Keeping one's eye on the target was most taxing. Mr. Delacroix lowered the scope for a moment and blinked his eyes.

"Can you stop the pitching, Captain?" he joked.

"I will try, Johnny," Will said and spun the wheel, slipping the *Reprisal* parallel to a deeper trough. "Try it now!"

The ship continued forward but was still for a moment from the rolling. Soon Mr. Delacroix shouted, "Small crew from what I can see on deck. Cannons were right, but they have a big sixteen-pounder mounted on the stern, facing rearward. They'll be no following, nipping at her heels, with this ship, Captain."

Will was relieved that they were able to see that cannon mounted at the rear—for he was about to follow and fire into the rear of the ship again. But even one well-placed sixteen-pound shot from their prey could cripple the *Reprisal*.

It will be a full frontal attack, Will plotted, *so the English noblewoman and whatever church dignitary might be on board will know the full brunt of my revenge.*

"Quartermaster, do you reckon we are faster than the English ship?" William asked.

"By five knots at least, Captain. She must be riding heavy—or she needs a careening. We can overtake her in much less than an hour."

Will held a steady course, well off her port stern. The winds were shifting slightly as the day warmed and were becoming stronger from the southeast. The *Reprisal* sailed well at broad reach with the wind, which on this day meant sailing from the south, heading northwest.

Will faced the warm breeze, closing his eyes for a moment, letting it spill around his features. Then he called out, "Cannon Masters!" Those crewmen gathered about, as did Mr. Delacroix and, of course, Luke.

"She is not well armed and has a meager crew. If we sail alongside her and trade cannon volleys, we risk injury and worse. She has some bark to her guns, to be sure. Rather than a battle of attrition, let us be bold. I want all cannons ready with double shot and double charges— we will have one round to make our presence felt. We will arc about first to the south, then catch the wind and head broad reach with it. That tacks our bow into her side—and very quickly. We are a small target face on, and we will have to trust their ineptitude and our luck to see us through."

"And God's protection, too, Mr. Hawkes. The Almighty will protect us," said a crewman.

Will sighed silently. "Yes, and God's protection. And to help him, we will sail bow first at them to a distance of two hundred yards, I will spin to starboard, and each gunner will have the merest chance to aim and fire a broadside. I want that broadside to be accurate and quick. As soon as all four guns discharge, we will reverse tack, spin to port, and in a moment our port guns will have her in view. You will have a moment longer to fire—and as you do, we will move to board her. Perchance there may be time for a second round, but with this wind, I doubt the time will be there."

Will looked at the ship they were pursuing, fat and lumbering. He looked at the grim faces of his crew. They all knew it was an English ship they were about to attack, yet not one man—save Mr. Delacroix when the plan was first proposed—had said a word in opposition. Their dark and bronzed faces reflected loyalty and confidence in their captain.

"Any questions?" he asked.

No word was uttered.

"Gentlemen, shall we commence?"

One sailor called out, "We should pray before this battle. We always 'ave in the past, and God has blessed us."

"Very well," Will said. "Please, gather yourselves for that prayer."

"It be up to you, Captain, to do it for us." Golder Ramsey, who had the job of leading prayers, was belowdecks attending to munition supplies.

William stood there, his hand on the wheel, and a desperate, terrified look on his face.

Luke stepped from behind him. "I pray. God don' know I black man." He turned to the crew, staring at them with narrowed eyes. "And nobody tell him I been slave."

Luke looked at each man's face. Most had received medicine from him, and some had been cured of injuries that oft killed others. No one raised a word of objection to his praying.

"Almighty One, we be your children. You help us here if you want. If you don', we don' get angry. We happy we know 'bout you. We thank you for all things—and most we thank you for Captain Hawkes. Amen."

Breaking the silence that followed that simple prayer, Will calmly said, "Gentlemen, prepare for battle."

▪ ▫ ▪ ▫ ▪

Kathryne was escorted to her cabin and locked the door as the sailor left. A quick tapping soon was heard, followed by a muffled voice through the door. It was Vicar Petley, calling her name.

"Kathryne! Kathryne! What is going on?"

She ran and unlocked the latch, pulled him in with a lurch, and shut the door behind her. "We are soon to be set upon by pirates, Giles."

"Pirates! Lord have mercy! How can this be? This cannot be happening. This is a civilized country! How can pirates attack a ship of England? Are they sure they have not made a mistake?"

His voice now measured a higher pitch, and his breath came in short puffs. "Where is this ship?" he squeaked.

Kathryne took him by the hand to the window. When she opened it, the pirate ship could be seen slicing away, heading south from the *Plymouth Spirit*.

"Well then, it seems to be sailing off. Perhaps they realized the error of their ways—coming up like that to a ship under the English flag."

Kathryne watched in amazement as the ship grew smaller by a bit. It did appear that it was pulling away. But then, with the wind, it turned and began to race towards them, bow first.

The pair jumped as they heard a sharp rap at the door. "Lady Spenser! The captain has instructed me to place you and the vicar in the captain's cabin now. I have prepared the wardrobe. Please, if you will, unlatch your door."

Kathryne unlocked the door and allowed herself to be escorted to the captain's cabin. The wardrobe was emptied of its clothing and uniforms. A small door in the back was open, and a space—no bigger than a coffin—was cleverly installed behind the hidden panel at the rear of the wardrobe.

"In here, my lady," the sailor instructed. "Pull the door tight after you, and we will place the clothing back in. No one will ever find you."

She stepped into the darkness, which smelled quite strongly of cedar. She slipped in, wedged herself into the tight space, and pulled the door shut. The sailor gave the door a final push to latch it tight.

"Now, Vicar, if you would, let us return the clothin'."

They put the red dress uniforms back in place, as well as the wool overcoats and breeches with gold braiding.

Kathryne tried to pray, but her thoughts were racing too fast to be coherent. She willed herself to remain composed, for the air was musty and would soon stale.

I will be calm, she told herself, *for the Almighty will let no harm befall me. He will provide protection. He will look after his child.*

She began to recite in her mind a familiar psalm. *He that dwelleth in the secret place of the most High shall abide under the shadow of the Almighty. I will say of the Lord, He is my refuge and my fortress: my God; in him will I trust. Surely he shall deliver thee from the snare of the fowler and from the noisome pestilence. He shall cover thee with his feathers, and under his wings shalt thou trust: his truth shall be thy shield and buckler. . . . For he shall give his angels charge over thee, to keep thee in all thy ways.*

"Vicar, I would suggest that you stay here," explained the sailor. "It is safer since we're not expectin' 'em to attack from the rear or the starboard side. Lock the door after I leave."

"Wait! What is going to happen? What do I do if we are attacked?" cried the vicar, his voice near tears.

"Vicar, I would suggest that you pray—like the rest of the crew."

62

17 October 1641
The Atlantic Ocean

The *Reprisal* was on a direct course with her prey. The wind was stronger now, and she was flying closer and closer. William, now at the helm, anticipated that the *Plymouth Spirit* would fire at her bow, but he hoped their marksmanship would be poor. Most merchant sailors seldom practiced with cannon fire.

At a distance of five hundred yards, the *Plymouth Spirit* fired its guns on the port side in a furious roar. All shots fell to the side, and most overshot their target.

They will not hit us—and they will not have time enough to reload, Will thought.

At two hundred yards, Will spun the wheel, and the rudder jerked to the side. The ship canted and then was speeding in the opposite direction.

The cannon master cried, "Fire!" and five guns roared to life in one unified voice. Each shot struck the *Plymouth Spirit* with a splintery crash. One mast tumbled into the sea, and a cannon port disappeared in a bellow of white smoke. The *Reprisal* port gunners cheered their accuracy.

Will spun the wheel in the opposite direction, and within the time a man can hold his breath, Will's vessel had drawn up alongside the *Plymouth Spirit*. As her wooden hull came into range, the *Reprisal*'s five cannons roared, their double shot and double charges ripping through the hull of her prey in five places. All five shots were elevated, and they tore through the second and top decks, ripping and shredding the decks and hull, the wood shrieking as if in agony.

As the cannons' roar echoed across the open sea, Will called for the grappling hooks. They clanged to the decks, and within a moment the two ships were locked together, bobbing in unison, wood scraping against splintered wood.

"Boarding party!" Will called, and three dozen men, some with pistols, some with sharpened pikes, all with swords and clubs, scrambled up the ropes to the enemy's deck. A dozen men with muskets skittered up the masts to afford a better angle to their aim.

A small fire had erupted where the cannon had exploded on the *Plymouth Spirit,* and Will saw some sailors passing buckets to douse the flames. Will spotted an officer in a red coat standing boldly on the quarterdeck just as a musket shot tossed him backwards, dropping him to the deck, clutching his thigh.

A sailor charged at Will brandishing a long sword. His first thrust was easily parried, and Will butted the enemy's head with the hilt of his cutlass. The man crumpled onto the deck. Will stepped over the prone figure, searching for combat, relishing the swirling tempest of the battle. To his right another defender rushed at him with a long pike held waist high. Will jumped to one side, caught the pike with the cutlass and deflected him past, again lashing out with the heavy hilt of his blade.

The battle spun about the vessel, and yet to William it was a battle of slow moving combatants. To his left a man with a club lunged at him, and a step to the rear sent the chap sprawling on deck. To his right another man with a long sword swung at him. The heavy blade took what seemed like hours to complete its long arc, and William feinted to the side, slashing at his opponent's right. His blade found its mark, and a thin red line sliced above the man's waist—not deep enough to kill, but the man dropped like a stone in water.

The three dozen crewmen from the *Reprisal* fought like wild, uncaged animals, shrieking and flailing at their rivals.

Within minutes Will had slashed his way to the first gangway that led to belowdecks. Guarding the stairs was an immense hulk of a sailor holding a pistol in his left hand and long rapier blade in his right.

I hope he is right-handed, Will thought, *and that his aim is off with his left hand.*

The sailor raised his pistol and aimed it at Will's forehead. Will clearly saw the enemy's finger tighten round the trigger, then tug, ever so gently, at its release, as if he desired to wait until the last possible moment to end Will's life. The gun howled, and the exploding powder encased the man in white smoke. Will felt the charge race past his left temple, the air crackling from the speed of the ball. He reached up and felt a trace of blood that followed the ball's path as it grazed his scalp.

The smoke, carried away by a gust of wind, left both men staring into each other's face. Will's piercing blue eyes narrowed, and he charged at his rival, sword at parry point. His enemy, using the thin rapier, had no defense, and Will found the soft flesh of his shoulder with the tip of his cutlass. The man screamed, dropped both the pistol and the blade, and tumbled backwards to the deck below, clutching at his shoulder as he bounced down the steps.

Will called out to the red-coated captain, still lying on the deck in front of him. "Sir! You have fought well. It is time to call your crew to cease. If they continue to fight, more will die. I ask you to order them to lay down their arms. We have our cannons reloaded and will fire a killing volley into your hull if we must. I insist, Captain Blake."

Captain Blake looked up, his face smeared with blood and grime. His leg continued to bleed, but less vigorously than when the musket ball first struck.

"If you call to cease, I will guarantee the safety of all. Continue to battle, and I will not issue such a guarantee," Will shouted.

Captain Blake struggled to one knee, sweat marking lines in the dirt on his forehead. "Men of the *Plymouth Spirit!* This is Captain Blake!" he called out over the din of men's shouts, the scream of wood as the two ships scraped together—both still under full sail—and the occasional musket shot. "Cease fighting! We are striking the flag! Raise the white banner!" he shouted to a junior officer.

Within moments the noise ceased. Men stood, alone, panting, clutching at wounds, calling for water or aid.

Will turned back to his ship. "Call for Luke to come aboard and treat the wounded," he said to Johnny Delacroix at his side.

Will turned back to Captain Blake. "We have a remarkably skilled healer—a former slave—who is most adept at treating wounds such as yours, Captain Blake. I shall send him to your side first."

Captain Blake, pain clouding his eyes, nodded in agreement, then looked back at William. "Have we made acquaintances, sir? I recall your looks, but I am at a loss—owing perhaps to the wound—to recall your name."

"I am William Hawkes. You attempted to hire me on as navigator several years prior."

"You are English!"

"Of course."

"What right do you have to attack an English ship?"

"By the right that I have established at the tip of my sword, dear

Captain Blake. And now, if you would be so kind as to tell me where the gold is hidden?"

Luke was at the captain's side, tearing through his blood-soaked breeches, washing the wound off with fresh water.

Captain Blake grimaced from the pain, then laughed. "Gold? On this ship? Captain Hawkes, I believe it is the other way around. Gold comes from the New World to home. We do not bring it back to the islands."

"And you are telling me that there are no funds on board to complete the church in Barbados?"

"None, Captain Hawkes," he grimaced again, "and I speak as one captain—one Englishman—to another. There is no gold on this ship."

Will closed his eyes and hoped that Captain Blake was not speaking the truth, but he was most fearful that he was.

"And there is no daughter of the governor of Barbados on board as well?" *Was that a flicker of fear in his eyes?* Will thought.

"Captain Hawkes, would Lord Spenser be foolish enough to send his daughter on a poorly armed merchant ship—and not call for a fleet of naval ships to transport such a precious passenger? There is no woman aboard this ship, Captain."

There still may be treasure on board, Will thought, *and I intend to find it.*

"Men of the *Reprisal!* You have fought bravely! This ship is now ours for plunder! Please begin your search!"

With that, Will stepped back and half-bowed to the fallen captain.

With Mr. Delacroix at his side, Will made his way to the second deck. Lying at the stern of the ship were the officers' quarters. Will selected the door with the most ornate carving, suspecting it to be that of the captain. He walked up to it, lifted his leg, and kicked solidly at the latch. The door splintered open and slammed against the wall with a bang. Will walked into the room to face a vicar, at the very edge of panic, dressed in a proper black frock, holding in front of him a shining, eight-inch blade of polished steel.

"Do not come any closer. I am not fearful of using this against you," the clergyman wavered.

Will looked at the blade, which was trembling, wobbling in the air like a new butterfly just out of its cocoon.

With his sword still held in his right hand, Will raised his hand to shoulder height, took a sudden step towards the vicar, and clubbed him soundly on the temple with the dull hilt of his cutlass. The vicar crumpled to the floor.

"And I, Vicar," Will said derisively at the prostrate figure, "am not fearful of using this either," brandishing his sword.

Will tore through the drawers, under the bed, and through the chart cabinets. He turned to hear a whistle at the door.

"Captain Hawkes, the English captain lied to you." A young sailor smirked. "There are women on board."

And with that he held up a lacy chemise and modeled it against himself.

Will turned back to the captain's cabin. The skinny wardrobe, built into the wall, was hardly sufficient for even a child to stand upright in. Then Will noticed that a small triangle of red was peeking through the door—the end of a uniform, perhaps. Captain Blake did not seem to Will to be the sort of man who would leave a coat stuck in a wardrobe door.

Will nodded silently to Mr. Delacroix, and they made their way over to opposite sides of the wardrobe. Each placed a hand on a door, and with a sudden jerk they flung both doors open, expecting a pistol to crash out in response.

But there was no pistol shot, just red, brass-buttoned waistcoats and breeches hanging there, softly swaying to the roll of the ship. Will stood back, puzzled. He poked his blade into the closet and found no hiding spot.

Will turned away, having no interest in stealing fancy officer's uniforms.

At the corner of his eye, as he turned, he noticed a spot of blue, different from any uniform he had ever seen. He turned back, unsure of what it was that he had seen.

He reached in and roughly pulled the uniforms out, dumping them on the floor. At the very bottom of the closet was a tiny trace of sea-colored fabric wedged between a nearly hidden seam in the wood.

Will nodded again at Delacroix, smiled, and took a step forward.

At that moment, the vicar, now roused from the blow to his head, jumped up to the left of William, steadying himself on the captain's chair.

"I must ask you again to leave this cabin at once!" he cried out. "There is nothing of value in this room. I have knowledge that there is no treasure here. I assure you that you will waste your energy searching further."

"Well, Vicar. It is Vicar, is it not?" Will asked, toying with him as a cat toys with a mouse. "You say there is nothing of value left in this cabin."

"That is true. Nothing of value," the vicar said, his voice high and tense.

Will slipped his cutlass into its scabbard and gently stroked at his chin.

"And we will waste our time searching here."

"Yes, that is correct," replied the vicar, who had begun to relax, thinking he had fooled this barbaric intruder.

Will lowered his hand to the belt on his waist and curled his fingers about the butt of his pistol. He slowly removed it from his belt. "Well, Vicar, if there is nothing of value here, you will find no harm in a single pistol shot, fired for practice, that is."

With that, Will raised the barrel of the pistol and leveled it at the back of the wardrobe. He slowly pulled back on the hammer, locking it into place. He looked over at the vicar.

"No harm in a single shot, is there?" Will repeated.

The vicar jumped between William and the wardrobe, his face white and bloodless.

"You will not fire your pistol into this! You will fire through me first!" he cried.

"A most remarkable piece of furniture—one that is worthy of your life, Vicar?"

Will raised the pistol until its barrel was aimed directly at the vicar's forehead.

"I wonder if a man's head will stop a pistol's discharge at such close range?" Will asked with an evil menace in his voice.

The vicar closed his eyes, yet he remained motionless between Will and the rear of the wardrobe.

"Well, I surmise that we will soon find out."

Suddenly the back of the wardrobe crashed outward, and an ashen-faced Kathryne Spenser tumbled into the room, dressed in a sea-blue dress, gasping for breath.

"You cutthroat heathen devil!" she shouted at Will. "I will allow no man to die on my behalf! If you desire to end a life, then fire into me! I am a willing target!"

The gun remained aimed at the vicar until now as Kathryne roughly shoved him to the side and stood where he had been standing.

"Well?" she shouted, her voice a rising fury. "Why do you not fire? You want to see someone die, do you not? Then fire! See my life ended! That is the only thing that will satisfy your bloodlust, is it not?"

Kathryne had no rational thought as to the origin of her bravado. She only knew that she was guided.

"Well, then, you heathen pirate, if you cannot fire your pistol, perhaps you may slice my heart with your cutlass! You do take pleasure in that, do you not? Do it then. Run the blade through my being. Do it!"

Will was stunned into speechlessness.

Kathryne was breathing fast, her color rising, her eyes flashing. She felt sweat on her forehead, her blood pumping fast, her breath swelling in her chest.

A sailor from the *Reprisal* came to the open doorway. "Captain, we have searched, and I believe what the English captain said is true. Other than a few trinkets, there is no treasure on board."

William smiled. "I believe you are wrong, sailor. I believe I have found the treasure."

He returned his pistol to shoulder height and spun his arm to the right. Without truly looking, he fired a shot that roared past the vicar's head, missing it by perhaps half a foot. The bark of his pistol filled the small room like a peal of thunder. As the echoes died, both Vicar Petley and Kathryne collapsed in dead faints.

"The real treasure has been found," Will added a final time.

■ ■ □ ■ □ ■

Those eyes, thought Will as he left the captain's cabin. *I have seen those eyes before.*

His mind raced back to a dim memory of a fall day many years prior. *The leaves had just turned crimson and gold, and Hadenthorne was bathed in sun, yet it was those eyes that lit up the afternoon sky.*

His heart wrenched, for it was a time when he still could feel love.

■ ■ □ ■ □ ■

The *Reprisal* untied the ropes that held the two ships together. Kathryne had been brought aboard first, still in a faint. Luke carried her over, as gently as a mother cat carries her kittens. The vicar had been handled less gently by the Tambor brothers, who were more accustomed to hauling barrels and sacks of grain.

Will walked over to the seated Captain Blake. "We are taking the Lady Kathryne Spenser as hostage," he explained. "The governor has one month to raise ten gold bars of standard measure for her ransom. If it is not met, she will be killed. We are taking the vicar as her chaperone. I will have no man accuse William Hawkes of taking liberties with an unwilling woman. She will not be harmed in any way up until that date, I assure you of that, provided our demands are met.

"See to it that the governor meets us at this point on this map—a two days' sail west from Bridgetown—by the first full moon of November."

Will had marked the rendezvous site with a thick, red X—an unnamed maze of shallow channels, dangerous shoals, and islets no more than a day's sail from the *Reprisal*'s secret base.

"If he does not, he will never again see his daughter taking breath. Sir, I take my leave of you now."

Will walked away and headed back to his ship, now waiting to cast off.

Captain Blake called to him. "Captain Hawkes!"

Will stopped and turned.

"Captain Hawkes? What transpired to change you? I called you less than a cutthroat in Weymouth—but this? A pirate? A kidnapper? I do not understand the descent. What happened? How did you lose the way?"

"I lost no way, Captain Blake. I have chosen to pursue this. It is my destiny. It is the path that God has willed for me."

Captain Blake looked down at the deck where he sat, stained with his own blood, and shook his head slowly. He looked back up at Will's cold and lifeless eyes. "God's will? Well, perhaps so, Captain. If God can will the death of innocents, perhaps he can will the birth of a pirate."

CHAPTER

63

18 October 1641
The Caribbean Sea

Kathryne awoke slowly, her eyelids fluttering like a tiny butterfly after a rain. Her head swam, and her thoughts were in a frantic jumble. Before she let light into her eyes, she placed her palm on her forehead, checking for fever.

Was this a dream I have had? It is a most unsettling dream if so, she thought. *It must have been, for I am still in this small sleeping alcove. . . . Though the color of the curtain seems to be different. . . . Perhaps it is merely a trick of the light. But why would I be still in my day gown if I have been to bed?*

Realizing that there was only a single method to settle her questions, Kathryne extended her hand to the curtain, and after a moment's hesitation she drew them back, filling the bedchamber with a blaze of sunlight.

This room is different! her brain screamed.

And as her eyes scanned the small space, she all but overlooked one vast difference. In the corner, by the window, a long-legged black man sat, or squatted on his haunches, if the truth be told. His bony knees were visible as his ragged canvas breeches had frayed to that length. He sat there calmly, with an impassioned look on his ebony features.

At first, Kathryne considered the strange form as no more sentient than another piece of furniture, but when he perked up and raised his head, craning his neck and smiling, Kathryne grasped at the curtain, drawing it around her fully clothed body, struggling with every ounce of her strength to not scream and shriek at his presence.

In a voice teetering on the gulf of panic, Kathryne asked in a warbling voice, "W-w-w-who are you? W-w-w-where am I? H-h-how did I get here?"

"Ahh good, you wake now. Luke fear de spirit dead and left de body. But you back now. Luke happy you back."

His most curious speech, almost childlike, had Kathryne puzzled. And amazingly a smile sought to crease her lips. She leaned forward to the black man with the beatific grin. In a small, whispery voice, she asked, "What has happened? How did I come to be here—in a strange cabin with a black man watching me?"

She heard a familiar chirping and looked to see that her Williamson thrush's cage had been hung from a peg in a ceiling rafter. "And who brought my bird with me?"

The lanky black man stood up, filling the room from floor to ceiling—and then some. "I am Luke. I was slave till Captain Will set me free. He bought me, den gave me away. I am healer on dis ship."

"What ship?"

"It be called de *Reprisal*. I not for sure what dat word is."

The pirate ship! I am captive on the pirate ship! Kathryne's thoughts raced.

Her voice quivering, she asked, "What will your captain do with me?"

Luke's brow furrowed. He nodded and stared at the floor, trying to remember. He brightened as he remembered the proper words. "He be gettin' ransom for you. He get gold from de English."

"Luke? There was a man in my cabin—a preacher. Was he . . . was he killed? I remember your captain firing a pistol at his head. Is he dead?"

"Oh no—he be alive. Captain bring him here, too. He protect your . . . your . . . honor? He protect you, lady."

"Yes, for my honor—that is right."

Thank you, Lord, she quickly prayed, *for sparing Giles' life at the hands of the heathens.*

Kathryne struggled to the end of the bed. She was still wearing her shoes. *Just like an uncivilized pagan to allow shoes on a bed.* "Luke, will I be allowed to see your captain?"

Luke looked puzzled.

"I want to talk to Captain . . ."

"Will. William Hawkes be his name. He be here, lady. He be here soon."

■ ■ ■ ■

The *Plymouth Spirit* limped toward Barbados. During the pirate attack, only two sailors had been killed, and that was in the explosion of the cannon. It was not apparent if the shot had caused the discharge or if a loose spark from a previous shot caused the powder bags to explode. But a score were injured and lay in sick bay.

Captain Blake, holding a long cane, trudged about the quarterdeck in foul humor. His ship—his pride—had been besmirched. A mast was down, and the decking in several places had been ripped to shreds by the pirates' cannon shot. Most despicably, though, was that his prize cargo, Lady Kathryne Spenser, was gone. How would he explain this to the governor?

He paced the deck, angry at their slow pace. Despite his injury, his leg was virtually pain free. *Whatever that black man did has surely worked miracles of healing,* Blake thought.

I am still most puzzled why Hawkes took aim at my ship on the journey into the Antilles—and why he thought there was gold aboard. It was almost as if someone had planted that information. But who? Surely the governor would do no such thing. But Radcliffe perhaps. But to put his only niece is such jeopardy is . . . a terrible thought.

Blake looked west and saw a green slice of earth—Barbados—rising from the turquoise sea just as it was announced from the remaining crow's nest.

If any man had the depraved will to do such a thing, it would be Radcliffe. And I wonder if enough money will be raised to free such a beautiful woman as Lady Spenser?

■ ■ ■ ■ ■

Kathryne remained in the small cabin, guarded by Luke. He had called for food, and a sailor brought in fresh fruit, biscuits, and cheese on a rough wooden plank. A small knife was on the board to cut the fruit. As Kathryne picked it up and felt the weight of it in her hand, she wondered if she could hide it on her person to defend herself from crude advances, if necessary. Or better yet, she thought, she could use it against her captor, Captain Hawkes.

No, she quickly concluded, *that is not a godly response. If I trust in the Almighty's leading, he will protect me. This knife will do little against any evil, but God has more weapons than this. I will leave it in his hands.*

She saw Luke watch her as she sliced through the strange yellow fruit with the thick skin. The knife was indeed sharp and would be a potent weapon.

Kathryne was about to place an entire yellow disk into her mouth when Luke stopped her by grabbing her hand. "No lady—only eat da inside. Da skin be bitter."

She peeled off the thick yellow skin, and the fruit carried indeed a most pleasant mild taste.

"What is this named, Luke?"

"It called banana, lady. Most do not slice till skinned."

With that he picked one off the board, peeled it back with a few easy strokes, then commenced eating it in front of her, taking large mouthfuls of the fruit, chewing loudly and with obvious enjoyment.

Kathryne and Luke ate much of the rest of the fruit and biscuits. Kathryne had not realized how hungry she had become.

"When will Captain William talk with me, Luke?"

"When we home. Four days."

"And I am to remain a prisoner in this horrid, foul cabin the entire time?"

"Dat what Captain Will says, and he be de captain."

Kathryne spent the next several days confined to that small room aboard Will's ship. Luke brought her food and drink, more than she could possibly eat and of good quality, much better than the fare on the *Plymouth Spirit*. She had a stack of books to read, many of a nautical nature, but a few of the classics were in the captain's library as well. Luke assured her that when they arrived home, everything would be explained. The captain, Luke claimed, was too busy sailing to talk.

"Plenty time when we gets home, lady. You talk den. You see—plenty time den. Da sea be full of danger, so we get home fast."

It was the afternoon of the fourth day when she heard the crew begin to talk in louder voices, excited and higher-pitched. From a distance, she heard the sound of waves crashing against shore, and the ship pitched and rolled more intensely than before. She had remained sitting in the small alcove and reached out with both hands to brace herself.

Luke, who had kept a private vigil most of the past four days with Kathryne, was squatting on the floor swaying in rhythm to the pitch of the ship. Then a sound of brush, or tree limbs, scraping against the side of the ship was followed by a smooth, quiet forward motion for perhaps a minute. Then a loud hiss, and the ship lurched forward, almost banging an unprepared Kathryne into the forward wall.

"We home, lady. We home now," Luke stated with finality.

He stood up and extended his hand for Kathryne to take. She hesitated for a brief moment. His childlike smile convinced her, and she placed her small, white hand in his wide, black, bony hand, and he escorted her through the unlocked door to the upper decks.

She stepped up the last few steps to the quarterdeck of the tiny ship, picking her long blue skirt up and folding it in her hand to prevent tripping over it. She stepped gently into the sun, blinking her eyes, adjusting to the riot of greens and blues and vibrant hues that splashed about the environment all around her.

Will had been handling a large crate of linen that had been liberated from the *Plymouth Spirit*. He looked up and saw the villagers on the island stop, dead still in their tracks, their eyes focused behind him.

The crew, normally loud and playful when returning from a battle, were stunned into silence. Jaws dropped, and eyes opened wide. Will spun about to investigate the cause of their astonishment, and there stood Kathryne, tall and regal Kathryne. The ivory, almost porcelain, skin of her face and demure open bodice was set off by the cascade of dark, silken hair that curled and spiraled along her pink cheeks and neck. She was wearing a gown of delicate blue, trimmed in white lace. Her eyes, dark green—greener than emeralds—were wide and inviting. She held her full lips to a thin line, not wanting to grimace in fear.

For many of the young villagers, it was the first white woman they had seen, and certainly for most others it was the most elegant and beautiful woman they had ever beheld.

The breeze fluttered her hair, and from the jungle beyond the beach a wild bird cawed loudly.

"Captain Hawkes? I am Kathryne Spenser. I would like a word with you."

Will stood up suddenly, brushing the dirt and dust from his clothes, and took an unfortunate step backwards in order to stand further away, feeling a bit unwashed. He caught his heel on a deck stanchion and tumbled, head over heels, into the shallow waters of the bay. As he splashed to an inglorious landing, the villagers and crew burst into giggles and laughter. Will sputtered as he stood up in the knee-deep water, his wet shirt clinging to his muscular body, and looked up at the glorious woman on the deck of his ship.

A quick smile trembled quickly across Kathryne's tightly closed lips.

By that afternoon, Kathryne had been situated in William's hut on the beach, along with her possessions that had been taken from the *Plymouth Spirit*.

The vicar, situated in a smaller hut next to hers, was suffering greatly from the sea maladies caused by the rolling and rocking of the ship. Luke had prepared a remedy for him at the outset, which he had refused to take, and he had spent most of the last four days green and in bed. The Tambor brothers had carried him, like a limp doll, from the ship to his hut.

Kathryne stood by her door, watching as Giles was gently placed in his cot. Will approached the portal where she stood.

"Lady Spenser," he said, "may I now explain your situation?"

Will stammered and searched for the proper words to communicate with such a noble beauty. "You are being held in custody until the full moon of November—a month hence—until a certain sum is presented to us for your safekeeping."

Kathryne interrupted, her voice stern and cold. "Being held hostage—a prisoner for ransom, Mr. Hawkes. Shall we call this practice what it truly is?"

Will looked sheepish. "Yes, well, . . . however, in this interim period, we will endeavor to make your stay here as pleasant as possible. Lady Spenser, I will assure you on my word of honor—"

She snorted a caustic laugh.

"—on my word of honor, no harm will befall you while in my care. No member of my crew will do anything . . . untoward . . . to you or the vicar."

"As if that will help me sleep at night in this forsaken jungle."

"Luke will sleep outside your door, Lady Spenser. He has insisted on it. There is no one who will dream of taking advantage of you with Luke as your guardian," Will replied, trying to set things right.

"And where are the remainder of my trunks?"

"We managed to bring a few of them with us. Pardon us for not knowing what might be important to you. All of them have been placed in your hut."

"And do you mean us to starve, Mr. Hawkes? Or will you be feeding us scraps?"

Kathryne, who was quite amazed at the articulate and proper language of this Captain Hawkes, was speaking colder, firmer, harsher than she felt. *But, after all,* she told herself, *I have been kidnapped.*

"You will dine with us when we take our meals. Whatever foods we have procured, you are welcome to all you desire."

"And then, in the meantime, I am confined to this hot, squalid little hut?" she demanded.

"Please, Lady Spenser, you have freedom about this village, the clearing, and the beach. I would advise not wandering into the brush, for it is most easy to become lost, and there are snakes and insects out there that are most unpleasant."

Her skin crawled when he mentioned snakes. *How I wish I hadn't asked that question,* she shuddered silently.

"And Vicar Petley? Shall he be in confinement as well?"

"No, Lady Spenser. He has the same freedoms as you."

As William and Kathryne negotiated the terms of her captivity, Luke squatted near the doorway of the hut. The sun had dipped close to the tops of the palms, and the children from the small village began arriving. To Kathryne, it appeared as they were waiting for some event, even though most of them continued to stare at her with an undiluted intensity.

"Lady Spenser, I must ask that I be able to remove a few books from my hut. The children are waiting for me."

Kathryne snipped, "It is *your* hut, after all. Who might I be to stop you?"

Will walked into the darkened space to retrieve his books. Several of Kathryne's trunks were open, and on the top of one, nearest the door, was a waterfall of silks and lace, most likely underthings of some sort. Will felt his throat tighten and the blood rush to his face when gazing upon such intimates. He turned his head quickly and walked abruptly out the door, with the wake of children following in his path.

Kathryne stood by the threshold as he walked away. She studied Will at length for the first time. While with him by the hut, she had noticed his penetrating blue eyes that stood out from his well-chiseled face. She now observed that he was a finely built man—neither excessively tall nor short, broad-shouldered, small-waisted and muscular, well-bronzed by the sun, with a generous mane of sun-lightened blond hair tied in a thick tail at his neck.

Around his legs leaped a dozen small black children, like excited puppies. When she was sure he was out of earshot, she leaned to Luke and asked, "What is Captain Hawkes doing? Why are the children following him?"

"Lady," Luke replied without moving, "he be schoolin'."

"Schooling?"

"Word I not know—but dey be openin' books and talkin'."

"Schooling?" Kathryne placed her hands on her hips, her eyes wide in surprise. "A pirate . . . and a schoolteacher?"

CHAPTER

64

21 October 1641
Barbados

"Kathryne! My poppet! A hostage! How can this be?"

Lord Aidan was pacing the room in a near panic, shouting and crying and staring up at the heavens, all at the same time.

"Captain Blake—how could you allow her to be taken? Had you no defenses? Could you not have battled with greater vigor? She is my daughter, for the Almighty's sake! What are we to do?"

The captain was standing in the finished library, empty of books as of yet, at Shelworthy. His leg was bandaged, and he carried a cane, but the musket wound was proving no great discomfort.

"My lord, we were set upon by a larger force. The pirates may have numbered two hundred." From the corner, Blake saw Radcliffe roll his eyes. *The blasted traitor knew!* Blake's thoughts screamed. *He bloody well knew!*

"And the ragabashes had greater firepower as well—perhaps forty large cannons." With this statement, Blake stared directly at Radcliffe, daring him to smirk or acknowledge his complicity.

Radcliffe sat at his brother's side, his face a perfect mask of terror and outrage. "How perfectly awful for you, Captain Blake—and wounded in the brave defense," Radcliffe oozed.

"We are but a poor merchant ship," Blake explained to Lord Aidan, "and our defenses are slight. But it was an Englishman who did this deed—an Englishman who possessed letters of marque from you, my lord."

Aidan froze in place, mouth agape, then resumed his pacing about the room. Radcliffe felt dizzy from watching and stared out the window instead.

"Why did I let you steer me to this course, Radcliffe? I knew that such a plan of action would eventually return regrets upon our heads. And, alas, it has. I knew that legal piracy would be the first step to illegal acts such as this!"

Radcliffe looked over at his brother with raised eyebrows. "Why a man turns to evil one can never predict," Radcliffe stated. "But now that this most dreadful thing has happened, what shall we do in response? Surely we must form a rescue voyage at once."

"Yes, yes, that is most certain, Radcliffe. But who shall lead such a voyage. And how shall the money be raised—in gold bars, yet? Imagine a heathen pirate making such demands."

Radcliffe stood and walked behind the massive desk. He pawed through the stack of papers and maps, extracting a sheet of parchment. "This, dear brother, is your payment. Only a few weeks ago, Mr. Hawkes voyaged to Barbados and left behind the Crown's share of his most recent plunder. It was before he let the evil take his soul."

Blake glared at Radcliffe. *So that's when you recruited him, you weasel. I will see your poltroon hide nailed to my mast before I leave this cursed place,* Blake steamed to himself.

"I should have seen it then, for his eyes were sunken and his demeanor possessed. But he left with me a sum of forty gold bars for the Crown. And that, dear brother, is more than sufficient to meet his ransom demands."

Lord Aidan paced to the windows, still smelling faintly of paint, then to his desk, then to the open door and back again. "I am vexed to the limit!" he exploded. "I must save my daughter. I must use that gold. See to it that the transfer is recorded, Radcliffe. And see to it that a ship is chartered as well. We have only three weeks to make arrangements."

Radcliffe and Blake bowed to Lord Aidan, whom they left slumped in the massive chair behind his desk.

As Radcliffe closed the huge door behind them, Blake grabbed Radcliffe by the collar, spun him around, and pinned him to the wall with his forearm. Blake squeezed Radcliffe's throat with near enough force to choke the man.

"I should slit your guts open here, you bloody mercenary," Blake venomously whispered in his ear. "But it would stain the new floors, and your death isn't worth the work of cleaning them."

Radcliffe, turning red, sputtered and grabbed at Blake's thick arm. "I did nothing, . . . you must believe me. I said nothing to Hawkes. Ask anyone at the alehouse as we met. I told him nothing," he choked.

"Then how did he know when and where to set upon me?" Blake demanded.

"He could have heard it from a thousand sources," Radcliffe wheezed, his breath growing shorter. "Now let me down, for I have a most interesting proposition for you."

After another moment Blake backed away, and Radcliffe doubled over, inhaling huge lungfuls of fresh air, rubbing at his bruised neck. He straightened up.

"Besides," he gasped, "what benefit do I have if Kathryne is killed or ransomed? What would I gain in this?"

"I am sure that you have found a way, Radcliffe."

The two men made their way out the elaborate front doors, tended by two uniformed doormen, sweating in starched white collars under heavy red woolen coats with gold buttons and braiding.

"But as I think about this dreadful situation, I do see a way that will enable *both* of us to profit—more profit than you ever dreamed possible, Captain Blake. Are you interested?"

"How much profit?"

Radcliffe thought as they walked down the path lined with crushed oyster shells, glints reflecting the hot sun.

"Twenty thousand pounds and an estate—would that be of interest?"

"You are bloody well joking, are you not, Radcliffe? That be a true king's ransom."

"Captain Blake, I never joke about money or power. Now then, are you interested?"

"For that much treasure I most assuredly would be. I believe I would bend my own rules for that sum—as flexible as they are."

It is so easy, Radcliffe thought, *to fish in the shallow waters of human nature. There is almost no sport left in it.*

CHAPTER

65

23 October 1641
An Unnamed Island
The Caribbean Sea

The village children were jumping with expectation as they gathered around William by the rock at the shore of the bay—perhaps a distance of fifty yards from where Kathryne stood at the door of Will's hut, intently watching.

"Luke, would you accompany me? I would like to walk to the water's edge."

"Yes, lady," he said as he stretched upright.

Just then a voice called out, "Kathryne! You are safe as well!"

Kathryne turned to see a wobbly vicar in the doorway of his hut, a few steps further inland from Kathryne's. *I had almost stopped thinking of him,* she thought, ashamed. *It is indeed the stress of recent events that gave me pause in my concern for the poor man.*

"Vicar! You are back with us. I am so relieved," she said as she walked toward him. "Is your stomach well?"

"It still roils when I think of food, but I believe standing on firm earth will settle it after a spell."

She went to his side and embraced him in as sisterly a manner as she could, not wanting to upset his constitution more than necessary.

"I am so relieved that you have recovered from the blow to your head as well. Does it cause you much pain?" she asked, gently touching the small welt at his temple.

"Not so much now, Kathryne dear, that we are together again. But what has happened to us? Where have we been placed? What is this vile spot?"

Kathryne took him by the hand, and they sat under the small roofed porch over the doorway to Will's hut.

Kathryne, in a calm voice that she had employed with the children of the free school, laid out the progression of events as she understood them. The vicar winced as she described parts of the battle and abduction.

She glanced over at the rocks and the children and saw William as he stood amidst them, acting out some sort of story. The children were shrieking with joy and excitement as Captain Hawkes danced from rock to rock. At some point, the story must have called for a tremendous rain, for Will removed his shirt and used it as a wrap about his forehead, allowing it to drape down his back. His chest was exposed, as well as his flat stomach, toasted golden from the sun. His arms were held out at angles from his body as the children leapt at them, hanging as from tree limbs, his muscles hardening to hold the children aloft.

"Don't you agree, Kathryne?"

"W-w-what . . . what was it you asked, Vicar? I must still be . . . suffering from this heat," she said as she raised the back of her hand to her forehead.

She hesitated, then turned away from the beach and looked directly at the vicar, who was sweating profusely in his wool clothing.

"I simply asked if your father is the type of man who will comply with these nefarious men's wishes? Will he send the ransom or a fleet of ships to take you back?"

Kathryne was flustered. *What response would be appropriate? What would her father do?*

"Well, Vicar, I am not sure of his course of action. Perhaps it will be the ransom. It would appear to be the safer, less hostile course."

The vicar crossed his arms over his chest, annoyed. "I would prefer that the British navy attend to this matter. They would cannon these blackguard heathens to the reward they deserve."

"Vicar," Kathryne replied, "I am shocked. That is not a godly response."

"These are not men of God, Kathryne, and deserve little mercy," the vicar spat.

▪ ▫ ▪ ▫ ▪

Kathryne slept fitfully during her first night on the small island. The jungle, a mere arm's length from her reclining form, was filled with chirps and calls and buzzes and howls. At one point a surprising loud racket of squeals and animal shouts erupted, it seemed to her, at the door of her hut. She leapt up, clutched her robe about her, and peeked out from the door. Luke lay on a small mat with barely a thin strip of linen covering himself from the elements.

Her breathing slowly calmed. *Well, if he has not become alarmed, then neither shall I,* she told herself as she returned to bed.

In the morning, Kathryne awoke to the most glorious sunrise she had ever seen. The sun rose directly through the small opening of the hidden cove and spilled its reds and golds in a surge of brilliant warm colors onto the cool blues of the bay. Kathryne felt the first heat of the day, the gold rays reflecting from the water onto her face. Soon the sun was higher than the ocean palms and flooded the cove with a liquid radiance.

Her Williamson thrush, Willy, his cage hung with care from a roof support, was silent this morning, save for a few polite chirps as Kathryne cooed at him. He looked perplexed, Kathryne imagined, that none of his plaintive songs was answered by the call of a single fellow thrush.

As she looked about, she saw a small child at the water's edge using a small pointed stick to trace in the wet sand. Kathryne looked around the beach and saw no one. Being fully dressed and most proper, she stepped over the still-sleeping Luke. As she turned to look, his eyes were bright and open.

"No run, lady."

She whispered back, "No run—just to the water."

"Good lady," he said and closed his eyes again.

She walked to the small child, a boy of about eight years old, she guessed, with huge brown eyes and a curly thatch of black hair. "Hello," Kathryne said in a most friendly manner.

"Bonjour," he replied.

Was that French? "Parlez-vous français?" she asked.

"Oui," the boy replied.

Kathryne had her hands on her knees and was bent to the boy, her jaw open in surprise.

"I know little English. Captain Will teach us," he added, nodding.

"And what marks are you making in the sand?"

"There," he pointed with pride. "My name."

Albert was etched into the sand in bold, childlike strokes.

"My prize pupil, Albert," came a voice from behind her.

Kathryne leapt up, her hand at her throat. Will, silent as a shadow, stood a few feet from her, barefoot in the wet sand.

"Lady Spenser, I did not mean to frighten you. I saw you speak with the boy and was not sure you spoke enough French—or that Albert yet spoke enough English—for you to understand each other."

Albert was beaming at both of them.

"We have understood each other as well as might be expected," Kathryne said, trying her best to maintain the stiff distance the situation seemed to require.

"Captain Will," Albert said as he tugged at the fabric of Will's breeches, then launched into several moments of such a strange language that Kathryne tilted her head at the sound, trying to understand even a single element.

Will squatted down next to the boy, gently put an arm about his shoulder, then chatted back in apparently the same odd language.

In a moment, the young boy nodded sagely, looked at Kathryne and smiled, then ran back to the small gathering of huts on the other side of the cove.

"What language is that, Mr. Hawkes?" Kathryne asked primly.

"It is the language of their home in Africa. I am not positive of the exact location so as to place it in the proper country, but they call their land the Home of the Sun."

"And how is it that you know their language? Do you sell slaves?"

"I do not, Lady Spenser. It was the children who have taught me much of their native language. It would seem that I have an innate facility with foreign tongues. It has served me well on the seas."

"What did Albert ask of you?"

"Just a childish question."

"No, Mr. Hawkes—you may tell me. What did he ask?"

"He asked if you were the queen from England, for you are most beautiful," Will answered, looking at her evenly.

Kathryne felt her smile grow and a faint blush come to her cheeks. "Queen?" she asked.

"The children have quite an imagination," replied Will.

"Queen. . . . Yes, they do, do they not?"

■ ▨ ■ □ ■

An hour later, after the sun had climbed higher, the vicar stumbled out of his hut, looking pale and wan.

"Kathryne," he said breathlessly, and he sank to the sand by where she sat. "My strength is most dissipated. I slept nary a moment all of last evening, for the screams of animals in pain and the rushing noises of the waves crashing on the shore. How I may survive on this wretched place for more than an entire month will be beyond my ability to predict."

He propped himself up on his elbow, still wearing a heavy shirt, covered by a dark baize coverlet from the ship. "Kathryne," he whispered, "will they feed us breakfast?"

"You silly goose," she answered, trying to be lively. "Of course they will."

She stood up and whistled, and two young boys ran over. Kathryne smiled at them. "Jooba?" she said with a bright smile.

And with that single word, the two ran off back to the village.

"Most remarkable, Kathryne, but what on earth have you said?"

"It is their word for food, I think—or perhaps breakfast. At any matter, they will soon be back."

In a moment, they came running with a large, thick, glossy leaf held between them, as big as a woman's frock. It was filled with fruits—bananas, Kathryne saw, some odd-looking green and red items, and two smoked fish.

They set it all carefully on the ground and stepped back. "Jooba," the taller of the two explained.

Kathryne reached into her pocket and pulled out two shillings. She knew that coins had no value on a remote island as this, but they were shiny bits of metal. She placed one in each of the boys' hands, and they ran off, laughing and grinning.

"Kathryne, I must say—two shillings for this odd . . . assortment. I would call that extravagant," Vicar Petley complained.

Kathryne merely smiled in return, sat on a smooth rock, and watched as the vicar carefully and most fastidiously picked through the tumbled array of fruit and fish.

* * *

"Mr. Hawkes!" Kathryne called as she saw William exit the belowdecks of the beached ship.

Will pulled his loose shirt over his head as he made his way toward her. "Yes, Lady Spenser. Do you require something?"

Kathryne again slipped into a snippy, terse tone with William. "How far a walk is that mountain over there?" she asked while pointing inland.

Why am I becoming so spiteful? Kathryne! He has not harmed you, she scolded herself. *You have stopped speaking like a Christian woman.*

"The base of that mountain, which is an extinct volcano, Lady Spenser, is perhaps an hour's walk."

"Is there a clear path?" she queried primly.

"Clear path? Through the jungle? Hardly, but the way is not too narrow nor overgrown."

"Will you escort me there?" she asked in a crisp voice. As his face showed surprise, she added, "If I am to be held captive for a month, I may as well expose myself to nature and to the topography of this place."

Kathryne! Why are you being such a horrible person? You are sounding every bit as mean as Celia Althorp.

"Lady Spenser, I would be glad to do so. But it is too late in the day to start such a journey. I prefer to sleep in a hut, rather than a jungle, and the dark does come quickly here."

"Tomorrow would be acceptable," she answered somewhat tersely.

William turned away and after a few steps, turned back again. "Lady Spenser, the vicar will need accompany us as well. I will not let you be the subject of unsubstantiated accusations."

"A most prudent assessment, Mr. Hawkes. I will inform him of such plans."

For a moment, I had forgotten about Vicar Petley. Such a wanton woman I have become!

Later that evening, as Kathryne prepared for sleep, she knelt by her canvas bed and began to pray. "Dearest Almighty Father, I thank thee for thy blessings and for keeping me from harm. It is by thy grace that I am alive. Please assure my Papa that I am well. Please provide me with the ability to show thy love to these poor villagers—and to the sailors as well. Amen."

She climbed into bed and tossed fitfully until the first glint of dawn.

66

24 October 1641
An Unnamed Island
The Caribbean Sea

The morning broke, and Kathryne looked out from the door of the captain's hut. In the dawn's mist that rose from the cove, she saw a figure by the water's edge holding what appeared to be a telescope. She leaned forward and squinted. It was William, on the sand, focusing on a nest of birds on the other side of the cove, removed from the huts and the village activity. They were large white birds—egrets perhaps, Kathryne thought. He folded up the instrument, opened a book, and began to write on its pages.

Who is this Mr. Hawkes? So far he has been a pirate, a kidnapper, a schoolteacher, a linguist, a man who loves children, and now an ornithologist.

Before he turned about, she drew her head back inside to wait for the dawn to fully break.

The crew had not brought all the trunks she had traveled with ashore, and she was unsure of what to wear for their walk to the volcano. *Volcano!* The word itself broke a tremble of anticipation to her being. *I have never been this close to a volcano before.*

Within the hour others had risen and were soon about the day's activities. Kathryne had selected a plain yellow nankeen dress with lutestring ribbon trimming that hung just above her ankles and that was not fully cut, but still allowed her legs free movement and required no petticoats. The bodice was buttoned to the neck—*too warm for the day,* she thought, *but more discreet than others I might have chosen.*

She fastened the gown to her neck, then looked down. She paused, closed her eyes, slowly brought her hand to her throat, and deliberately undid the first three ivory buttons of her bodice.

I will think no more of this, she told herself, *for I have undone them as a result of this heat. That is all. Because of the tropical heat of this island.*

Will came striding up to the hut, his arms full of fruits and a small slice of cheese.

"Lady Spenser?" he called. "Lady Spenser? Will you want breakfast? I have brought some fruit and cheese."

She came out, head held a little too high. "I suppose I shall." *Kathryne! Be civil!*

Her one nature was urging her to be aloof—after all, the man was a pirate and a killer, no doubt. And he had kidnapped her for ransom. But another side of her was intrigued and warmed by this complex man full of amazing contradictions and astounding opposites.

How could such a tender teacher exist in the same frame as a heartless pirate? The combination does not seem possible. And yet, here he is.

She also knew nothing of his spiritual condition, which was perhaps most important of all the questions that buzzed through Kathryne's thoughts that morning.

She made a point of praying, longer than usual, over her breakfast. William waited silently, she noticed, until she had finished, then quietly served himself a sliced melon and a wedge of cheese. Kathryne nibbled at the fruit, which tasted sweeter than any she had ever eaten before.

"Mr. Hawkes," she asked, attempting to keep the harder edge from her voice, "are you a praying man?"

William looked at her tender face and opened his mouth as if wanting to answer the question, but no words were formed.

Luke looked up brightly. "Massa not pray. I pray for Massa. I pray for all de sailors." The grin slid from Luke's face, and his visage grew serious. "Lady? Do I pray for you? You want Luke prayers?"

Kathryne touched her hand to her heart. "Why, Luke, that would be the most caring thing you could do for me."

"So I pray?" he asked again, a childlike smile on his face.

"Yes, please."

And with that, Luke began to softly speak, just above a whisper, and in a laughing, singsong tone. Kathryne bent close to hear, but the words were a garble of odd sounds. Luke closed his eyes and rocked back and forth, as if a boat bobbing in the waves.

William softly explained to Kathryne. "He prays in his native language—I think he is afraid it will disappear if he stops using it. He will pray—almost chant—for an hour or two at a time."

She whispered back, "What is he saying?"

"It is too speedy for me to comprehend it all. But I believe he prays for everyone he has ever met or known and retells their stories to God. He wants God to understand who these people are—there, he mentioned you as the lady from the water with the . . . beautiful eyes."

Will stared at her green eyes.

. . . and a pirate who understands the prayers of an old black African, she thought as she looked into his.

He stared back at her, as a child stares at their world, full of wonder and delight, innocence and joy. *In all my life I have never beheld a creature that made me so forget myself as this woman,* Will marveled, her beauty near blinding him.

The vicar walked over to Kathryne and William and glanced at Luke chanting softly.

"What is that frowsy heathen doing?" he asked with a caustic bite to his voice.

Kathryne looked annoyed. "Giles, he is praying."

"To what god?" he laughed, with a scowl on his face. "Truly, does he think that gibberish will be heard by the almighty God of the Bible?"

Both William and Kathryne tried to ignore the comment and rose quickly.

"Mr. Hawkes, shall we depart on our hike?"

"Lady Spenser, I am ready to leave. Vicar, have you eaten? Are you ready to depart as well?"

"I have eaten hardly at all since arriving here. This food is quite distasteful, Mr. Hawkes. Is there any chance of finding decent sustenance on this island?"

"Perhaps a wild hog may be more your liking. Roasted pork meat on a skewer?"

The vicar perked up. "Yes, that would be most tempting. Is there a possibility of such a dish? Soon?"

William nodded. "We will depart in a moment, after a few instructions to my crew, if you would allow me."

Kathryne nodded, and the vicar sighed loudly and tapped his foot.

"Mr. Delacroix, if you please," Will called out, and his second-in-command came up immediately. The two began to discuss quietly the list of tasks that Will needed to have the ship's crew accomplish in his absence.

Will had noticed how Kathryne addressed the vicar by his Christian name. Will spoke a little louder to Mr. Delacroix. "And John, perhaps discretion may be the best face of valor. Perhaps we should take further steps for defense if the ship is beached. Can you hoist two—no, four cannon from the ship and set them facing our channel that accesses the sea? If we were to host uninvited guests, we will be equipped to provide a hot welcome for them."

"Four cannon, Mr. Hawkes?" asked Delacroix. "That is indeed a great deal of work."

"We will need a lighter vessel when we . . . when we meet with the English," Will explained, trying to lower his voice so Kathryne would not hear and become upset. "When the English come to the rendezvous point, the waters are shallow there, even for the *Reprisal*. We will require the shallowest draft we can muster—several cannons removed will help, as well as less ballast."

"We will accomplish your preparations. And, Captain, the chief has asked if you would speak to him this morning. He wants Lady Spenser to accompany you as well."

William turned to Kathryne and Vicar Petley, with his palms held up, and shrugged. The vicar appeared annoyed at the delay, as if he were to miss his carriage bound for London if they tarried.

Kathryne nodded, then said, "I have never met an African chief. I would be delighted."

"Lady Spenser," Will explained as they began to walk to the other side of the cove where the former slaves had built their huts, "Sapua is not a chief as you may have imagined following your reading of the latest lurid descriptions and observations by Englishmen in the jungles. Sapua is an old man with knowledge of the past and is quite revered by the tribe."

"Mr. Hawkes, how did these people come to be on this desperate place?" Kathryne asked.

Will spoke of the shipwreck and the slave ship's subsequent attempts to recapture them and their long struggle to survive, lacking any outside help.

"To be truthful, Lady Spenser, even now, with the small assistance we provide, life on this island is difficult. I am certain that they would have clearer chance at surviving in a more civilized place, but to do that would entail returning them as slaves. And I am simply loathe to see any man in chains."

A pirate with a firm conscience. This Mr. Hawkes continues to surprise, Kathryne thought.

In a few moments, with a bouncing entourage of yelping, laughing children at his feet, Will stopped at the front of a small hut. Above the door was mounted the jaw of a sea beast, studded with rows of dangerous, sharp teeth.

Will noticed Kathryne's wide-eyed stare at the bones. "From a white shark," he whispered. "*Carcharodon carcharias.*"

And he knows Latin, she thought with amazement as she stared at him, stunned by his knowledge.

The chief walked out into the sunlight and squinted. A small man, the color of dark coffee, he stood a few inches shy of five feet. He was wearing a robe that to Kathryne looked as if it had been sewn from a deep blue textured drapery material.

He saw William, and the two embraced. Then he stepped back and peered intently at Kathryne, squinting one eye at her, much like a bird peering at an insect. He then turned back to William and began chattering in an odd language, looking first to William, then gesturing to Kathryne. He spoke for perhaps five minutes without allowing Will to answer.

Kathryne noticed that William stood by the old man with his hands crossed in front and his head slightly bowed. It was only after the chief stopped speaking and Will had waited several seconds in which no one spoke that he offered a reply. Will spoke in the same tongue, but his was a slower, less melodic speech, with a less animated quality.

The old man listened politely, then chattered on again. He finally turned to Kathryne, and with a more deferential tone, addressed her for a moment. When he finished, he tilted his head slightly, as if awaiting an answer.

William, in a loud whisper, said, "Tell him that you will do what he has asked. I will translate for you."

"But what did he say? What did he ask?" Kathryne queried.

"It will take too long to translate now, and he has not quite grasped that not everyone can speak his language," Will explained.

Kathryne looked a bit flustered but gamely replied, "Yes, sir. I will do all that you ask."

The vicar, who had wandered over and at this point stood five steps behind in the conversation, piped up in a petulant tone, "But Kathryne, you have no idea as to what you have agreed. For what you know of this . . . person, he may have asked if he might serve you for Sunday dinner. Perhaps he is a cannibal—I have heard that many of his kind are."

Kathryne turned with a scowl, as did William.

"But I have heard it was true," Vicar Petley replied in defense.

Will turned back and translated Kathryne's response, to which the chief smiled wide and nodded his head with vigor.

The chief then peered over Kathryne's shoulder to the vicar, and chattered to Will for a moment. Will responded, then the chief chattered again, and Will answered. The chief made a curious squeaking noise, then shrugged, began to laugh, and stepped back into his hut.

"What in blazes was that gibberish about?" the vicar demanded. "What did he want of me?"

William began to walk back toward the ship and his hut, saying, "Perhaps you may not want to know."

"Listen, you pagan pirate," the vicar insisted, grabbing at William's shoulder. "I have a right to know what was said about me—and what Lady Spenser has agreed to. I demand that you tell us."

Will looked as if he were about to knock the vicar's hand away in anger, but he saw Kathryne and instead slowly took the vicar's wet palm from his shoulder.

"First of all, he berated me for bringing such a beautiful woman to this harsh place. He understands that a great worth has been placed on the beautiful lady's safety, but he has ordered me never to do such a thing again. It is a dishonor to the entire tribe, he said."

The vicar snorted, "I never in my wildest dreams thought I would be in agreement with a black savage, but I am."

Will ignored him and continued, turning to Kathryne. "He said that if I, or any sailor from my ship, did anything that brought the lady pain or dishonor, that the lady must tell the chief immediately, and he will have the offender beheaded."

Kathryne gasped, "Would he truly do that?"

"I believe he would try. His offer is most sincere. And when you said that you would follow his wishes, I repeated that promise to him."

Kathryne was most surprised. "Does the crew know of his threat?" she asked.

"They will when I speak of it. And I am honor bound to tell them."

"Then Captain Hawkes, I will sleep even more soundly this evening knowing I have such a vengeful and powerful protector—that is in addition to the protection of the Almighty."

Will nodded, and smiled.

"But what did he say of me?" the vicar asked. "He spoke at length of me."

"It was a trifling, Vicar."

"Trifling? No. I demand that you tell me of his words. Perhaps I am to be so protected as well?"

"He asked, if you must know," Will said, his impatience rising, "what pursuit you had."

"And you said?"

"I called you a man of God—a preacher."

"And?"

"And the chief asked again. I said, 'A preacher.'"

"But he laughed. Why?"

Will smiled again. "He laughed because he said that God must smile when he hears your high-pitched voice—like a woman's, he said."

"High-pitched voice? The savage!" the vicar cried.

From the corner of Will's eye, he thought he saw that same faint smile slip over Kathryne's beautiful mouth again. But when he looked, it was gone—replaced by tightly pursed lips.

She smiled. I know she smiled, Will realized, his heart curiously buoyant. *A smile like that is no less a miracle than the sun.*

Will turned and began to walk back to his hut. *And the sun is smiling today.*

▪▫▪▫▪

The three had walked for two hours through the green of the jungle, Will guiding the way through the often dense landscape. He carried a thick sugarcane scythe and cut through the vines and clawlike tendrils that reached from the dark corners of the path or that clutched at their heads with waving fingers from above.

When the path grew less tortured, Will would point out the plants that he knew and that Luke used to make his medicines. As they came upon birds, Will would identify them by name, such as the black-and-white anhinga, the coppery-tailed trogon, and the thick-billed popinjay, its red and green plumage iridescent in the sun. Often only their wailing, haunting cries could be heard, echoing through the leafy, templelike underbrush, and Will named them from their calls if he could.

The sun was nearing its zenith when the vicar asked how much longer they might be walking. "My feet are most unfamiliar with such undulating topography and are becoming fatigued. And this beastly heat—I do not understand how one can endure its punishment on a regular basis."

"If you must know," Will said, "it becomes even hotter next month—and a little wetter, with a mist of heat forming about the lowlands. This may be warm, but it becomes more intense with the wetter air."

"My word, hotter still?" the vicar complained.

"And Bridgetown—on Barbados—is worse. The winds are slight, for it sits in a bowl of land that holds the heat about it longer," added Will.

A desperate look spread across the vicar's face.

Kathryne began to fatigue as well. "Mr. Hawkes, how much longer shall we walk—" *Keep your tongue civil, Kathryne,* she told herself— "for if it is to be much further, I would like to rest a moment."

Will looked about and walked a few yards from the path to a thick, sturdy tulip tree and proceeded to climb it, simply by grasping about its girth, to a distance halfway up its height. After surveying the jungle from that height, he shimmied down and leaped the last half dozen yards to the soft earth.

My goodness—how lithe and limber he is, Kathryne mused, her eyes following him closely.

"I was momentarily unsure, but we have only a quarter mile to travel," Will said.

"Well," Kathryne said with a mock theatrical tone, "I should be prepared to traverse that far without swooning."

In fifteen minutes they veered from the darkened jungle path into filtered sunlight and climbed a series of short stone escarpments, each several feet in height. Will helped Kathryne with each long rise, extending his hand so she could step up. She held his hand with one of hers and raised slightly the bottom of her dress, exposing a flash of ivory flesh, as she climbed. Will was glad the vicar had fallen behind.

"This is not too strenuous for you, is it Lady Spenser?" Will asked. "If it is, you will please inform me, for I am not accustomed to knowing the sensibilities and resources of a woman such as yourself—being from noble lineage and all."

"Mr. Hawkes," Kathryne snipped, "my nobility has nothing to do with my physical ability. I will keep up."

What did I say? William thought, confused.

They reached the last barrier at the height of the treetops—a tall, sheer rock face of shiny black stone, about eight feet high. There was a small rock outcropping at a third of the distance from the bottom. If one was skilled, one could leap to that ledge, then scramble up to the top to a large, flat plateau.

Kathryne looked at the ledge, her eyes shifting from the top of the ledge to the bottom again. "Well, Mr. Hawkes, nobility or not," Kathryne said with finality, "I believe this obstacle will stop me. It appears to be more than I may overcome."

Will examined it through the eyes of a weaker, yet willing, climber. "No, Lady Spenser. I did not allow you to travel this great distance to be denied the final pleasure. The vista will make the pain of the journey disappear."

"But it is too steep—too high and difficult for me."

Will leaped with ease to the first ledge. If he stood back, there would be barely enough of a foothold for two persons—if they were to stand in an intimate fashion.

He bent deeply at the waist, both hands extended out to Kathryne. "Come here, Lady Spenser. I will help you up safely."

Kathryne looked at Will and then bent toward him, arms outstretched. She heard a rustling on the path and turned to see the vicar, who had just arrived at the last rock ledge, his dark hair matted in skinny rivulets about his face, his brow dripping with sweat, his cheeks flushed.

She took a step forward into the reach of Will's arms. She looked into his blue eyes and felt a momentary rush of a strange desire to leap, blind, into the pleasure and safety of his embrace. But, instead, she placed her hands on the top of his forearms, still unsure of what he required of her.

How soft is the hair on his arms—like that of a kitten, she said to herself, enjoying the new sensation.

He reached out further and placed his hands on her carefully, his fingers under her shoulders in the crook of her arms and torso, his thumbs, straight up, nearly touching the tops of her shoulders. He tightened his grip sharply.

What power he has in his hands, she thought.

With the slightest of efforts, Will pulled her straight up into the air and placed her delicately on the small rock perch with him.

For a moment, the pair stood on the narrow ledge, face-to-face, their bodies nearly touching. Perhaps a thin leaf could have passed between them, but barely.

I can feel his warmth, she thought, *and he smells of the sea and salt.*

And with a sudden lift, he raised her up again, into the air, to the top plateau above him, turning her so she faced outward, away from the rock.

In an instant she found herself seated, now above Will's head, on the rock ledge, her knees out, her palms flat on the rock behind her. She pulled herself further back to a safer position. And for another brief heartbeat, the hem of her dress caught and bared several inches of her leg, just above her laced boot.

Will looked down, then looked up at Kathryne's face, which was reddening as she smoothed at her hem.

Kathryne stood up, smoothing her dress, and soon forgot her discomfort as she gazed into an unforgettable panorama.

At her feet was a carpet of lush verdant jungle of every hue of green known to God. The carpet led to an endless azure sea that encompassed the island. The sun's reflection looked to be of diamonds, with thousands upon thousands of waves catching the light and passing it back in colors of blue, aquamarine, and gold. To the west, shrouded in mists and clouds, were the peaks of several mountains, thrusting boldly from the ocean. In the sky, white and rounded clouds—as sheep on a distant meadow—floated by on hidden winds. From the darkened jungle below sounded a symphony of bird, frog, and insect calls, all underscored by the ever-so-faint roar of the sea as it met the rocks on the craggy shore below.

Kathryne stood and breathed deep, the air tinged by the salt and the scent of a thousand orchids hidden in the green denseness at her feet.

She blinked at the splendor, one of few humans to have drunk in such magnificence.

A voice behind her, as clear as if a man had been standing behind her, called out in a calm and soothing voice. *"The earth is the Lord's and the fullness thereof; the world, and all that dwell therein. For he hath founded it upon the seas, and established it upon the floods. Who shall ascend to the hill of the Lord? or who shall stand in this holy place? He that hath clean hands, and a pure heart."*

She listened, then spun about to locate the source and saw no one. In a flash she realized that she had heard from the living God. Ready to drop to her knees, she closed her eyes and let the soft island mosaic of scent and sound wash over her as a rain—and then heard again: *"Let the earth fear the Lord; let all the inhabitants of the world stand in awe of him."*

She bowed her head. All of nature about sang to the glory of God, and she was alone in his great creation. For the first time in her spiritual life Kathryne knew, with every fiber in her being, that God was God of every creature and every living thing. His power filled her willing spirit with an awareness of his overwhelming magnificence.

But then, pulling her spirit back to earth, she heard a deep rustling grunt interrupting her worshipful thoughts, and she saw a hand scrabble onto the ledge where she stood, followed by a black sleeve. The vicar's face and shoulders followed. He was still groaning and sweating.

After a few agonizing moments, he made the crest and lay on his side, panting. "My heavens . . . first kidnapped," he said between pants, "then forced to hike in a torrid jungle . . . then made to crawl like a reptile over rocks. What more fiery trials could lie in wait for me?"

Kathryne saw two more hands at the edge, and then in one fluid motion William shot up, spinning lithely to land facing outward in a seated position.

The vicar struggled to his knees and looked out at the view. "Quite untamed, is it not? How much more civilized it would be if there were fences, farms, and polite fields."

"Wildness is neither civil nor proper," Will said, "but I have grown to appreciate it—almost desire it—for what it is, not what it might become."

He paused, looked down, then recited in a clear voice:

> " 'Bless the Lord, O my soul. O Lord my God, thou art very great; thou art clothed with honor and majesty: who covereth thyself with light as with a garment: who stretchest out the heavens like a curtain: who layeth the beams of chambers in the waters: who maketh the clouds in his chariot: who walketh upon the wings of the wind: who maketh his angels spirits; his ministers a flaming fire: who laid the foundations of the earth, that it should not be removed for ever. Thou coveredst it with the deep as with a garment: the waters stood above the mountains. At thy rebuke they fled; at the voice of thy thunder they hasted away. They go up by the mountains; they go down by the valleys unto the place which thou hast founded for them. Thou hast set a bound that they may not pass over; that they turn not again to cover the earth. He sendeth the springs into the valleys, which run among the hills. They give drink to every beast of the field. . . . For the Lord is a great God, and a great King above all gods. In his hand are the deep places of the earth: the strength of the hills is his also. The sea is his, and he made it; and his hands formed the dry land. O come, let us worship and bow down: let us kneel before the Lord our maker.' "

Kathryne, stunned again, could only stare at the back of his torso, his damp shirt clinging to his fine frame.

A pirate quoting Scripture? she thought, astonished.

"And where is that from, Mr. Hawkes?" she asked, thinking that he was merely repeating well-known lines from another source.

"From the one hundredth and fourth and ninety-fifth psalms. Isn't that correct, Vicar?"

"Why, yes, I believe it is. Yes. I am sure of it now—as I ponder on it some."

Kathryne turned to William, having been completely astonished more often this day than any day before in her life. Her gaze fell into his eyes, wide and open. In them she saw a terrible sadness and pain.

"How do you . . . when did you memorize such . . . I am . . . ," Kathryne stuttered, unable to ask a proper question.

"They were among my mother's favorite psalms. She blended them and repeated them frequently," Will said, something in his voice kindred to that of a small, scared child.

He looked away from both Kathryne and the vicar, looking east to England. And as he stared off, his hand moved to his chest, tapping at the center, a gesture that Kathryne had no explanation for, yet that touched her very core.

67

*7 November 1641
An Unnamed Island
The Caribbean Sea*

Two weeks passed uneventfully. The normal routine of most of the sailors on the island consisted of lazing about after breakfast, playing a game of draughts, napping after the midday meal, and rousing only in time for supper. Several days of a heavy, drumming downpour kept natives and sailors alike closed up in their huts, save the children, who frolicked in the warm rain.

Kathryne passed much of her time praying, listening to the raindrops on the palm-thatched roof, marveling at its waterproofing properties, and reading through several of the books that William had left in his hut. It was a most pleasant diversion, she thought, to be able to read uninterrupted and without pause for hours.

On the first day that broke clear and dry, Kathryne asked if she might see the west side of the island—the side hidden by the volcano. "In the few weeks I have remaining on this isle, I would so much like to see the western vista," she explained. "Is there a simple way to achieve that?"

"Well, I, for one," the vicar snorted, "will not be foolish enough to traverse that mountain again. The multitude of insects and the odd jungle creatures were most unpleasant." He neglected to add that he was near exhaustion when returning and that he had numerous blisters on his feet.

"My apologies, Vicar," Will said. "To cross the island to the west is a full day's journey and requires a night spent on the beach—neither appropriate activities for Lady Spenser."

"Mr. Hawkes, may I remind you that the journey is not that difficult for me," Kathryne said with a hint of annoyance in her voice.

Will held up his hand in surrender and smiled. "We would be forced to bed down on the beach without proper shelter. And that, I believe, would be a violation of the chief's order for scrupulous, civilized behavior in regards to your treatment. And, Lady Spenser, I choose not to face beheading."

Is she smiling as well? Will asked himself. *Do I dare believe that she has become comfortable in my presence?*

"But," he added, "it is a simple matter to sail there. We could take one of our two longboats and sail near shore the entire trip. It would be a most scenic journey."

"Mr. Hawkes, that would be most enjoyable," said Kathryne. "I have never sailed in such a small boat. It is a half-day's journey there and returning? Perhaps we may take a small midday meal with us."

"Vicar," Will asked, "would that be enjoyable for you as well?"

At the mention of boarding a ship again, the vicar's color paled to a slight green. Despite this reaction, he answered, "If Lady Spenser desires to sail there, then by all means, we should do so. Let us visit this wild place if that will provide her some moments of happiness on this wretched island."

William stood, looked at the clouds, then faced the sun and felt for the wind at his face. A breeze was coming slightly from the east. It lifted his blond hair off his neck, and he jutted his chin into it to judge its strength. Will turned his face back in time to catch Kathryne's intense stare at its finely chiseled form and her subsequent quick stare at her own feet.

Will called out to Luke, who was seldom more than arm's length apart from him. "Luke, any rain today?"

Luke looked about, carefully, then said with a great finality, as if no other opinion could be existent, "No rain. Rain tomorrow. No rain today."

Will clapped his hands together once. "Then shall we ready a boat? I will see to it that we carry water and foodstuffs with us for the midday meal."

The longboat, capable of carrying twelve men in a pinch, was spacious for three people. It had a single mast with a long boom to the rear, a small foresail, and a jib sail to the forward. It could be rowed as well, and the small tiller was set at the rear.

John and Bryne Tambor wrestled the craft from its perch along the swaying palms and dragged it, huffing and laughing, to the water's edge. They then stepped back a half-dozen paces and watched in silent awe as Kathryne walked to the boat.

John nudged Bryne and in a loud whisper, said to his brother, "They say she be related to the king."

John responded, "Then the king must be a handsome man—for she be the prettiest woman I have yet to see."

Kathryne pretended not to hear, but she blushed slightly with pleasure.

"Lady Spenser, I shall help you board," Will said, extending his hand to her.

She grasped it and stepped over the high planking. He steadied her as she sat in the middle thwart, the widest seat in the boat, their eyes locking for a brief moment.

"It be best if you are placed amidships, for your slight weight will be bookended by the vicar and myself. She'll sail more cleanly this way."

The vicar stepped to the shoreline and lifted his foot, placing it onto the rear side bench by the tiller. A wave broke at him, and he hopped with the shore-bound foot and fell forward slightly, splashing into the knee-deep surf. He scrambled until he flopped into the boat, arms and legs akimbo.

"Oh, now this boot has been drenched by the sea! The blasted water will turn its fine leather to mold in a day, no doubt," he muttered ruefully as he stepped to the bow.

"Vicar," Kathryne said in a most clipped tone, "I am sure it will dry without problem. The sun will accomplish it in mere moments."

"Kathryne, I must say that you do not understand how careful one must be with one's footwear. A vicar is not a rich man. I must wisely use the resources God has given me. To waste good boots would be most foolish and irresponsible."

Kathryne sighed and said, "Yes, you are correct. One should care for one's boots."

As she spoke she rolled her eyes skyward, her back to the vicar, forgetting that Will remained at the stern, ready to push the boat into the water. She looked over and saw him looking at her with a slight smile. Kathryne was mortified that William had seen her being petty and rude, yet he made no comment on her behavior.

William saw her silent comment to the vicar and tried hard to suppress his grin. *Perhaps she is not the snobbish, condescending person that Radcliffe spoke of. It appears to me that she does not bear fools well.*

Kathryne watched Will intently as he gave a strong push, and the boat bobbed free of the shore. He pushed once more, then expertly hoisted himself to the stern seat, pulling out the long oars that were stored at the boat's sides. He set them in the oarlocks and began to row into the open sea.

Kathryne was facing the stern, staring straight at William as his muscles flexed with each stroke. Each time he reached back, the cords in his neck and chest muscles became taut, and his shirt, now unbuttoned to nearly his waist, fluttered in the breeze, revealing a bronzed smoothness. Her eyes darted over William's shoulder, then to the skies, then to the floor decking.

Will sensed her discomfort—though he attributed it to the boat's motion and not his own—and advised, "Lady Spenser, perhaps facing forward would be easier, for one seldom suffers from the rolling and pitching when one does so. Your eyes can then be fixed on a distant horizon."

Kathryne nodded silently and faced front.

A longboat could be fairly tossed in the rough surf at the southern shoreline of the small island. The reef was shallow here, and the waves crested quickly and chopped toward the shore. The vessel's sails were unfurled, and under Will's practiced hand at the tiller, the boat slipped through the waves with the grace of a sleek sea beast.

Kathryne seemed to greatly enjoy the sensation as the craft tilted with the winds, plowing forward with a spray.

The vicar, sitting far forward in the boat, held on to the sides with a white-knuckled grip. He appeared to be fighting another bout of seasickness. He turned to the stern and called out, "How much longer shall we ride in this tempest? It is far more unstable than the *Plymouth Spirit*. Please inform me that we are nearing our destination."

"We are," Will shouted over the wind. "See that promontory there, in front of us? That will be our destination, and we will be there in but a few minutes."

"Thanks be to the Almighty," the vicar cried.

Will steered the boat directly to a small strip of sand just south of the massive rock formation that thrusted out into the sea. He lithely jumped out into the waist-deep water and pulled the bow forward, anchoring the craft to the shore with a stout rope tied to a huge boulder.

He first helped Vicar Petley, who was in a great deal of distress, out of the longboat. The vicar took a few steps inland and sank to his knees, breathing in deep gulps of air. Then Kathryne jumped out, deliberately, Will thought, into the knee-deep water, soaking her boots as well as the bottom third of her gown.

William took her hand and walked her through the small waves to the shore. They both started inland when Will turned and called, "Vicar? You will accompany us, will you not?"

The vicar, still on his knees, waved him away with a petulant toss of his wrist. "I am afraid that I must remain here. The pitching and the tilting has done me in," he replied.

Will stopped and looked at Kathryne's bright face, then back to the vicar. "We will not proceed without Vicar Petley. I will give no man cause to speak ill of your honor, Lady Spenser."

Kathryne looked crestfallen. "But Mr. Hawkes, it is only to the end of the promontory. We will be in the full view of the vicar the entire walk—except for that small section hidden by the brush just there. Vicar, please say it meets with your approval. I do so want to experience this vista." She turned back to William. "It is indeed magnificent, is it not?"

"Yes, Lady Spenser. It is quite a view. But I will not besmirch your name."

She turned back to the vicar, calling, "Please indicate your approval, Giles. It is only the three of us here." Then she addressed Will. "Mr. Hawkes, you will do nothing to dishonor me, for I know you take Chief Sapua's warning to heart. And the vicar is in no condition to travel now. Please, Mr. Hawkes. There will be no honor maligned here today."

"Vicar? Will it meet your approval?" Will asked.

The vicar was now lying flat on his back, and he waved his arm again. "Yes, yes, it will be fine. I will observe you, Kathryne and pirate heathen. There is no need to worry."

He let his limp arm drop to the shore. "But before you depart, would you leave a flagon of wine you have brought with our provisions? I believe I may take a few sips to quell my churning stomach. That is most biblical, is it not? A little wine for the stomach's sake?"

"Well then, Mr. Hawkes," Kathryne said brightly. "Shall we go?"

Barbados

"Aidan, dearest brother, I do bring good tidings."

Governor Spenser had bravely tried to carry on in the wake of the horrific report of his daughter's abduction. He had supervised the final touches on Shelworthy, the governor's residence—a home, he thought with acute sadness, that Kathryne might never gaze upon. And he continued to plan and organize for the yearly assembling of the Barbados Parliament. The population of the island had burgeoned to ten thousand, and the loose confederation of plantation and landowners had found it increasingly difficult to self-police the rules and regulations that made for an orderly society.

"Good tidings, Radcliffe? This has been a month where no report has been good. I cannot wake nor sleep without thinking of what may be happening to my precious Kathryne."

How dreadfully tired I am of Aidan's histrionics, Radcliffe thought. *I will be immensely relieved when this affair is over and all the players have left the stage.*

"But, Brother, it is good news. We have located and secured a Dutch fluyt—a vessel perfectly suited to navigate the shallow waters of the pirates' appointed rendezvous."

"Who will be captain of this mission? Do we have an experienced man?" Lord Aidan queried.

They were in the governor's study, the heat of the day increasing the temperature on a moment-by-moment basis. Radcliffe kept his wide straw hat on, even indoors, for the sun had become more and more troublesome to his eyes.

"We have secured the service of our good Captain Blake, who is most familiar with the waters and has the daring and cunning that will put any pirate to shame. I believe we can rescue our Kathryne with no risk. He is most eager to do what needs to avenge himself on these dastardly pirates."

"But he will do nothing that would place Kathryne in harm's way, will he?" Aidan demanded, voice at the edge of panic again. "I will endorse no foolhardy plan that puts my daughter in peril."

Please, Radcliffe sneered to himself, *will you cease with your whining and caterwauling?*

"Yes, Brother," Radcliffe calmly assured him. "We will do nothing that would place little Kathryne in jeopardy. Captain Blake will follow my orders to the letter, no matter how distasteful he may find them to be personally. I have every assurance of his total compliance," Radcliffe said with a most curious smile.

Aidan calmed and asked, "And we will still depart in a fortnight?"

"We will, Brother. You and I and my brave crew will find Kathryne, and she will be rescued into your open arms."

Governor Spenser laid his head on his desk and began to weep softly.

An Unnamed Island
The Caribbean Sea

Kathryne and William hurried through the dozen yards of brush where their forms were hidden from Vicar Petley's observation. In a long moment they appeared at the edge of the promontory and began to walk up the steep rocks to the flat, waterworn finger of land pushing into the sea. The vicar was still prone, sipping at the wine, and gave no indication that he cared what either Lady Spenser or William did.

Kathryne carefully picked her way along the moss- and fern-covered rocks. The last flat rock finger was square, no wider or longer than two tall men laid end to end.

From that spot, Kathryne looked out to the western horizon and saw nothing but infinite sunlight dappled on the water. From this height, the sea appeared as a pale green, endlessly faceted gemstone. Each small wave caught the sun and winked back at the shore in forever-intensifying colors until the sea disappeared in the west. Off to the north and south, Kathryne saw a shallow reef of white coral just below the water's surface, like a hidden, jagged necklace ringing the island. When she turned, the volcano rose above her like a spout of black obsidian pointing to the heavens. The mountain's top disappeared into the faint mist that ringed its black surface like a halo.

She stood between the sea and the mountain—the rolling waves crashing below her feet, the mountain looming above her, its shadow threatening to engulf her every inch. She turned, arms extended out to each as an angel, closed her eyes, and thought she felt the pull of the depths and the heights at her open fingertips. Will watched in an almost holy silence as she reveled in the beauty around them.

"Mr. Hawkes, I believe that there may not be a more powerful location in the world," she said reverently. "Do you feel that pull of sea and rock as well?"

"Yes, Lady Spenser, I do, and I must say that this sight—one seen by few humans—has become a cherished location for me. It is a most wondrous place."

Kathryne then sat down on the canvas that Will had brought in his bag. He had pulled out fruit, cheese, manioc biscuits, and a flagon of weak red wine to drink.

Kathryne helped herself to a banana, a biscuit, and some cheese.

Neither spoke much, letting nature provide the music. From her spot, Kathryne could see the vicar, who had roused to a sitting position, his back against a rock, staring out to sea while nipping at the wine.

"Mr. Hawkes, I do not wish to appear forward, but I feel that in light of my position—on this island and with you—I have the need to ask a question that I would have deemed so terribly impolite in . . . more civilized settings."

She stopped and folded her hands in her lap. "I do not call this uncivilized to be spiteful, Mr. Hawkes, but I know no other way to describe where I am and who you appear to be."

"Lady Spenser, I have taken no offense, I assure you. Your characterization of this place—and me—as uncivilized is accurate. Please, continue with your question."

Without raising her eyes to him, she asked, "How did a man such as yourself, who appears to be quite educated and civil, become a pirate on this forgotten isle? I have struggled mightily in coming up with a rational discourse as to a possible reason, and I am afraid none suits you. Would you pardon my boldness if I ask you for a history of your travels?"

William stood and scanned the western horizon. Kathryne looked up at his fine form, then at his tanned face.

He turned and saw her lovely face, upturned, bright with promise, and her eyes so deep that a man might drown . . . *It was those eyes I saw that day in England as well! In Weymouth, in that carriage! It must have been her,* his memory assured. *Those eyes are indeed unforgettable.*

Will stood there, silent for a moment, as the sea crashed about the rocks below. *A woman of such beauty and grace and goodness,* he thought, his conscience crashing about his scarred soul as well, *and I have placed her in peril. In my wildest dream, I would scarce have thought that this be possible.*

Kathryne stared back, guileless and unaffected, her eyes penetrating deep into his heart. *If I could believe in the Almighty, I would pray that I could be the equal of this woman,* Will's thoughts cried out, *for in her I recognize something I need.*

"Lady Spenser, I first want to . . . apologize for this trial I have put you through. The course of action seemed appropriate when it unfolded those several weeks prior. But now . . . I am regretful and see no course of action that can stem the tide of events I have initiated."

Kathryne nodded and murmured, "I understand."

"But you ask of how I came to be on this place—a pirate, a kidnapper, a brigand."

He sat back down on the rock, his legs dangling over the precipice more than forty feet above the foaming waves.

"The journey was most unplanned, Lady Spenser. At no time in my life did I calmly plan to be a common thief, sailing in the tropical seas. But . . . here I am, doing just that."

He pitched a small rock into the waters below and watched as it disappeared into the mists. He thought about how, as a child, he played ducks and drakes on the river Taw, spending carefree hours skipping flat stones across the babbling water.

"I was born in Hadenthorne, an ordinary village in Devon. . . ."

As William spoke the word *Hadenthorne,* an image so strong came upon Kathryne that she felt transported.

There was a small boy on a tall chestnut horse . . . with the deepest, clearest, and most honest blue eyes I have ever seen. Are these the eyes I have seen in my dreams?

She closed her eyes and shook her head to clear the images that filled her consciousness. When she opened them again, the world had settled and returned to an even keel. *Such eyes,* she recalled, *are never to be forgotten.*

For the next hour, Will spoke of his childhood, the vicar, the deaths of his parents, his tour with the Royal Navy, his journeys aboard the merchant ship, the attack of the Spanish pirates and the kidnapping of Vicar Mayhew, the letters of marque issued by her father, the raids and attacks and his increasing wealth, omitting his association with her uncle, Radcliffe Spenser.

Kathryne listened carefully, without comment, her vibrant green eyes focused on his unforgettable blue eyes and fine mouth. As she heard him describe the death of his mother and the locket she had given to him, tears crept to her eyes, recalling her own mother's passing at a similar age.

When he had finished his narrative, he turned and took a long sip of wine, then looked down to the vicar, who was sleeping, curled in a ball at the water's edge. The tide was coming in slowly and was about to begin lapping at his precious boots.

"Mr. Hawkes, may I ask another question?" Kathryne asked softly. William nodded.

"You are an educated man. You know of the Scriptures. You know of God. Why have you turned your back on his mercies? Why have you abandoned him?"

Will struggled up from his sitting position and stood above her, his face in a scowl.

"Abandoned God? Lady Spenser, I did no such thing. I had a mother who loved me—who was taken by God. I had a devoted father—killed by a drunken nobleman. Vicar Mayhew, my most trusted friend and mentor—taken by pirates and lying at the bottom of the sea, no doubt. What makes you think I abandoned God?

"Where was your God when all these people in my life were being taken from me? Was your God smiling at the tests he was placing in my path? Even your own Vicar Petley has claimed that the trials we endure are from God and that suffering brings out our character. If that be true, then I want no part of a deity who takes sainted people such as my mother to improve a poor lad's character. Let him find some other way to construct spiritual fiber."

Kathryne looked up at his angry, pained face. She reached up her hand to him, extending the fingers as far as they could stretch. Her palm was open, upward. Her fingers curled slightly, inviting his hand to join hers.

He stood, legs spread wide as if ready for an attack, arms loose and open at his sides. His shoulders were tensed, as if to do battle. He looked down, and after but a few moments, her hand began to tremble, and he reached out, suddenly taking her tender fingers in his roughened hand. His hand engulfed hers, fingers wrapping fully about its width. For a brief moment, Kathryne felt swallowed by his presence. She pulled slightly, drawing him toward her, drawing him to sit at her side.

"Please, Mr. Hawkes. Please sit." Her face was drawn and pleading, her brows arched in concern.

He closed his eyes, then opened them and sat down, an arm's length from her on the canvas spread.

"God does not take those we love for sport," soothed Kathryne gently. "We live in a broken world, Mr. Hawkes. Disease and death is all around us. Do not blame God that Adam and Eve broke that first perfect covenant. It is our legacy—as Adam's children. People die and crimes are committed, Mr. Hawkes, but God does not desire these things. Perhaps out of this pain some good may result. But God is not its author."

Will looked deeply into her face, into her beautiful eyes filled with concern. "I cannot obey a deity who seems to allow blessings and curses to fall capriciously on sinners and saints alike. My mother would still be alive—and being a tender comfort to those around her—if God were just."

"My mother, as well, Mr. Hawkes, whom I lost at near the same age as you."

William gulped and lowered his head. "I am sorry, Lady Spenser. I did not know of your loss."

For a moment, Kathryne heard the loud beating of her heart, even above the sound of the waves below. "But Mr. Hawkes, we will all perish in this world. You will, as will I. If your mother was the wonderful Christian woman you describe—and I believe she was—then she is with God, watching you now. Would you surmise that she would want her son to live a life of evil and sin? Would you presume that she would want her only son to be separated from her for all eternity? Would she not tell you now to turn away from your sin and turn back to the Almighty, begging for forgiveness?"

Kathryne spoke bolder than she had ever spoken before, for she had never given witness to such a person. Before this day she had never knowingly conversed with a man who lived in such depths of sin. All of her conversations were with civilized people who, if they be not Christian, were much too polite to indicate their lack of faith.

William turned away as a tear—or what Kathryne thought a tear—formed at the corner of his eye, the liquid catching the reflection of the sun.

"Mr. Hawkes, you have focused for these many years on what you have lost. It grieves me that you have lost much, but you do not see what you have gained."

Without turning to face her, he replied, his voice near cracking, "Gained? What have I gained?"

Kathryne replied in a firm manner, "You have a crew who literally worships you. You have officers that respect you as an honest, committed man, as do your crewmen. No, Mr. Hawkes, they have said nothing to me, but I can see it in how they speak to you, how they respond to your orders, how they are almost . . . reverent in your presence. There is an entire village of former slaves who owe their freedom, their very existence, to you. The village children worship you and love you, as well."

She paused, looking at the side of his face. "Mr. Hawkes—look at me."

William obediently turned to face her, tears on his cheeks, unashamed, his emotions apparent.

"You are a much-loved man, most in keeping with who your mother was. That is what you have gained. You have passed her legacy of care and, yes—love—on to others. Your mother's image lives in you, and you have gained much from that.

"But Mr. Hawkes, what is most painful in this is that you have turned your back on your mother's God, who is with her at this very moment. Can you not see that? Can you not forgive? Can you not accept God and his gift? Must you fight on? You will lose, Mr. Hawkes, for you are not as powerful as he."

In a small voice, that Kathryne had to lean close to hear, William asked, "But is it not true that so few may make entrance to heaven? I heard your vicar tell some of the crew that the path to heaven is like taking a camel through the eye of a needle. I have done too much evil, Lady Spenser, to be forgiven. I have ordered men killed, and with my own hand have taken a man's life. My path is too far from God for him to find me."

Kathryne reached over and took both of his hands in hers. "No, Mr. Hawkes. God is bigger than that. For the Scriptures say that he never sleeps, nor does he slumber, and if we ask for his forgiveness, he will hear and it will be so. Is not your heart weary of the battle, Mr. Hawkes? Are you not fatigued by the fight? Can you not lay down your arms before the Almighty?"

"Lady Spenser, how I wish I could . . . but I am not able to. . . ." His voice trailed off to a whisper.

Kathryne sensed that what William had lacked his entire life was a tender heart beating next to his—listening, nurturing, loving the small boy. His mother's death had deprived him of that. And his father, a kind man, and Vicar Mayhew, a godly man—they were not tender men. There was no one to pull the small child close and whisper words that soothed the fears, the hurts, and the tears.

Kathryne was about to raise her arms and pull this broken man to herself and to cradle him in her love when from the shore below came a loud and profane bellowing.

The tide had rolled ever upward, and by the time Vicar Petley was awakened, the water had come to his calf, streaming down his boot tops.

He was up now, howling at the water, swinging at the air with an empty flagon in his hand, shouting that he was left on shore to drown, shaking his clenched fist at Kathryne and William.

They had both turned to look at the figure, staggering at the water's edge. In a moment of stunned silence, Kathryne began to giggle—quietly at first, then her laughter erupted in pleasant birdlike chirps.

Even William forgot his pain and began to smile through his tears.

As they gathered up the canvas and food, Kathryne turned to William and spoke in earnest. "Mr. Hawkes, you must dwell on the truth. Trust me, we will speak of this again."

10 November 1641
An Unnamed Island
The Caribbean Sea

William's presence was scarce in the small island village the following several days. Kathryne saw him early one morning with his leather bag, striding into the jungle toward the mountain. He carried a musket, and she assumed he was in search of wild game. He did not return home that evening, and she asked after him as dusk neared.

The following afternoon, the children came to her hut, asking for Captain Will.

"But he is not here," she said sadly, looking with dismay at their crestfallen faces.

One small boy asked, in unaccented French, "Then no school to-day?"

There were a dozen sad expressions peering up at her.

"Well, since Captain William is not here, would it be to your liking if *I* read to you a story?"

For a moment, the children turned heads sidelong, to gauge each other's reaction, all remaining mute. Then a tall boy, perhaps near the age of seven or eight, broke into a huge smile. "Lady, we like that."

Kathryne ducked into the hut and scanned Will's small shelf for a book that might have children's stories, but all she saw were science or navigational titles or dense classical books.

"Children, I find no books to read from. May I *tell* you a story?"

The children answered with excited squeals and laughter.

"Shall we sit by the water?" she said and turned and walked to the rocks at the edge of the bay where Will held his classes. Selecting a large, dry boulder, she gathered up her skirts and folded her hands in her lap. The children spread out in a circle about her.

Now what shall I tell them? She looked at their faces and smiled. "I was born on a large island far, far away," she began in a happy voice, "and lived in a house made of stone that had one hundred rooms."

She told the story of her life. Luke walked over to listen as well, and when Kathryne's French failed and the English word was unknown to the children, Luke would translate it back into their native tongue. For the following two hours, until dusk, Kathryne told them stories, in French, English, and scattered words of the Dahomey language—stories of gala balls and theater and foxhunts and all sorts of exotic tales of the English nobility.

Never had the children been so enchanted.

■ ▫ ■ ▫ ■

They came to her the following day and begged for another story, a request that Kathryne was honored to accommodate.

As she told the tale of King Arthur and Camelot, William returned from the forest, pulling two large boars on a skid of bamboo. He laid his catch by his hut and stood at a distance, with crossed arms, watching the glow on Kathryne's face as she spun the tale. Every dozen sentences, she would stop, lean toward Luke, who squatted by her feet, and whisper a few words. Luke would whisper back, and she would insert several words in the children's native language into her story, much to their delight. She waved her hands in the air, then crouched down, close to their faces, and roared like a lion, to their laughter and cries of joy.

As William watched, he felt in his heart a strange stirring, a longing that had been hidden and unused. *What is this feeling?* Will wondered, uncomfortable. It persisted through that day and into the night as well.

At dusk that evening, the boars were roasted over a fire by the shore, and the entire island feasted on the juicy meat.

In the dark of that night, Will stood alone by the water and watched the advance of the silver moon, as it added to itself nightly, sliver by pale sliver. Within a few days it would be full—and he would have to exchange Kathryne for mere gold.

20 November 1641
An Unnamed Island
The Caribbean Sea

Kathryne arose before the first purple light of dawn and waited at her
door for William to awaken, listening to the rhythmic lap of the waves
on the cove-cradled beach. He appeared at the threshold of his small
hut, a score of yards distant, with his hair tousled and sleep evident on
his face. She watched intently as he stretched his fine, taut body in the
morning sun.

Kathryne called brightly. "Mr. Hawkes! May I have a word with
you?"

He quickly tried to smooth his hair and tuck in his shirt, which was
loosely hanging about his waist.

Kathryne took a few steps forward, and William came at a fast walk.

"Yes, Lady Spenser?" he inquired.

"Mr. Hawkes," she said with an efficient note in her voice. "You at
one time mentioned that there were *three* vistas on this island that were
memorably beautiful. You have taken me to two of them. Before I leave
this place, which will be a day or so hence, I believe, I would most
appreciate seeing the third."

William scratched his temple and edged his toe in the sandy soil.
"There are three, Lady Spenser, but the third is also a short trip in the
longboat. Do you think the vicar is up to a second voyage? The first was
most unpleasant for him. That is the reason I did not suggest the third
trip."

Kathryne smiled, for the first time unafraid of letting her true emotions show. "He was into his cups, as they say, was he not?" she giggled.

"For a man of the cloth, he danced in the water most admirably."

"And he spent the rest of the trip back and that night—and all the following day—in abject distress. He claimed the wine was tainted."

"Yes. I heard his complaint several hundred times, I'm afraid. And his boots—I have never seen a man so distraught over a pair of wet boots."

Kathryne giggled again. "May we go, Mr. Hawkes?" Kathryne asked. "I believe the vicar is sufficiently recovered. Is the trip as long?"

"No. We could walk there in two hours, if it were not for the sheer cliffs north of this cove. But the time at sea is less than a single hour. I believe that the vicar could endure even that."

"After breakfast, can we go? Can that be arranged, Mr. Hawkes?" Kathryne asked again, looking up into his blue eyes.

Did I blink my eyes at him on purpose, Kathryne asked herself, *or was there a mite of sand dust in them?*

"Yes. Yes, we can. I shall arrange to have the longboat readied."

After the morning meal, the Tambor brothers again prepared the boat, again staring reverently as Kathryne passed close to them. She had various scented waters, powders, and lotions in her trunks and had used them liberally this morning. Both Tambor brothers breathed in deeply as Kathryne passed, savoring the intoxicating fragrances of a noble-born woman.

"Did you smell that?" Bryne asked softly as he nudged John.

"That is what heaven will smell like," John said with firmness as he nodded.

The vicar gingerly entered the boat a few moments later. Once the Tambor brothers pushed the longboat out into the water, William began to pull on the oars, breathing in more deeply than was needed, as he looked at her. *Have I not noticed how lovely she smells before?* William wondered as he inhaled.

Kathryne smiled gamely, folded her hands in her lap, and looked back at the receding shoreline, now finding less discomfort in looking backward than forward.

In an hour, the small craft bumped onto a rocky shoal at the mouth of a large stream—or small river—emptying into the sea.

Vicar Petley, even on this short trip, had tinted green again. Luke had prepared a concoction that was to cure the malady, which the vicar swallowed with a grimace. Not only did the potion work quickly, it relaxed the vicar greatly. As William tied off the boat, the vicar spread a canvas sheet on a patch of soft moss and was snoring loudly within but a few moments.

Kathryne tried vainly to rouse the vicar. "Mr. Hawkes, it appears that the medicine serves as a sleeping potion as well, for I cannot pull him from his slumbers. Please do not say we cannot travel inward to the special view. I do so want to see it."

"But, Lady Spenser, here lies our chaperone. What of your honor?"

"You have given me no cause to worry thus far. And I believe that our Lord will watch over me in the vicar's absence."

William looked at the prone figure, then at Kathryne's pleading, upturned face, then at the path that led inland. "Very well. The walk is but a few minutes in duration. We do not have to spend more than a moment at the final destination, and we can then return here to his side."

William had seen this concoction work previously, and its effects were evident for several hours at the minimum. Without comment, though, he gathered his leather bag full of food and drink and extended his hand to Kathryne, helping her stand. They looked at each other for a long, silent moment.

"Shall we proceed?" he finally said, his voice barely breaking the silence.

They left the shore, walked through a dense layer of underbrush for a few yards, and then came upon the clear bank of the river. Delicate stems of sun-flamed heliconias arched gently above. Emerald green, turquoise blue, and ruby red hummingbirds darted among the foliage, stopping to feed now and again on tender blossoms.

"In the rainy season the waters flood to where we walk now," William explained. "This is not a massive river, as rivers go, for the length of its run is short—several miles from the foothills of the mountain to here. But what it lacks in breadth, it makes up in drama."

From the distance, they could hear a slight rumbling sound. Will was amused as Kathryne looked to the sky, checking for the storm clouds responsible for the thunderous sound.

"Only a few steps farther to our first stop, Lady Spenser," William said.

They followed the river for a few moments and then ducked under a canopy of tangled lianas and ferns. From the dark, cool moistness, the pair emerged into a sunlit clearing. Kathryne blinked a few times, and before her eyes lay an extraordinary sight.

From a high escarpment, perhaps a hundred feet in height, poured a waterfall. The water dropped two-thirds of the distance, then crashed in a pool of foam and mist into a small cleft in the rock. From there, the waterfall broke into three separate spouts, each pouring into a larger pool at the base, across which Will and Kathryne now stood. Mist filled the air, and the sunlight effervesced through the water droplets, as if one were entering an all-encompassing rainbow.

Kathryne spun about, twirling in the mist about her, clapping her hands in sheer delight. The mist eddied and swirled round her movements as well. "This is what the Garden of Eden must have been like," she cried out. "It is a most breathtaking and beautiful place."

William smiled, watching her pleasure. "Come, Lady Spenser, it becomes even more pleasurable."

He led her, taking her hands at times, to the rocky cliff and to a series of nature-carved steps. After a few minutes' climb they were at the pool partially up the cliff. The ledge was wide enough for two people to pass, but Kathryne hugged at the inner edge nonetheless. Will took her hand and pulled her toward the heavy stream, then ducked behind it into a small hollow cavern, cut from the sheer rock by a million years of water rushing against it. The mists were swirling about in a frenzy, providing a most pleasant cooling sensation. The water's roar was like that of a great beast, filling the small space with a totality.

Kathryne was enthralled. "I am standing behind a waterfall!" she cried to William, trying to be heard over the roar. "I would never have dreamed this possible!"

William gestured her forward again. A small cavern was cut around the entire width of the pool and exited at the other side, where a similar path traversed the rock. At the other side, a series of steeper steps were broken into the rock face, and with a few minutes' effort, both William and Kathryne made their way to the very top of the rock, to the origin of the falls.

At the summit of the cliff lay a broad expanse of flat land, the size of a small English meadow. The floor of this meadow was a dense carpet of ferns, waist high. Surrounding the meadow of ferns was a jungle of thick, jade green foliage. The small stream flowed out of that jungle, through the meadow, and into a shallow pool. The stream paused there for a moment, then, like a tipped teakettle, the water cascaded down the rock face, rainbows flashing and blinking as the cottony clouds overhead played with the sun's rays.

The noise was greatly muted here. All that remained of the water's roar was a most pleasant hissing tumble of liquid sounds.

Kathryne spun about again, drinking in the vista, her mouth agape and eyes wide with joy. "This is the most marvelous spot on the earth, Mr. Hawkes. How privileged I feel to have seen it."

Her wet hair hung about her throat and face, making a dark frame, highlighting her delicate features. Her emerald eyes sparkled and danced, her lips, red from laughter, were full and open.

"How I envy you, Mr. Hawkes, for having such a dazzling jewel on your own private island."

But the dazzling jewel is not the waterfall, he thought, admiring her beauty.

Nodding, Will spread out the thick canvas sheet over a thick carpet of pangola grass at the edge of the stream, several yards from the verge of the cliff. He sat down, looking at the enchanting mists below him, and then stared out to the azure seas beyond.

Kathryne sat at the other side of the canvas, breathing deeply, pushing her hair back from her forehead, gently shaking out her wet sleeves and skirt.

Will stared at her, his thoughts in confusion. Then, as the sun bursts through a cloud, Will's thoughts slowed and gathered in a precise manner. *I have never been in the presence of a woman—or anyone— who has this effect on my heart. It is as if my heart is at peace when I am at her side. That is the truth—my heart is at peace. With her my heart has stopped hurting.*

Will gulped and his hand went to his heart. This time the gesture was not unconscious, but deliberate.

Kathryne had pulled her long hair into a tail and draped it over her left shoulder, gently combing it through with her hands, trying to dry it in the sun. There were droplets of water shining at her throat, exposed by the collarless dress she wore. She turned and caught William's direct and unabashed stare. She held his eyes for a moment, then looked away.

"Mr. Hawkes, may I share with you a memory I have of my mother?" she asked.

William looked startled, then replied, "I would be honored."

"Our home is large, Mr. Hawkes, and my father is a wealthy man. As I grew up, I was used to having servants. Various servants would clean my bedchamber and look after my clothing and cook my meals and care for my horse. I can offer no apologies for such a life, for I did nothing to choose it.

"I was most accustomed to doing little in terms of work, Mr. Hawkes. I am sure that comes as no surprise to you—knowing your feelings about the noble and wealthy."

William coughed an interruption. "I have known so few as to be unfair, I believe, in my estimations of all."

Kathryne smiled at his comment, then continued. "One day—I was no more than five or six years of age—I came upon my mother, in a very elegant taffeta gown, placing cooked meats, ale, and breads into a hamper. I asked what she might be doing. She replied that she was preparing a meal for the Thompsons, who were tenant farmers on our lands. She said that the mother was ill and that the family was in need. I asked why *she* was doing it and not letting Mrs. Cole—our head cook—handle such affairs.

"She knelt down to me and replied that a gift is not a gift if it does not cost the giver. She was not suited for kitchen tasks, and this was a difficult thing for her to do. And the Thompsons were not pleasant people. They were rough and crude and nasty, as I recall.

"I asked her, 'Why them?' She replied that God did not instruct us to pay attention to differences, but only to help and to serve. She took me with her as she walked to their small hovel—perhaps a walk of a mile—in the cold, blustery air of winter.

"My mother, in her ermine-lined coat, tapped at the door and presented the father with this oilskin bag with a meal well beyond their humble means. The man did not say a word of thanks. He just grabbed the bag and shut the door.

"My mother only smiled. And we walked back—in the cold—in silence. When we returned, my mother helped me off with my coat. I must have looked puzzled, for she knelt to me again and said, 'A true Christian is a person who serves, Kathryne, regardless of thanks or reward. We served today, for that is what we are called to do, as Christ served us when he gave his life as atonement for our sin.'

"She died when she contracted consumption from another family to whom she delivered food. She died of serving others. And yet as she died, it was with a smile on her face, for she knew that others had known the Almighty through her service. And that was reward enough."

Kathryne stopped speaking for a moment, wiping at the tears rolling down her face. "To her, to die in service of the living God was the supreme gift to give."

Kathryne wept quietly for a moment before continuing. "I have told that story to no man before. But her last words to me are what I carry with me now. I need to serve, Mr. Hawkes. I need to serve."

William looked at her tear-lined face. His brow wrinkled, for he knew not how to soothe her or answer her need.

"But Lady Spenser, how can you serve me? I am a pirate. I have kidnapped you. I am holding your very life in my hands in exchange for gold. There is no service you can render to me."

"Mr. Hawkes, if I perish in this jungle or perish in a storm at sea—if I must give up my life—I will awaken in the arms of the almighty God, for I have allowed Christ's death to be the atonement for my sin, as well."

She wiped at the tears on her face with her open palm. "And with that, I have peace. It is a peace that I can see your heart yearns for. It is a peace your mother possessed. You are searching for tenderness, Mr. Hawkes, and you will never find it unless you give yourself to Christ. You will not recognize the tenderness of true love until then. And until that moment, for you there will be no true peace." She paused, then said gently, "You can have all that, Mr. Hawkes, if you lay down your arms."

Will looked away as tears came to his eyes as well. His heart began to pound, and he felt a Presence surround him, one of warmth and security. He blinked his eyes and tried to fight it off.

And in the distance, he heard a voice calling, faint and far away, *"Be still and know that I am God."*

He looked down, the reality of his sin and rebellion a crushing, silencing weight.

"Lady Spenser, it is no good to try and save me. It is a hopeless crusade. If I were to give in to God, I would need turn away from my evil ways as a pirate. I would need refuse the gold that I promised the crew for your release. I would be condemning these men—if I give myself up—to the gallows. With the ransom from your kidnapping I can set these men free. It will provide them, if they choose, with a new start. If I refuse to continue with this plan, they will have no new start but will wash up in any number of ports in the Caribbean Sea with a price on their heads and the hangman in their future. I cannot, Lady Spenser—nor will not—condemn the entire crew to death to save my soul. I cannot."

"Perhaps if you negotiated with my father—"

"No, Lady Spenser. I have constructed a thousand different plans, and each plan, save the original, leads every man to his death. I am trapped, Lady Spenser, like a fox set on by a pack of hounds. I must fulfill the original scheme—or all will die."

"But can you not accept God's gift? Can you not put it all in his hands and trust him to provide a path, a way out for you?" she pleaded.

William bowed his head and felt the warmth and security surround him again. "Not since my mother died have I felt as secure as I do at this moment. I trust that it is her presence that I feel. If I am to do what you ask, I will do it with the foreknowledge that I will still need follow the arrangements for your release. It may be evil, but I will not condemn others to death for my faith. Is that understood?"

"William," she said, for the first time using his Christian name, "I understand completely. But I also believe completely that the Almighty has more wisdom than you or I. A way will be presented. There will be a sign."

After she spoke those words, she began to pray, *Lord, please allow these things to transpire as I have spoken. I beseech you, my heavenly Father, to provide a path out of this jungle for William. I have no ability to see such a path, but you must. Dear God, please save this man.*

William bowed his head, and after a long moment of silence, repeated the words that he thought appropriate—the Lord's Prayer—that he had memorized as a child. *"Our Father which art in heaven, hallowed be thy name. Thy kingdom come. Thy will be done in earth, as it is in heaven. Give us this day our daily bread. And forgive us our debts, as we forgive our debtors. And lead us not into temptation, but deliver us from evil: for thine is the kingdom, and the power, and the glory, for ever. Amen."* He then softly added his own words to the centuries-old prayer. *"God, I trust it is your peace that I have been searching for and have finally found. I've done many vile and unforgivable things, yet I ask you to forgive me them. And I ask not for my sake, but for that of my men, that there be a way out of this dilemma that we are in. Amen."*

When he finished praying, Will raised his head, and the tears in his eyes were dried, his heart beating calmly.

Kathryne looked at the new William Hawkes and opened her arms to embrace him. He responded, and the two—on their knees—held each other tight for many precious moments.

After a time, they parted. Their eyes then locked, and slowly, ever so slowly, their faces moved toward each other. Kathryne tilted her head to the right, and their lips met. The pounding of two hearts drowned out the sound of the rest of the world.

‡‡‡

On the rocky shoals, the vicar awoke in a stupor. He stood up, wobbly, and began to bellow out, "Kathryne! Hawkes—you dog of a pirate heathen! Come back at once!"

But the roar of the sea against the shore overwhelmed his cries.

70

20 November 1641
An Unnamed Island
The Caribbean Sea

Kathryne and William spoke little on their return to the longboat as they walked hand in hand down from the waterfall. In their eyes was a sparkle that outshined the blues and greens of the sea and jungle that surrounded them.

By the time they reached Vicar Petley that afternoon, who had continued to bellow and rant until their return, the sun had begun to dip over the western edge of the mountain. Its dark peak wore a misty tiara as it rose against the sky.

As they reappeared at the water's edge, the vicar nearly leapt at them. "Where in the name of the almighty God have you been?" he shouted. And wagging a finger at William's nose, he cried, "And you, you heathen pirate! What have you done to Lady Spenser? If the chief does not have you beheaded for this—I shall."

Kathryne placed a hand on his shoulder. "Vicar, calm yourself. The potion that you took to relieve the sea illness must have disoriented you. It has only been a short while since we left. We went to get fresh water upstream. You took the medicine when we arrived here, and you were awake until an hour ago, when you began to swoon. You have been asleep for no more than a few minutes. We went to retrieve water for you, thinking that it would be of help."

The vicar glared at her and then at William. "But Kathryne, it was morning when we left the village. It is now afternoon. What, pray tell, happened to the rest of the day?"

"It must be the potion that is causing you to react this way, Vicar. You have been asleep for no more than a few minutes."

The vicar looked confused and muddled. "But why both of you to fetch water? Answer me that, you blackguard pirate!" the vicar shouted.

Will looked at Kathryne, and hiding every trace of his complicity, he replied, "Lady Spenser was unwilling to drink from the same flagon as I and requested I accompany her to where she could sip water at the source. I allowed her to do so, knowing that we would not tarry."

Vicar Petley snorted, "She shows good sense in avoiding close contact with you, you heathen."

The vicar wobbled back to the boat, and Will saw Kathryne unsuccessfully struggle to keep a smile from her lips and a giggle from her throat.

"What was that, Kathryne? What did you say?" the vicar demanded as he plopped down in the front of the longboat.

"I was asking how you felt, Giles. Has the potion worked to eliminate the illness?"

"*Now* you care—after I suffer through a lost afternoon at the hands of a black savage and his voodoo medicine! Kathryne, I am stunned at your lack of concern. As a woman you are to have a servant's attitude, but your behavior is most ungenerous."

The vicar slouched backwards against the bowsprit of the boat. "I am glad that we have seen what the tropical heat does to the female of the species," he said in an undulating voice. "It makes them weak and unpredictable. A whole new facet of your character has been revealed, Kathryne. And I must say that I do not like it one bit."

Kathryne was sitting in the boat on the middle seat, with her back to the vicar, as his woozy rampage continued. Her smile was that of a schoolgirl caught in a prank and unable to extract herself. Will bit at his lower lip, almost drawing blood, as he watched Kathryne struggle not to laugh.

▪▪▪▪

Kathryne remained awake until late into that night, sitting at the door to her hut, watching the reflection of the moon upon the calm waters of the cove. The moon was a few days from its fullness. The night was mild and still, so she sat, in the quiet, recalling the events of the day, still trembling as she thought of William's lips on hers, his strong arms around her.

How can I consider what I am considering? she pondered. *He is a common-born pirate. He is a criminal who will be hanged if caught. How has he affected me as he has? But yet I do so desire him—and I know God will punish me for these thoughts. . . .*

But I have led him to the knowledge of you, dear Lord, she prayed. *He will have eternal life. That is cause for the angels to celebrate. So why am I so confused?*

Kathryne stood and walked slowly to the shore where William taught his children. She sat on a smooth boulder and watched the moonlight on the rocks in the water. The cove was still that night—a slight cat's-paw wind scarce caused a single ripple.

Kathryne tossed a pebble into the water and watched the circles form and radiate away from the splash. She put her hand on the smooth rock that William stood upon to teach, running her palm over its cool surface. She remembered the feeling of her hands against his hard back when she had her arms around him. She looked back at the sleeping little village lit in whites and grays by the moon as it rose in an ink-black sky sprinkled with thousands and thousands of stars.

Lord, she prayed, *I beg of you to provide a path for me. I am torn between my feelings for this man and what I know to be right and proper. What am I to do, Lord? What am I to do?*

She hung her head and silently wept, her tears dropping soundlessly onto the sand and washing away to the water's edge.

Kathryne looked up to see a dark figure walking toward her. She could tell in an instant that it was William by his purposeful stride, broad shoulders, and narrow waist.

"Lady Spenser, I looked for you in your hut and was alarmed to see you gone. Are you feeling ill? Is anything wrong?"

"No Mr. Haw—William. I am not ill. And there is nothing . . . and everything . . . wrong."

And with that, her tears began to fall again. She made no attempt to hide them, nor did William make any attempt to comfort her.

"William," Kathryne sniffed, "what will become of you in a few days—when the moon is full?"

He sat in the pale light and looked to the stars. "Do you see that star up there in the northern sky—the one that shines brighter than the rest—where I am pointing my hand?" he asked.

Kathryne wiped at her eyes and followed his direction. "Yes, I see the star."

"It is Polaris, the last star in Ursa Minor—the constellation of the Little Bear. It is called the North Star, for it always hovers above true north. It is a constant in a sailor's life. When one is at sea—in the middle of a trackless ocean of dark and rolling waters—if a sailor can look up into the heavens and see that star, then he is comforted, for he knows that he is not lost but found. When the night on the open water is black—so black that a man can forget what light looks like—that star can be his anchor to the world.

"Until this day, Lady Spenser, I thought I knew what direction I was traveling. But I did not. I was at error in my belief. I was looking at a tiny blink of light—myself—and calling that Polaris. I was by no means a beacon. Like Paul—yes, I know who Paul was, for one cannot live with Vicar Mayhew for many years and not—the scales fell from my eyes today. It is at God who I must aim my sextant—not at myself."

William paused and cleared his throat, gulping to prevent tears from forming. "I do not think I will ever be able to repay the debt I feel I owe to you. Nothing I may do, nothing I may say, nothing I may give you will reconcile that debt."

Kathryne, through her tears, cried, "William, you owe me nothing! I have only done as the Scriptures demand—I am to be a servant. It is not *my* doing that changed your soul, but almighty God's."

"Lady Spenser—Kathryne—I understand that. But still, I am in your debt."

She thrilled to have him call her by her Christian name at last.

The quiet of the evening seemed to fill in the open areas of the island like a thick blanket covering a small child, muffling the noises, muting the animals' cries, and stilling the calls of the insects.

"William, you did not answer my question. In two days, what will happen?"

Will stood, took a short step into the water, and looked out at the open sea. "Kathryne, I have been reborn. My life is changed. It is as if my heart has at last begun to beat. And it is not only our Lord for whom it beats—but . . . I am not certain how these words will be taken . . . it beats for you. From the first moment I opened my eyes to you, I knew. I have seen your face before me in my dreams. My heart is truly at peace only when it beats near yours."

"But, William, what will occur two days hence? You have not said." Tears were streaming down her cheeks.

"Kathryne, I will not tell you falsehoods. What course history shall take is beyond my power to influence. My wants will not shift the way of fate."

Kathryne turned to him, face upturned, "But William, I believe God would have a future for us. He must. For I, too, have dreamed of your face."

"Were that so, Kathryne, I would sleep easy. But I am afraid God's plans are not always kind to people such as we. And as for our dreams . . ."

"Then what happens?" she cried.

"It is most improbable that a person such as you—a woman of standing and breeding—would even deign to speak to one such as I, with my common background and criminal ways. I cannot see how such a future would be accomplished. What we have shared these few days and weeks has been the start of a new life for me. But it cannot be more than that. It cannot be a new life for *us,* together."

Kathryne's tears continued to fall. Will bent down to her and took her hands in his. "If I had the power of the supernatural, I would alter my past to correct the present and insure our future. But I cannot.

"This is what I know to happen. We will sail from this island by the afternoon of tomorrow. We will reach our destination in a day's journey. The moon will be full that night, and then on the morrow you will see your father again."

"And you, William? What about you?" she cried.

"You will not see me again."

Her tears began to fall faster.

"But, Kathryne, that star I pointed to—the constant in the sky. I would beg this one thing of you, that in the evening, when the air is cool and the noise of the day has ceased, you will step outside your elegant mansion and look up at the dark, star-filled heavens. And when you see that bright star hanging overhead, I would ask that you think of me, for I, too, will be gazing at it at the same time. As long as it burns, it will bond us together forever, Kathryne. As the Almighty has promised us eternity, I will promise myself to you, for the rest of my days faithful to your name."

He paused as her tears fell more slowly now.

"That star, there," Will said, pointing to it, releasing Kathryne's hand. "That is the star that seals my oath to you. Just gaze upon it when your heart is sad, and I will be there, Kathryne. When your sight has grown dim, the star will still be there in your vision. It will be as I will—a constant light too distant to touch but always with you."

He paused again, the stillness enveloping them both. "That will be what happens in two days when the moon is filled, my dear Kathryne."

Her tears had ceased, for she realized that a good-bye was best done with dry eyes. She held both his hands once again. "William, God will find a way," Kathryne said in a small, little voice. "I have prayed, William. Our Father will give you a sign. He has promised to be with us when we pray. He will answer the cries of his children."

"Let us not think of us apart from this evening," William answered. "I have looked for God's signs too long to think that the Almighty will always enter history at our request. I will be satisfied by the memories of you—your sweet face in this moonlight, your laughter on the mists of a rainbow, your heart beating next to mine, your kind and gentle ways."

He put his strong arms around her and drew her close, her head nestled on his broad shoulder. They knelt together for a moment, matching heartbeats in the dark. He drew back. He put his rough hand beneath her smooth chin and held it, staring into her eyes. He tenderly pulled her to him and gently, as gently as a butterfly upon a rose, set his lips to hers. The kiss she returned was yearning and insistent.

"There is no tomorrow for us, Kathryne," he said softly as he finally broke away, "but we will have the perfection of this moment forever. That is what God has given us this night."

He stood up, pulled her to her feet, then began to walk away—away from the village toward the darker edges of the cove. After three steps, he stopped and turned. "Go back to your hut, Kathryne. Prepare for tomorrow's voyage. And perhaps, before the moon dips and the sun arrives, you will look at the heavens again—at the constant star—and remember, for I will be there with you."

He turned and walked slowly and silently away.

71

22 November 1641
Barbados

On board the *Serendipity,* Captain Blake made his preparations as well. He had spent the last three weeks recruiting, from any ship that visited Bridgetown, a crew handpicked for their ruthlessness and their ability to keep a quiet tongue. He and Radcliffe Spenser sat in the cramped, hot, and rancid-smelling officer's cabin of the ship.

"Captain Blake," Radcliffe had whispered to Blake as they planned, "are you quite positive these crewmen will remain closemouthed following the exchange? Are you prepared to insure their silence, if need be?"

Blake looked at Radcliffe. He squinted his eyes into slits. "For my share of this venture, I would slit the throat of my own brother," he said evenly. "I am quite prepared to do what this business requires. And the crew is well apprised of such terms."

Radcliffe sat back, leaning against the wall of the room, his feet tucked under a small stool. He had a clay pipe in his mouth and was filling the quarters with a blue haze. "That, my dear Captain Blake, is music to my ears," he hissed through the smoke.

Blake, his eyes bloodshot from the sleepless rush of preparations needed in such a short time, took a healthy swallow of island rum. He winced and gave his head a slight shake. "I'll be happy when it is all finished."

"Ah, but Captain Blake, old chum, the fun is in the execution."

Blake tilted his head back and drained the last of his tankard full of spirits. "And when will your brother be arriving? We will need to sail with the morning tide if we are to make the rendezvous on time."

Radcliffe leaned forward, and his chair clunked loudly on the floor. The pipe in his mouth was jostled, and sparks and embers floated out into the already heated air. "He will arrive here at dawn, as instructed, with the ten gold bars."

Blake brightened, adding, "And I am sure that all ten bars will be returned to us—if my assumptions are correct as to Hawkes's navigational plans. Our three sister ships, lying in wait for him at the western edges of those shoals, will set the perfect trap."

"True, Captain. One can hope for an even happier ending to our plot."

Blake coughed a few times, then began to laugh, a deep rumbling laugh that erupted from the very depths of his soul.

Radcliffe almost joined in, but instead he only allowed a smile to curve upward on his slim lips.

Dawn arrived, pale blue and reedy, with the sun a translucent scarlet ball in the east. Lord Aidan arrived at dawn's initial glimmer in a royal carriage, followed by a livery team hauling a sturdy sea chest bearing a large padlock.

Lord Aidan stepped out and strode to the ship, followed by a servant carrying two large valises. A team of sailors retrieved the trunk under Radcliffe's watchful eye.

Captain Blake met the governor at the gangway and greeted him with a wobbly, but outstretched hand. "Welcome aboard the *Serendipity,* my lord," he crowed. "We'll be shoving off in a trice, Lord Aidan. And soon enough you'll have your dear daughter returned."

"I trust that to be true," he said. "I have thought of little else for these last weeks. If they have done anything to harm Kathryne, I will have them hunted down like dogs and killed. I will see to it that all will be made to suffer."

Blake wrapped his arm about Aidan's shoulder. "They'll be no need, Governor. For we will have her back. We will see to it that she is taken care of. And, of course, yourself as well. Come with me, my lord, and I will show you to your cabin."

Radcliffe stood on the rear deck, watching first the gold being loaded, then the captain and his brother. It would soon be time to depart on the most monumental voyage of his life.

An Unnamed Island
The Caribbean Sea

The *Reprisal*'s crew formed a line along the beach and passed, hand to hand, the supplies they needed to bring with them. They brought aboard some food, a barrel of roasted boucan meat, a barrel of green fruit, and two barrels of fresh water. Captain William reminded them that the route would carry them over very shallow reefs and that all unneeded items were to be left on the island.

The tide was nearly at its highest flow, and the vessel sat, incongruously, almost cheerfully buoyant, in the warm, shallow waters. They had cut the ballast weight by a third, in the process cleaning out the rancid water, dead rats, and mold. Removing it breathed a freshness into the interior of the ship.

They carried only six cannon on this trip, leaving six on the beach. Both Captain Hawkes and Mr. Delacroix, normally pessimistic planners, felt that the chance of cannon fire during the exchange would be virtually nonexistent. On their approach, the English would not risk injury to Kathryne, and on their departure, the *Reprisal* would have benefit of better wind and a more thorough knowledge of the dangers of the reefs and shoals. They carried a small amount of shot and powder in case their escape route was blocked by a second or third English vessel awaiting them at the western edge of the shallows.

William had told Mr. Delacroix that he had located a fresh, uncharted exit—a narrow channel that led north, rather than west, from the rendezvous location—so their departure could not be thwarted, short of an armada of English ships.

The vicar had gathered his few items and was fussing and fuming with last-minute packing and rearranging. "I simply cannot wait until boarding," he sputtered to no one in particular. "For the sooner I leave this forsaken island the better. Oh, to be back in civilization and away from the insects and the bloodcurdling noises of this infernal jungle!"

Kathryne heard his ranting from her hut as she finished putting away the few items of clothing she had used during her stay. As she closed the final trunk, snapping the latch secure, she sat down on her canvas bed of palm fronds. She folded her hands and looked about the darkened hut, waiting for sailors to come and fetch her things, for she heard them shouting and calling from the water's edge.

She shut her eyes tight, and tears came, this time a small torrent, even though she had imagined that all the tears she had were shed in the last nights, awaiting this day.

William tapped softly at the door. "Lady Spenser? Are you prepared to depart?" he asked softly as he entered. "We must load your trunks aboard now so as to catch the highest tide."

Kathryne merely nodded, noticing his formal address, not willing to trust her voice, her eyes moist, her heart beating rapidly.

A dozen men trooped in, all silent and grave, shouldered the trunks and cases and trooped out, saying nary a single word. The sadness of their captive was thick in that small hut.

"Load these onto the longboat on deck," Will explained to them, "We will not risk dropping them into the sea when the transfer is made."

William stayed in the hut, silently watching the crew remove the trunks. When the last man had left, Will turned to Kathryne and held out his hand. "It is time now, Kathryne. We must leave now."

Kathryne leaped up and into his arms, crying as hard as she had in all her short life.

As she clung to him, she said, "William, please. Is there not another course of action we can consider? My heart is being rent in two."

William held her tenderly, stroking her hair, feeling her sweet, hot, tearful breath on his chest. "Kathryne, we are of two different worlds. These worlds collided for a mere moment, and perhaps that is all the taste of you I shall have. There is no need for further words. You have opened my eyes to God. That is riches uncounted." A tear formed at Will's eye, and he wiped it dry. "Remember to look to that star, Kathryne, for that bond between us will never be sundered, by man nor God."

He bent down to her face, flushed with sadness and despair, gently kissing the tears from her cheeks, and then, in a gracious ending, he placed his lips firmly on hers for a long moment. Kathryne closed her eyes again and prayed that it would never end.

But after a brief moment more, Will pulled her from his embrace, took her hand gently, and said, "These hours with you have breathed life into my soul. Because of you, Kathryne, I live. Without you, my heart would be dead."

He lifted her hand to his mouth and tenderly kissed it, as he imagined nobility must do to seal a vow. "Kathryne, out of all of the harsh acts I have committed, this is the most hateful and brutal thing I have ever done. But I must do it. I must send you away. Please, let us go now. We must be boarding before the tide leaves."

And with that he escorted her to the ship, helping her up to the deck and calling out, in a voice just at the edge of cracking, "Cast off!"

▪ ▪ ▪

Luke stood at the bow of the ship as it crashed into the light surf outside. His heart felt the most free when the sea spray wet his face in the wind. He watched as the *Reprisal*'s sails filled with air and she was pulled, speeding, into the deep water south of the island. After several leagues of travel, he walked back to William, who was standing at the wheel, his face into the sun.

"Massa Will, you be sad?"

"No, Luke. Everything will be fine in two days."

"Luke see sad in Massa's eyes. Do not tell lies. God hate lies."

Will neither smiled nor frowned.

"Sad for white lady? She leave soon."

"Yes, Luke. I am sad for her to go."

"You love white lady?"

Will laughed—not loud nor hard, but brittle, as if it hurt his soul to laugh. "Luke, a pirate cannot love a lady such as Lady Spenser."

"Why? God don' care who be what. You can love white lady. God say it good."

"Luke, she must be returned to her father. You know that. And by tomorrow, she will be."

"Luke don' care what you say, Massa Will. I pray for white lady and you."

And with a great flourish, Luke knelt by William, bowed his head, and began to pray in his native language and in his chanting tone. Will heard the words for "white lady" and "love" and "happy" and "together" and "path," and lowered his head as well—out of deep sadness and out of deep despair.

Kathryne, who had left her cabin for some fresh air, had come to the small hatch, just behind the wheel of the ship. She saw Luke kneel, and William bow his head alongside him, and watched from the shadows of belowdeck as the black ex-slave prayed for the freedom of his master.

72

27 November 1641
Rendezvous Point
The Caribbean Sea

By late afternoon Will and the crew maneuvered the *Reprisal* to the rendezvous spot. The reefs were even higher than Will had recalled, and at several points, under half-sail, the crew used long poles to push the ship from the jagged coral edges. Will struggled to keep her moving forward. Tacking was often an impossibility, and occasionally Will only had the jib sail set. Progress was slow, but without the protection of the reefs Will's small ship would have been a open target for any English vessel.

The anchor was dropped with an angry splash, and the crew, using poles, set the boat facing west, so that with a quick command her sails could be lowered and their escape could be made.

Vicar Petley lurched up on deck. He was less green than usual, for he had taken a smaller dose of Luke's potion to combat the seasickness. At half-power, the concoction caused the vicar to appear as if drunk, and he spun from mast to rail to mast again in a zigzag line of motion, his feet wobbly beneath him and his knees swaying.

"Mr. Hawkes! Where are you, you heathen pirate?" he called.

"Vicar," Will said, waving his hand, "I am right here by the wheel station."

The vicar pushed back from the rail and wobbled over to the wheel, grasping at it, but forgetting it spun easily. As he leaned against it, it turned with his weight, and the vicar stumbled, dropping in a heap to the deck.

"Brigand! Treacherous villain!" he cried as he struggled to regain his footing.

William was laughing quietly as he helped the vicar to sit at the rear rail bench. As William released him, the vicar reached up and grabbed Will's shirt, pulling him close.

"What have you done to Lady Spenser?" the vicar wheezed into William's ear. "She has stayed in her cabin, crying, this entire voyage. I have tapped at her door, and she tells me to leave her alone. Me! The vicar! The man who has kissed her not once, but twice! She has told me to leave! What have you done to her, you perfidious heathen?"

William grabbed the vicar's arms and squeezed them.

The vicar silently mouthed *ouch* and released his grip on William's shirt.

William stood, and the vicar lolled back against the rail. He raised a wobbly arm toward Will, extending his finger at him. "Well, infidel? How have you bewitched her? Have you used the African savage witch doctor to bedevil her in some manner? I demand that you release her. In the name of all that is holy and pure—in the name of God—I demand it!"

Will fought back an urge to simply strike the vicar with his hand and toss him into the sea.

Did she kiss him as well? Is Kathryne the pure woman I think she is? Will's thoughts raced, but he forced the image from his mind.

He stood, bent forward, and placed his hands on the vicar's knees. He squeezed again, and the vicar was even more animated as he mouthed another *ouch* in response to William's strength.

"Listen, you hypocrite! I have done nothing to Lady Spenser, whom you do not deserve to even know, much less kiss. I have not bewitched anyone. I have been honest with her and treated her as a proper lady—with respect and kindness. Perhaps you should try having those Christian attitudes yourself. And I will not have you invoke the Almighty like he is your personal assistant. The Almighty will do what he chooses when he chooses—without orders from a whimpering, sniveling man such as yourself. Now if I hear you say one more ill-mannered remark of Lady Spenser, I will have no alternative than to heave you into the waters to become supper for the sharks." Will squeezed again. "Do you understand?"

"Yes, yes, I understand—now, please . . . release my legs," the vicar wheezed.

Will stood up and walked off, leaving the vicar to rub at the red marks, soon to be bruises, just above his kneecaps.

Late that evening, after the crew had eaten and most had bedded down, the full moon rose above the tranquil waters, its reflection a liquid sphere flickering on the surface.

Will was sitting, legs on each side of the bowsprit, facing west, seeing only the reflection of the moon. The smell of lilacs filled the air, and he knew Kathryne had approached.

He turned to face her, seeing and feeling her concern, her sadness, her despair.

"William, I could not stay hidden until tomorrow. I had to speak with you one last time."

Will turned back around and stared into the dark western horizon. "Why not seek comfort with Vicar Petley. I understand that you are close to him as well," he said with a hint of bitterness.

Kathryne stood silent for a moment. "I heard what he told you of me, William. I was at the hatch door as he spoke. And it is true."

His heart took a small, angry leap. *Is this yet one more treasure that is held before me, then removed? Can I not even hold a mere memory as dear and pure?* he wondered.

"But William, all that happened a lifetime ago—at home in England when I still thought as a child. I cannot excuse it any other way. That Kathryne Spenser was a different person than I am now. I have been transformed. Can a few weeks so radically alter a person? I believe it can—for I am proof. Before I set foot on your island, I believed that God was a God who inhabited proper churches and civilized people's hearts. But now I see God as one who inhabits all of nature, all of his creatures, and who is as concerned with my soul as he is with your soul or the soul of a black ex-slave named Luke. I would have never felt God's presence with me as I do now had I not seen how God's presence came to you, my dear William."

He continued to stare westward.

"William, you asked if our bond, sealed on the North Star, would be forever. I will answer you now. It *will* be forever. I do not know how God will work, but there will be a sign—a path, an open door—that will allow us both to enter."

William gave a small, almost derisive, laugh.

"It is true," Kathryne continued, "for Luke just came to pray with me in my cabin. His faith is indeed that of a child, as our Lord asks, and he prayed that your heart and my heart will be happy in God together."

She reached over and touched his shoulder. "I believe God can make it happen, William. I believe a path will be lit."

William did not stir.

"Do you believe, William? Do you believe it to be so?"

For the longest moment he did not move. He first turned only his head to her slightly, then was about to turn and embrace her with all of himself. But at that moment a crewman shouted out, "Lights off to the stern, Captain, Lights off at stern!"

At a few leagues' distance there was a faint flickering. It was the light of two large lanterns, hung at the fore and aft of a fluyt, as it was poled through the shallow waters, making its slow progress to the rendezvous.

Will slept on the deck that night and spent most of the dark hours staring out to sea. At the loneliest point of the night, he prayed a brief prayer. *Lord, I am not accustomed to seeking your face, but I merely ask that tomorrow . . . your will be done and that I can follow whatever path you should choose.*

CHAPTER

73

28 November 1641
Rendezvous Point
The Caribbean Sea

False dawn came early, the first weak light spilling across the channel from the east. Each vessel became more evident to the other, both bobbing peacefully in the calm waters. The wind was modest that day—a few knots at most—and the sky was opaque, yielding the promise of stronger winds by noon.

Captain Blake came to the forward deck and looked at the rocks and shoals a few feet beneath the waterline. *Curse that pirate for selecting this site! This channel could be no more narrow. I believe we will both have difficulty extracting ourselves from this maze.*

▮▮▯▮▮▯

From the *Reprisal,* an ensign was being raised. It called for the longboats to be lowered from both ships—the English ship's with the gold and the *Reprisal*'s with Kathryne and Vicar Petley.

Will had called out the order on his ship. "Set it up, Mr. Delacroix. There is no need to tarry further."

Mr. Delacroix came to Will's side and placed a hand on his shoulder. "We can tarry," he said softly, "if there be more words you might say to Lady Spenser. We have hours before the tide recedes."

"No, John. A pain deferred is no less painful when one experiences it. Let us follow through now before our English friends become nervous."

The crew winched the longboat into the water. Already loaded with Lady Spenser's trunks, the boat sat heavy in the light swell. Her small birdcage, woven of vines by the children of the village, was perched on top with Willy, her thrush, flitting about inside.

Vicar Petley scrambled down the rope rigging to the craft, a distance of but a few feet, muttering under his breath and glaring at William and the rest of the crew. As he set foot in the boat, he turned back and shouted, "God will punish you for all your sins, you heathen dogs! Do not think he has not seen your evil hearts. Such evil must be punished—and none of you can hope to avoid the fiery gates of hell, rest assured of that!"

And with that, a small wave hit the boat, and the vicar lost his balance and tumbled backward to the forward bench, his legs pointing to the sky.

Kathryne came from her cabin, silent and pale, and walked directly to the rail by the longboat. Will stood a few feet away at the wheel stand.

For a moment, the crew, who had gathered about, thought that she would leave without looking back. They stood, to a man silent as a tomb, watching her prepare to leave. The two Tambor brothers were in the longboat, with oars at the ready, staring up at her anguished face.

She turned about suddenly and faced Will. Their eyes locked. A tear was seen glinting off her cheek in the morning sun. Will looked close to tears as well, but remained stoic and unmoved in front of his crew.

For a moment, Kathryne stared at William, memorizing his features. Another moment passed, and no one breathed. Yet another moment went by. A tear, large like a pearl, fell from Kathryne's cheek to the deck.

She walked to William, stood almost as if she were to embrace him, and looked up at his face, lined with pain. Then gently, almost unsure of the movement, as if a bird first learning to fly, her hand moved to his cheek. With the barest of touches, she grazed his cheek, trailing her faint fingertips along his face to the very swell of his mouth. There she lingered for a moment, her finger braced at the valley of both lips, bridging the gap, calling for silence. A heartbeat later, she let her hand drop, as a partridge would fall to the ground, shot through the heart with a musket ball.

She turned and walked to the rail. A crewman picked her up, gently, delicately, with the ease of picking up a child's china doll, and handed her to Bryne Tambor in the longboat, his bearded, sun-creased face washed with tears of his own.

She sat down on the rear seat, facing backward.

Captain Hawkes walked to the rail, stared down at her now up-turned face for the longest moment, and then called out, "Cast off."

He stood unmoving as the oars dipped into the water. The Tambor brothers pulled mightily against the waves, and the small vessel began to slip away from the *Reprisal*.

The longboat began to cut through the light swells with ease as the two powerful brothers began to stroke through their tears. Kathryne and William could not cease staring directly at each other's eyes, not even after the distance made such contact impossible.

At the same time that Kathryne's longboat was slipping from the *Reprisal,* a longboat laden with the gold was being rowed from the side of the *Serendipity.* The two would meet halfway, and the crew would step from one boat to the other so as to not risk dropping a gold-filled case into the sea. The wind would be at the back of the *Reprisal's* returning longboat, so if treachery was detected, they would arrive to safety sooner. And the wind from the east would be with Will so that he would be able to speed westward at a shout. The *Serendipity* would need to sail north for half a league first, then navigate a series of mazelike reefs in order to catch the *Reprisal.* It would be an impossible task for them, as William had known when he carefully selected the rendezvous point.

When the two longboats met, the Tambor brothers jumped easily into the English longboat and opened the trunk. Within a moment it was noted that the treasure was indeed there. Bryne waved to William, who signaled that they should return.

Within minutes they were back at the *Reprisal,* and the gold was raised to the deck to an oddly quiet crew. Normally such a treasure would be greeted with wild shouts of glee and happiness. But on this day, they merely lowered it into the bottom holds and made ready their departure. The longboat was hauled to the deck, dripping saltwater over the small wet dashes of Kathryne's tears.

William, Mr. Delacroix, and the helmsman were at the stern, each with a telescope trained on the English ship.

Bryne Tambor came to the small group and quietly asked, "Captain, should we be about raisin' the anchor now—for our escape and all?"

Will held up his free hand to indicate Bryne was to wait. "I would like to see her returned safely before we depart, Bryne," Will said softly. "It will be only a moment more."

Bryne stood behind them and waited to receive the order.

Through the telescope, William watched as the longboat, with Kathryne as precious cargo, reached the English ship. She was quickly hauled aboard, in a rather rough manner, William thought. *Do they not understand who she is?* he wondered.

Then he saw another man—light-haired, perhaps silver—rush to her and embrace her. *That must be her father,* Will thought. *At least she is back in loving arms.*

He was within a heartbeat of lowering his glass, the others already having done so, when he saw a crewman roughly grab at the governor's shoulder. The crewman wrenched father and daughter apart and pulled Lord Aidan's hands behind him, securing them with irons and manacles.

On the longboat, Will saw the sailors toss some of Kathryne's luggage into the sea. The birdcage fell to the decking, and the small thrush flew out and away from the English ship.

"Mr. Delacroix! Helmsman! Refocus your glasses on the English ship!" Will cried urgently.

Both telescopes hissed to extension, and all three watched the silent drama unfold.

Lord Aidan, his hands indeed in irons behind his back, was pulled and locked to a ring on the mast.

Kathryne spun about, her face in terror, and shouted to another. Radcliffe came up to her and struck her cruelly across her face with the full force of the back of his hand. She fell to her knees on the deck.

Was that blood? Will's eyes demanded.

Two crewmen on either side of her lifted her up roughly, pulled her hands behind her, and secured them in irons as well, placing her next to her imprisoned father. Then Vicar Petley was roughly pulled from the boat and led at knifepoint to a forward hatch, then tossed into the darkness.

Radcliffe then moved to Kathryne and spoke closely to her face as her head dropped to her chest. He roughly placed his hand under her chin and made her look at him while he spoke.

Kathryne's father was struggling to be released from his chains until a crewman came beside him and rapped him sharply at the temple with the butt of a pistol.

William lowered his glass, his eyes wide with disbelief—stunned, shocked. "Have I seen in error, John? Have my eyes lied?" he asked in a trembling voice.

Mr. Delacroix said somberly, "No, Captain. They have been taken prisoner."

"The man who struck her was Radcliffe Spenser, was he not?"

"Aye. I believe it was, Captain."

William looked ashen. "Then, no doubt he will have them both put to death. I must assume that he means to usurp his brother's role as governor. And along with the position, whatever estate his brother has will be Radcliffe's."

Mr. Delacroix nodded. "That would be my opinion as well, sir. It appears that Lady Spenser and her father are in the greatest peril."

The ship was silent, and William waited only a score of heartbeats. "There is no other course to be decided. I must save her," Will said coldly. "But how can I put the crew in peril for this?"

Mr. Delacroix leaned close to Will and said with a tenderness, "Sir, these men would follow you to the very gates of hades. All you need do is ask."

The crew had gathered closely around the captain, pressing ever closer for information.

William turned about to face his crew. He stood on the rear bench so all could see him. He looked at each man's face and saw cold, resolute determination. He spoke quickly.

"Men, I believe that Lady Spenser and her father will be killed unless we intercede on their behalf. I have always operated this ship with your votes equal to mine. I dare not presume that you'll participate in her rescue, for if we are not successful, we will all hang. I will not presume that you'd put your lives at risk for me in such a matter."

An old crewman looked up at Will and said, "Captain, to a sensible man every day is a day of reckonin'. If today be the day the Almighty says enough, and we are sent to Abraham's bosom, it be enough no matter whether we sail west or east. We need no vote on this. We sail east to the Lady Spenser! None of us would face the morrow with joy if we leave her to die—regardless of the gold in that trunk."

Will stood for a moment, realizing that every man was willing to lay down his life to provide freedom for a noble-born woman.

"The rest of you say aye to his words?"

"Aye!" erupted all around.

"Anyone say no? If so, I promise that no ill be thought of that man." The ship was quiet, save the gusting of the wind.

"Then raise anchor, set sails, and bring her about! Mr. Delacroix! Cannon Master! Prime the cannon, but fire only into the waterline or their canvas. I will not have Lady Spenser injured by my hand. Assemble the muskets, pikes, and grappling hooks on deck!"

And in an instant the ship came alive with rushing men scrambling to their appointed tasks.

Radcliffe stood at the rear of the *Serendipity,* smiling, rubbing his hands together, gloating over his most audacious and successful plan.

"Captain Blake, well done!" he called. "Soon you will have your estate—and I will be governor, even if only for a few months. But it will be sufficient time to adjust my funds as necessary. And I will soon have Broadwinds as well. All in all, Captain, a most rewarding day."

Captain Blake looked ill, but he nodded with Radcliffe's enthusiastic assessment. "We will both be rich men, Lord Radcliffe, and that is a great freedom," Blake said with little feeling. And as he spoke, he turned to see the pirate ship unfurl their sails and catch the wind.

That is most curious, he thought. *If I did not know better, I would say that they are sailing directly east—at us. Now why would that be? They have our gold, and we have Kathryne. What more can they want—Oh, please . . . no!*

Blake turned calmly to face his coconspirator. "Radcliffe, how did you describe Captain Hawkes to me once? Did you not call him a pirate with a conscience?"

Radcliffe, who was looking east, absently said, "I may have called him that. What of it? Why do you ask now?"

"It appears as if our moral pirate is sailing against us. Perhaps he has seen his kidnap victim in chains."

Radcliffe spun about and ran to the rail. The *Reprisal,* now under full sail, was indeed cutting the waves towards them.

"Blast them to the heavens! Curse them, the devils!" Radcliffe shouted.

The entire crew turned to see what Radcliffe was shouting at.

"Well, do not stand there like ignorant slaves!" Radcliffe shrieked at them. "Get us away from here! And do so now! *Now!* Ready cannon, pass out muskets! I will not have my scheme thwarted by some looby sailor!"

Radcliffe strode, imperially, to Kathryne. "You think your pirate can foil my plans? Think again, you trollop," and he reached back and struck her again. "No one will stand in my way—not even you, my dear Kathryne. Not even you."

A thick run of blood appeared at the corner of Kathryne's mouth. Her eyes darted from Radcliffe looming before her, to her father, and then to Will's small pinnace growing larger with each passing heartbeat.

The *Reprisal* had gained an edge in preparing to sail first, even though the wind was at her face. In a few moments she entered a stretch of clear, deep water and headed to the narrow channel where the English ship lay.

Blake ordered the anchor raised, the ship poled about, and the sails lowered. *If we are lucky, we may be able to outsail her, for I know our vessel is faster,* Blake thought. *If we win the race back to Bridgetown, then the fort will fire upon the pirates, and this complication will be solved.*

Will had ordered all the *Reprisal*'s sails lowered in spite of the risk of running aground. He had but one chance to close the distance, for he knew that the English ship was faster. Will did not think she would stop and offer battle.

The small channel came up quickly, and William had only one chance to set a course. If he missed any turn or if the wind became strong then faded, the hull would be ground against the razor-sharp coral and rocks.

At a distance of five hundred yards, the *Reprisal* sat at broadsides to the English ship, at least for a moment.

"Cannon Master! Fire at will, but only through her canvas!" Will shouted.

All three cannons barked, and the double shots ripped through the mainsail of the *Serendipity* with a hiss. Blake's gunners fired back at the *Reprisal,* but as Will surmised, the crew was a ragtag team, not accustomed to the guns or the ship's handling, and missed all shots.

The *Serendipity* was still well in the lead and sailing with the wind off the starboard. She was faster at broad reach with the wind than the *Reprisal*. The channel was no more than fifty yards wide, and it required every bit of skill to place the vessels, sailing at list with the wind, in the middle of the channel, away from danger. The open sea was mere minutes away, and if they both reached it at their current distance, the English ship would quickly speed away, the *Reprisal* having no chance to match her speed. Whichever ship reached Barbados first would be the victor. Radcliffe could execute his evil plan at any point in the journey.

Mr. Delacroix called to Will, "Our only chance to slow them is to use the offense we employed against the Spanish warship."

"Too risky, John!" William shouted back. "The channel is too narrow!"

The quartermaster called out from the port side, "No other way, Captain. We'll place ourselves on either side to tell you our margin of deep water."

William looked about at the grim, set faces of the crew. He saw the *Serendipity,* under full sail, inching away from them. He knew the fate of Kathryne if he failed. "Very well," Will called. "Are the cannons primed?"

"Aye, sir!"

"You will have but a heartbeat to fire—and only at the sails. Do you understand? At the sails only! And with double powder!"

"Aye, sir."

Will angled the ship to the starboard reef, coming within an arm's length of it before spinning the wheel and going broadside against the English ship's stern.

In an instant the three cannons fired, sending double shots, bound together with a short length of chain, through the sails.

As soon as he heard the cannons' roar, Will spun in the reverse direction to allow the other side to fire. On this tack, the channel closed tighter, and Will caught an edge of the reef. With a sickening grumble of splintering wood, the ship pitched a bit, then righted itself.

A carpenter popped through an open hatch. "Just a scratch, Captain. A few buckets of water is all. We'll get her patched."

As the *Reprisal* sat behind the *Serendipity,* she was at risk of musket fire, which Will's men were returning, as well as cannon fire from two small six-pound guns mounted on the *Serendipity*'s stern deck. Because of her unfamiliar crew, most of the *Serendipity*'s shells went long, but a few found their targets. Several of Will's crewmen were hit by a splintery explosion amidships, and it appeared that two others were simply swept away as a section of railing exploded. Many shots whistled through their canvas as well, pulling rigging down and slowing them slightly.

Two more times Will made the tack, coming broadside to the English ship's stern, and two more times the cannons reported. The second time, he caught coral on the port bow, and again a grinding, splintery scream of wood was heard from belowdecks.

From an open hatch, the same carpenter popped up, his hair matted to his head with seawater. "We can patch her, Captain, but another scrape on the port side may be more threatenin'."

The open water of the ocean was just ahead, no more than a two minutes' sail. The *Serendipity* had slowed some, but not enough to offset her possible speed.

"We have one more chance, men! Make it count!" Will shouted.

He spun the wheel again, and the cannons roared. And as Will turned the ship back to the middle of the channel, he watched, as did the rest of the crew, to see the rear mizzen sail of the *Serendipity* slowly tilt, then tumble, to the starboard side of the ship, its mast snapped one-third of the way up. As it collapsed, it pulled part of the mainsail down as well, just as the ship entered the deep waters beyond the reefs.

Will lowered his head and offered a brief prayer of thanksgiving. The race was done, but the battle remained.

In a moment, the *Reprisal* was at the English ship's stern. Grappling hooks flew, linking the two ships in a web of ropes and iron and musket fire.

Will was one of the first to scale the side of the *Serendipity,* pistol in his left hand and sword in his right. An English sailor came rushing at him with a long pike tipped with a curved metal spike. Will jumped to the left and fired a single shot into the sailor's thigh. The attacker fell in a screaming clump.

Will leaped right as another sailor came at him from his left. He dropped the pistol—there would be no time to reload now—clubbed the man soundly with the hilt of his sword, grabbed at his shirt collar, and flung him in a shallow arc overboard into the sea.

From behind Will came sounds of a march of musket shots. Musket balls whizzed past his head and thumped into the deck, bits of splinter falling at his feet. He parried and thrusted through the defense, and a sailor to his right dropped to the deck, his left arm a mangled bloody mess. Will parried another sailor's attack, swords clanging loudly. Another volley of musket fire erupted—this time from his side. Will was not aware if the fire was from friend or foe, yet he charged blindly ahead into the smoke, the screams, the carnage.

Will battled his way to the railing of the upper port gundeck. He looked out over the middle deck, looking for the base of the mainmast. Smoke from a small fire of cannon shots poured through the air, turning the bright morning to a nightmare of darkness. Canvas and rigging hung loose as spider webs above their heads.

A gust of wind cleared the deck for a moment, and Will caught sight of Kathryne, still chained to the mast, next to her father. Her face was bloodied, and she was ashen, white with shock.

She looked up at William, her eyes pleading, knowing that his actions may have doomed himself as well as his entire crew.

"Kathryne!" he screamed over the din.

She responded by standing taller and leaning towards him, the chain about her wrists stretched to the limit, cutting into the soft and tender flesh.

"God has sent me a sign!" he cried. "The sign was you!"

He struck out at a sailor brandishing a thick iron pike.

"William!" she shouted back, "you must not sacrifice yourself for me! Leave while there is time!"

"No, Kathryne! I cannot! A man is only as good and as noble as whom he loves!"

He jumped to the top of the railing, narrowly missing being impaled by another defender with a sharpened pikestaff.

And at that moment Radcliffe stepped calmly from the smoke and stood next to Kathryne. He was carrying two pistols and a sword in a scabbard at his waist. He turned to Kathryne.

"Say farewell to your pirate savior," he snarled, then turned and leveled both pistols at William, firing them simultaneously, the recoil sending his arms flaying backward.

Kathryne shrieked and pulled at her chains, cutting deeper gashes in her wrists, as William toppled from the rail.

"You devil!" she screamed. "How black is your heart to do this to your own brother and niece."

He tossed one pistol aside and raised the other to strike at her again. She closed her eyes for the blow, but did not move to avoid it.

"You touch her, and I will see you die a thousand horrible deaths!"

Kathryne opened her eyes and watched as Radcliffe slowly lowered his pistol. It finally dropped, clattering to the deck. William had appeared at the top of the short staircase leading to the gundeck. His left shoulder was bloodied, but he was alive. He carried his cutlass in the forward position in his right hand. He jumped the last few steps to stand between Kathryne and Radcliffe.

"To harm her, you demon, you will need kill me first." William held his cutlass at arm's length in front of him.

"Why, that will be my pleasure, Mr. Hawkes."

And with that Radcliffe swung his long sword in a high arc, clanging it against Will's. Again and again, he thrust at Will's left, knowing that the wound would cause him a momentary pause in response to that side. With each parry, Will was a moment slower bringing his blade back to a defensive position.

Radcliffe placed both hands on the hilt of his sword and again put his entire weight behind the arc. Again it smashed into Will's weapon with a metallic clang, and again Will staggered a bit more, not having the strength to respond in kind.

As the battle swirled about them, Will's only intent was to protect Kathryne. In his mind, a question came flashing through his thoughts again and again. *Can I kill this man? Can I kill this man?* Will's mind raced.

As a child of God, would killing a man in defense of the defenseless prove such a sin that even God would not forgive? Until this point, at his hand only one man had died—the Spanish captain of the *El Diablo,* and that was nearly as accidental as Will could imagine. He had given the orders that caused other deaths, but none other had died by his own hand.

Radcliffe swung again, the arc of his blade starting at the deck, then following around in a huge circle over his head, and pivoting downward, his full weight behind the blade, aimed at William's left shoulder.

William held up his blade in defense, gripped by his right hand only, his left hanging loose and dead at his side.

The swords clashed together again, sparks flying in all directions. Will managed to deflect the attack, but his blade was forced to within inches of his exposed neck. Will's strength was ebbing as the battle pitched about him.

William gathered what reserves remained in him and jabbed sharply at Radcliffe's unprotected left side, slicing a thin cut into his lower arm. Radcliffe howled like a beast in an iron trap.

"You worthless peasant! It will give me the greatest pleasure to see your guts spilled out at my feet!" Radcliffe bellowed as he lurched his blade toward Will's middle.

Will deflected most of the thrust with his blade, yet Radcliffe's attack nicked a deep wound in his side, blood seeping quickly through his shirt to his belt.

God, what am I to do? he thought, as again he met a furious sweep of Radcliffe's sword with his own. *Help me, O God.*

Radcliffe lunged again, and Will feinted to the right, Radcliffe slipping past him. Will spun about and cut at Radcliffe's legs. His thrust met only air, and William staggered to his left, trying to find solid purchase on the slippery deck, now greased with human blood.

Radcliffe turned, sweating, his face streaked with dirt and grime, blood flecks coloring his forearms.

"I will smile as I slice your heart in two, you worthless scum, and I'll feed you and the trollop to the sharks," Radcliffe wailed, his voice booming from a dark and horrid place near his soul.

With his left hand, he wiped his brow on his sleeve and grinned. He then swung again at William, catching him off balance, knocking him to his knees. William struggled to rise, his vision dimmed by the wound, faintness clouding his actions.

Radcliffe raised his blade again, poised to sweep through William's exposed neck. William slipped back to his knees and focused his eyes on Kathryne. *At least I will leave this world with beauty filling my eyes,* Will thought, his mind curiously objective and calm.

At that moment, from the yardarm came a cracking, creaking sound. The upper mast, just below the maintop, had been hit by a cannon shot, and half of the wood had been torn away. With a groan, the yardarm finally gave way and plummeted to the deck. The rigging arced it away from the mast, yet it swung faster and faster downward. The yardarm, as thick as a man's waist, swept across the deck, sweeping Radcliffe and three other sailors across the narrow ship, tearing through the rail, and spewing them into the water off the port side. The oak beam had missed William's head by inches. If not for kneeling, Will would have been swept away as well.

On the forecastle deck, Captain Blake lay prostrate, grimacing and cursing. He had fallen early, hit by a volley of shots.

The English crew watched as Radcliffe was swept overboard, and several ran to the side to see if he struggled up to the surface. The water about the boat was filled with crates, wooden spars, pieces of decking, barrels—standard residue of a battle of wooden ships. They scanned the debris and could see no one.

The battle seemed to halt at that moment. The remaining English crew looked about. Blake was down, Radcliffe was swept into the sea—and they were leaderless. Quickly they laid down their arms and held their hands in the air.

Mr. Delacroix rushed to Will's side. "You've been shot! Let me call for Luke."

William, who had raised himself slightly upright, still on his knees, dropped his sword with a clang to the deck. "Not yet, Johnny. First you will see that Lady Spenser and her father are released and cared for."

"Aye, sir."

"And will you assist me to my feet? I seem to be a bit weakened."

Mr. Delacroix tenderly wrapped his arms about William and helped him stand, legs locked beneath him.

Will turned just in time to see Kathryne embrace her father. "It appears, Mr. Delacroix, that we have accomplished our mission here."

And with that Will slumped to the deck, with Mr. Delacroix shouting for Luke as he cradled the captain's head in his arms.

74

28 November 1641
Rendezvous Point
The Caribbean Sea

It was noon, the sun high in the middle of the sky. The shadows had shortened, and the smoke had long since cleared.

The *Serendipity* and the *Reprisal* sat side by side, rocking gently in the breeze. The wood and crates and barrels and debris from the battle had slowly floated away in the soft current. Both longboats had been cast aside during the fight, and all of Kathryne's clothing and possessions were drifting toward the islands off the Venezuelan coast.

Luke tended to the wounded on both ships, carefully bandaging the deep cuts on Kathryne's wrists, rubbing a stinging lotion made from ginger and aloe on them before he wrapped them. "Dey be hurtin' now, but dey heal soon."

"Thank you, Luke," Kathryne said when he finished. She reached out and touched his forearm. "What of . . . what of Captain William?"

Luke shook his head. "Much blood spilt. He be weak, but should live."

"And what of Vicar Petley?" Kathryne asked.

"He be down in cabin, Lady. He be fine soon. He don' wan' talk to no one. He green and make mess."

Kathryne then replaced Mr. Delacroix at Will's side. They had laid him on a pallet of rough canvas hammocks. She sat quietly by, offering heavenward as many prayers as she could compose. She held his hand, cradling it as one might cradle a fallen baby thrush.

As a gull cawed overhead, Will's eyelids fluttered, then opened. He saw Kathryne and smiled weakly. "Is this heaven?" he asked.

Kathryne smiled and squeezed his hand tightly.

After a few moments, she said, "My father wants to speak to you, if you are capable of conversation."

Will nodded again and asked that Mr. Delacroix attend them as well.

Lord Aidan knelt next to his daughter, face-to-face with William. "Captain Hawkes, we owe you our lives. If it had not been for your courageous actions, Kathryne and myself would be dead."

"But sir, if it were not for us, you would not have been put in peril," answered Will.

"Perhaps not, Captain Hawkes, but if Radcliffe's evil intentions had not transpired today, they would have transpired some day in the future—when the outcome may have proved even less to our liking."

Will nodded.

"Captain Hawkes, as governor I have a proposition to put to you."

"Yes?"

"I gave you the letters of marque that began these actions. That order I am officially rescinding as of this moment. I am placing Captain Blake and his crew under arrest, and they will stand trial when we return to Bridgetown."

"Yes, Governor," William said contritely.

"And as reward for your bravery, I am offering a governor's pardon for you and all your crew, providing that you cease your piracy on the seas. Your men may keep what funds they have accumulated to date, with the exception of the gold that was provided for my daughter's ransom."

Will looked at Mr. Delacroix, who nodded and leaned to whisper in Will's ear. "A most generous offer, William, but we need to allow the crew to accept or decline as they see fit."

Edging his elbows to the bed and struggling to prop himself up, Will replied. "I will take your offer, sir. I believe God has opened this door for me to leave the life of a pirate. But I cannot answer for the entire crew. I must allow them the choice. If they do not accept your pardon, I will allow them to sail off with their share of the ransom—with no official pursuit—on board the *Reprisal*. Will you allow them that option, sir?"

Lord Aidan looked about at the faces of the crew that surrounded their captain. "Yes, Captain Hawkes. That is fair."

After a few minutes of discussion, the crew made their choices. Nearly thirty decided that the allure of gold was too strong and opted to sail off on the *Reprisal* with their shares. The rest would take the pardon and sail back to Barbados aboard the *Serendipity* with William.

It took the rest of the afternoon to transfer possessions between the ships. Will made sure that his books, charts, and maps were brought over. William also made certain that the *Reprisal* would not depart the shallows by the obvious means—for there were most likely ships of Radcliffe's plot lying in wait for them. The northern route would be safest.

The gold was divided, and the men clamored aboard the *Reprisal*. William insisted on standing to salute his departing crew, and Kathryne helped him to rise.

"You have all proven your worth and bravery," Will called in a weak voice. "I ask that you do nothing to dishonor the memory of the noble *Reprisal*. God speed you on your journey. And if you will, stop at our cove and tell Chief Sapua I have been delayed but will send supplies to him as soon as I am able. Will you promise me that?"

"Aye, sir," one of the departing sailors called. "We promise on our honor to do so."

Another man shouted, "Godspeed to you as well, Captain Hawkes. It has been our privilege to sail with you."

The crew then saluted each other in a ragtag fashion and then cast off the ropes between the two ships. Several sailors used pikes and poles to separate them, and at last, the *Serendipity* began its slow voyage back to Barbados, Mr. Delacroix at the helm.

━ ▪ ▪ ▪ ▪ ▪ ━

It was near dusk, the sun slipping to the western horizon and the shadows lengthening across the deck of the ship. Kathryne sat by William's side and said only a word or two, her bandaged hand on his chest, content to see its rhythmic rise and fall as he breathed.

"I am sorry, Kathryne," Will said softly.

"For what, William?"

"For allowing your thrush to be lost in the battle."

"His name was Willy, and—" Kathryne was about to say that the safety of a small English bird was insignificant to the safety of her father and the foiling of Radcliffe's evil plan, when a brown flutter caught both their attention.

On the railing, by Kathryne's head, landed the Williamson thrush. He perched there, eying them each intently, hopped closer to Kathryne, then broke out in the most joyous song either William or Kathryne had ever heard.

75

30 November 1641
Barbados

The *Serendipity* had been badly damaged in the battle, and only the foremast had escaped unscathed. Enough of the mizzenmast remained to allow the hanging of a wide mizzen course sail. She returned to port at a slow, but steady pace. The winds were gracious, for they blew from the northeast and allowed her to sail, almost without tacking, directly to Barbados.

It was a time of relief as well as deep sorrow for Lord Aidan and Kathryne Spenser, for they could think of little else but their shock at Radcliffe's evil and of his being swept into the sea.

Will offered what little comfort he could give to them in their grief. "I have seen men who had been thrown overboard reappear—washed up on an island shore after several days at sea, having clung to an item of nautical debris."

At Kathryne's insistence, father and daughter spent time in prayer together for the soul of their brother and uncle.

In light of Radcliffe's actions against them, it was difficult for Kathryne and Lord Aidan to sort out if they could find it in themselves to hold out hope of the improbable survival of Radcliffe, but they prayed that if by some miracle he was still alive, God would have mercy on his soul. Despite all the grim events of the past few days, the two shared a deep sense of peace that comes from an abiding faith in God. The hours were a bittersweet mix of profound sadness over their brother and uncle and unbounded happiness with being in each other's presence again.

It was early in the afternoon of the second day of the trip when the *Serendipity* slipped into a quiet Bridgetown harbor. The Dutch fluyt possessed a draft shallow enough to pull to the deepest pier. Mr.

Delacroix neatly executed a precision maneuver and slid gracefully alongside the wooden gangway. Sailors leaped to the pier and began to tie the ship secure.

There were only a few citizens about the pier that day, and most rushed to the *Serendipity,* first curious over the arrival of an unscheduled ship, next wanting to inspect the damage, then incredulous over the scene that awaited them.

Within only a few minutes the briefest of stories was laid out—the foiled plot of Radcliffe, the kidnapped and ransomed daughter Kathryne, the noble pirates sailing to her rescue, the imprisoned Captain Blake, and the safe return of their official governor, Lord Aidan Spenser. It was an amazing tale that quickly grew and magnified upon itself.

The few witnesses of the *Serendipity*'s return took off at a gallop to spread the word, and within an hour a large party of perhaps a hundred people had formed at the harbor. Drink, food, and a crowd of curious islanders soon followed, and by midafternoon it seemed as if all of Barbados was at the harbor, celebrating a most courageous story of good triumphing over evil.

A band made up of slaves playing fiddles and flutes was brought to the harbor to provide music to augment the festivities.

■■■ ■■

Not long afterward, Geoffrey Foxton arrived at the harbor on an elegant Arabian horse. Most assuredly the celebrants knew of the intended relationship between the handsome planter and the governor's eligible daughter.

He was clad in a smart blue weskit, tan calfskin breeches, and knee-high leather boots the color of warm butter. He had shorter chestnut hair, pulled back in a small tail at his neck, a strong jawline and deep-set blue eyes. It appeared to Will—who had remained lying on his pallet on the rear deck of the *Serendipity,* his left shoulder bandaged and his arm bound tightly in a sling—that the crowd parted, like the waters parted for Moses, as Foxton's long strides carried him along the pier and to the ship.

Geoffrey Foxton spoke briefly to Lord Aidan, Will saw, as he craned his neck to follow Foxton's progress. And then, as Will watched, Lord Aidan called Kathryne over to Foxton, and the two met.

Kathryne kept one bandaged hand at her throat while her other attempted to smooth her hair, loosened and snarled during the battle.

Geoffrey Foxton took her hand gently and bowed elegantly, kissing it with the utmost civility. He stood back up and spoke a few words into Kathryne's ear. She smiled, then pointed at the injured William, who was struggling to rise above his prone position, angling himself up using his one good arm and shoulder to watch.

Foxton walked directly to the *Serendipity* and boarded. He approached William and knelt beside him, extending his large, open hand. "Sir, I am Geoffrey Foxton. Am I to understand correctly that Lady Spenser and her father owe their lives to your bravery?"

William was surprised and struggled to answer. "I . . . I simply did what . . . I did what any man in my position would have done. There was a wrong that needed to be righted."

Foxton shook his hand vigorously, William fighting the urge to wince or cry out from the jostling his wound was being given.

"Nonsense, Mr. Hawkes. You are a hero, and the entire island owes you a huge debt of gratitude. And I owe you even more. For saving Lady Spenser's life, I will be eternally in your debt. If you require anything while you remain on Barbados, I want you to call on me for assistance. Do you understand, Mr. Hawkes? Anything at all."

"Why, yes, I suppose I do . . . but . . . but . . ."

"There will be no buts about my offer." He stood, turned abruptly and said, "We must celebrate this monumental occasion.

"Attention everyone! Attention!" he shouted to the people gathered about. Slowly the crowd stopped its buzz and turned to face Foxton. "In honor of Governor Aidan's and the Lady Kathryne's safe return, we will celebrate at my estate—with drink and food for all—for days if need be! Let us make plans now and reassemble there at dusk. The entire island is invited to attend."

The crowd cheered, hats flying in the air. Will's remaining crewmen were ecstatic, for this was the first time they had been well treated by civilized persons.

Kathryne edged toward Geoffrey Foxton, elbowing her way politely through the crowd.

"Mr. Foxton," she called. As he turned to her, she said, "I will not be able to attend such an event, for during the battle my entire wardrobe was lost. I have no clothing other than the tatters I am wearing now, and they are most unsuitable for any purpose."

Foxton looked Kathryne up and down—more slowly, Will thought, than he had a right to do, his eyes stopping at places where the garment had torn to reveal the lace beneath. "Nonsense, Lady Spenser. I will have no honored guest of mine missing their own celebration."

Foxton looked about, then called out, "Lady Carrington, Lady Wycliffe! Could you attend me for a brief moment?"

The two ladies, not much older than Kathryne, came hurriedly to his side.

"Lady Carrington, Lady Wycliffe—this is Lady Kathryne Spenser. She is in need of a wash and a change of clothing. You are of approximately the same frame as she. Will you see to it that she is properly attired for this evening?"

Both women giggled excitedly and held Kathryne at arm's length for a moment, then nodded vigorously.

"I have the perfect gown for you, Lady Spenser. I would be delighted to present it to you," said an excited Lady Carrington.

"And my home is but five minutes from here," Lady Wycliffe cooed. "You may freshen there while the dress is being brought."

They took her by the arms and swept her from the pier. Just before she disappeared from view, she turned back to Will and mouthed the words, "I will return."

William struggled to gain purchase for his feet, but Luke came from nowhere and pulled him back to his bed. "Massa Will not leave bed. Not today. Stay!"

Geoffrey Foxton looked over at the black man restraining Will. "A darky talks to you that way, Mr. Hawkes?"

Will glared up at him. "Luke is a free man, Mr. Foxton. And he is the ship's doctor."

Mr. Foxton arched his eyebrows and shrugged. "Well, then . . . again, if there be anything you need, Mr. Hawkes, do not feel awkward in asking for my assistance. I will do what I can for you. And now, I must take my leave—for I believe I have guests soon to arrive! 'Tis a pity you will miss such a celebration."

He cut through the crowd without looking back.

The rest of the onlookers quickly followed, and within a quarter hour the pier and ship were near deserted, with the exception of the Tambor brothers, a few sailors still in sick bay, Will, and Luke, who was squatting nearby, watching his captain, making sure he attempted no escape.

Vicar Petley finally emerged from his cabin and was accompanied to the church parsonage by Vicar Coates, who was most eager for any and all details of the battle.

"Was it all terribly swashbuckling?" he was overheard to ask as the two made their way down the pier. No reply was heard from the other vicar.

The sun took an eternity to settle from afternoon to evening. And the moon took twice as long to rise, Will thought.

The harbor was quiet. Most everyone was at the Foxton estate, celebrating. Will gritted his teeth as he imagined the music and dancing, the food and spirits, the talk and laughter.

Would she dance with him? he thought, angry at the image that was flickering before his eyes. *Was she laughing at the peasant pirate who had dreams of respectability? Were Foxton and Kathryne already making plans for their intended wedding? Were the words she had spoken to him merely a facade? Was her tenderness to him yet another cruel dream left unrealized?*

Will looked over the waters and felt much too restive—and angry— to offer his voice to God. *Perhaps that is the best life for Lady Spenser. Perhaps I was only to rescue her,* Will told himself, trying to soften his fall, if that was to be the outcome. *We have shared much and I will always have those memories. Perhaps that is all the Almighty wants me to have in my life . . . memories.*

It was past midnight, and Will was about to close his eyes when he heard a clatter of hooves on the dock.

A carriage pulled to a stop, and a door opened. A small figure got out and walked to the ship, directly to William.

It was Kathryne, dressed in an elegant gown of white and green with a beautiful gold necklace about her neck, resting on the slight rise of chest well below her bared throat. Will could feel his mouth going dry.

"Mr. Hawkes, perhaps you would care to see me home?" she asked.

Luke rose to stop his captain from rising, but Will stared deep into his eyes. After a moment, Luke nodded.

"Massa Will—you go wit de lady, den come back to de ship. No dance."

Kathryne laughed.

That laugh—like the music of angels, Will thought.

"Aye, sir, Luke. Just a ride to the governor's estate and back."

"Good, Massa. That I allow," Luke said as he helped Will up and then into the carriage.

The carriage clattered away, carrying William and Kathryne. Their ride was silent for a time.

"Was the celebration enjoyable?" Will asked finally.

"Quite," Kathryne responded pleasantly. "It will go on for days, I am sure. But I am simply exhausted and must have some sleep, or I will simply collapse."

Silence filled the carriage once more as it clattered up the hill to Shelworthy.

"Mr. Foxton seems . . . pleasant," Will stated with little enthusiasm.

"Yes, Mr. Foxton is a most pleasant gentleman," Kathryne agreed evenly, without emotion.

In the darkness of the carriage, with the moon the only light visible, as the intoxicating scents of the island filled the small space, Kathryne reached out and placed her hand atop William's right hand. With the lightest of pressure, she stroked his wrist and gently, slowly, softly slipped her hand into his. They were now palm to palm, skin to skin, the delicate smoothness of hers pressing hard against his rough and calloused hand. She slipped her fingers into the gaps between his and entwined his hand with hers, their fingers cleaving together as if one entity. She pressed tightly, and he pressed back. Will could feel the blood pound in his heart.

Kathryne leaned against him and gently laid her head upon his right shoulder, holding onto his hand as if being rescued from a dark, swirling tempest.

The horses' pace slowed, and the carriage came to a sluggish stop. Their hands separated, unwilling. William carefully climbed out and walked around to open the opposite door for Kathryne.

Kathryne took Will's hand again and stepped down from the carriage, and with a sigh looked up, for the first time taking in the sight of her new home, bathed in the warm light of its many lanterns and rush torches.

She and William walked up the drive to the governor's mansion. Each slow step on the roadway, made of sparkling crushed oyster shells, filled the stillness of the warm night with an echoed crunch.

William turned his head toward Kathryne as a glint of the moon sparkled off the water below. In the glow of the lanterns, he saw a warm and comforting light reflected in her emerald eyes.

They approached the massive wrought iron gate that encircled the entry, just before the front walk to the steps. An elegant soldier in a stiff, red coat slipped from the gatehouse, shouldered his musket, and swung the gate open, allowing the pair through.

Kathryne stopped and turned her face toward William, her hands gentle at her sides.

William stood woodenly and looked down at his scuffed and worn boots. He lifted up his face and stared into the now luminous eyes of the governor's only daughter.

"Lady Spenser," he said softly. "May I see you again?"

She stood for a moment, then suddenly turned on her heel and stepped away.

Will's heart lurched at her withdrawal.

Kathryne then stopped, turned back to him, and said quietly and calmly, "Mr. Hawkes, you may. I would so very much look forward to that."

The hardness dissolved, and his heart began to beat again. Will noticed a small glint on her cheek. *Was that a tear?* he wondered.

Kathryne met Will's eyes and quickly turned away. Over her shoulder, as she walked up the steps of her new home, she added, "You will have to speak to the governor, of course. And I have heard that he will be seeking a new captain for Fort Charles."

Captain William Hawkes stood, still as a stone, in the darkness, listening to the crickets serenade the night and watching as Lady Kathryne Spenser disappeared inside, slipping into the darkness with his heart.

1 December 1641
Barbados

The following dawn broke clear, cloudless, and with a warm wind blowing in from the west. There was a scent of grain in the air, William imagined, and the very thought reminded him of the fields of Hadenthorne, the fields he had not seen for years. In his thoughts he could see Vicar Mayhew strolling next to a vast expanse of freshly cut hay.

William had spent the night aboard the ship, alone except for Luke and the Tambor brothers, who insisted on guarding the vessel from the brigands they were sure had followed them home.

Will smiled at the two, who had slept on the top deck, wrapping themselves in the torn and ripped canvas sails that had been shot away during the final chase of the battle. Their snoring rippled across the harbor water. It was one of the louder sounds that early in the morning.

William splashed some cold water on his face and gently shook out his coat, brushed some threads and dust from the gold braiding along the sleeves, and slipped into the comfortable garment.

"Might as well become accustomed to wearing a proper coat to work," he said to himself. "It does a harbor captain right to present himself well dressed."

He looked down at his torn breeches and well-worn boots. *It appears to be time to recast my wardrobe,* William thought, and gathered up some gold coins to do his shopping in Bridgetown.

William had treasured Kathryne's words of last evening, her voice lilting through his thoughts for hours until sleep silenced it. He had heard it again when he awoke, *"Mr. Hawkes, you may. I would so very much look forward to that."*

His heart was warmed by her gentleness and acceptance. He took her invitation to speak to her father about the Fort Charles position as a sign—a sign that he should stay in Barbados, could court Kathryne, should try to win her hand, and someday marry the woman who had stolen his heart.

For a disquieting moment, an image of the handsome face of Geoffrey Foxton, polished and mannered, the governor's choice for Kathryne, entered Will's thoughts. He willed himself to discount the interloper's presence, but Foxton's fluid grace and the way the other women had watched him walk past on the dock were troubling indeed. And then the face of Vicar Petley swam before him.

It is of no matter, Will reassured himself in the manner of a young man who whistles all the louder as he passes a graveyard in the dark of a hidden moon.

He slipped quietly down the wooden gangway of the pier and slowly walked along the Careenage toward Eggington's Green and the surrounding labyrinth of small streets and shops that lined the waterfront.

He made his way to a public house and ordered a massive repast for his morning meal—biscuits, ham, gravy, beans, coffee, fruit. He ate rapidly, accustomed to downing a quick meal at odd times.

Exiting the darkened establishment, Will squinted into the bright morning sun. He strolled east along Broad Street, amid the street vendors and small shops that ringed the harbor area. Tiny stalls and pushcarts lined the way, offering fruits, vegetables, fresh fish, woven mats, and cloth. Ebony-skinned natives sang out the benefits and quality of their wares as Will passed by.

"Mornin' sir! Do ya care fo' a pretty sea bass dis mornin'?"

"Mistah, you'll be wantin' some fine linen today, true?"

Will strolled through the market area, not knowing exactly what he was looking for nor where he was going. He knew that he would go to the tailor's shop on Jemmott Lane and then to the shoemaker on Oxley Street, but he was too preoccupied with his thoughts at the moment to decide on colors and fashions.

He turned a corner, walking along James Street, past the square where the church was being built. He then headed west, where the town began to give way to fields of sugarcane, which could be seen just over the last set of low buildings and shanties. He stopped and looked about. He seldom had come to this area populated with itinerant workers and a few freed slaves.

The air was quieter and a little hotter. The sea breeze was cut off by the more impressive buildings that looked out to the harbor.

Will turned to head back to the main part of town. Just then a street peddler, encamped at the corner of the street, caught his eye. On a rough canvas patch in front of the old, gray-haired Arawak was a small scattering of trinkets and jewelry, no doubt made of cheap metal and glass bits.

He had thought it would be advantageous to present Kathryne with a small gift signifying his proper intentions. While a street peddler would not have anything that would be nearly acceptable to such a fine woman, Will paused nevertheless.

He almost turned away. Still, there was something that was curious here, William thought, something that drew him closer. He stood over the peddler's meager offerings, his tall frame casting a long shadow over the man.

The wizened old native looked up and smiled a toothless grin. "What be your pleasure, suh? Der be lots of pretty bits for de ladies."

William nudged at a piece of gold-colored jewelry with the toe of his boot, and then in a flash, knelt before the man, picking up the small, solid circle of gold. With his hand he rubbed the dust from the piece, turning it over in his trembling fingers.

William's eyes filled with immediate tears as he opened the small locket and once again gazed at the dark-haired portrait of his mother. A tear tumbled from his cheek and splashed the dirt away from her image.

The familiar Scripture from the Psalms reassured William's heart: *Be still and know that I am God. Psalm 46:10.* Seeing her image filled William's soul with undiluted, overwhelming joy.

His fingers felt a roughness on the back of the locket, and using the moisture of his tears, he rubbed away the grime and dust.

On the back, in small, delicate, and deliberate scratches, William read these tiny words: PSALM 61, T. MAYHEW.

The Atlantic Ocean

In the captain's cabin of the *Bellaguarda,* bound for England from the Virginia colonies, there sat a small carved wooden chest, crafted from Carolina pine and polished until it glowed like the afternoon sun in summer. Locked in that small, sturdy chest was a stack of official correspondence and a small bundle of personal letters tied together with a stout length of twine.

In that bundle was a letter addressed to one William Hawkes, in care of the vicar of St. Jerome's Church in Hadenthorne, in the shire of Devon, England. At the bottom of that envelope was written in bold black letters, the words: PLEASE FORWARD. MOST URGENT.

At the top left-hand corner of the envelope was inscribed a name in delicate and flowing script. Written with a new feather pen were the following three simple words: Missy (Holender) Cavendish.